TABLE TITANS CLUB

Story and art by **Scott Kurtz**

Color by **Steve Hamaker**

HOLIDAY HOUSE · NEW YORK

For Miranda

Text and illustrations © 2024 by Scott Kurtz
Color by Steve Hamaker
Color assists by Cole Roberts, Deon Parson, and Faby Saturn
All Rights Reserved
HOLIDAY HOUSE is registered in the U.S. Patent and Trademark Office.
Printed and bound in November 2023 at Toppan Leefung, DongGuan, China.
www.holidayhouse.com
First Edition
1 3 5 7 9 10 8 6 4 2

Library of Congress Cataloging-in-Publication Data is available.

ISBN: 978-0-8234-5316-0 (Hardcover)
ISBN: 978-0-8234-5681-9 (Paperback)

CHAPTER ONE

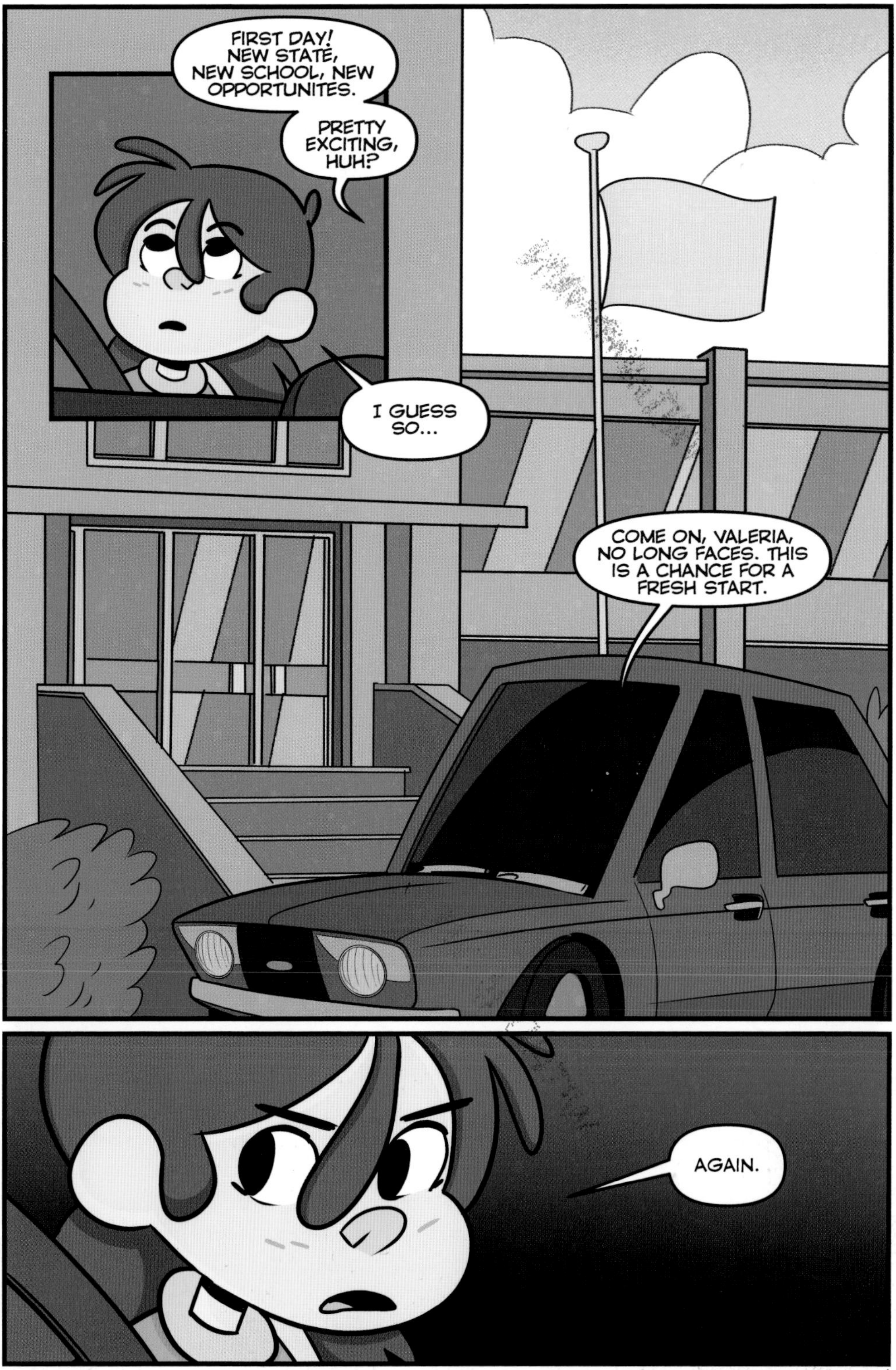
FIRST DAY! NEW STATE, NEW SCHOOL, NEW OPPORTUNITES.
PRETTY EXCITING, HUH?
I GUESS SO...
COME ON, VALERIA, NO LONG FACES. THIS IS A CHANCE FOR A FRESH START.
AGAIN.

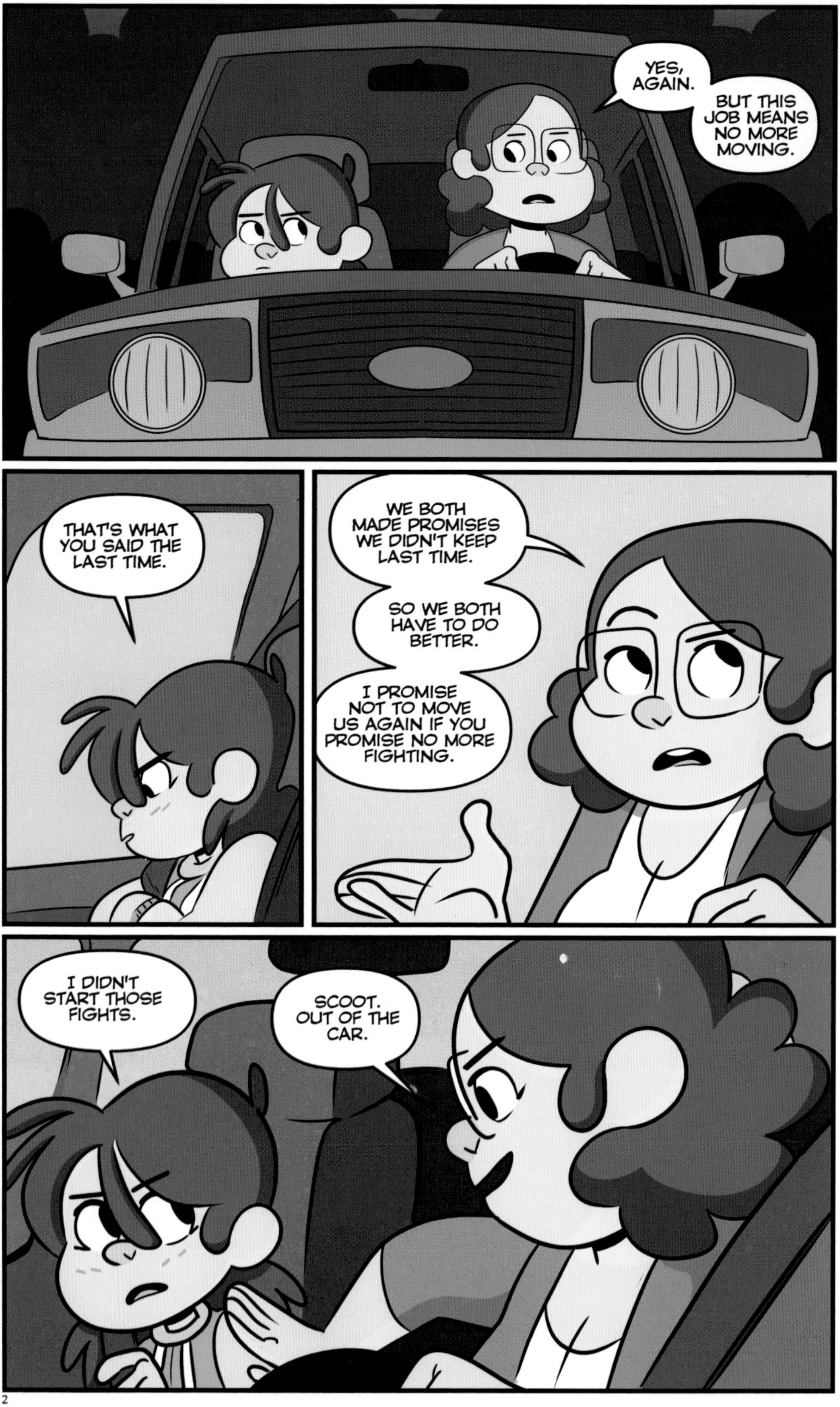
YES, AGAIN.
BUT THIS JOB MEANS NO MORE MOVING.
THAT'S WHAT YOU SAID THE LAST TIME.
WE BOTH MADE PROMISES WE DIDN'T KEEP LAST TIME.
SO WE BOTH HAVE TO DO BETTER.
I PROMISE NOT TO MOVE US AGAIN IF YOU PROMISE NO MORE FIGHTING.
I DIDN'T START THOSE FIGHTS.
SCOOT. OUT OF THE CAR.

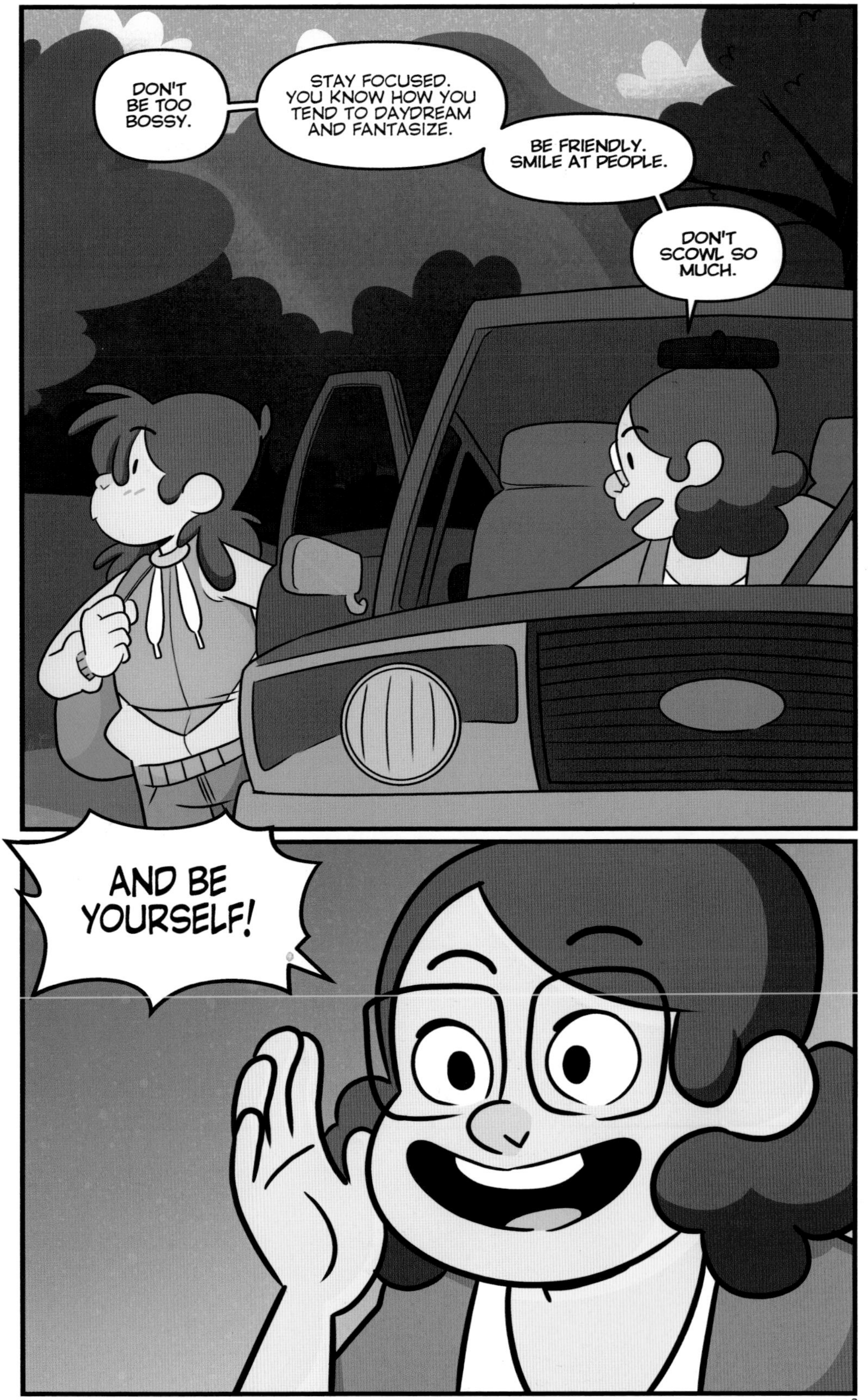
DON'T BE TOO BOSSY.
STAY FOCUSED. YOU KNOW HOW YOU TEND TO DAYDREAM AND FANTASIZE.
BE FRIENDLY. SMILE AT PEOPLE.
DON'T SCOWL SO MUCH.
AND BE YOURSELF!

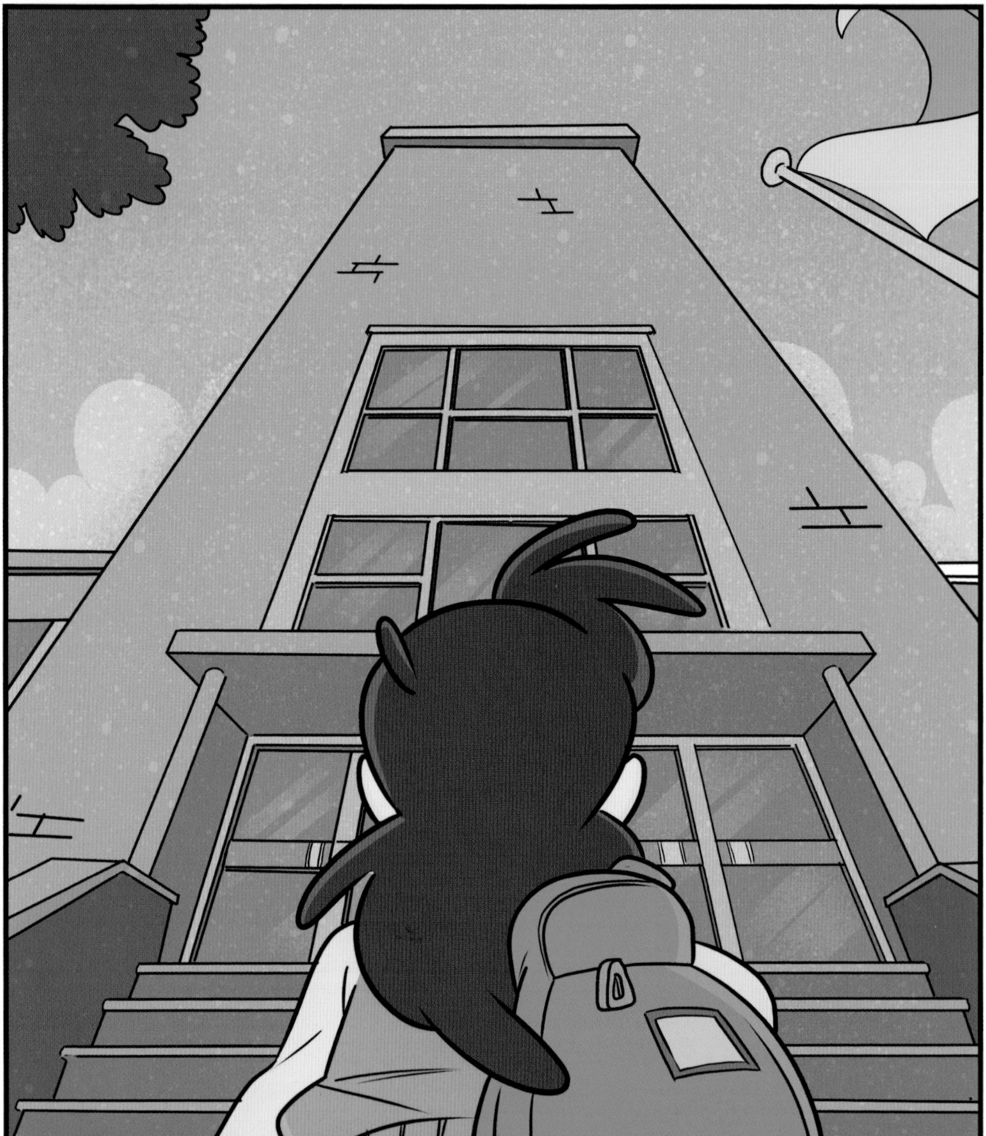

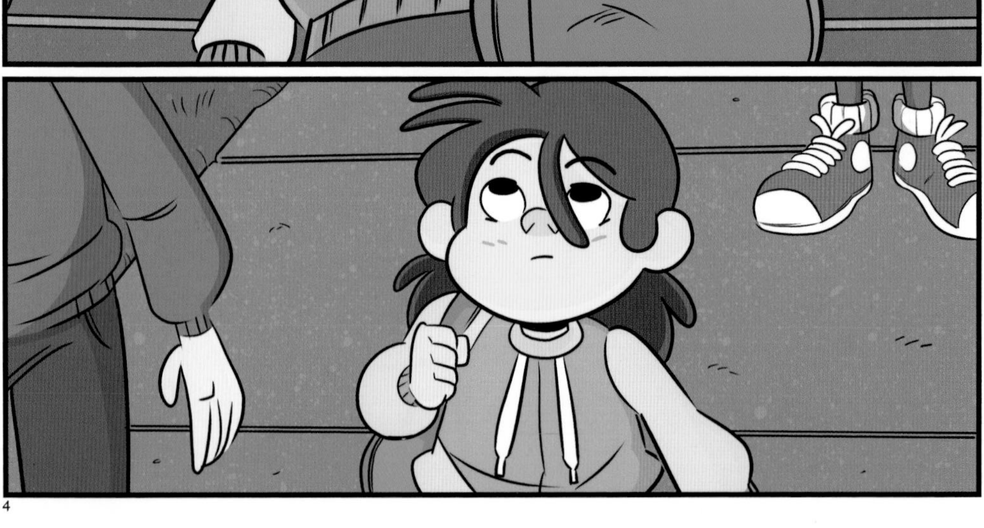

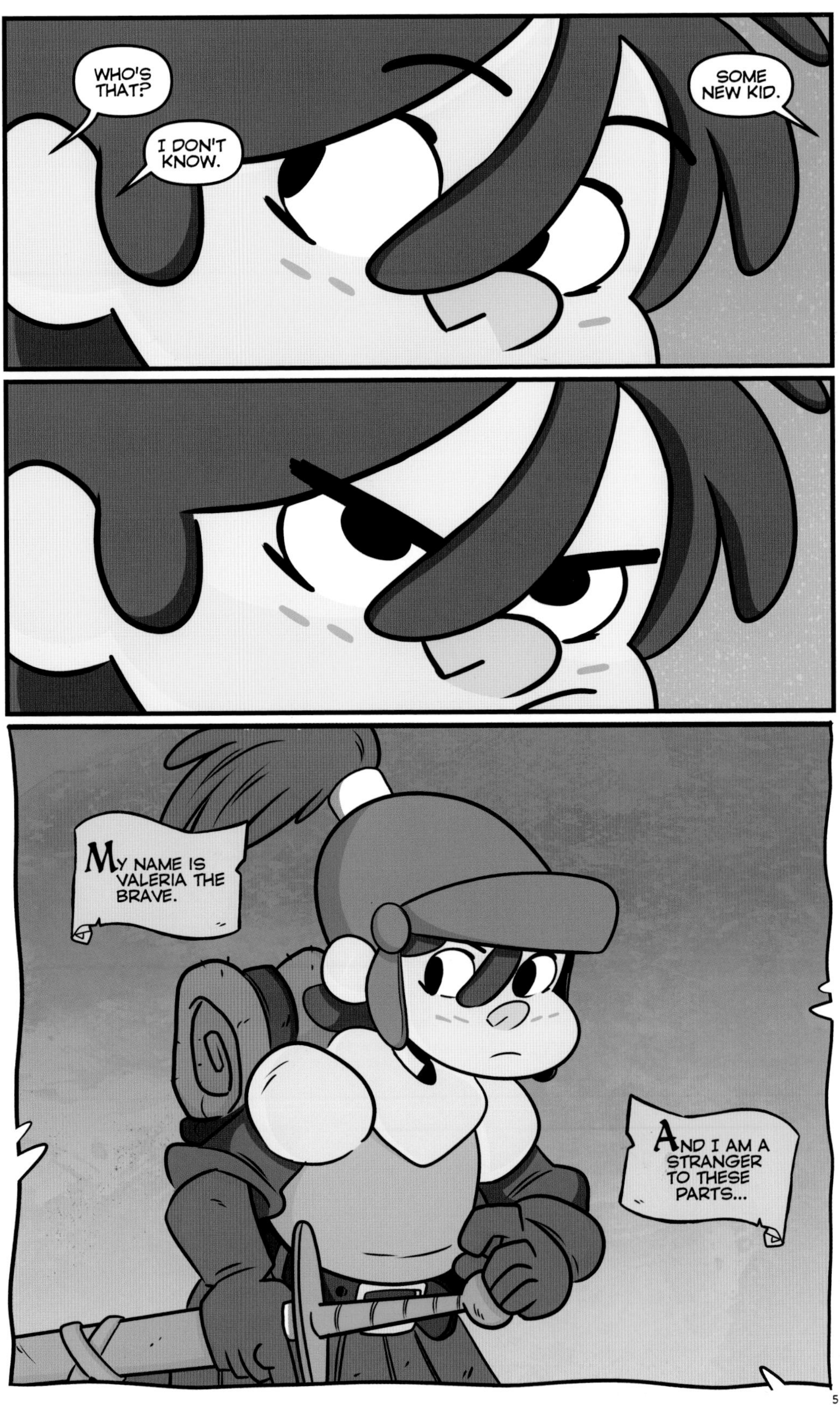
WHO'S THAT?
I DON'T KNOW.
SOME NEW KID.
MY NAME IS VALERIA THE BRAVE.
AND I AM A STRANGER TO THESE PARTS...

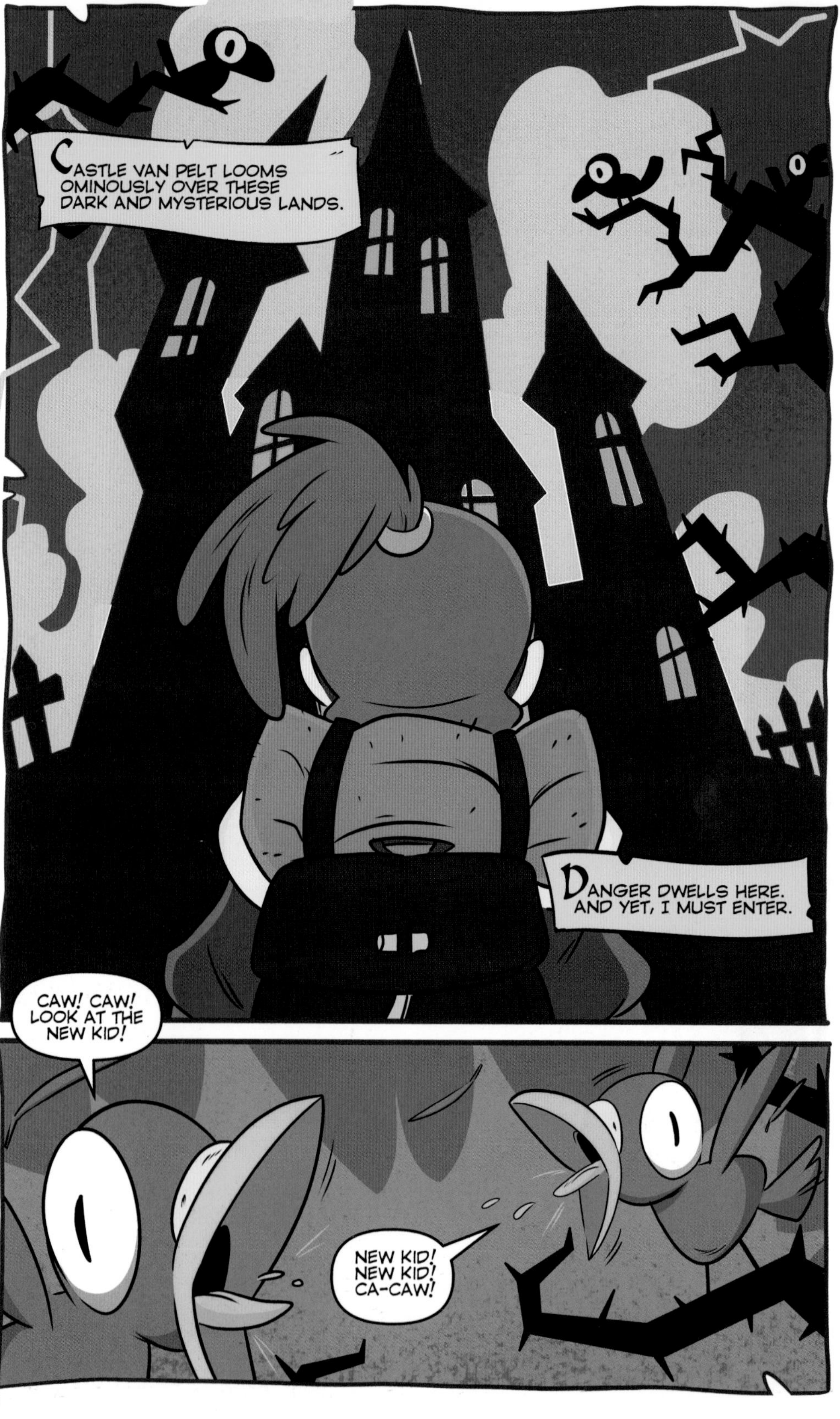
CASTLE VAN PELT LOOMS OMINOUSLY OVER THESE DARK AND MYSTERIOUS LANDS.
DANGER DWELLS HERE. AND YET, I MUST ENTER.
CAW! CAW! LOOK AT THE NEW KID!
NEW KID! NEW KID! CA-CAW!

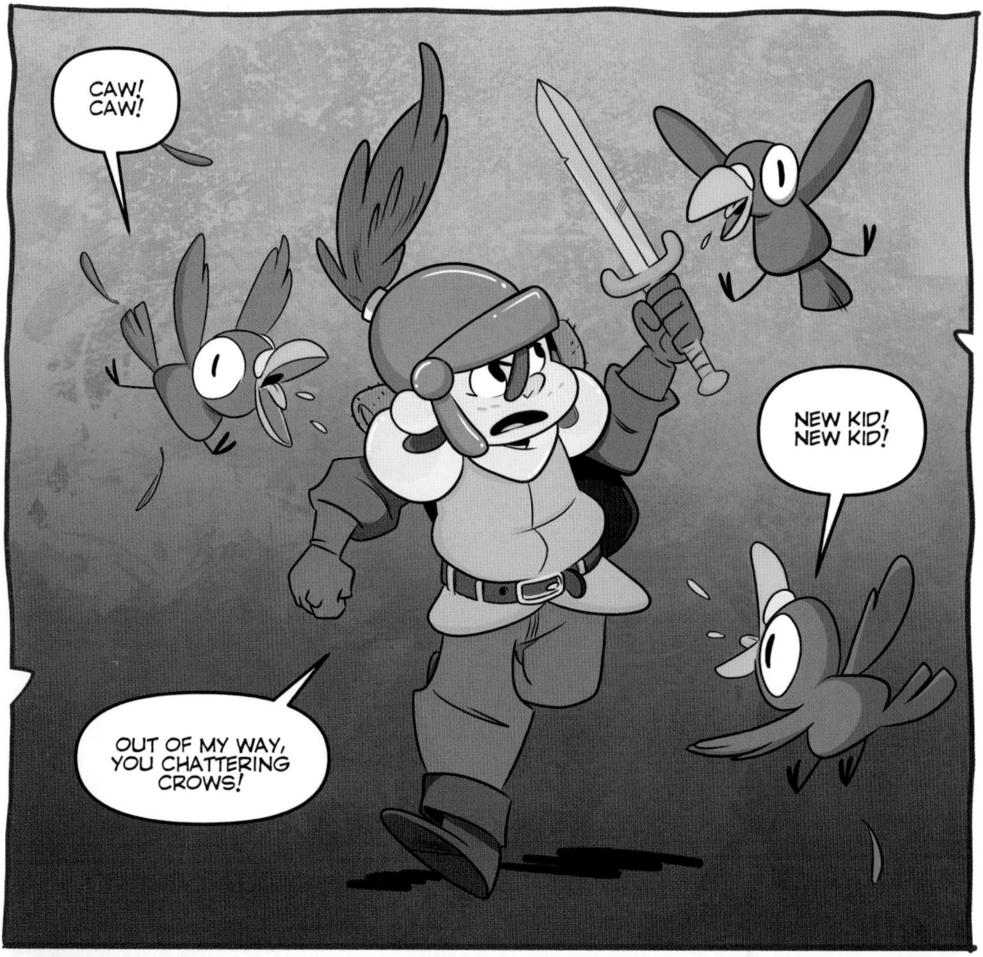
CAW! CAW!
NEW KID! NEW KID!
OUT OF MY WAY, YOU CHATTERING CROWS!

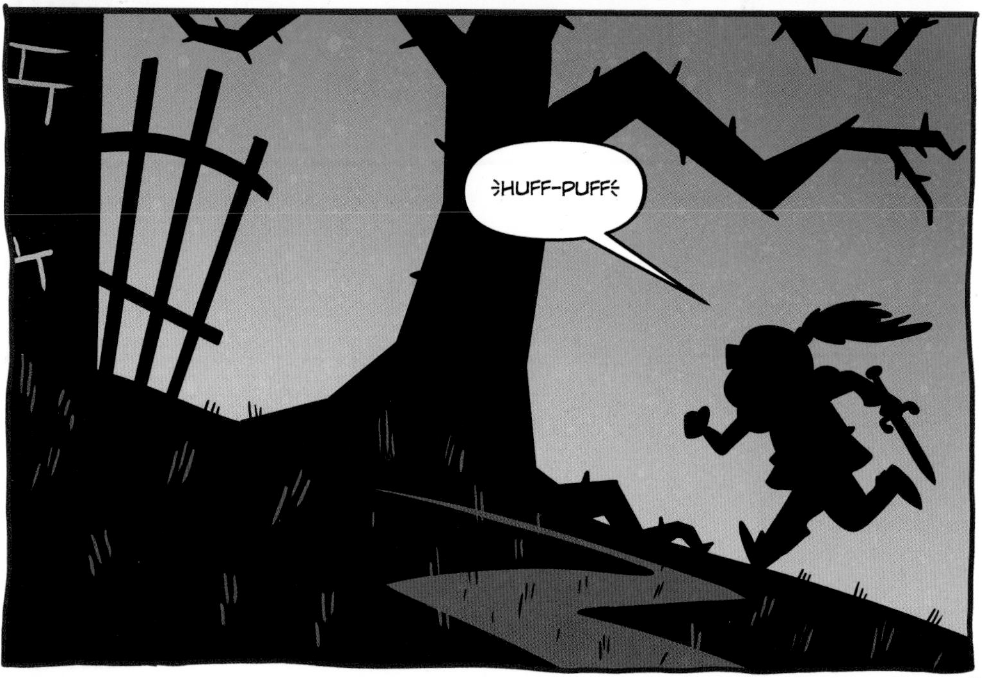
HUFF-PUFF

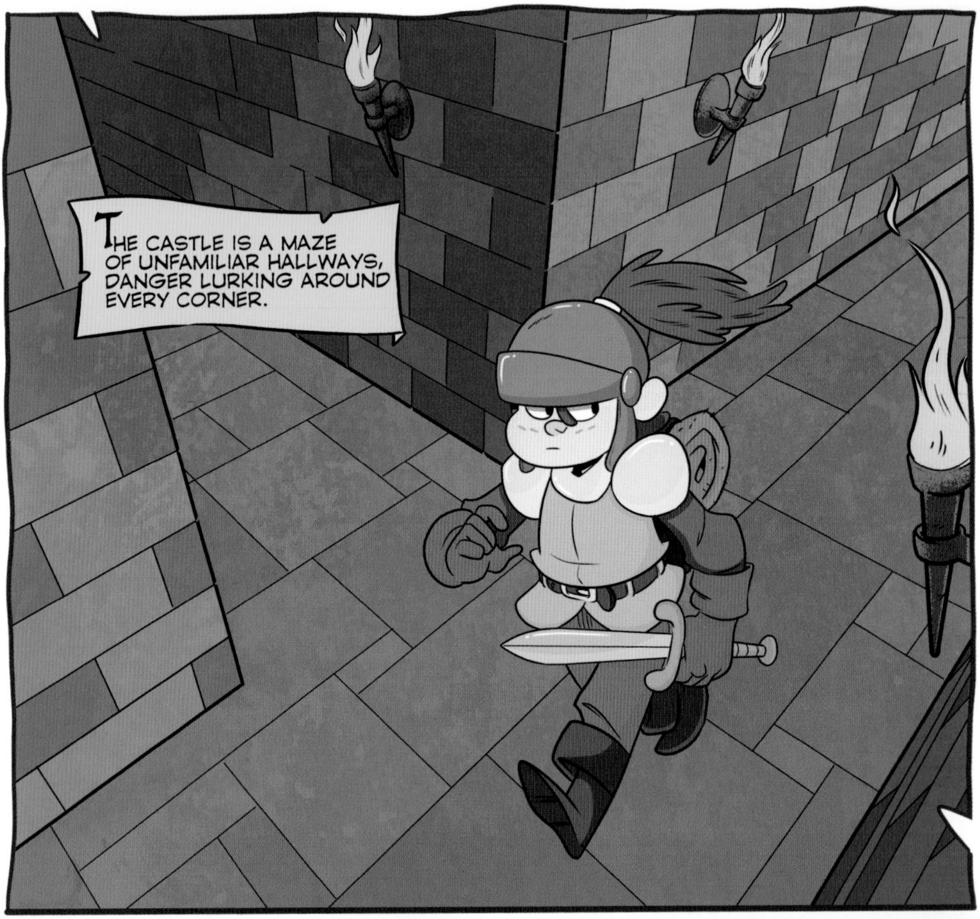
THE CASTLE IS A MAZE OF UNFAMILIAR HALLWAYS, DANGER LURKING AROUND EVERY CORNER.

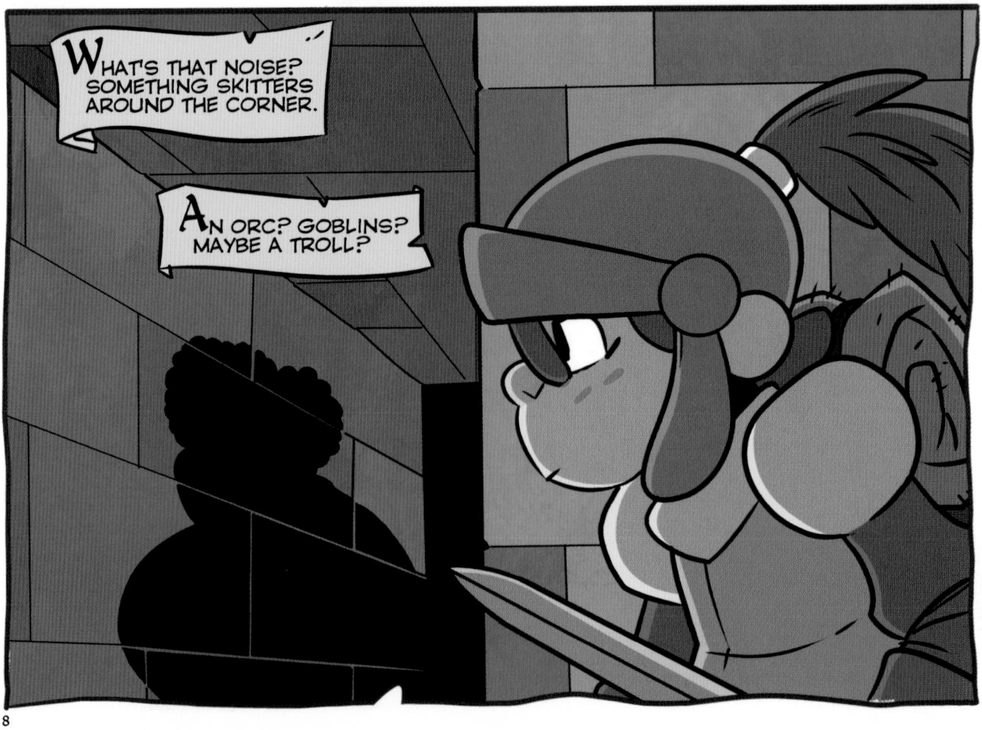
WHAT'S THAT NOISE? SOMETHING SKITTERS AROUND THE CORNER.
AN ORC? GOBLINS? MAYBE A TROLL?

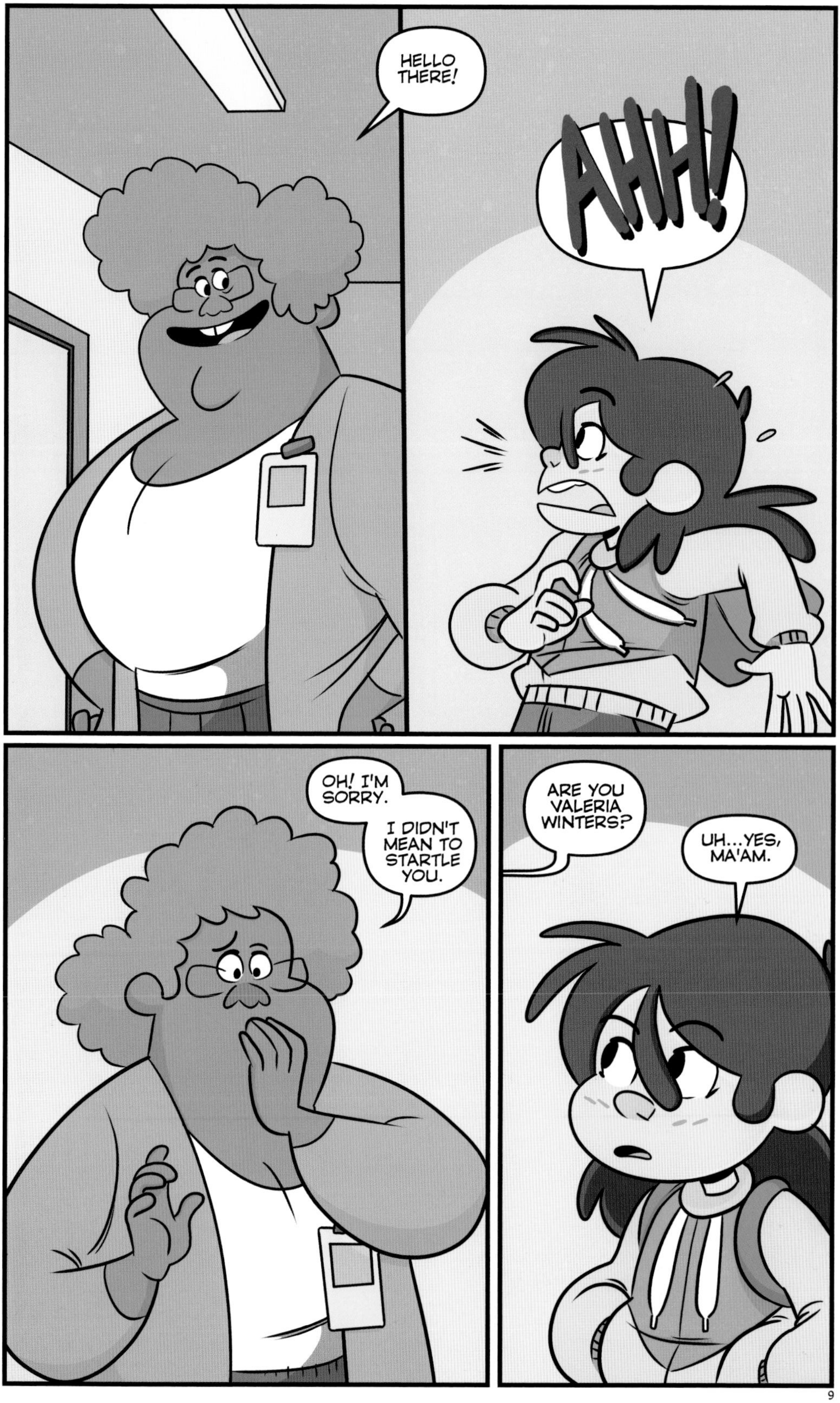
HELLO THERE!
AHH!
OH! I'M SORRY.
I DIDN'T MEAN TO STARTLE YOU.
ARE YOU VALERIA WINTERS?
UH...YES, MA'AM.

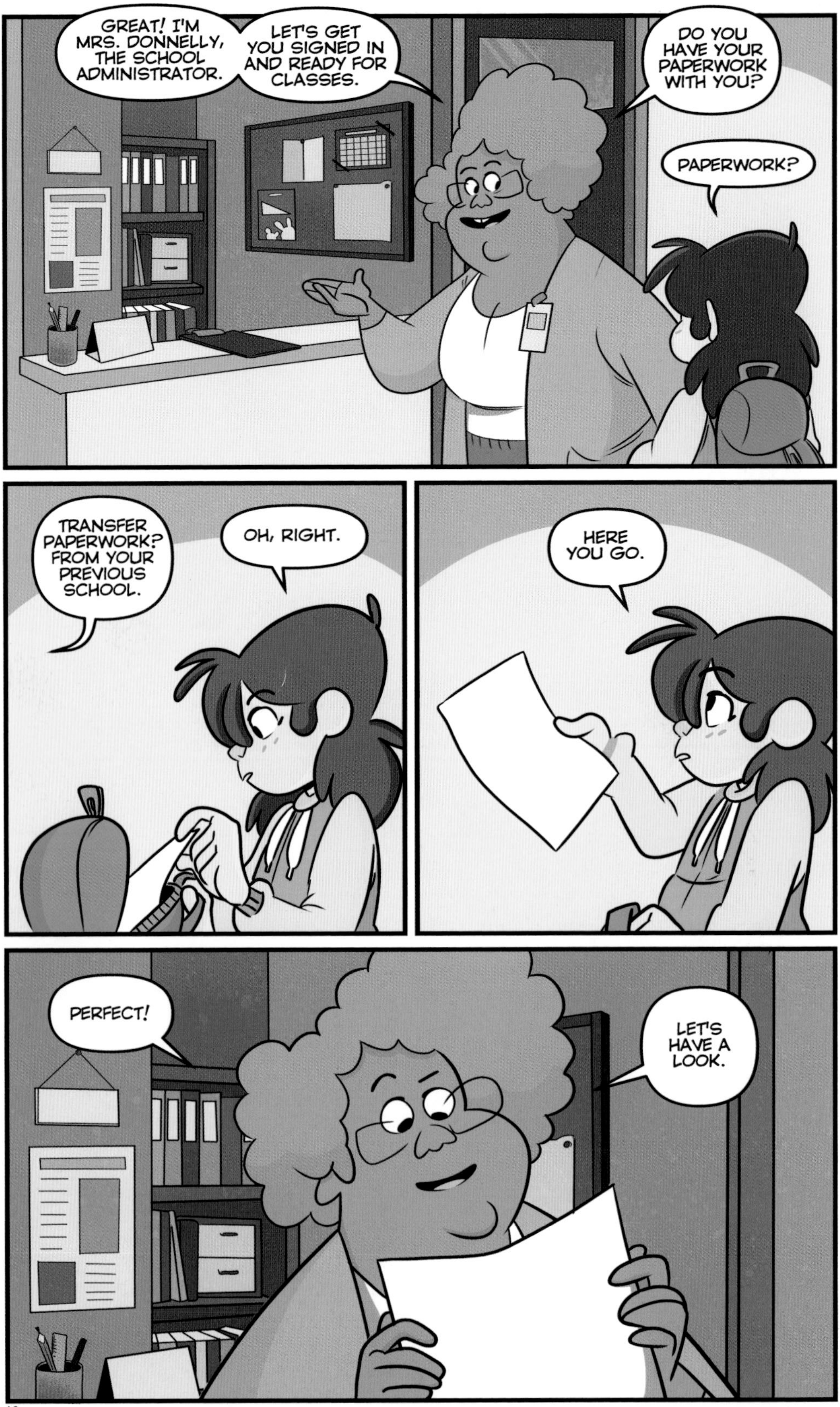
GREAT! I'M MRS. DONNELLY, THE SCHOOL ADMINISTRATOR.
LET'S GET YOU SIGNED IN AND READY FOR CLASSES.
DO YOU HAVE YOUR PAPERWORK WITH YOU?
PAPERWORK?
TRANSFER PAPERWORK? FROM YOUR PREVIOUS SCHOOL.
OH, RIGHT.
HERE YOU GO.
PERFECT!
LET'S HAVE A LOOK.

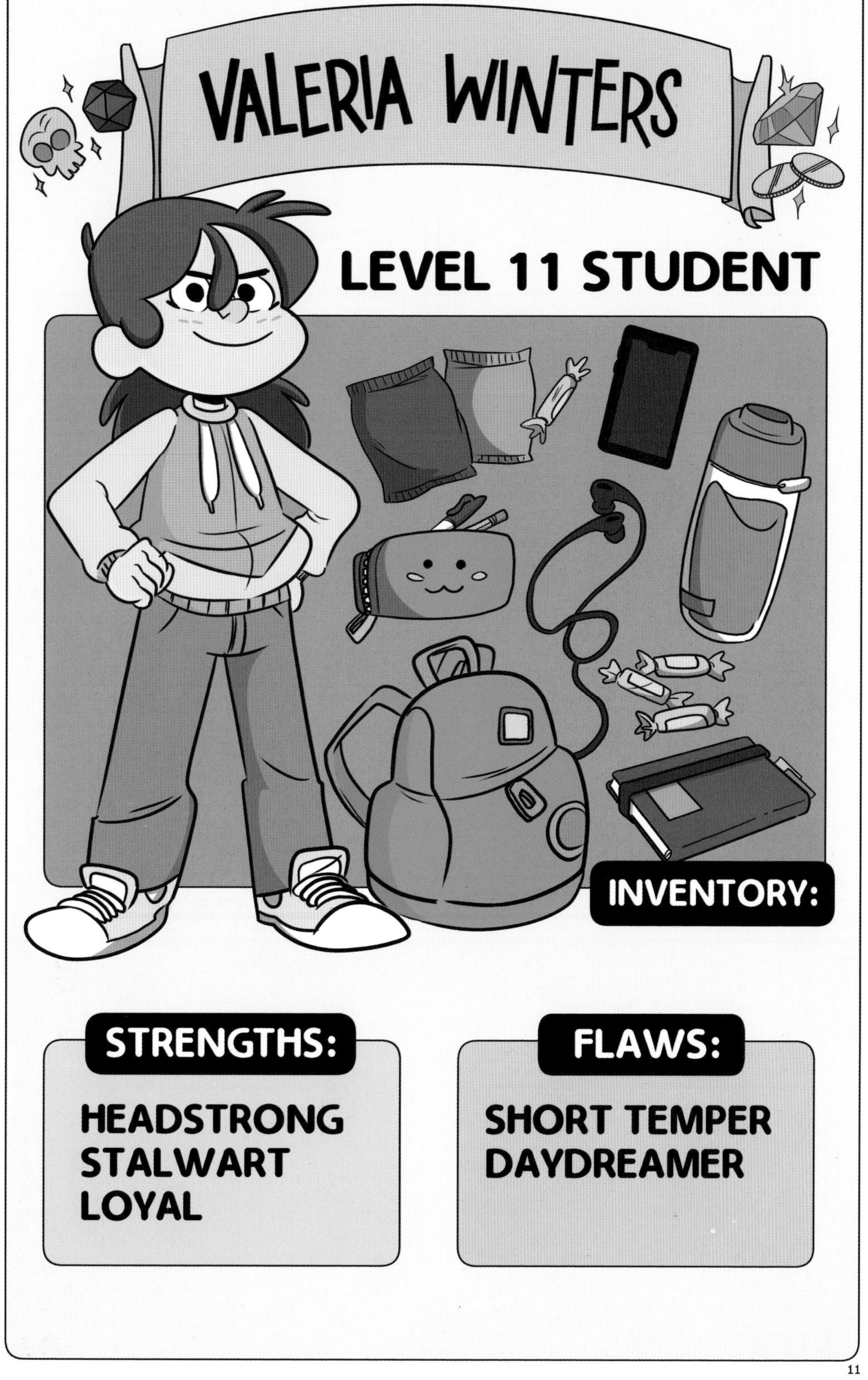
VALERIA WINTERS
LEVEL 11 STUDENT
INVENTORY:

STRENGTHS:

HEADSTRONG
STALWART
LOYAL

FLAWS:

SHORT TEMPER
DAYDREAMER

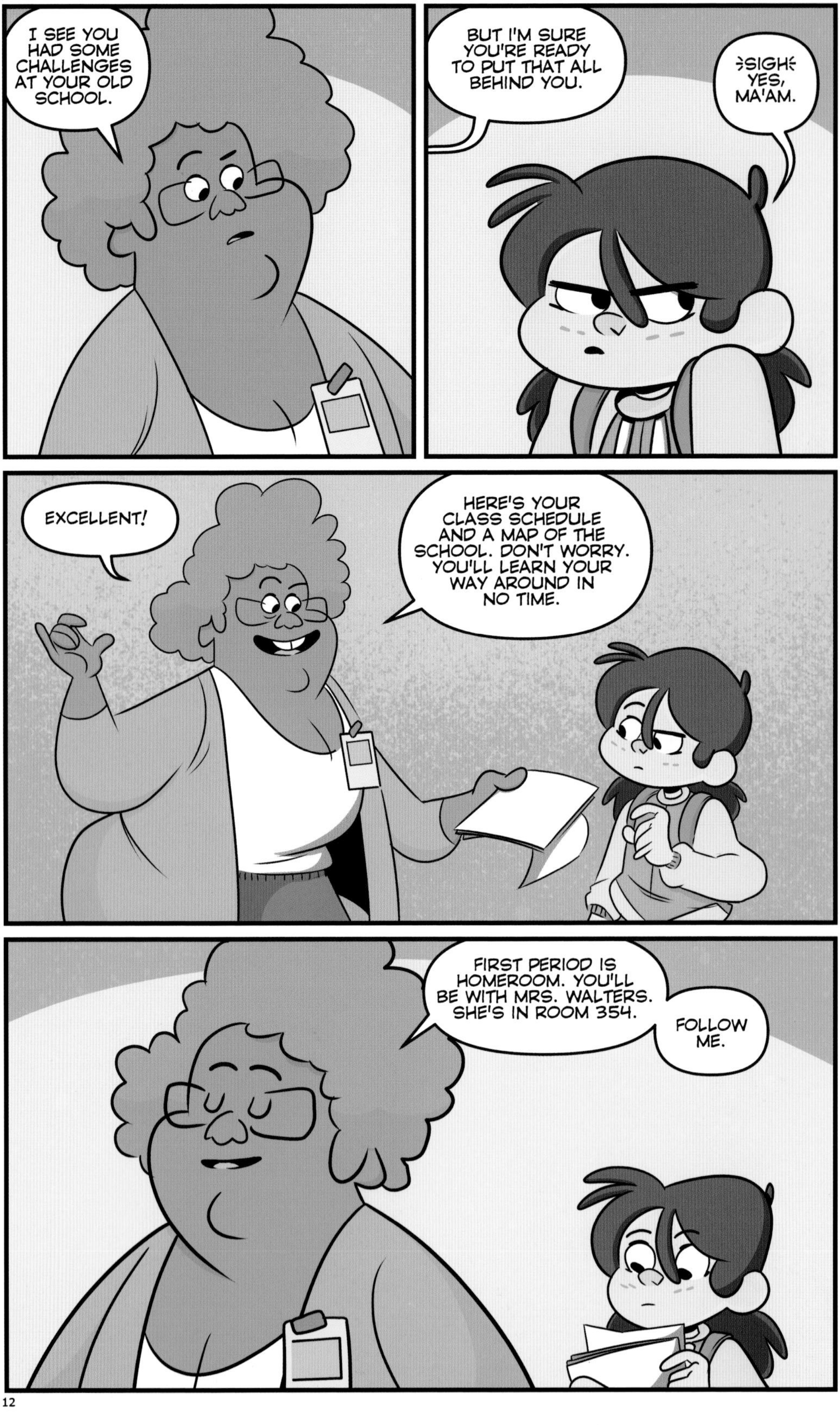
I SEE YOU HAD SOME CHALLENGES AT YOUR OLD SCHOOL.
BUT I'M SURE YOU'RE READY TO PUT THAT ALL BEHIND YOU.
SIGH
YES, MA'AM.
EXCELLENT!
HERE'S YOUR CLASS SCHEDULE AND A MAP OF THE SCHOOL. DON'T WORRY. YOU'LL LEARN YOUR WAY AROUND IN NO TIME.
FIRST PERIOD IS HOMEROOM. YOU'LL BE WITH MRS. WALTERS. SHE'S IN ROOM 354.
FOLLOW ME.

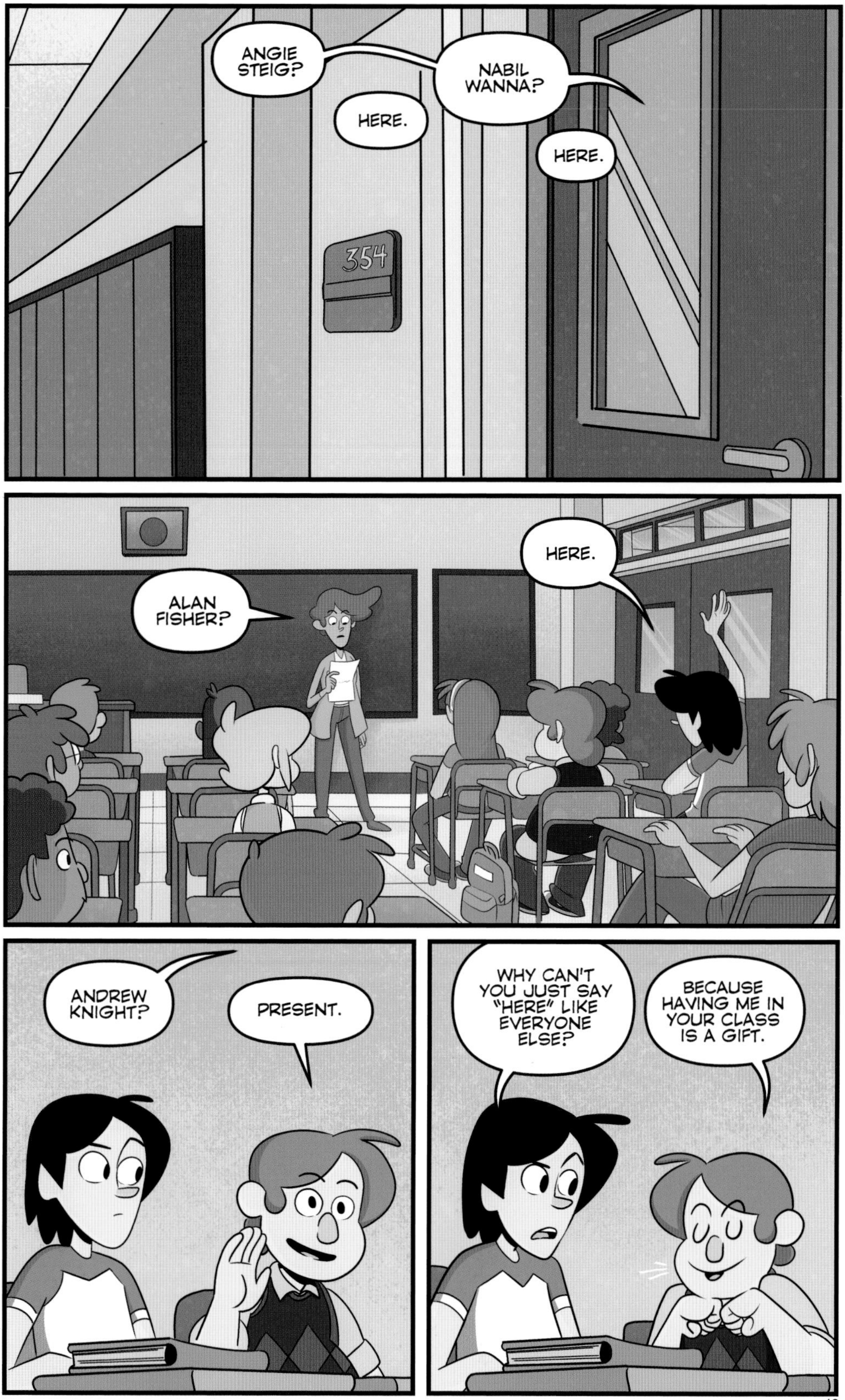
354
ANGIE STEIG?
HERE.
NABIL WANNA?
HERE.
ALAN FISHER?
HERE.
ANDREW KNIGHT?
PRESENT.
WHY CAN'T YOU JUST SAY "HERE" LIKE EVERYONE ELSE?
BECAUSE HAVING ME IN YOUR CLASS IS A GIFT.

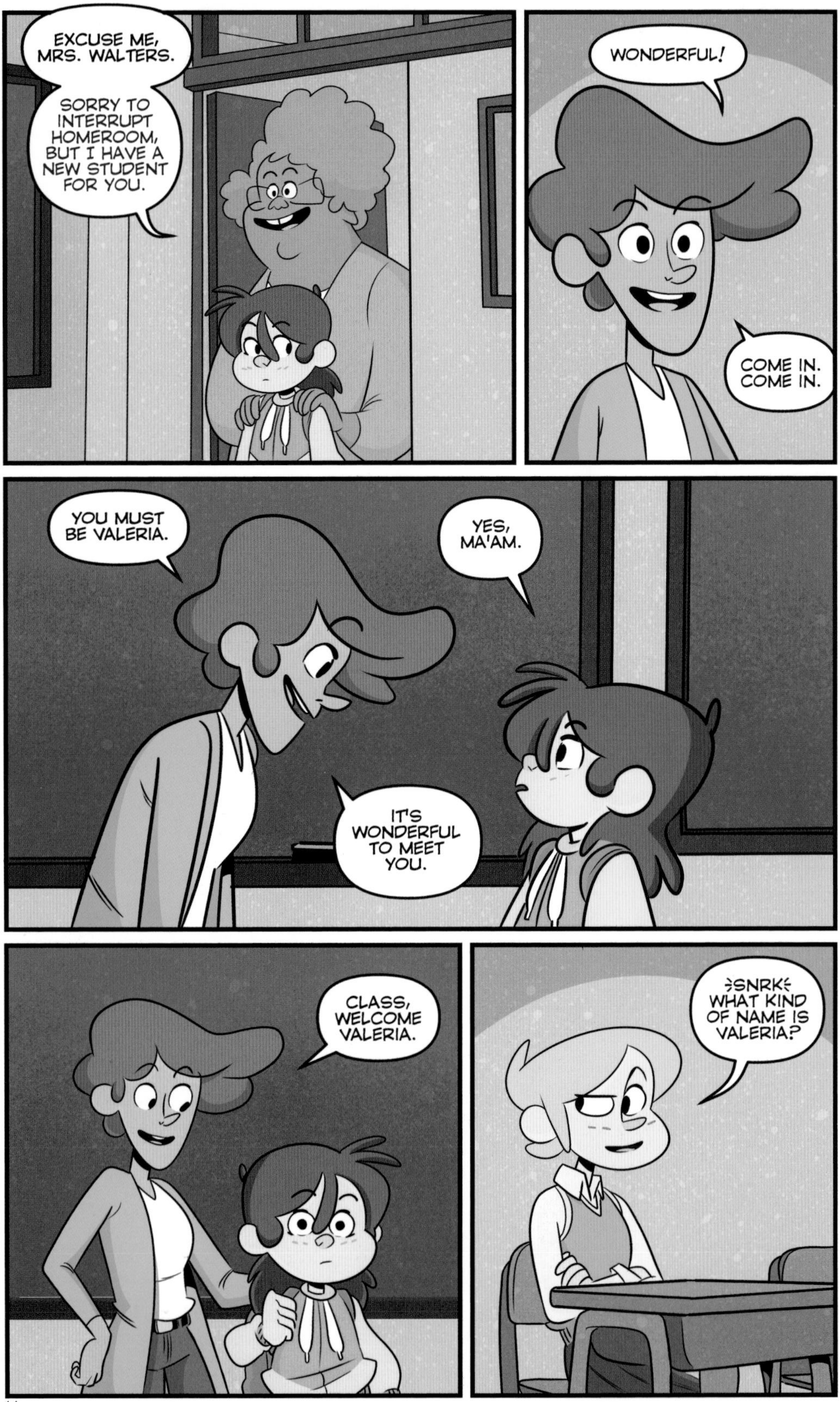
EXCUSE ME, MRS. WALTERS.
SORRY TO INTERRUPT HOMEROOM, BUT I HAVE A NEW STUDENT FOR YOU.
WONDERFUL!
COME IN. COME IN.
YOU MUST BE VALERIA.
YES, MA'AM.
IT'S WONDERFUL TO MEET YOU.
CLASS, WELCOME VALERIA.
SNRK WHAT KIND OF NAME IS VALERIA?

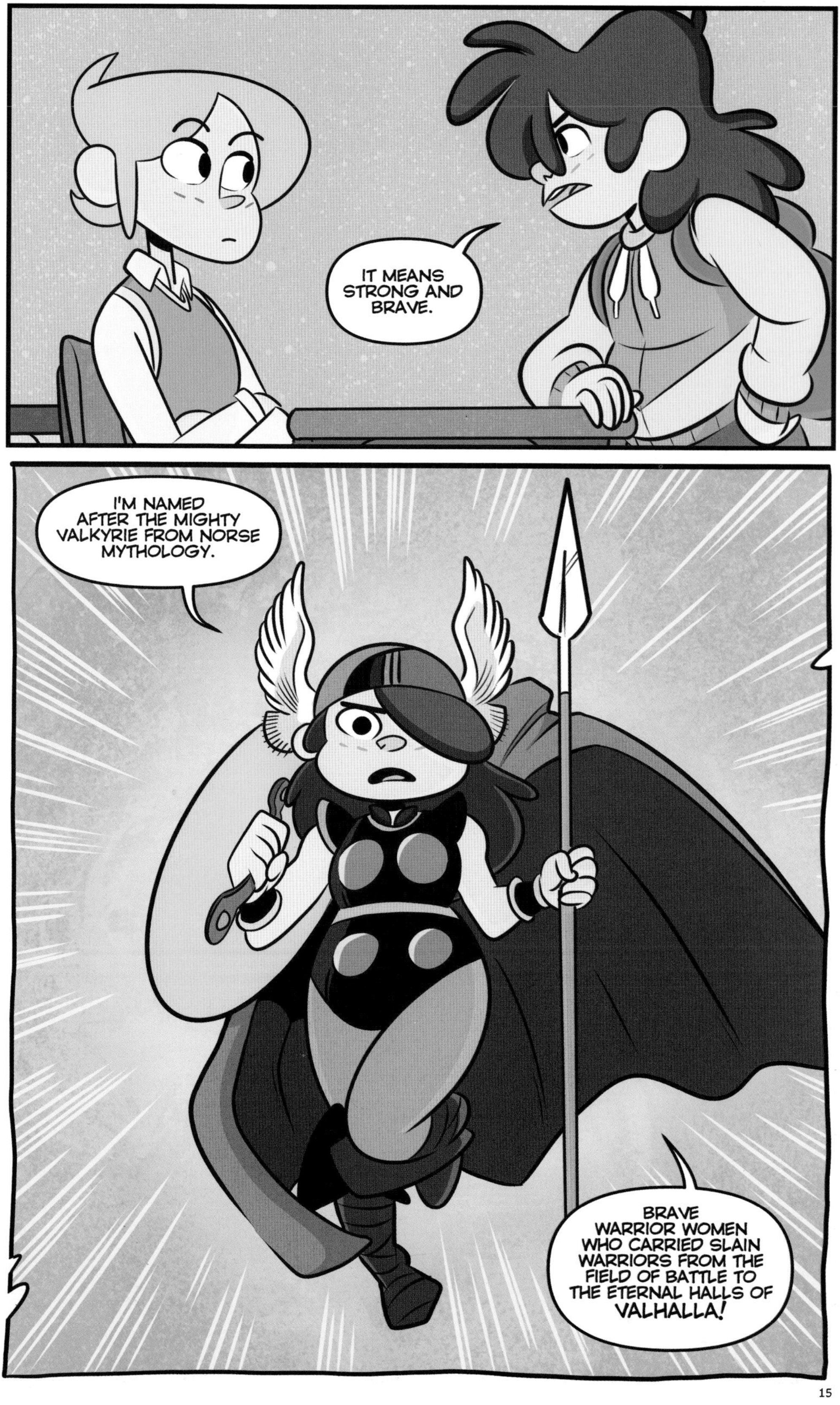
IT MEANS STRONG AND BRAVE.
I'M NAMED AFTER THE MIGHTY VALKYRIE FROM NORSE MYTHOLOGY.
BRAVE WARRIOR WOMEN WHO CARRIED SLAIN WARRIORS FROM THE FIELD OF BATTLE TO THE ETERNAL HALLS OF VALHALLA!

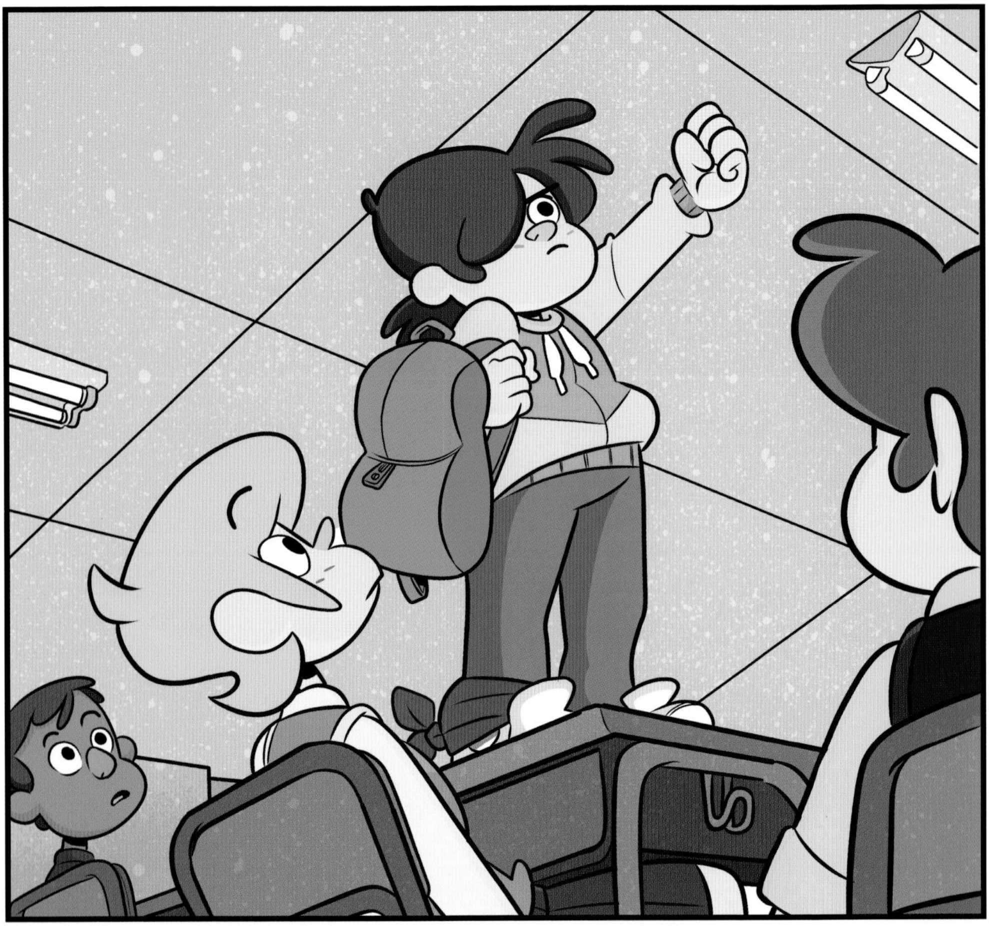

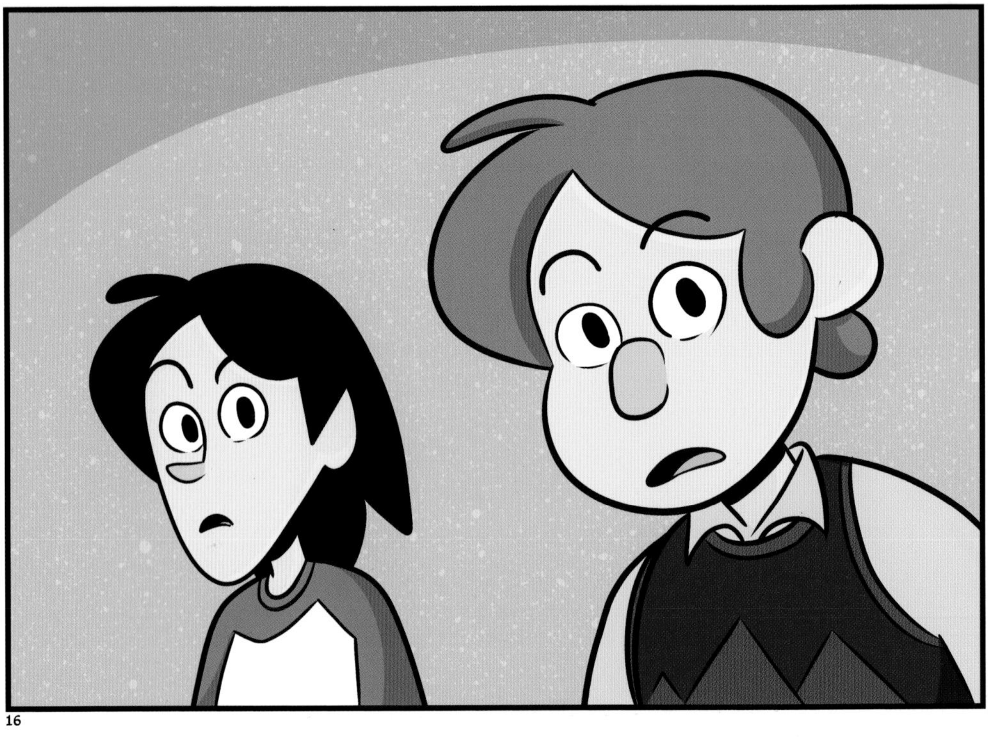

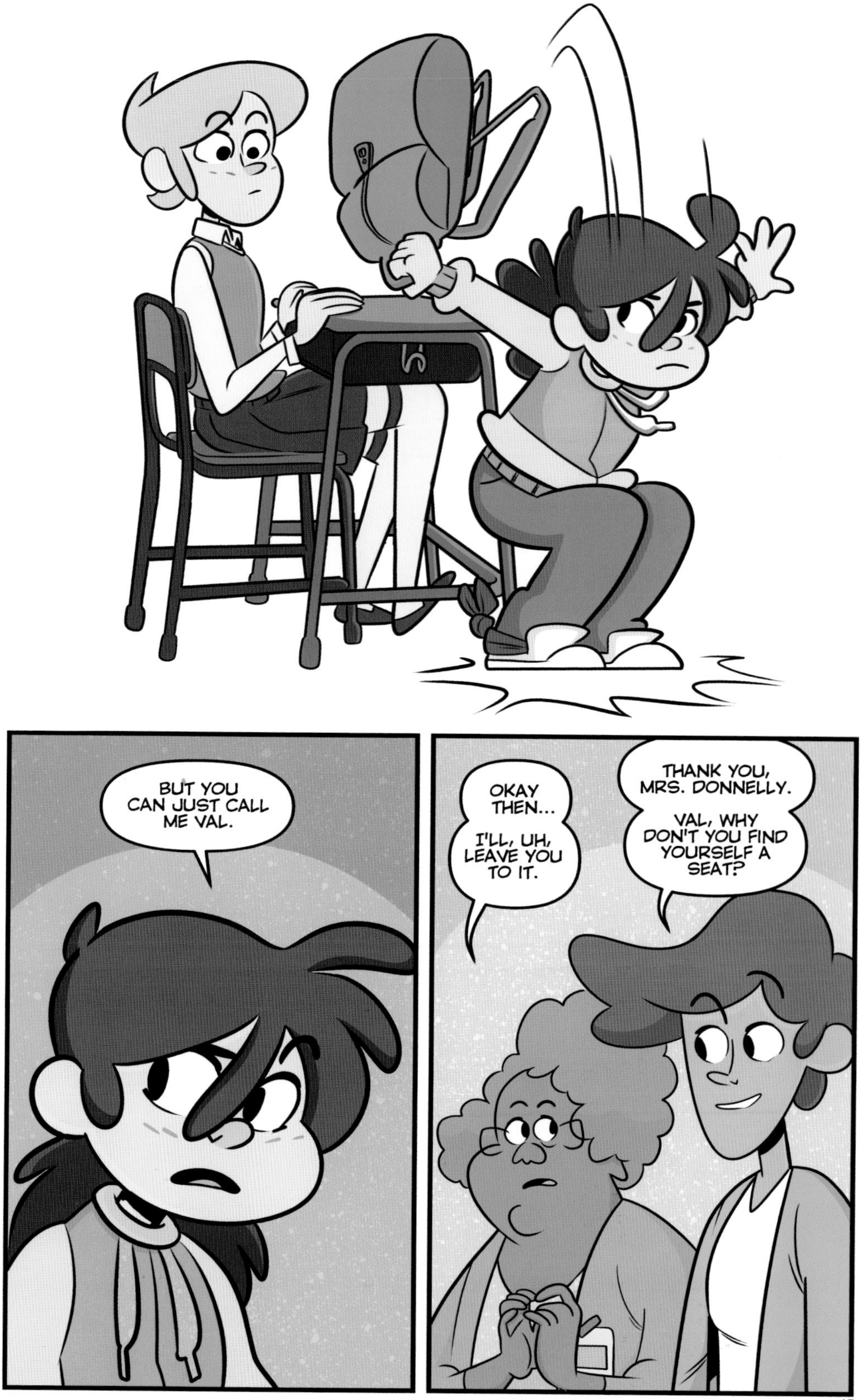
BUT YOU CAN JUST CALL ME VAL.
OKAY THEN...
I'LL, UH, LEAVE YOU TO IT.
THANK YOU, MRS. DONNELLY.
VAL, WHY DON'T YOU FIND YOURSELF A SEAT?

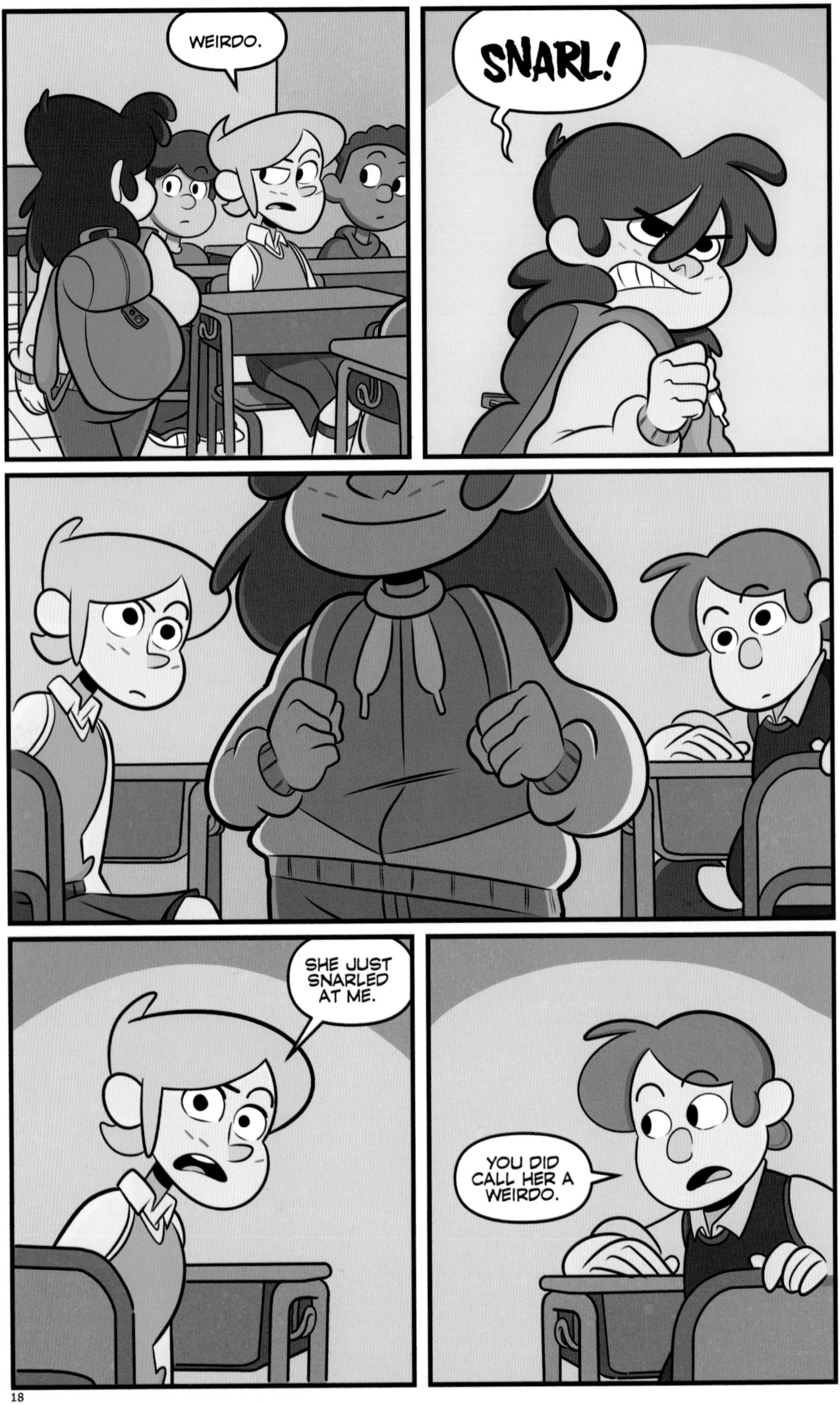
WEIRDO.
SNARL!
SHE JUST SNARLED AT ME.
YOU DID CALL HER A WEIRDO.

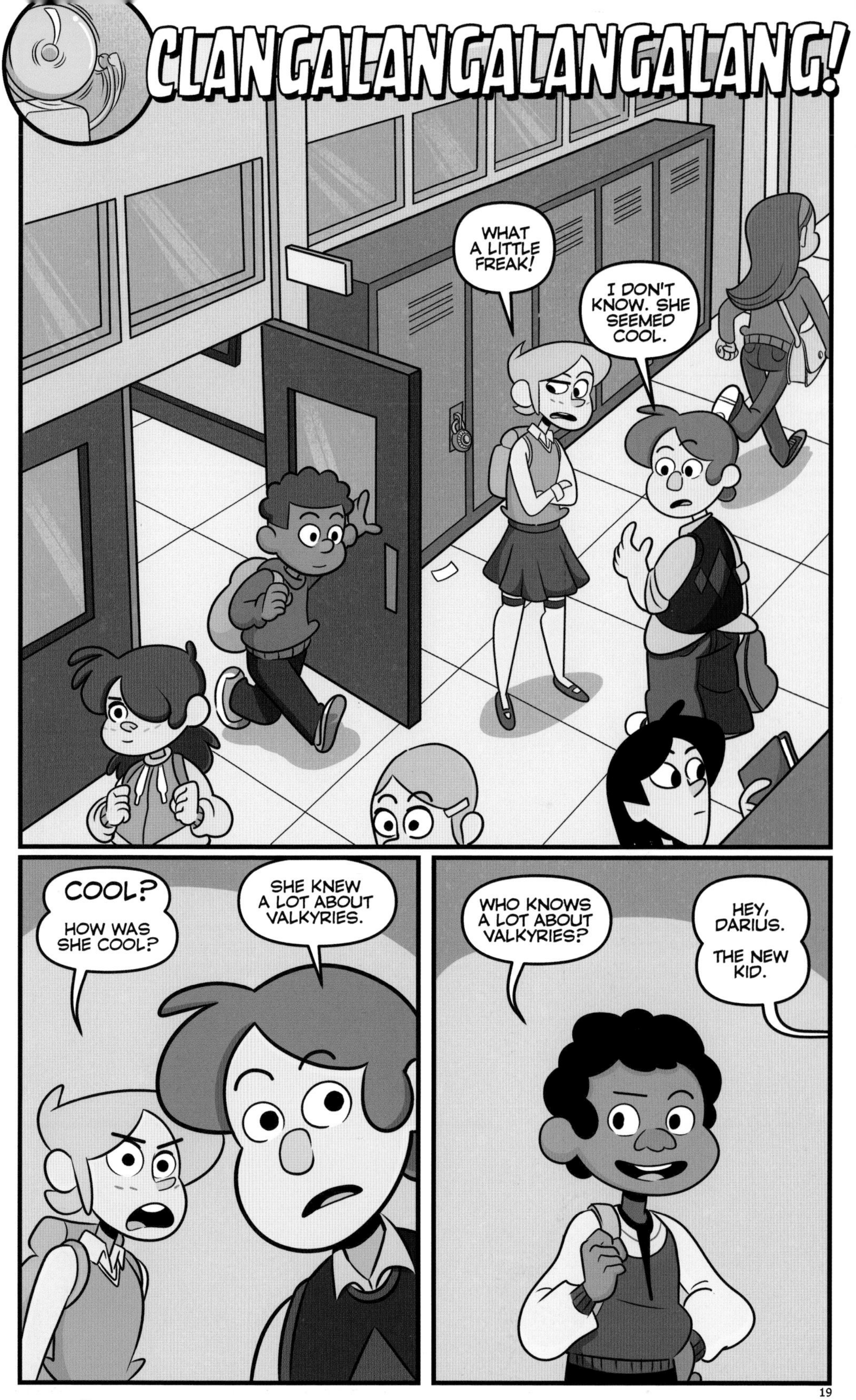
CLANGALANGALANGALANG!
WHAT A LITTLE FREAK!
I DON'T KNOW. SHE SEEMED COOL.
COOL? HOW WAS SHE COOL?
SHE KNEW A LOT ABOUT VALKYRIES.
WHO KNOWS A LOT ABOUT VALKYRIES?
HEY, DARIUS. THE NEW KID.

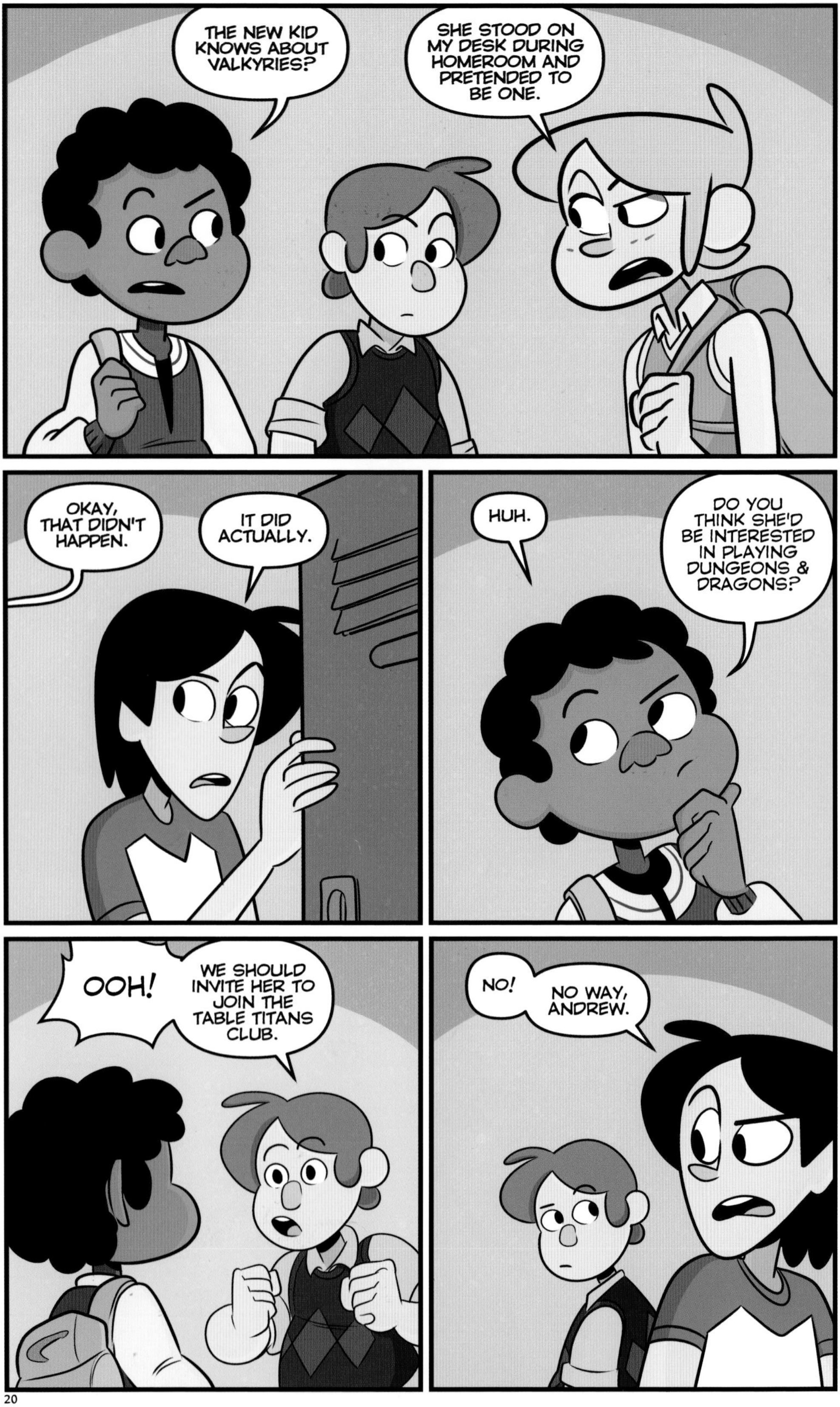
THE NEW KID KNOWS ABOUT VALKYRIES?
SHE STOOD ON MY DESK DURING HOMEROOM AND PRETENDED TO BE ONE.
OKAY, THAT DIDN'T HAPPEN.
IT DID ACTUALLY.
HUH.
DO YOU THINK SHE'D BE INTERESTED IN PLAYING DUNGEONS & DRAGONS?
OOH!
WE SHOULD INVITE HER TO JOIN THE TABLE TITANS CLUB.
NO!
NO WAY, ANDREW.

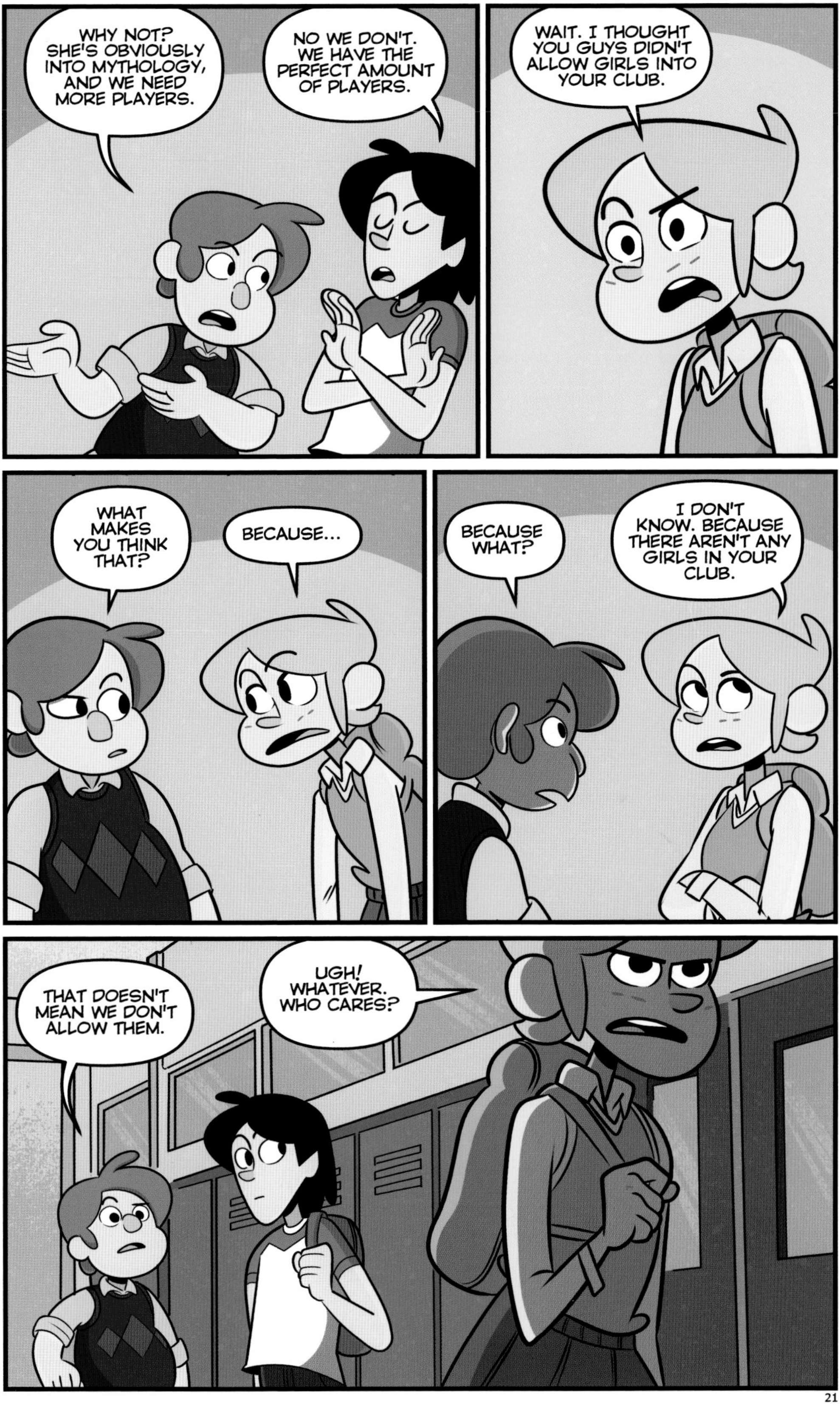
WHY NOT? SHE'S OBVIOUSLY INTO MYTHOLOGY, AND WE NEED MORE PLAYERS.
NO WE DON'T. WE HAVE THE PERFECT AMOUNT OF PLAYERS.
WAIT. I THOUGHT YOU GUYS DIDN'T ALLOW GIRLS INTO YOUR CLUB.
WHAT MAKES YOU THINK THAT?
BECAUSE...
BECAUSE WHAT?
I DON'T KNOW. BECAUSE THERE AREN'T ANY GIRLS IN YOUR CLUB.
THAT DOESN'T MEAN WE DON'T ALLOW THEM.
UGH! WHATEVER. WHO CARES?

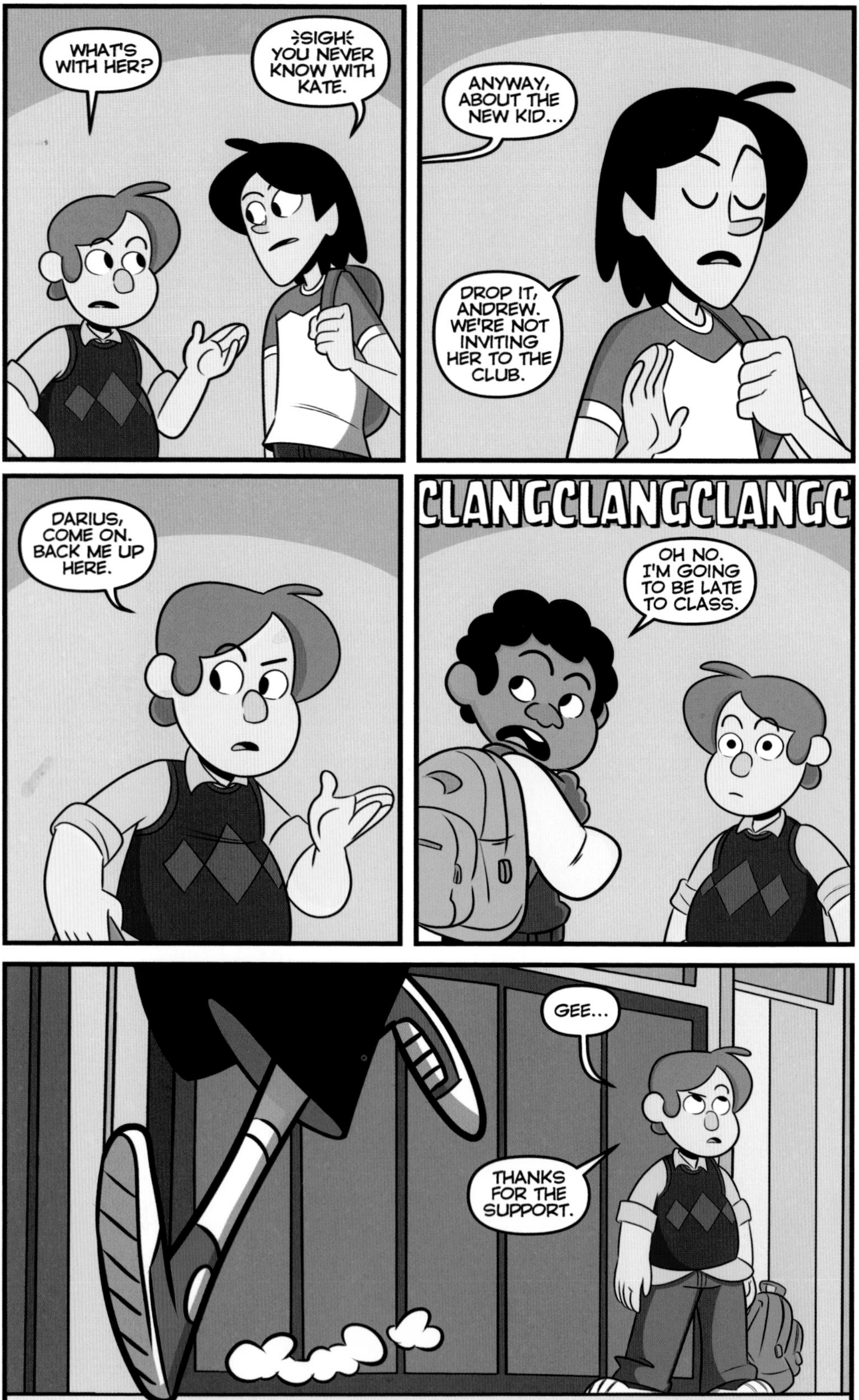
WHAT'S WITH HER?
SIGH YOU NEVER KNOW WITH KATE.
ANYWAY, ABOUT THE NEW KID...
DROP IT, ANDREW. WE'RE NOT INVITING HER TO THE CLUB.
DARIUS, COME ON. BACK ME UP HERE.
CLANGCLANGCLANGC
OH NO. I'M GOING TO BE LATE TO CLASS.
GEE...
THANKS FOR THE SUPPORT.

HISTORY: MR. SCHWEIZER

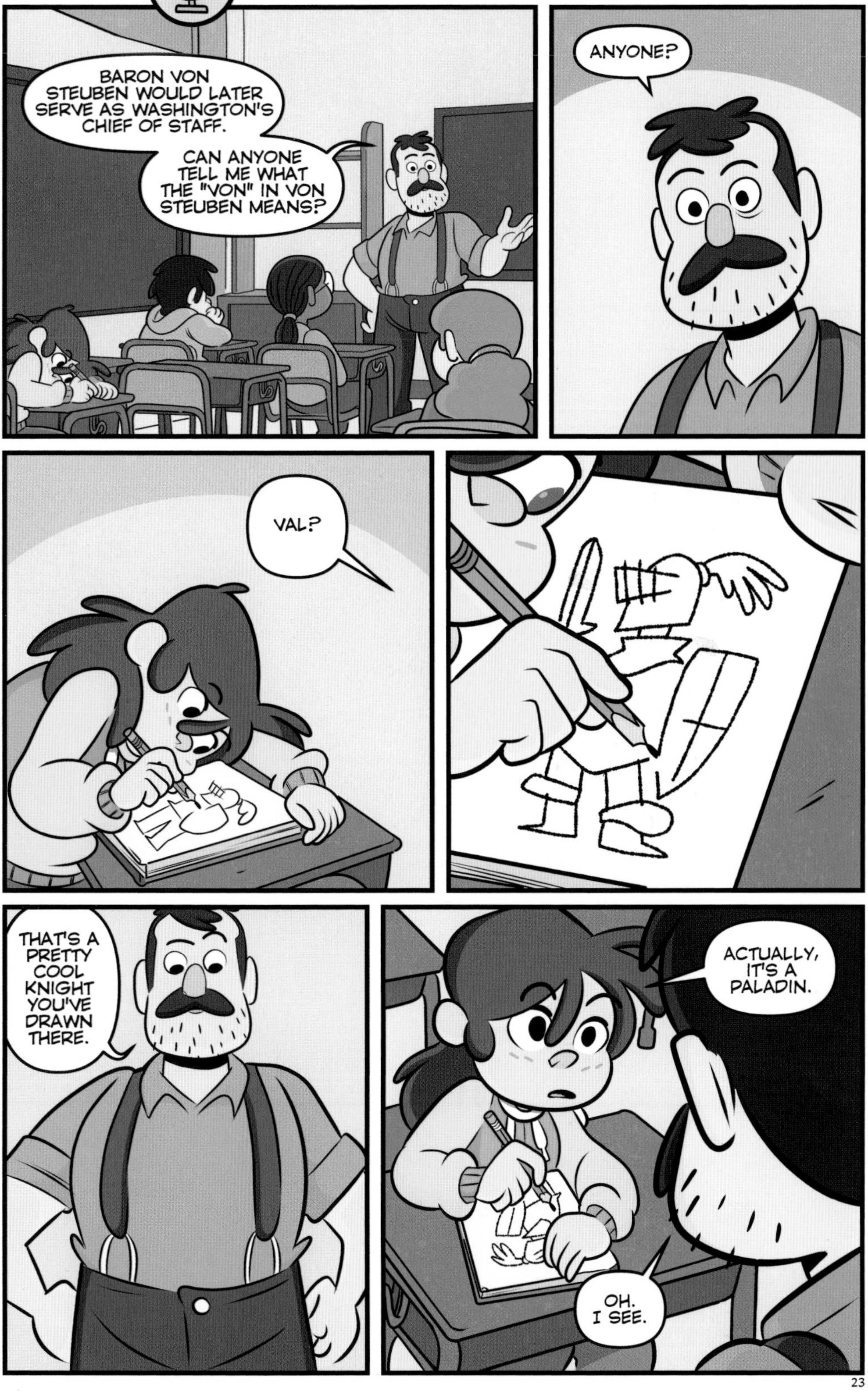
BARON VON STEUBEN WOULD LATER SERVE AS WASHINGTON'S CHIEF OF STAFF.
CAN ANYONE TELL ME WHAT THE "VON" IN VON STEUBEN MEANS?
ANYONE?
VAL?
THAT'S A PRETTY COOL KNIGHT YOU'VE DRAWN THERE.
ACTUALLY, IT'S A PALADIN.
OH. I SEE.

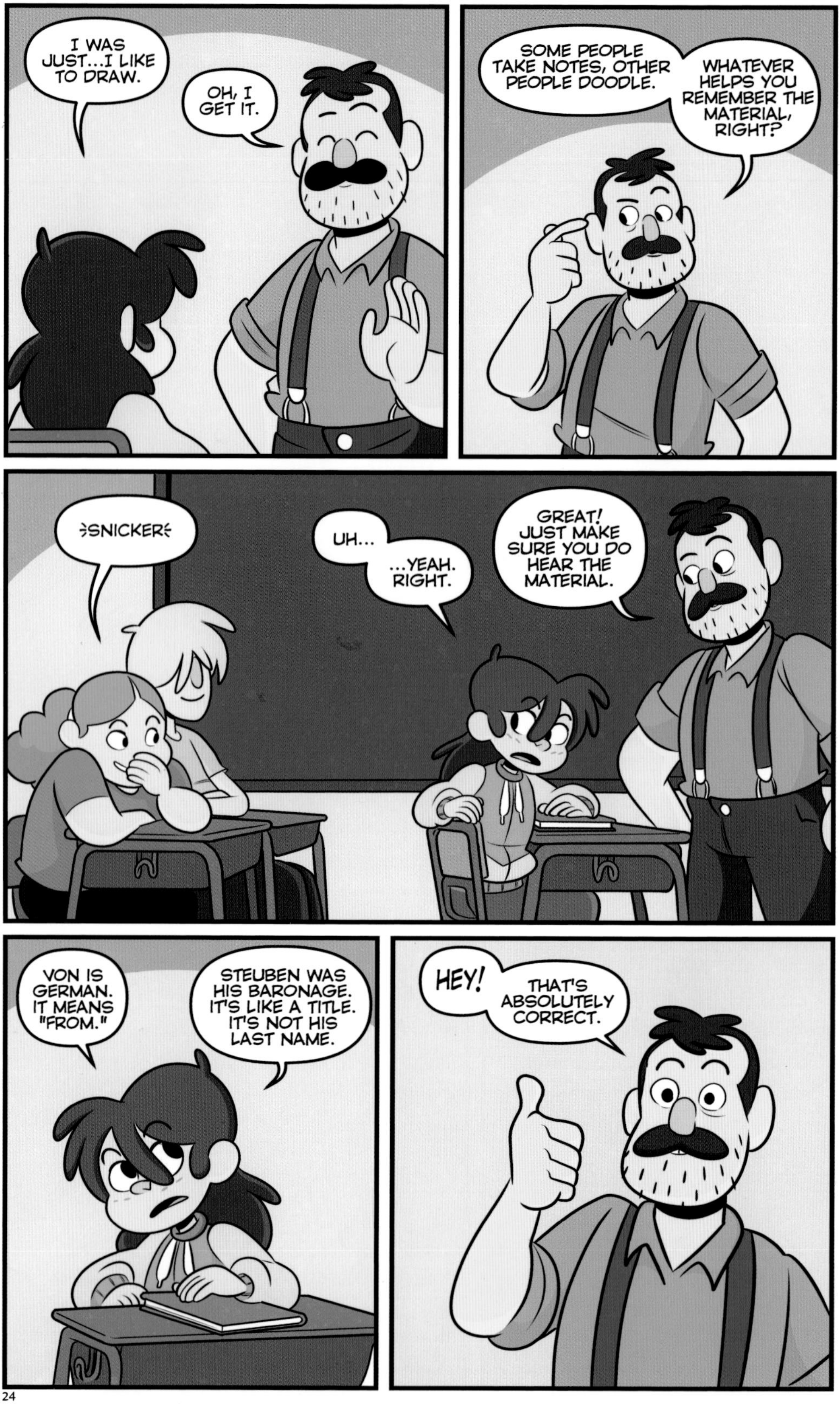
I WAS JUST...I LIKE TO DRAW.
OH, I GET IT.
SOME PEOPLE TAKE NOTES, OTHER PEOPLE DOODLE.
WHATEVER HELPS YOU REMEMBER THE MATERIAL, RIGHT?
SNICKER
UH...
...YEAH. RIGHT.
GREAT! JUST MAKE SURE YOU DO HEAR THE MATERIAL.
VON IS GERMAN. IT MEANS "FROM."
STEUBEN WAS HIS BARONAGE. IT'S LIKE A TITLE. IT'S NOT HIS LAST NAME.
HEY!
THAT'S ABSOLUTELY CORRECT.

LUNCHTIME

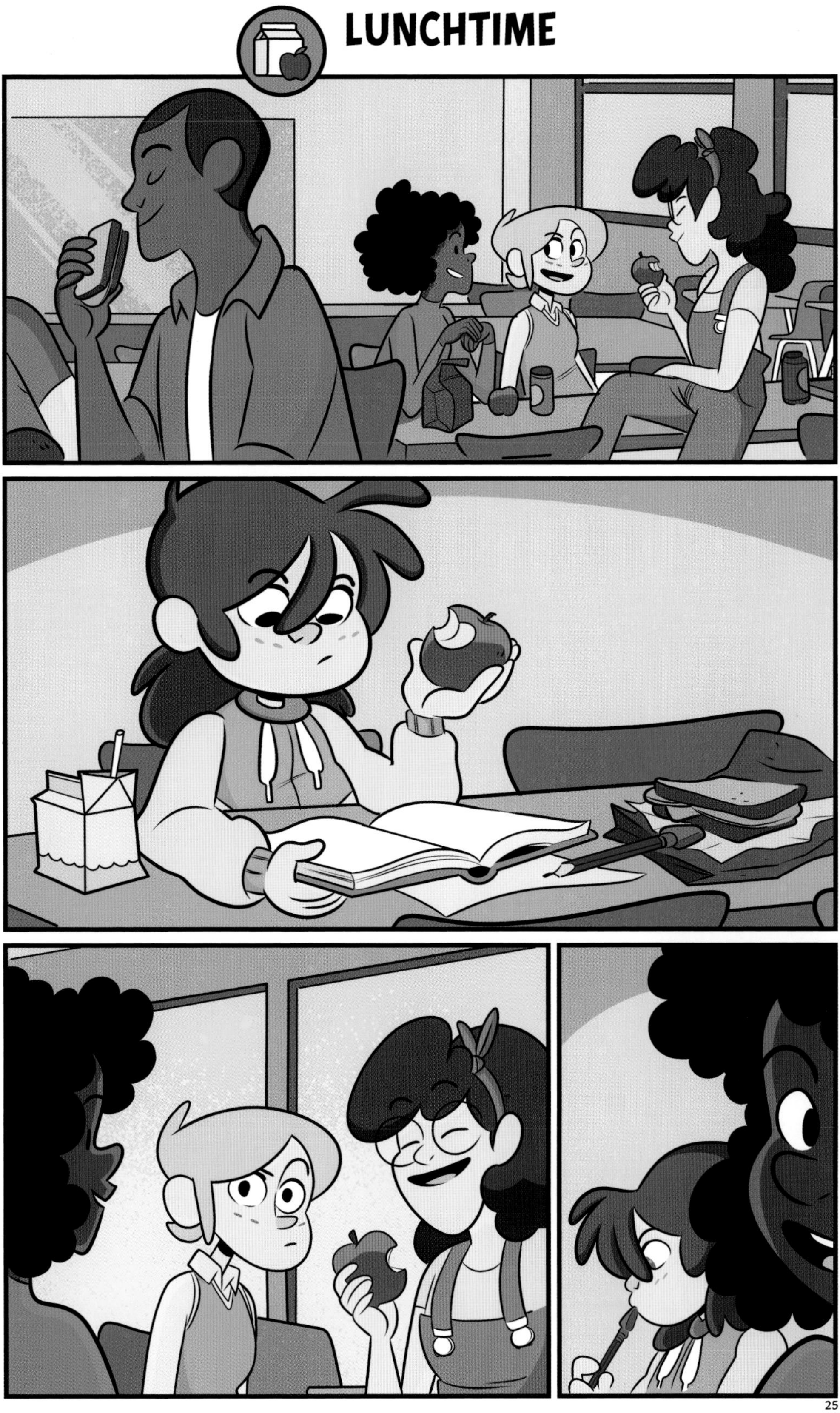

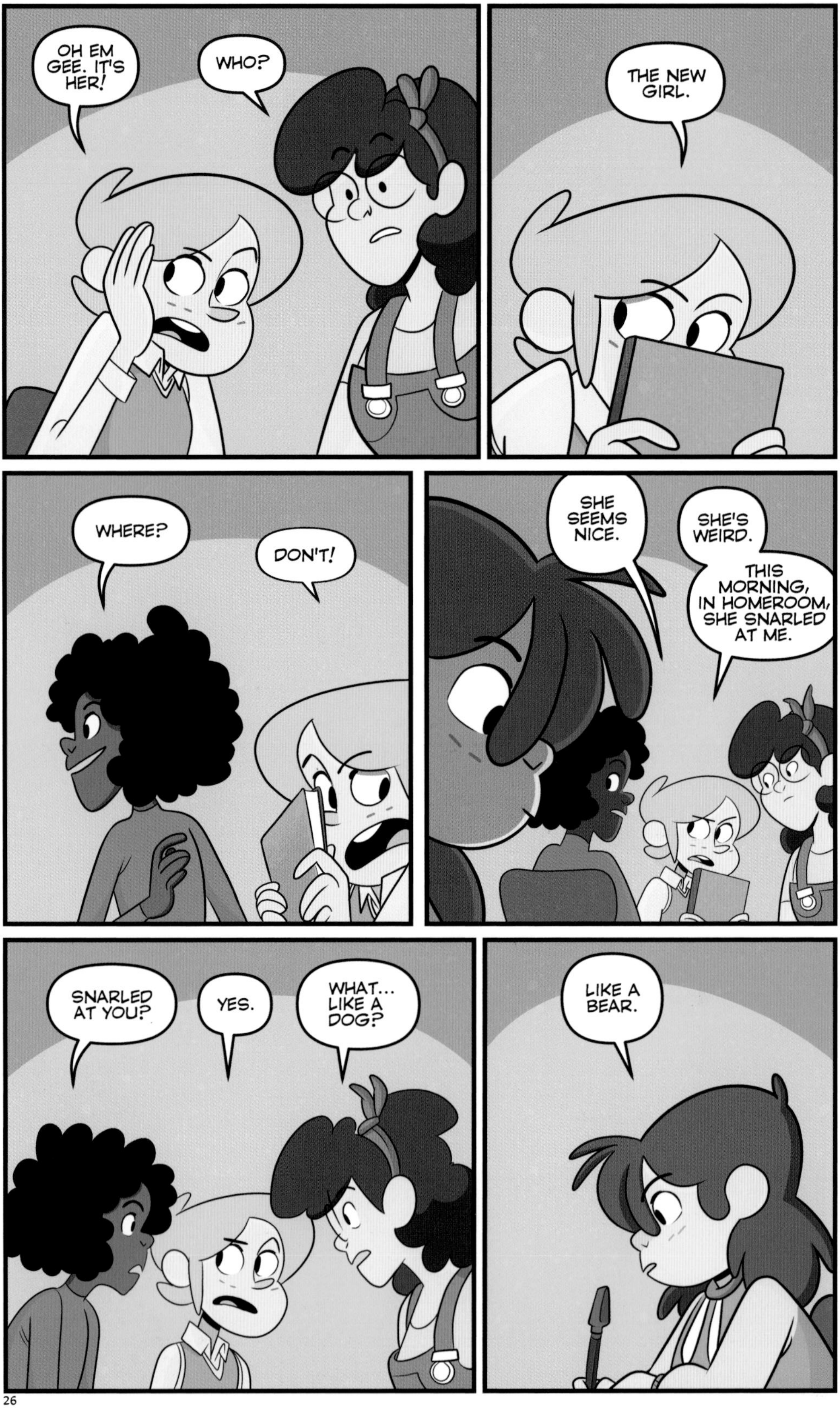
OH EM GEE. IT'S HER!
WHO?
THE NEW GIRL.
WHERE?
DON'T!
SHE SEEMS NICE.
SHE'S WEIRD.
THIS MORNING, IN HOMEROOM, SHE SNARLED AT ME.
SNARLED AT YOU?
YES.
WHAT... LIKE A DOG?
LIKE A BEAR.

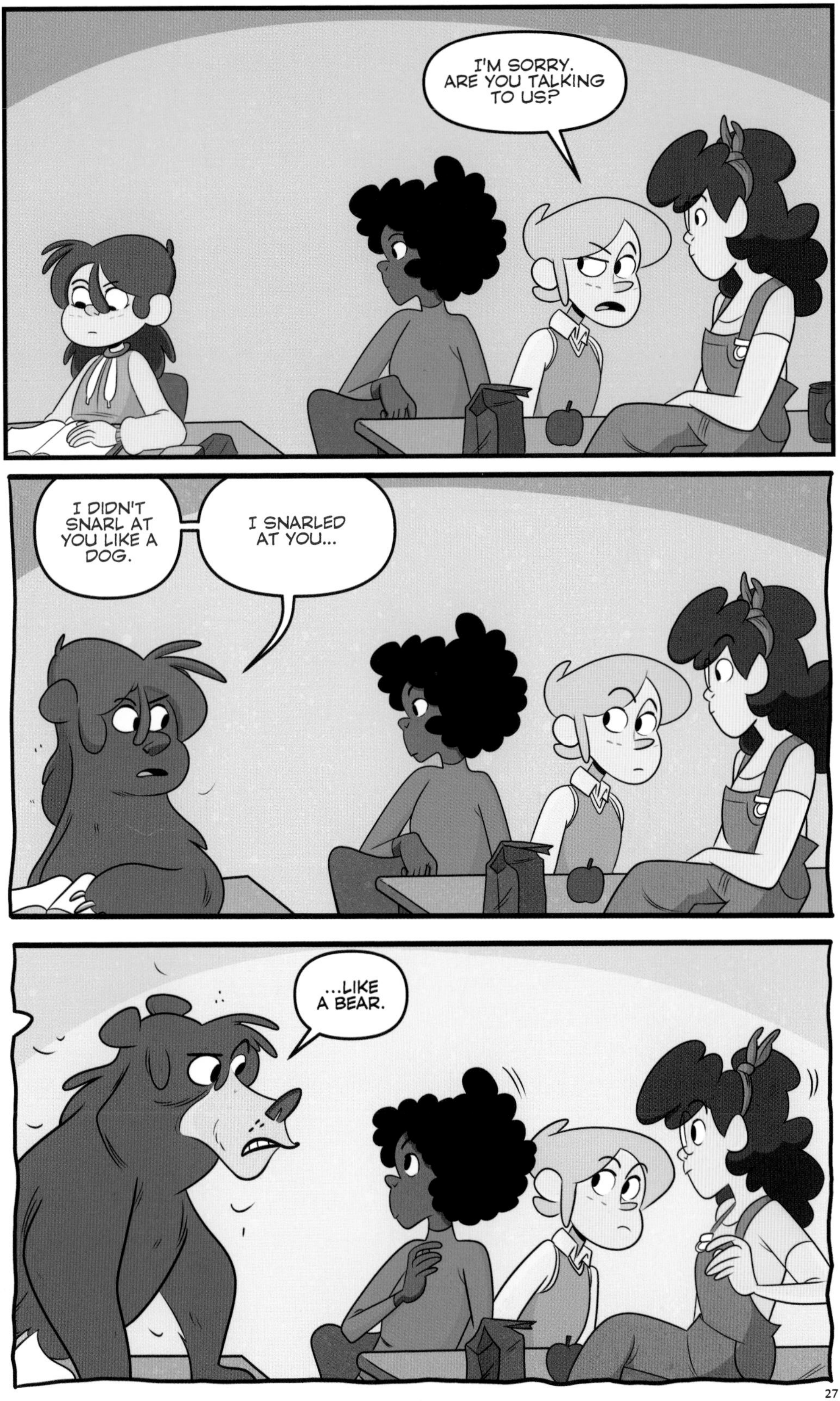
I'M SORRY. ARE YOU TALKING TO US?
I DIDN'T SNARL AT YOU LIKE A DOG.
I SNARLED AT YOU...
...LIKE A BEAR.

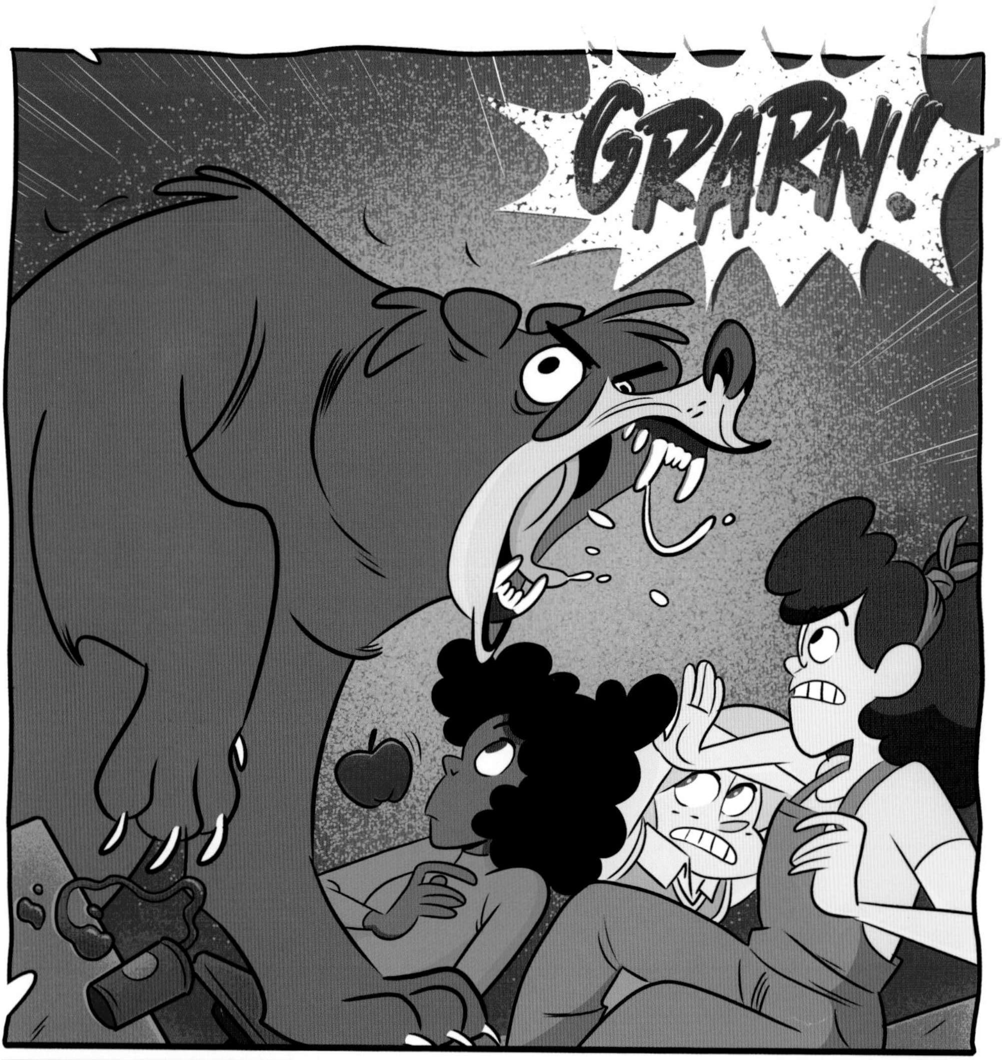
GRARN!

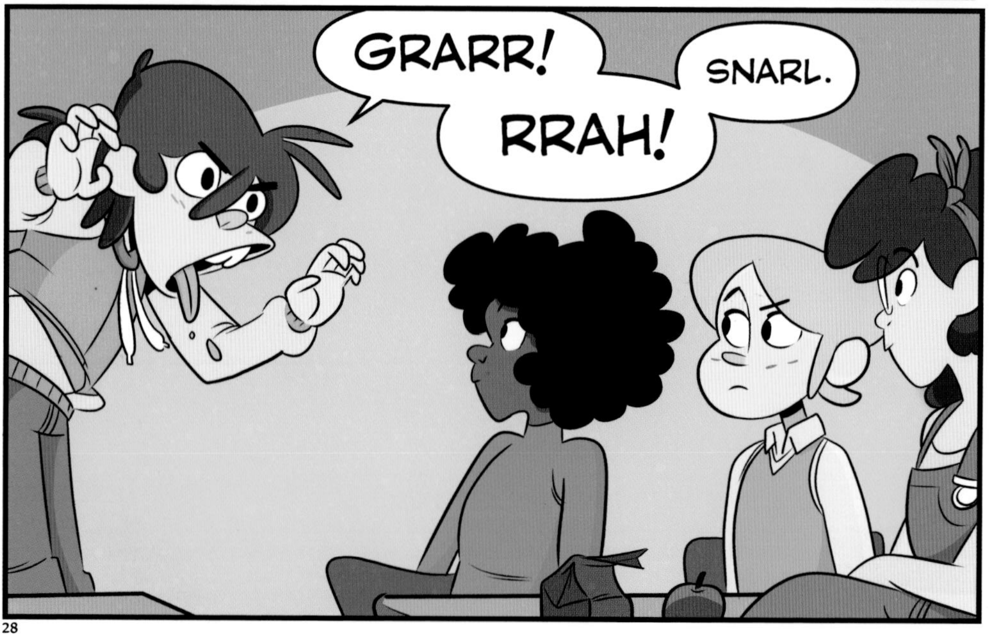
GRARR!
RRAH!
SNARL.

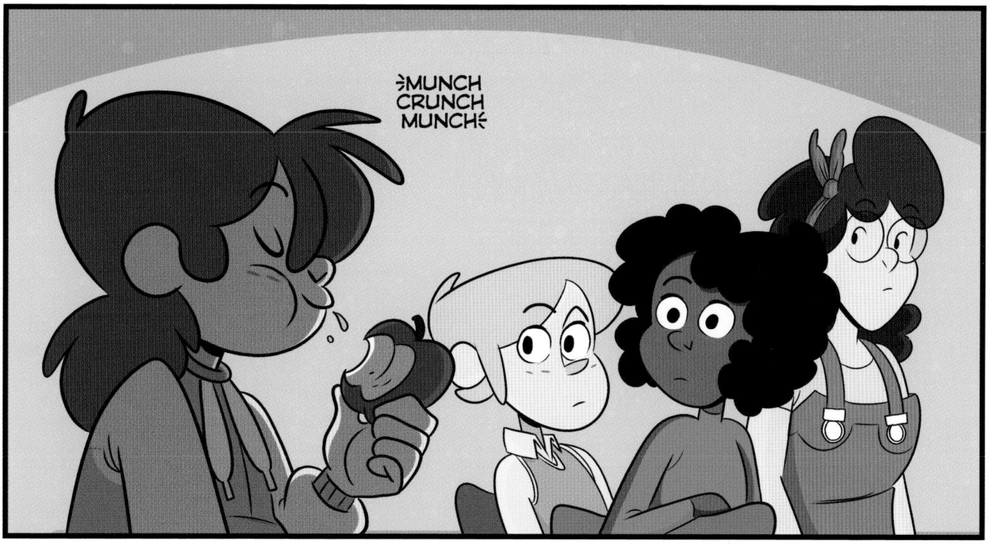
MUNCH
CRUNCH
MUNCH

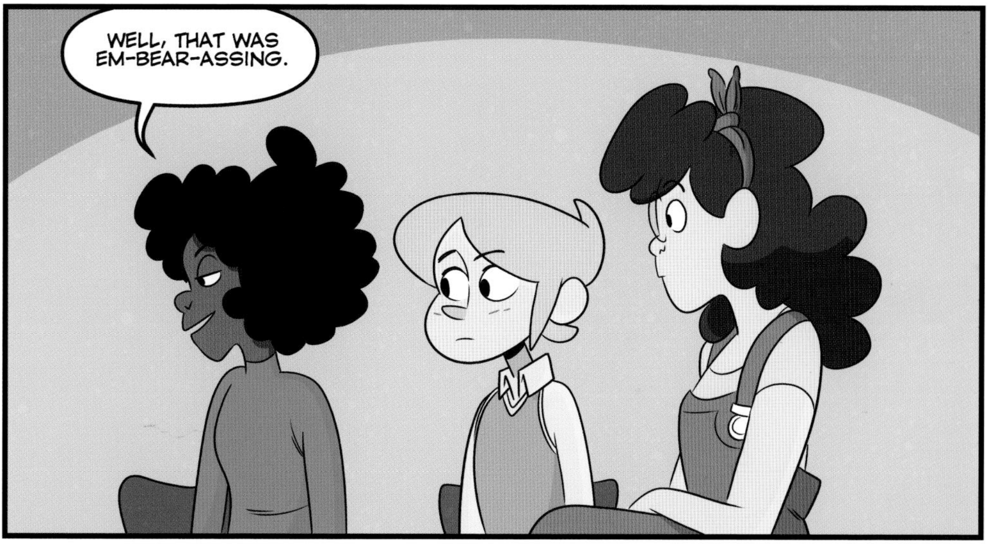
WELL, THAT WAS EM-BEAR-ASSING.

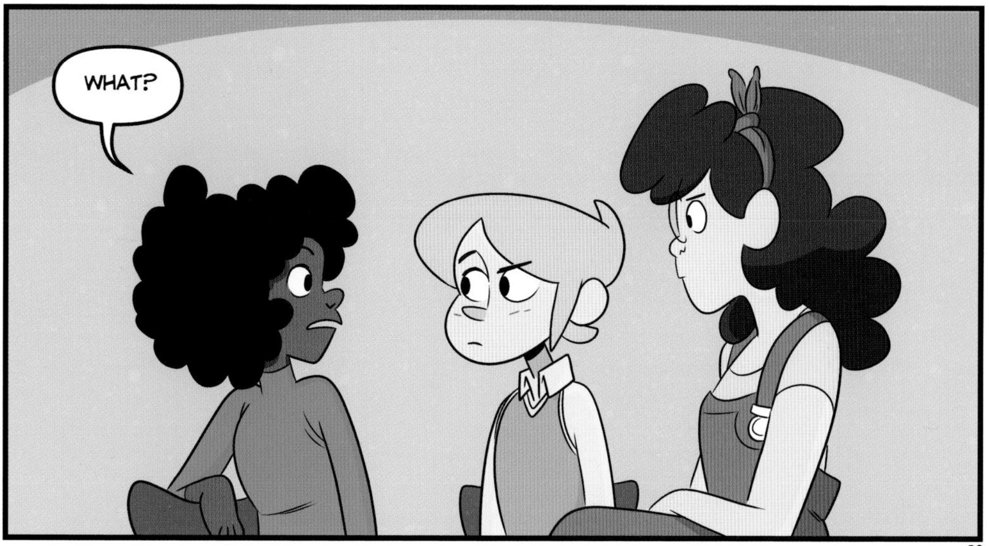
WHAT?

ENGLISH LIT: MR. STONE

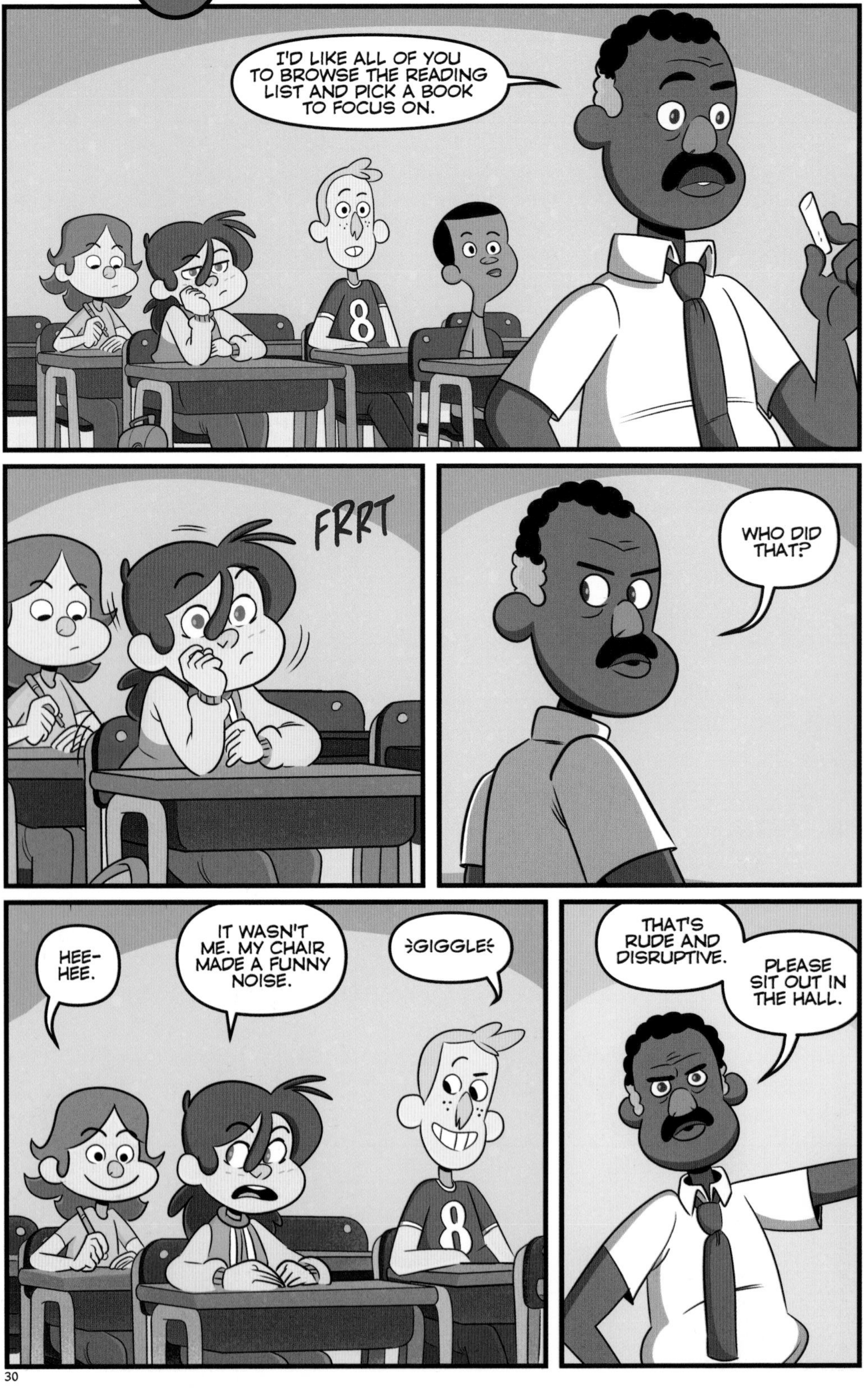
I'D LIKE ALL OF YOU TO BROWSE THE READING LIST AND PICK A BOOK TO FOCUS ON.
FRRT
WHO DID THAT?
HEE-HEE.
IT WASN'T ME. MY CHAIR MADE A FUNNY NOISE.
GIGGLE
THAT'S RUDE AND DISRUPTIVE.
PLEASE SIT OUT IN THE HALL.

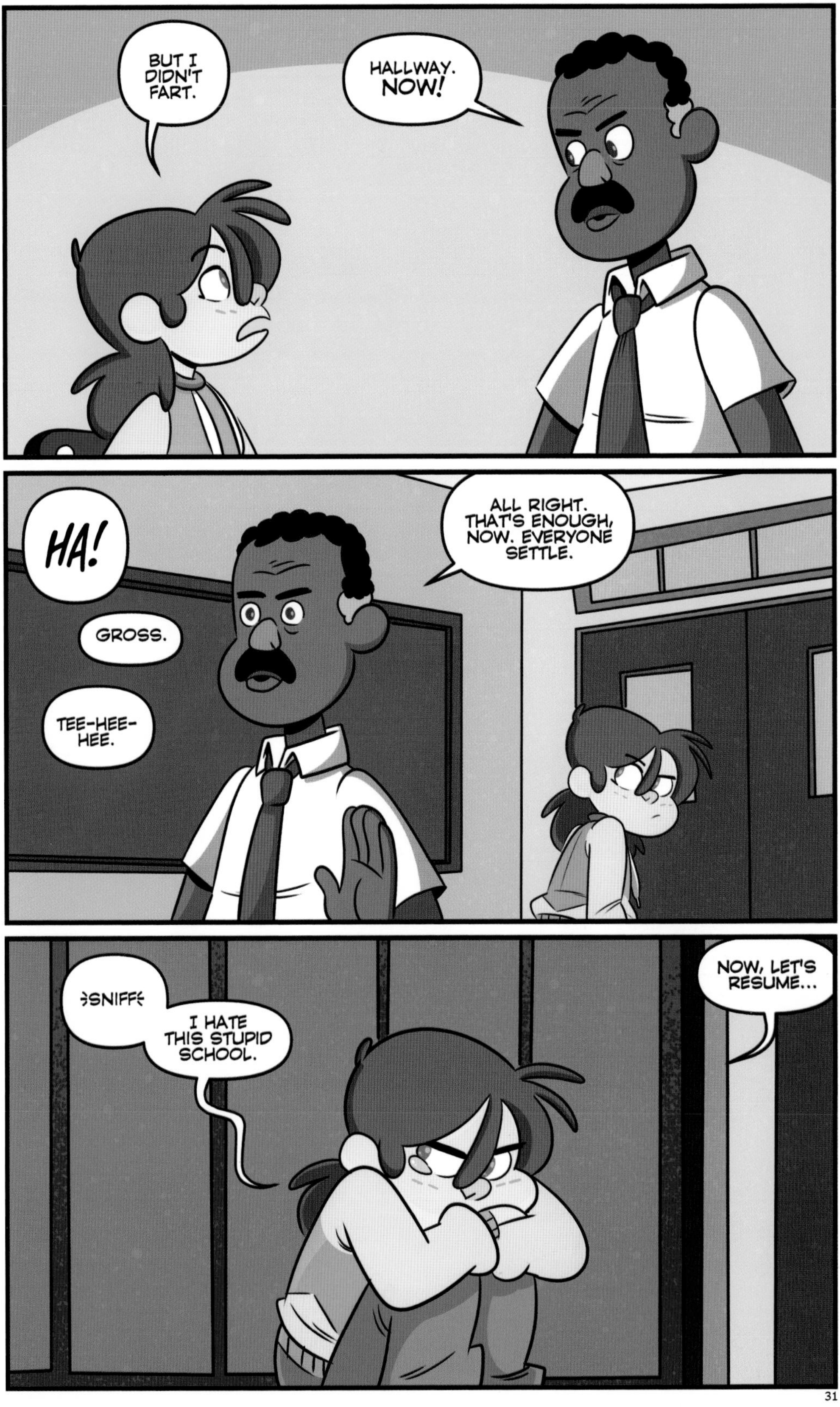
BUT I DIDN'T FART.
HALLWAY. NOW!
HA!
GROSS.
TEE-HEE-HEE.
ALL RIGHT. THAT'S ENOUGH, NOW. EVERYONE SETTLE.
NOW, LET'S RESUME...
SNIFF
I HATE THIS STUPID SCHOOL.

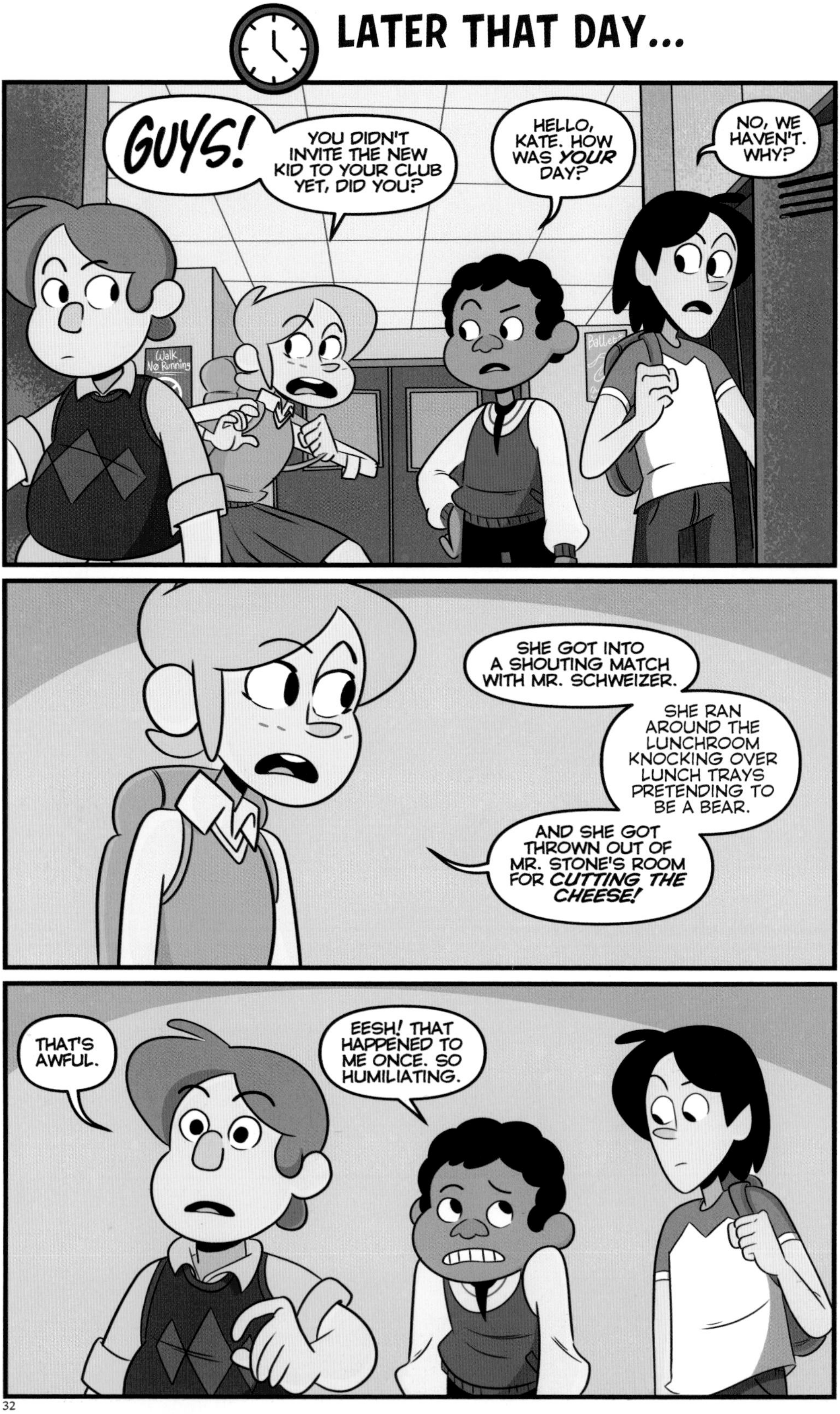
LATER THAT DAY...
GUYS!
YOU DIDN'T INVITE THE NEW KID TO YOUR CLUB YET, DID YOU?
HELLO, KATE. HOW WAS YOUR DAY?
NO, WE HAVEN'T. WHY?
Walk No Running
SHE GOT INTO A SHOUTING MATCH WITH MR. SCHWEIZER.
SHE RAN AROUND THE LUNCHROOM KNOCKING OVER LUNCH TRAYS PRETENDING TO BE A BEAR.
AND SHE GOT THROWN OUT OF MR. STONE'S ROOM FOR CUTTING THE CHEESE!
THAT'S AWFUL.
EESH! THAT HAPPENED TO ME ONCE. SO HUMILIATING.

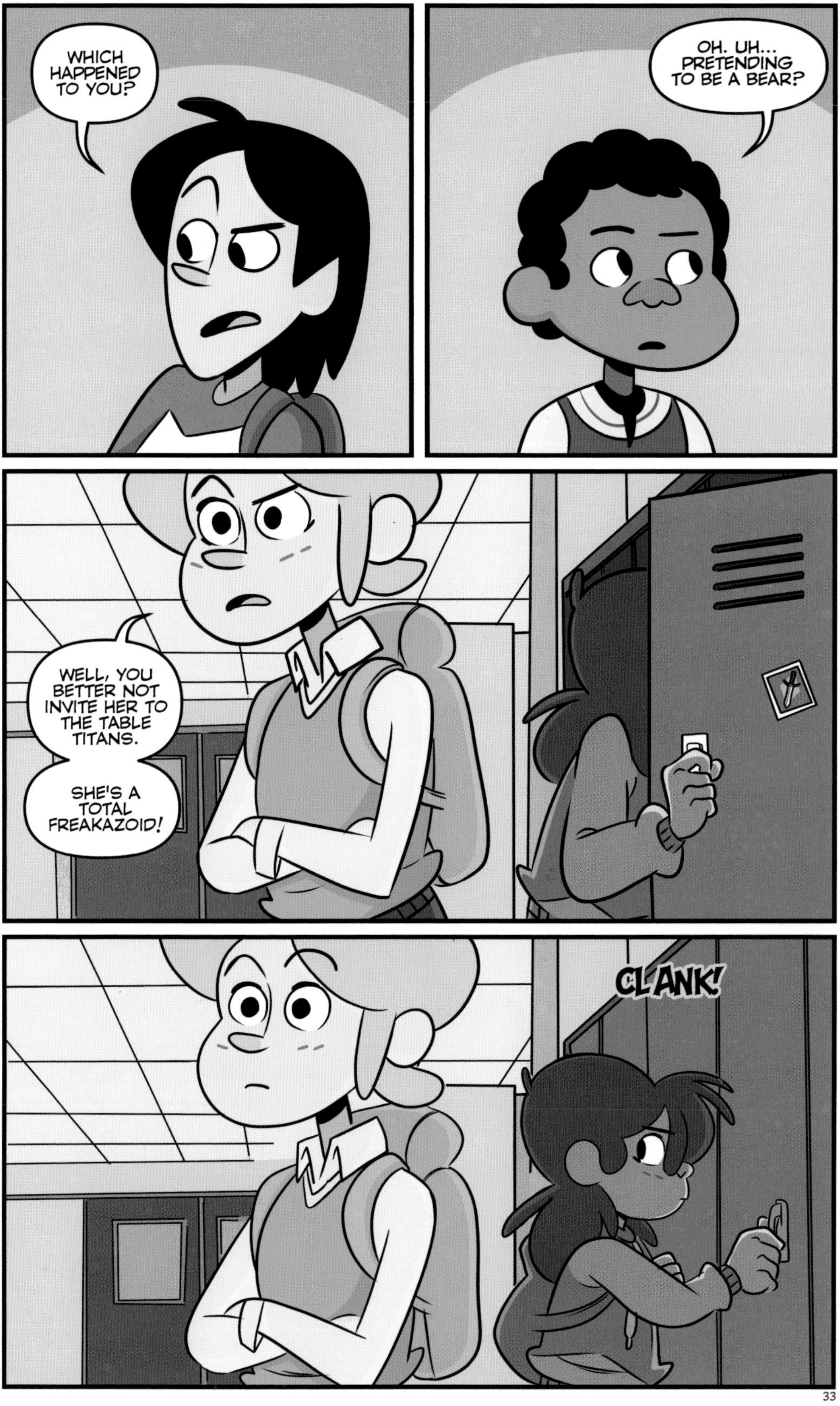
WHICH HAPPENED TO YOU?
OH. UH... PRETENDING TO BE A BEAR?
WELL, YOU BETTER NOT INVITE HER TO THE TABLE TITANS.
SHE'S A TOTAL FREAKAZOID!
CLANK!

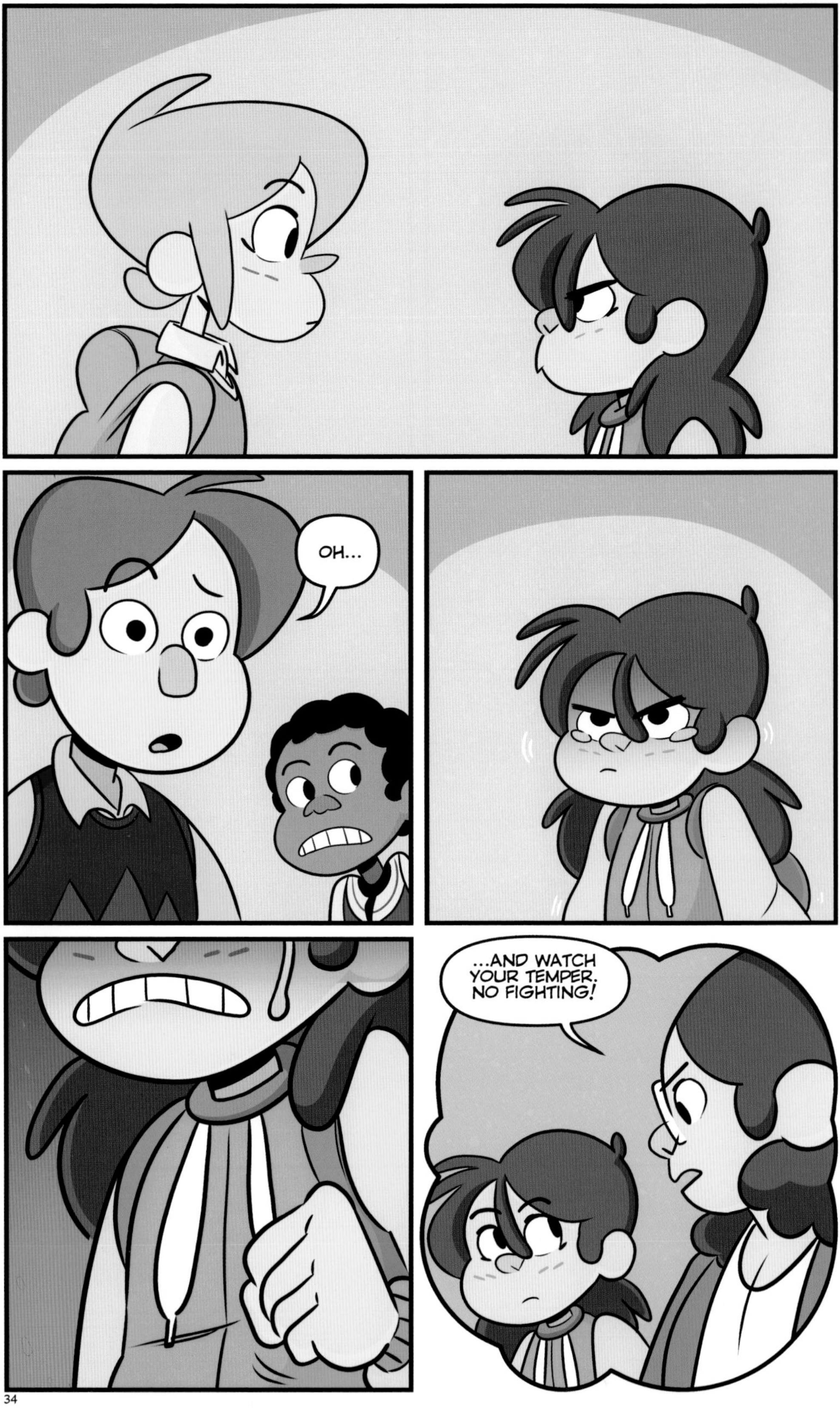
OH...
...AND WATCH YOUR TEMPER. NO FIGHTING!

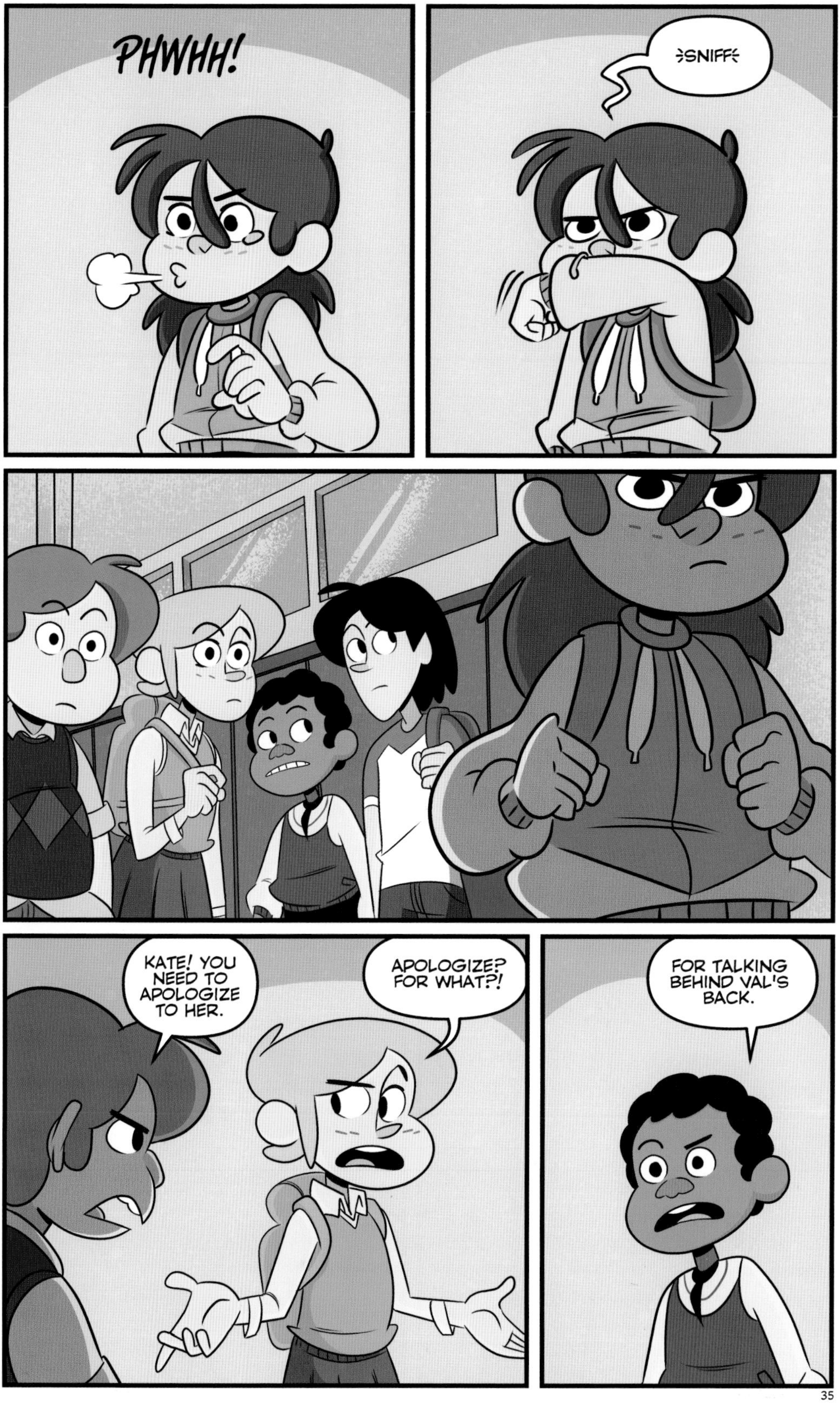
PHWHH!
SNIFF
KATE! YOU NEED TO APOLOGIZE TO HER.
APOLOGIZE? FOR WHAT?!
FOR TALKING BEHIND VAL'S BACK.

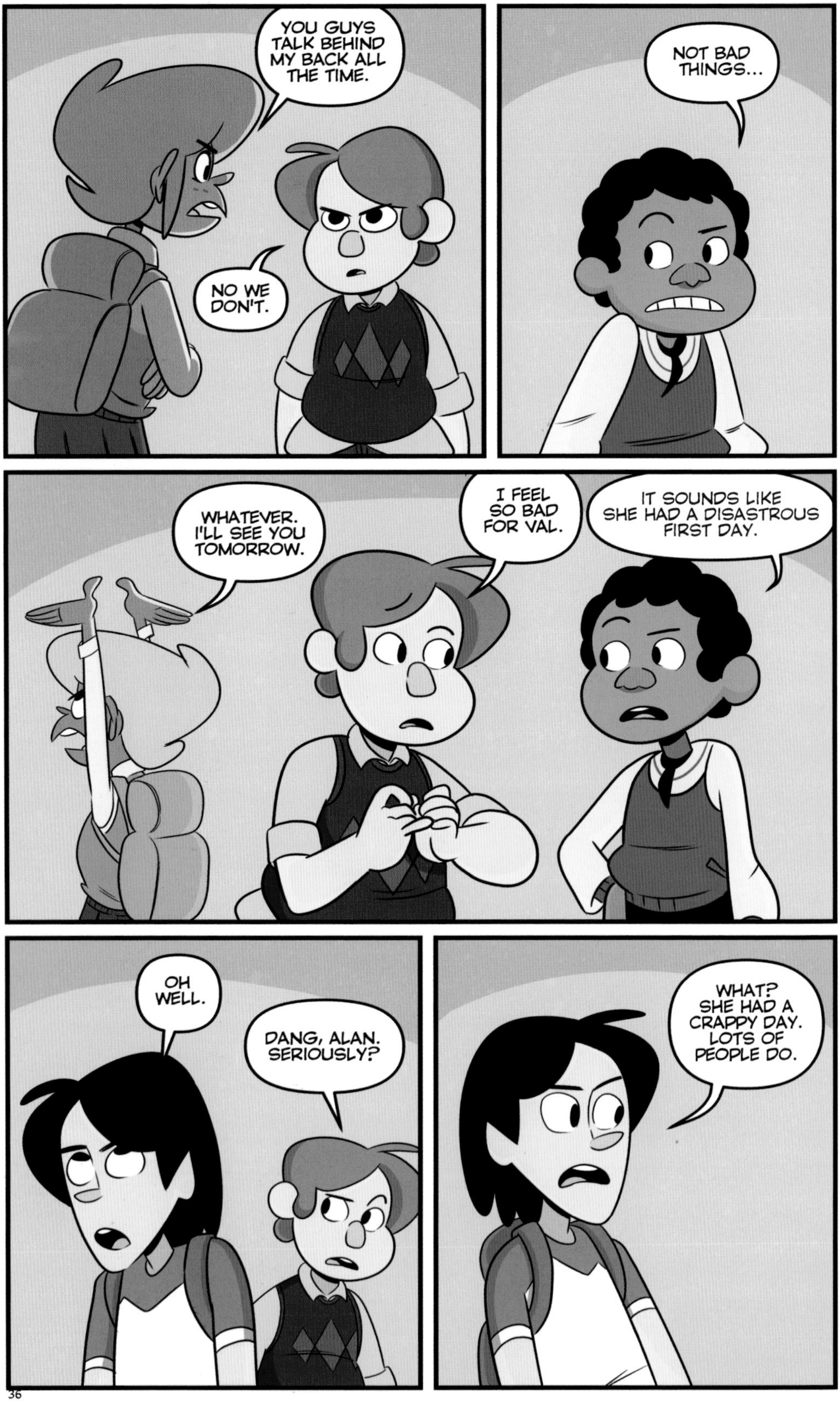
YOU GUYS TALK BEHIND MY BACK ALL THE TIME.
NO WE DON'T.
NOT BAD THINGS...
WHATEVER. I'LL SEE YOU TOMORROW.
I FEEL SO BAD FOR VAL.
IT SOUNDS LIKE SHE HAD A DISASTROUS FIRST DAY.
OH WELL.
DANG, ALAN. SERIOUSLY?
WHAT? SHE HAD A CRAPPY DAY. LOTS OF PEOPLE DO.

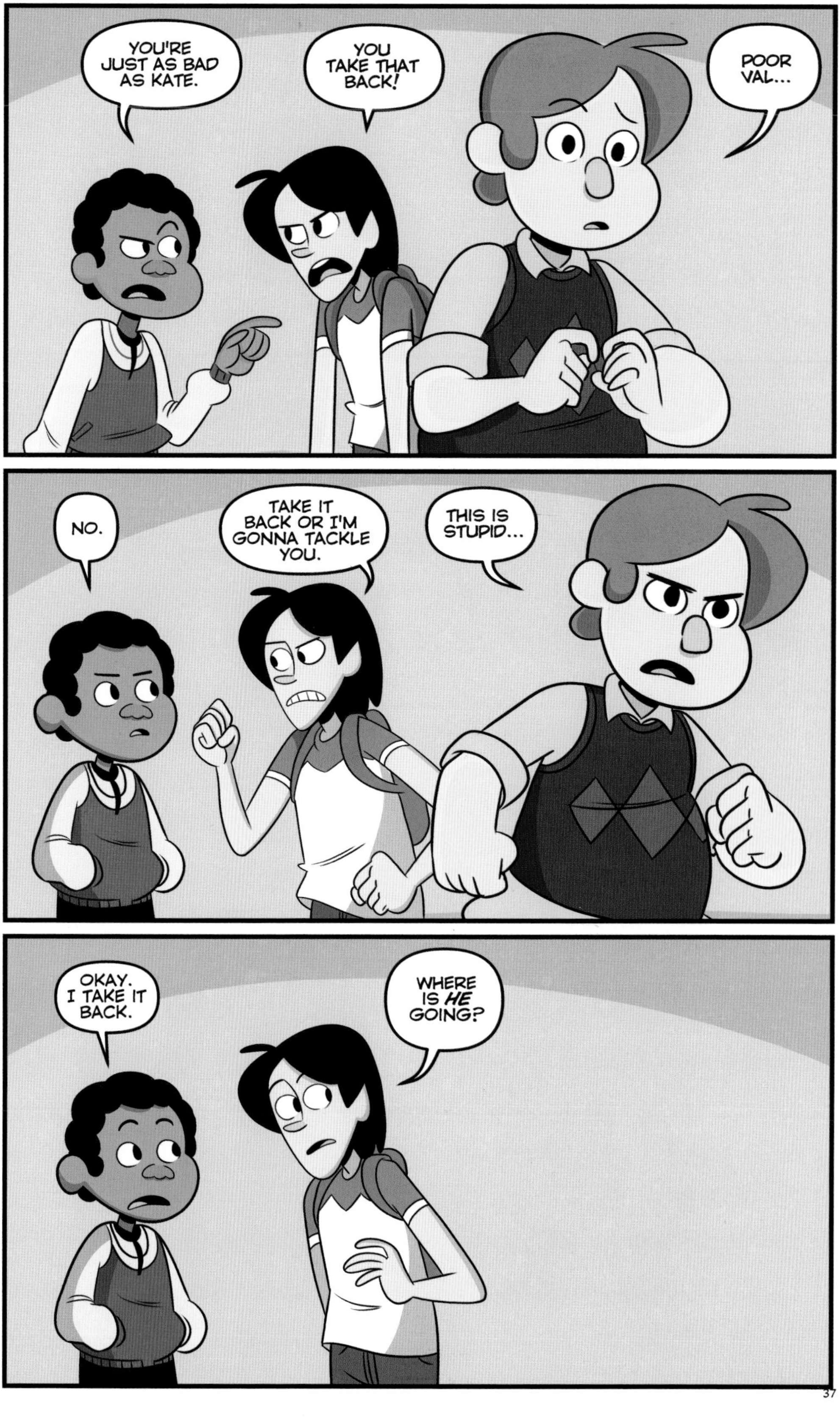
YOU'RE JUST AS BAD AS KATE.
YOU TAKE THAT BACK!
POOR VAL...
NO.
TAKE IT BACK OR I'M GONNA TACKLE YOU.
THIS IS STUPID...
OKAY. I TAKE IT BACK.
WHERE IS *HE* GOING?

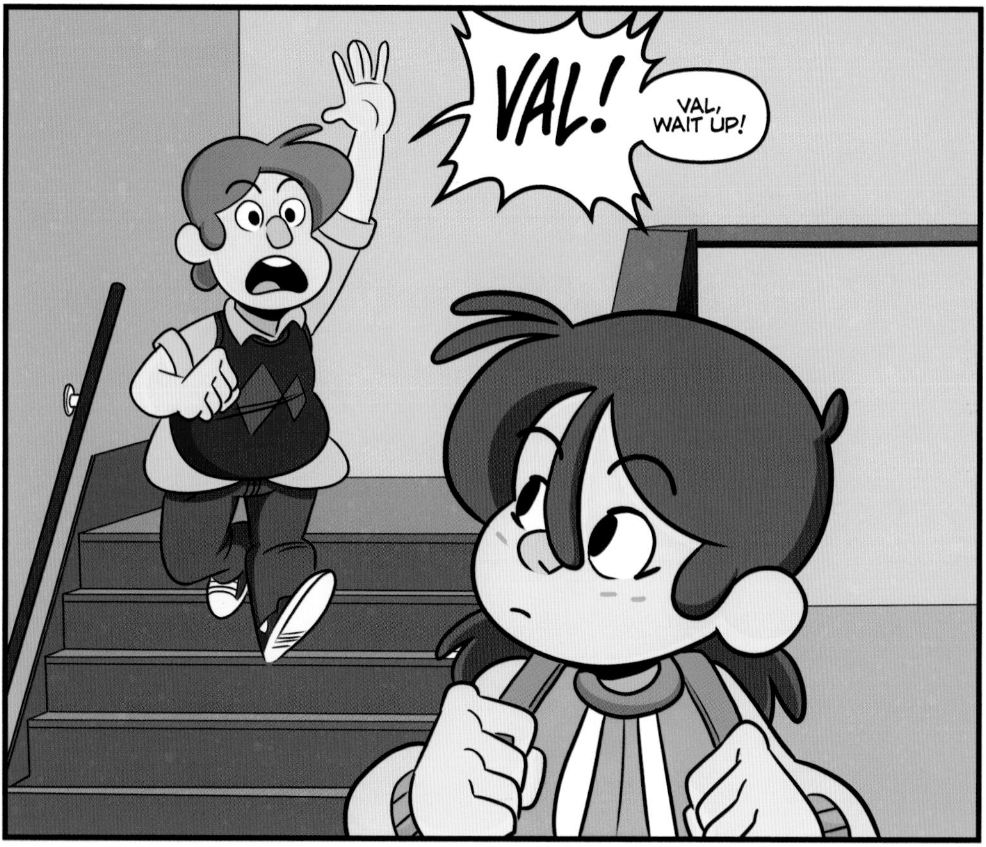
VAL!
VAL, WAIT UP!

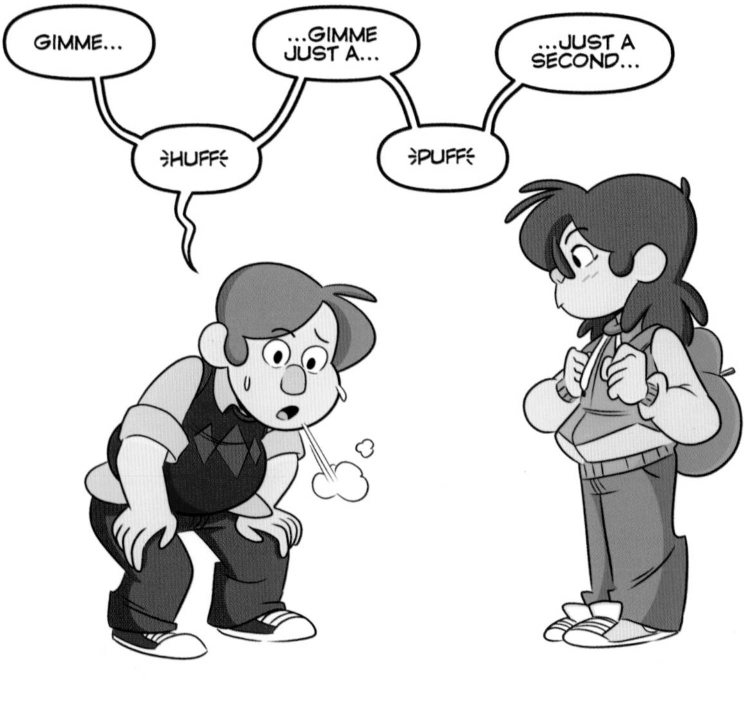
GIMME...
HUFF
...GIMME JUST A...
PUFF
...JUST A SECOND...

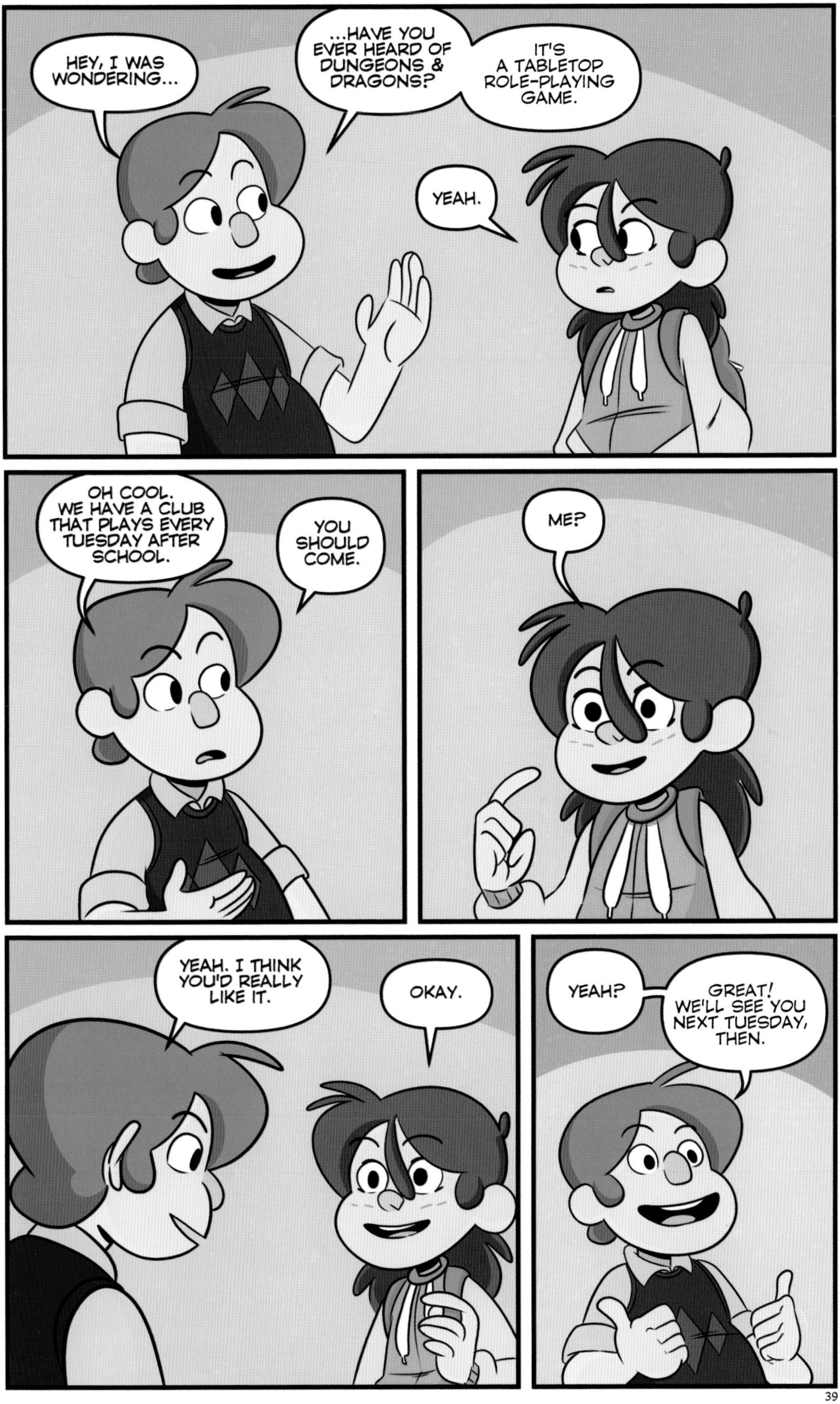
HEY, I WAS WONDERING...
...HAVE YOU EVER HEARD OF DUNGEONS & DRAGONS?
IT'S A TABLETOP ROLE-PLAYING GAME.
YEAH.
OH COOL. WE HAVE A CLUB THAT PLAYS EVERY TUESDAY AFTER SCHOOL.
YOU SHOULD COME.
ME?
YEAH. I THINK YOU'D REALLY LIKE IT.
OKAY.
YEAH?
GREAT! WE'LL SEE YOU NEXT TUESDAY, THEN.

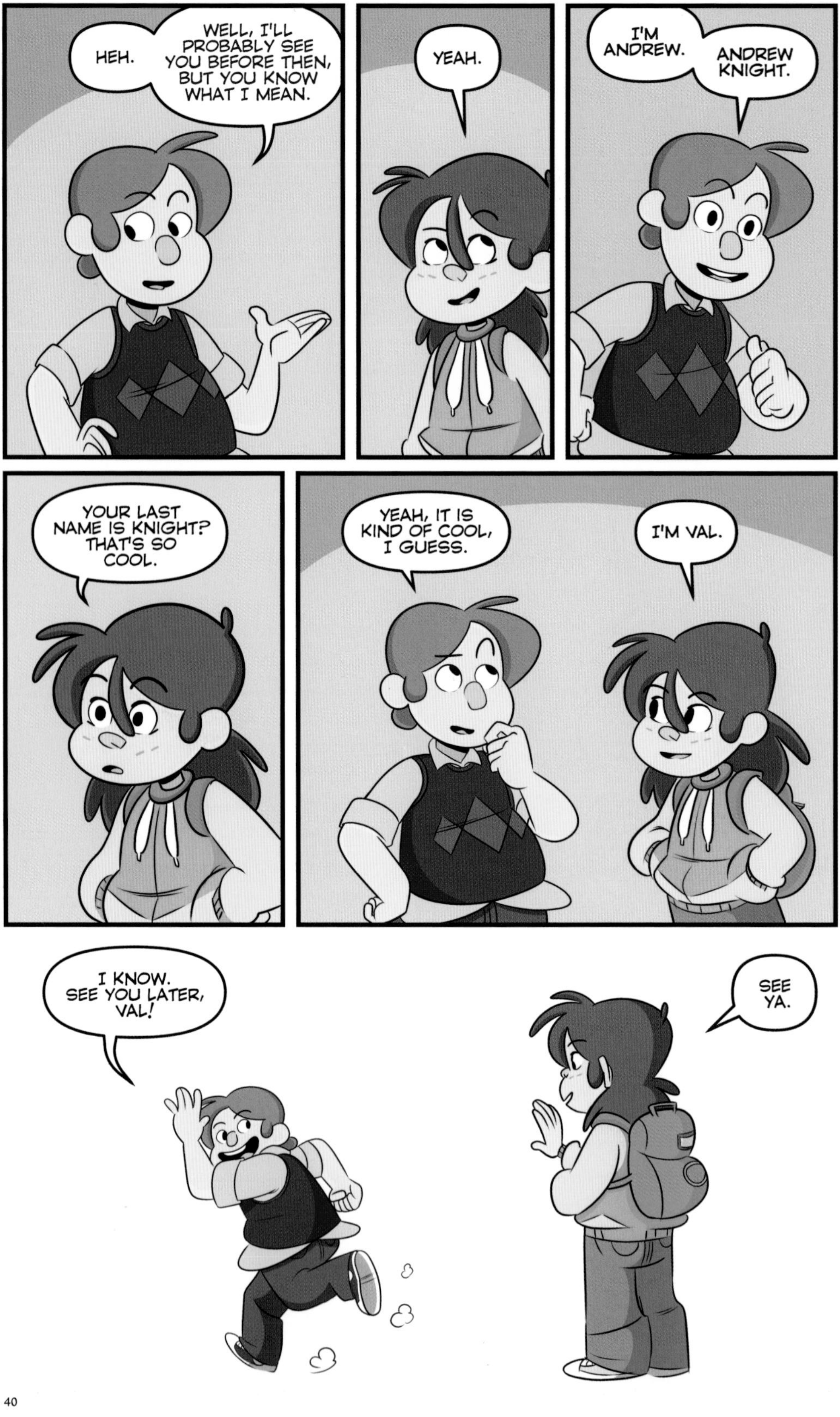
HEH.
WELL, I'LL PROBABLY SEE YOU BEFORE THEN, BUT YOU KNOW WHAT I MEAN.
YEAH.
I'M ANDREW.
ANDREW KNIGHT.
YOUR LAST NAME IS KNIGHT? THAT'S SO COOL.
YEAH, IT IS KIND OF COOL, I GUESS.
I'M VAL.
I KNOW. SEE YOU LATER, VAL!
SEE YA.

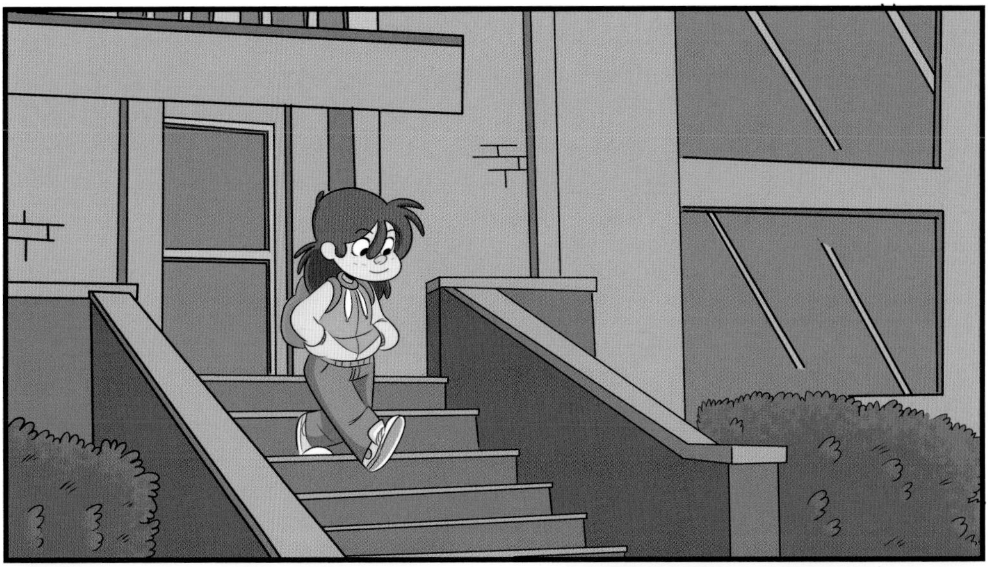
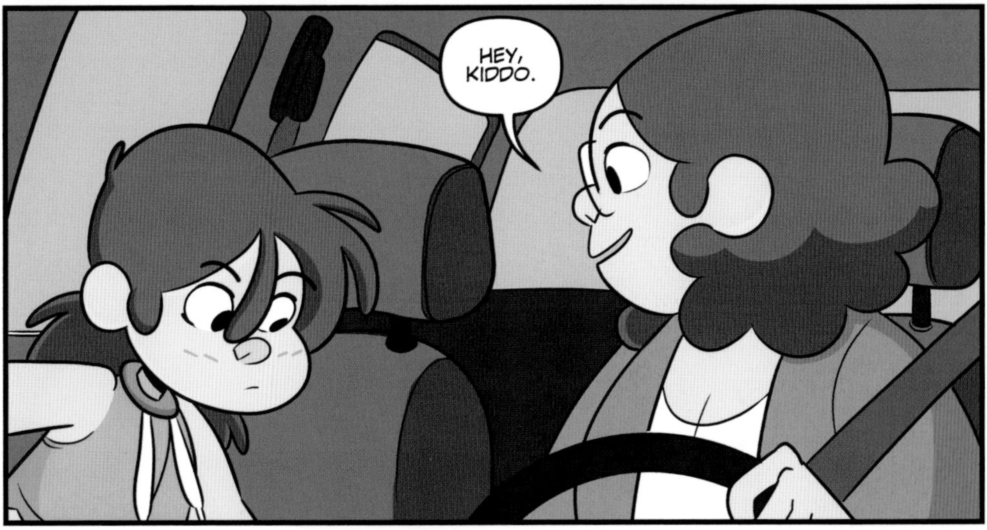
HEY, KIDDO.
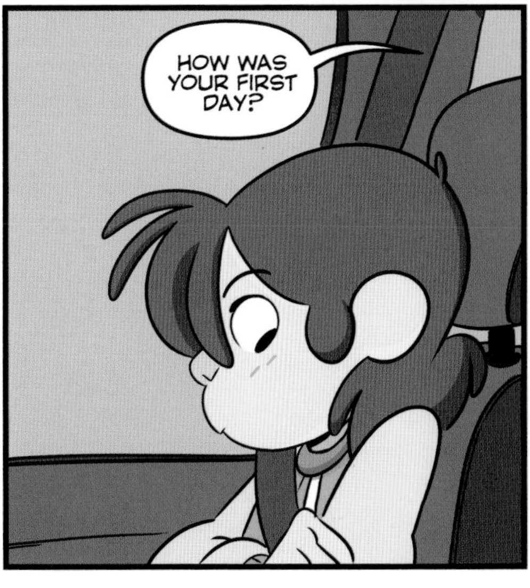
HOW WAS YOUR FIRST DAY?
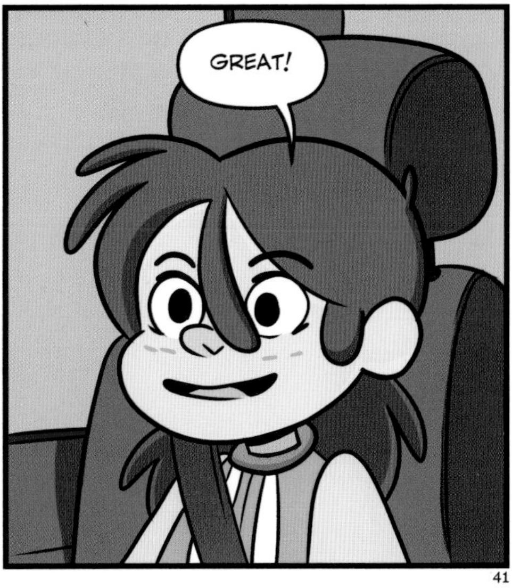
GREAT!

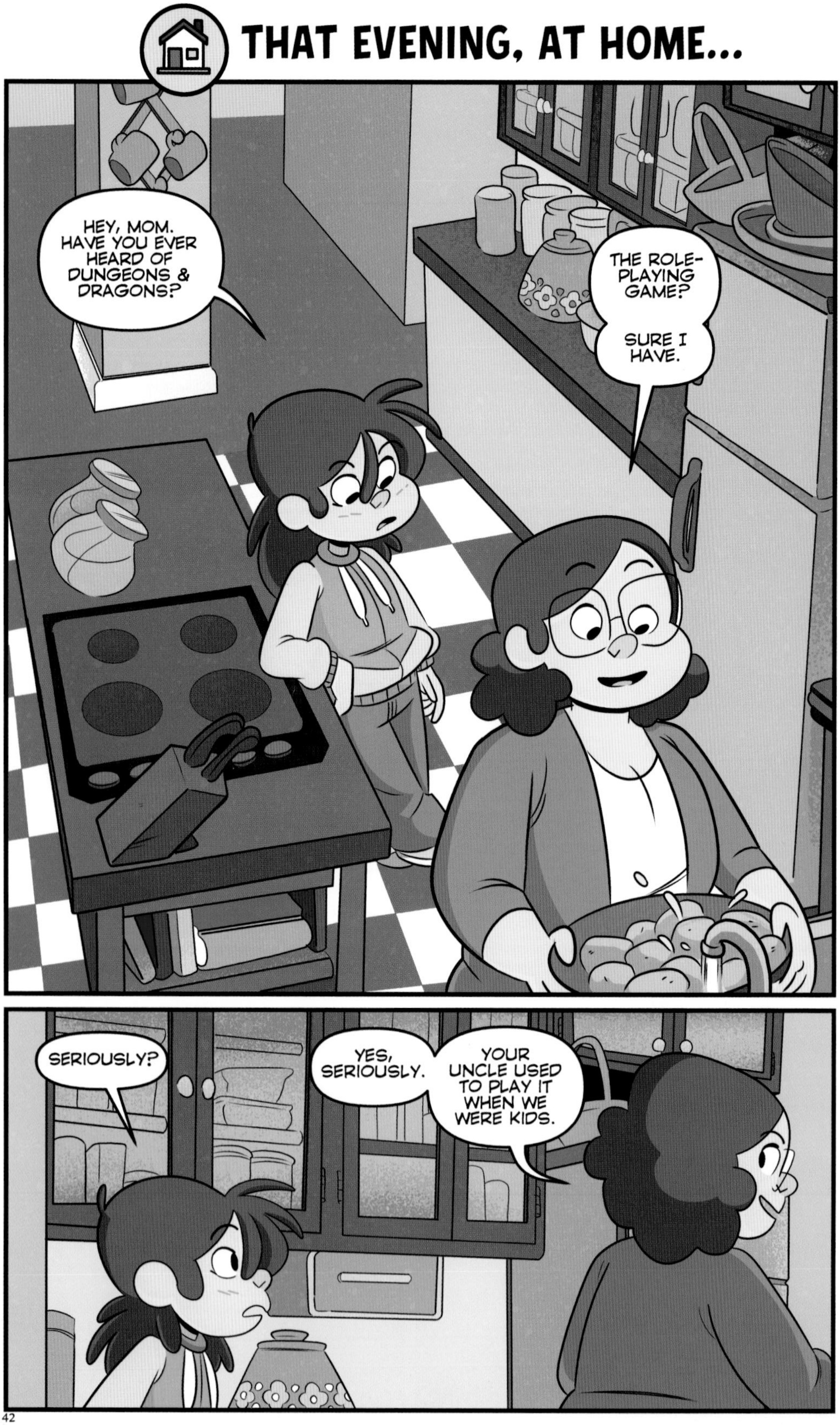
THAT EVENING, AT HOME...
HEY, MOM. HAVE YOU EVER HEARD OF DUNGEONS & DRAGONS?
THE ROLE-PLAYING GAME?
SURE I HAVE.
SERIOUSLY?
YES, SERIOUSLY.
YOUR UNCLE USED TO PLAY IT WHEN WE WERE KIDS.

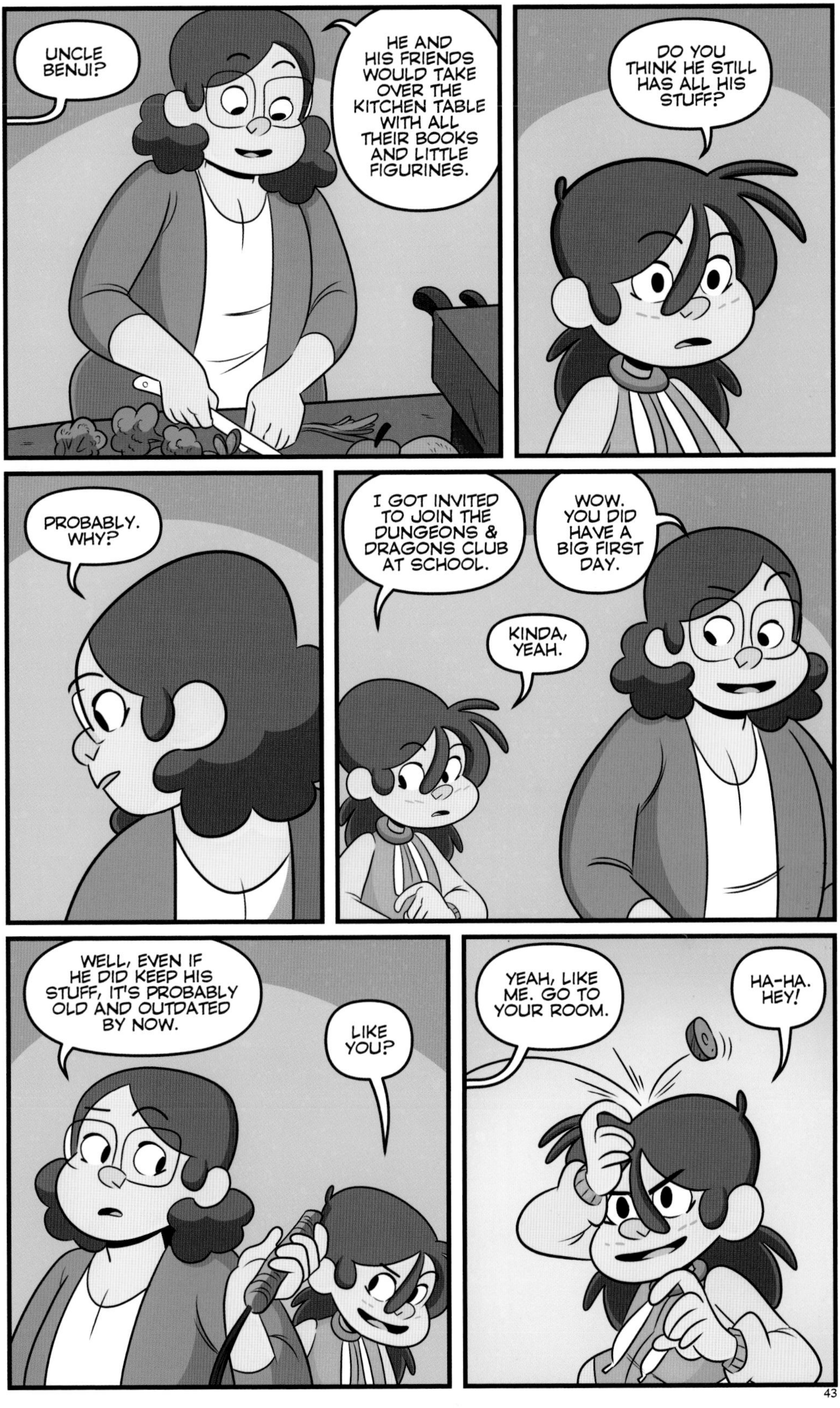
UNCLE BENJI?
HE AND HIS FRIENDS WOULD TAKE OVER THE KITCHEN TABLE WITH ALL THEIR BOOKS AND LITTLE FIGURINES.
DO YOU THINK HE STILL HAS ALL HIS STUFF?
PROBABLY. WHY?
I GOT INVITED TO JOIN THE DUNGEONS & DRAGONS CLUB AT SCHOOL.
WOW. YOU DID HAVE A BIG FIRST DAY.
KINDA, YEAH.
WELL, EVEN IF HE DID KEEP HIS STUFF, IT'S PROBABLY OLD AND OUTDATED BY NOW.
LIKE YOU?
YEAH, LIKE ME. GO TO YOUR ROOM.
HA-HA. HEY!

CHAPTER TWO

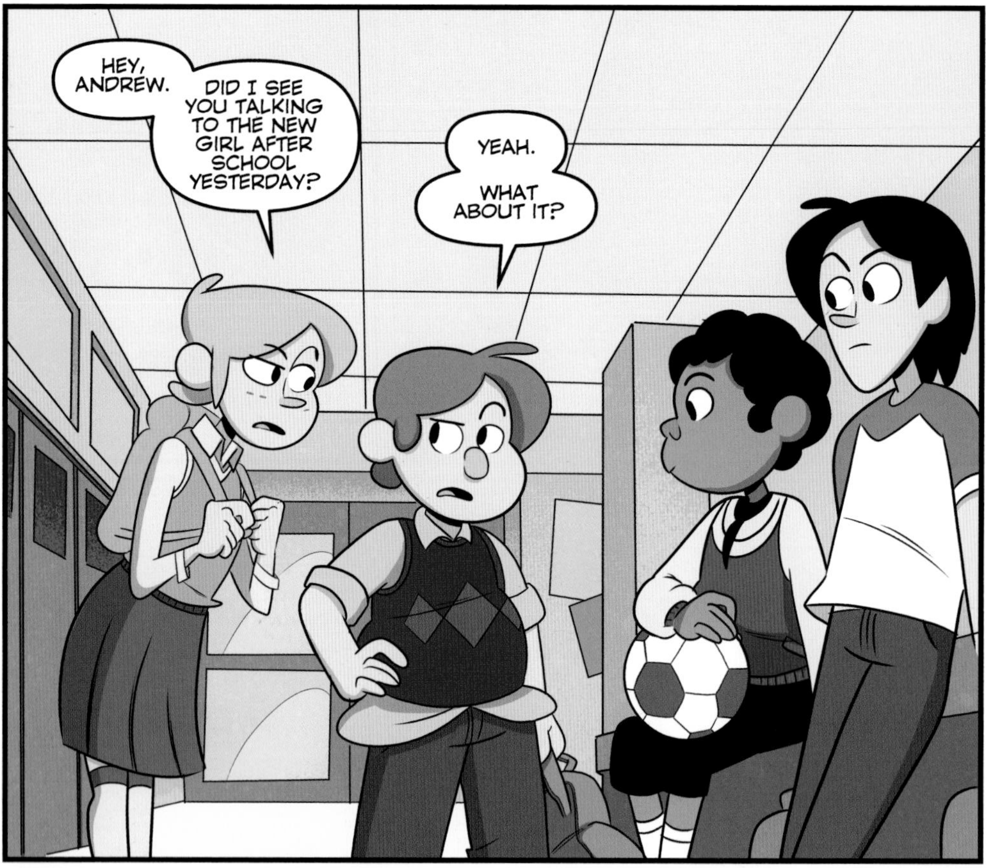
HEY, ANDREW.
DID I SEE YOU TALKING TO THE NEW GIRL AFTER SCHOOL YESTERDAY?
YEAH.
WHAT ABOUT IT?

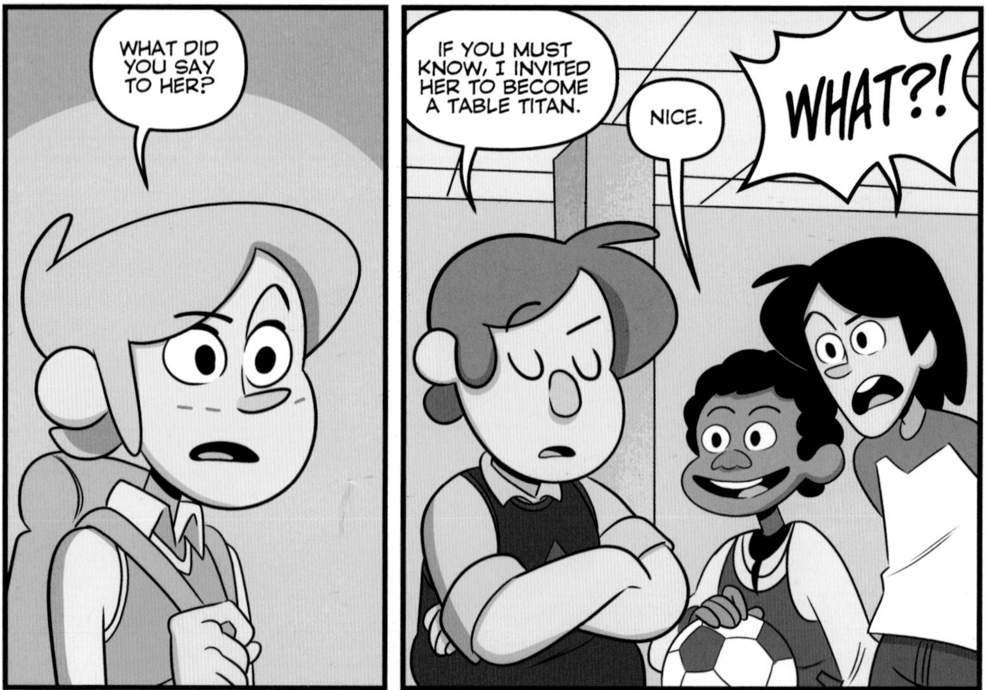
WHAT DID YOU SAY TO HER?
IF YOU MUST KNOW, I INVITED HER TO BECOME A TABLE TITAN.
NICE.
WHAT?!

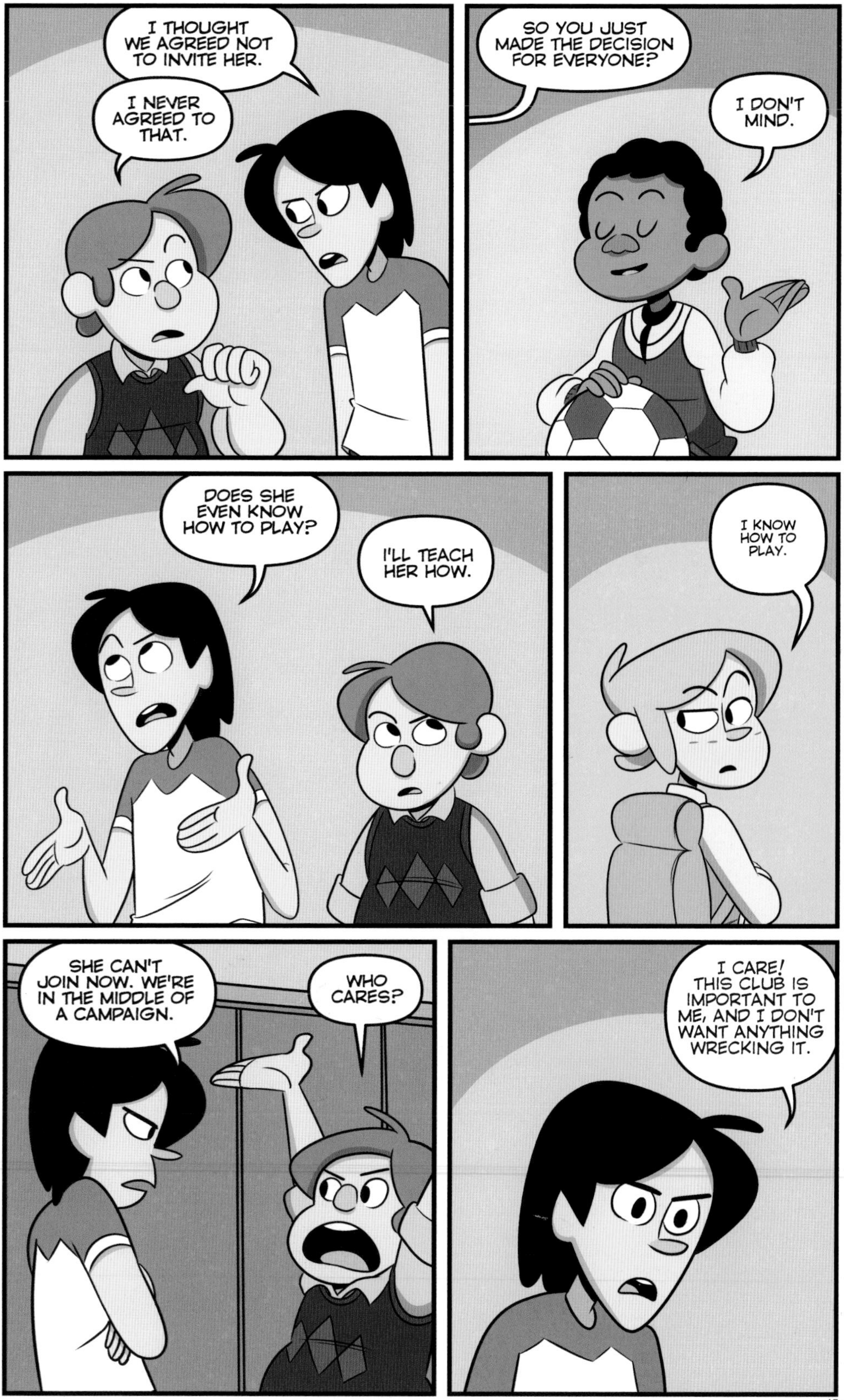
I THOUGHT WE AGREED NOT TO INVITE HER.
I NEVER AGREED TO THAT.
SO YOU JUST MADE THE DECISION FOR EVERYONE?
I DON'T MIND.
DOES SHE EVEN KNOW HOW TO PLAY?
I'LL TEACH HER HOW.
I KNOW HOW TO PLAY.
SHE CAN'T JOIN NOW. WE'RE IN THE MIDDLE OF A CAMPAIGN.
WHO CARES?
I CARE! THIS CLUB IS IMPORTANT TO ME, AND I DON'T WANT ANYTHING WRECKING IT.

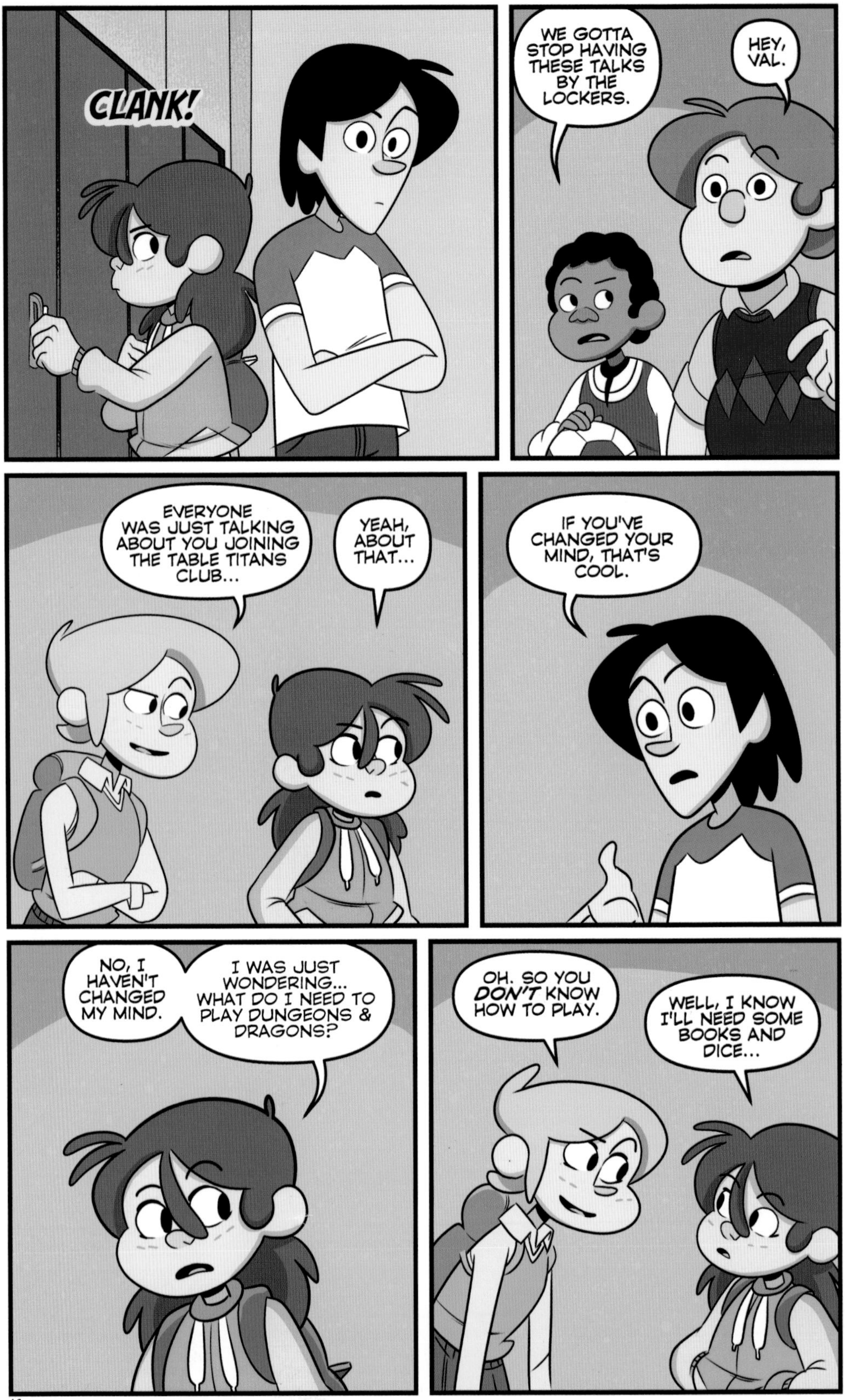
CLANK!
WE GOTTA STOP HAVING THESE TALKS BY THE LOCKERS.
HEY, VAL.
EVERYONE WAS JUST TALKING ABOUT YOU JOINING THE TABLE TITANS CLUB...
YEAH, ABOUT THAT...
IF YOU'VE CHANGED YOUR MIND, THAT'S COOL.
NO, I HAVEN'T CHANGED MY MIND.
I WAS JUST WONDERING... WHAT DO I NEED TO PLAY DUNGEONS & DRAGONS?
OH. SO YOU *DON'T* KNOW HOW TO PLAY.
WELL, I KNOW I'LL NEED SOME BOOKS AND DICE...

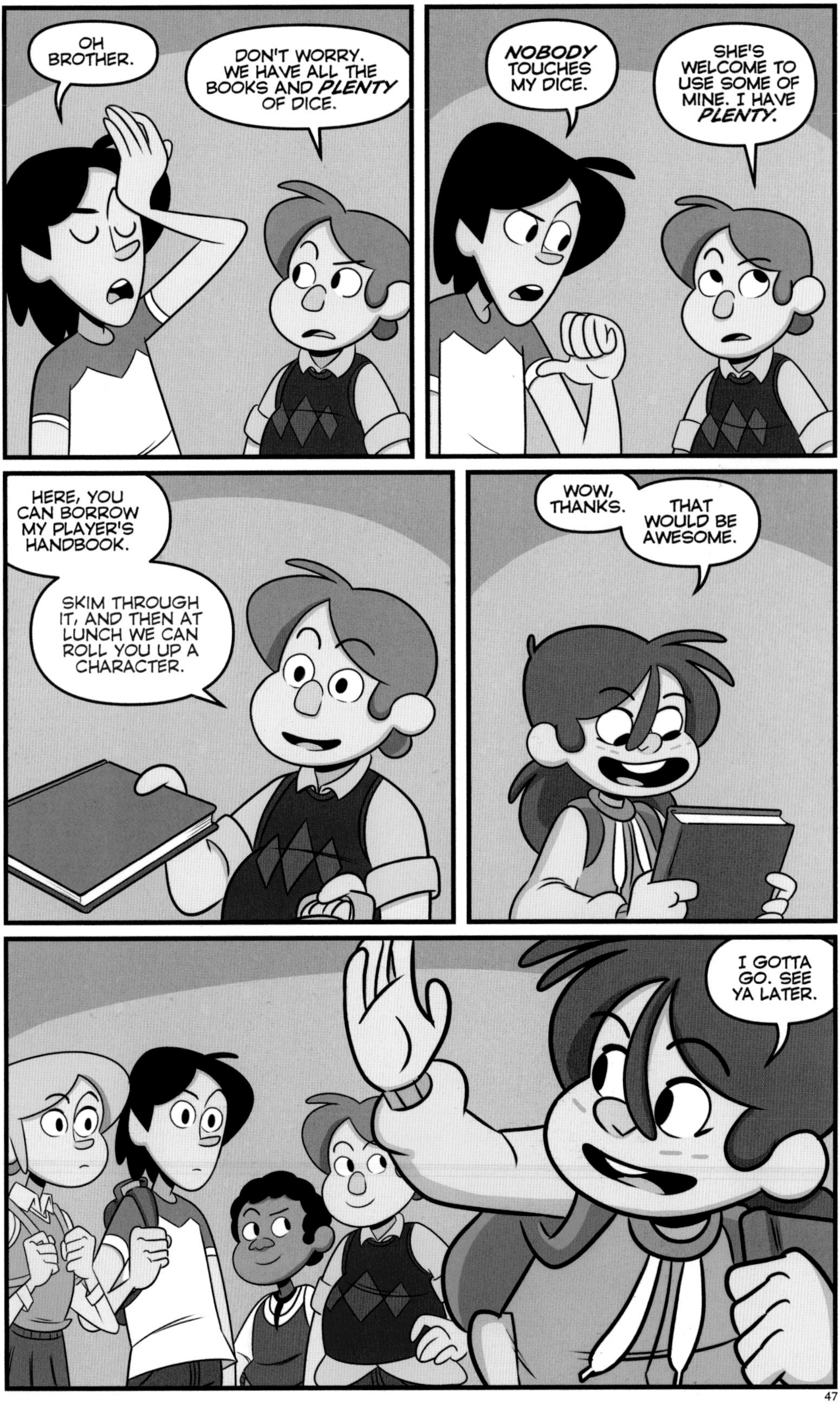
OH BROTHER.
DON'T WORRY. WE HAVE ALL THE BOOKS AND PLENTY OF DICE.
NOBODY TOUCHES MY DICE.
SHE'S WELCOME TO USE SOME OF MINE. I HAVE PLENTY.
HERE, YOU CAN BORROW MY PLAYER'S HANDBOOK.
SKIM THROUGH IT, AND THEN AT LUNCH WE CAN ROLL YOU UP A CHARACTER.
WOW, THANKS.
THAT WOULD BE AWESOME.
I GOTTA GO. SEE YA LATER.

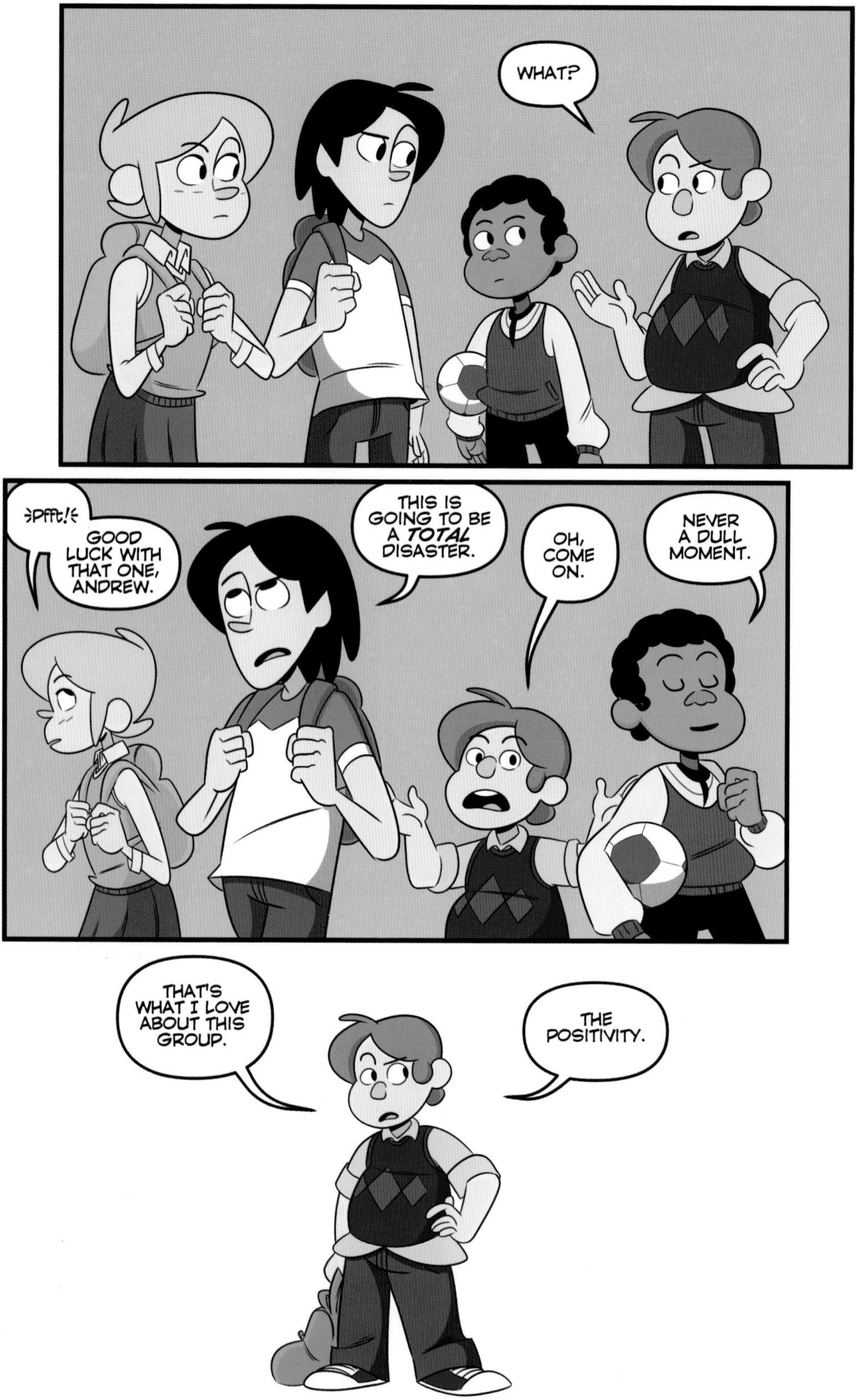
WHAT?
>PFFT!<
GOOD LUCK WITH THAT ONE, ANDREW.
THIS IS GOING TO BE A TOTAL DISASTER.
OH, COME ON.
NEVER A DULL MOMENT.
THAT'S WHAT I LOVE ABOUT THIS GROUP.
THE POSITIVITY.

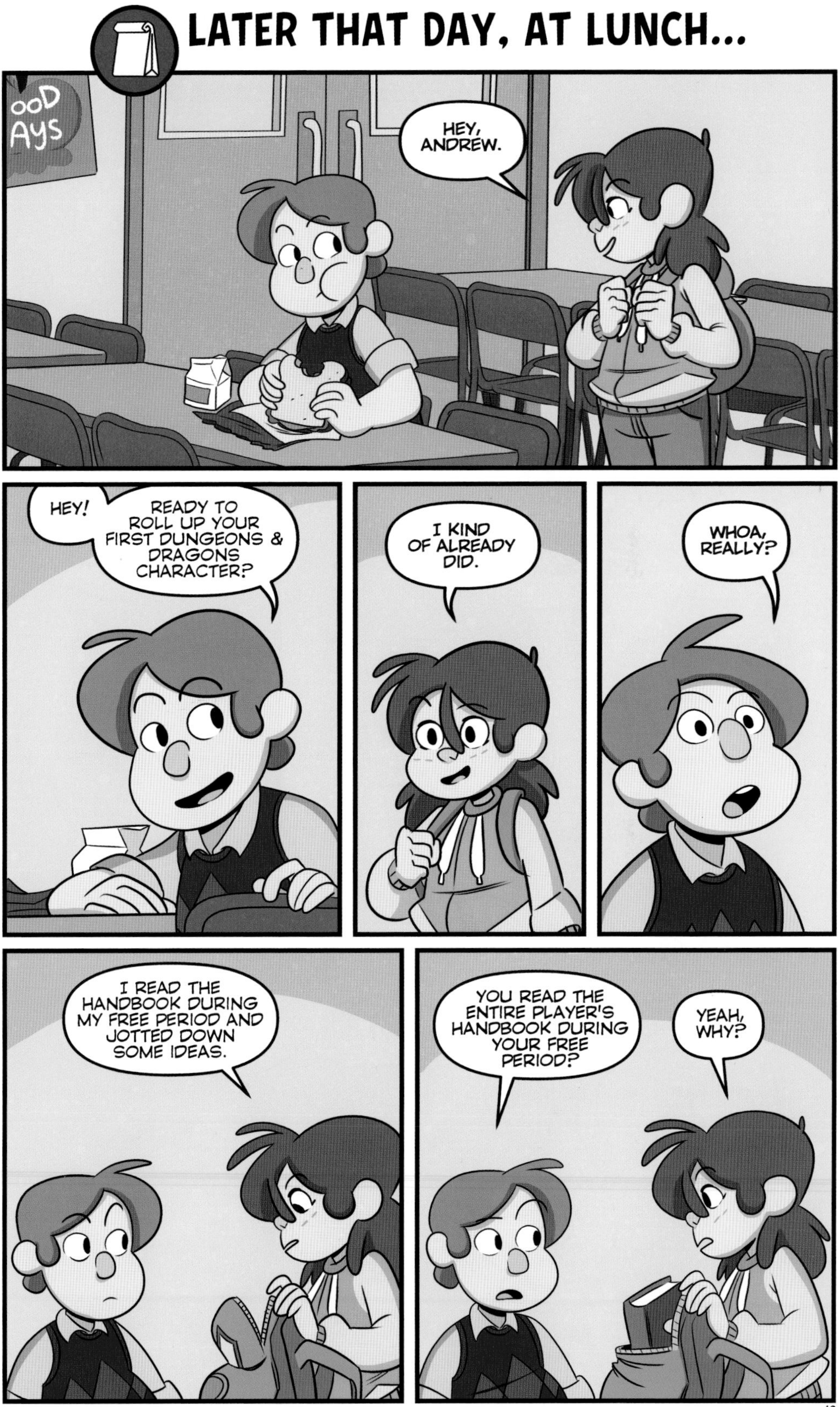
LATER THAT DAY, AT LUNCH...
HEY, ANDREW.
HEY!
READY TO ROLL UP YOUR FIRST DUNGEONS & DRAGONS CHARACTER?
I KIND OF ALREADY DID.
WHOA, REALLY?
I READ THE HANDBOOK DURING MY FREE PERIOD AND JOTTED DOWN SOME IDEAS.
YOU READ THE ENTIRE PLAYER'S HANDBOOK DURING YOUR FREE PERIOD?
YEAH, WHY?

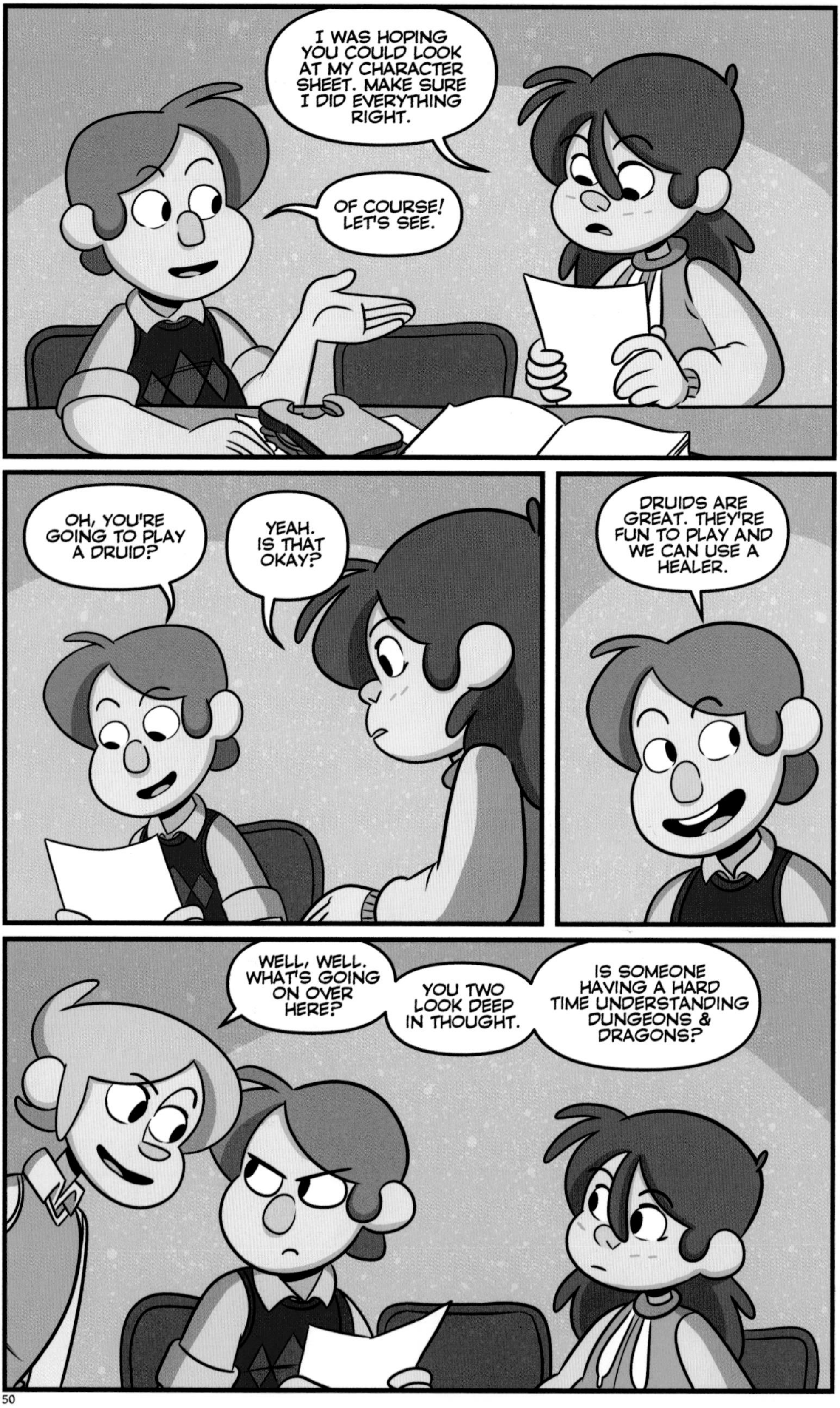
I WAS HOPING YOU COULD LOOK AT MY CHARACTER SHEET. MAKE SURE I DID EVERYTHING RIGHT.
OF COURSE! LET'S SEE.
OH, YOU'RE GOING TO PLAY A DRUID?
YEAH. IS THAT OKAY?
DRUIDS ARE GREAT. THEY'RE FUN TO PLAY AND WE CAN USE A HEALER.
WELL, WELL. WHAT'S GOING ON OVER HERE?
YOU TWO LOOK DEEP IN THOUGHT.
IS SOMEONE HAVING A HARD TIME UNDERSTANDING DUNGEONS & DRAGONS?

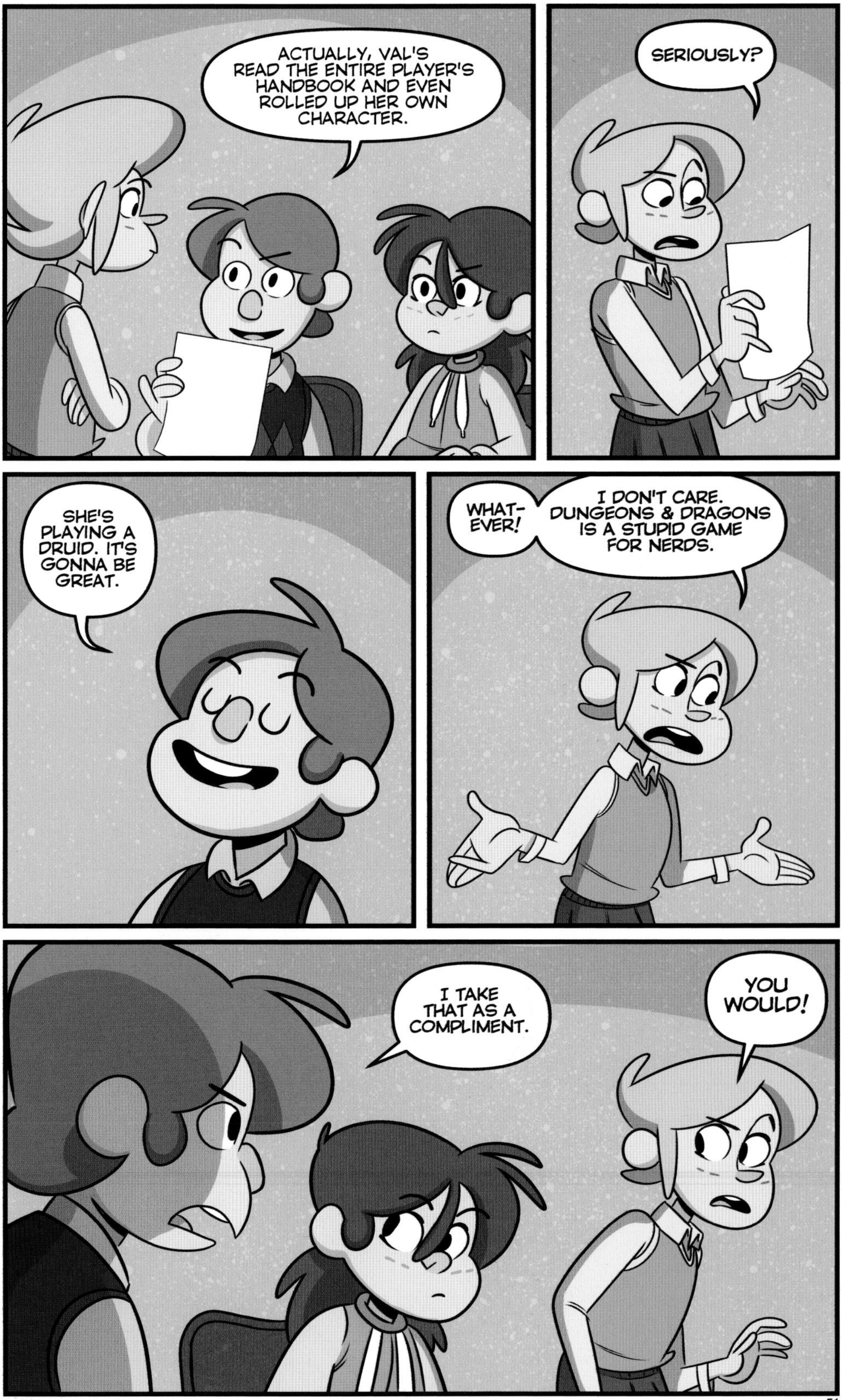
ACTUALLY, VAL'S READ THE ENTIRE PLAYER'S HANDBOOK AND EVEN ROLLED UP HER OWN CHARACTER.
SERIOUSLY?
SHE'S PLAYING A DRUID. IT'S GONNA BE GREAT.
WHAT-EVER!
I DON'T CARE. DUNGEONS & DRAGONS IS A STUPID GAME FOR NERDS.
I TAKE THAT AS A COMPLIMENT.
YOU WOULD!

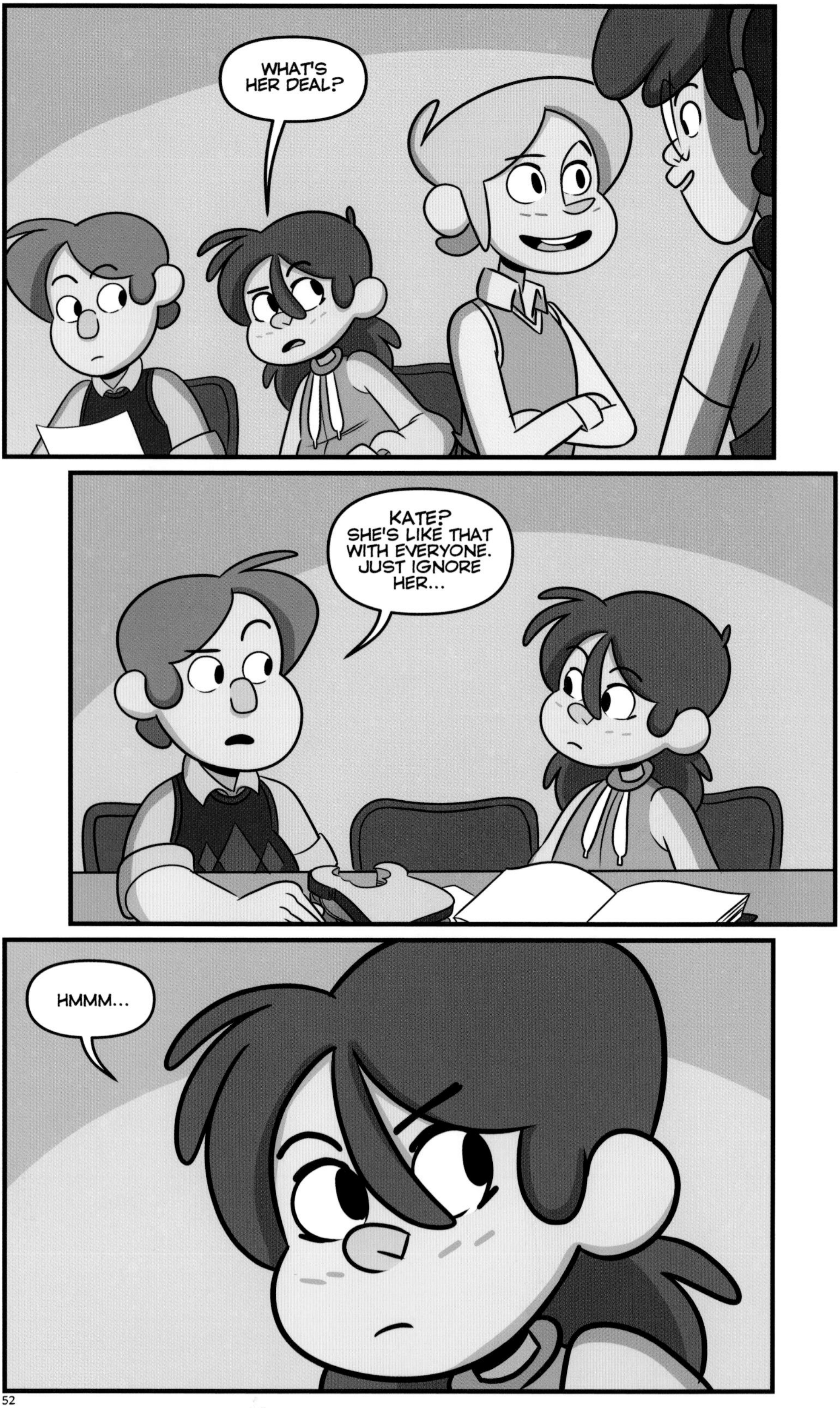
WHAT'S HER DEAL?
KATE? SHE'S LIKE THAT WITH EVERYONE. JUST IGNORE HER...
HMMM...

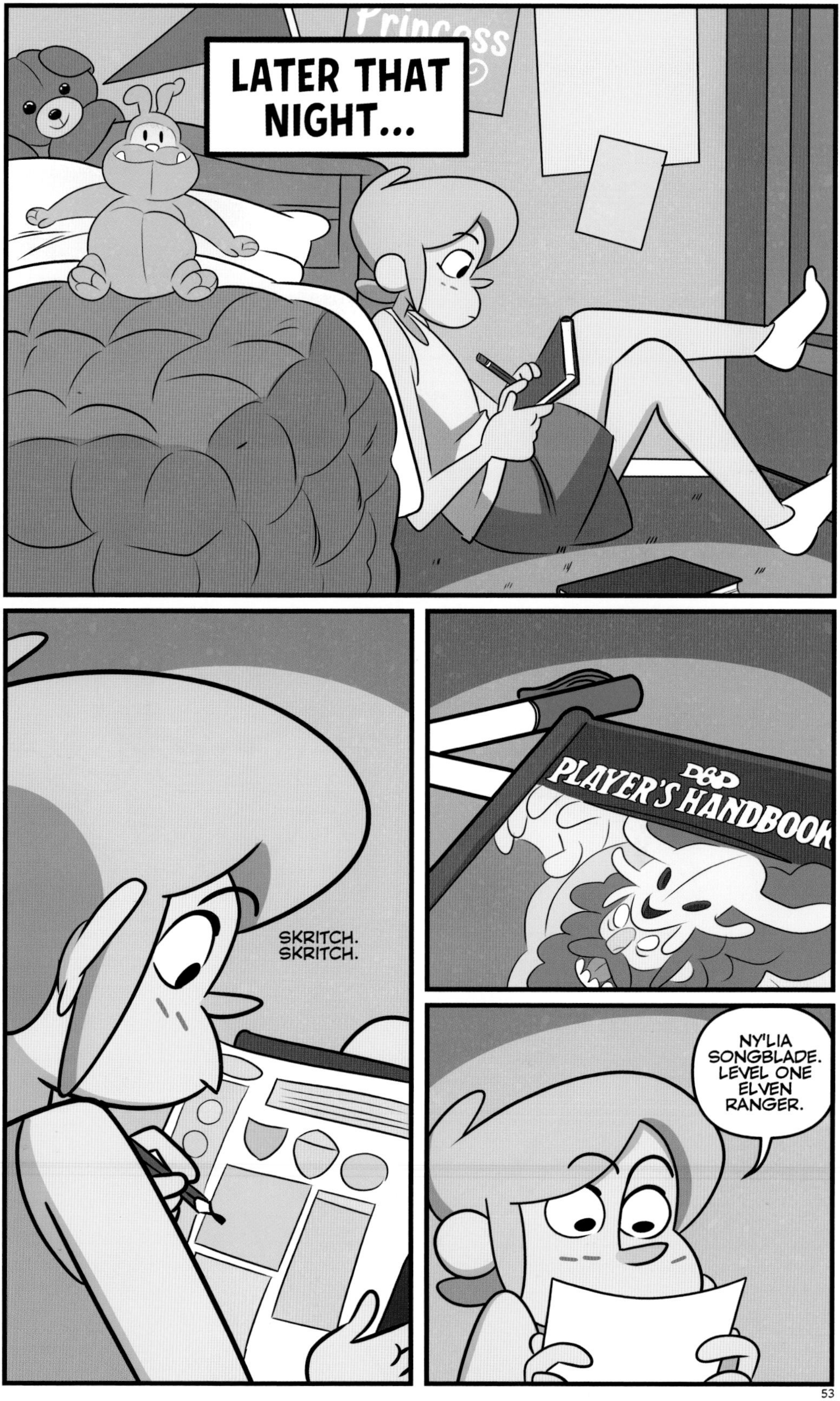
LATER THAT NIGHT...
Princess
SKRITCH. SKRITCH.
D&D PLAYER'S HANDBOOK
NY'LIA SONGBLADE. LEVEL ONE ELVEN RANGER.

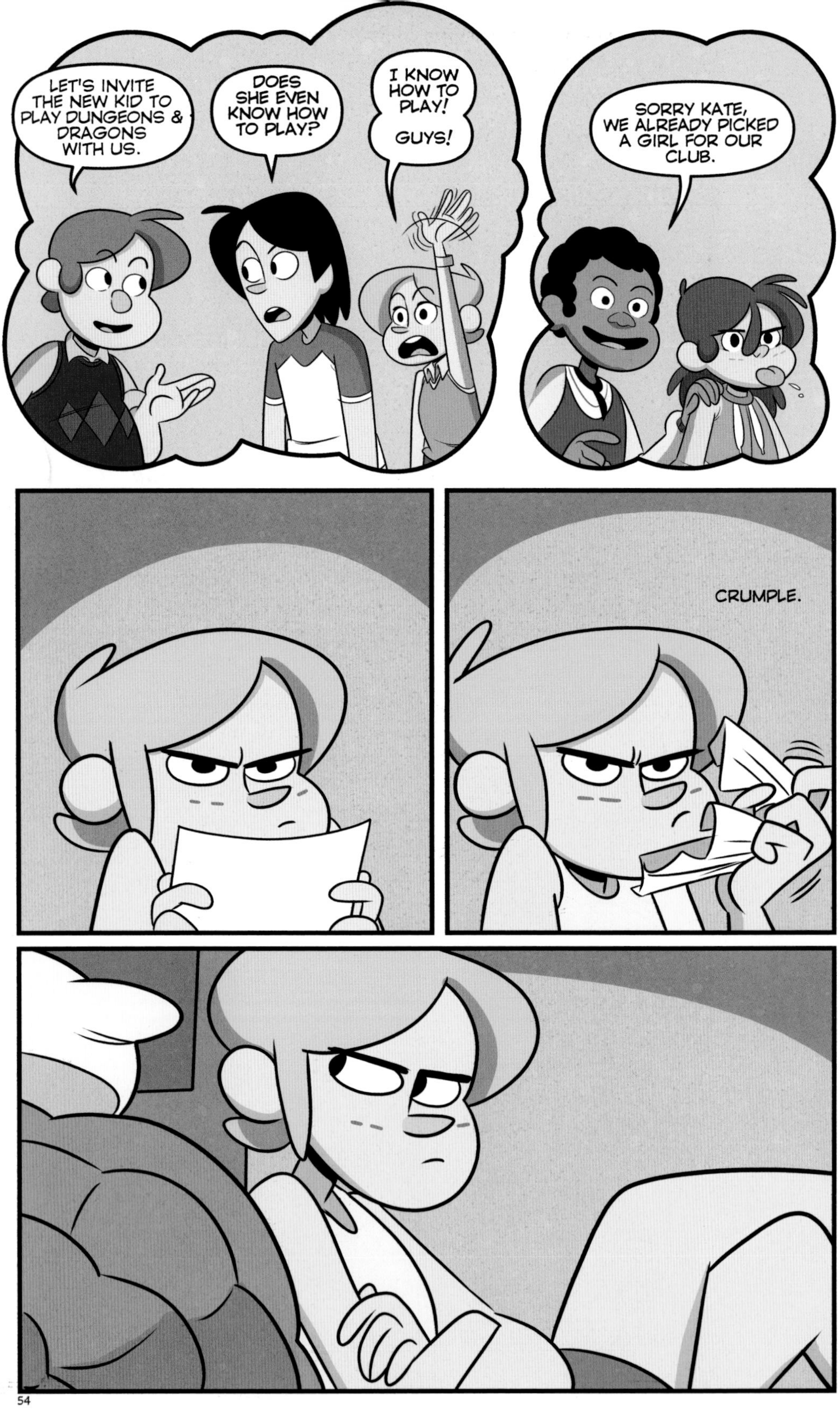
LET'S INVITE THE NEW KID TO PLAY DUNGEONS & DRAGONS WITH US.
DOES SHE EVEN KNOW HOW TO PLAY?
I KNOW HOW TO PLAY!
GUYS!
SORRY KATE, WE ALREADY PICKED A GIRL FOR OUR CLUB.
CRUMPLE.

CHAPTER THREE

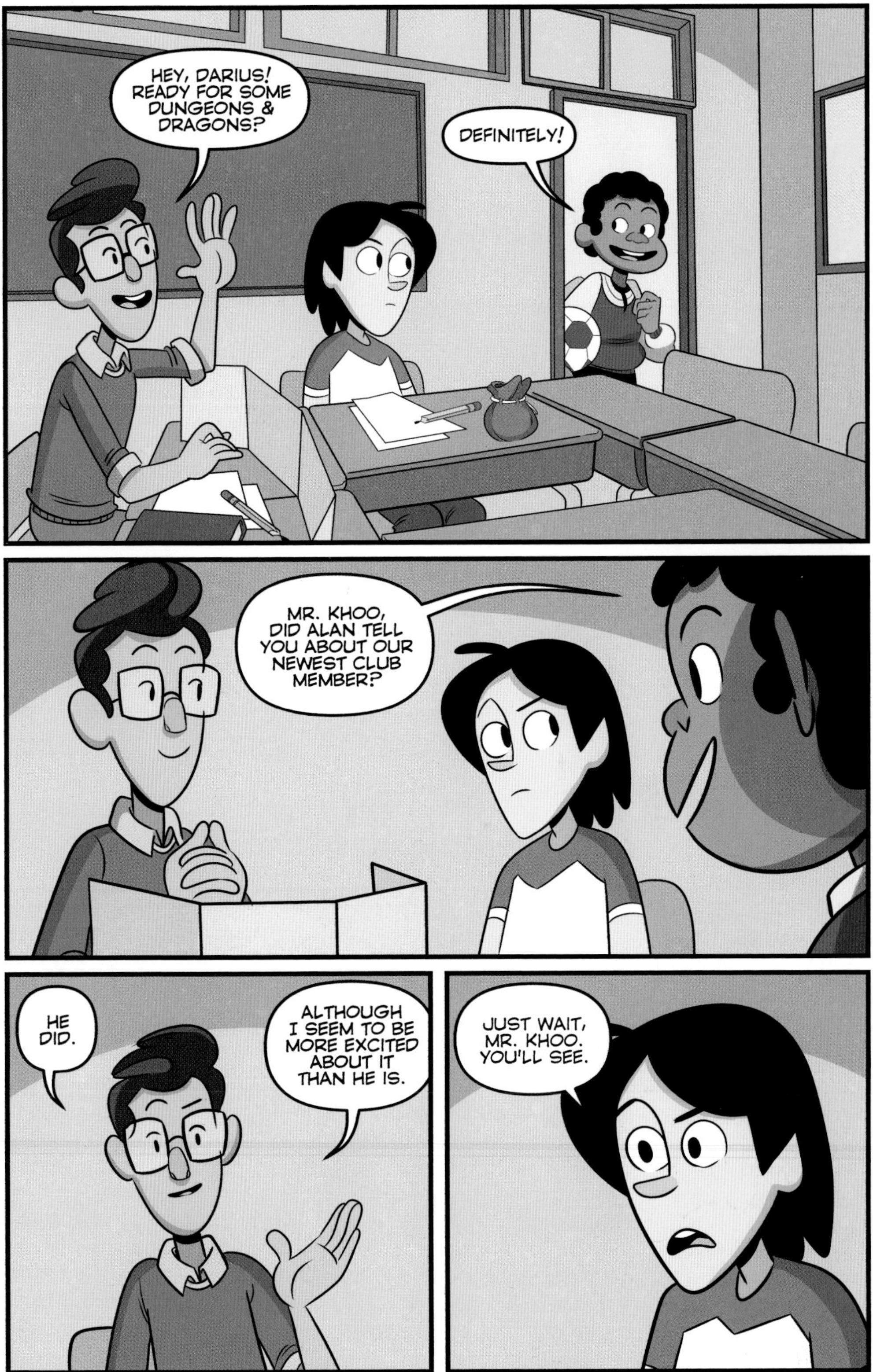
HEY, DARIUS! READY FOR SOME DUNGEONS & DRAGONS?
DEFINITELY!
MR. KHOO, DID ALAN TELL YOU ABOUT OUR NEWEST CLUB MEMBER?
HE DID.
ALTHOUGH I SEEM TO BE MORE EXCITED ABOUT IT THAN HE IS.
JUST WAIT, MR. KHOO. YOU'LL SEE.

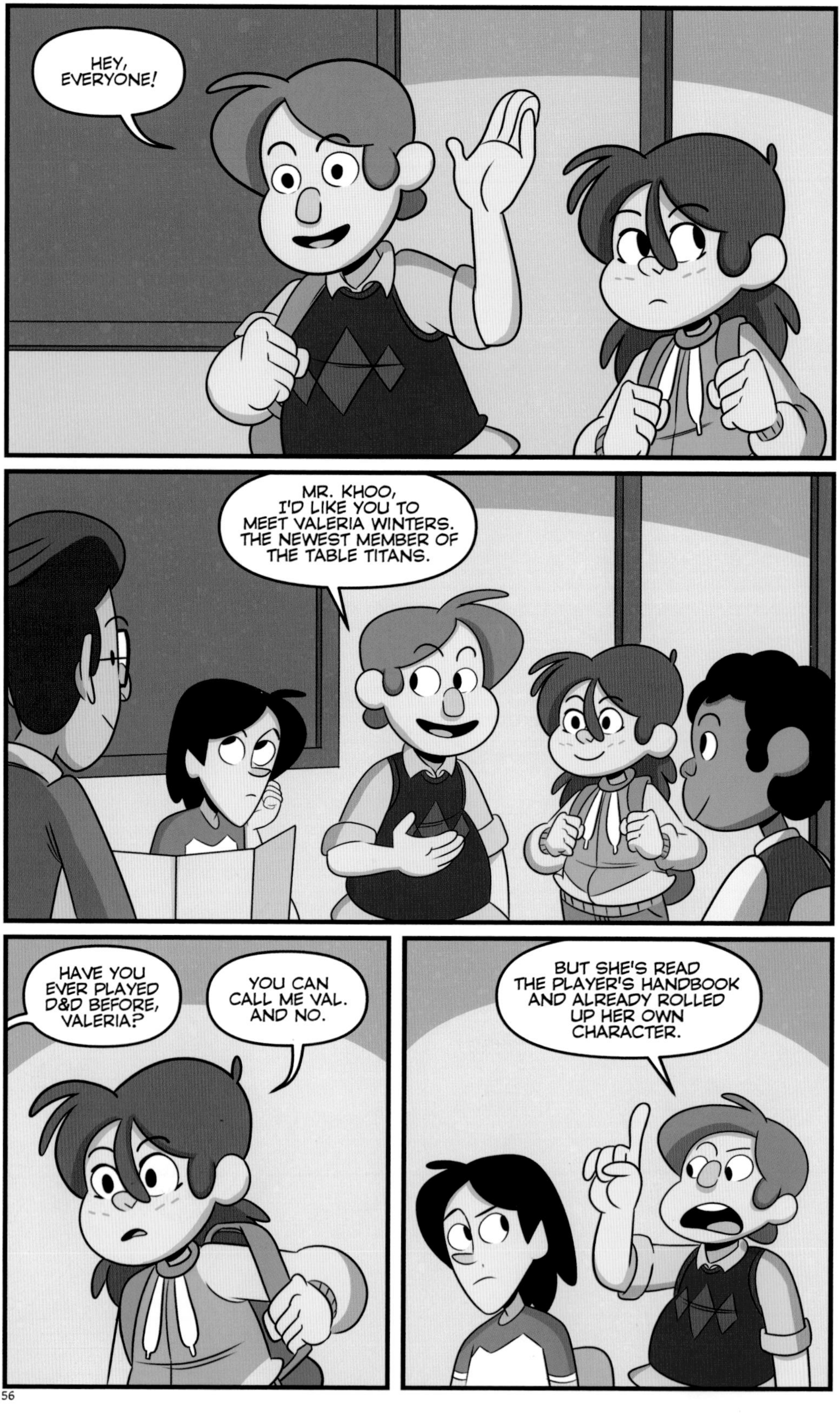
HEY, EVERYONE!
MR. KHOO, I'D LIKE YOU TO MEET VALERIA WINTERS. THE NEWEST MEMBER OF THE TABLE TITANS.
HAVE YOU EVER PLAYED D&D BEFORE, VALERIA?
YOU CAN CALL ME VAL. AND NO.
BUT SHE'S READ THE PLAYER'S HANDBOOK AND ALREADY ROLLED UP HER OWN CHARACTER.

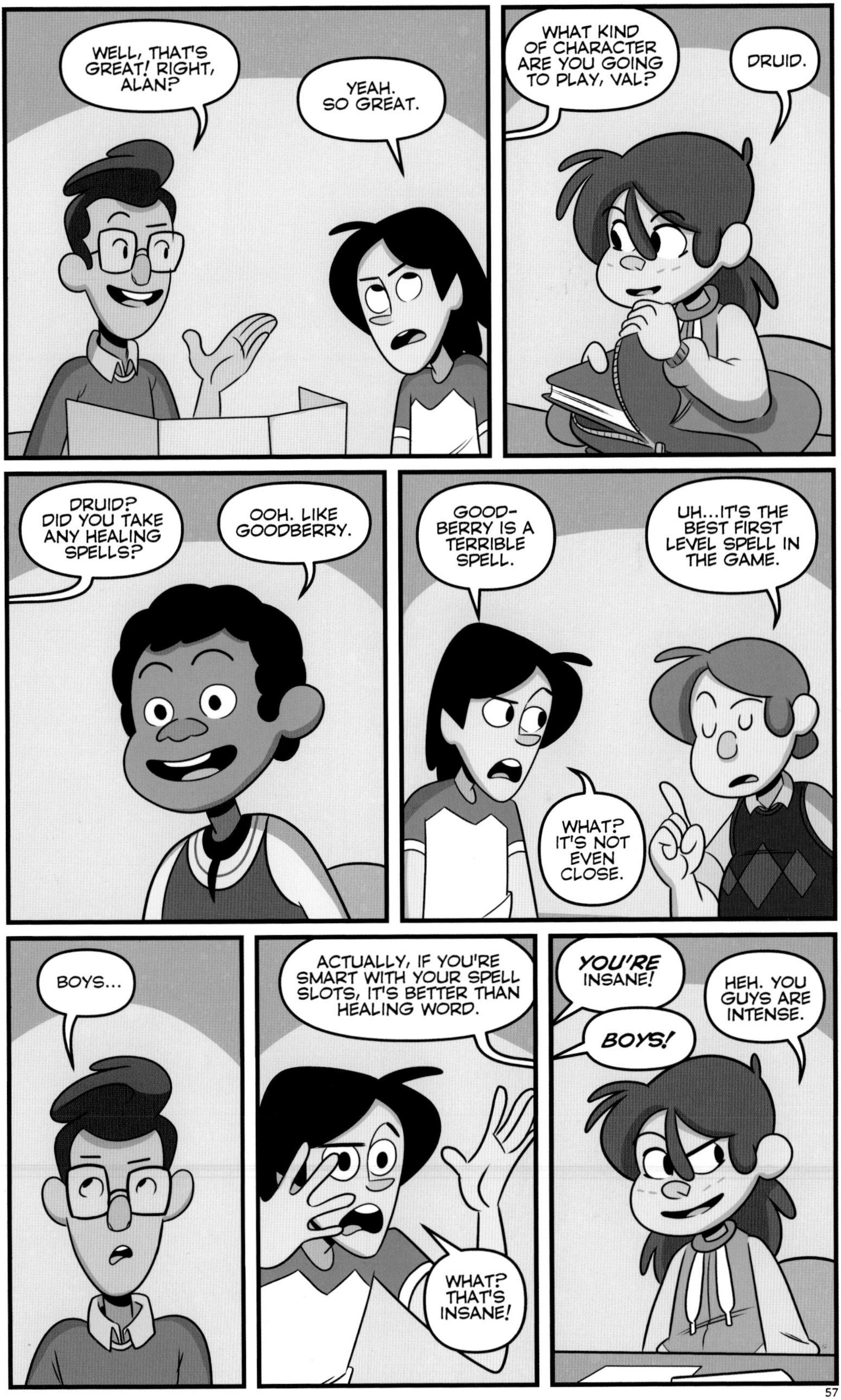
WELL, THAT'S GREAT! RIGHT, ALAN?
YEAH. SO GREAT.
WHAT KIND OF CHARACTER ARE YOU GOING TO PLAY, VAL?
DRUID.
DRUID? DID YOU TAKE ANY HEALING SPELLS?
OOH. LIKE GOODBERRY.
GOOD-BERRY IS A TERRIBLE SPELL.
UH...IT'S THE BEST FIRST LEVEL SPELL IN THE GAME.
WHAT? IT'S NOT EVEN CLOSE.
BOYS...
ACTUALLY, IF YOU'RE SMART WITH YOUR SPELL SLOTS, IT'S BETTER THAN HEALING WORD.
WHAT? THAT'S INSANE!
YOU'RE INSANE!
BOYS!
HEH. YOU GUYS ARE INTENSE.

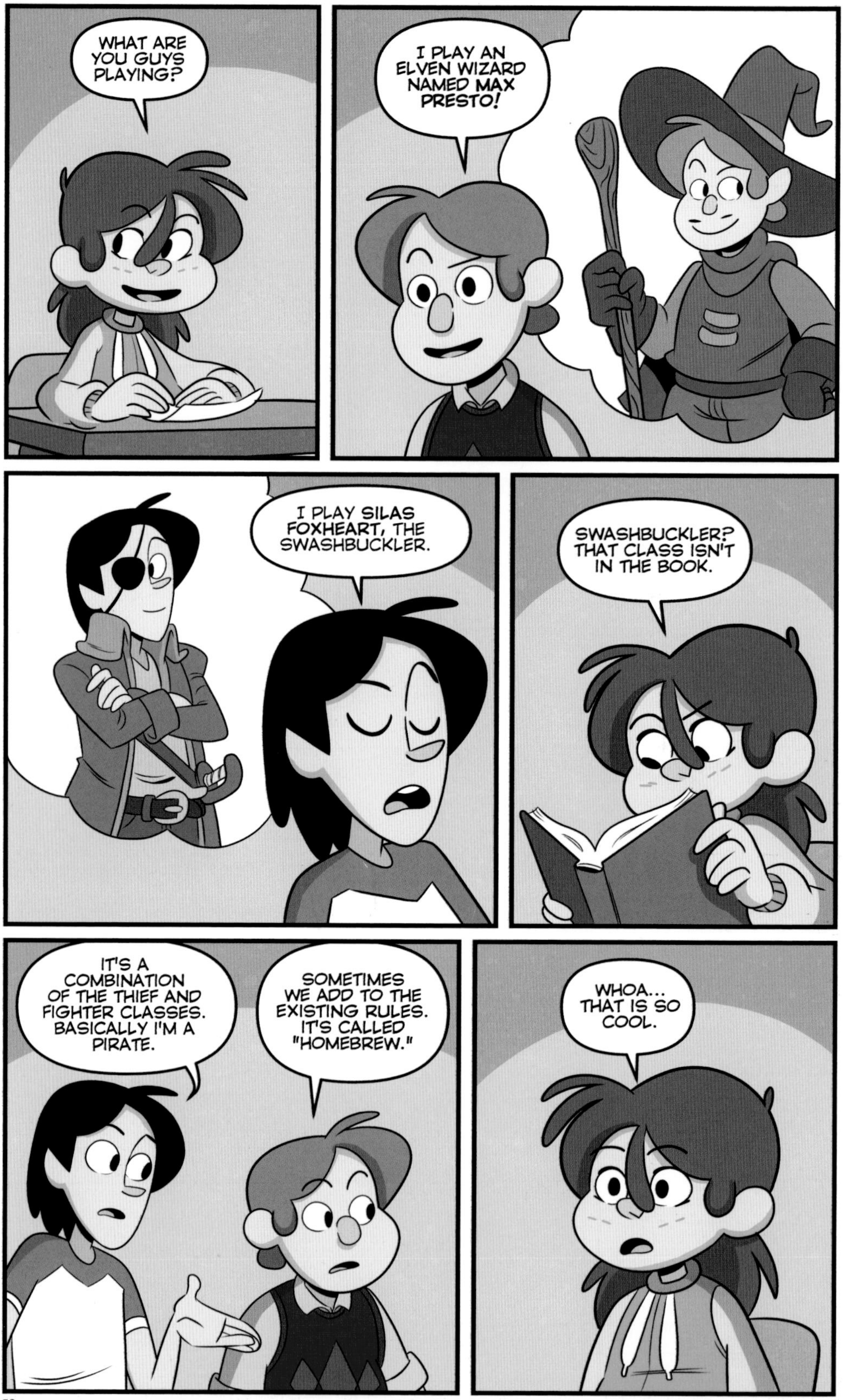
WHAT ARE YOU GUYS PLAYING?
I PLAY AN ELVEN WIZARD NAMED MAX PRESTO!
I PLAY SILAS FOXHEART, THE SWASHBUCKLER.
SWASHBUCKLER? THAT CLASS ISN'T IN THE BOOK.
IT'S A COMBINATION OF THE THIEF AND FIGHTER CLASSES. BASICALLY I'M A PIRATE.
SOMETIMES WE ADD TO THE EXISTING RULES. IT'S CALLED "HOMEBREW."
WHOA... THAT IS SO COOL.

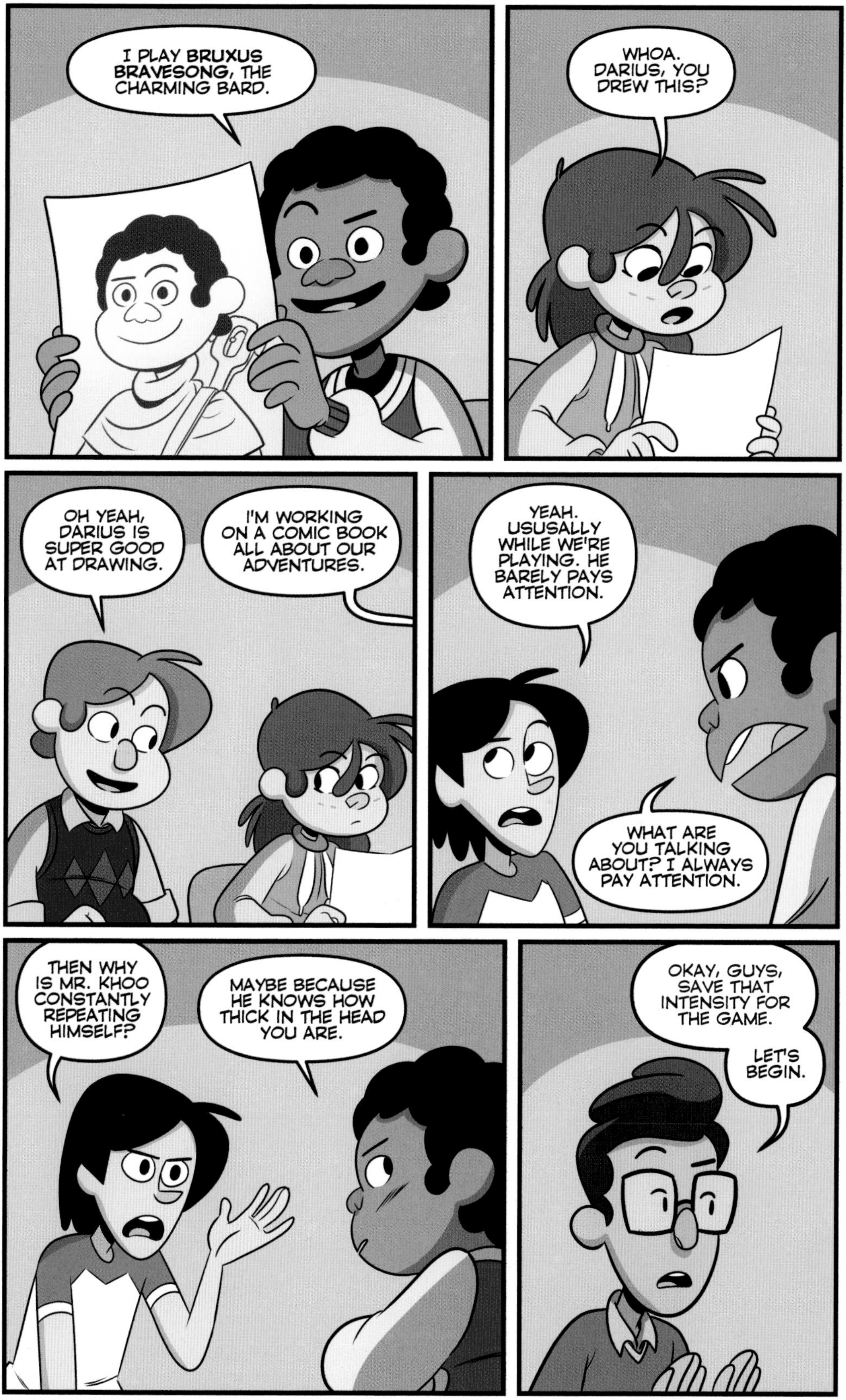

I PLAY BRUXUS BRAVESONG, THE CHARMING BARD.
WHOA. DARIUS, YOU DREW THIS?
OH YEAH, DARIUS IS SUPER GOOD AT DRAWING.
I'M WORKING ON A COMIC BOOK ALL ABOUT OUR ADVENTURES.
YEAH. USUSALLY WHILE WE'RE PLAYING. HE BARELY PAYS ATTENTION.
WHAT ARE YOU TALKING ABOUT? I ALWAYS PAY ATTENTION.
THEN WHY IS MR. KHOO CONSTANTLY REPEATING HIMSELF?
MAYBE BECAUSE HE KNOWS HOW THICK IN THE HEAD YOU ARE.
OKAY, GUYS, SAVE THAT INTENSITY FOR THE GAME.
LET'S BEGIN.

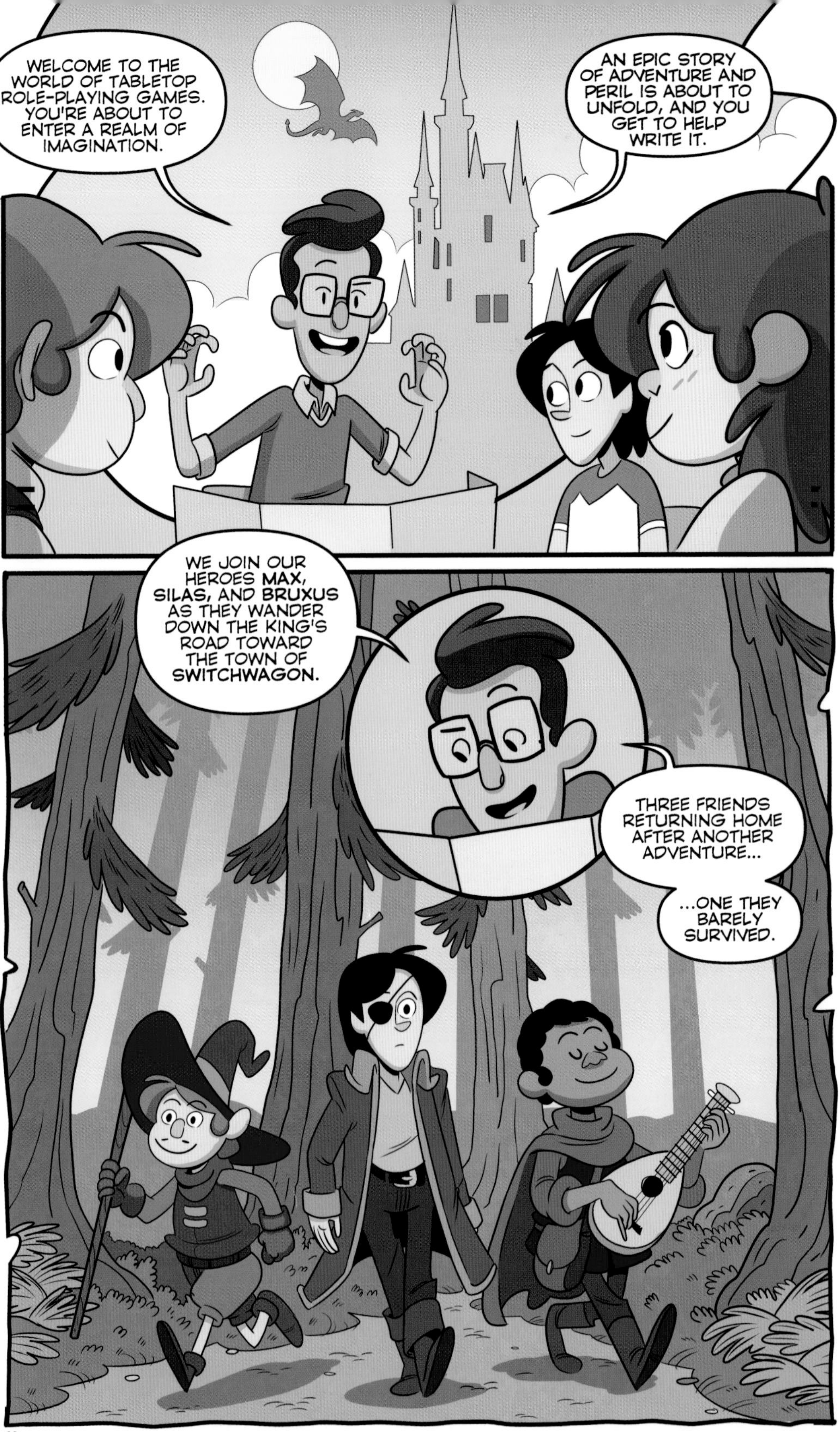
WELCOME TO THE WORLD OF TABLETOP ROLE-PLAYING GAMES. YOU'RE ABOUT TO ENTER A REALM OF IMAGINATION.
AN EPIC STORY OF ADVENTURE AND PERIL IS ABOUT TO UNFOLD, AND YOU GET TO HELP WRITE IT.
WE JOIN OUR HEROES **MAX**, **SILAS**, AND **BRUXUS** AS THEY WANDER DOWN THE KING'S ROAD TOWARD THE TOWN OF **SWITCHWAGON**.
THREE FRIENDS RETURNING HOME AFTER ANOTHER ADVENTURE...
...ONE THEY BARELY SURVIVED.

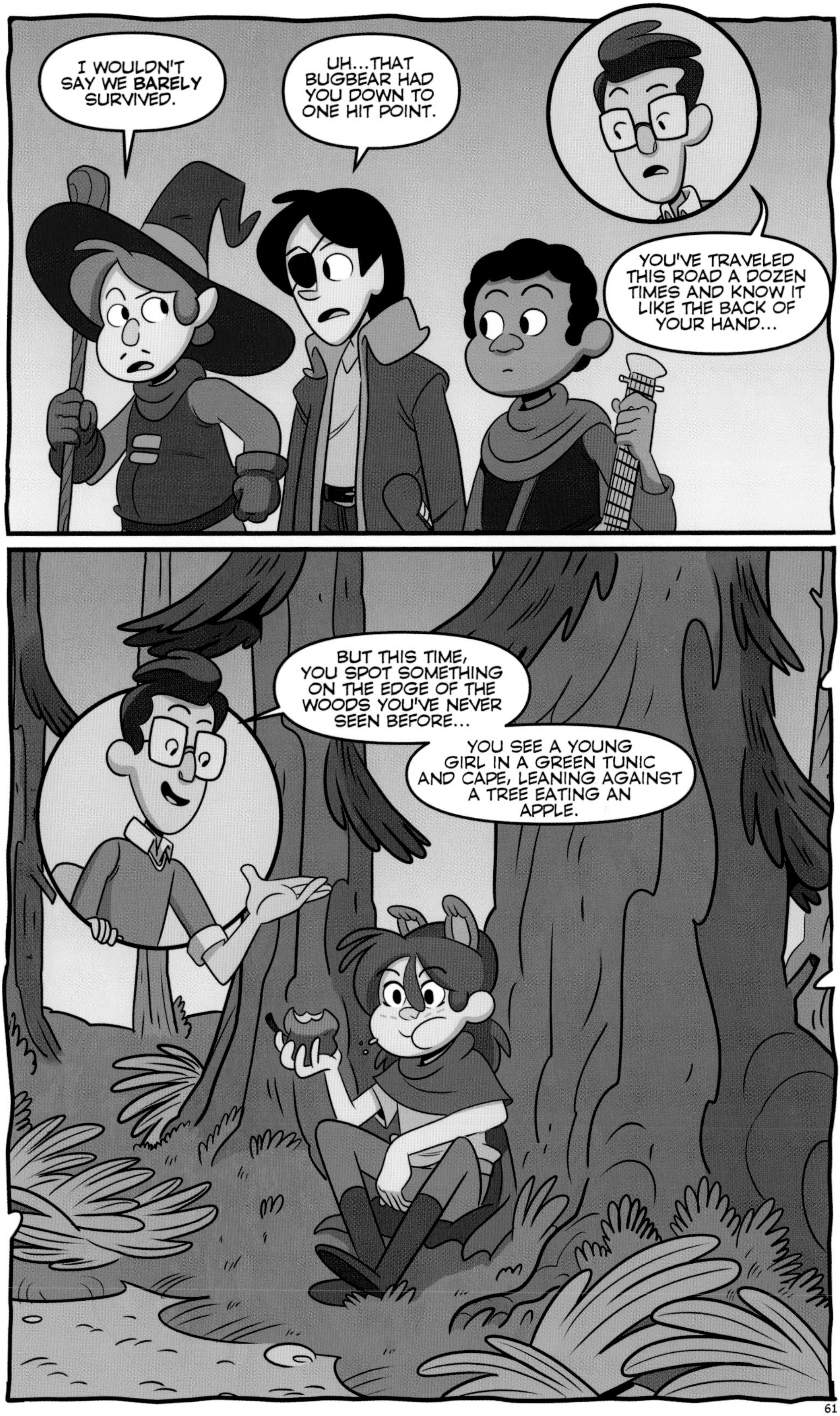
I WOULDN'T SAY WE BARELY SURVIVED.
UH...THAT BUGBEAR HAD YOU DOWN TO ONE HIT POINT.
YOU'VE TRAVELED THIS ROAD A DOZEN TIMES AND KNOW IT LIKE THE BACK OF YOUR HAND...
BUT THIS TIME, YOU SPOT SOMETHING ON THE EDGE OF THE WOODS YOU'VE NEVER SEEN BEFORE...
YOU SEE A YOUNG GIRL IN A GREEN TUNIC AND CAPE, LEANING AGAINST A TREE EATING AN APPLE.

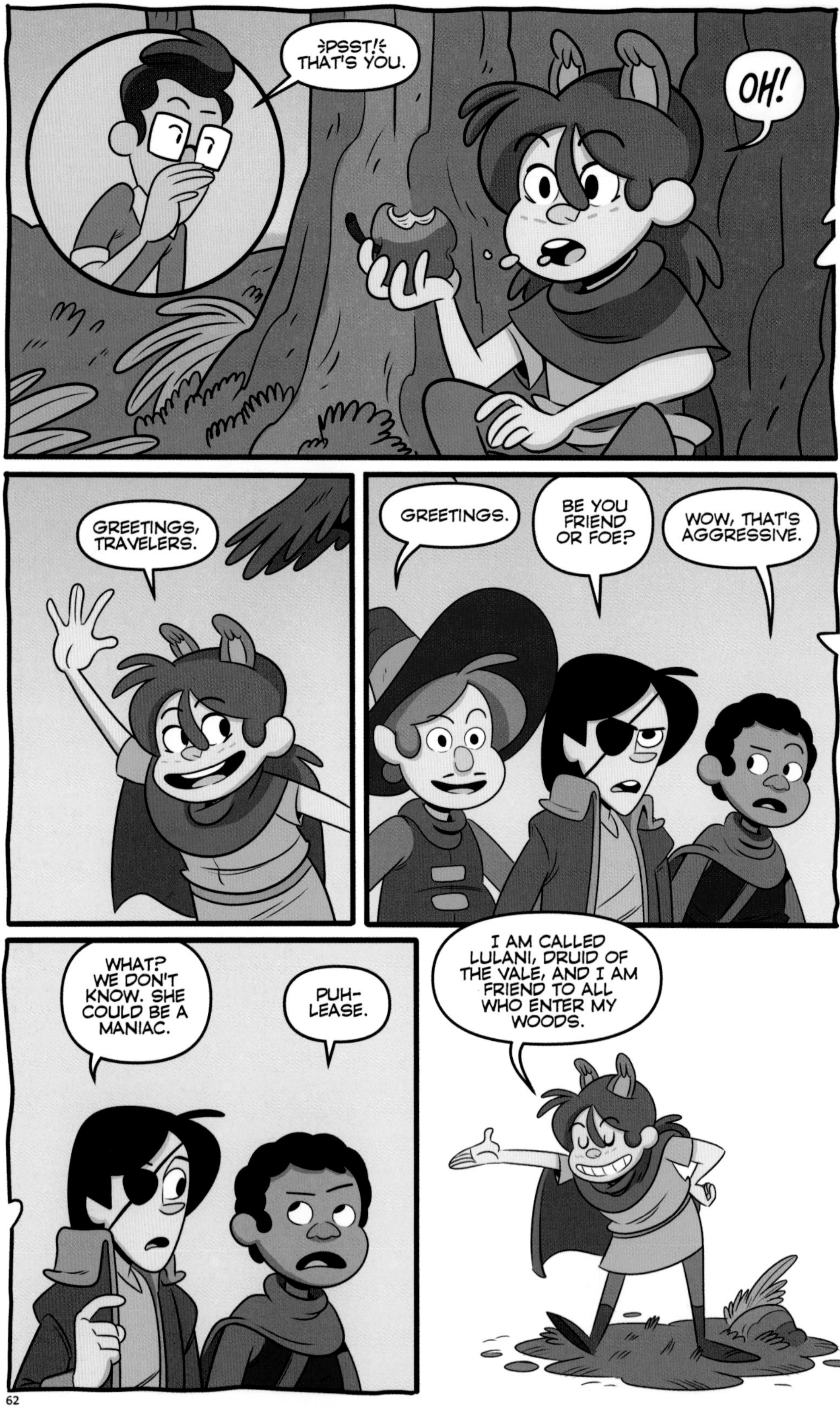
PSST!
THAT'S YOU.
OH!
GREETINGS, TRAVELERS.
GREETINGS.
BE YOU FRIEND OR FOE?
WOW, THAT'S AGGRESSIVE.
WHAT? WE DON'T KNOW. SHE COULD BE A MANIAC.
PUH-LEASE.
I AM CALLED LULANI, DRUID OF THE VALE, AND I AM FRIEND TO ALL WHO ENTER MY WOODS.

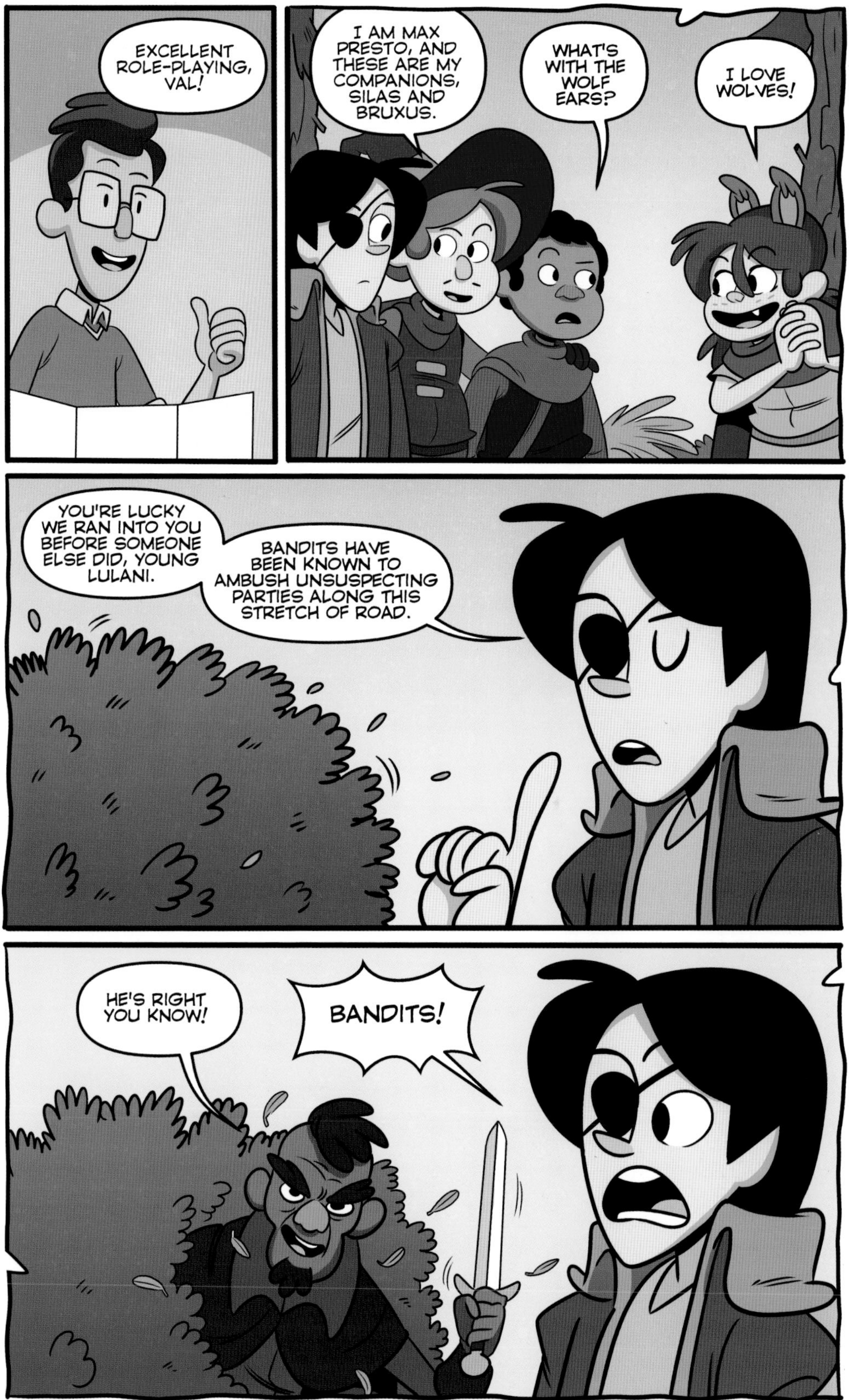
EXCELLENT ROLE-PLAYING, VAL!
I AM MAX PRESTO, AND THESE ARE MY COMPANIONS, SILAS AND BRUXUS.
WHAT'S WITH THE WOLF EARS?
I LOVE WOLVES!
YOU'RE LUCKY WE RAN INTO YOU BEFORE SOMEONE ELSE DID, YOUNG LULANI.
BANDITS HAVE BEEN KNOWN TO AMBUSH UNSUSPECTING PARTIES ALONG THIS STRETCH OF ROAD.
HE'S RIGHT YOU KNOW!
BANDITS!

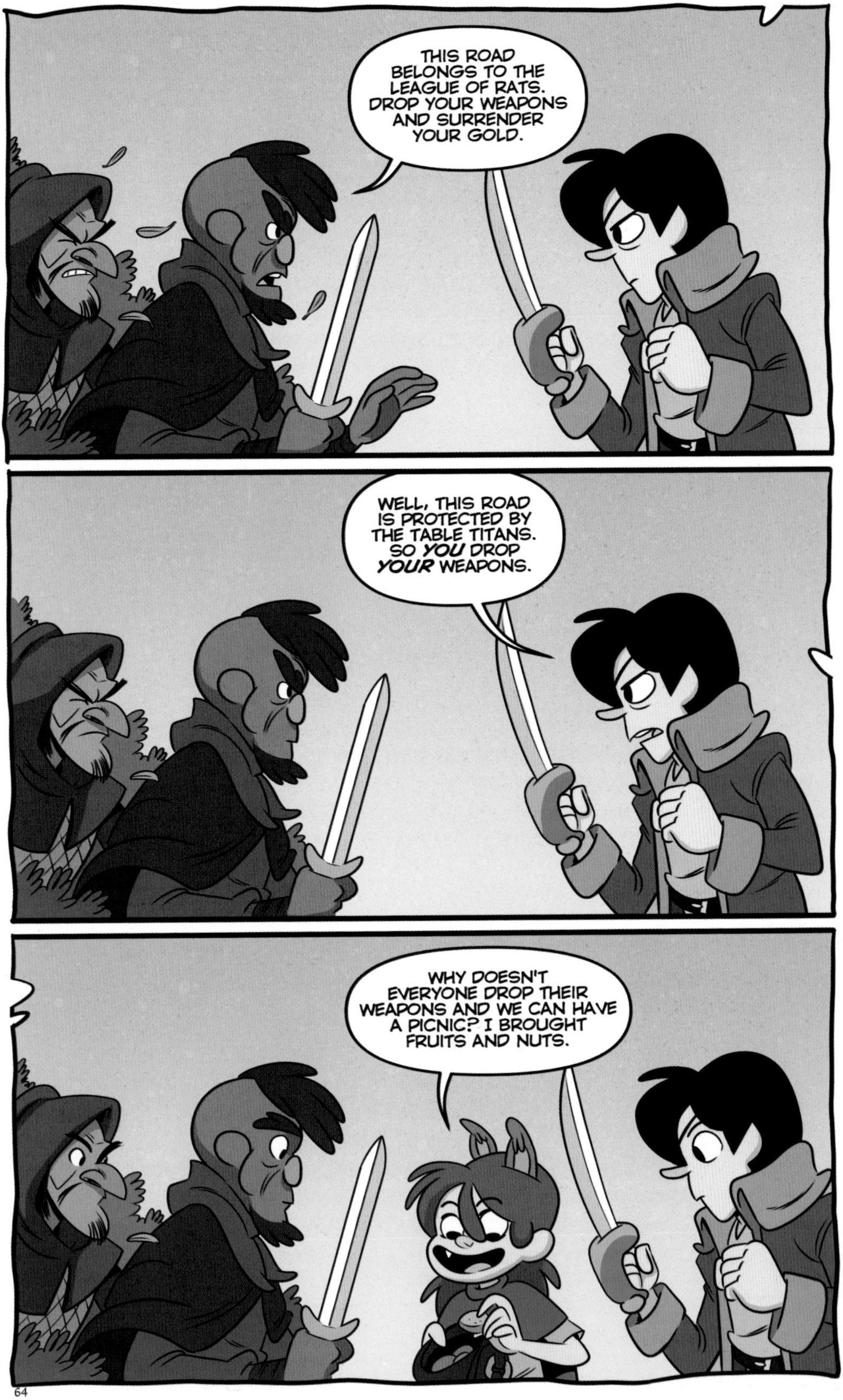
THIS ROAD BELONGS TO THE LEAGUE OF RATS. DROP YOUR WEAPONS AND SURRENDER YOUR GOLD.
WELL, THIS ROAD IS PROTECTED BY THE TABLE TITANS. SO *YOU* DROP *YOUR* WEAPONS.
WHY DOESN'T EVERYONE DROP THEIR WEAPONS AND WE CAN HAVE A PICNIC? I BROUGHT FRUITS AND NUTS.

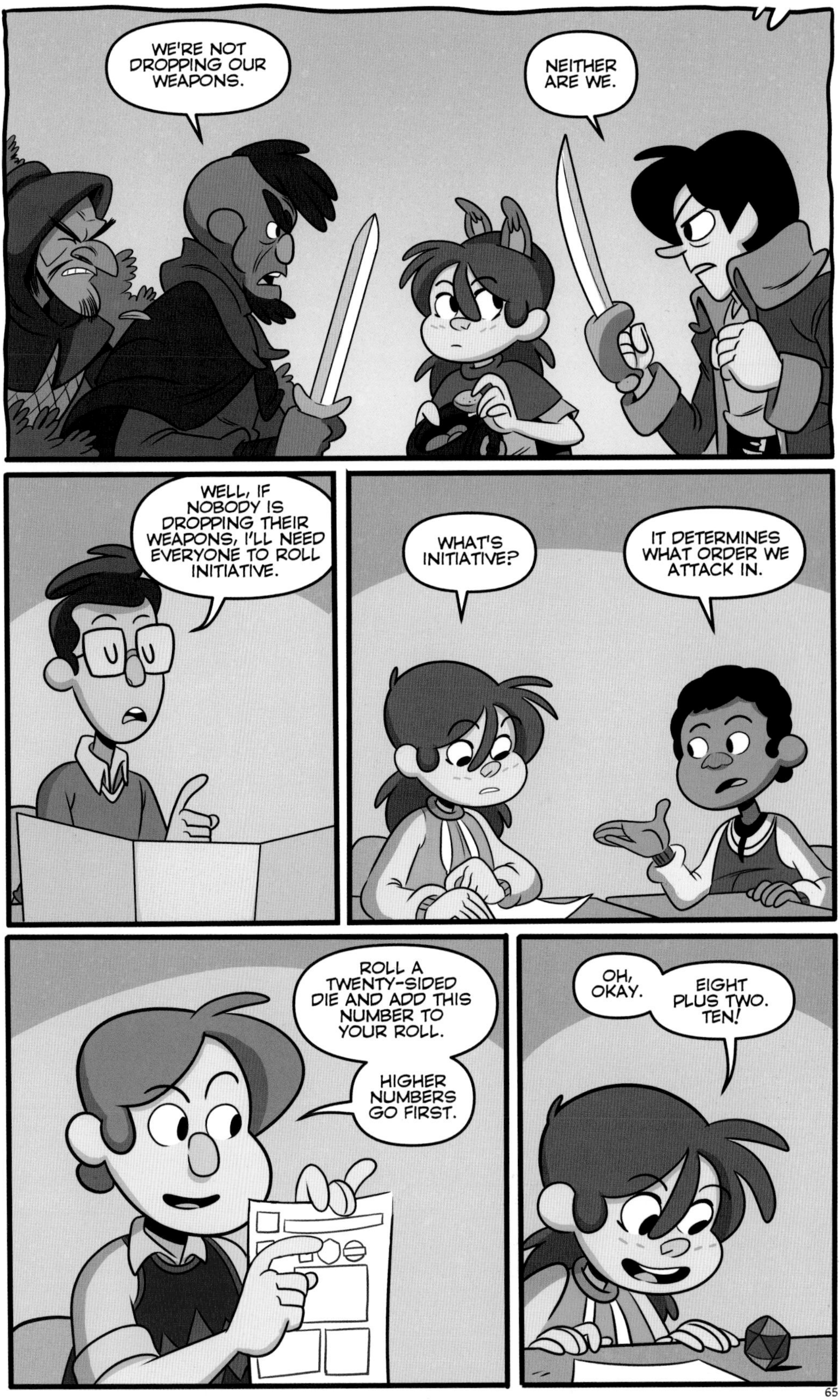
WE'RE NOT DROPPING OUR WEAPONS.
NEITHER ARE WE.
WELL, IF NOBODY IS DROPPING THEIR WEAPONS, I'LL NEED EVERYONE TO ROLL INITIATIVE.
WHAT'S INITIATIVE?
IT DETERMINES WHAT ORDER WE ATTACK IN.
ROLL A TWENTY-SIDED DIE AND ADD THIS NUMBER TO YOUR ROLL.
HIGHER NUMBERS GO FIRST.
OH, OKAY.
EIGHT PLUS TWO. TEN!

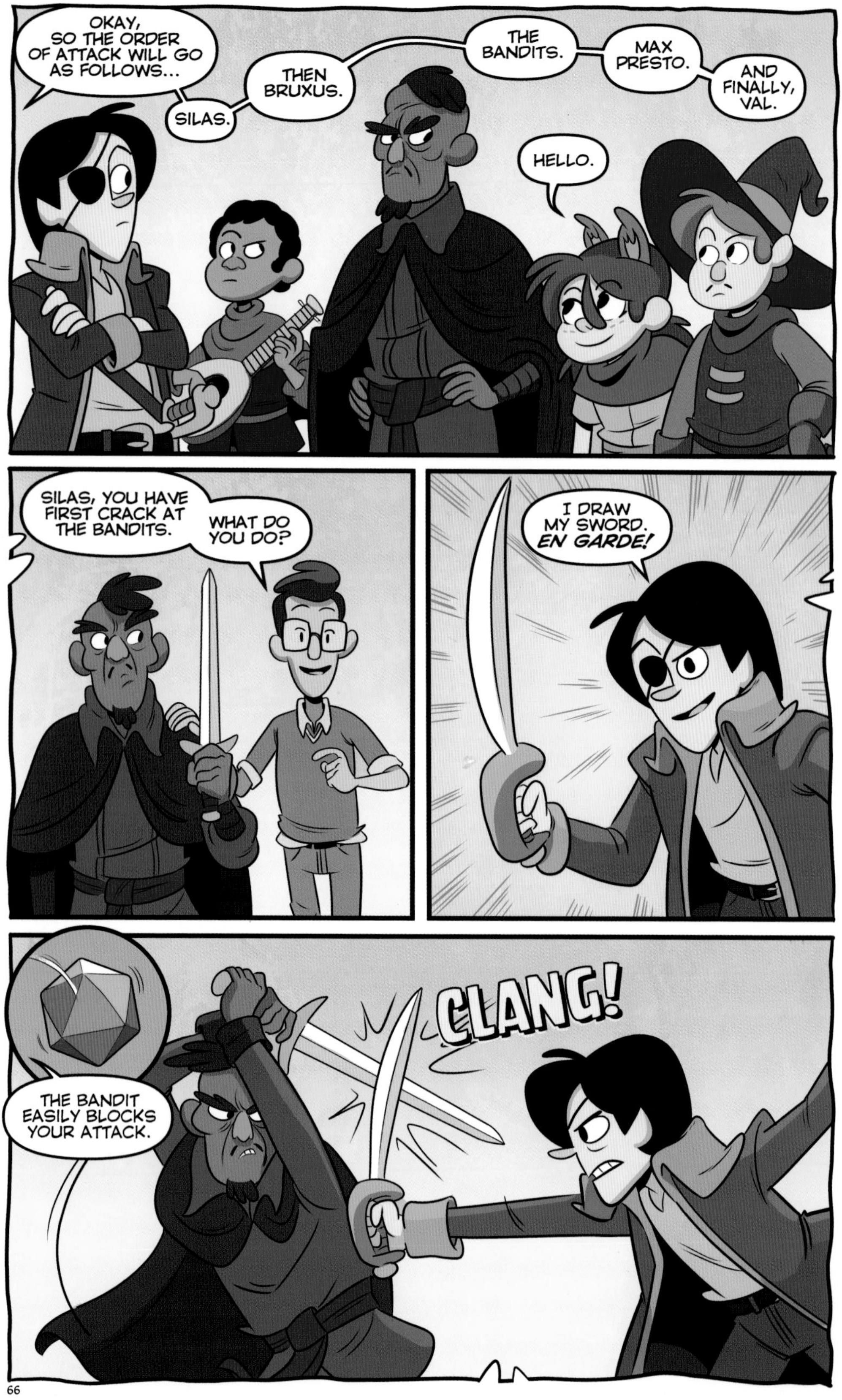
OKAY, SO THE ORDER OF ATTACK WILL GO AS FOLLOWS...
SILAS.
THEN BRUXUS.
THE BANDITS.
MAX PRESTO.
AND FINALLY, VAL.
HELLO.
SILAS, YOU HAVE FIRST CRACK AT THE BANDITS.
WHAT DO YOU DO?
I DRAW MY SWORD. *EN GARDE!*
CLANG!
THE BANDIT EASILY BLOCKS YOUR ATTACK.

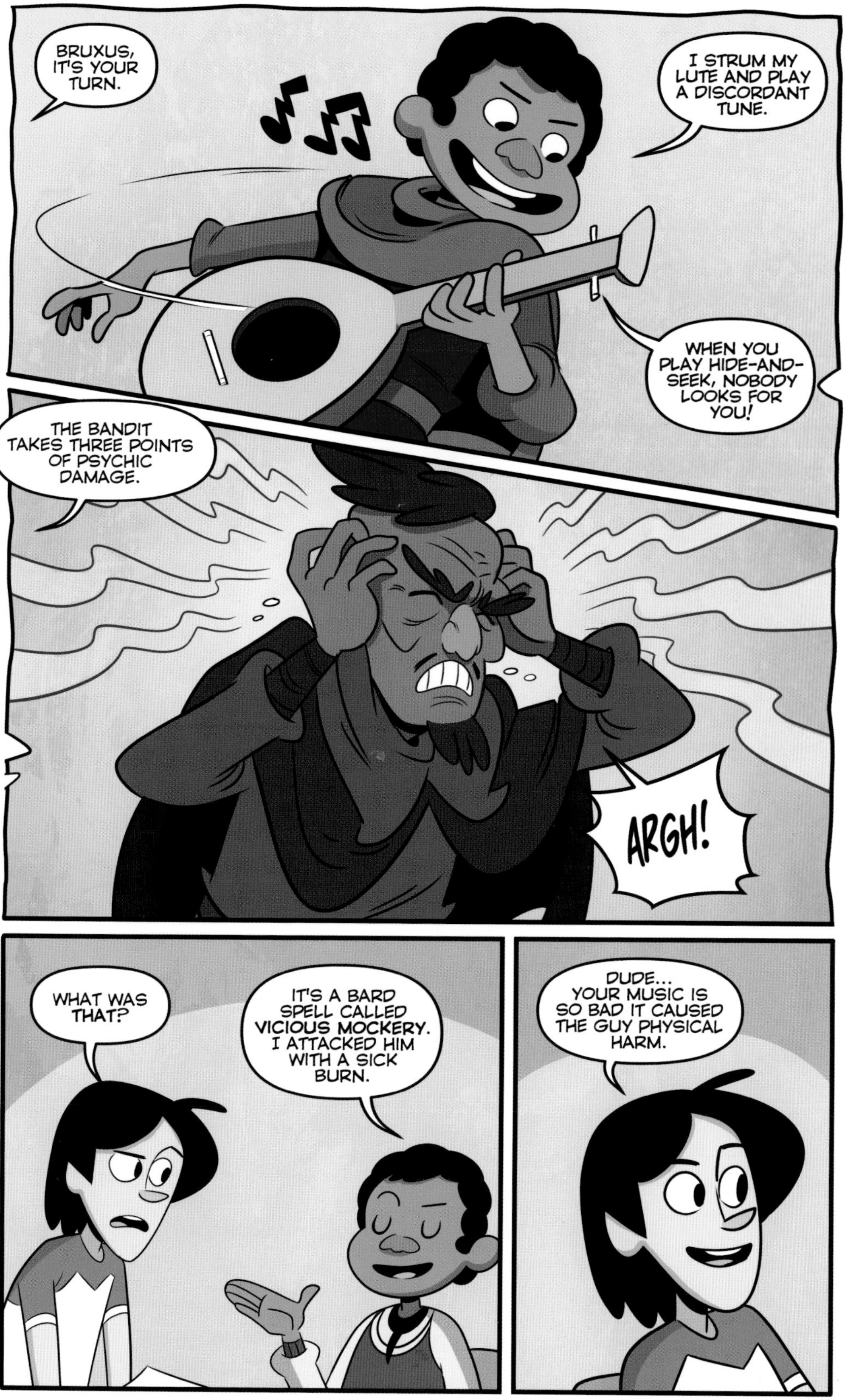

BRUXUS, IT'S YOUR TURN.
I STRUM MY LUTE AND PLAY A DISCORDANT TUNE.
WHEN YOU PLAY HIDE-AND-SEEK, NOBODY LOOKS FOR YOU!
THE BANDIT TAKES THREE POINTS OF PSYCHIC DAMAGE.
ARGH!
WHAT WAS THAT?
IT'S A BARD SPELL CALLED **VICIOUS MOCKERY**. I ATTACKED HIM WITH A SICK BURN.
DUDE... YOUR MUSIC IS SO BAD IT CAUSED THE GUY PHYSICAL HARM.

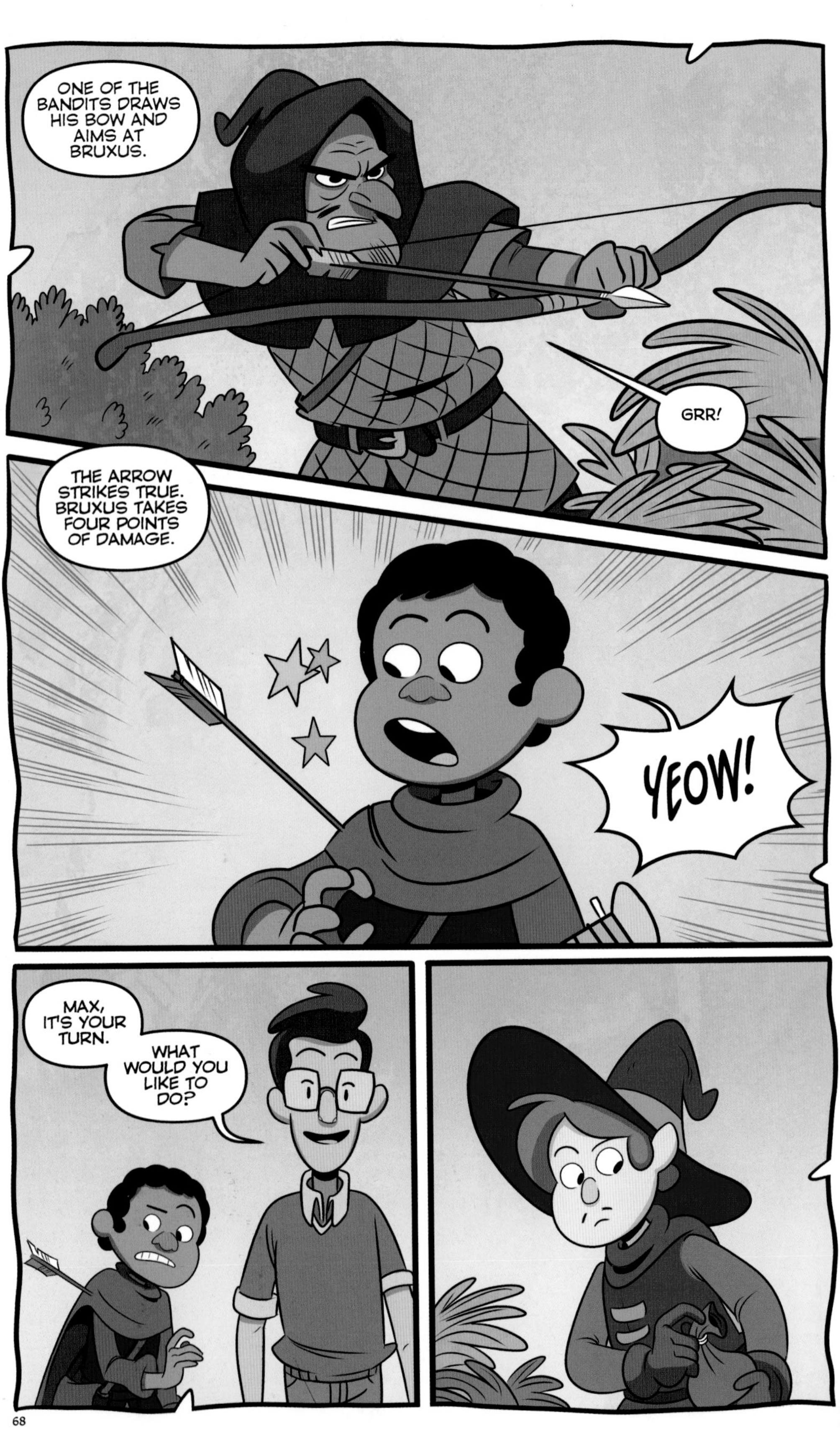
ONE OF THE BANDITS DRAWS HIS BOW AND AIMS AT BRUXUS.
GRR!
THE ARROW STRIKES TRUE. BRUXUS TAKES FOUR POINTS OF DAMAGE.
YEOW!
MAX, IT'S YOUR TURN.
WHAT WOULD YOU LIKE TO DO?

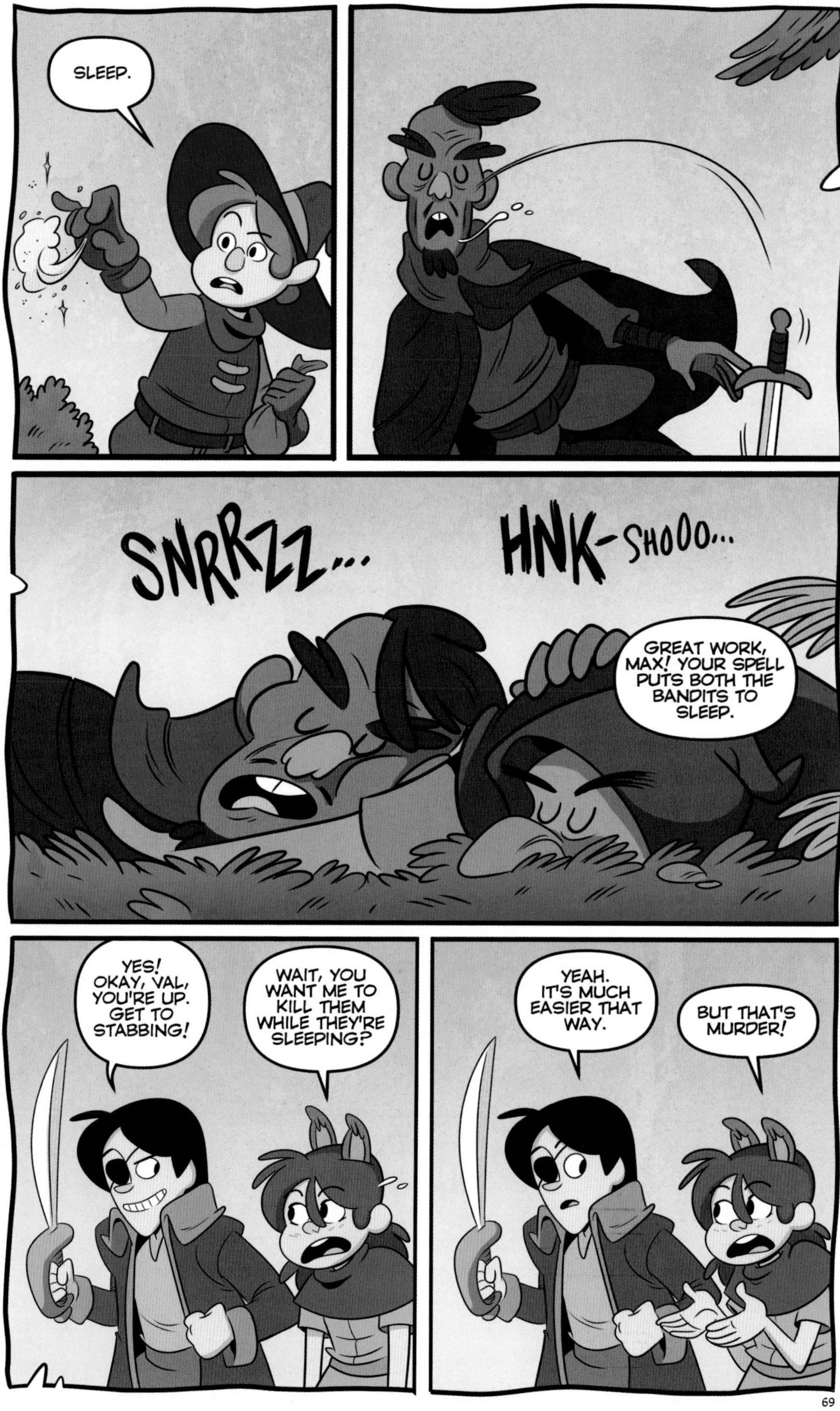
SLEEP.
SNRRZZ...
HNK-SHOOO...
GREAT WORK, MAX! YOUR SPELL PUTS BOTH THE BANDITS TO SLEEP.
YES! OKAY, VAL, YOU'RE UP. GET TO STABBING!
WAIT, YOU WANT ME TO KILL THEM WHILE THEY'RE SLEEPING?
YEAH. IT'S MUCH EASIER THAT WAY.
BUT THAT'S MURDER!

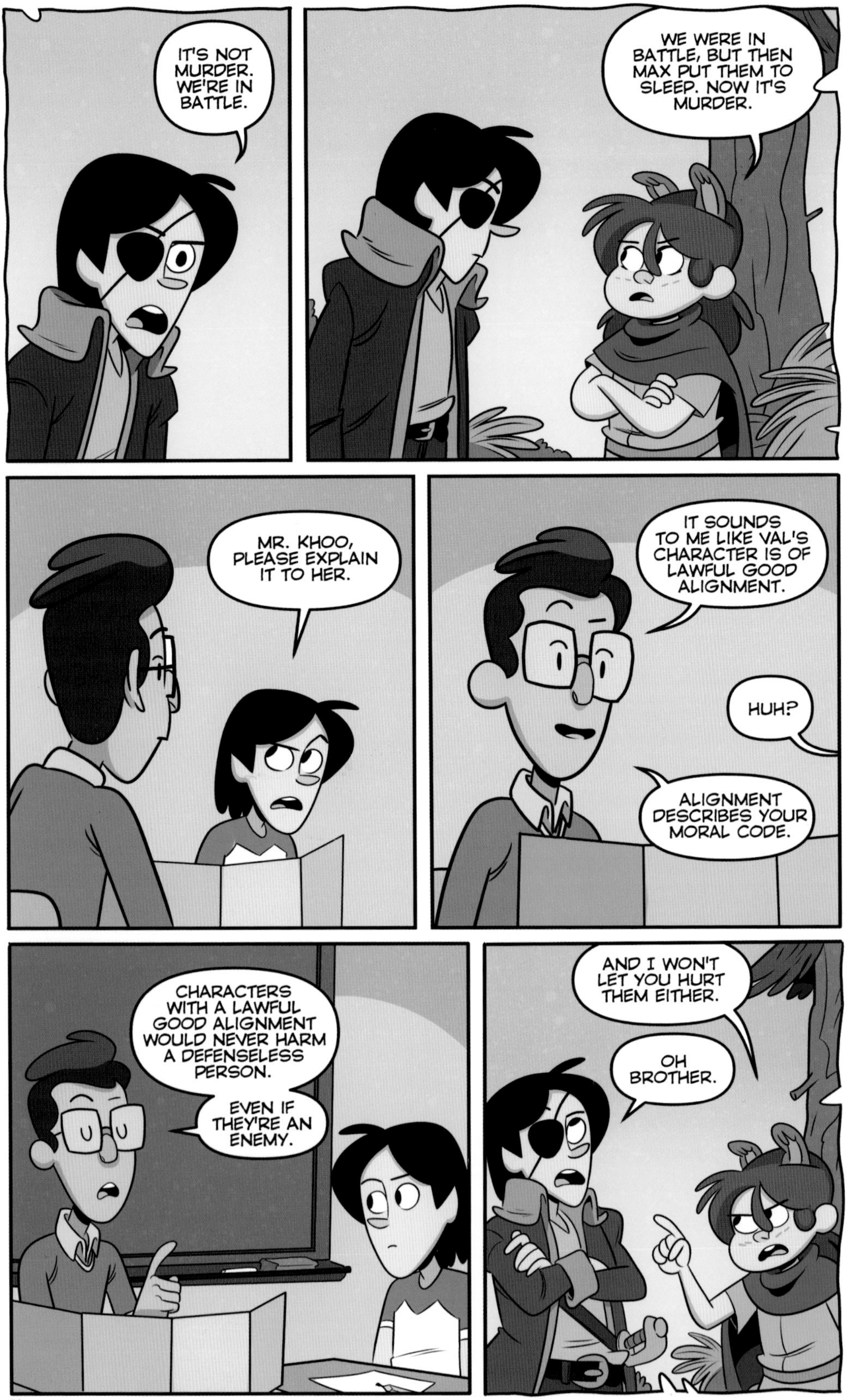
IT'S NOT MURDER. WE'RE IN BATTLE.
WE WERE IN BATTLE, BUT THEN MAX PUT THEM TO SLEEP. NOW IT'S MURDER.
MR. KHOO, PLEASE EXPLAIN IT TO HER.
IT SOUNDS TO ME LIKE VAL'S CHARACTER IS OF LAWFUL GOOD ALIGNMENT.
HUH?
ALIGNMENT DESCRIBES YOUR MORAL CODE.
CHARACTERS WITH A LAWFUL GOOD ALIGNMENT WOULD NEVER HARM A DEFENSELESS PERSON.
EVEN IF THEY'RE AN ENEMY.
AND I WON'T LET YOU HURT THEM EITHER.
OH BROTHER.

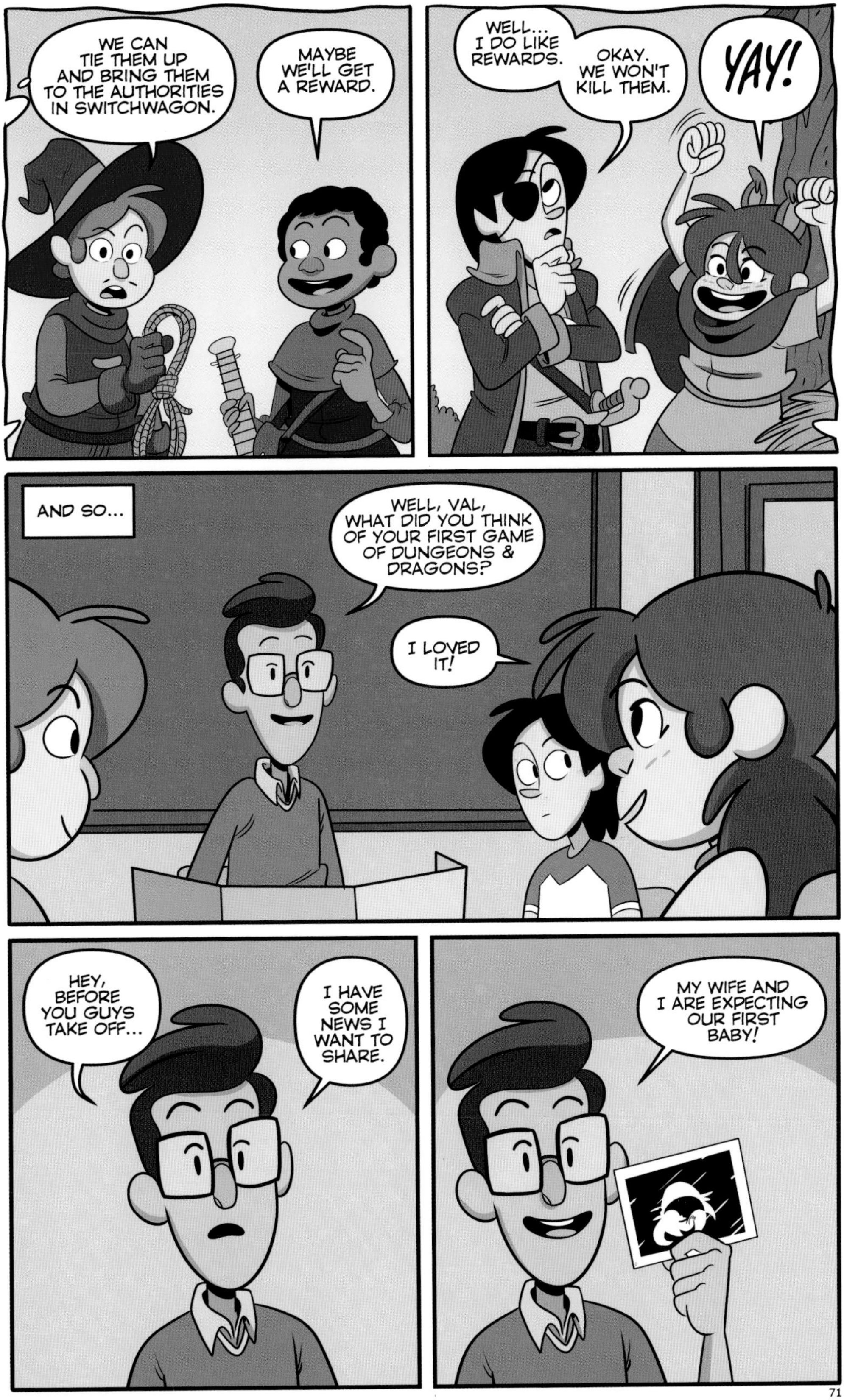
WE CAN TIE THEM UP AND BRING THEM TO THE AUTHORITIES IN SWITCHWAGON.
MAYBE WE'LL GET A REWARD.
WELL... I DO LIKE REWARDS.
OKAY. WE WON'T KILL THEM.
YAY!
AND SO...
WELL, VAL, WHAT DID YOU THINK OF YOUR FIRST GAME OF DUNGEONS & DRAGONS?
I LOVED IT!
HEY, BEFORE YOU GUYS TAKE OFF...
I HAVE SOME NEWS I WANT TO SHARE.
MY WIFE AND I ARE EXPECTING OUR FIRST BABY!

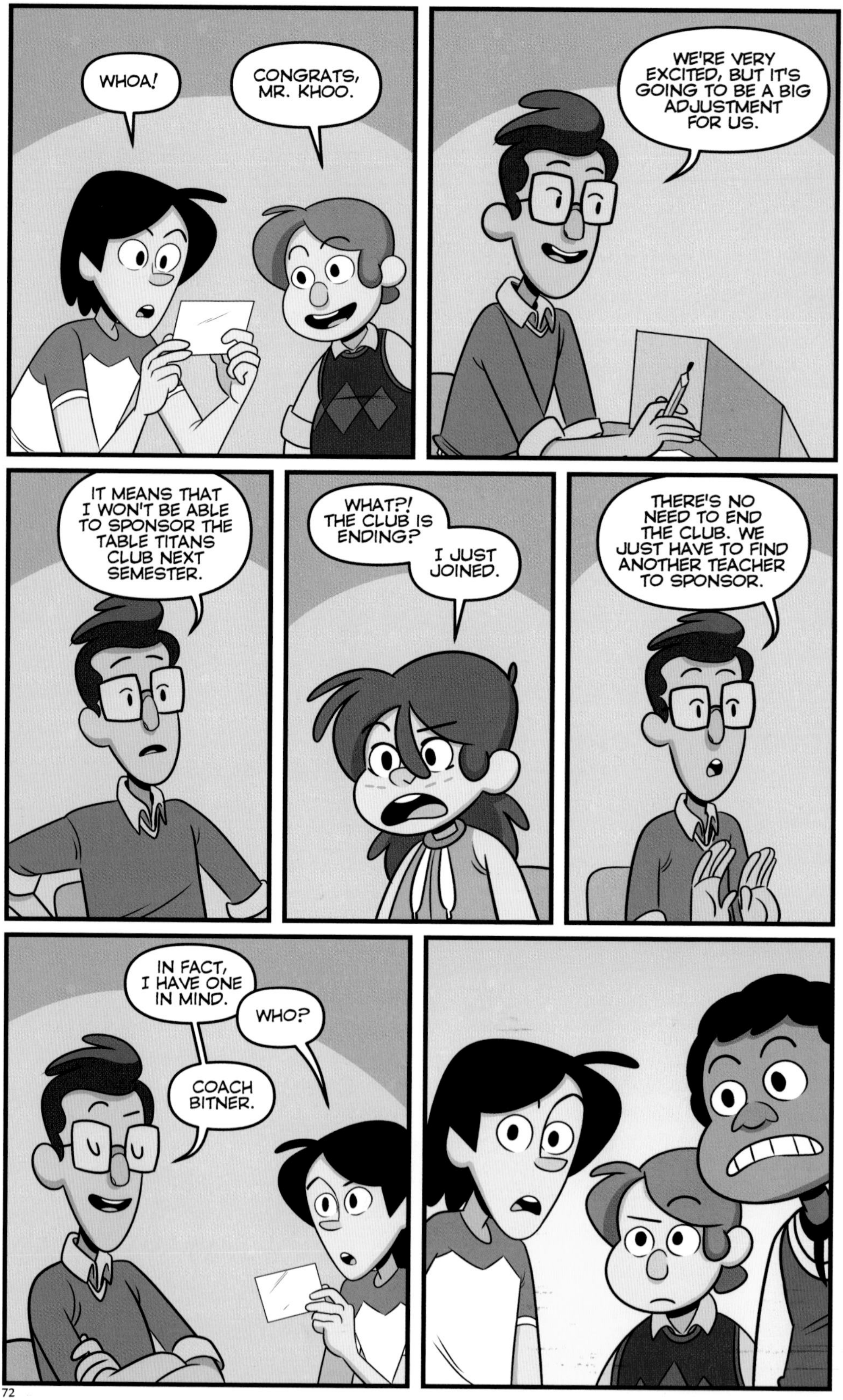
WHOA!
CONGRATS, MR. KHOO.
WE'RE VERY EXCITED, BUT IT'S GOING TO BE A BIG ADJUSTMENT FOR US.
IT MEANS THAT I WON'T BE ABLE TO SPONSOR THE TABLE TITANS CLUB NEXT SEMESTER.
WHAT?! THE CLUB IS ENDING?
I JUST JOINED.
THERE'S NO NEED TO END THE CLUB. WE JUST HAVE TO FIND ANOTHER TEACHER TO SPONSOR.
IN FACT, I HAVE ONE IN MIND.
WHO?
COACH BITNER.

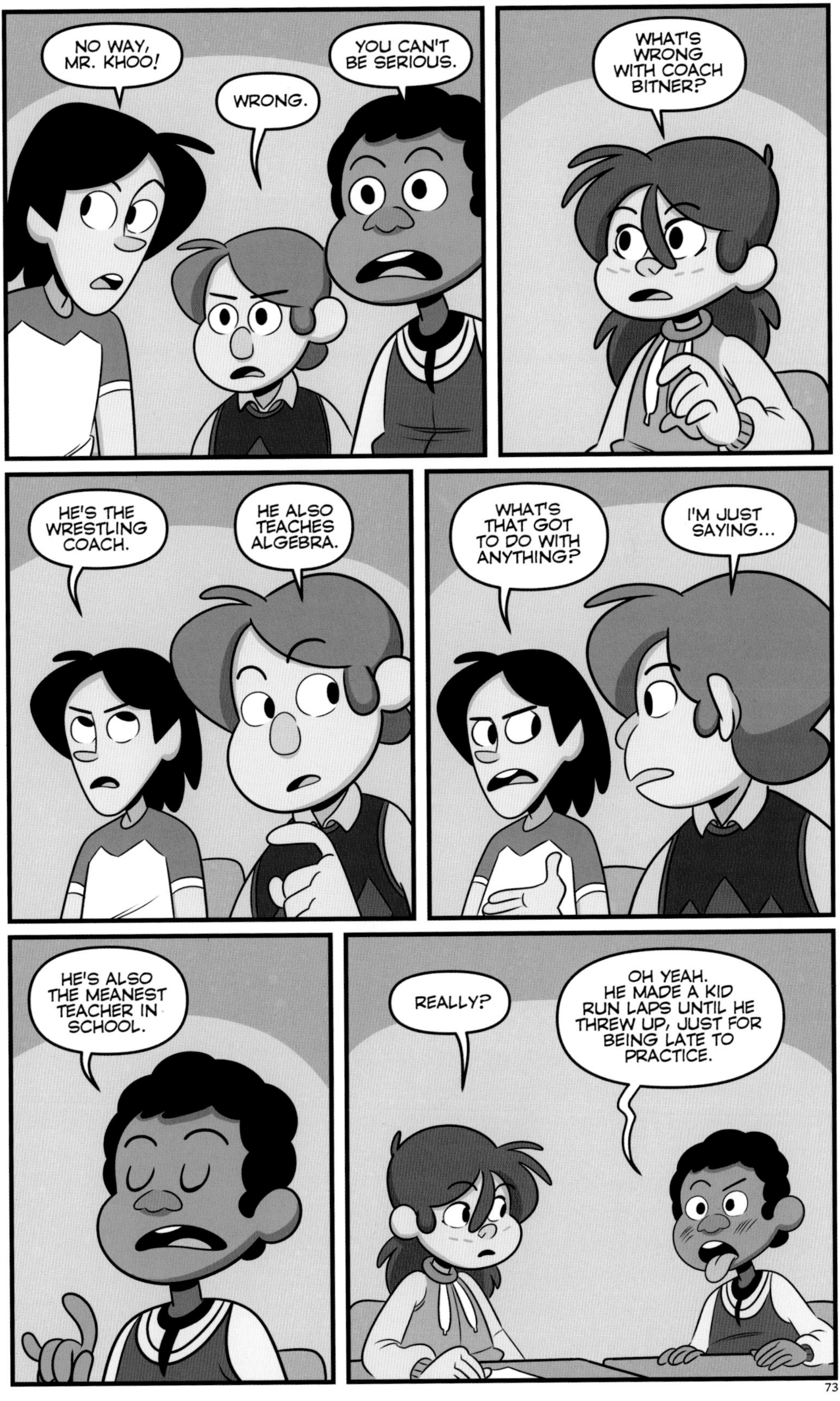
NO WAY, MR. KHOO!
WRONG.
YOU CAN'T BE SERIOUS.
WHAT'S WRONG WITH COACH BITNER?
HE'S THE WRESTLING COACH.
HE ALSO TEACHES ALGEBRA.
WHAT'S THAT GOT TO DO WITH ANYTHING?
I'M JUST SAYING...
HE'S ALSO THE MEANEST TEACHER IN SCHOOL.
REALLY?
OH YEAH. HE MADE A KID RUN LAPS UNTIL HE THREW UP, JUST FOR BEING LATE TO PRACTICE.

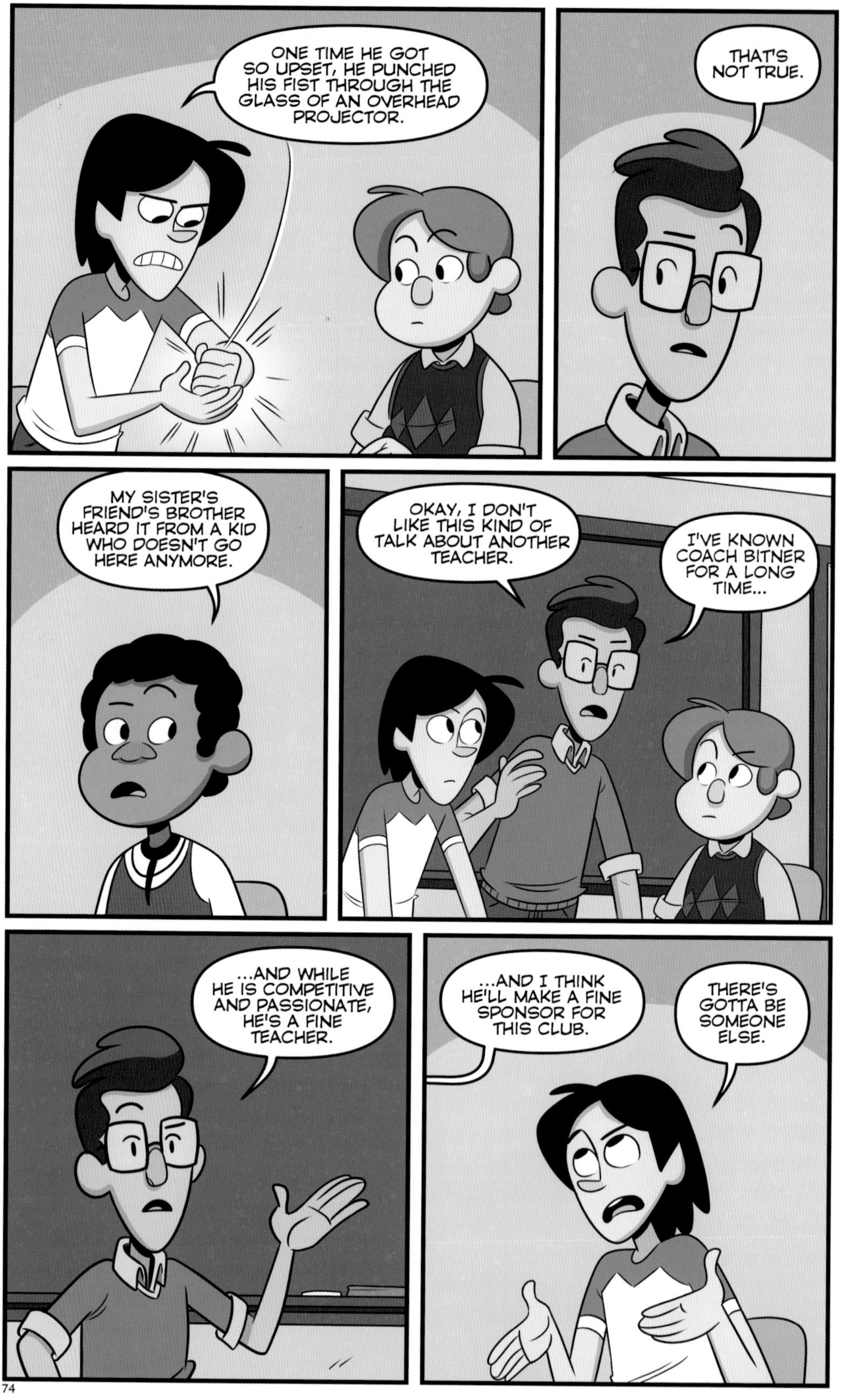
ONE TIME HE GOT SO UPSET, HE PUNCHED HIS FIST THROUGH THE GLASS OF AN OVERHEAD PROJECTOR.
THAT'S NOT TRUE.
MY SISTER'S FRIEND'S BROTHER HEARD IT FROM A KID WHO DOESN'T GO HERE ANYMORE.
OKAY, I DON'T LIKE THIS KIND OF TALK ABOUT ANOTHER TEACHER.
I'VE KNOWN COACH BITNER FOR A LONG TIME...
...AND WHILE HE IS COMPETITIVE AND PASSIONATE, HE'S A FINE TEACHER.
...AND I THINK HE'LL MAKE A FINE SPONSOR FOR THIS CLUB.
THERE'S GOTTA BE SOMEONE ELSE.

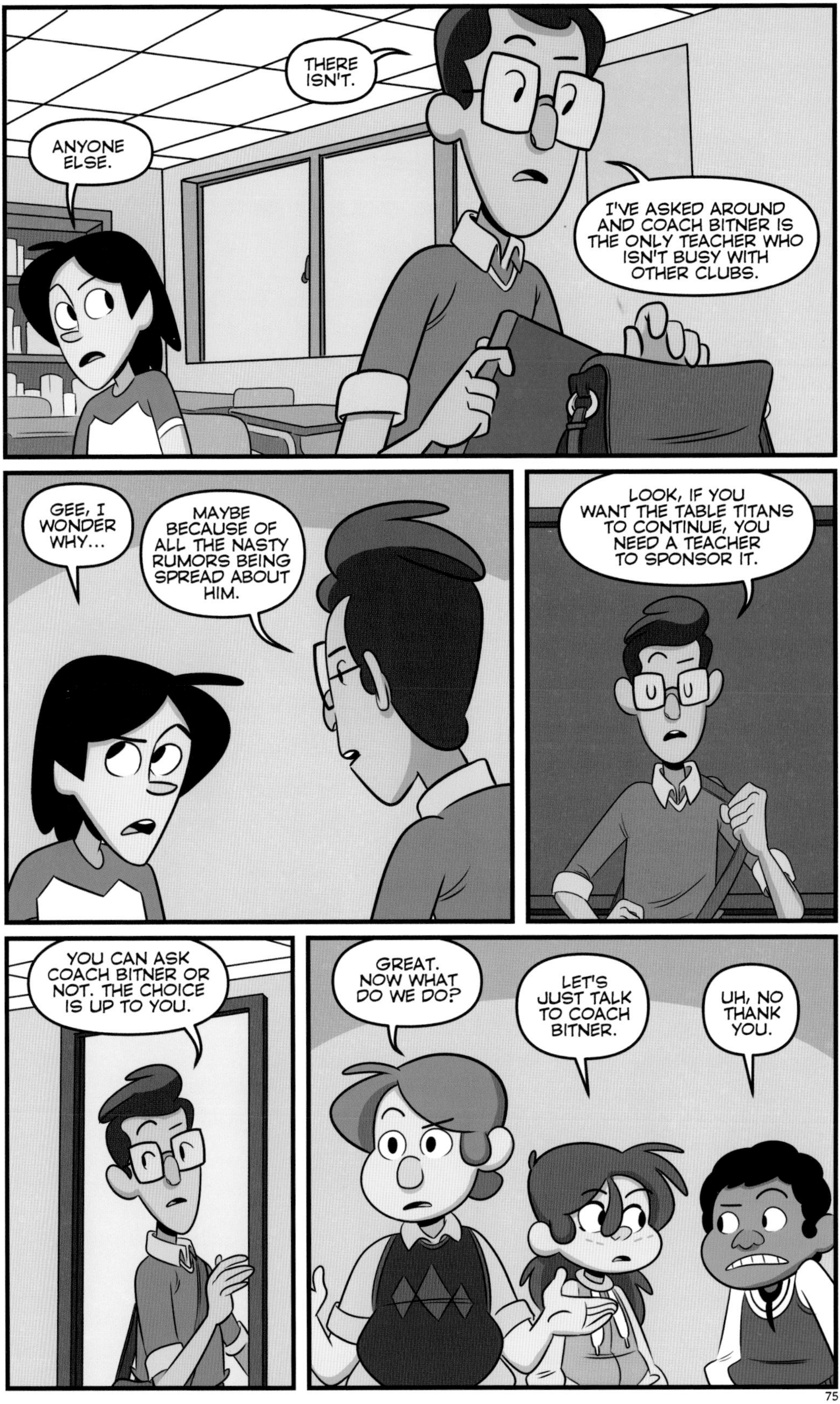
ANYONE ELSE.
THERE ISN'T.
I'VE ASKED AROUND AND COACH BITNER IS THE ONLY TEACHER WHO ISN'T BUSY WITH OTHER CLUBS.
GEE, I WONDER WHY...
MAYBE BECAUSE OF ALL THE NASTY RUMORS BEING SPREAD ABOUT HIM.
LOOK, IF YOU WANT THE TABLE TITANS TO CONTINUE, YOU NEED A TEACHER TO SPONSOR IT.
YOU CAN ASK COACH BITNER OR NOT. THE CHOICE IS UP TO YOU.
GREAT. NOW WHAT DO WE DO?
LET'S JUST TALK TO COACH BITNER.
UH, NO THANK YOU.

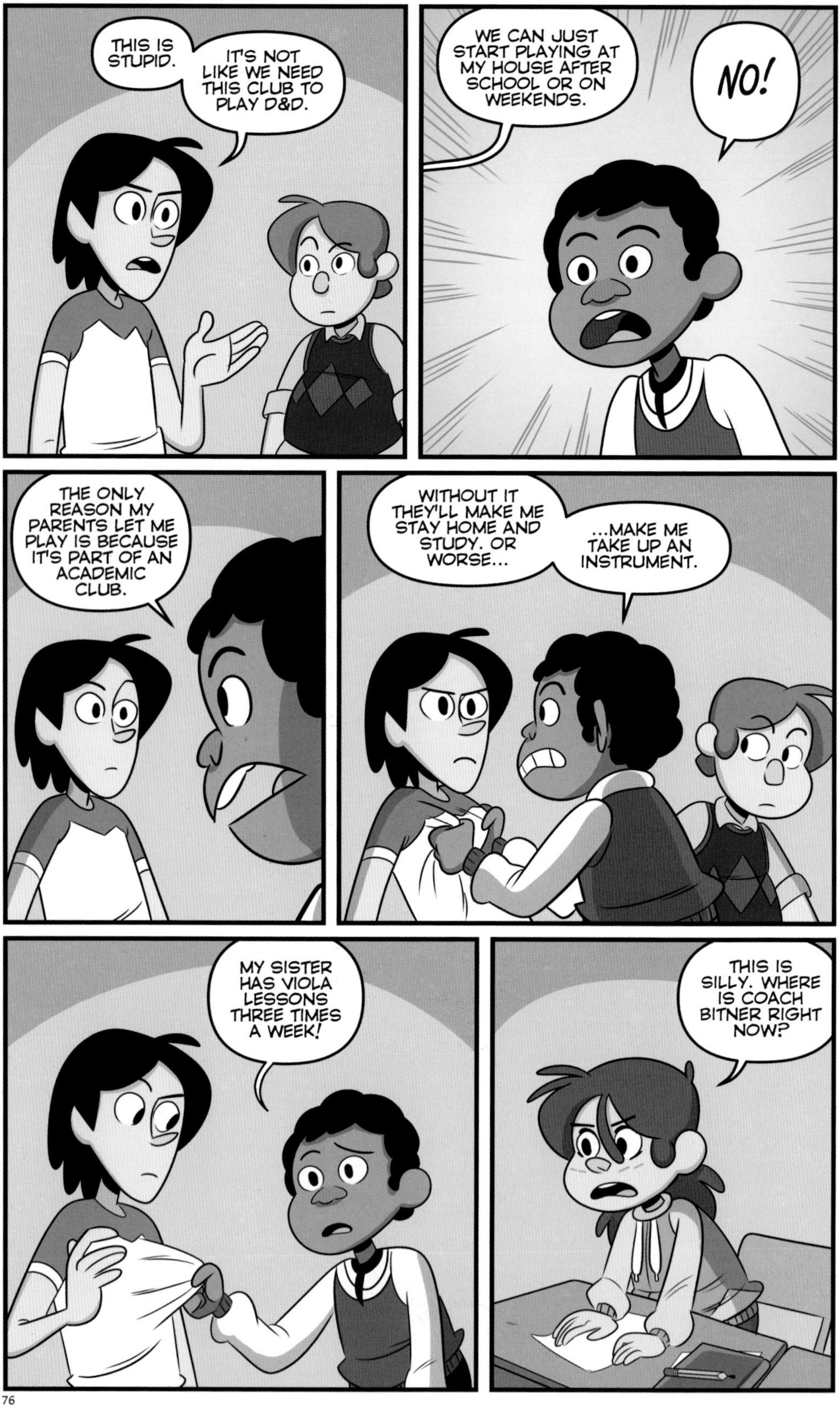
THIS IS STUPID.
IT'S NOT LIKE WE NEED THIS CLUB TO PLAY D&D.
WE CAN JUST START PLAYING AT MY HOUSE AFTER SCHOOL OR ON WEEKENDS.
NO!
THE ONLY REASON MY PARENTS LET ME PLAY IS BECAUSE IT'S PART OF AN ACADEMIC CLUB.
WITHOUT IT THEY'LL MAKE ME STAY HOME AND STUDY. OR WORSE...
...MAKE ME TAKE UP AN INSTRUMENT.
MY SISTER HAS VIOLA LESSONS THREE TIMES A WEEK!
THIS IS SILLY. WHERE IS COACH BITNER RIGHT NOW?

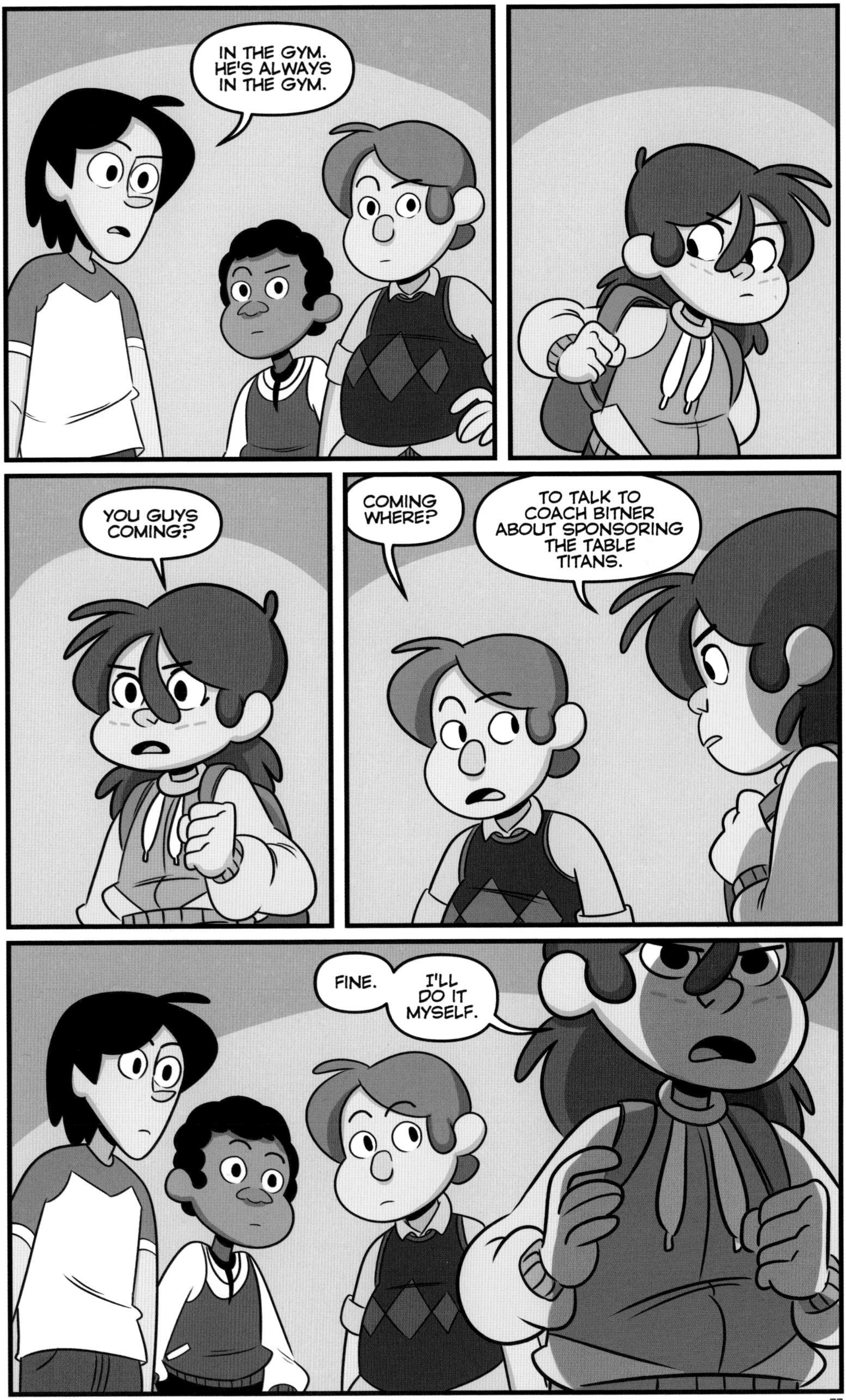
IN THE GYM. HE'S ALWAYS IN THE GYM.
YOU GUYS COMING?
COMING WHERE?
TO TALK TO COACH BITNER ABOUT SPONSORING THE TABLE TITANS.
FINE.
I'LL DO IT MYSELF.

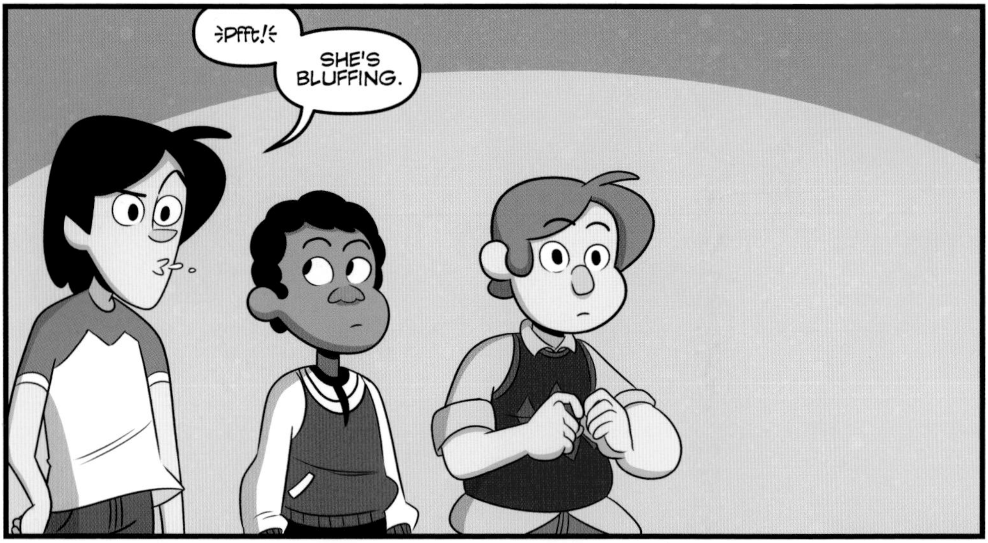
PFFT!
SHE'S BLUFFING.

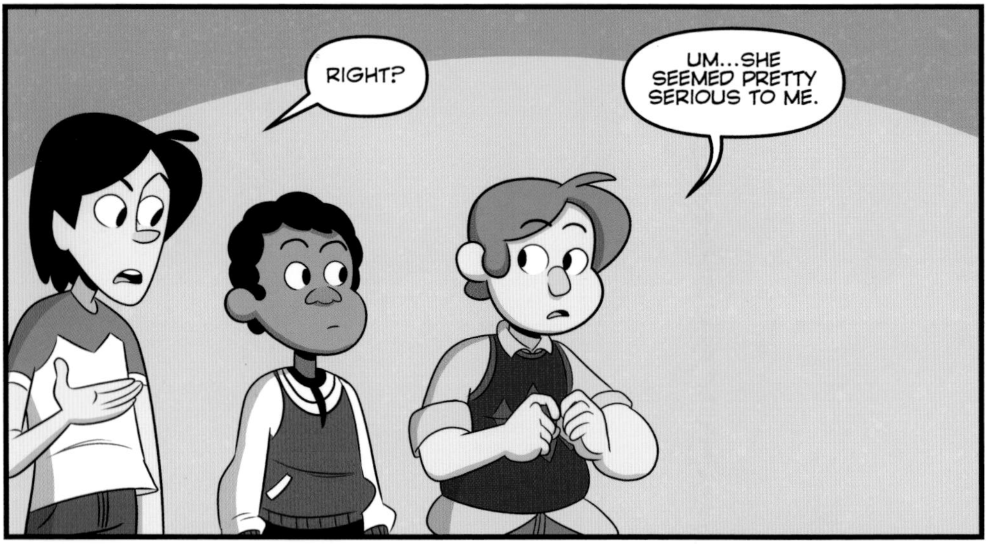
RIGHT?
UM...SHE SEEMED PRETTY SERIOUS TO ME.

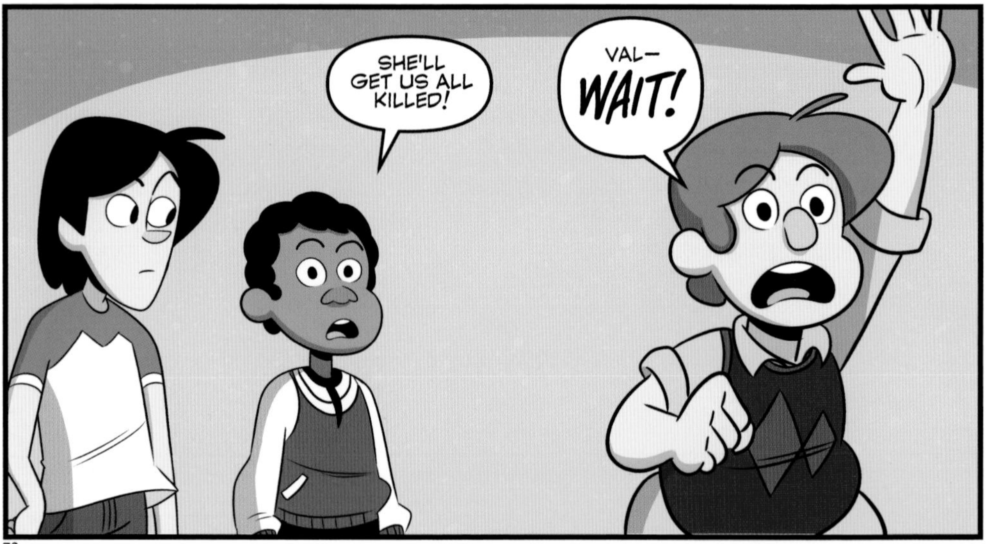
SHE'LL GET US ALL KILLED!
VAL—
WAIT!

GYMNASIUM: COACH BITNER

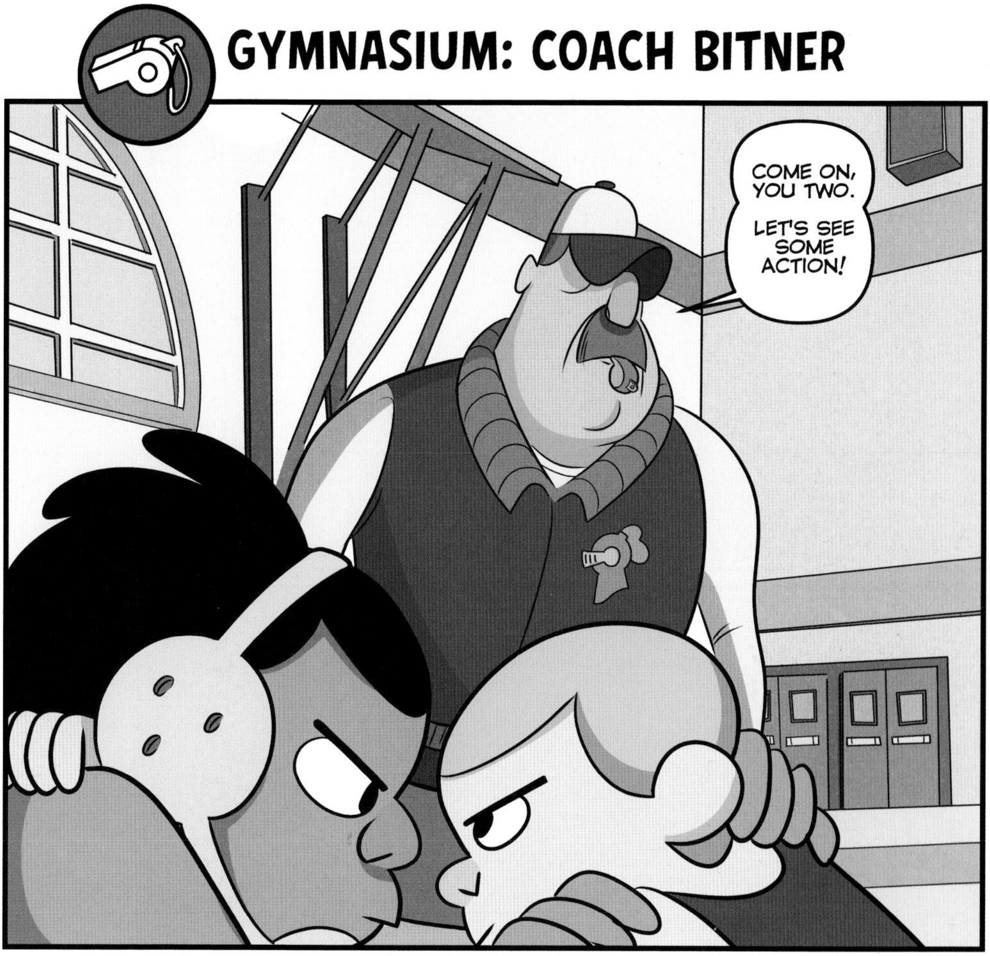
COME ON, YOU TWO.
LET'S SEE SOME ACTION!

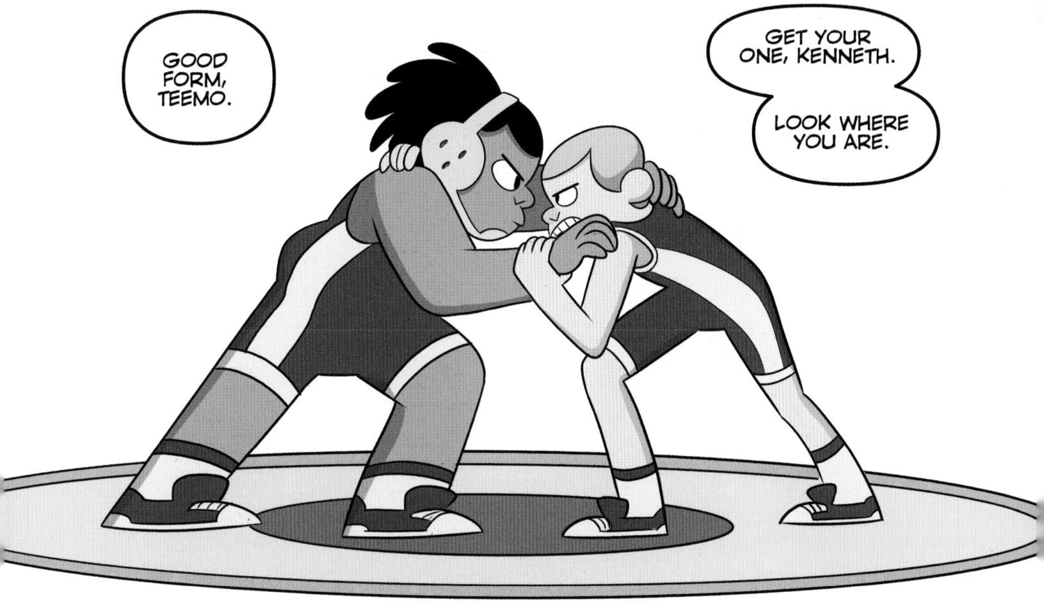
GOOD FORM, TEEMO.
GET YOUR ONE, KENNETH.
LOOK WHERE YOU ARE.

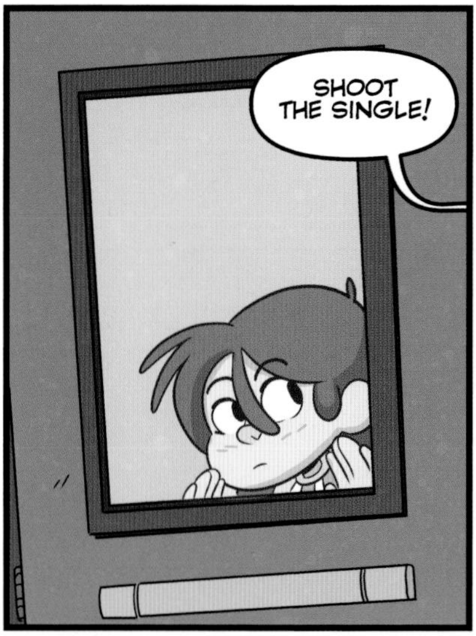
SHOOT THE SINGLE!

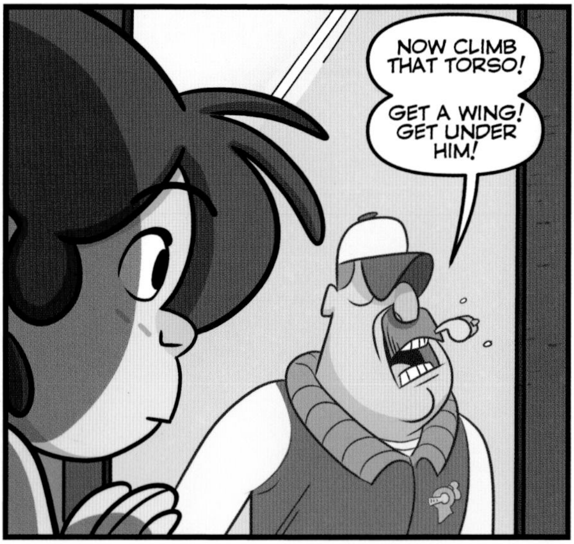
NOW CLIMB THAT TORSO!
GET A WING! GET UNDER HIM!

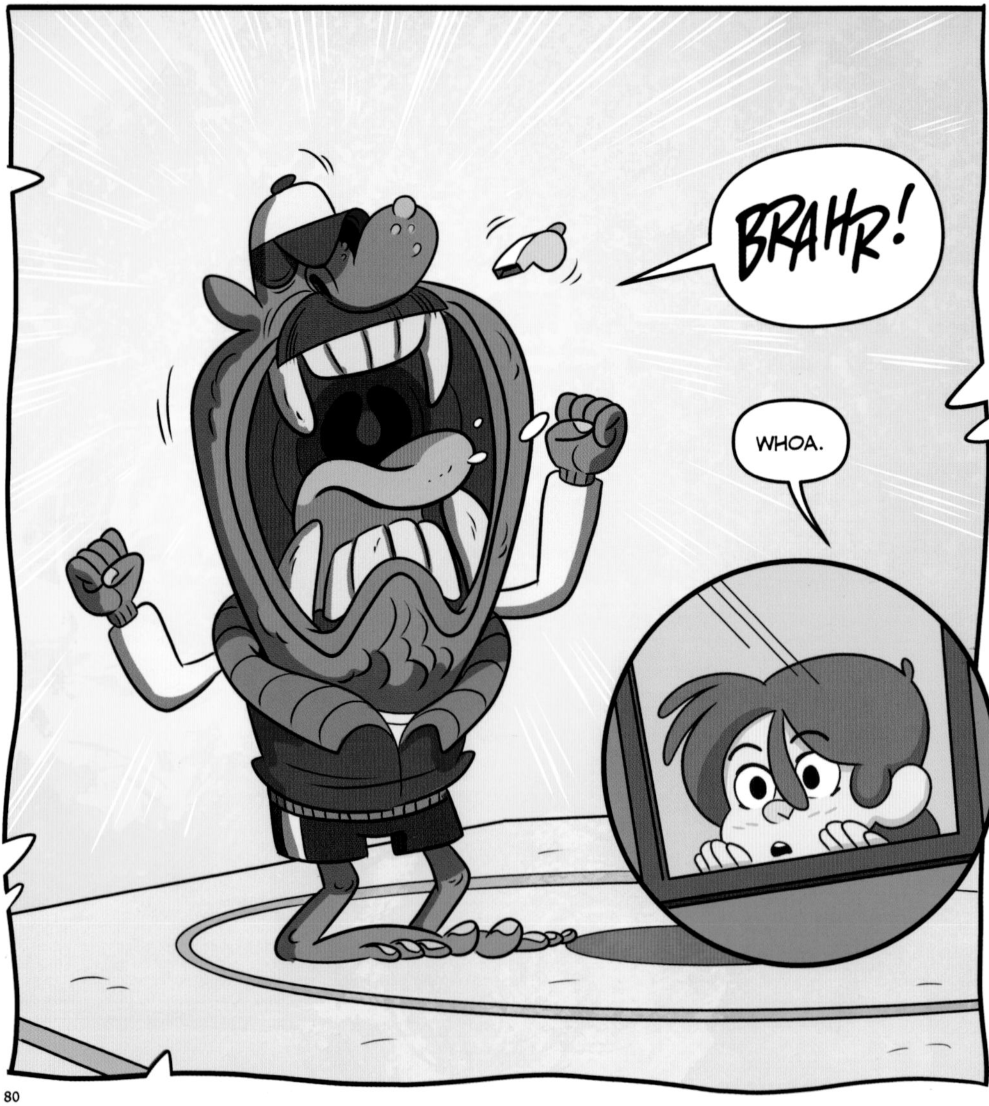
BRAHR!
WHOA.

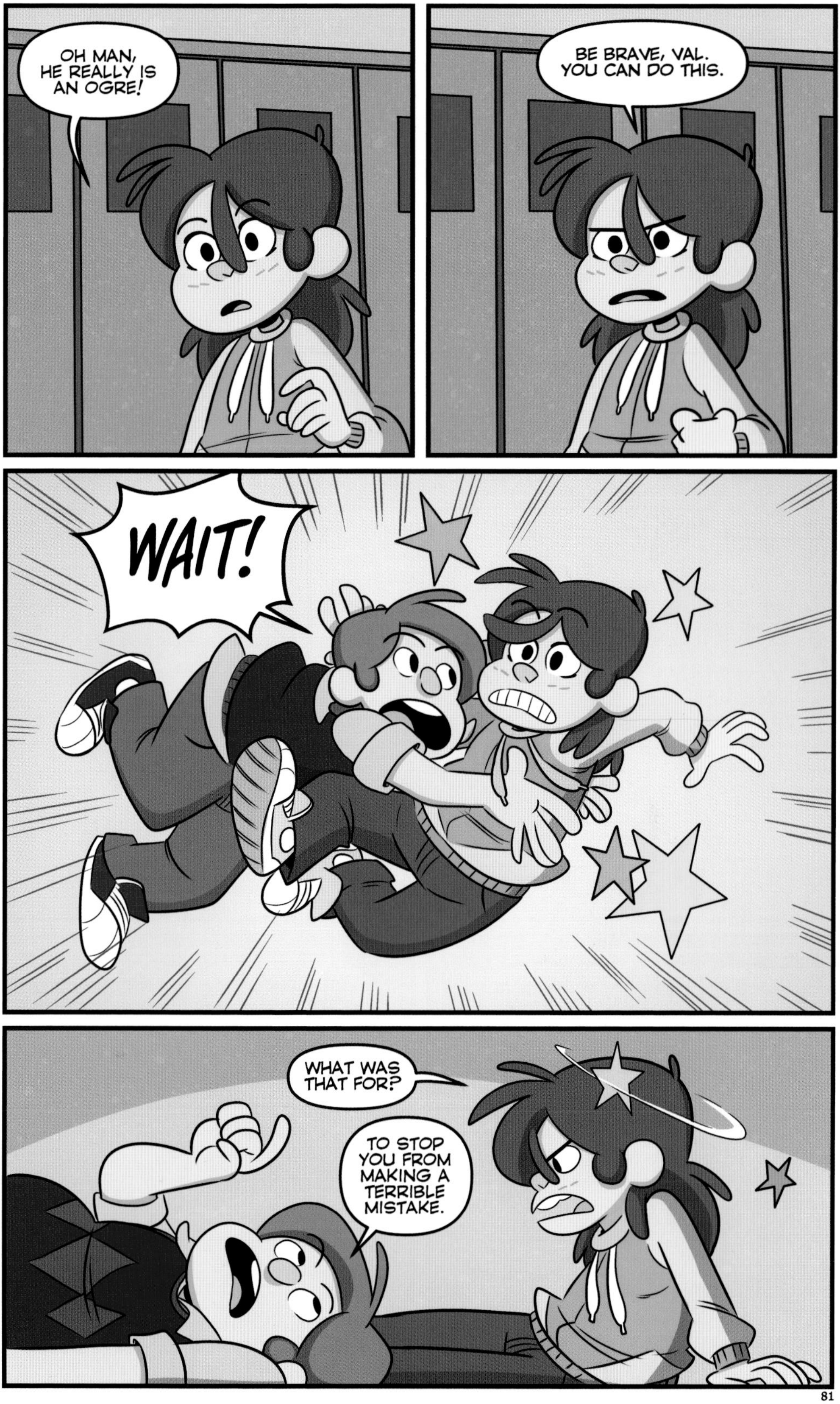
OH MAN, HE REALLY IS AN OGRE!
BE BRAVE, VAL. YOU CAN DO THIS.
WAIT!
WHAT WAS THAT FOR?
TO STOP YOU FROM MAKING A TERRIBLE MISTAKE.

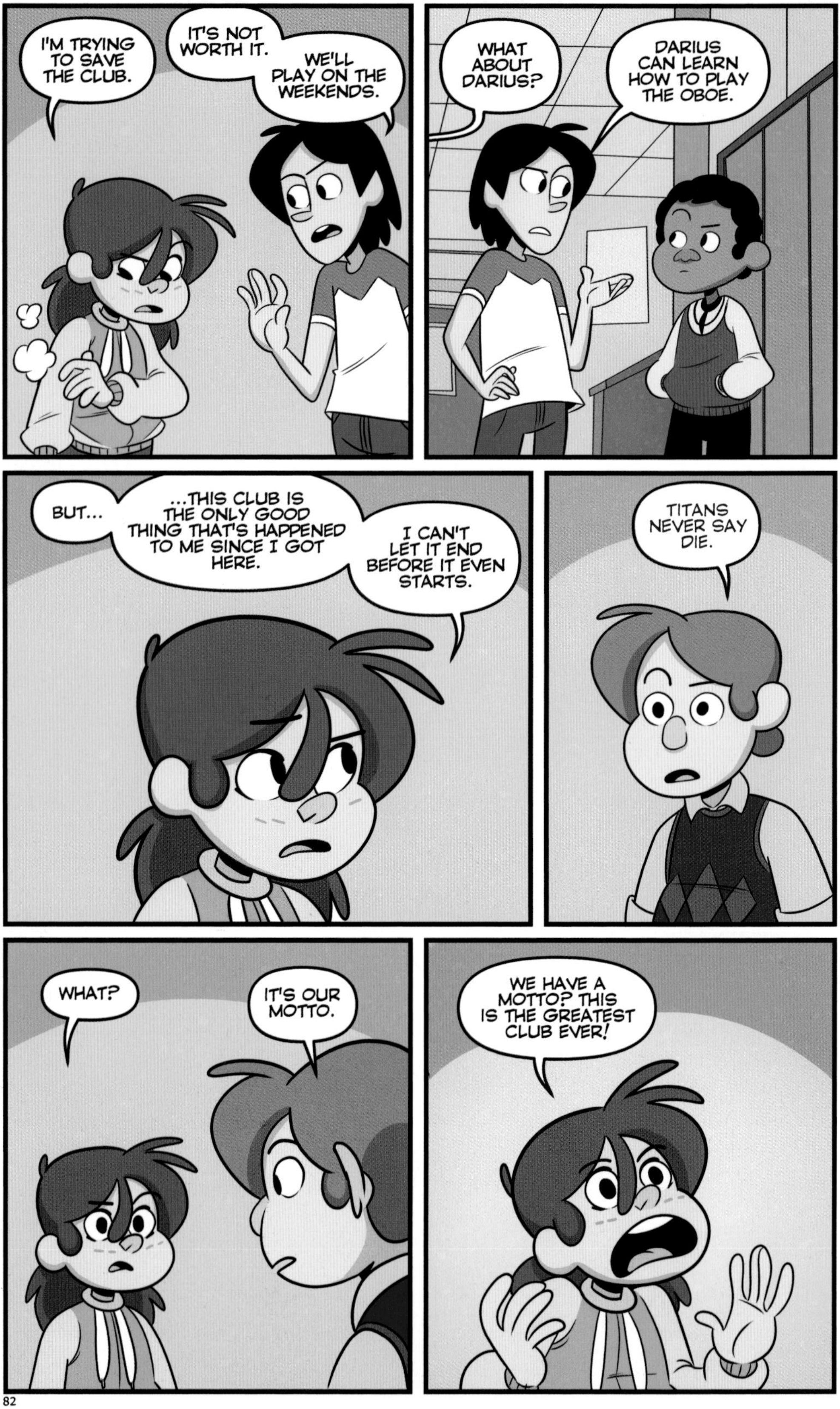
I'M TRYING TO SAVE THE CLUB.
IT'S NOT WORTH IT.
WE'LL PLAY ON THE WEEKENDS.
WHAT ABOUT DARIUS?
DARIUS CAN LEARN HOW TO PLAY THE OBOE.
BUT...
...THIS CLUB IS THE ONLY GOOD THING THAT'S HAPPENED TO ME SINCE I GOT HERE.
I CAN'T LET IT END BEFORE IT EVEN STARTS.
TITANS NEVER SAY DIE.
WHAT?
IT'S OUR MOTTO.
WE HAVE A MOTTO? THIS IS THE GREATEST CLUB EVER!

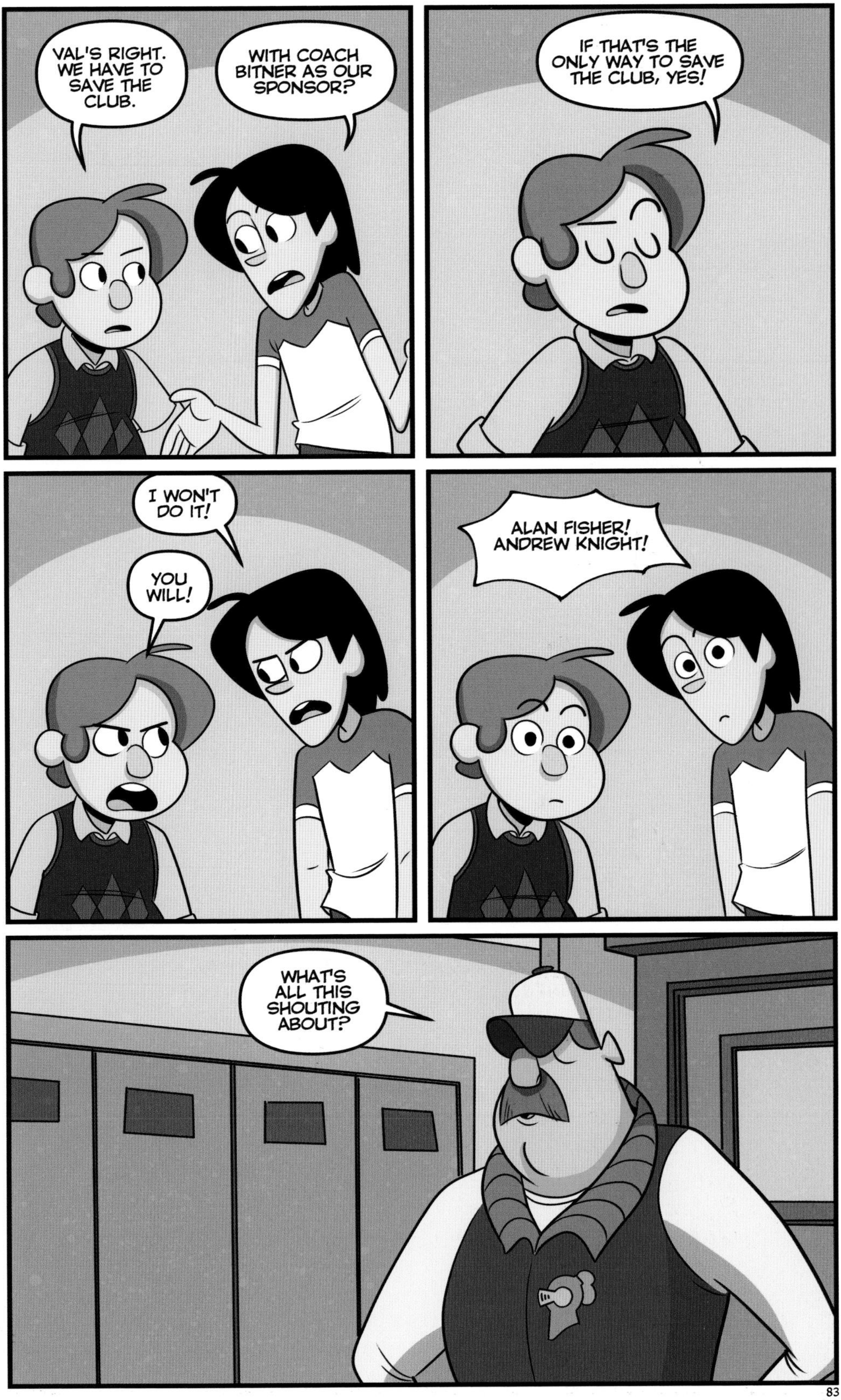
VAL'S RIGHT. WE HAVE TO SAVE THE CLUB.
WITH COACH BITNER AS OUR SPONSOR?
IF THAT'S THE ONLY WAY TO SAVE THE CLUB, YES!
I WON'T DO IT!
YOU WILL!
ALAN FISHER! ANDREW KNIGHT!
WHAT'S ALL THIS SHOUTING ABOUT?

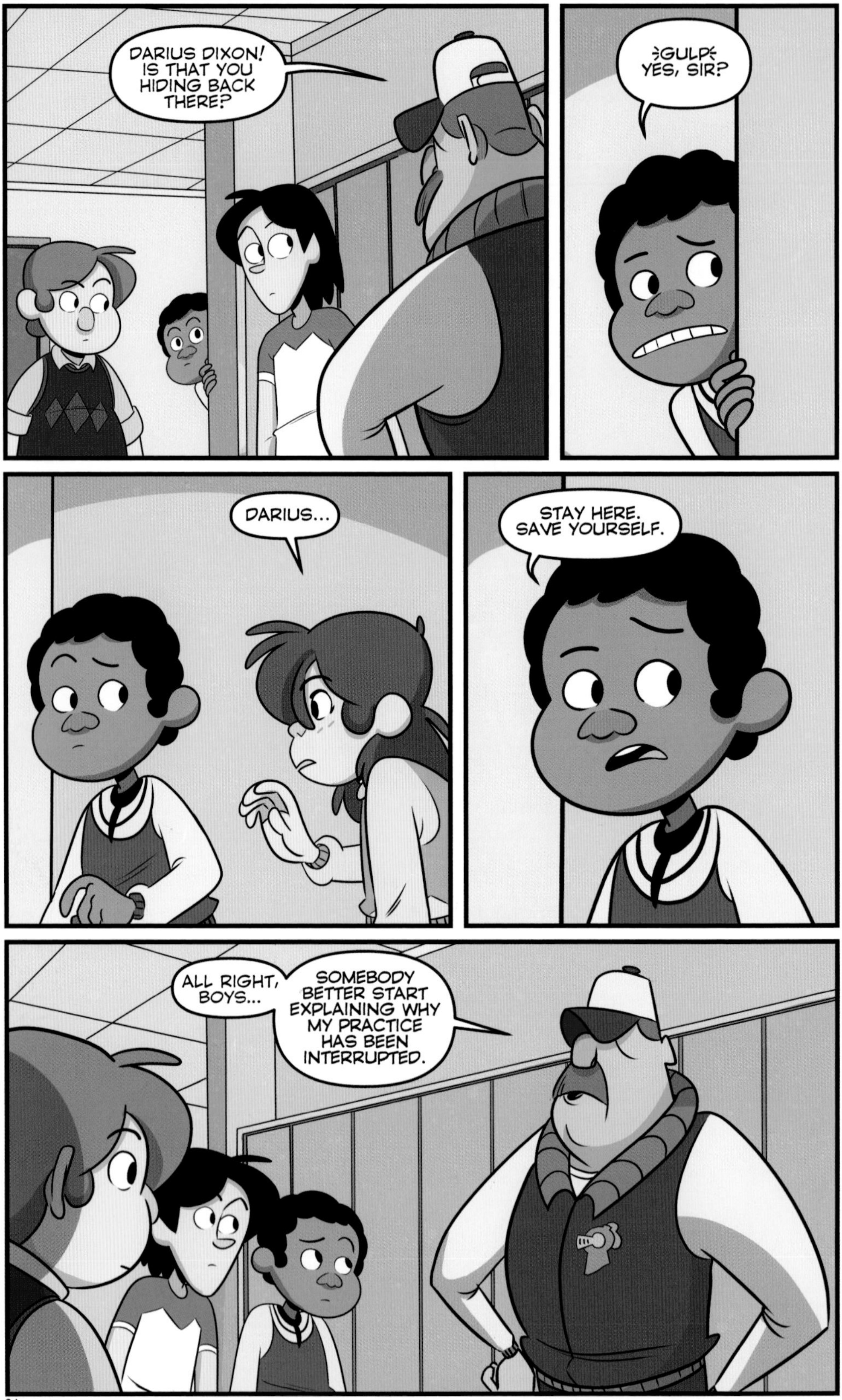

DARIUS DIXON! IS THAT YOU HIDING BACK THERE?
⊰GULP⊱ YES, SIR?
DARIUS...
STAY HERE. SAVE YOURSELF.
ALL RIGHT, BOYS...
SOMEBODY BETTER START EXPLAINING WHY MY PRACTICE HAS BEEN INTERRUPTED.

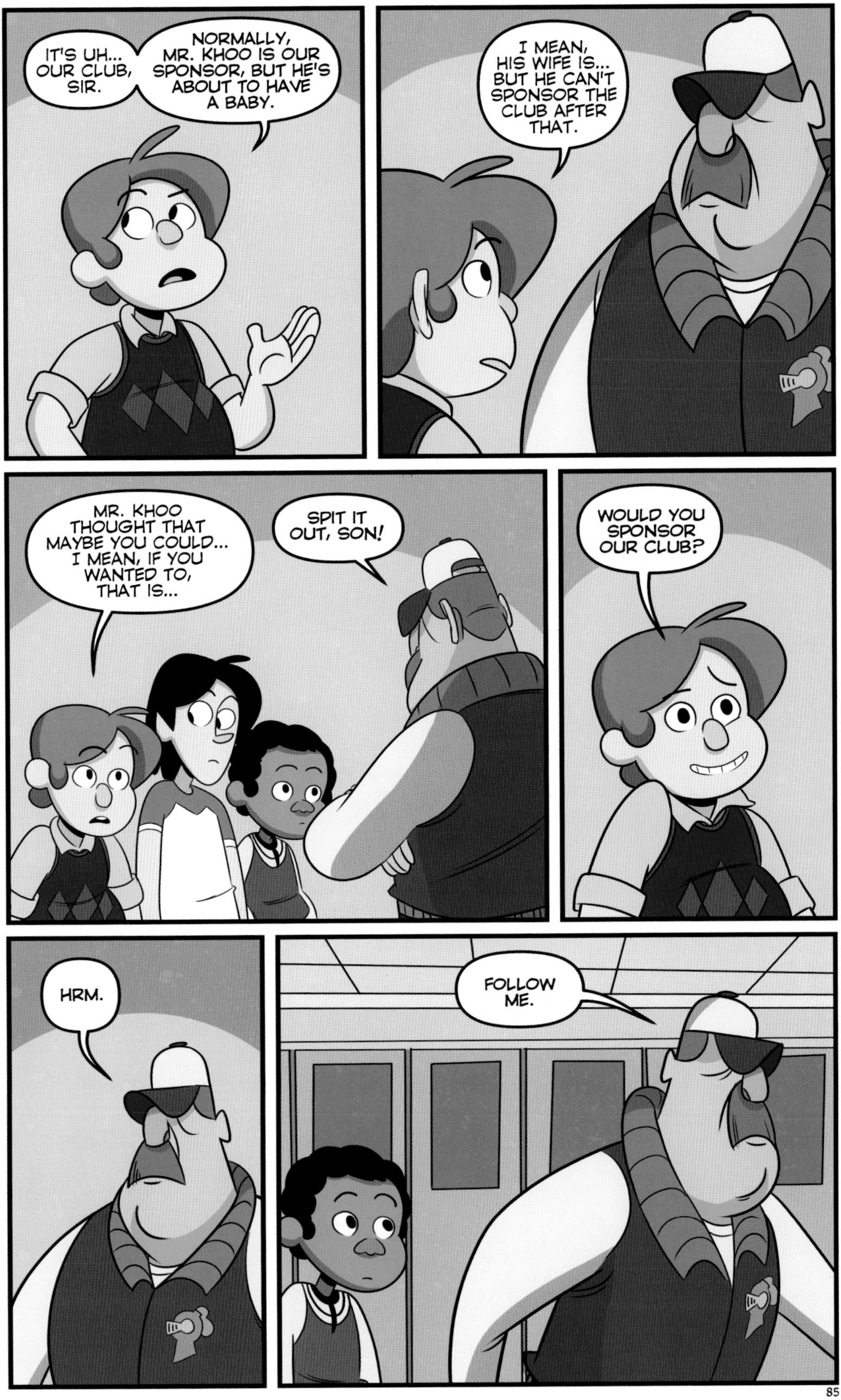
IT'S UH... OUR CLUB, SIR.
NORMALLY, MR. KHOO IS OUR SPONSOR, BUT HE'S ABOUT TO HAVE A BABY.
I MEAN, HIS WIFE IS... BUT HE CAN'T SPONSOR THE CLUB AFTER THAT.
MR. KHOO THOUGHT THAT MAYBE YOU COULD... I MEAN, IF YOU WANTED TO, THAT IS...
SPIT IT OUT, SON!
WOULD YOU SPONSOR OUR CLUB?
HRM.
FOLLOW ME.

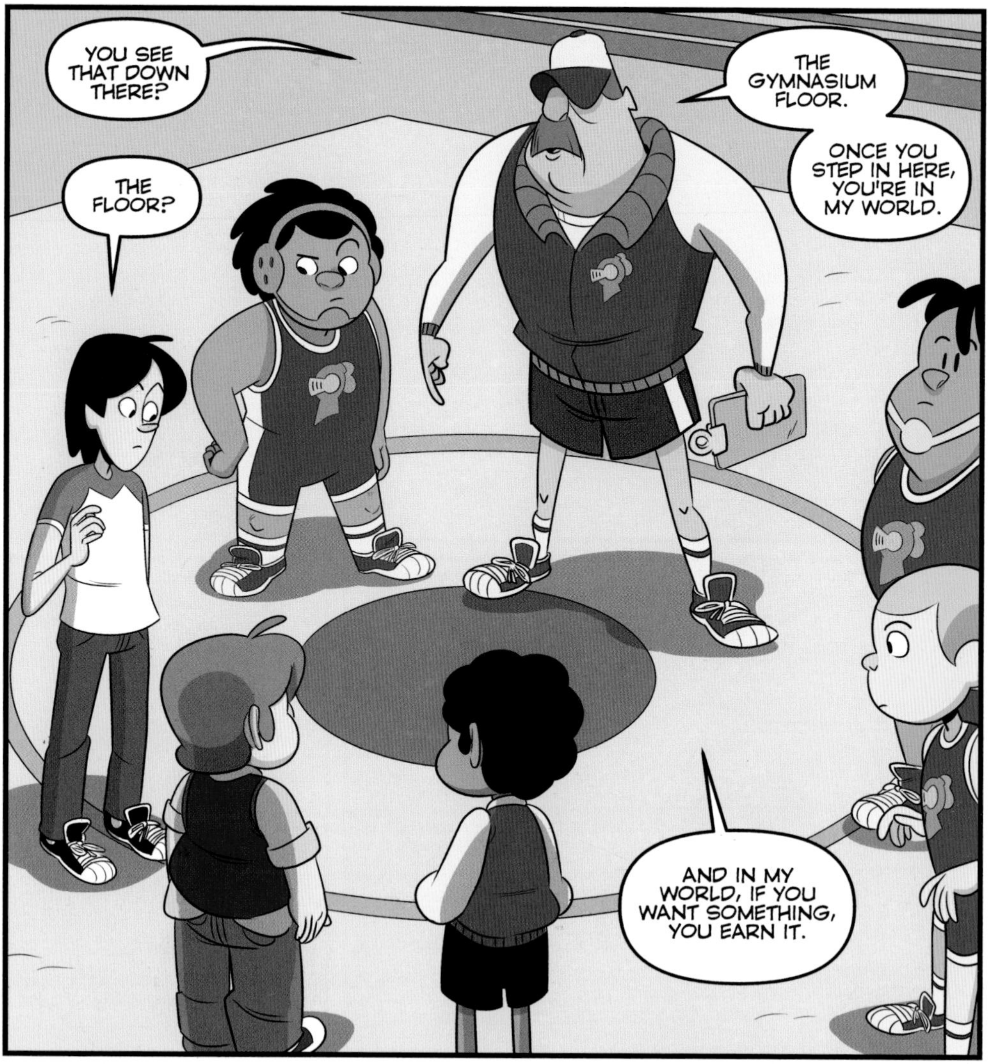
YOU SEE THAT DOWN THERE?
THE GYMNASIUM FLOOR.
ONCE YOU STEP IN HERE, YOU'RE IN MY WORLD.
THE FLOOR?
AND IN MY WORLD, IF YOU WANT SOMETHING, YOU EARN IT.

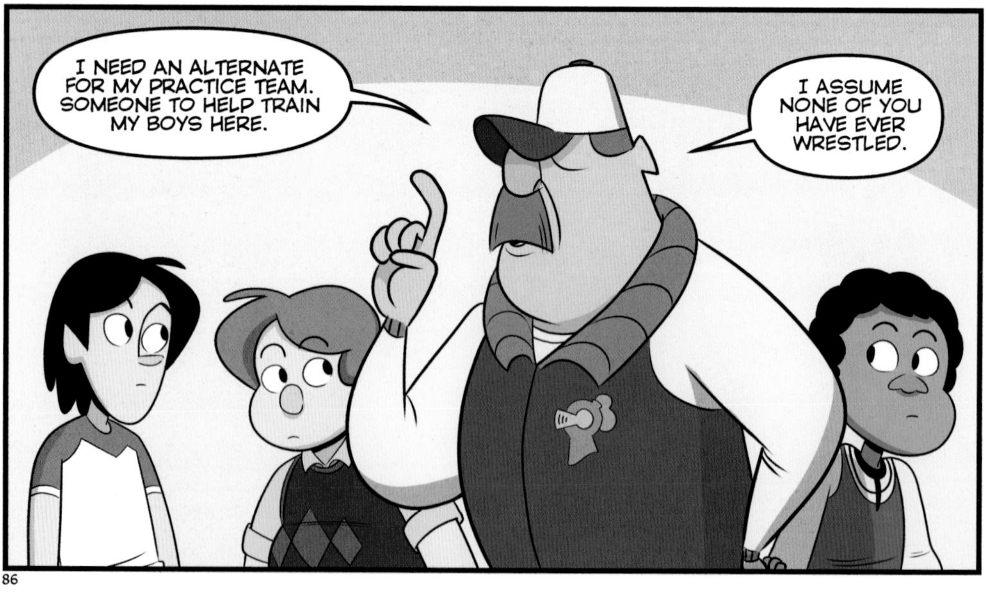
I NEED AN ALTERNATE FOR MY PRACTICE TEAM. SOMEONE TO HELP TRAIN MY BOYS HERE.
I ASSUME NONE OF YOU HAVE EVER WRESTLED.

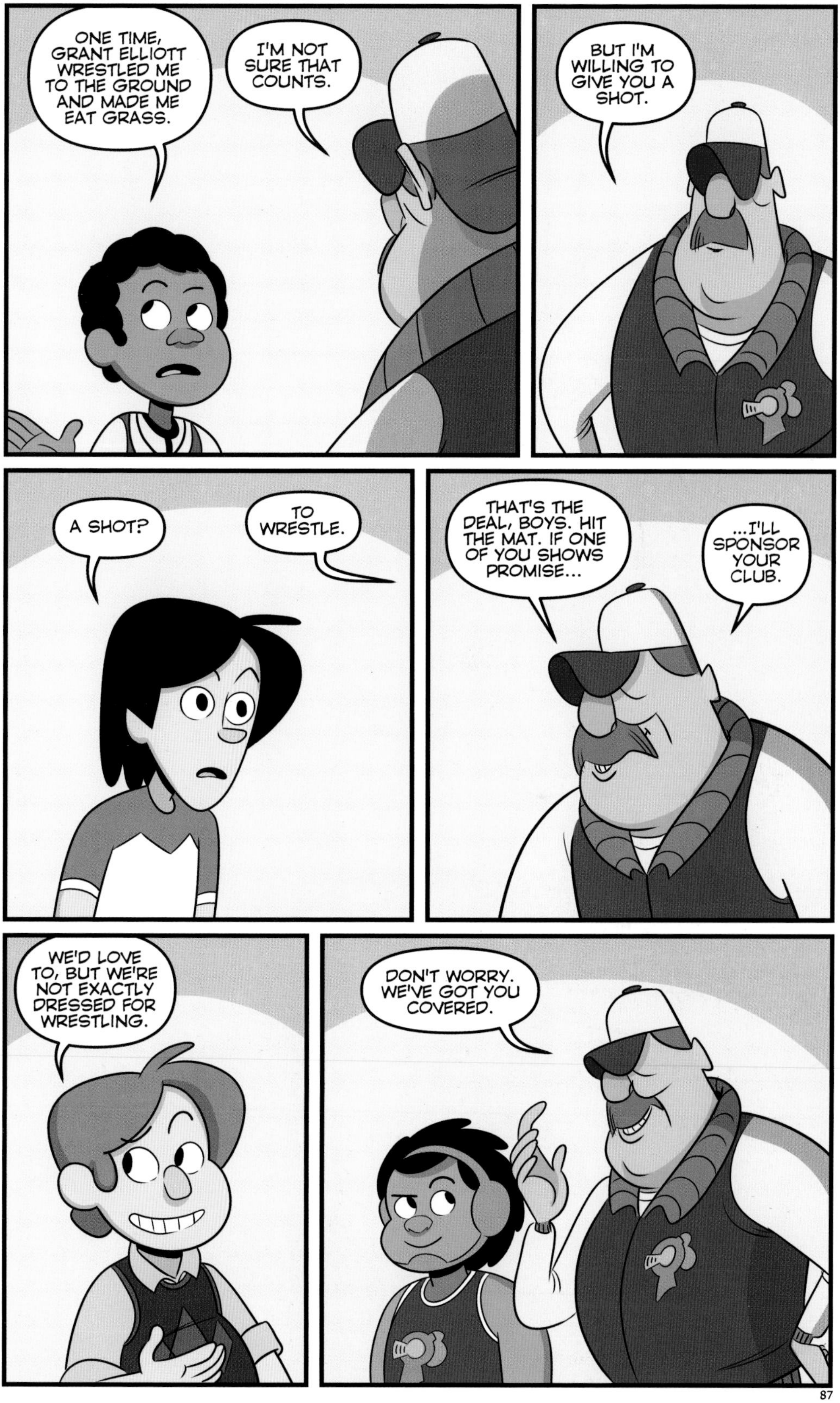
ONE TIME, GRANT ELLIOTT WRESTLED ME TO THE GROUND AND MADE ME EAT GRASS.
I'M NOT SURE THAT COUNTS.
BUT I'M WILLING TO GIVE YOU A SHOT.
A SHOT?
TO WRESTLE.
THAT'S THE DEAL, BOYS. HIT THE MAT. IF ONE OF YOU SHOWS PROMISE...
...I'LL SPONSOR YOUR CLUB.
WE'D LOVE TO, BUT WE'RE NOT EXACTLY DRESSED FOR WRESTLING.
DON'T WORRY. WE'VE GOT YOU COVERED.

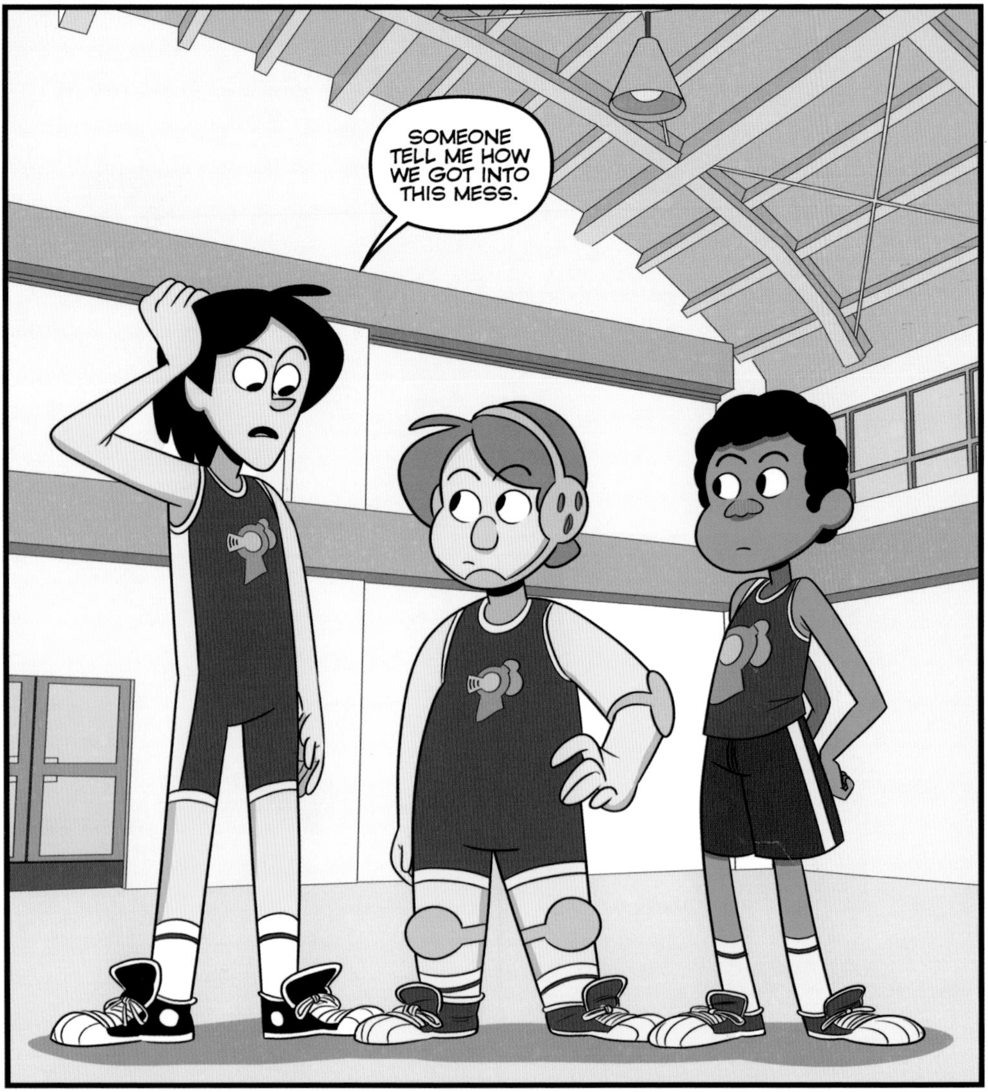
SOMEONE TELL ME HOW WE GOT INTO THIS MESS.

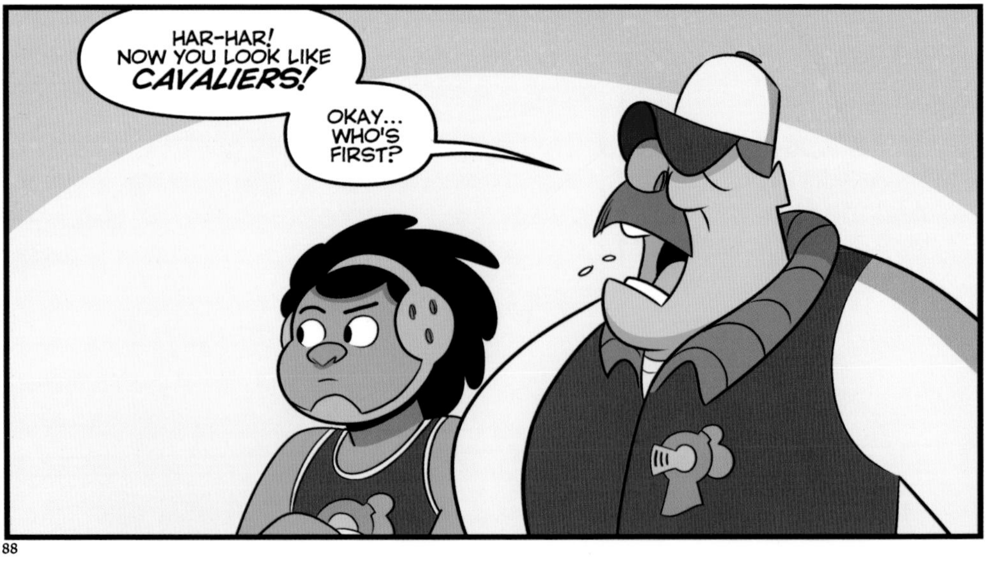
HAR-HAR! NOW YOU LOOK LIKE *CAVALIERS!*
OKAY... WHO'S FIRST?

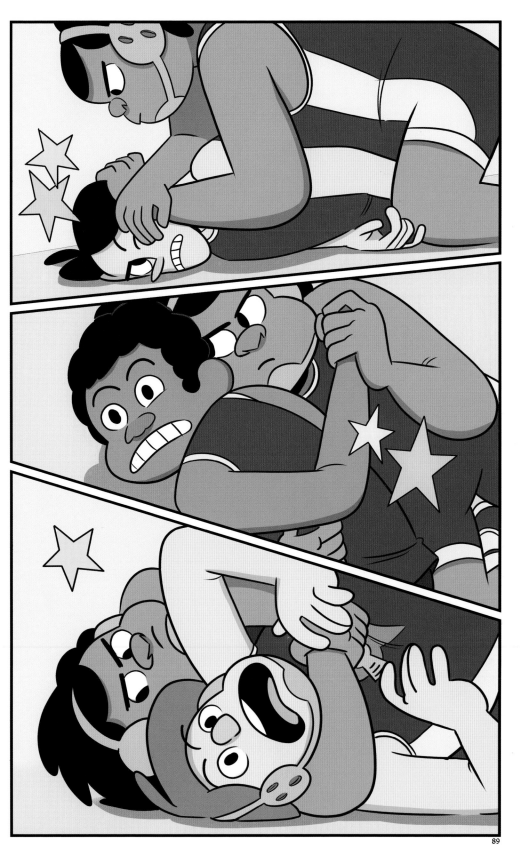

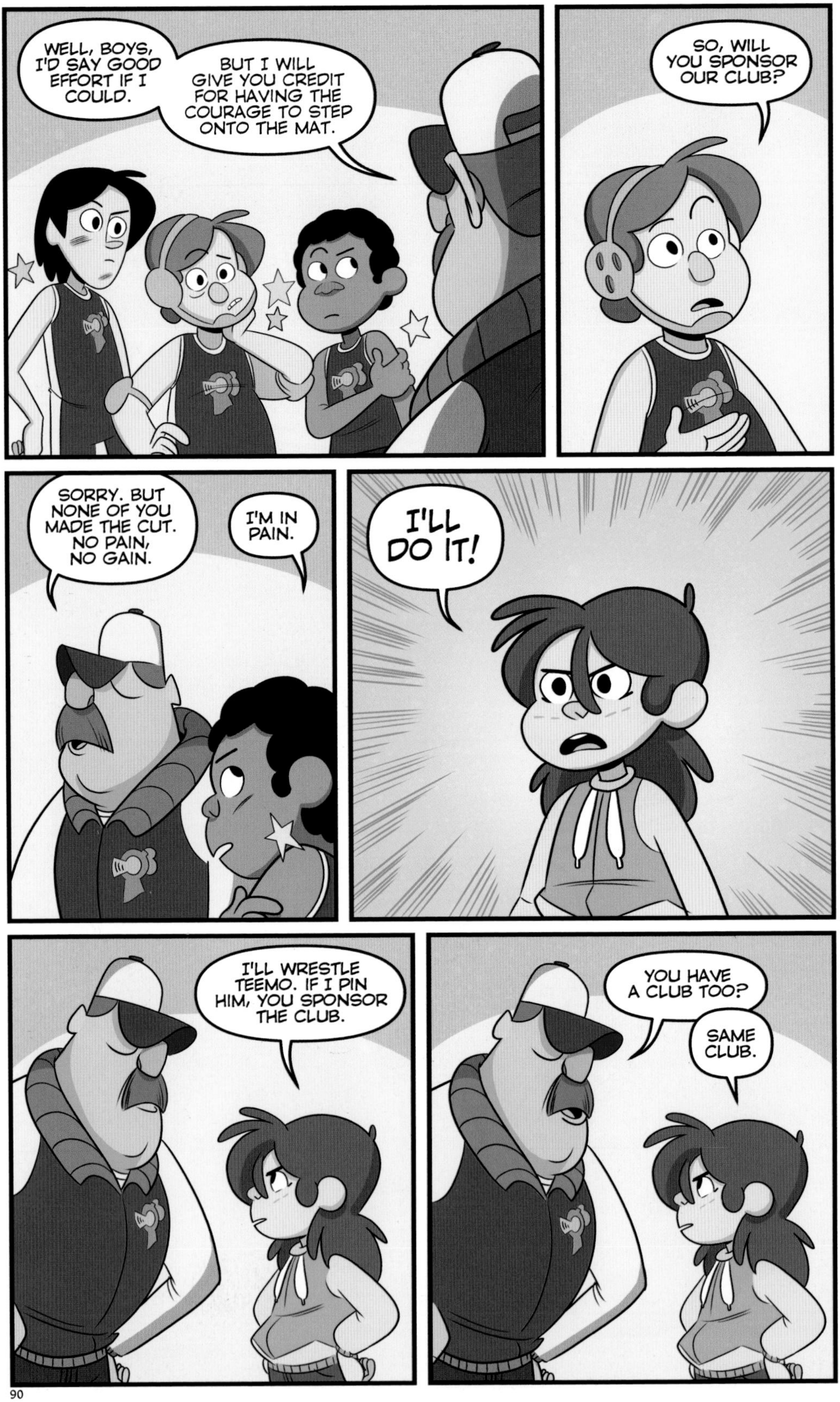
WELL, BOYS, I'D SAY GOOD EFFORT IF I COULD.
BUT I WILL GIVE YOU CREDIT FOR HAVING THE COURAGE TO STEP ONTO THE MAT.
SO, WILL YOU SPONSOR OUR CLUB?
SORRY. BUT NONE OF YOU MADE THE CUT. NO PAIN, NO GAIN.
I'M IN PAIN.
I'LL DO IT!
I'LL WRESTLE TEEMO. IF I PIN HIM, YOU SPONSOR THE CLUB.
YOU HAVE A CLUB TOO?
SAME CLUB.

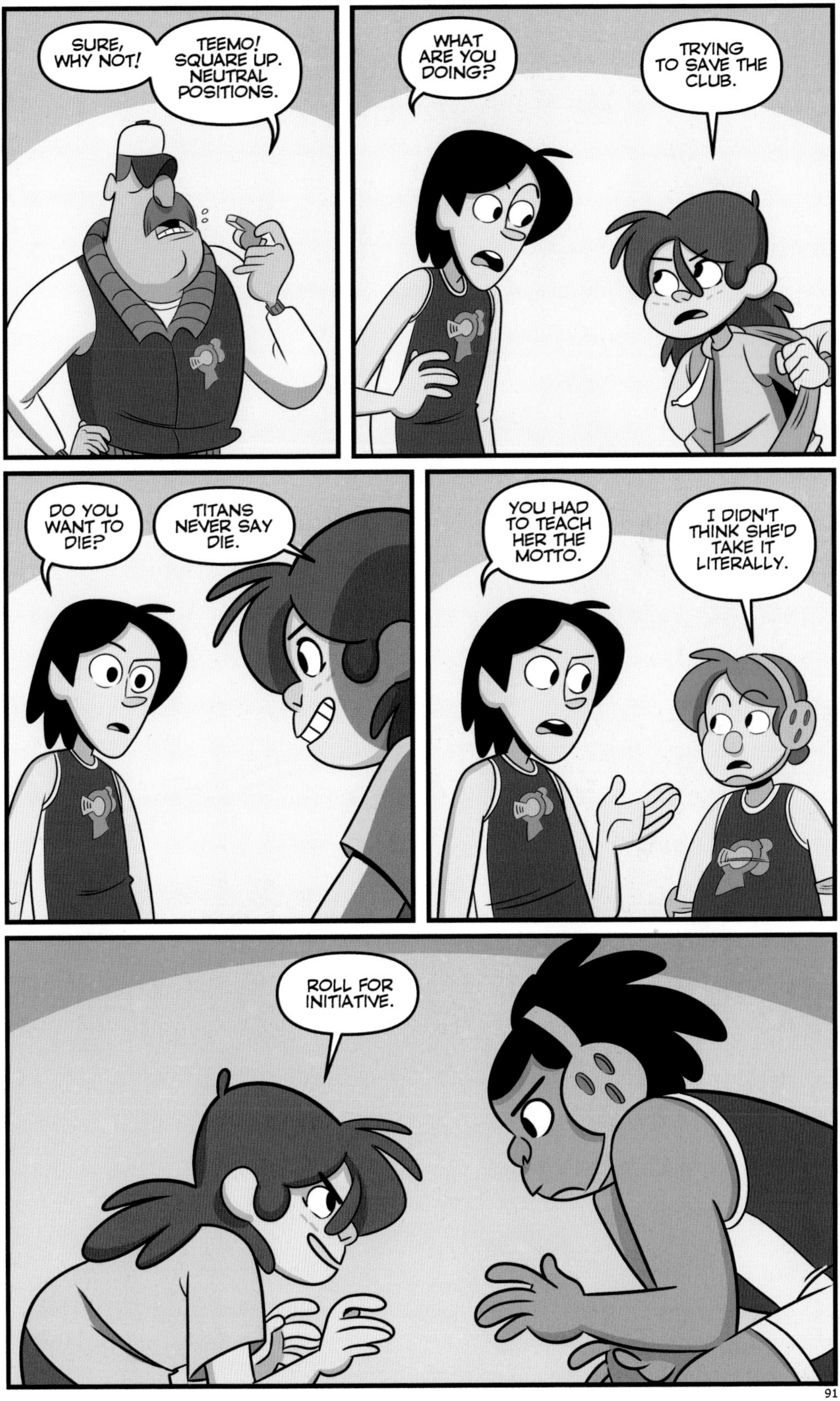
SURE, WHY NOT!
TEEMO! SQUARE UP. NEUTRAL POSITIONS.
WHAT ARE YOU DOING?
TRYING TO SAVE THE CLUB.
DO YOU WANT TO DIE?
TITANS NEVER SAY DIE.
YOU HAD TO TEACH HER THE MOTTO.
I DIDN'T THINK SHE'D TAKE IT LITERALLY.
ROLL FOR INITIATIVE.

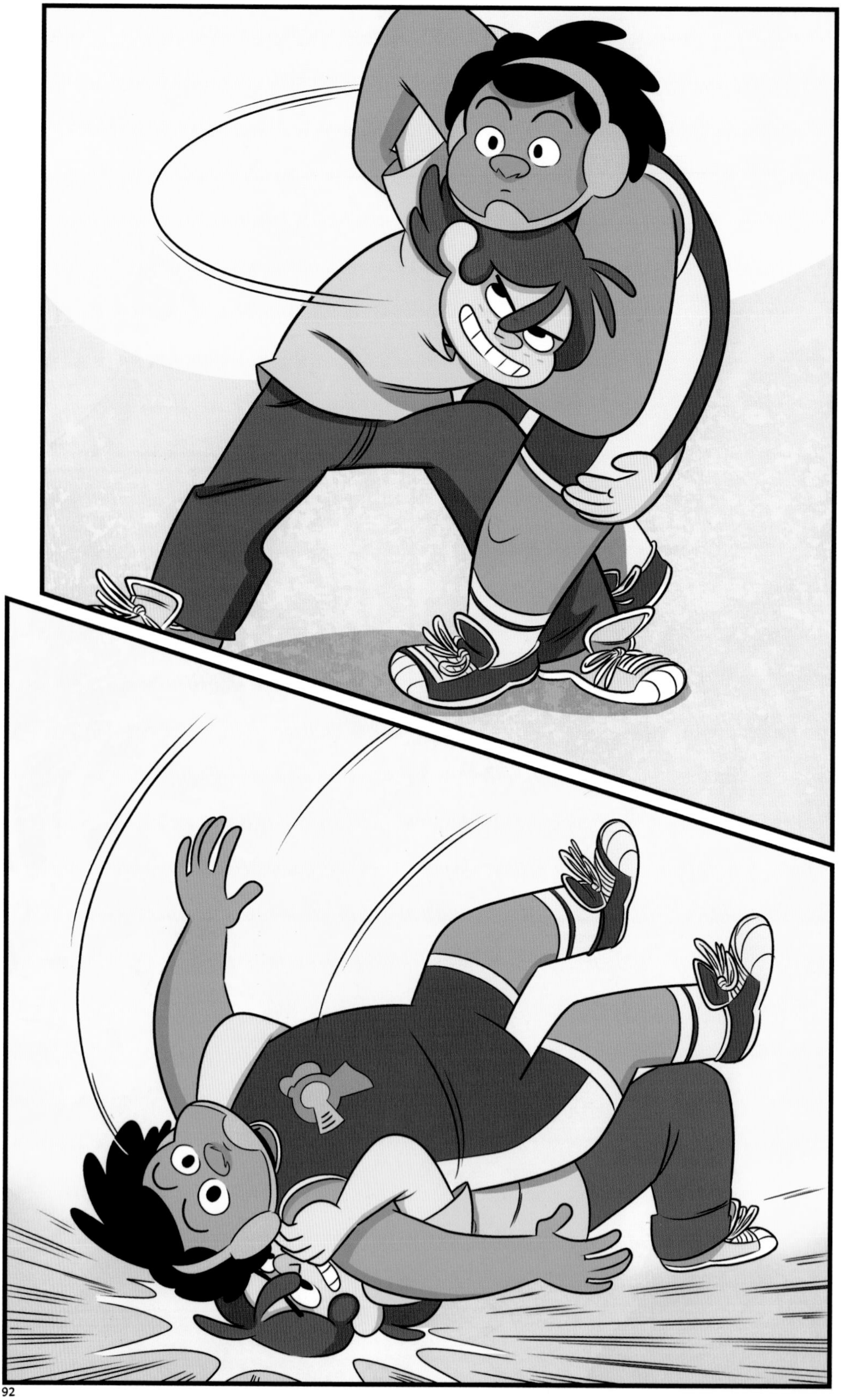

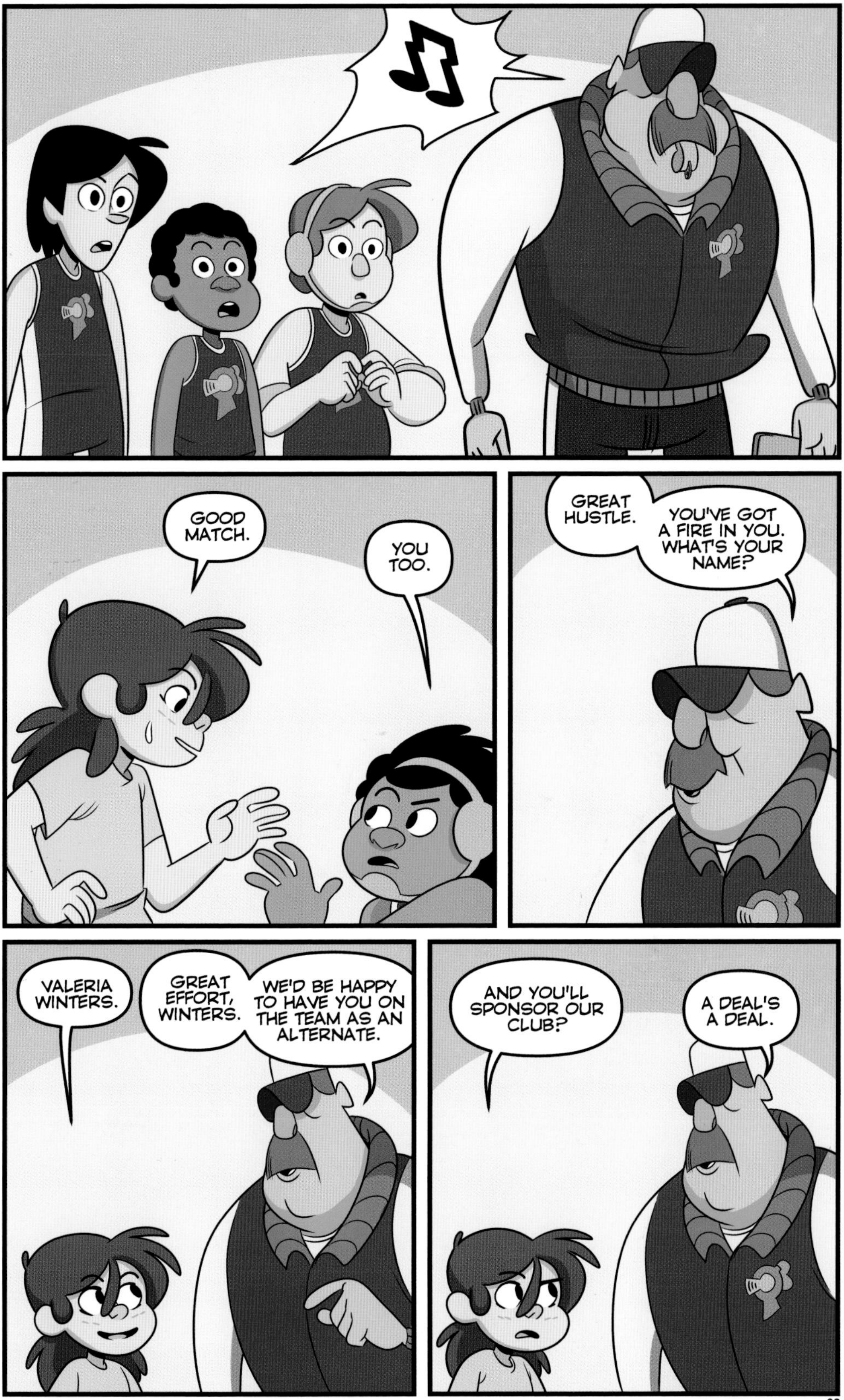
GOOD MATCH.
YOU TOO.
GREAT HUSTLE.
YOU'VE GOT A FIRE IN YOU. WHAT'S YOUR NAME?
VALERIA WINTERS.
GREAT EFFORT, WINTERS.
WE'D BE HAPPY TO HAVE YOU ON THE TEAM AS AN ALTERNATE.
AND YOU'LL SPONSOR OUR CLUB?
A DEAL'S A DEAL.

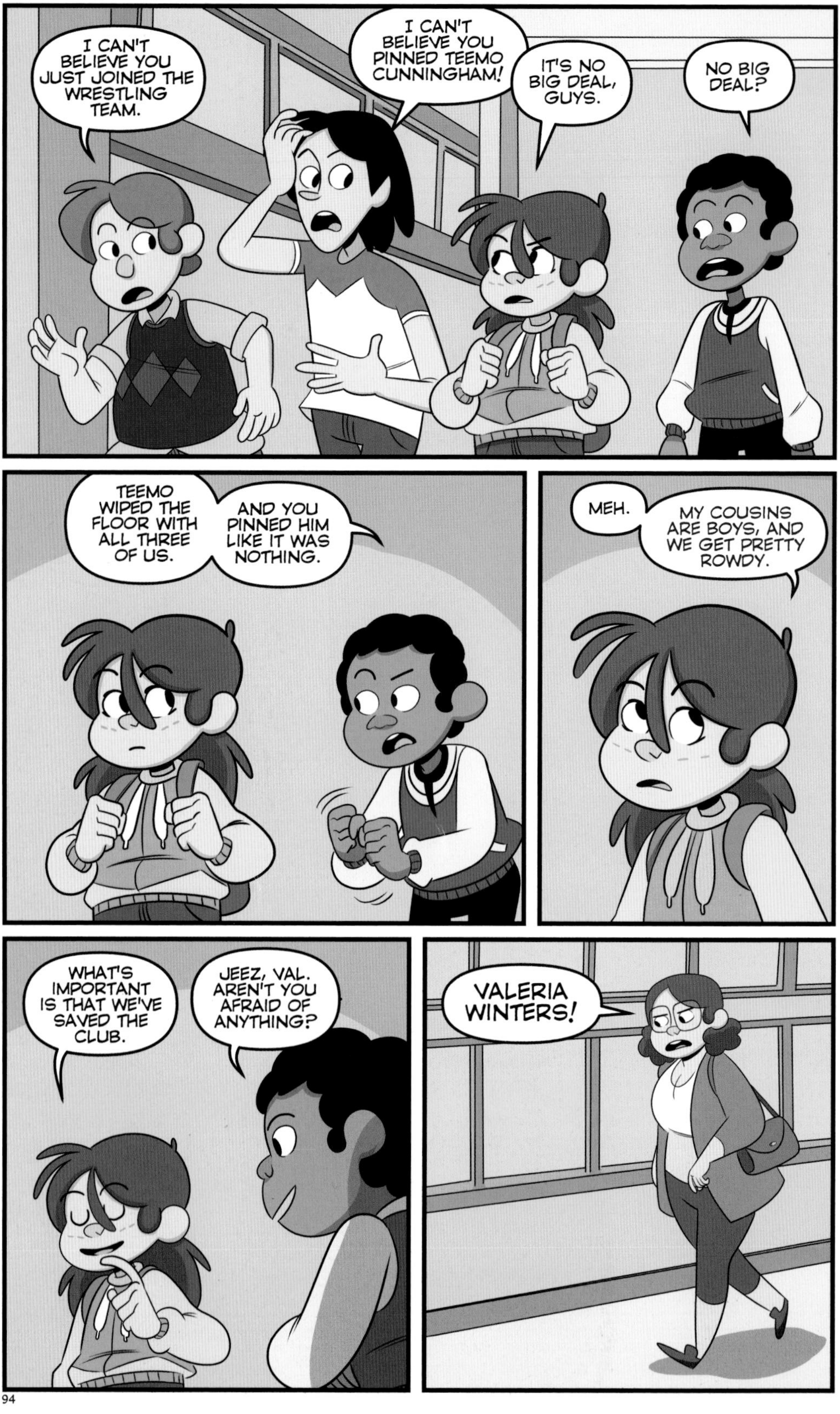
I CAN'T BELIEVE YOU JUST JOINED THE WRESTLING TEAM.
I CAN'T BELIEVE YOU PINNED TEEMO CUNNINGHAM!
IT'S NO BIG DEAL, GUYS.
NO BIG DEAL?
TEEMO WIPED THE FLOOR WITH ALL THREE OF US.
AND YOU PINNED HIM LIKE IT WAS NOTHING.
MEH.
MY COUSINS ARE BOYS, AND WE GET PRETTY ROWDY.
WHAT'S IMPORTANT IS THAT WE'VE SAVED THE CLUB.
JEEZ, VAL. AREN'T YOU AFRAID OF ANYTHING?
VALERIA WINTERS!

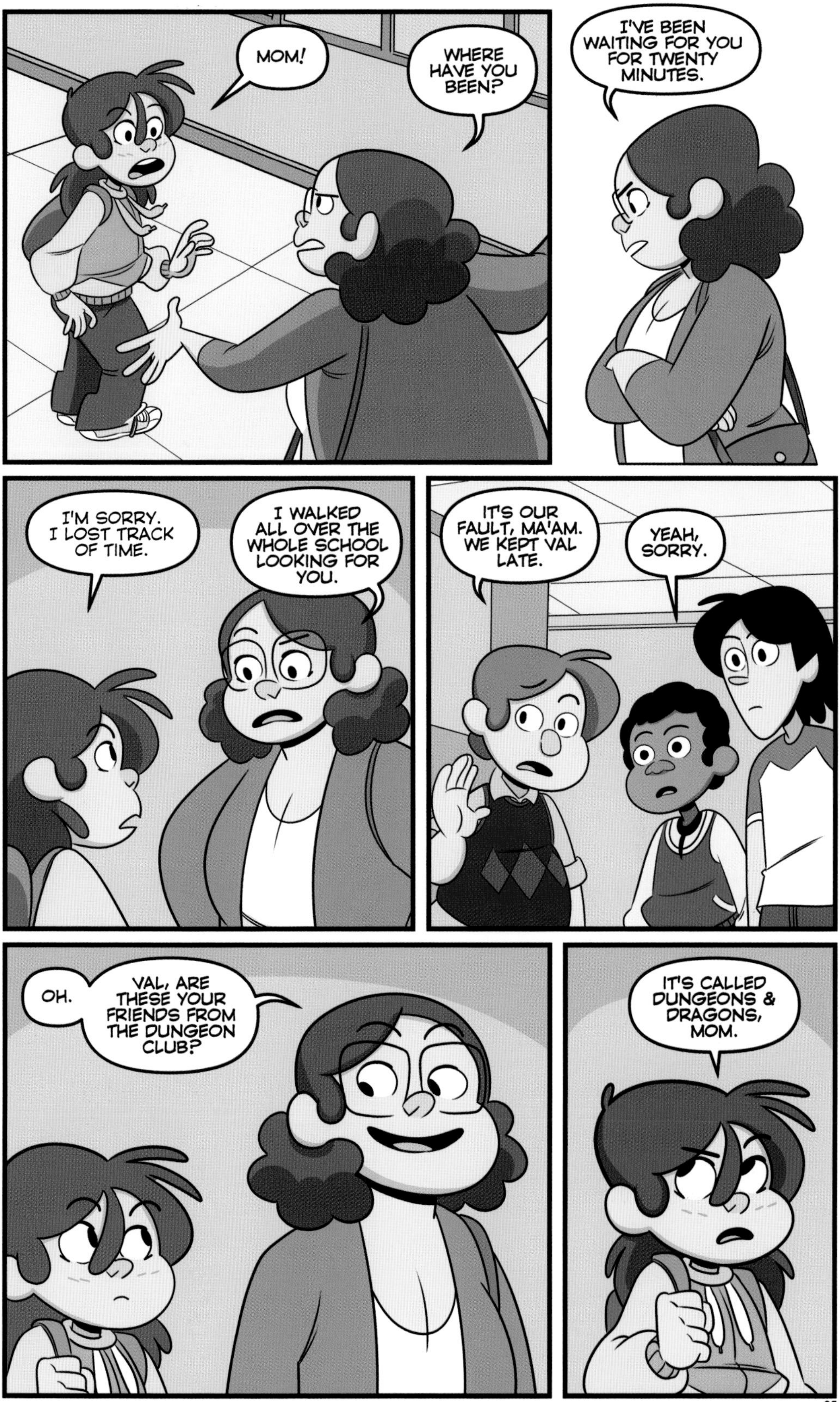
MOM!
WHERE HAVE YOU BEEN?
I'VE BEEN WAITING FOR YOU FOR TWENTY MINUTES.
I'M SORRY. I LOST TRACK OF TIME.
I WALKED ALL OVER THE WHOLE SCHOOL LOOKING FOR YOU.
IT'S OUR FAULT, MA'AM. WE KEPT VAL LATE.
YEAH, SORRY.
OH.
VAL, ARE THESE YOUR FRIENDS FROM THE DUNGEON CLUB?
IT'S CALLED DUNGEONS & DRAGONS, MOM.

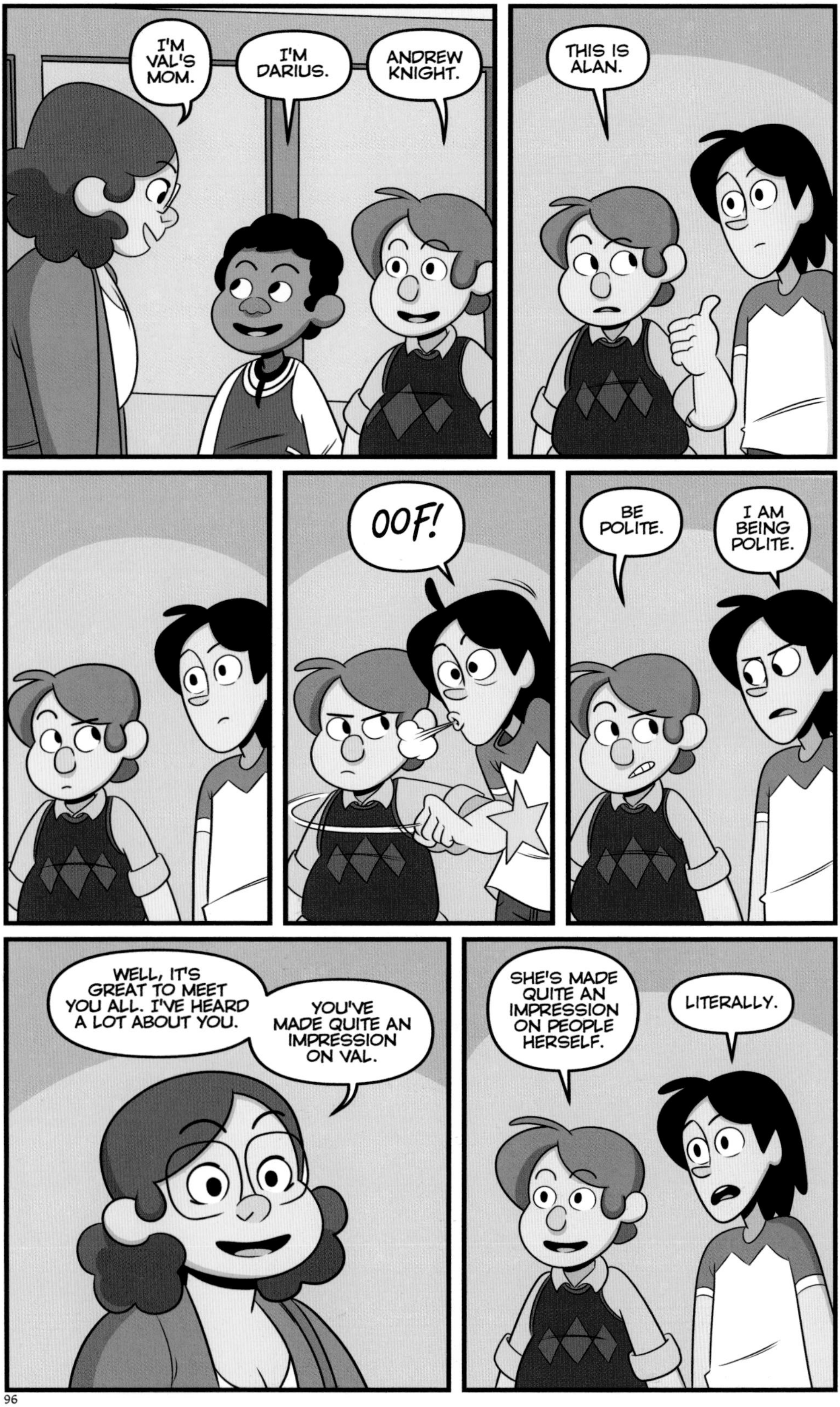
I'M VAL'S MOM.
I'M DARIUS.
ANDREW KNIGHT.
THIS IS ALAN.
OOF!
BE POLITE.
I AM BEING POLITE.
WELL, IT'S GREAT TO MEET YOU ALL. I'VE HEARD A LOT ABOUT YOU.
YOU'VE MADE QUITE AN IMPRESSION ON VAL.
SHE'S MADE QUITE AN IMPRESSION ON PEOPLE HERSELF.
LITERALLY.

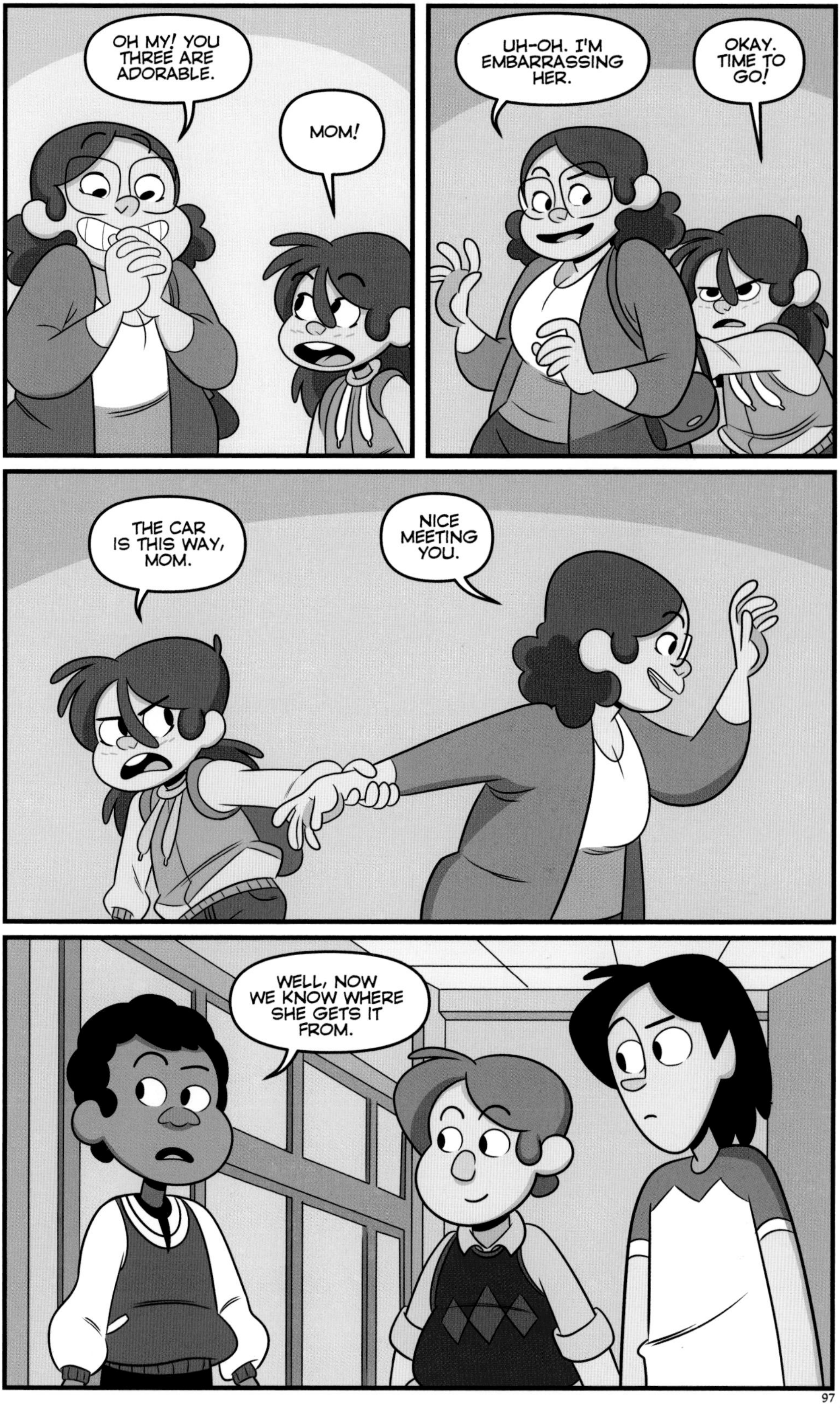
OH MY! YOU THREE ARE ADORABLE.
MOM!
UH-OH. I'M EMBARRASSING HER.
OKAY. TIME TO GO!
THE CAR IS THIS WAY, MOM.
NICE MEETING YOU.
WELL, NOW WE KNOW WHERE SHE GETS IT FROM.

CHAPTER FOUR

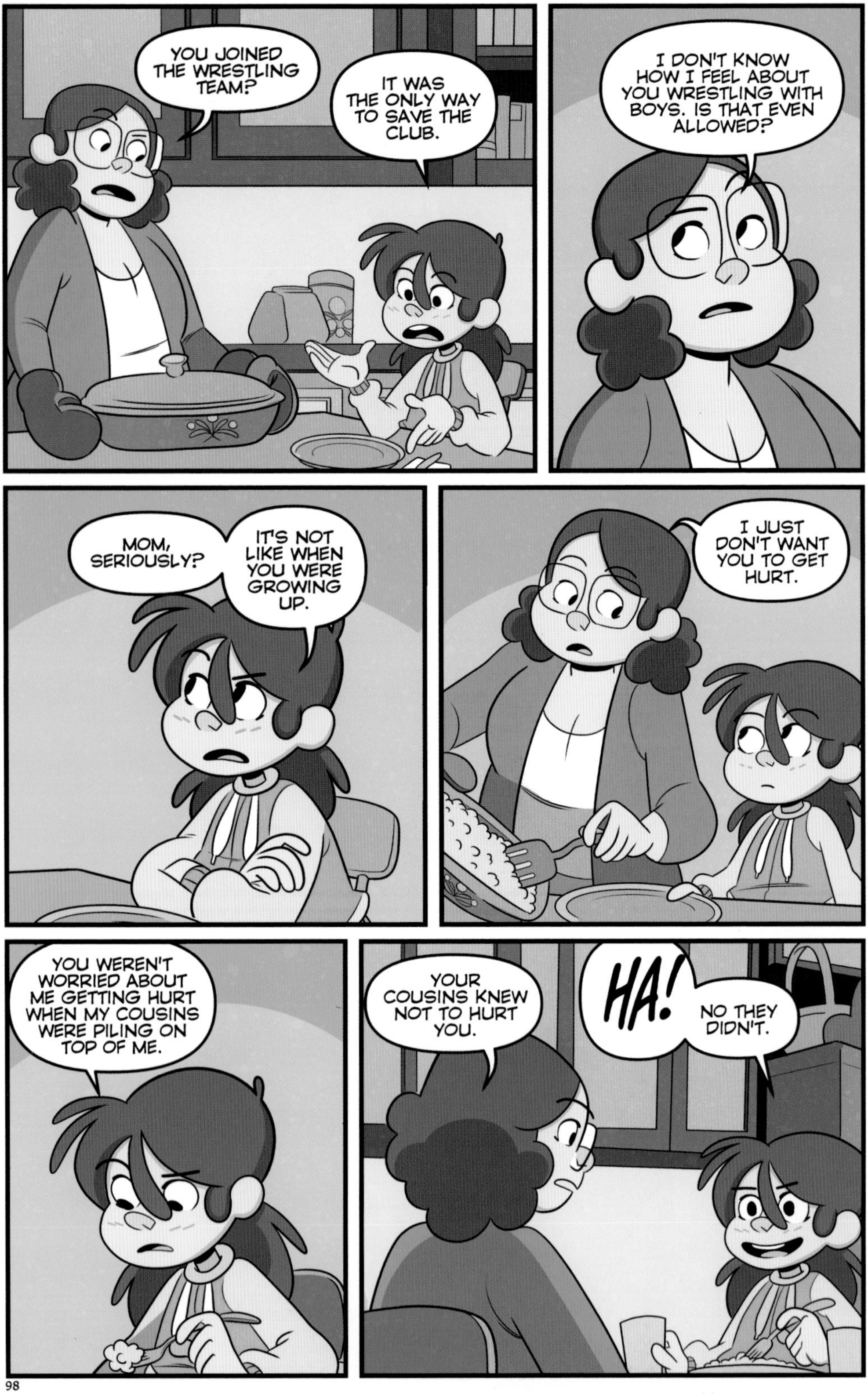

YOU JOINED THE WRESTLING TEAM?
IT WAS THE ONLY WAY TO SAVE THE CLUB.
I DON'T KNOW HOW I FEEL ABOUT YOU WRESTLING WITH BOYS. IS THAT EVEN ALLOWED?
MOM, SERIOUSLY?
IT'S NOT LIKE WHEN YOU WERE GROWING UP.
I JUST DON'T WANT YOU TO GET HURT.
YOU WEREN'T WORRIED ABOUT ME GETTING HURT WHEN MY COUSINS WERE PILING ON TOP OF ME.
YOUR COUSINS KNEW NOT TO HURT YOU.
HA!
NO THEY DIDN'T.

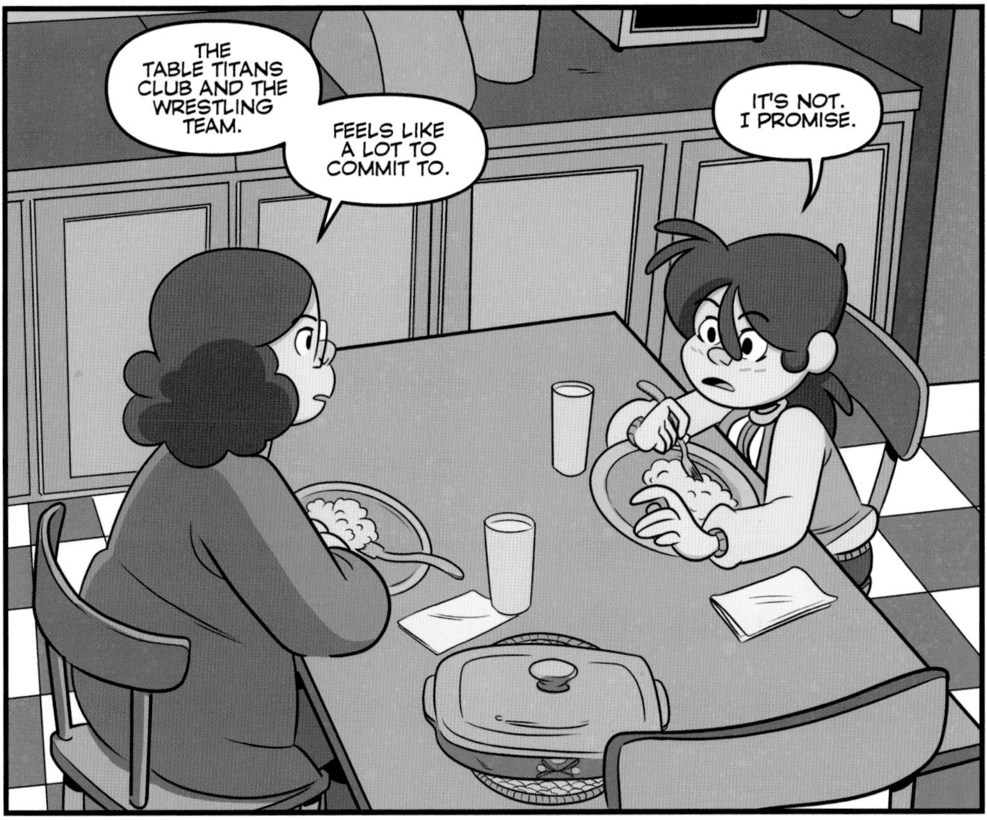
THE TABLE TITANS CLUB AND THE WRESTLING TEAM.
FEELS LIKE A LOT TO COMMIT TO.
IT'S NOT. I PROMISE.

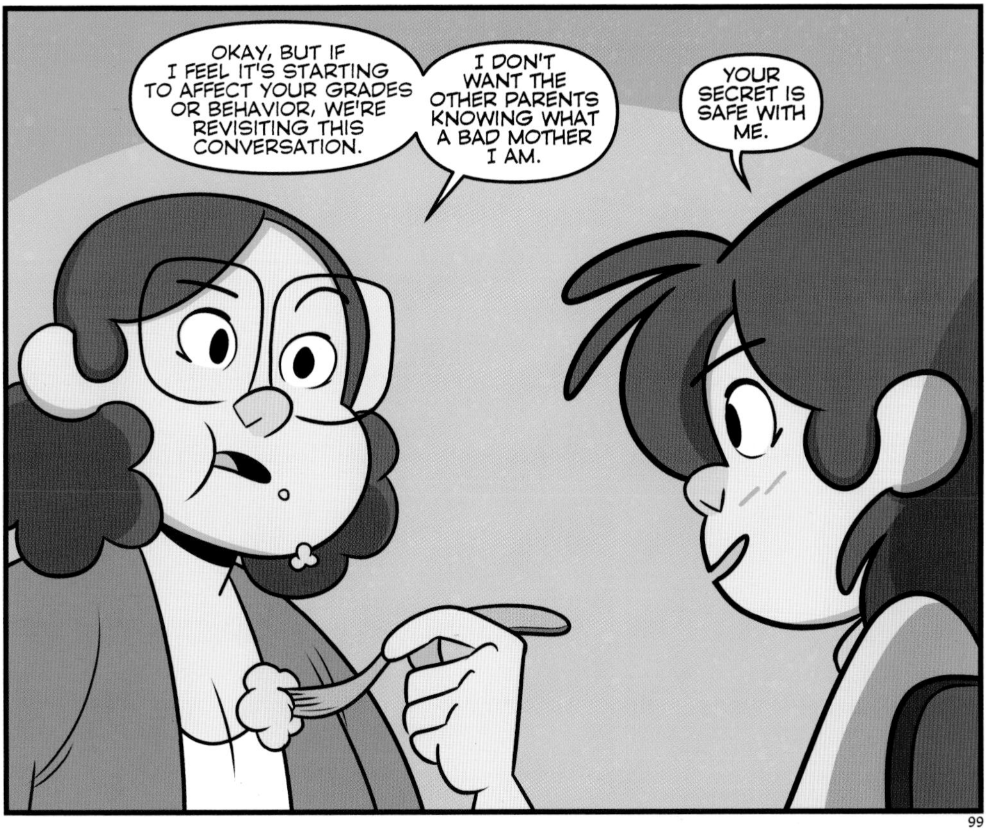
OKAY, BUT IF I FEEL IT'S STARTING TO AFFECT YOUR GRADES OR BEHAVIOR, WE'RE REVISITING THIS CONVERSATION.
I DON'T WANT THE OTHER PARENTS KNOWING WHAT A BAD MOTHER I AM.
YOUR SECRET IS SAFE WITH ME.

CHEMISTRY: MRS. WILSON

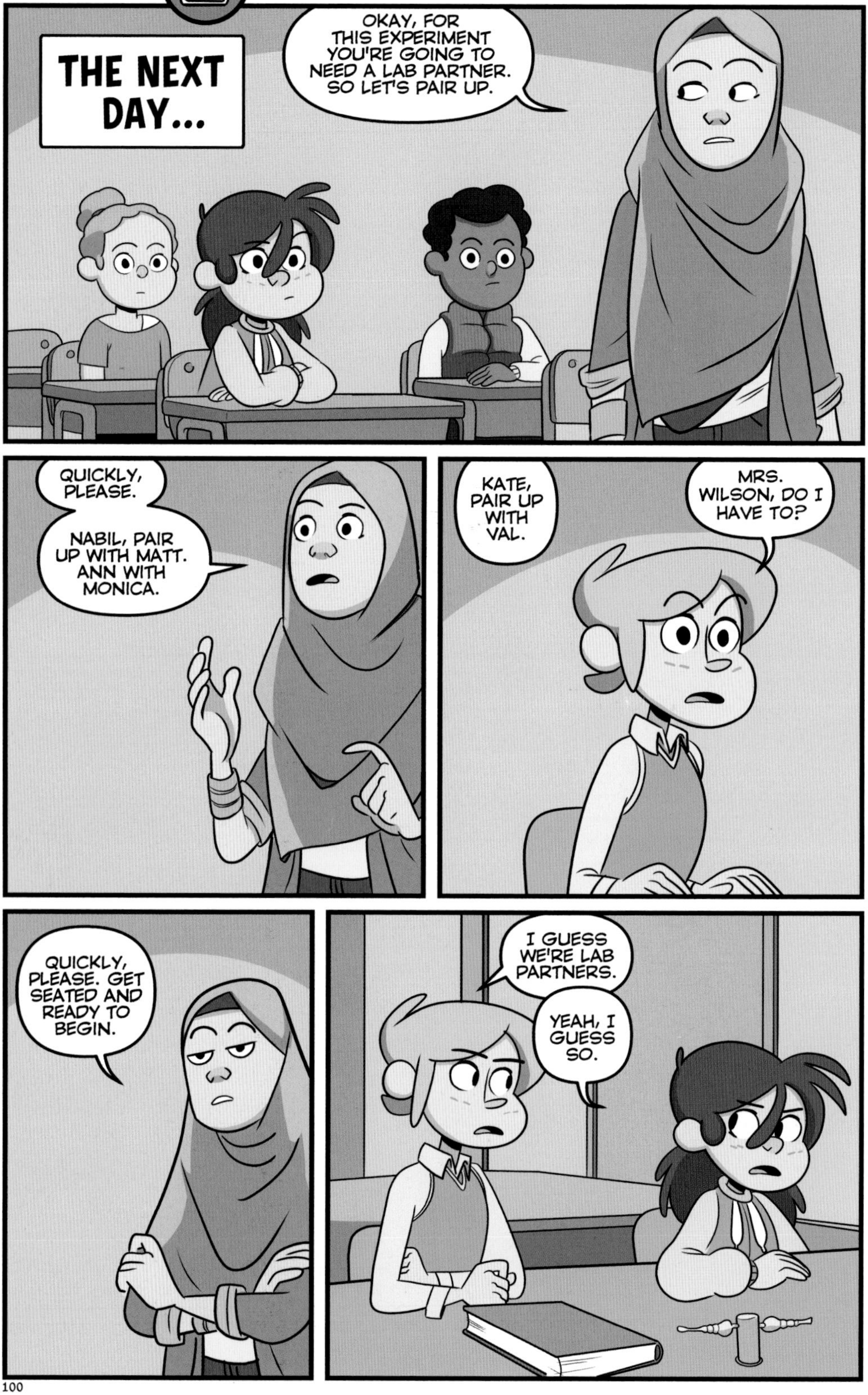
THE NEXT DAY...
OKAY, FOR THIS EXPERIMENT YOU'RE GOING TO NEED A LAB PARTNER. SO LET'S PAIR UP.
QUICKLY, PLEASE.
NABIL, PAIR UP WITH MATT. ANN WITH MONICA.
KATE, PAIR UP WITH VAL.
MRS. WILSON, DO I HAVE TO?
QUICKLY, PLEASE. GET SEATED AND READY TO BEGIN.
I GUESS WE'RE LAB PARTNERS.
YEAH, I GUESS SO.

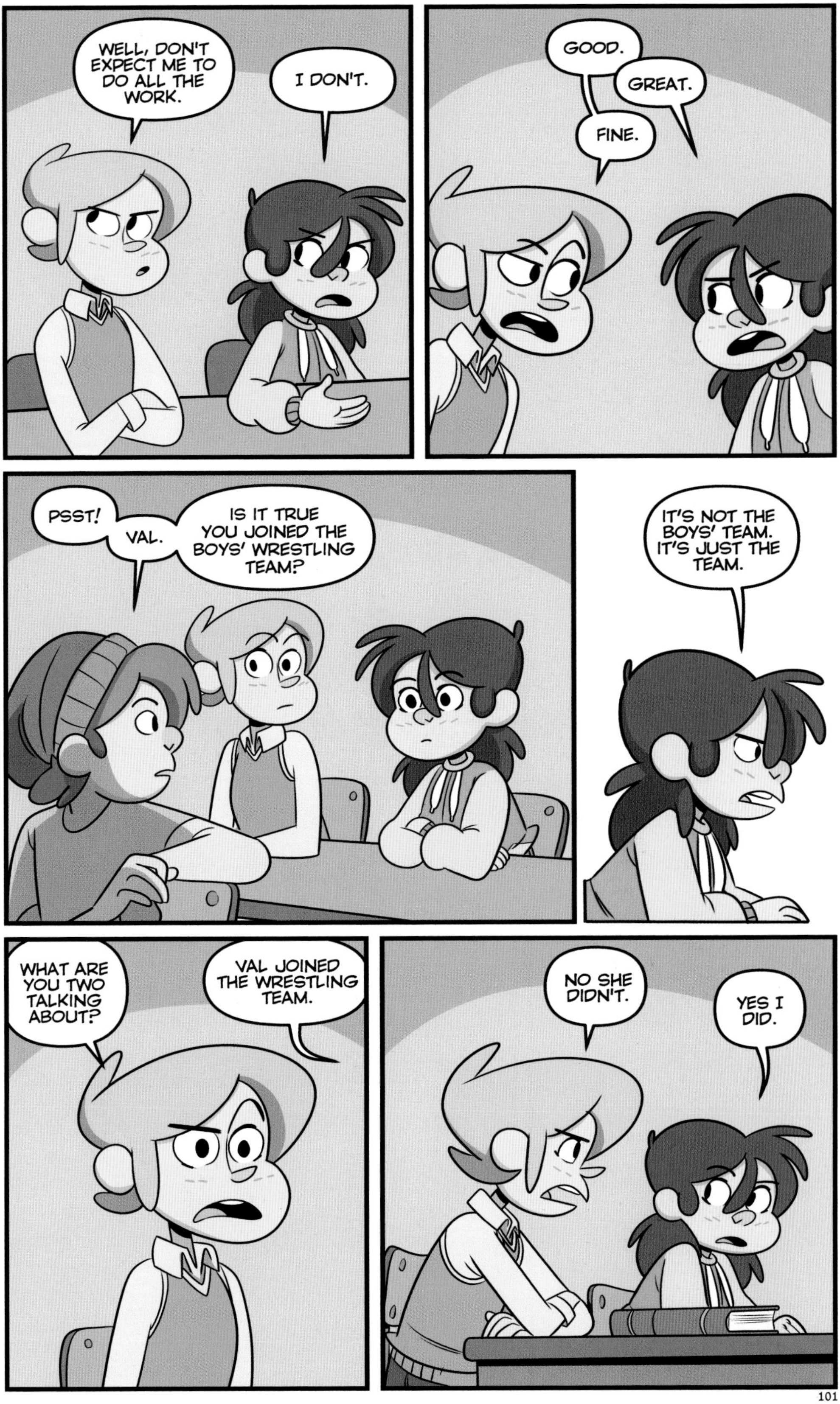
WELL, DON'T EXPECT ME TO DO ALL THE WORK.
I DON'T.
GOOD.
GREAT.
FINE.
PSST!
VAL.
IS IT TRUE YOU JOINED THE BOYS' WRESTLING TEAM?
IT'S NOT THE BOYS' TEAM. IT'S JUST THE TEAM.
WHAT ARE YOU TWO TALKING ABOUT?
VAL JOINED THE WRESTLING TEAM.
NO SHE DIDN'T.
YES I DID.

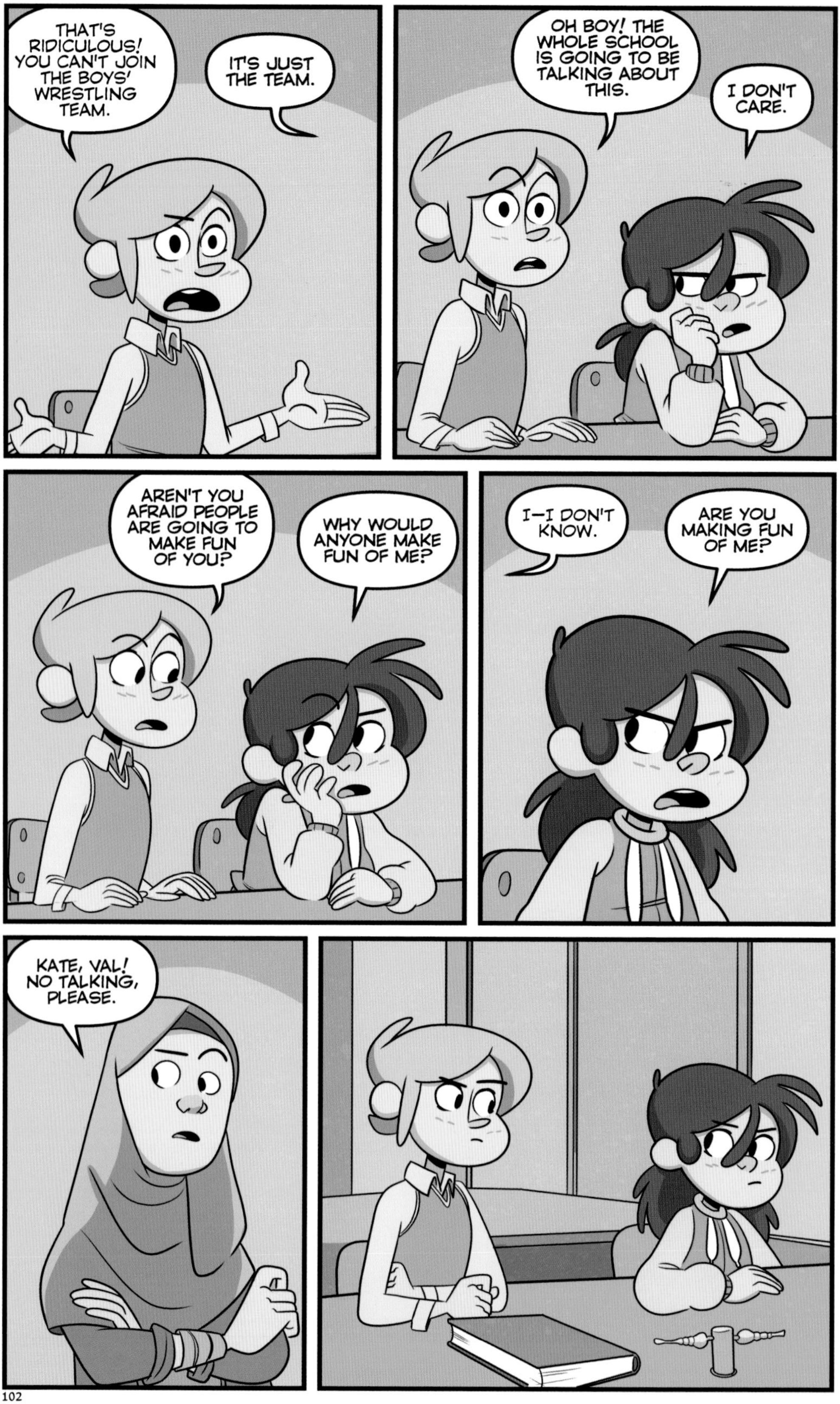
THAT'S RIDICULOUS! YOU CAN'T JOIN THE BOYS' WRESTLING TEAM.
IT'S JUST THE TEAM.
OH BOY! THE WHOLE SCHOOL IS GOING TO BE TALKING ABOUT THIS.
I DON'T CARE.
AREN'T YOU AFRAID PEOPLE ARE GOING TO MAKE FUN OF YOU?
WHY WOULD ANYONE MAKE FUN OF ME?
I—I DON'T KNOW.
ARE YOU MAKING FUN OF ME?
KATE, VAL! NO TALKING, PLEASE.

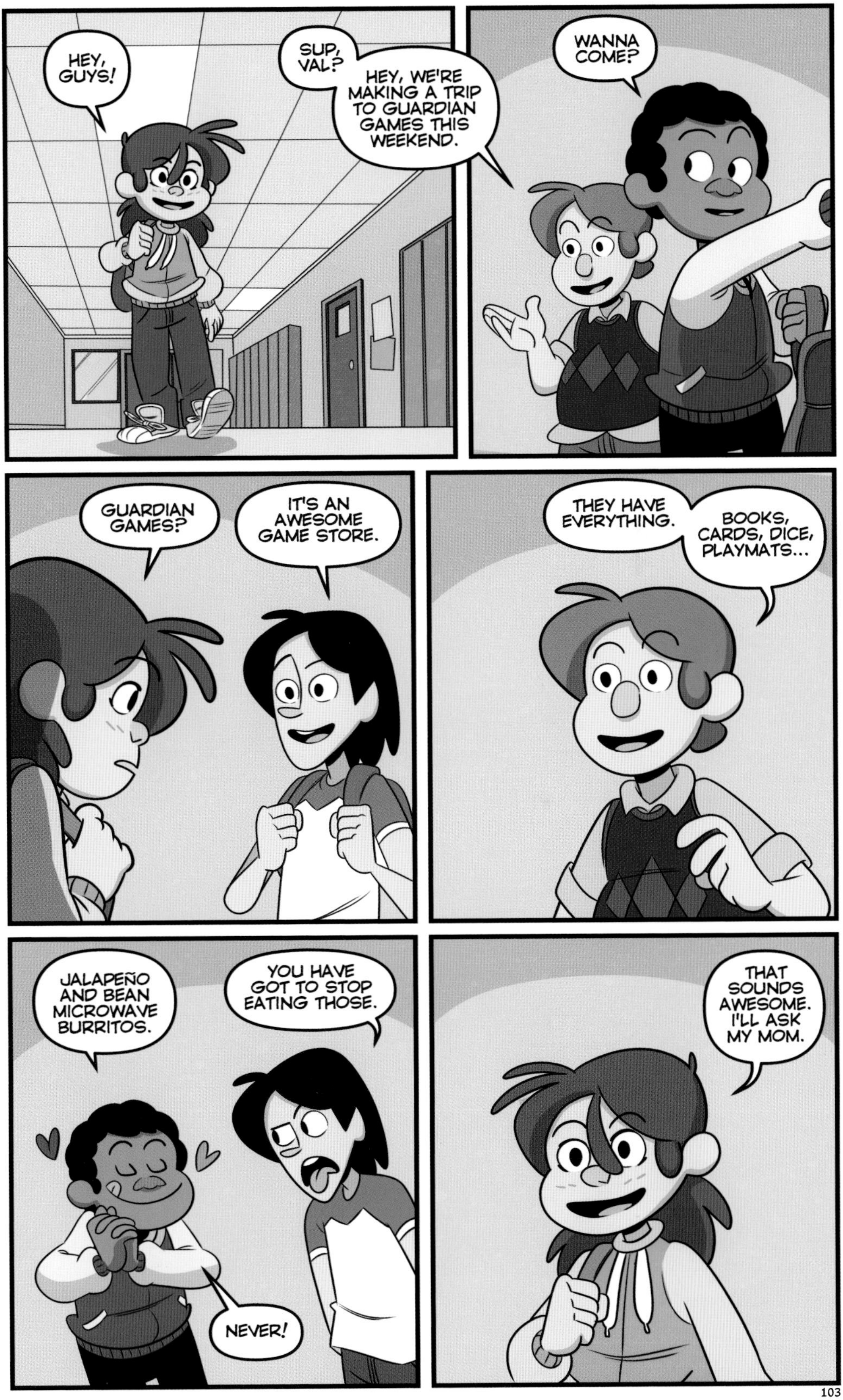
HEY, GUYS!
SUP, VAL?
HEY, WE'RE MAKING A TRIP TO GUARDIAN GAMES THIS WEEKEND.
WANNA COME?
GUARDIAN GAMES?
IT'S AN AWESOME GAME STORE.
THEY HAVE EVERYTHING.
BOOKS, CARDS, DICE, PLAYMATS...
JALAPEÑO AND BEAN MICROWAVE BURRITOS.
YOU HAVE GOT TO STOP EATING THOSE.
NEVER!
THAT SOUNDS AWESOME. I'LL ASK MY MOM.

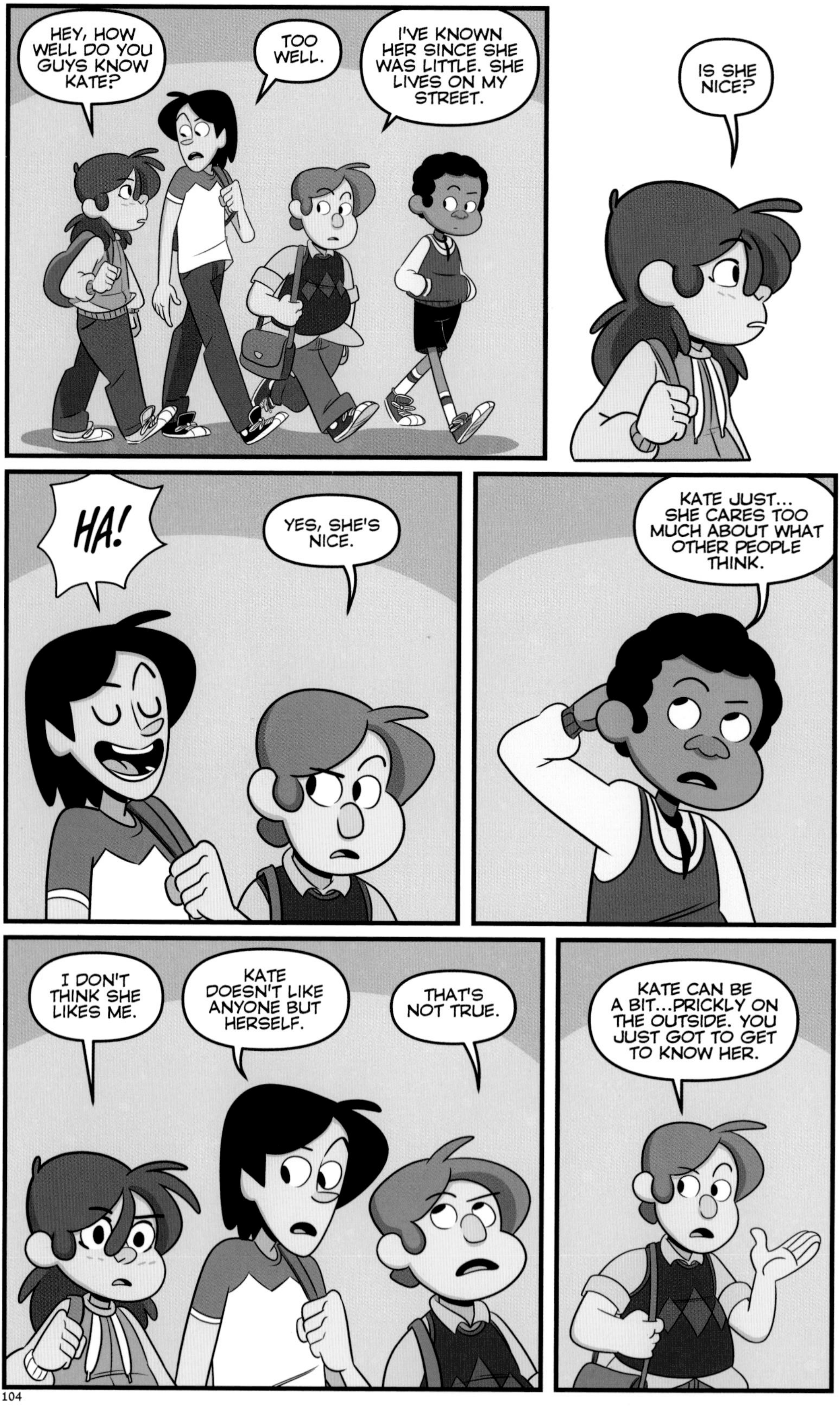
HEY, HOW WELL DO YOU GUYS KNOW KATE?
TOO WELL.
I'VE KNOWN HER SINCE SHE WAS LITTLE. SHE LIVES ON MY STREET.
IS SHE NICE?
HA!
YES, SHE'S NICE.
KATE JUST... SHE CARES TOO MUCH ABOUT WHAT OTHER PEOPLE THINK.
I DON'T THINK SHE LIKES ME.
KATE DOESN'T LIKE ANYONE BUT HERSELF.
THAT'S NOT TRUE.
KATE CAN BE A BIT...PRICKLY ON THE OUTSIDE. YOU JUST GOT TO GET TO KNOW HER.

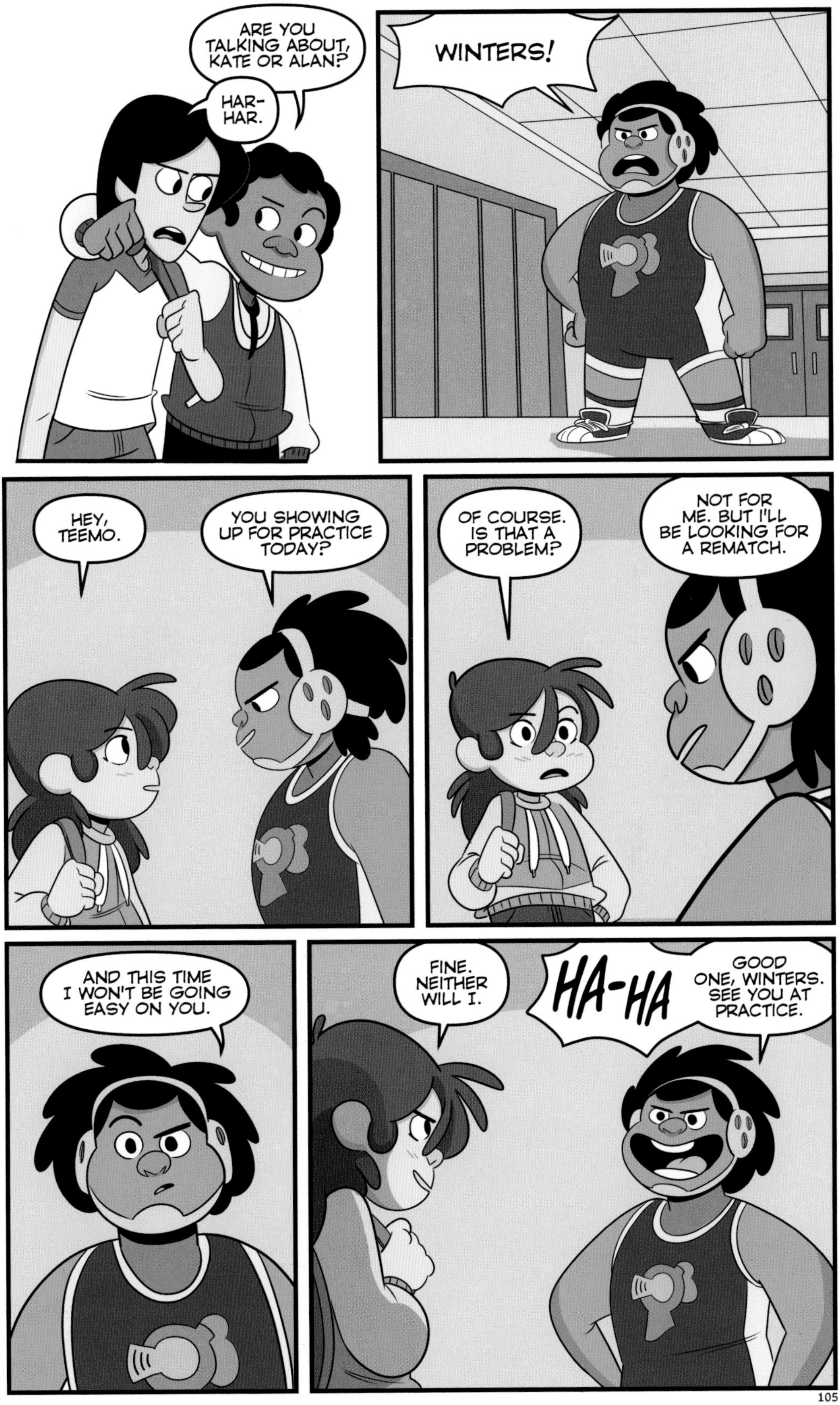
ARE YOU TALKING ABOUT, KATE OR ALAN?
HAR-HAR.
WINTERS!
HEY, TEEMO.
YOU SHOWING UP FOR PRACTICE TODAY?
OF COURSE. IS THAT A PROBLEM?
NOT FOR ME. BUT I'LL BE LOOKING FOR A REMATCH.
AND THIS TIME I WON'T BE GOING EASY ON YOU.
FINE. NEITHER WILL I.
HA-HA
GOOD ONE, WINTERS. SEE YOU AT PRACTICE.

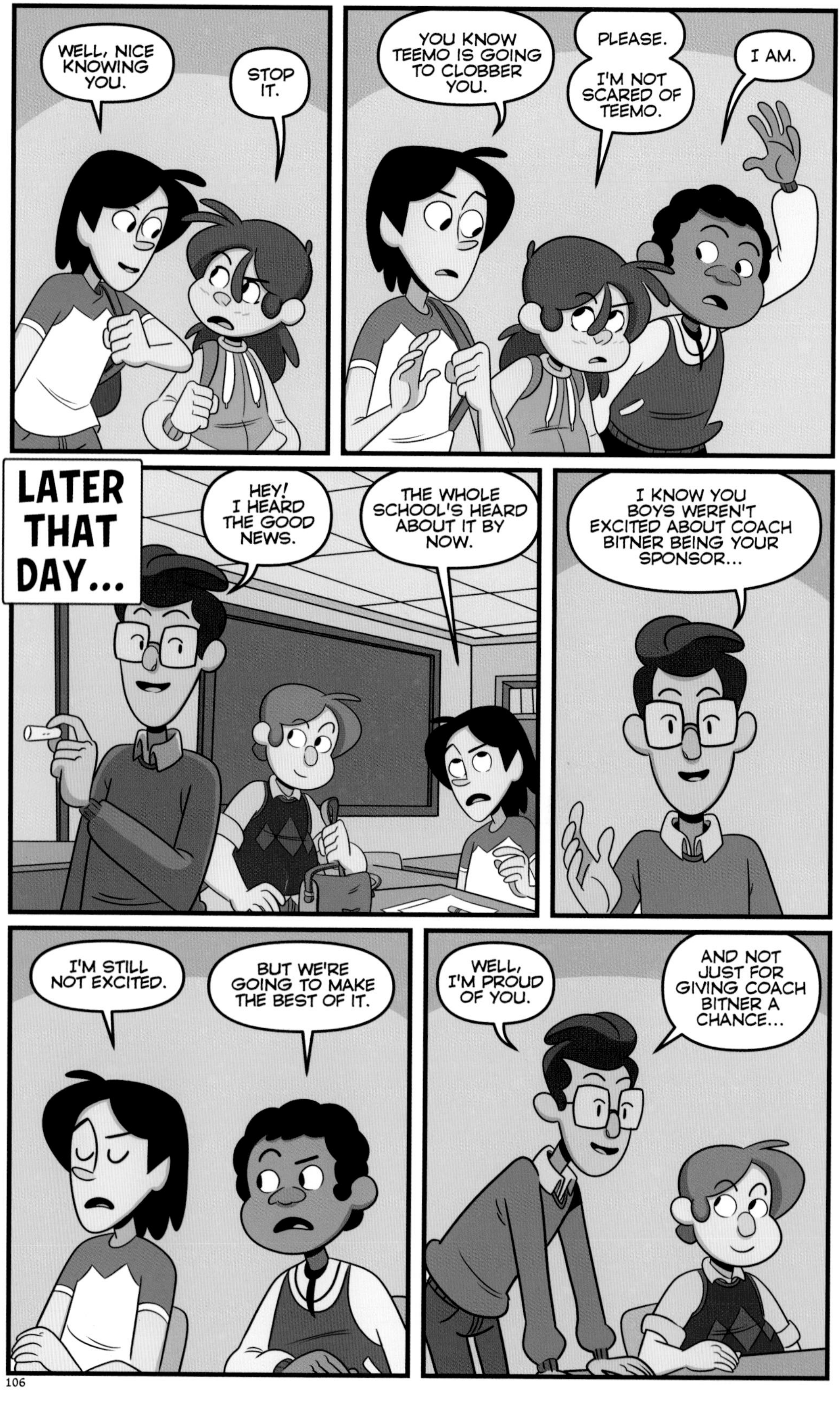
WELL, NICE KNOWING YOU.
STOP IT.
YOU KNOW TEEMO IS GOING TO CLOBBER YOU.
PLEASE.
I'M NOT SCARED OF TEEMO.
I AM.
LATER THAT DAY...
HEY! I HEARD THE GOOD NEWS.
THE WHOLE SCHOOL'S HEARD ABOUT IT BY NOW.
I KNOW YOU BOYS WEREN'T EXCITED ABOUT COACH BITNER BEING YOUR SPONSOR...
I'M STILL NOT EXCITED.
BUT WE'RE GOING TO MAKE THE BEST OF IT.
WELL, I'M PROUD OF YOU.
AND NOT JUST FOR GIVING COACH BITNER A CHANCE...

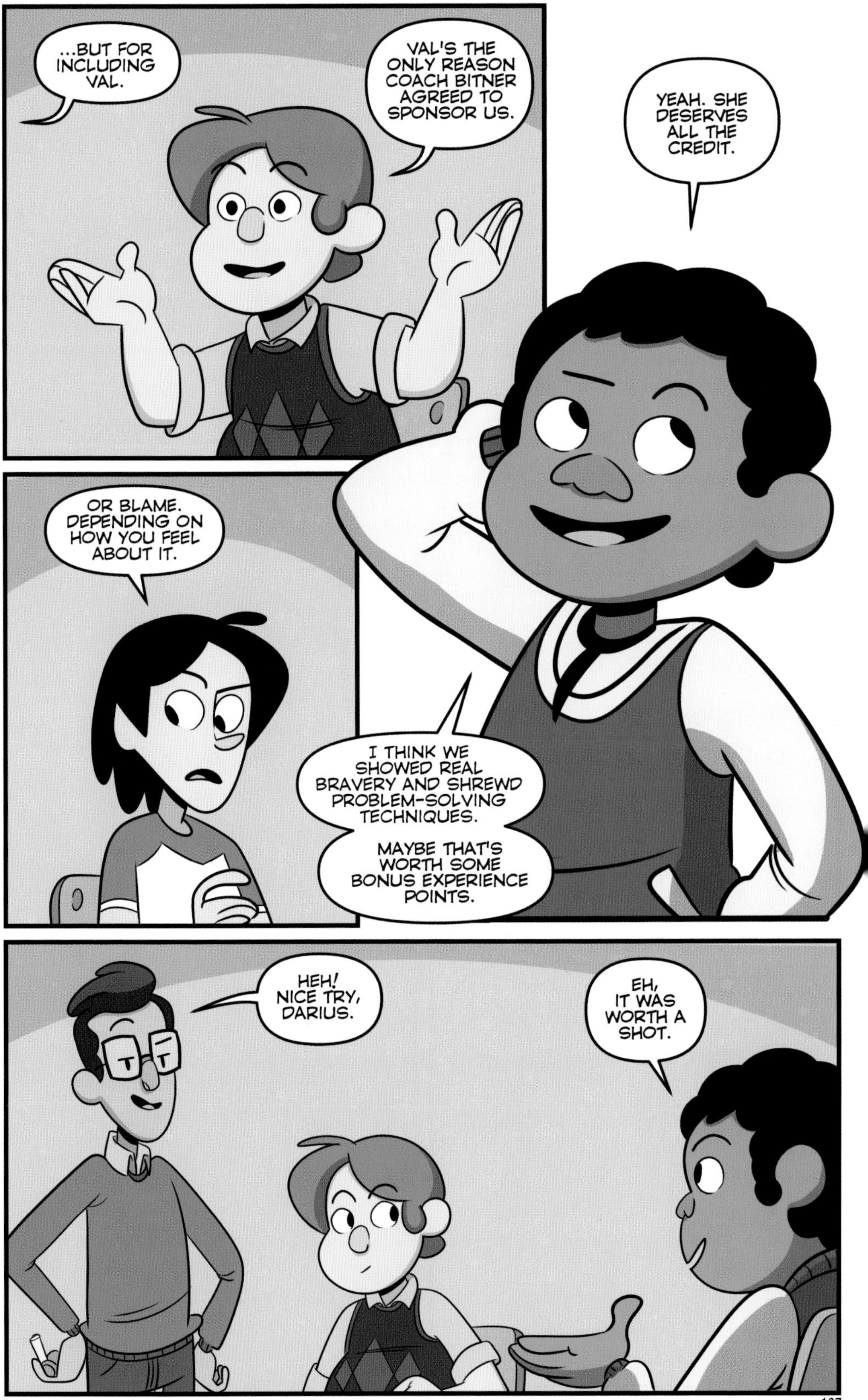
...BUT FOR INCLUDING VAL.
VAL'S THE ONLY REASON COACH BITNER AGREED TO SPONSOR US.
YEAH. SHE DESERVES ALL THE CREDIT.
OR BLAME. DEPENDING ON HOW YOU FEEL ABOUT IT.
I THINK WE SHOWED REAL BRAVERY AND SHREWD PROBLEM-SOLVING TECHNIQUES.
MAYBE THAT'S WORTH SOME BONUS EXPERIENCE POINTS.
HEH! NICE TRY, DARIUS.
EH, IT WAS WORTH A SHOT.

CHAPTER FIVE

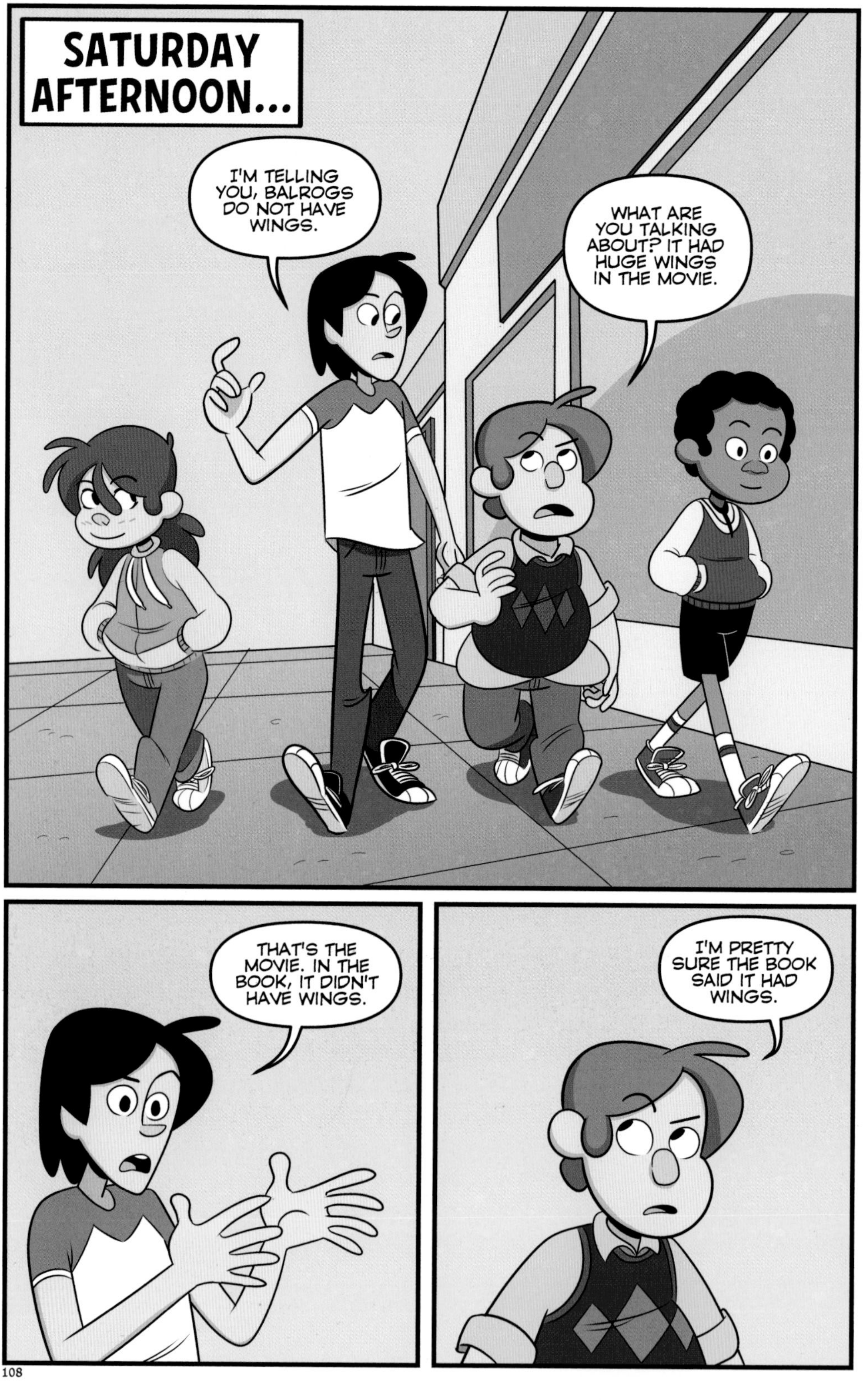
SATURDAY AFTERNOON...
I'M TELLING YOU, BALROGS DO NOT HAVE WINGS.
WHAT ARE YOU TALKING ABOUT? IT HAD HUGE WINGS IN THE MOVIE.
THAT'S THE MOVIE. IN THE BOOK, IT DIDN'T HAVE WINGS.
I'M PRETTY SURE THE BOOK SAID IT HAD WINGS.

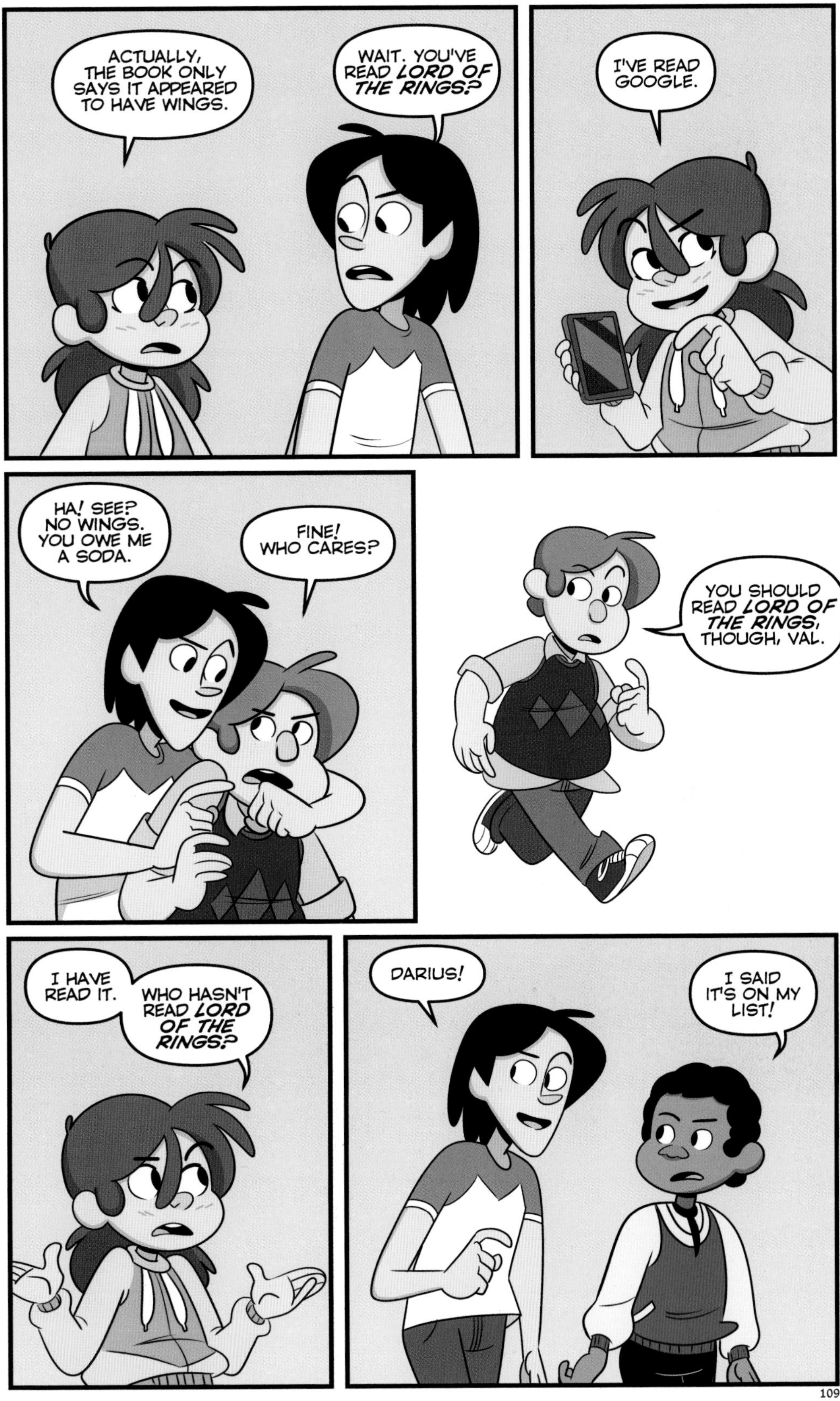
ACTUALLY, THE BOOK ONLY SAYS IT APPEARED TO HAVE WINGS.
WAIT. YOU'VE READ *LORD OF THE RINGS?*
I'VE READ GOOGLE.
HA! SEE? NO WINGS. YOU OWE ME A SODA.
FINE! WHO CARES?
YOU SHOULD READ *LORD OF THE RINGS*, THOUGH, VAL.
I HAVE READ IT.
WHO HASN'T READ *LORD OF THE RINGS?*
DARIUS!
I SAID IT'S ON MY LIST!

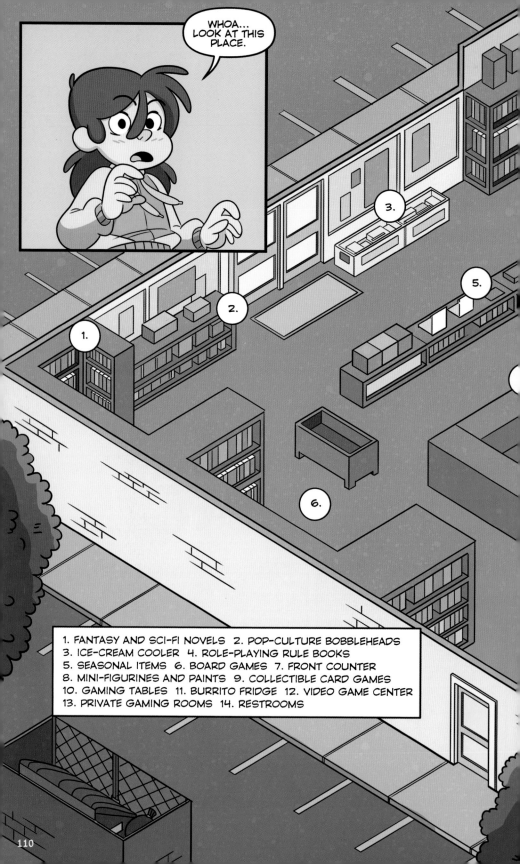

1. FANTASY AND SCI-FI NOVELS 2. POP-CULTURE BOBBLEHEADS
3. ICE-CREAM COOLER 4. ROLE-PLAYING RULE BOOKS
5. SEASONAL ITEMS 6. BOARD GAMES 7. FRONT COUNTER
8. MINI-FIGURINES AND PAINTS 9. COLLECTIBLE CARD GAMES
10. GAMING TABLES 11. BURRITO FRIDGE 12. VIDEO GAME CENTER
13. PRIVATE GAMING ROOMS 14. RESTROOMS

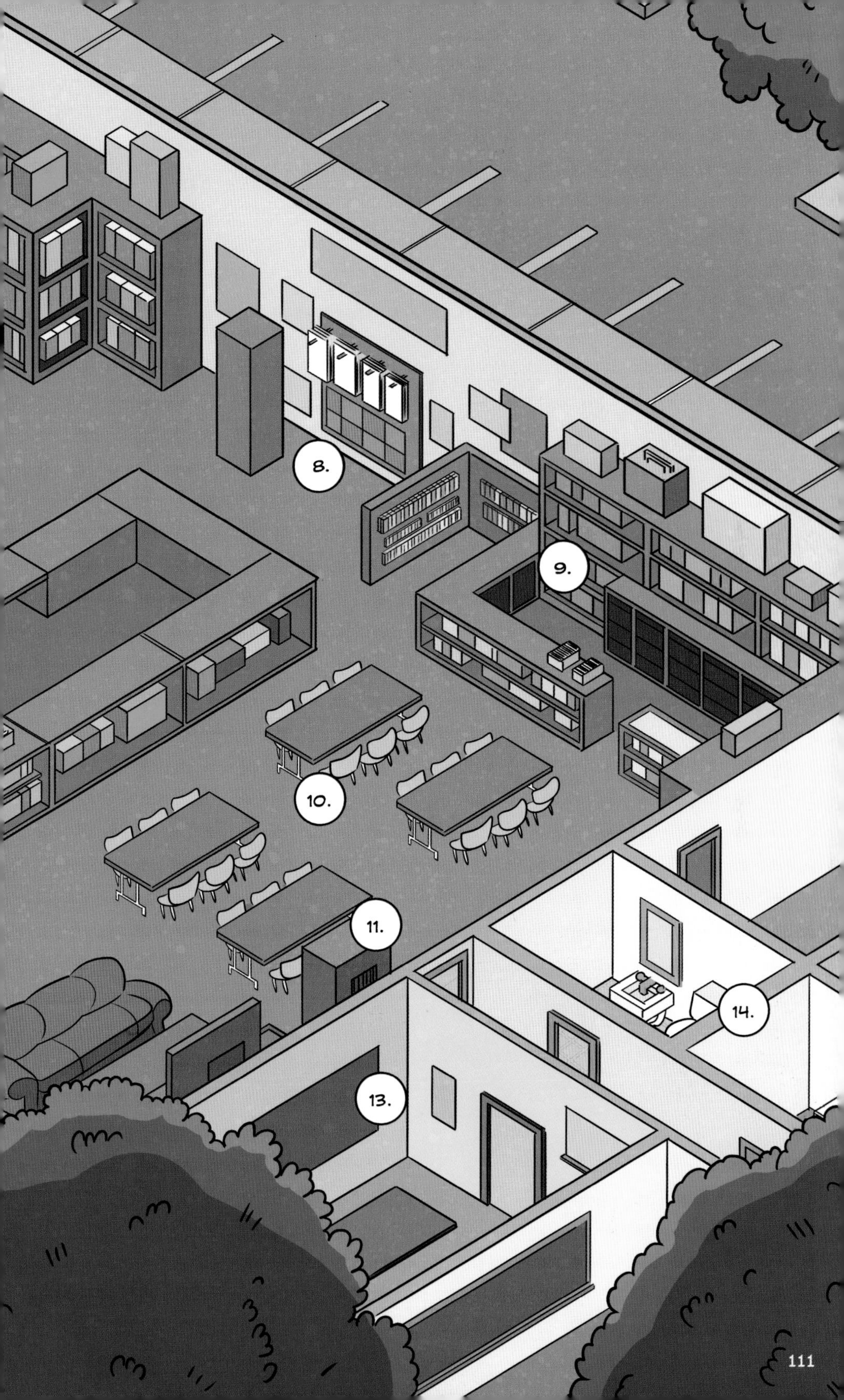
8.
9.
10.
11.
13.
14.

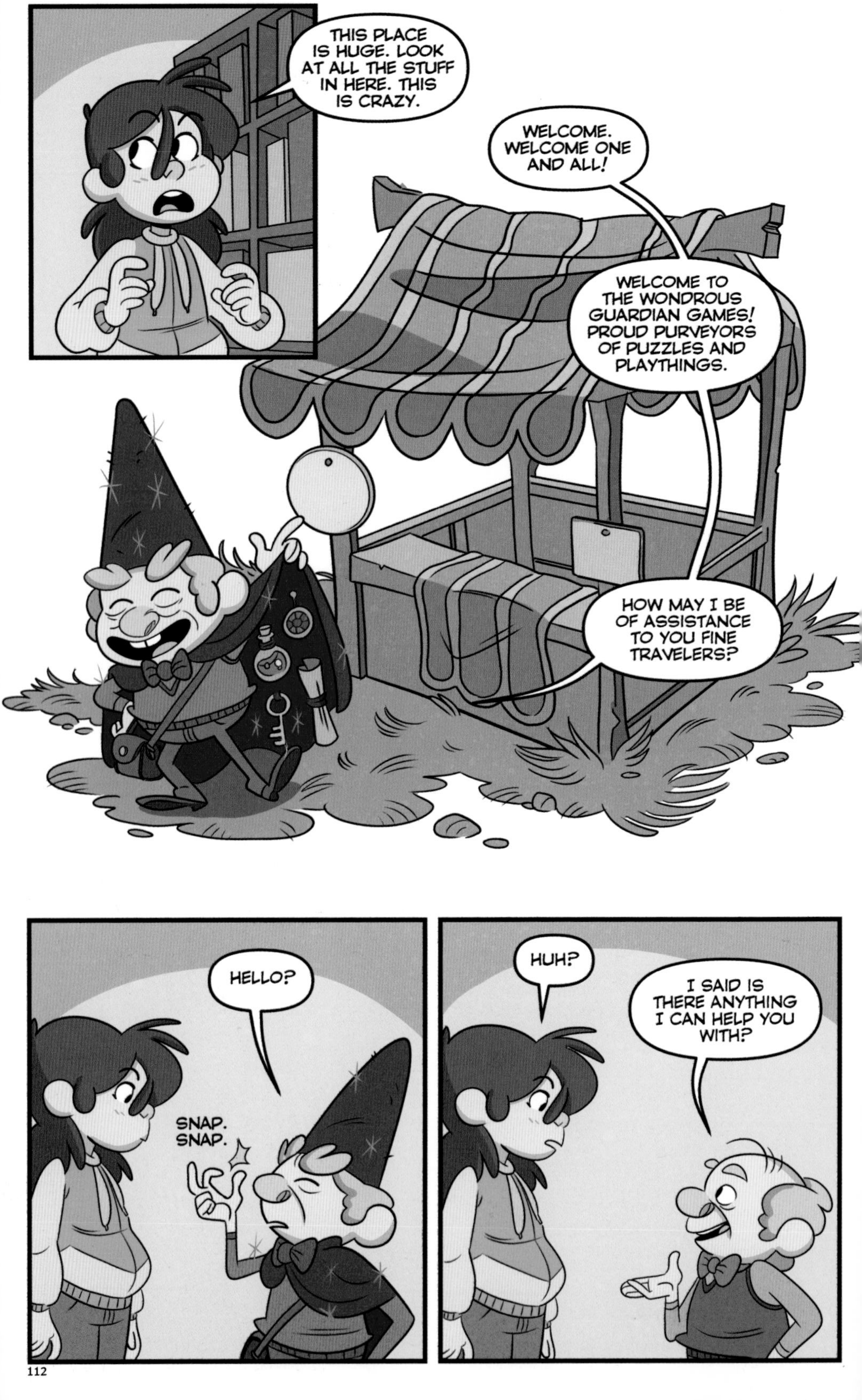
THIS PLACE IS HUGE. LOOK AT ALL THE STUFF IN HERE. THIS IS CRAZY.
WELCOME. WELCOME ONE AND ALL!
WELCOME TO THE WONDROUS GUARDIAN GAMES! PROUD PURVEYORS OF PUZZLES AND PLAYTHINGS.
HOW MAY I BE OF ASSISTANCE TO YOU FINE TRAVELERS?
HELLO?
SNAP. SNAP.
HUH?
I SAID IS THERE ANYTHING I CAN HELP YOU WITH?

OH. I'M JUST LOOKING AROUND.

WELL, LET ME KNOW IF YOU NEED ANYTHING.

YOU OKAY? YOU KIND OF SPACED OUT THERE.

YEAH. THIS PLACE IS JUST KIND OF OVERWHELMING.

VAL, THE ROLE-PLAYING BOOKS ARE OVER HERE.

WOOF!

THESE ARE REALLY EXPENSIVE.

THINK OF THEM AS AN INVESTMENT.

FORTY BUCKS FOR A BOOK?

VAL, THIS ISN'T A BOOK. IT'S A DOORWAY TO ANOTHER WORLD.

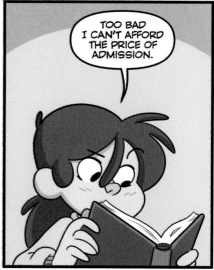

TOO BAD I CAN'T AFFORD THE PRICE OF ADMISSION.

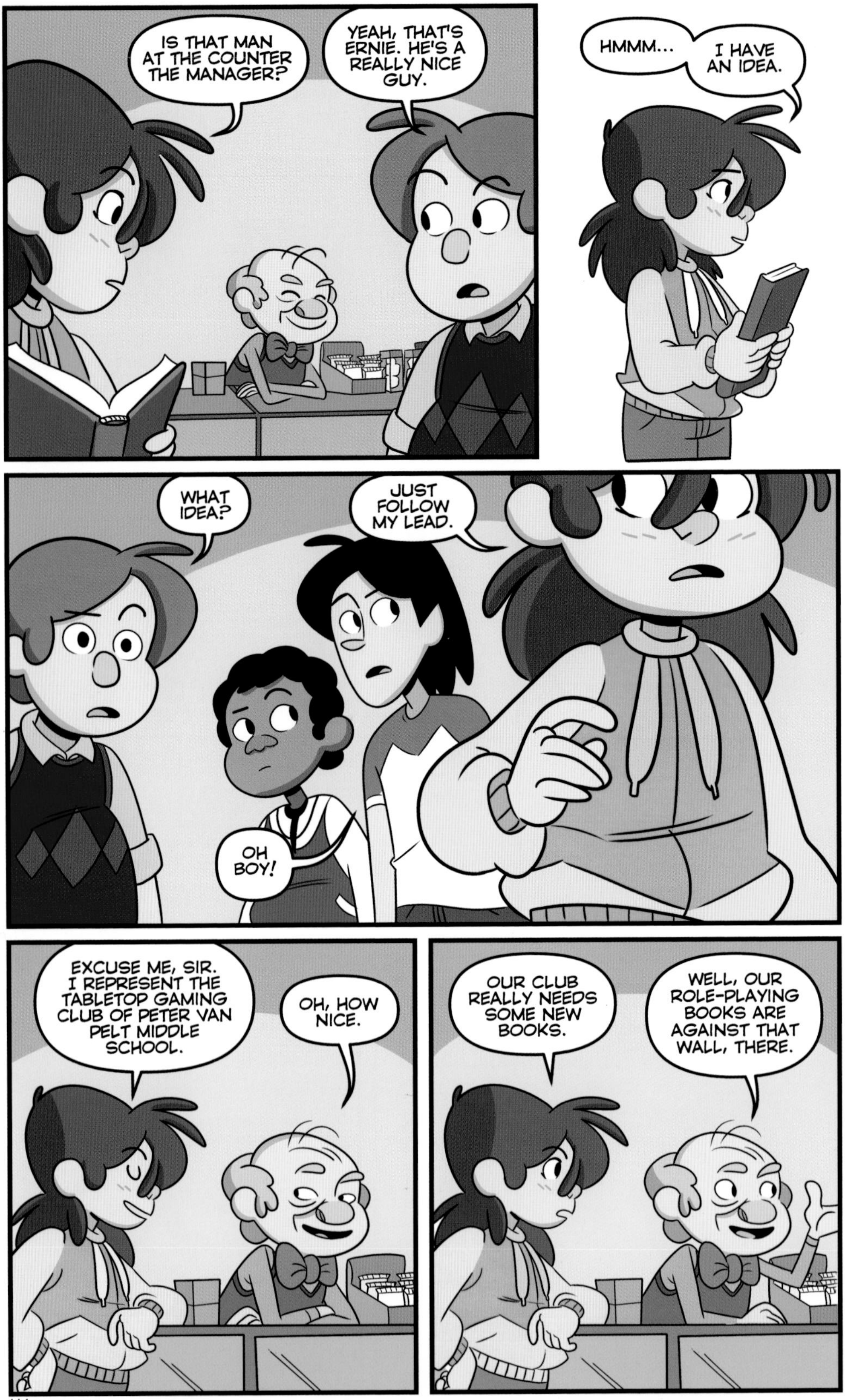
IS THAT MAN AT THE COUNTER THE MANAGER?
YEAH, THAT'S ERNIE. HE'S A REALLY NICE GUY.
HMMM...
I HAVE AN IDEA.
WHAT IDEA?
JUST FOLLOW MY LEAD.
OH BOY!
EXCUSE ME, SIR. I REPRESENT THE TABLETOP GAMING CLUB OF PETER VAN PELT MIDDLE SCHOOL.
OH, HOW NICE.
OUR CLUB REALLY NEEDS SOME NEW BOOKS.
WELL, OUR ROLE-PLAYING BOOKS ARE AGAINST THAT WALL, THERE.

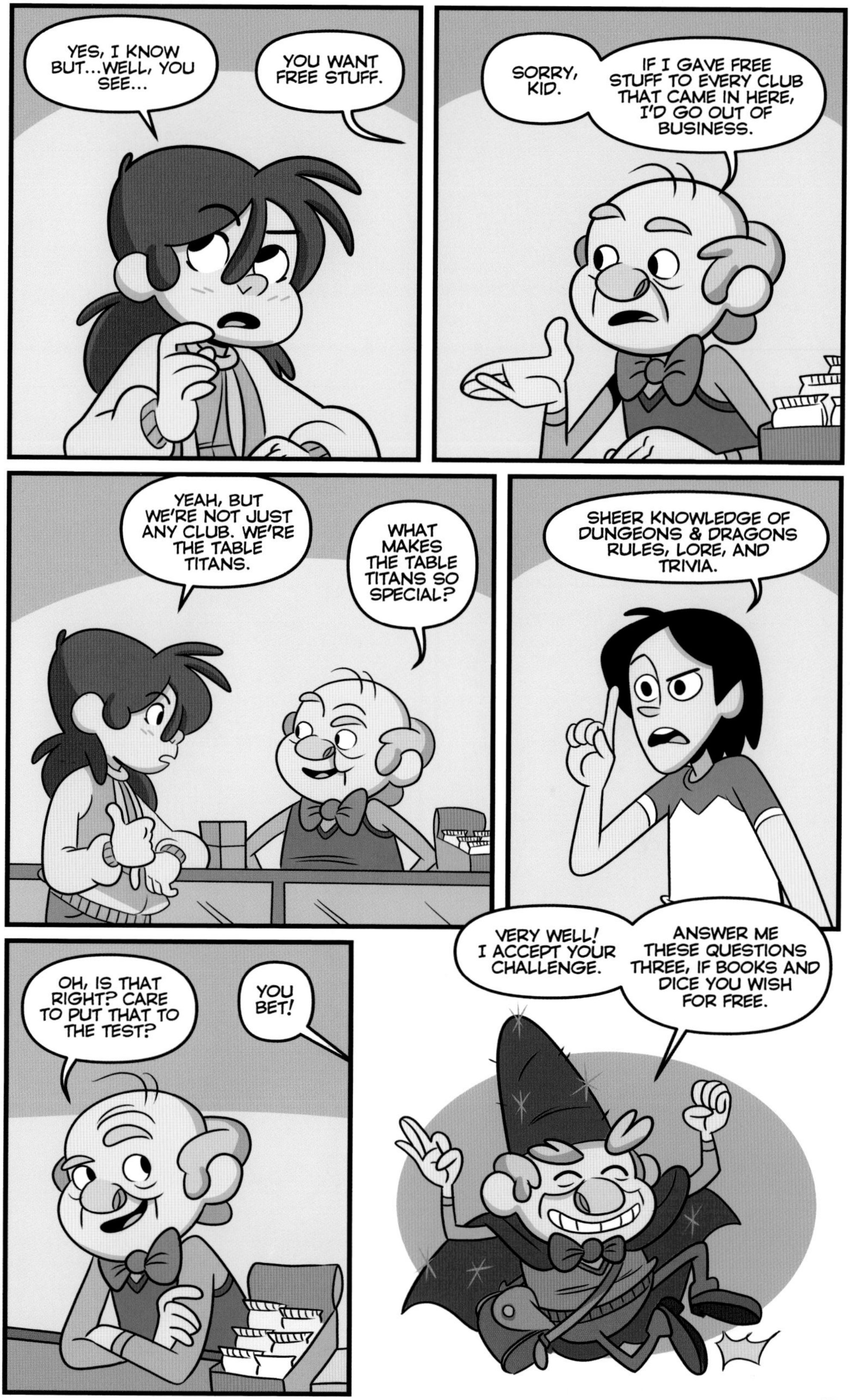
YES, I KNOW BUT...WELL, YOU SEE...
YOU WANT FREE STUFF.
SORRY, KID.
IF I GAVE FREE STUFF TO EVERY CLUB THAT CAME IN HERE, I'D GO OUT OF BUSINESS.
YEAH, BUT WE'RE NOT JUST ANY CLUB. WE'RE THE TABLE TITANS.
WHAT MAKES THE TABLE TITANS SO SPECIAL?
SHEER KNOWLEDGE OF DUNGEONS & DRAGONS RULES, LORE, AND TRIVIA.
OH, IS THAT RIGHT? CARE TO PUT THAT TO THE TEST?
YOU BET!
VERY WELL! I ACCEPT YOUR CHALLENGE.
ANSWER ME THESE QUESTIONS THREE, IF BOOKS AND DICE YOU WISH FOR FREE.

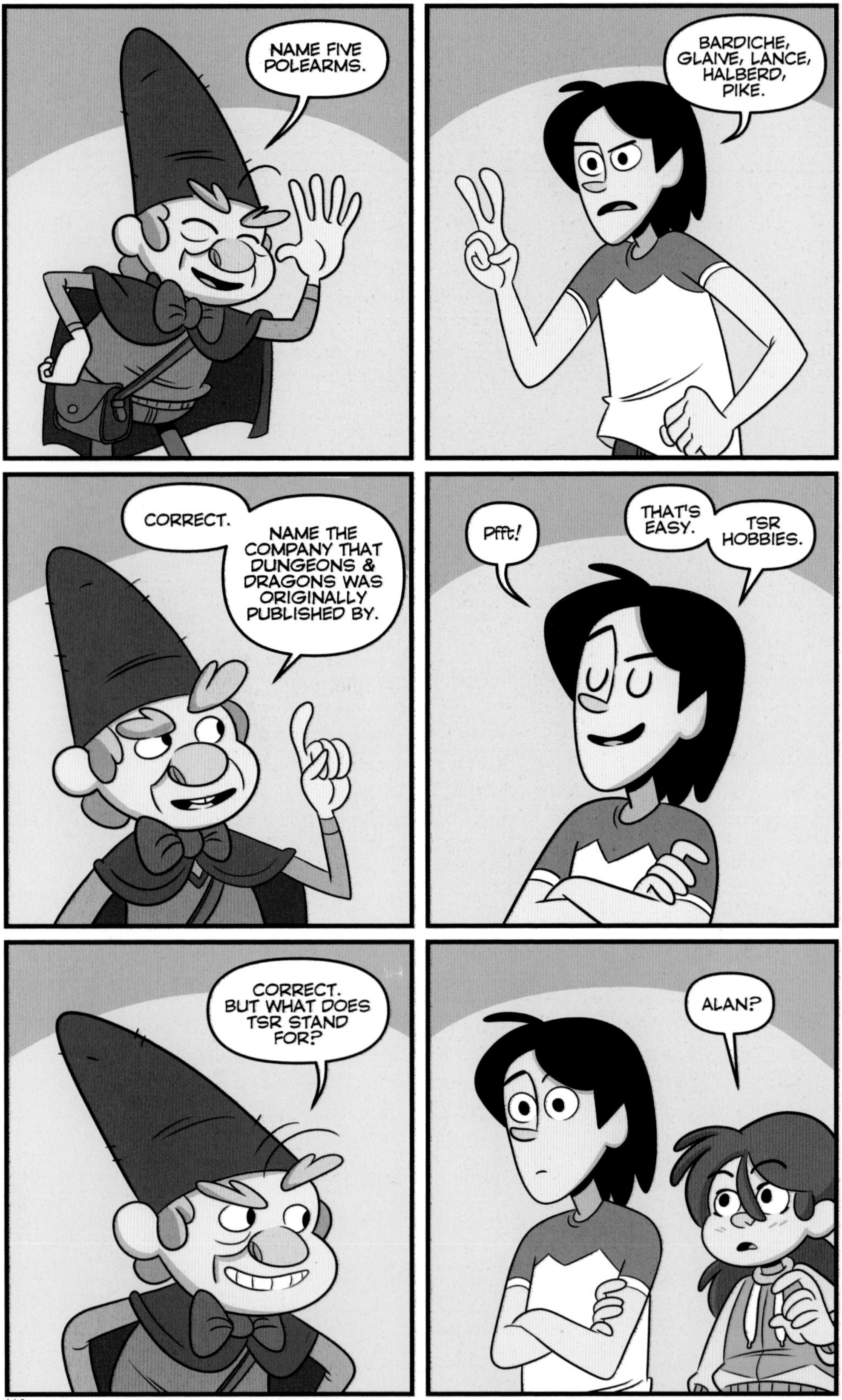
NAME FIVE POLEARMS.
BARDICHE, GLAIVE, LANCE, HALBERD, PIKE.
CORRECT.
NAME THE COMPANY THAT DUNGEONS & DRAGONS WAS ORIGINALLY PUBLISHED BY.
Pfft!
THAT'S EASY.
TSR HOBBIES.
CORRECT. BUT WHAT DOES TSR STAND FOR?
ALAN?

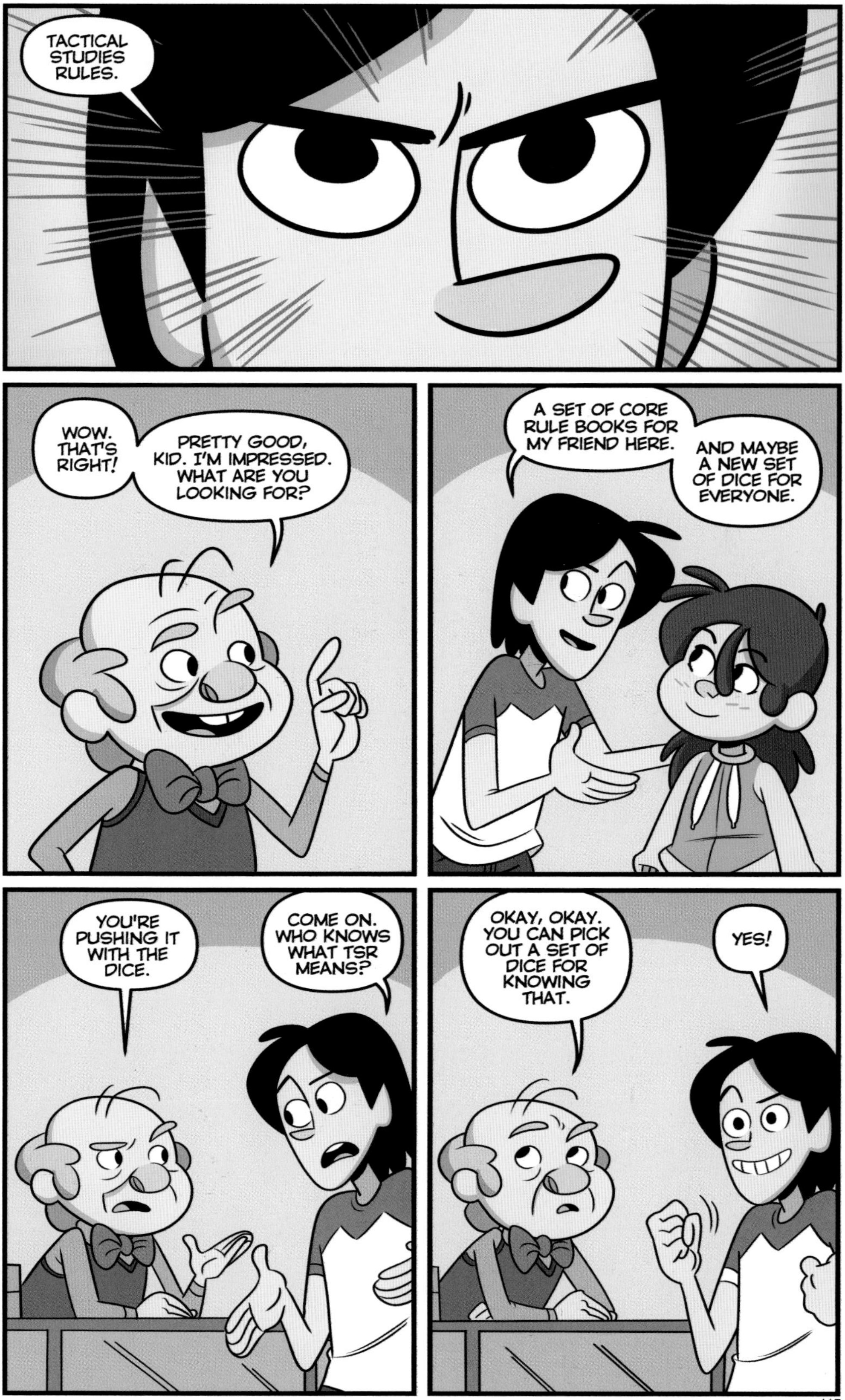

TACTICAL STUDIES RULES.
WOW. THAT'S RIGHT!
PRETTY GOOD, KID. I'M IMPRESSED. WHAT ARE YOU LOOKING FOR?
A SET OF CORE RULE BOOKS FOR MY FRIEND HERE.
AND MAYBE A NEW SET OF DICE FOR EVERYONE.
YOU'RE PUSHING IT WITH THE DICE.
COME ON. WHO KNOWS WHAT TSR MEANS?
OKAY, OKAY. YOU CAN PICK OUT A SET OF DICE FOR KNOWING THAT.
YES!

SNACK BREAK, NEXT DOOR...

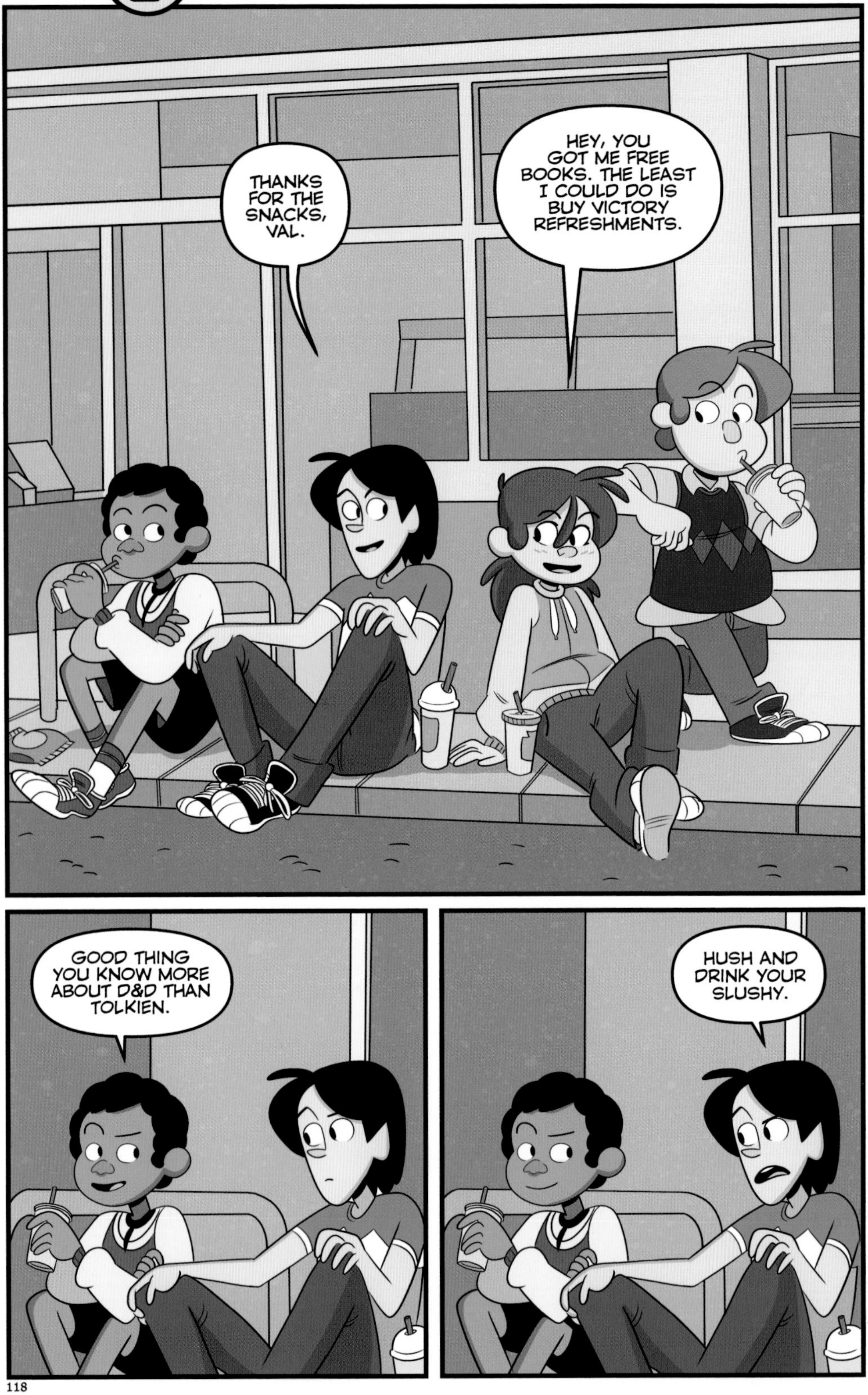
THANKS FOR THE SNACKS, VAL.
HEY, YOU GOT ME FREE BOOKS. THE LEAST I COULD DO IS BUY VICTORY REFRESHMENTS.
GOOD THING YOU KNOW MORE ABOUT D&D THAN TOLKIEN.
HUSH AND DRINK YOUR SLUSHY.

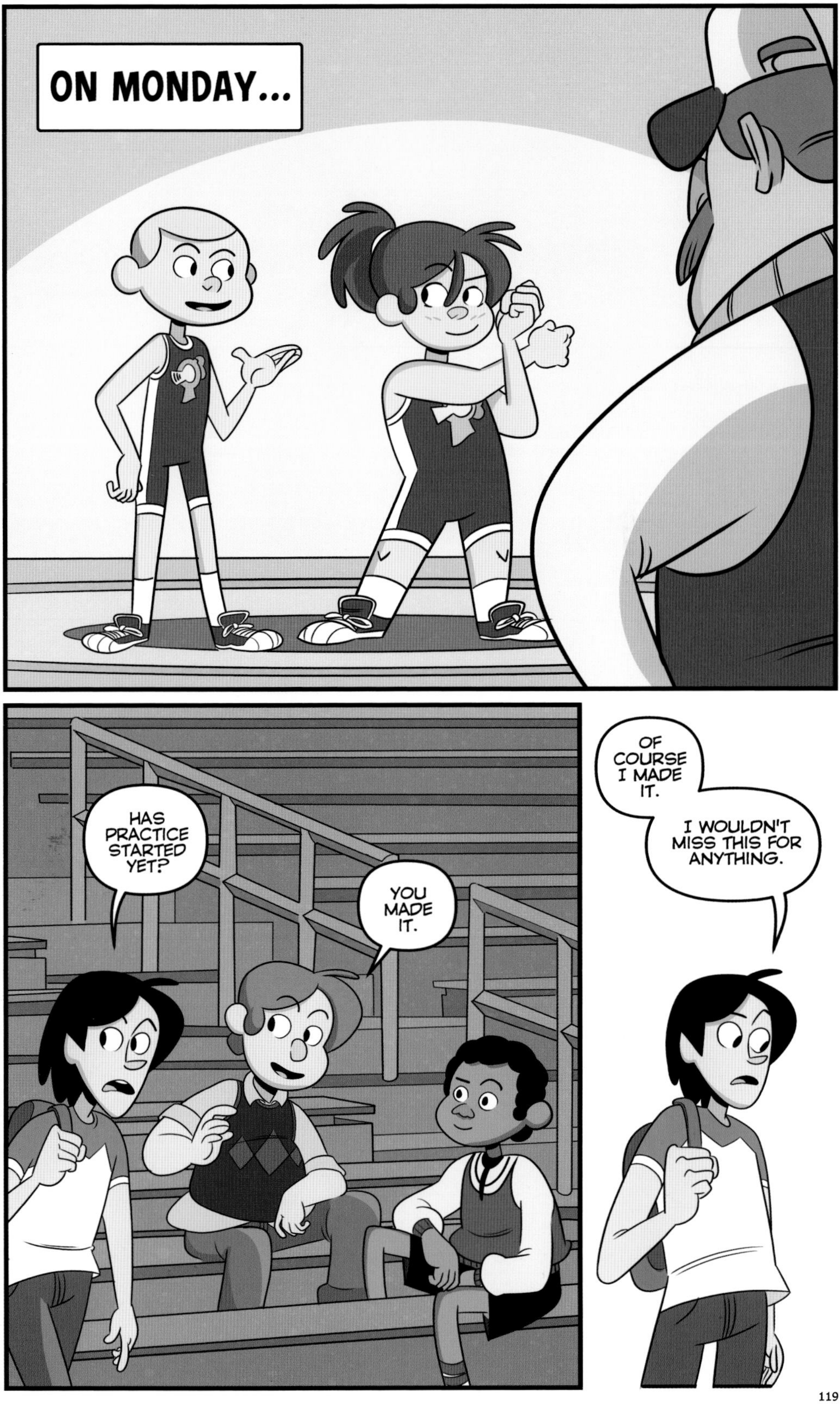
ON MONDAY...
HAS PRACTICE STARTED YET?
YOU MADE IT.
OF COURSE I MADE IT.
I WOULDN'T MISS THIS FOR ANYTHING.

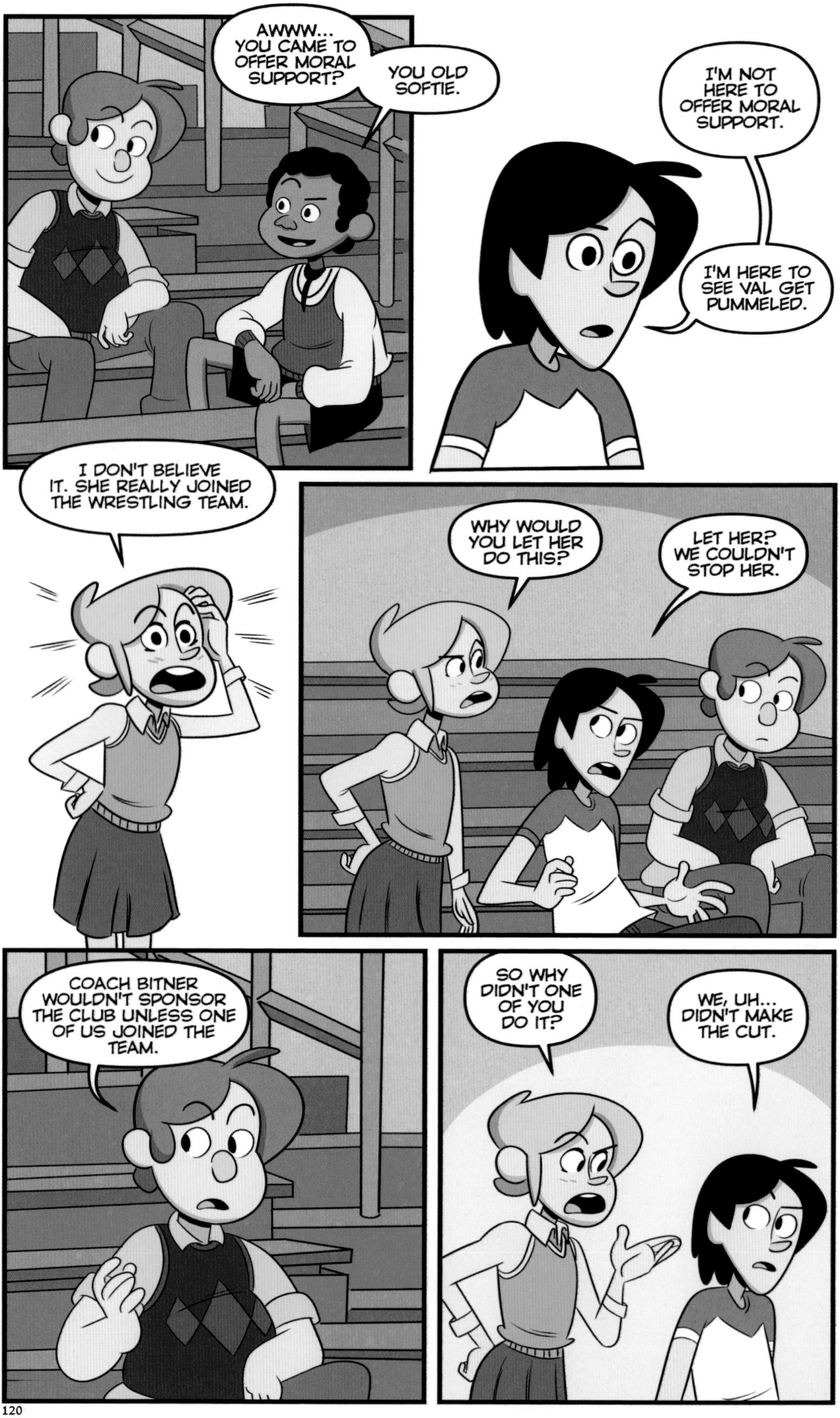
AWWW... YOU CAME TO OFFER MORAL SUPPORT?
YOU OLD SOFTIE.
I'M NOT HERE TO OFFER MORAL SUPPORT.
I'M HERE TO SEE VAL GET PUMMELED.
I DON'T BELIEVE IT. SHE REALLY JOINED THE WRESTLING TEAM.
WHY WOULD YOU LET HER DO THIS?
LET HER? WE COULDN'T STOP HER.
COACH BITNER WOULDN'T SPONSOR THE CLUB UNLESS ONE OF US JOINED THE TEAM.
SO WHY DIDN'T ONE OF YOU DO IT?
WE, UH... DIDN'T MAKE THE CUT.

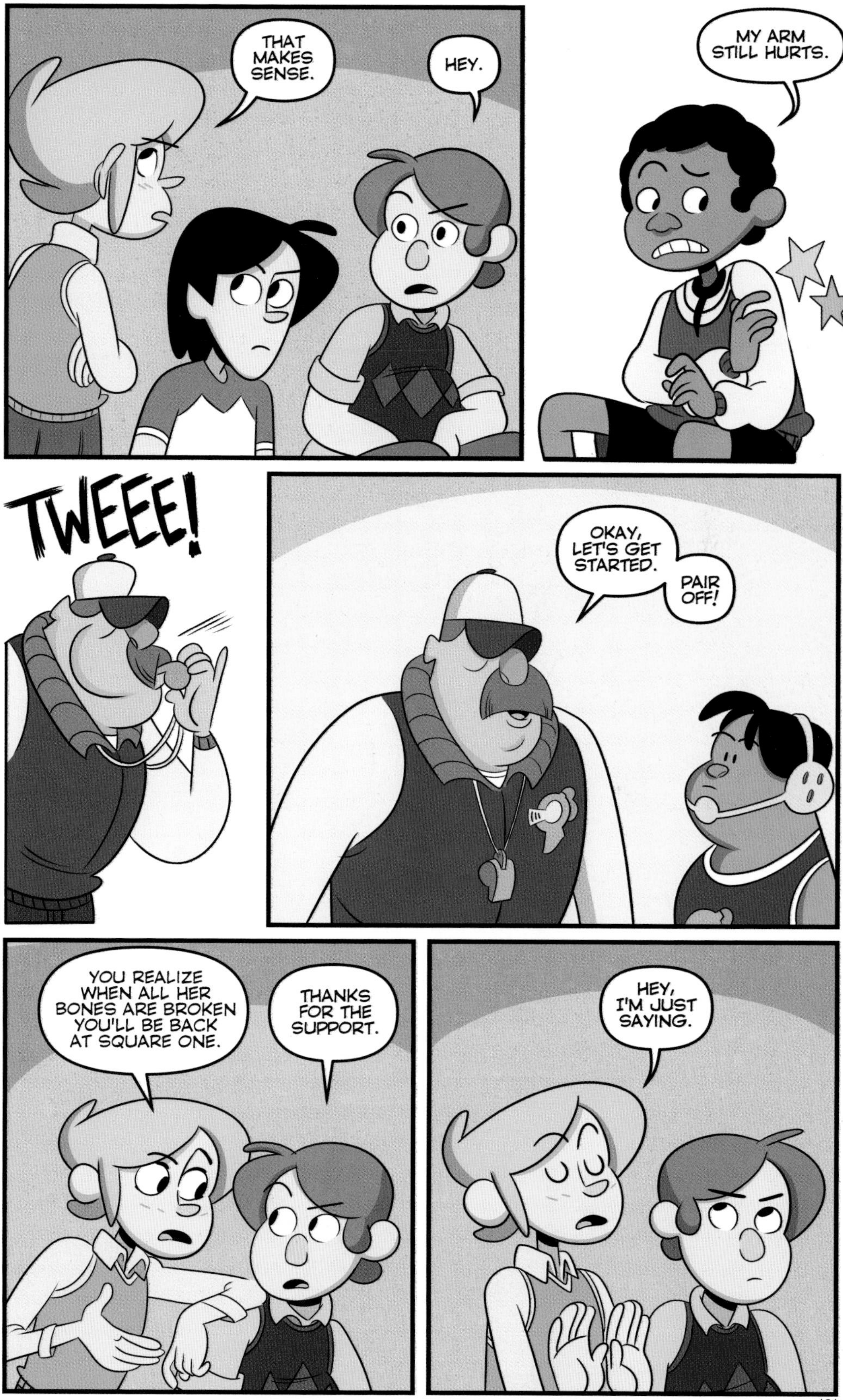
THAT MAKES SENSE.
HEY.
MY ARM STILL HURTS.
TWEEE!
OKAY, LET'S GET STARTED.
PAIR OFF!
YOU REALIZE WHEN ALL HER BONES ARE BROKEN YOU'LL BE BACK AT SQUARE ONE.
THANKS FOR THE SUPPORT.
HEY, I'M JUST SAYING.

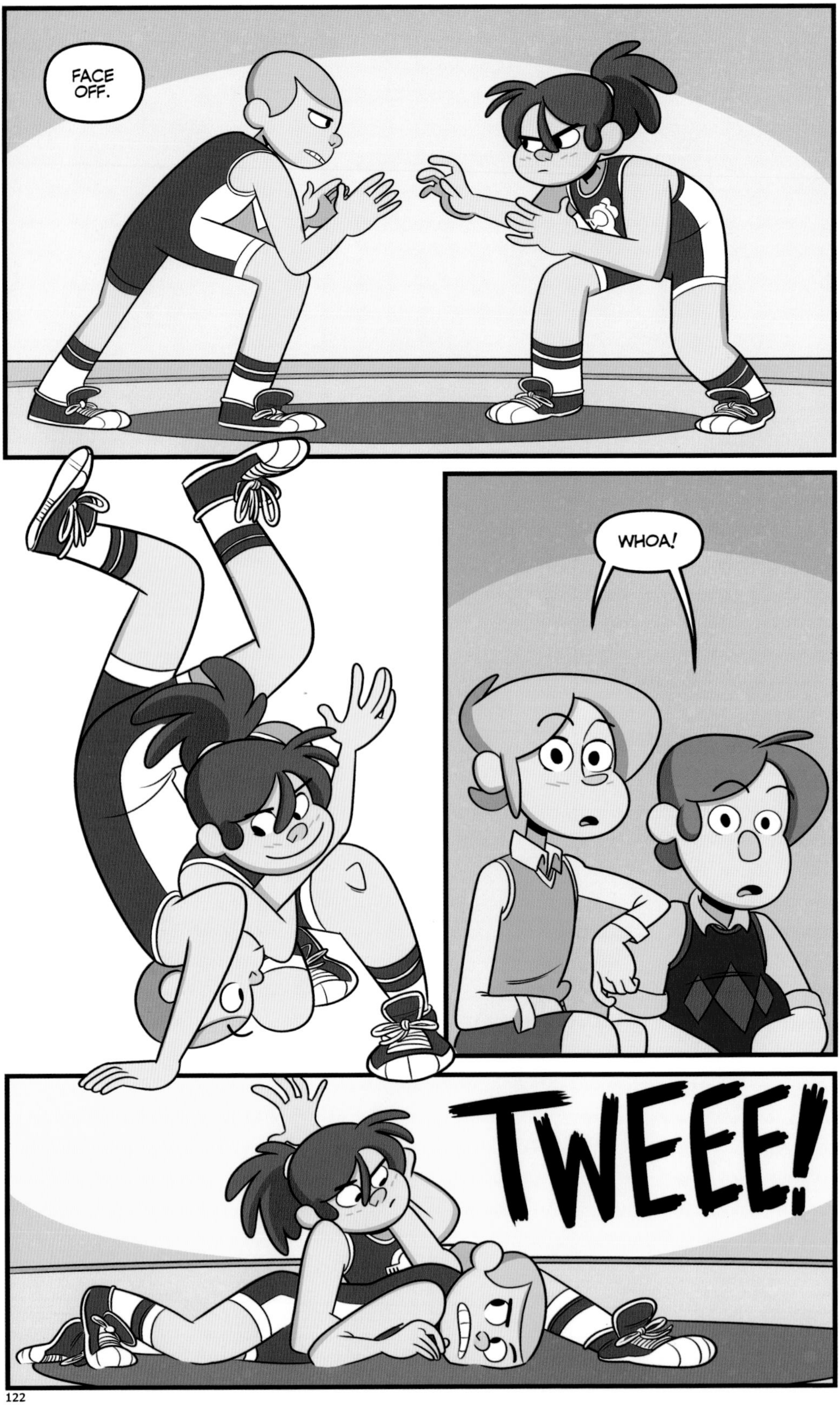
FACE OFF.
WHOA!
TWEEE!

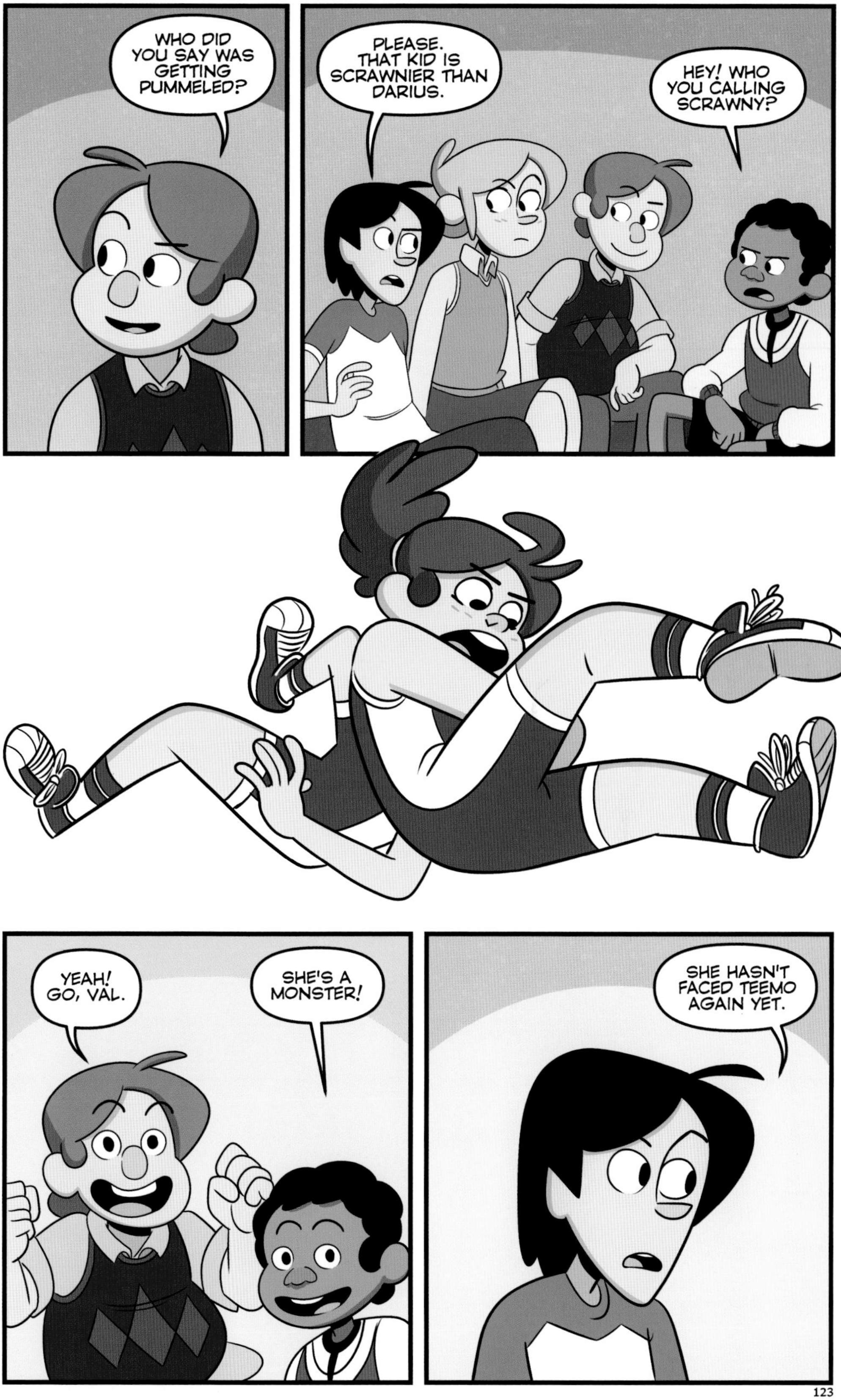
WHO DID YOU SAY WAS GETTING PUMMELED?
PLEASE. THAT KID IS SCRAWNIER THAN DARIUS.
HEY! WHO YOU CALLING SCRAWNY?
YEAH! GO, VAL.
SHE'S A MONSTER!
SHE HASN'T FACED TEEMO AGAIN YET.

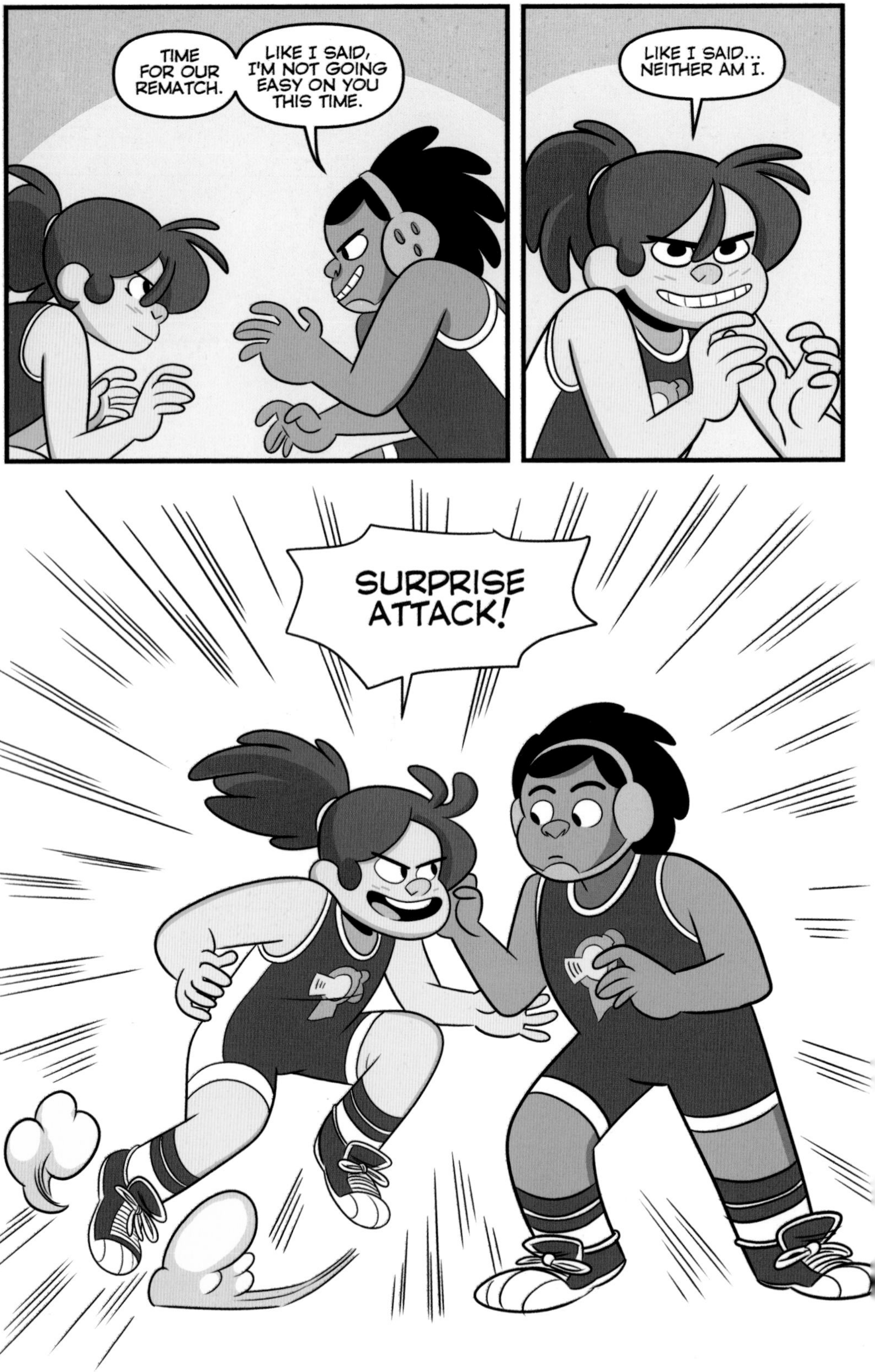

TIME FOR OUR REMATCH.
LIKE I SAID, I'M NOT GOING EASY ON YOU THIS TIME.
LIKE I SAID... NEITHER AM I.
SURPRISE ATTACK!

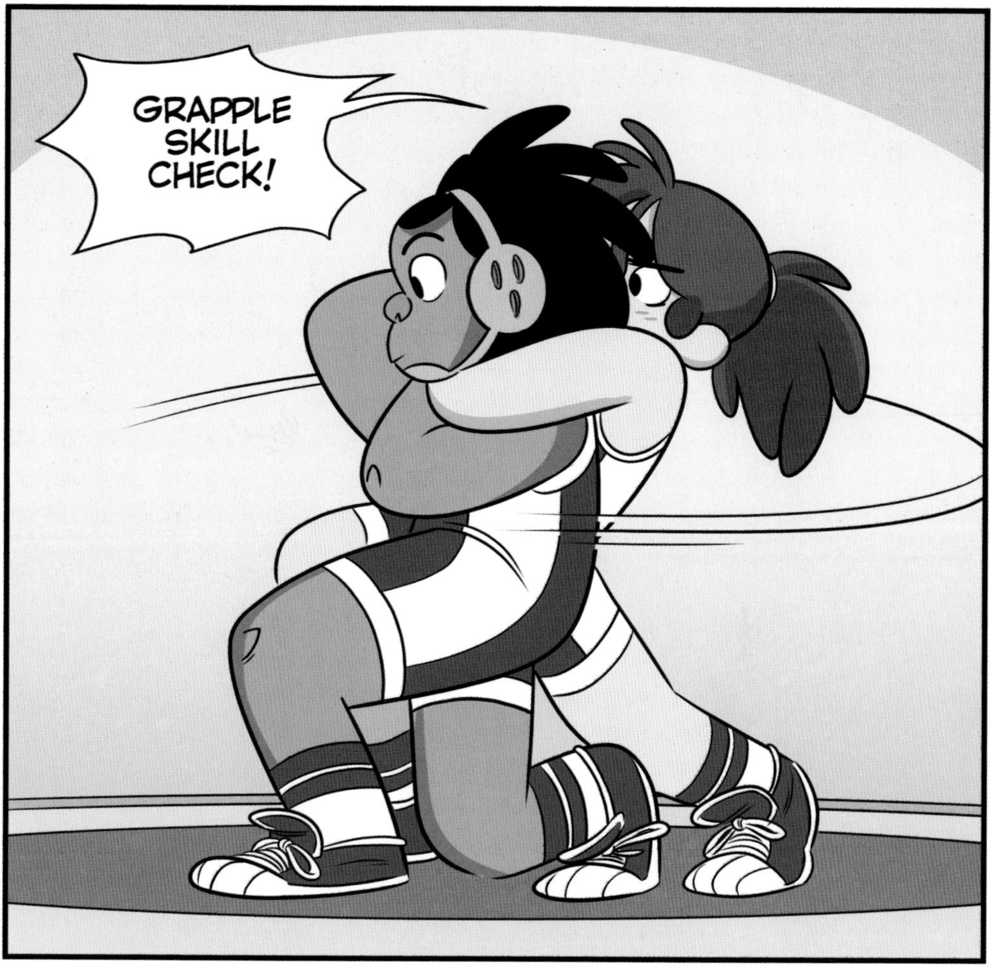
GRAPPLE SKILL CHECK!

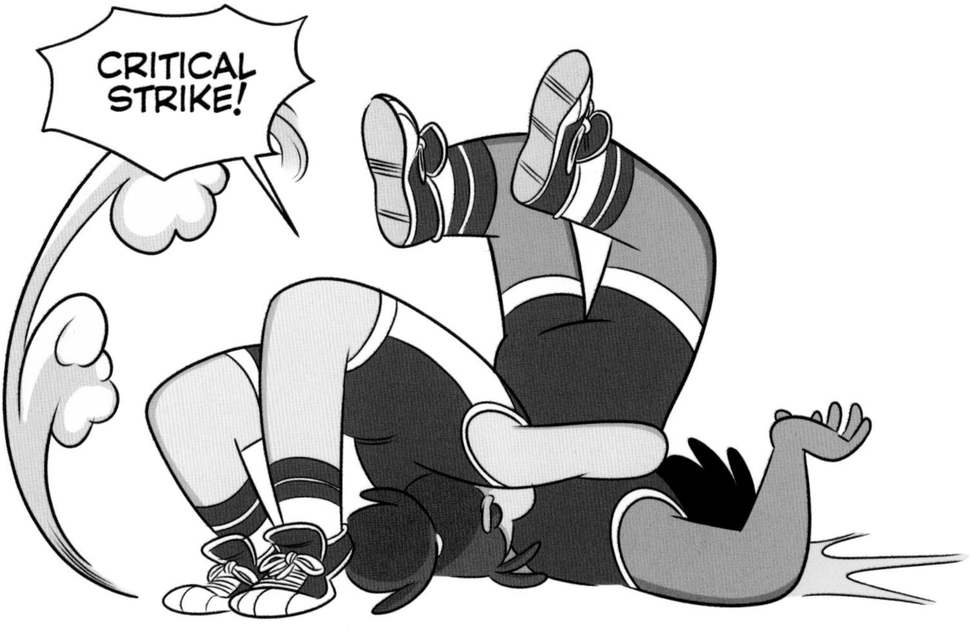
CRITICAL STRIKE!

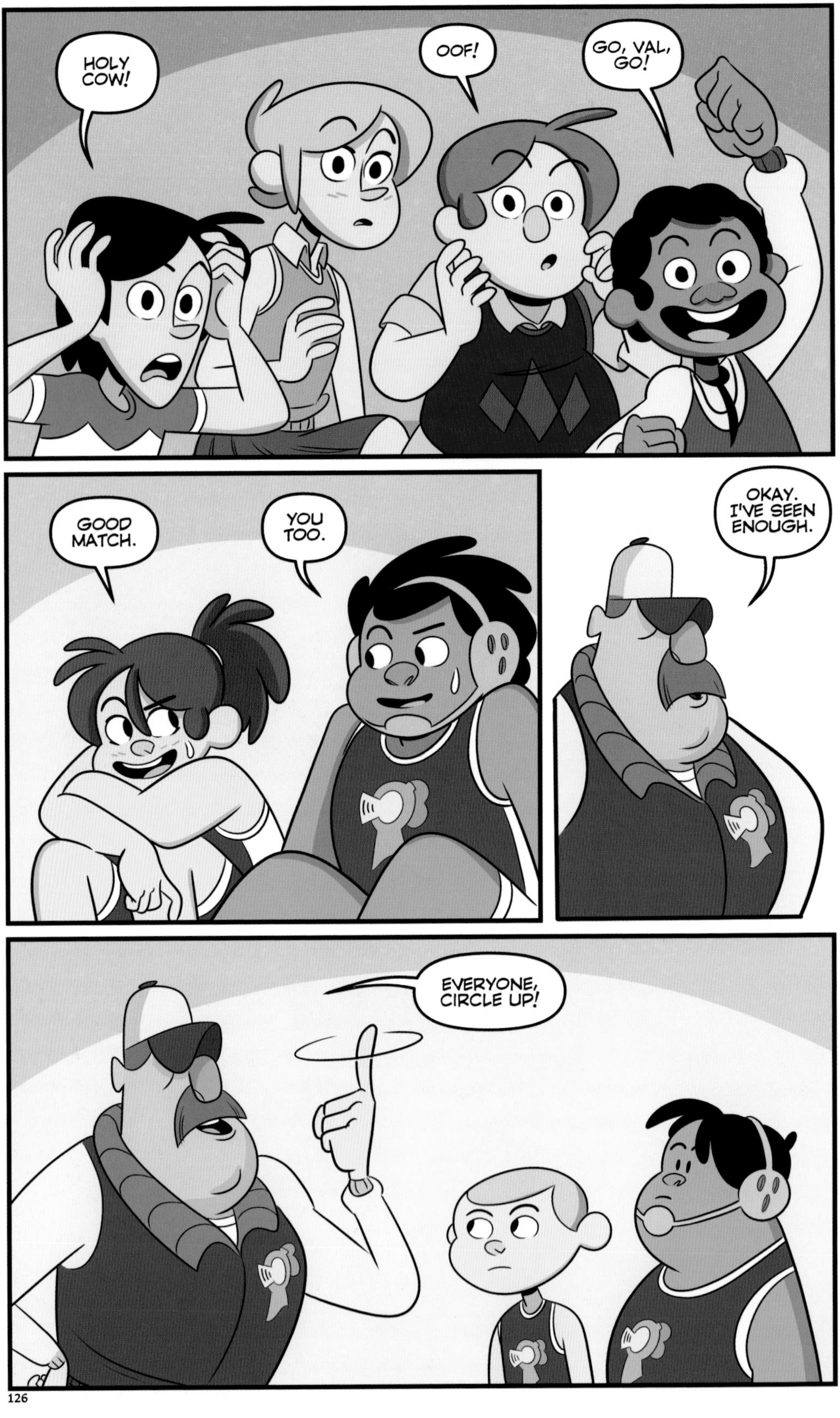
HOLY COW!
OOF!
GO, VAL, GO!
GOOD MATCH.
YOU TOO.
OKAY. I'VE SEEN ENOUGH.
EVERYONE, CIRCLE UP!

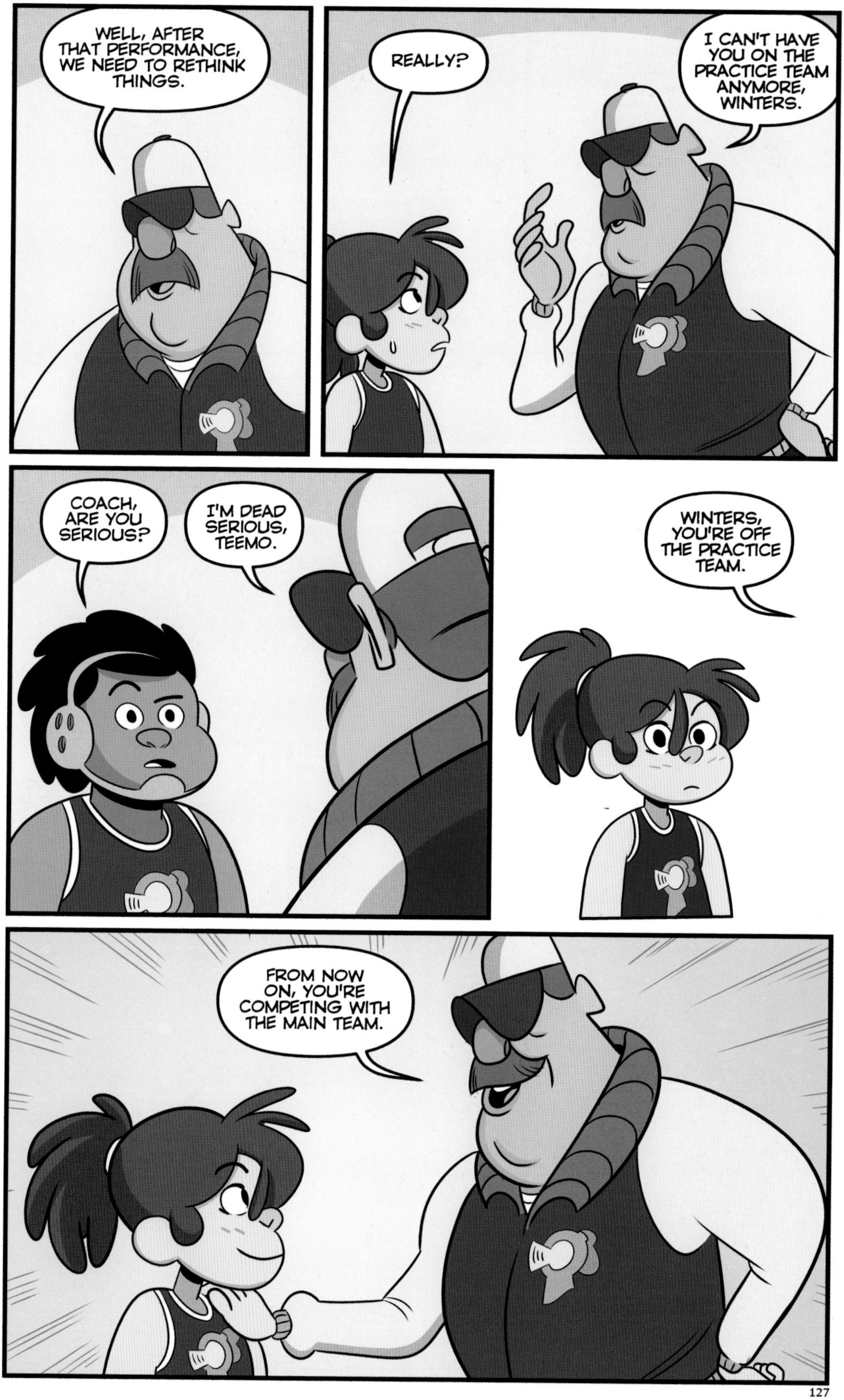
WELL, AFTER THAT PERFORMANCE, WE NEED TO RETHINK THINGS.
REALLY?
I CAN'T HAVE YOU ON THE PRACTICE TEAM ANYMORE, WINTERS.
COACH, ARE YOU SERIOUS?
I'M DEAD SERIOUS, TEEMO.
WINTERS, YOU'RE OFF THE PRACTICE TEAM.
FROM NOW ON, YOU'RE COMPETING WITH THE MAIN TEAM.

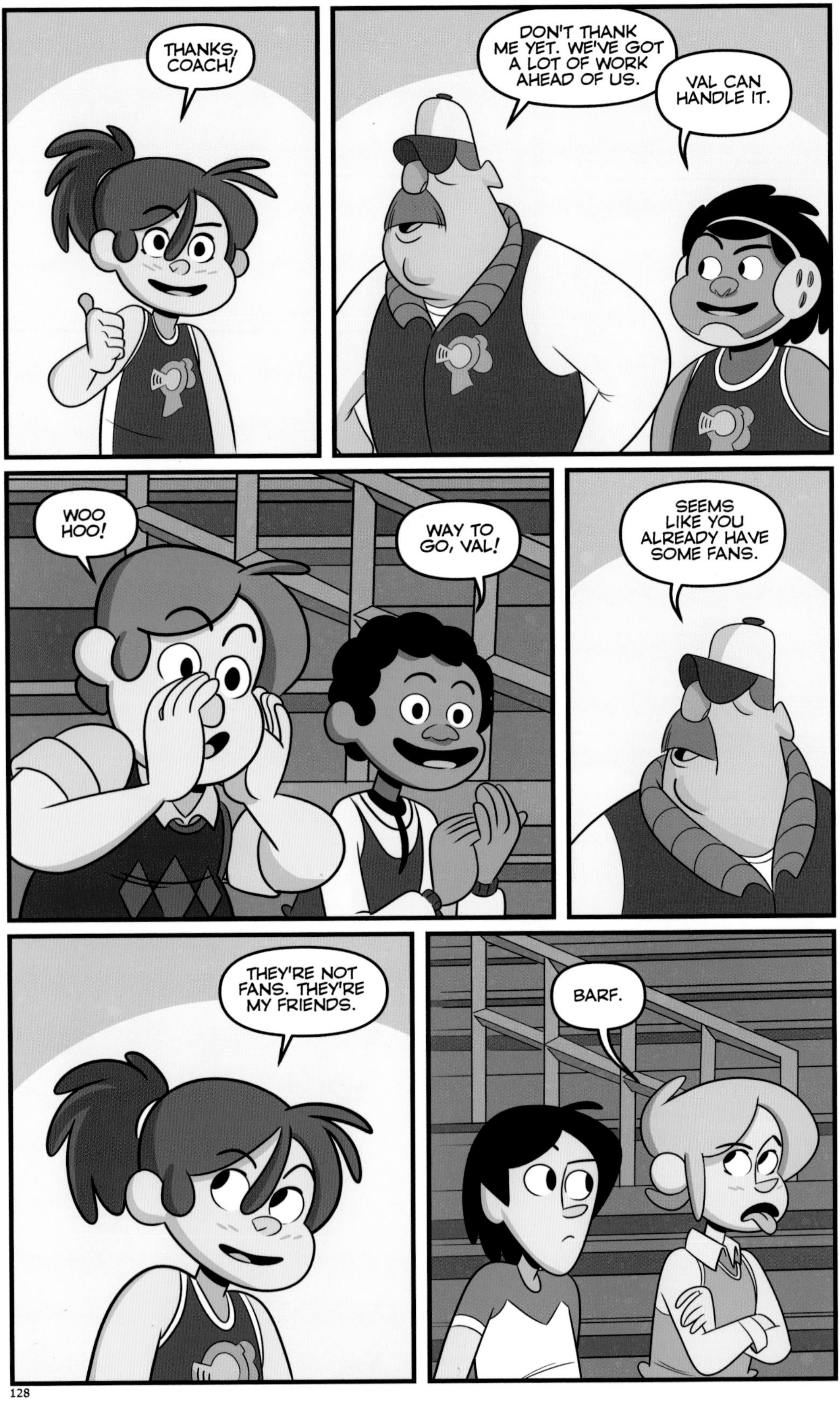
THANKS, COACH!
DON'T THANK ME YET. WE'VE GOT A LOT OF WORK AHEAD OF US.
VAL CAN HANDLE IT.
WOO HOO!
WAY TO GO, VAL!
SEEMS LIKE YOU ALREADY HAVE SOME FANS.
THEY'RE NOT FANS. THEY'RE MY FRIENDS.
BARF.

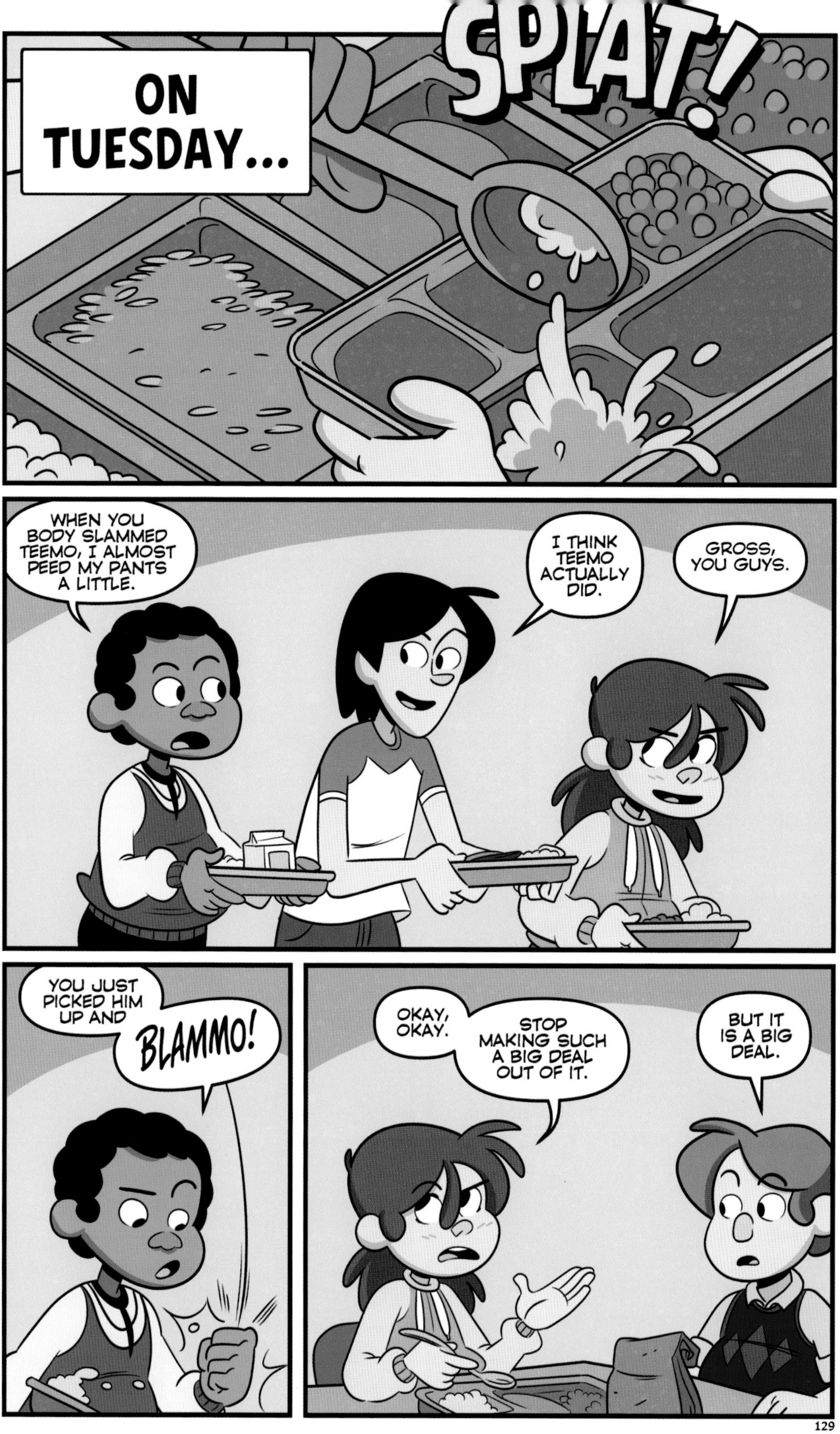
ON TUESDAY...
SPLAT!
WHEN YOU BODY SLAMMED TEEMO, I ALMOST PEED MY PANTS A LITTLE.
I THINK TEEMO ACTUALLY DID.
GROSS, YOU GUYS.
YOU JUST PICKED HIM UP AND
BLAMMO!
OKAY, OKAY.
STOP MAKING SUCH A BIG DEAL OUT OF IT.
BUT IT IS A BIG DEAL.

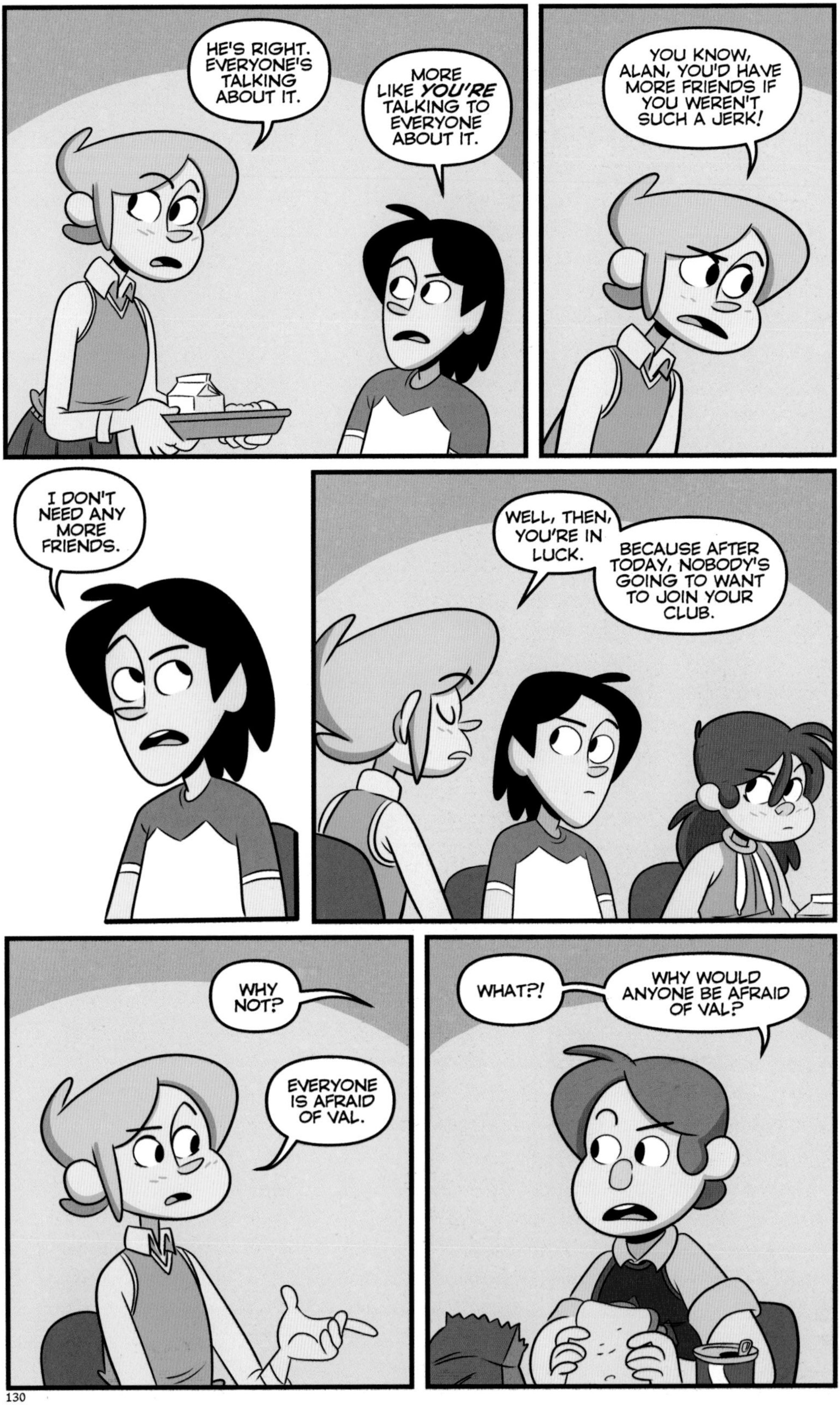
HE'S RIGHT. EVERYONE'S TALKING ABOUT IT.
MORE LIKE *YOU'RE* TALKING TO EVERYONE ABOUT IT.
YOU KNOW, ALAN, YOU'D HAVE MORE FRIENDS IF YOU WEREN'T SUCH A JERK!
I DON'T NEED ANY MORE FRIENDS.
WELL, THEN, YOU'RE IN LUCK.
BECAUSE AFTER TODAY, NOBODY'S GOING TO WANT TO JOIN YOUR CLUB.
WHY NOT?
EVERYONE IS AFRAID OF VAL.
WHAT?!
WHY WOULD ANYONE BE AFRAID OF VAL?

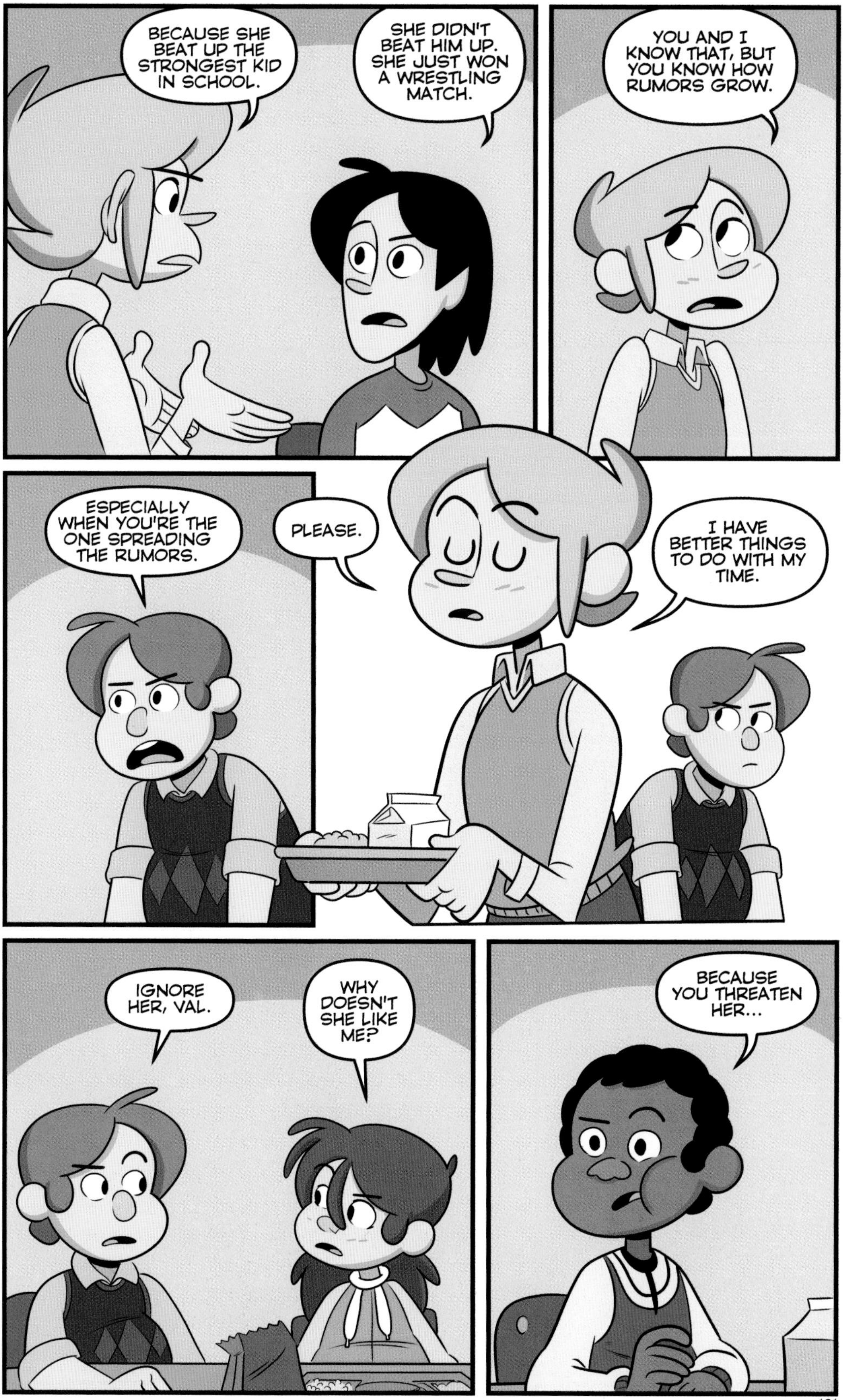
BECAUSE SHE BEAT UP THE STRONGEST KID IN SCHOOL.
SHE DIDN'T BEAT HIM UP. SHE JUST WON A WRESTLING MATCH.
YOU AND I KNOW THAT, BUT YOU KNOW HOW RUMORS GROW.
ESPECIALLY WHEN YOU'RE THE ONE SPREADING THE RUMORS.
PLEASE.
I HAVE BETTER THINGS TO DO WITH MY TIME.
IGNORE HER, VAL.
WHY DOESN'T SHE LIKE ME?
BECAUSE YOU THREATEN HER...

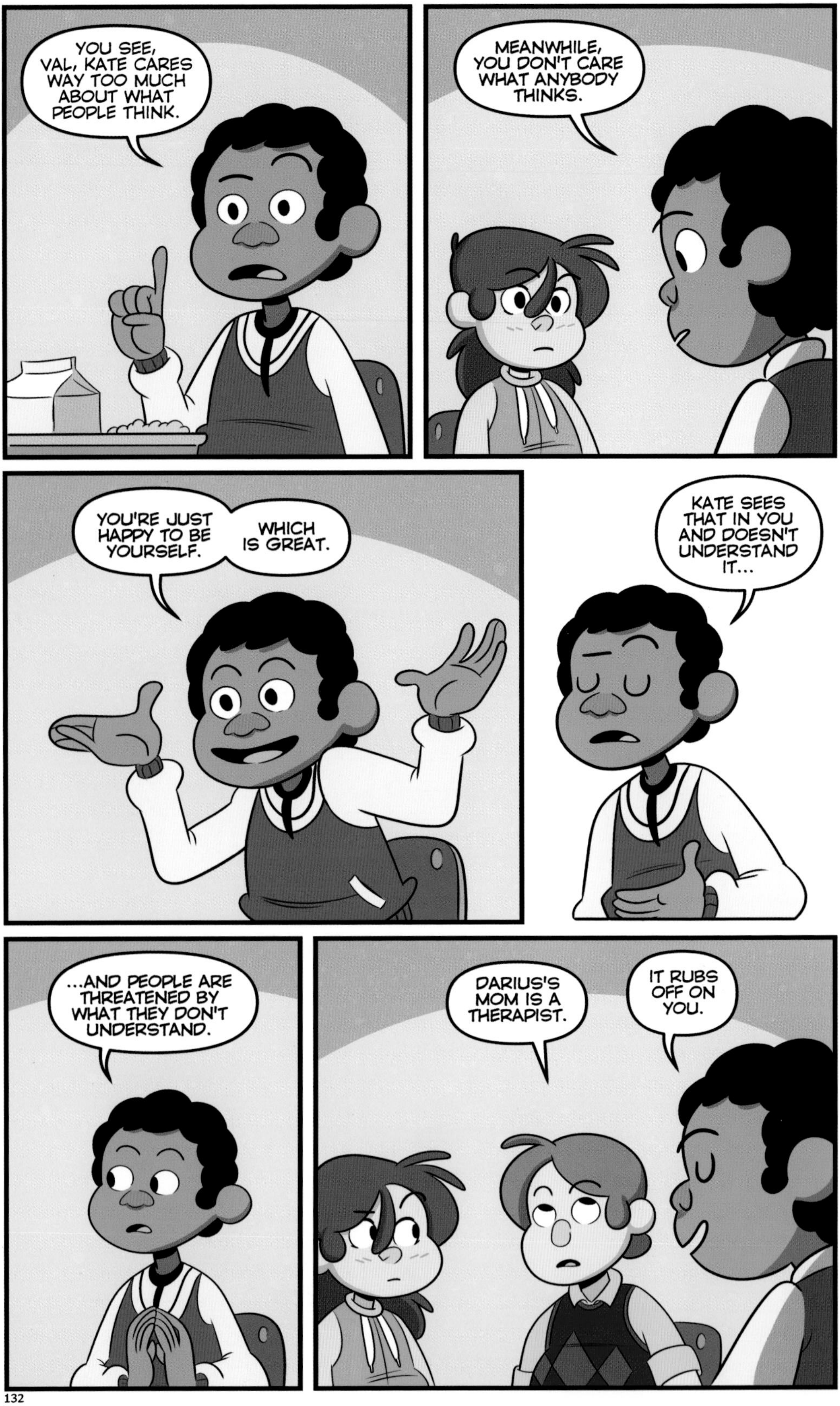
YOU SEE, VAL, KATE CARES WAY TOO MUCH ABOUT WHAT PEOPLE THINK.
MEANWHILE, YOU DON'T CARE WHAT ANYBODY THINKS.
YOU'RE JUST HAPPY TO BE YOURSELF.
WHICH IS GREAT.
KATE SEES THAT IN YOU AND DOESN'T UNDERSTAND IT...
...AND PEOPLE ARE THREATENED BY WHAT THEY DON'T UNDERSTAND.
DARIUS'S MOM IS A THERAPIST.
IT RUBS OFF ON YOU.

CHAPTER SIX

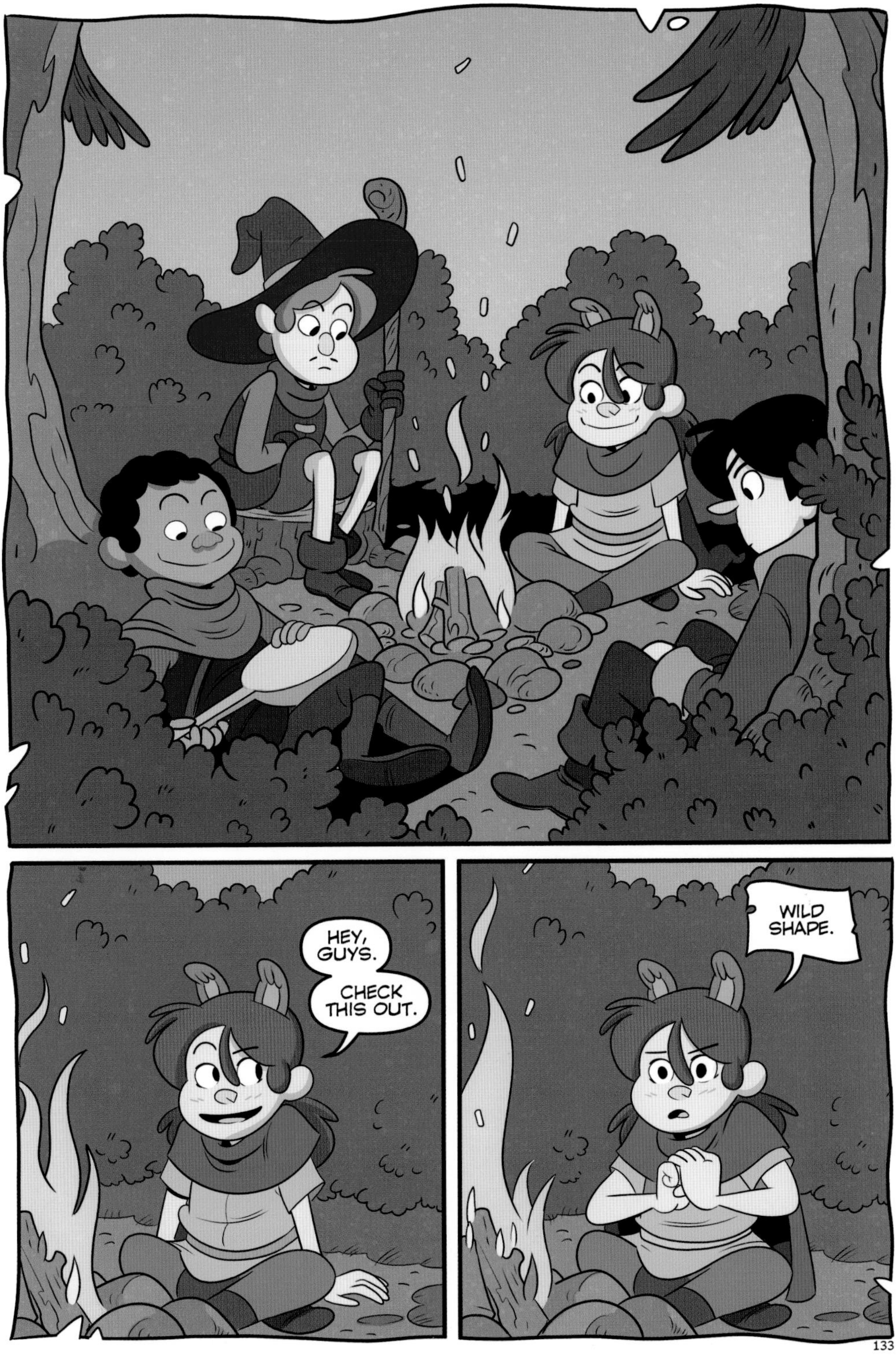
HEY, GUYS.
CHECK THIS OUT.
WILD SHAPE.

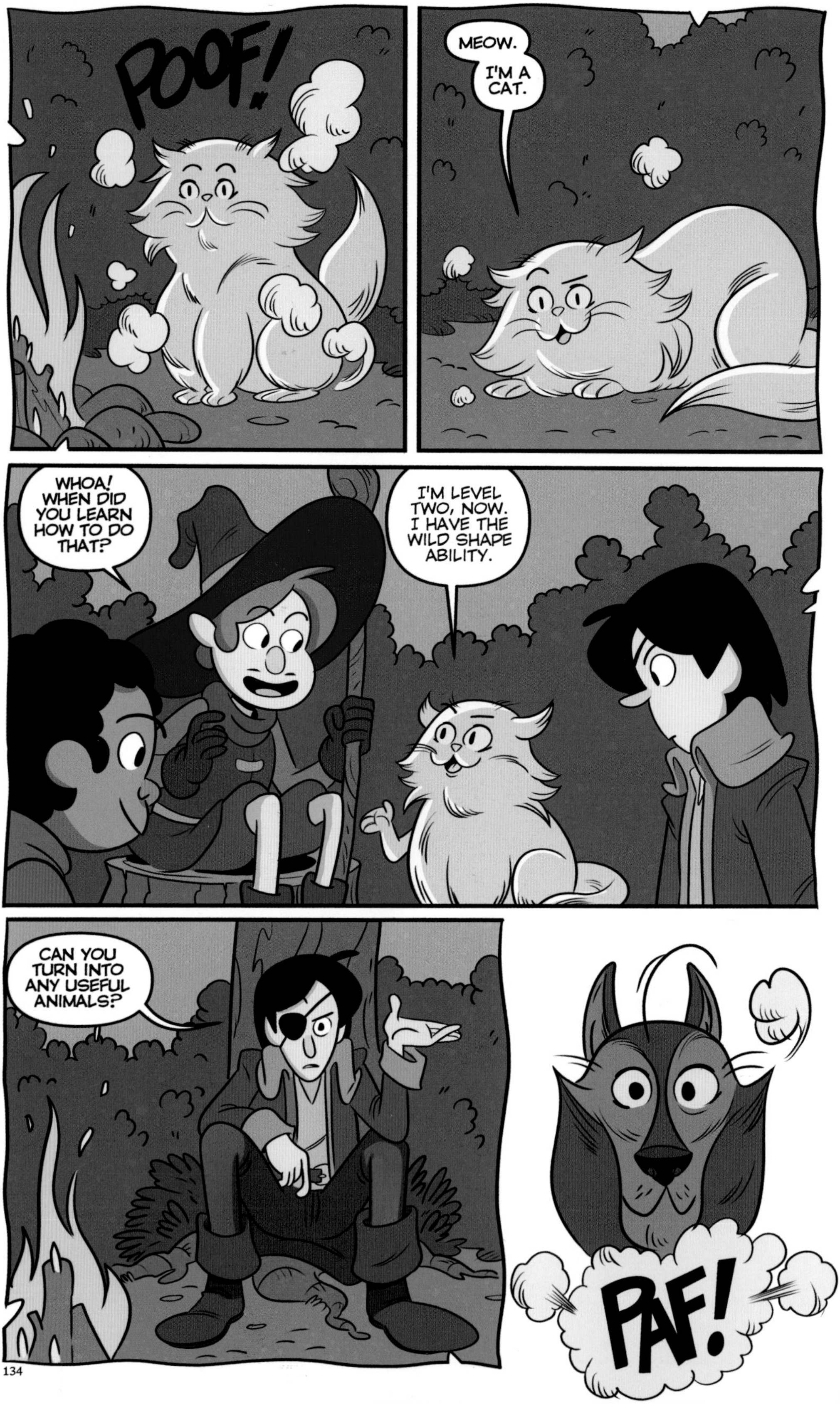
POOF!
MEOW.
I'M A CAT.
WHOA! WHEN DID YOU LEARN HOW TO DO THAT?
I'M LEVEL TWO, NOW. I HAVE THE WILD SHAPE ABILITY.
CAN YOU TURN INTO ANY USEFUL ANIMALS?
PAF!

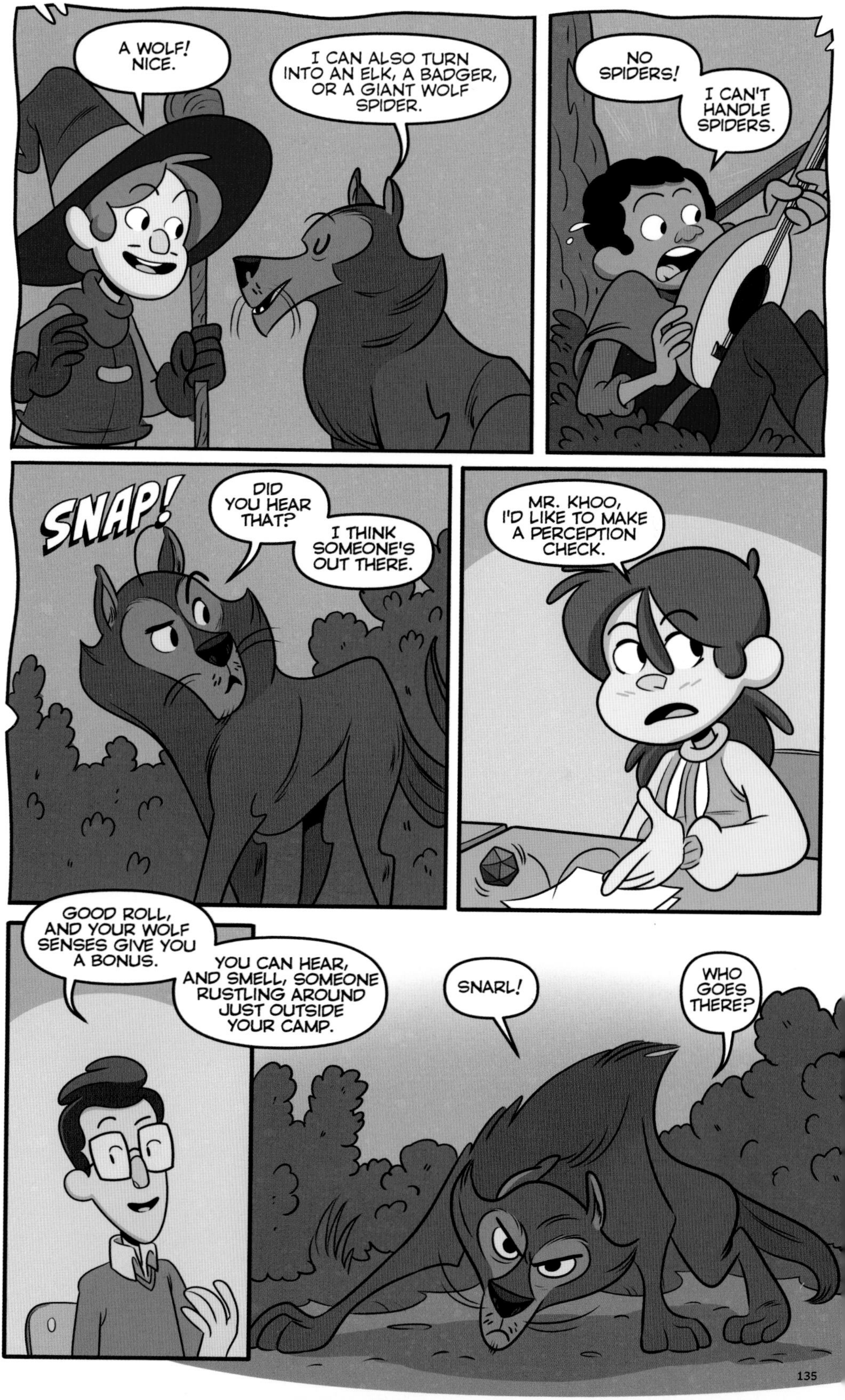

A WOLF! NICE.
I CAN ALSO TURN INTO AN ELK, A BADGER, OR A GIANT WOLF SPIDER.
NO SPIDERS!
I CAN'T HANDLE SPIDERS.
SNAP!
DID YOU HEAR THAT?
I THINK SOMEONE'S OUT THERE.
MR. KHOO, I'D LIKE TO MAKE A PERCEPTION CHECK.
GOOD ROLL, AND YOUR WOLF SENSES GIVE YOU A BONUS.
YOU CAN HEAR, AND SMELL, SOMEONE RUSTLING AROUND JUST OUTSIDE YOUR CAMP.
SNARL!
WHO GOES THERE?

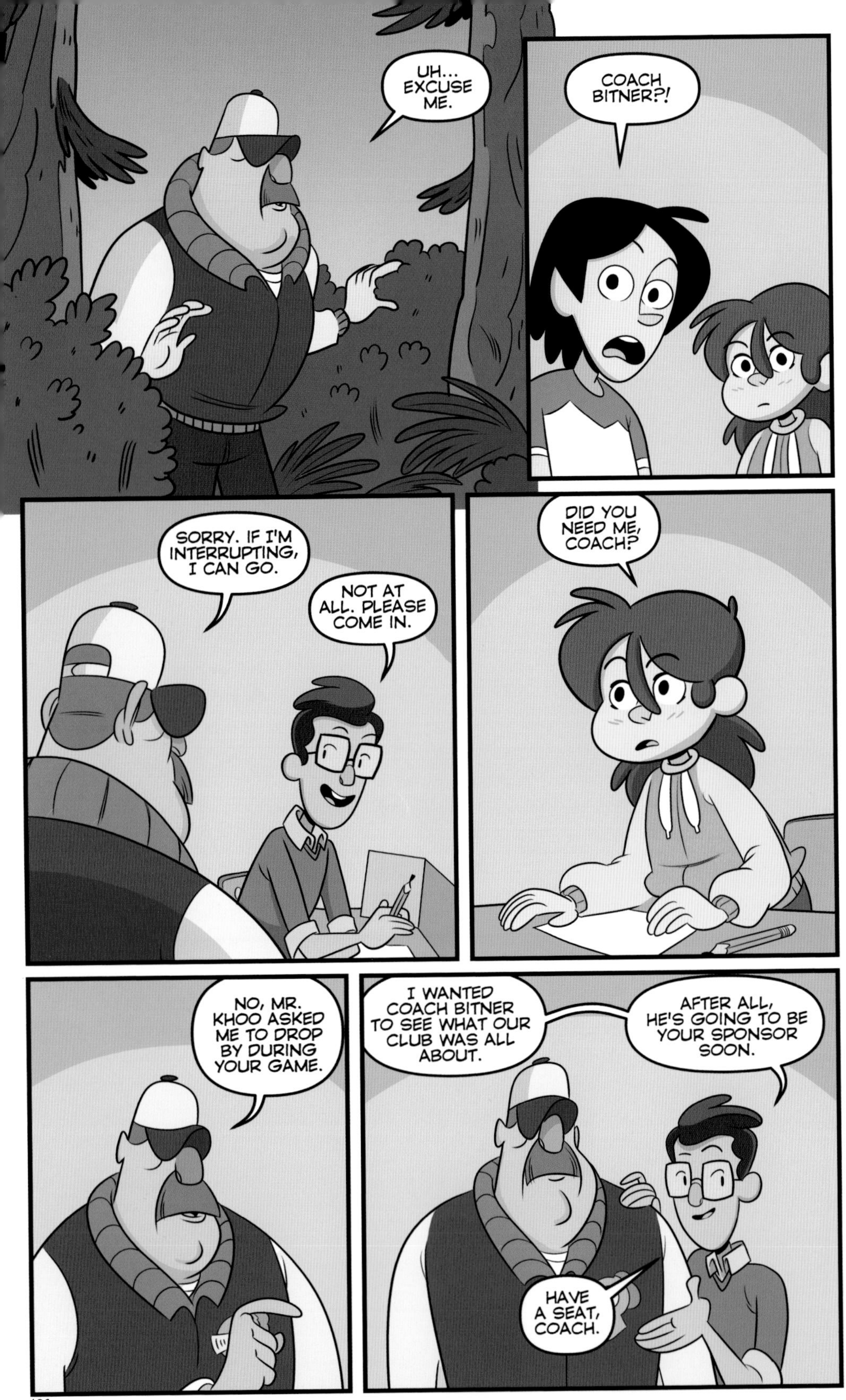
UH... EXCUSE ME.
COACH BITNER?!
SORRY. IF I'M INTERRUPTING, I CAN GO.
NOT AT ALL. PLEASE COME IN.
DID YOU NEED ME, COACH?
NO, MR. KHOO ASKED ME TO DROP BY DURING YOUR GAME.
I WANTED COACH BITNER TO SEE WHAT OUR CLUB WAS ALL ABOUT.
AFTER ALL, HE'S GOING TO BE YOUR SPONSOR SOON.
HAVE A SEAT, COACH.

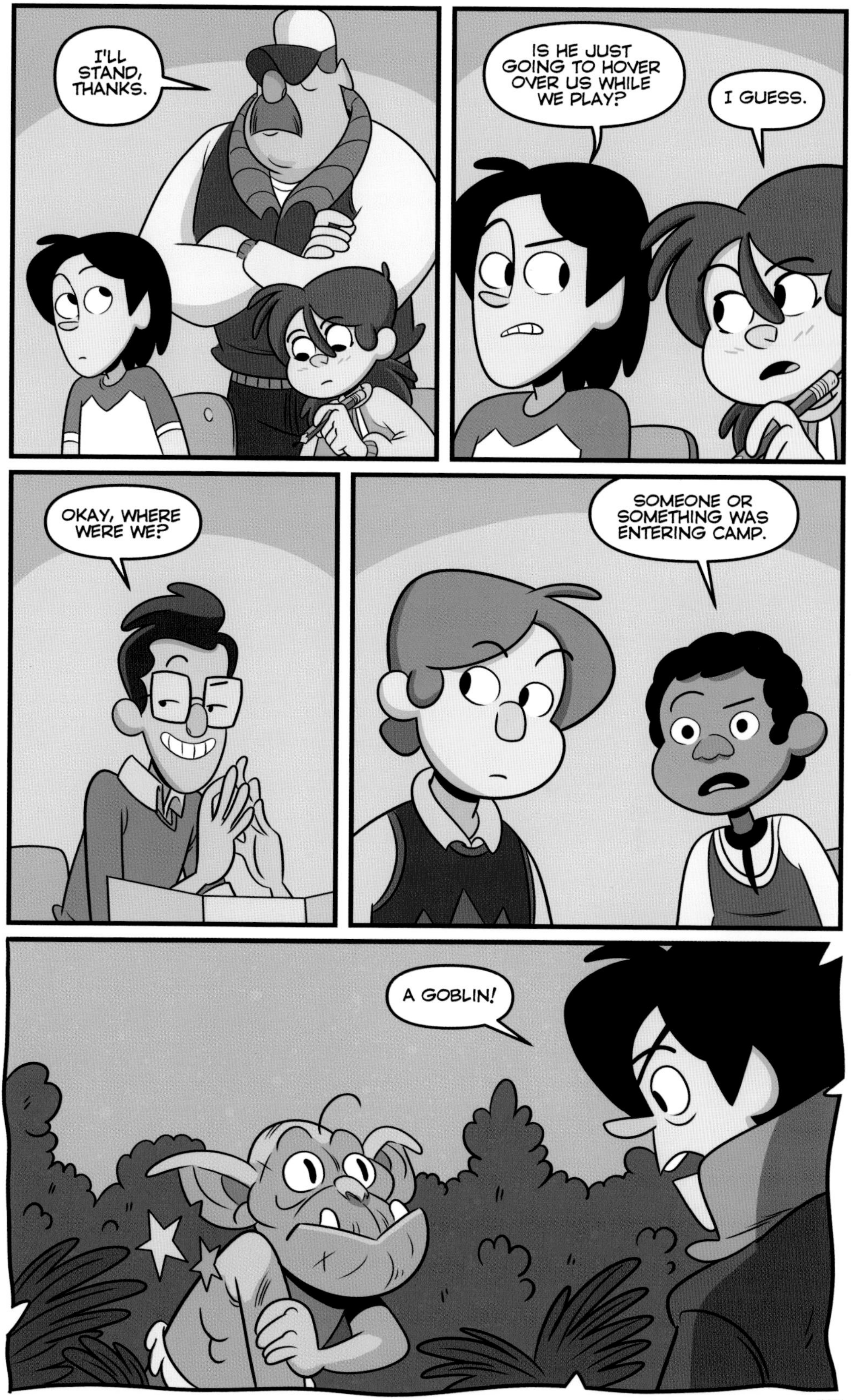
I'LL STAND, THANKS.
IS HE JUST GOING TO HOVER OVER US WHILE WE PLAY?
I GUESS.
OKAY, WHERE WERE WE?
SOMEONE OR SOMETHING WAS ENTERING CAMP.
A GOBLIN!

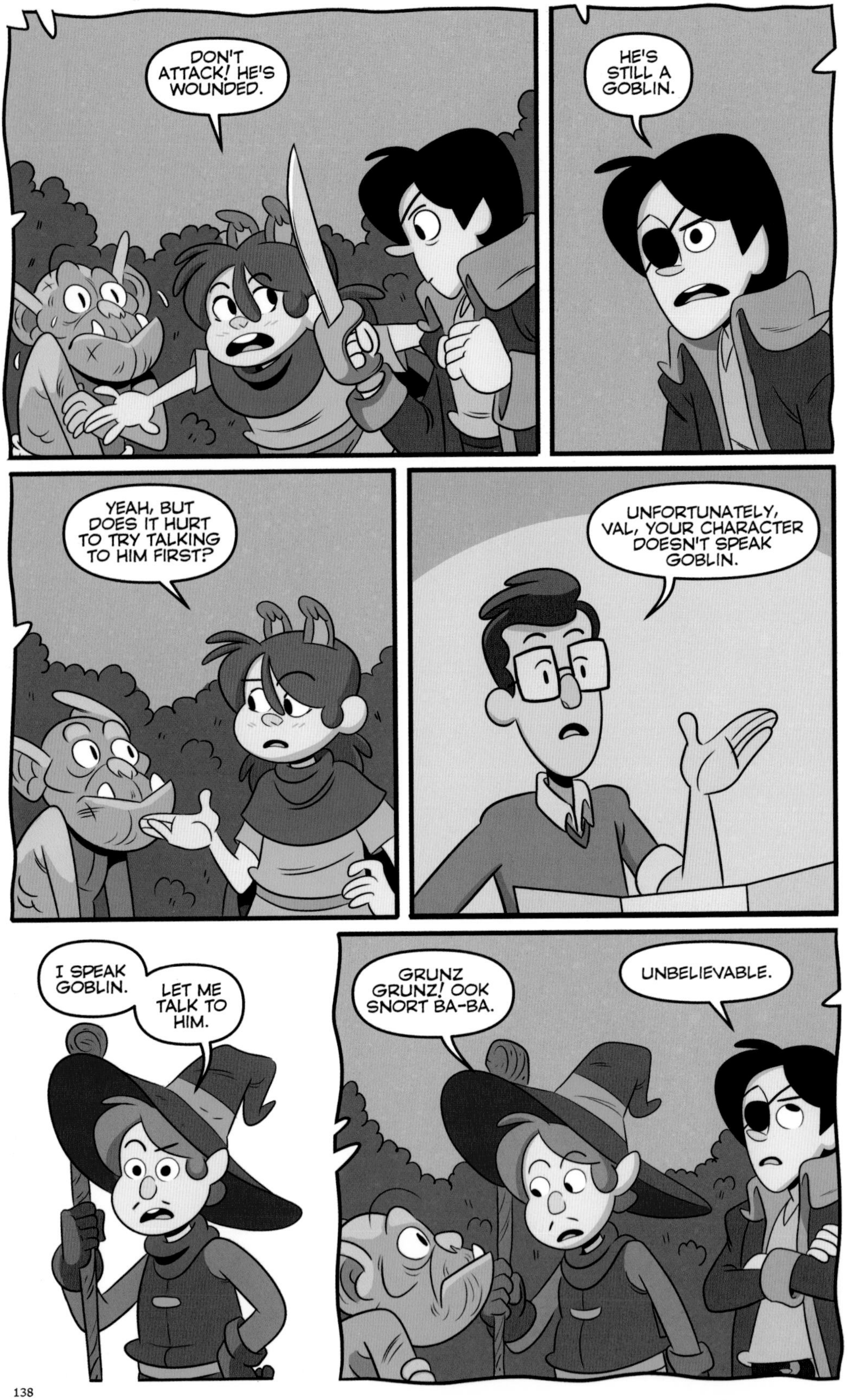
DON'T ATTACK! HE'S WOUNDED.
HE'S STILL A GOBLIN.
YEAH, BUT DOES IT HURT TO TRY TALKING TO HIM FIRST?
UNFORTUNATELY, VAL, YOUR CHARACTER DOESN'T SPEAK GOBLIN.
I SPEAK GOBLIN.
LET ME TALK TO HIM.
GRUNZ GRUNZ! OOK SNORT BA-BA.
UNBELIEVABLE.

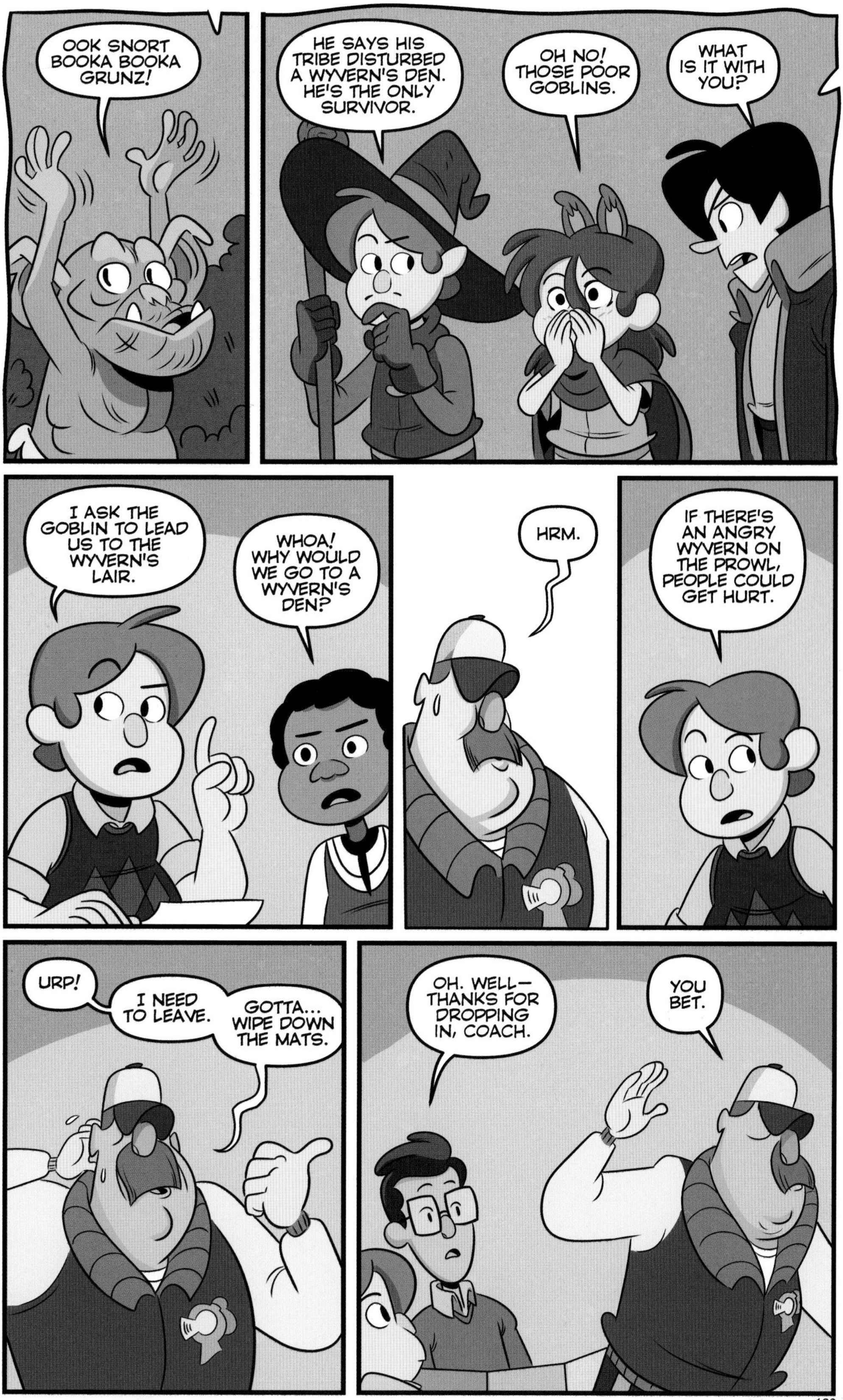
OOK SNORT BOOKA BOOKA GRUNZ!
HE SAYS HIS TRIBE DISTURBED A WYVERN'S DEN. HE'S THE ONLY SURVIVOR.
OH NO! THOSE POOR GOBLINS.
WHAT IS IT WITH YOU?
I ASK THE GOBLIN TO LEAD US TO THE WYVERN'S LAIR.
WHOA! WHY WOULD WE GO TO A WYVERN'S DEN?
HRM.
IF THERE'S AN ANGRY WYVERN ON THE PROWL, PEOPLE COULD GET HURT.
URP!
I NEED TO LEAVE.
GOTTA... WIPE DOWN THE MATS.
OH. WELL— THANKS FOR DROPPING IN, COACH.
YOU BET.

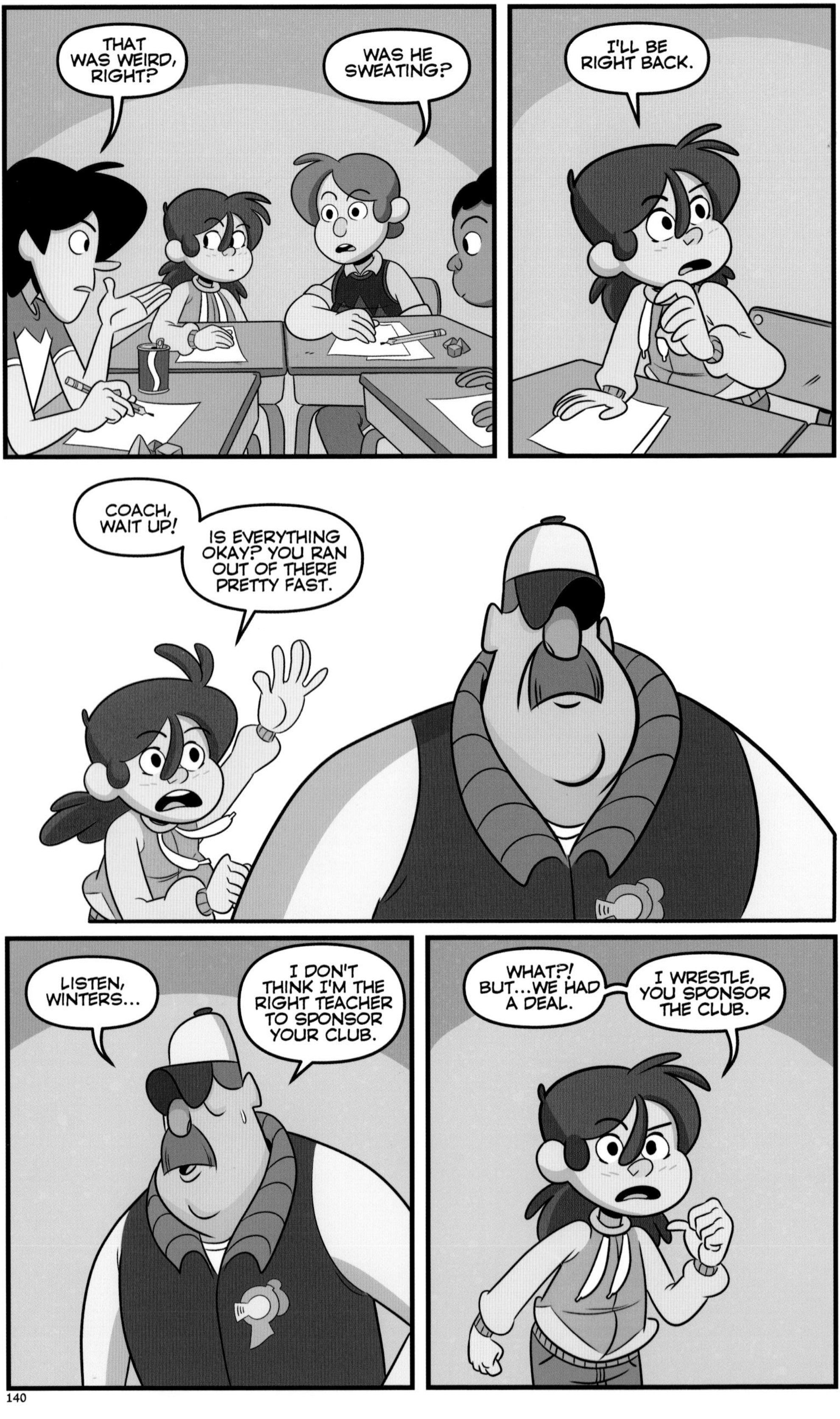
THAT WAS WEIRD, RIGHT?
WAS HE SWEATING?
I'LL BE RIGHT BACK.
COACH, WAIT UP!
IS EVERYTHING OKAY? YOU RAN OUT OF THERE PRETTY FAST.
LISTEN, WINTERS...
I DON'T THINK I'M THE RIGHT TEACHER TO SPONSOR YOUR CLUB.
WHAT?! BUT...WE HAD A DEAL.
I WRESTLE, YOU SPONSOR THE CLUB.

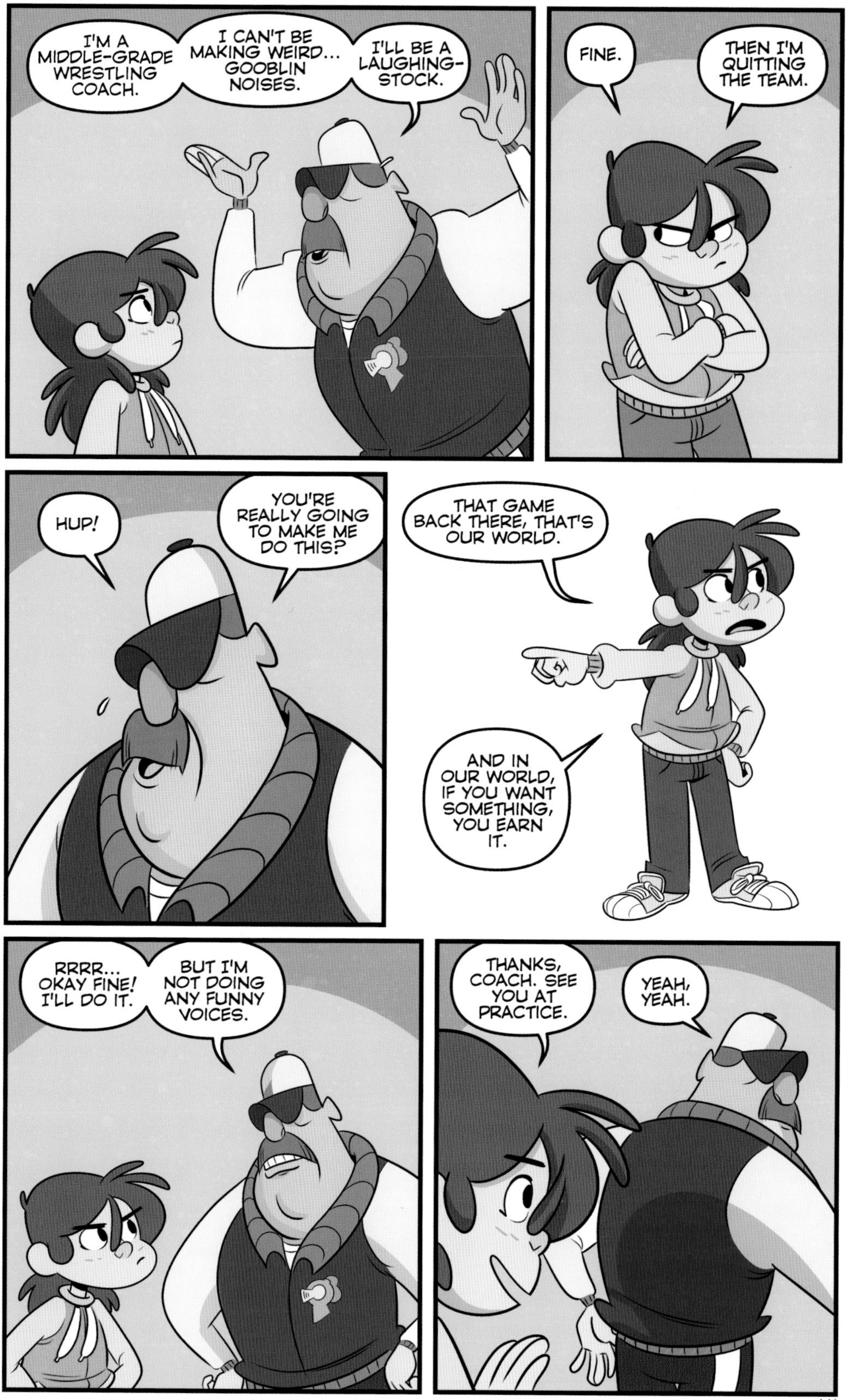
I'M A MIDDLE-GRADE WRESTLING COACH.
I CAN'T BE MAKING WEIRD... GOOBLIN NOISES.
I'LL BE A LAUGHING-STOCK.
FINE.
THEN I'M QUITTING THE TEAM.
HUP!
YOU'RE REALLY GOING TO MAKE ME DO THIS?
THAT GAME BACK THERE, THAT'S OUR WORLD.
AND IN OUR WORLD, IF YOU WANT SOMETHING, YOU EARN IT.
RRRR... OKAY FINE! I'LL DO IT.
BUT I'M NOT DOING ANY FUNNY VOICES.
THANKS, COACH. SEE YOU AT PRACTICE.
YEAH, YEAH.

CHAPTER SEVEN

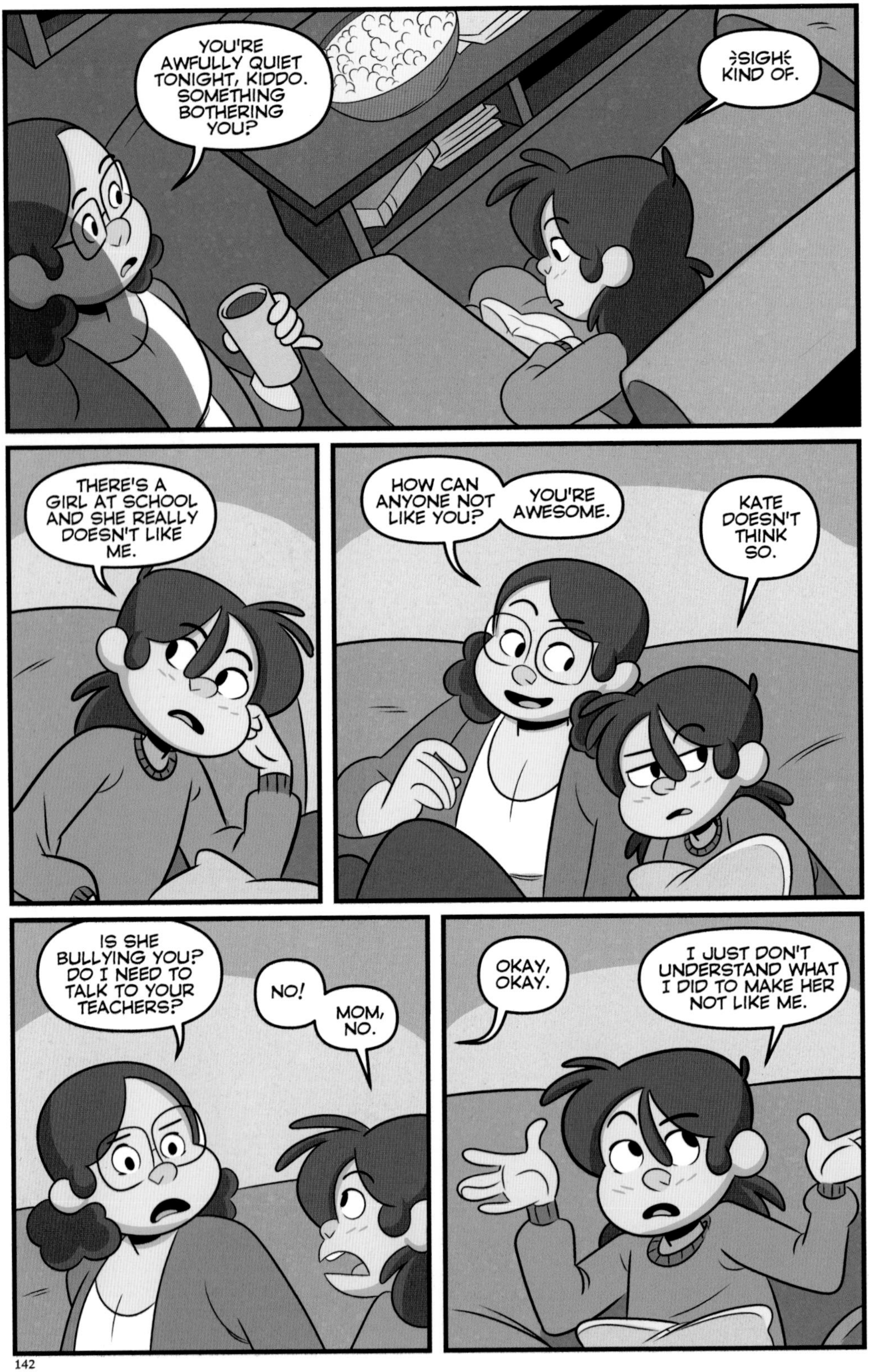

YOU'RE AWFULLY QUIET TONIGHT, KIDDO. SOMETHING BOTHERING YOU?
SIGH KIND OF.
THERE'S A GIRL AT SCHOOL AND SHE REALLY DOESN'T LIKE ME.
HOW CAN ANYONE NOT LIKE YOU?
YOU'RE AWESOME.
KATE DOESN'T THINK SO.
IS SHE BULLYING YOU? DO I NEED TO TALK TO YOUR TEACHERS?
NO!
MOM, NO.
OKAY, OKAY.
I JUST DON'T UNDERSTAND WHAT I DID TO MAKE HER NOT LIKE ME.

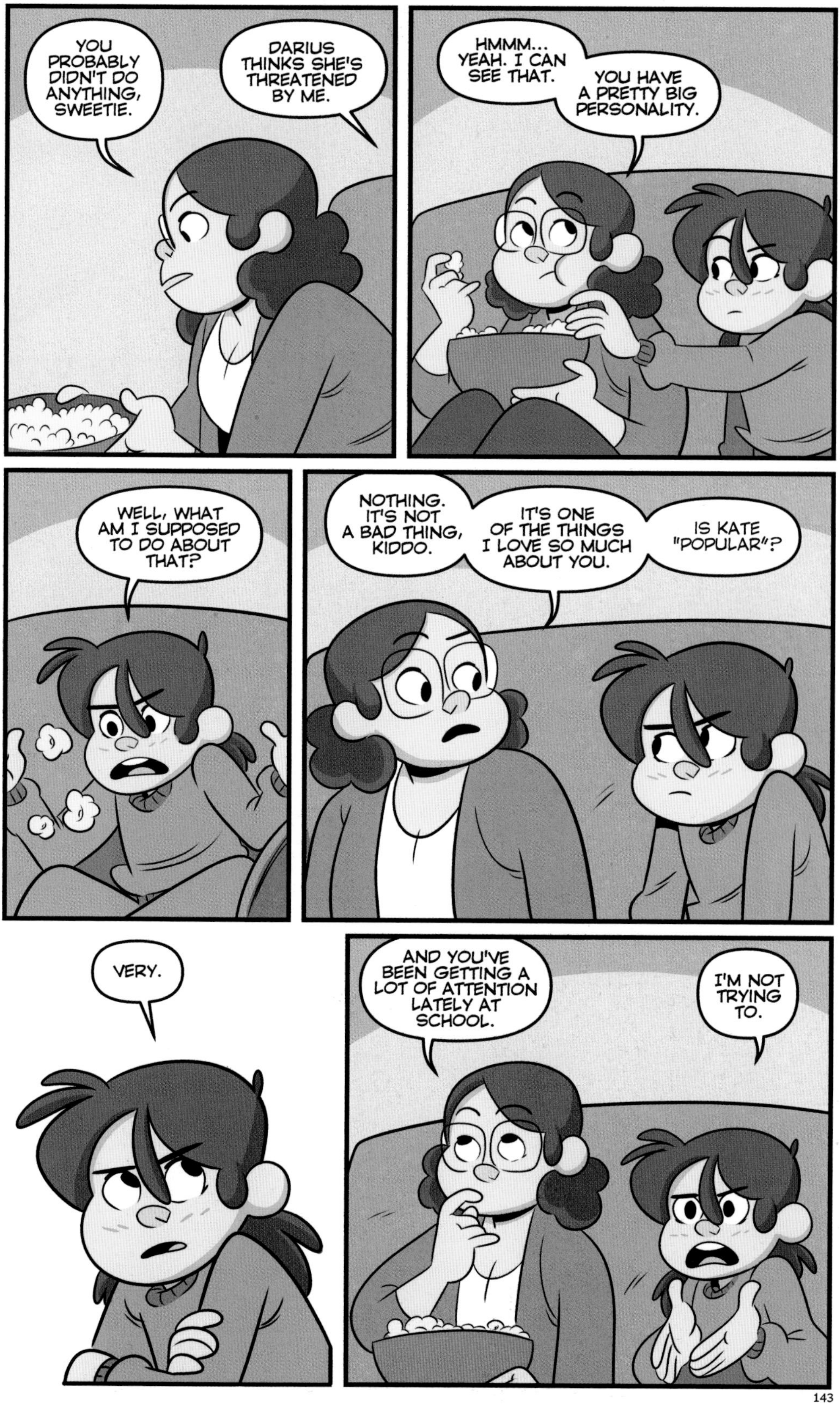
YOU PROBABLY DIDN'T DO ANYTHING, SWEETIE.
DARIUS THINKS SHE'S THREATENED BY ME.
HMMM... YEAH. I CAN SEE THAT.
YOU HAVE A PRETTY BIG PERSONALITY.
WELL, WHAT AM I SUPPOSED TO DO ABOUT THAT?
NOTHING. IT'S NOT A BAD THING, KIDDO.
IT'S ONE OF THE THINGS I LOVE SO MUCH ABOUT YOU.
IS KATE "POPULAR"?
VERY.
AND YOU'VE BEEN GETTING A LOT OF ATTENTION LATELY AT SCHOOL.
I'M NOT TRYING TO.

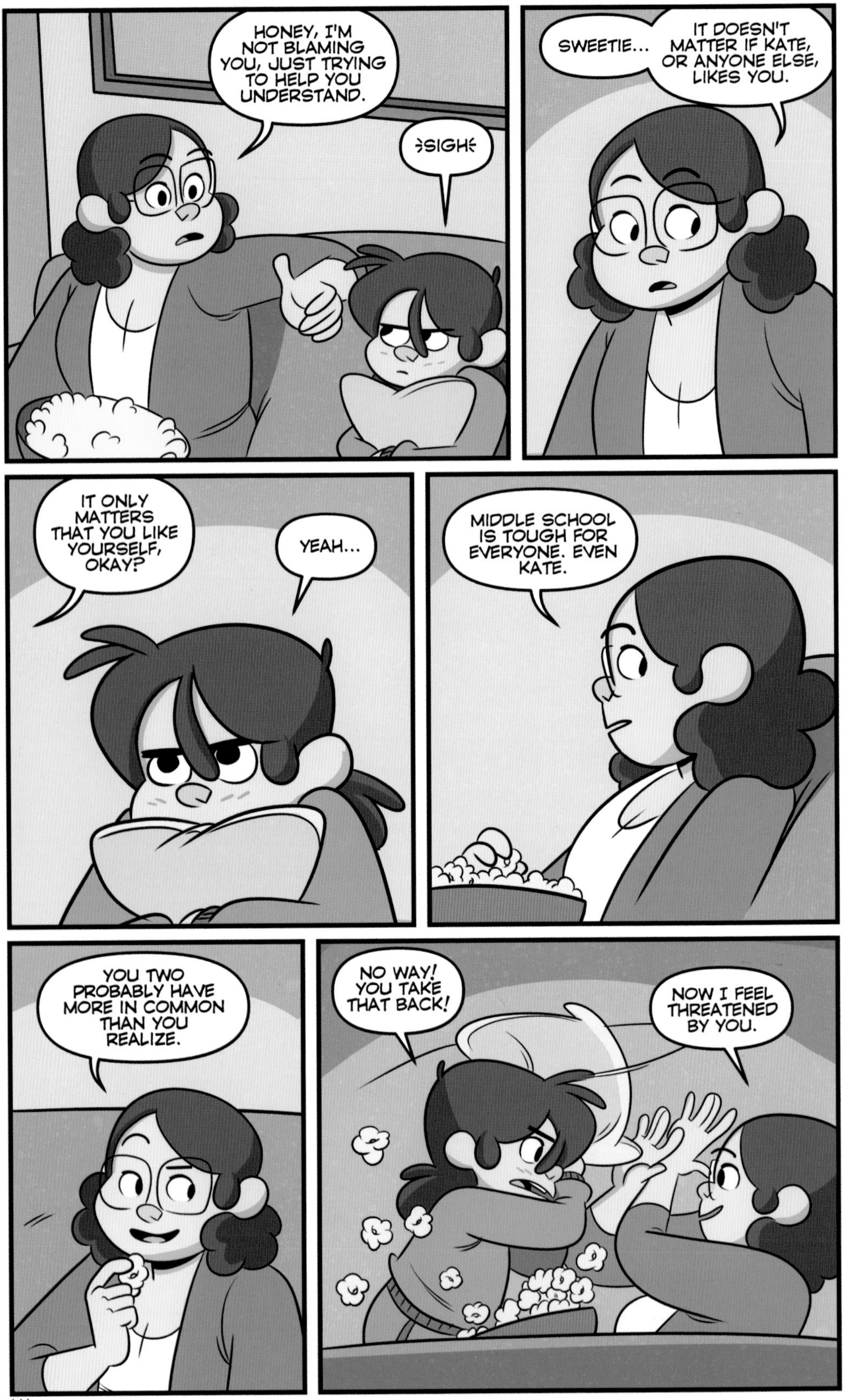
HONEY, I'M NOT BLAMING YOU, JUST TRYING TO HELP YOU UNDERSTAND.
SIGH
SWEETIE...
IT DOESN'T MATTER IF KATE, OR ANYONE ELSE, LIKES YOU.
IT ONLY MATTERS THAT YOU LIKE YOURSELF, OKAY?
YEAH...
MIDDLE SCHOOL IS TOUGH FOR EVERYONE. EVEN KATE.
YOU TWO PROBABLY HAVE MORE IN COMMON THAN YOU REALIZE.
NO WAY! YOU TAKE THAT BACK!
NOW I FEEL THREATENED BY YOU.

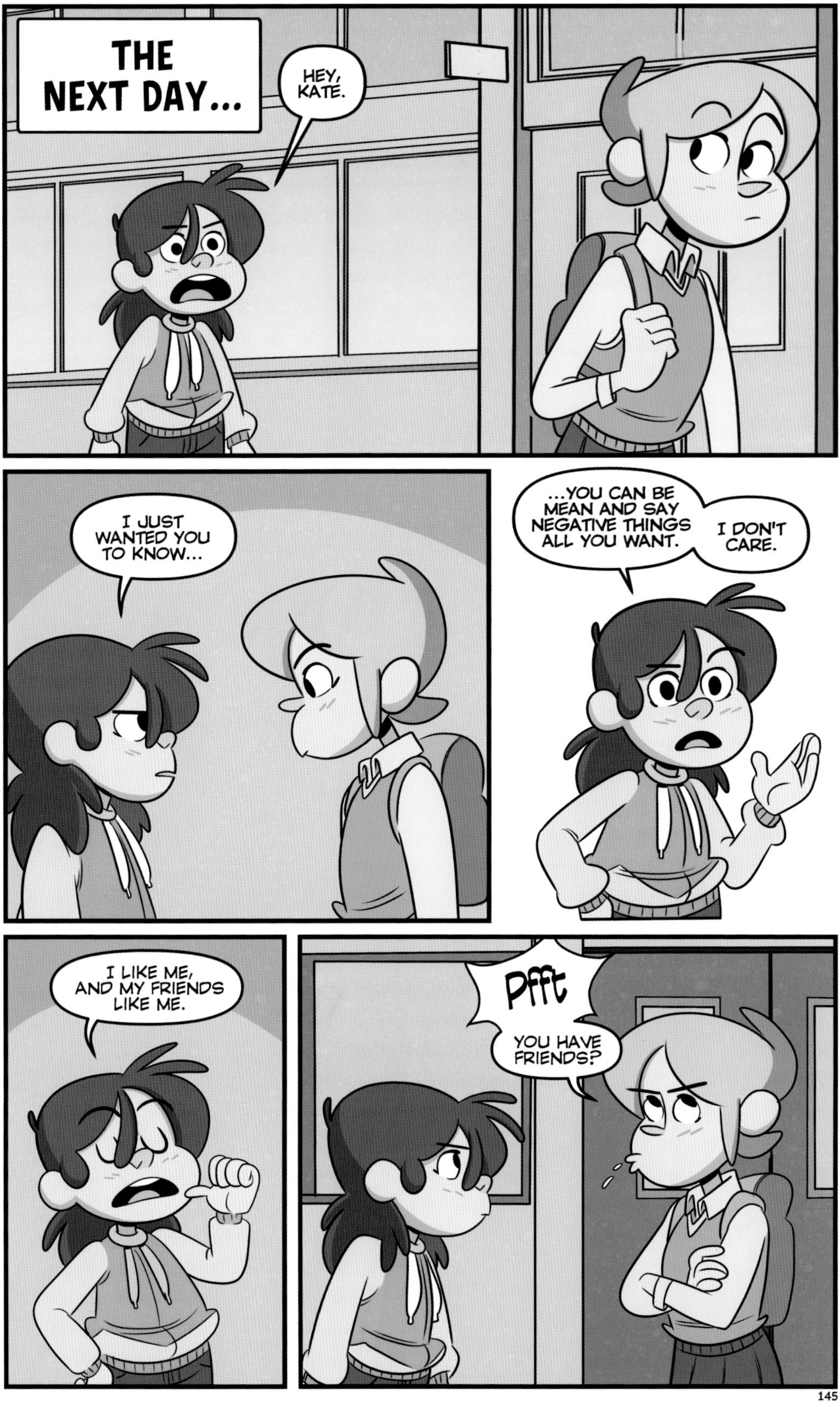
THE NEXT DAY...
HEY, KATE.
I JUST WANTED YOU TO KNOW...
...YOU CAN BE MEAN AND SAY NEGATIVE THINGS ALL YOU WANT.
I DON'T CARE.
I LIKE ME, AND MY FRIENDS LIKE ME.
Pfft
YOU HAVE FRIENDS?

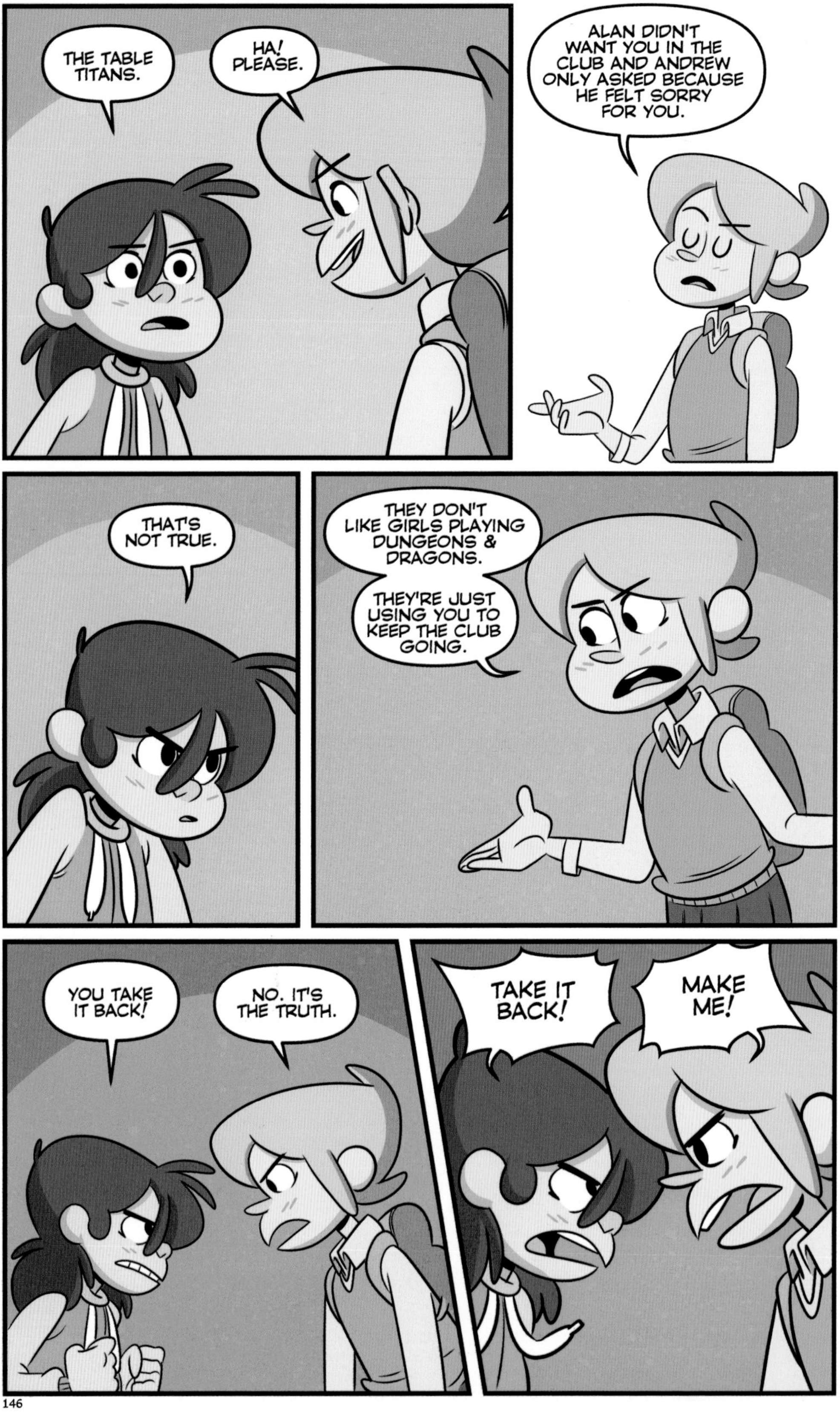
THE TABLE TITANS.
HA! PLEASE.
ALAN DIDN'T WANT YOU IN THE CLUB AND ANDREW ONLY ASKED BECAUSE HE FELT SORRY FOR YOU.
THAT'S NOT TRUE.
THEY DON'T LIKE GIRLS PLAYING DUNGEONS & DRAGONS.
THEY'RE JUST USING YOU TO KEEP THE CLUB GOING.
YOU TAKE IT BACK!
NO. IT'S THE TRUTH.
TAKE IT BACK!
MAKE ME!

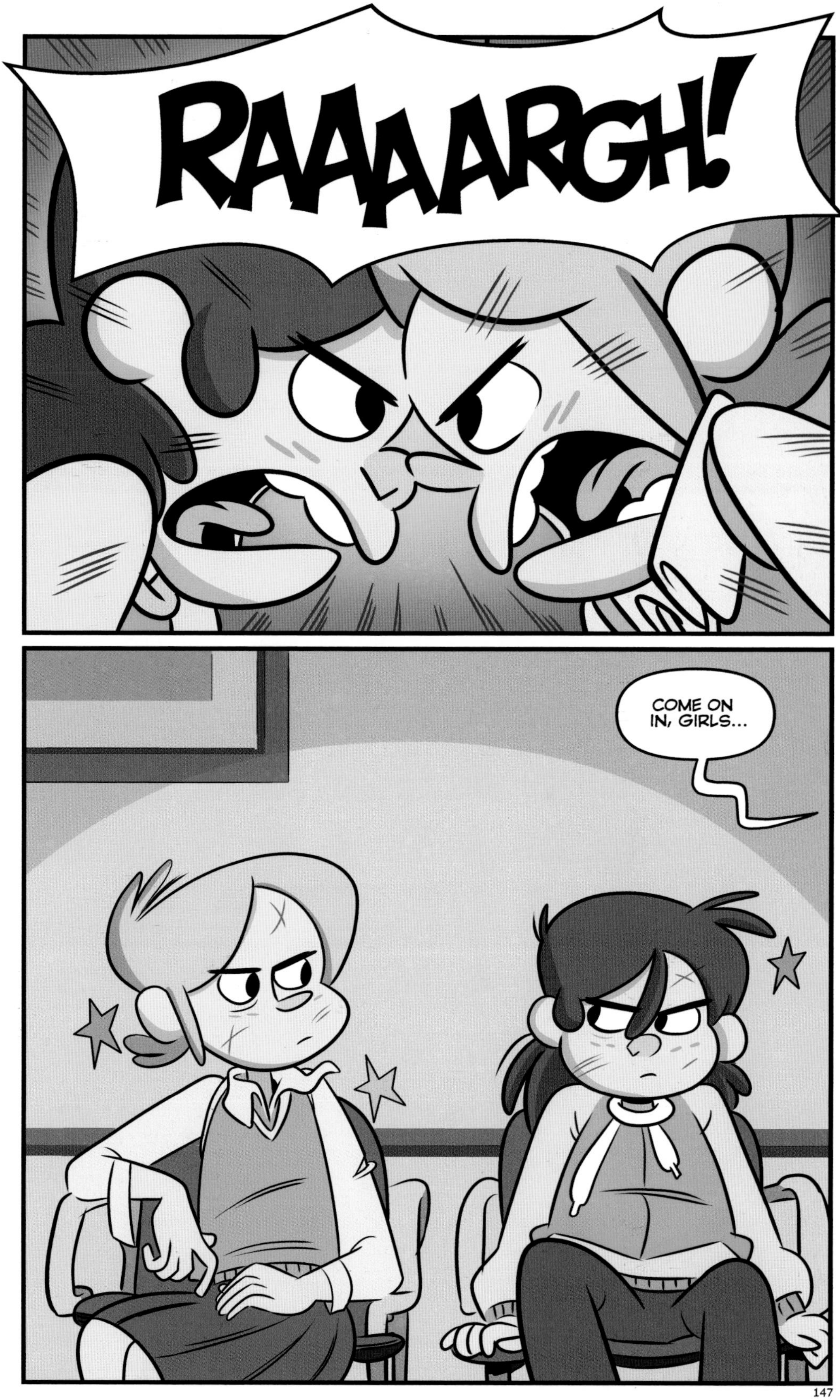
RAAAARGH!
COME ON IN, GIRLS...

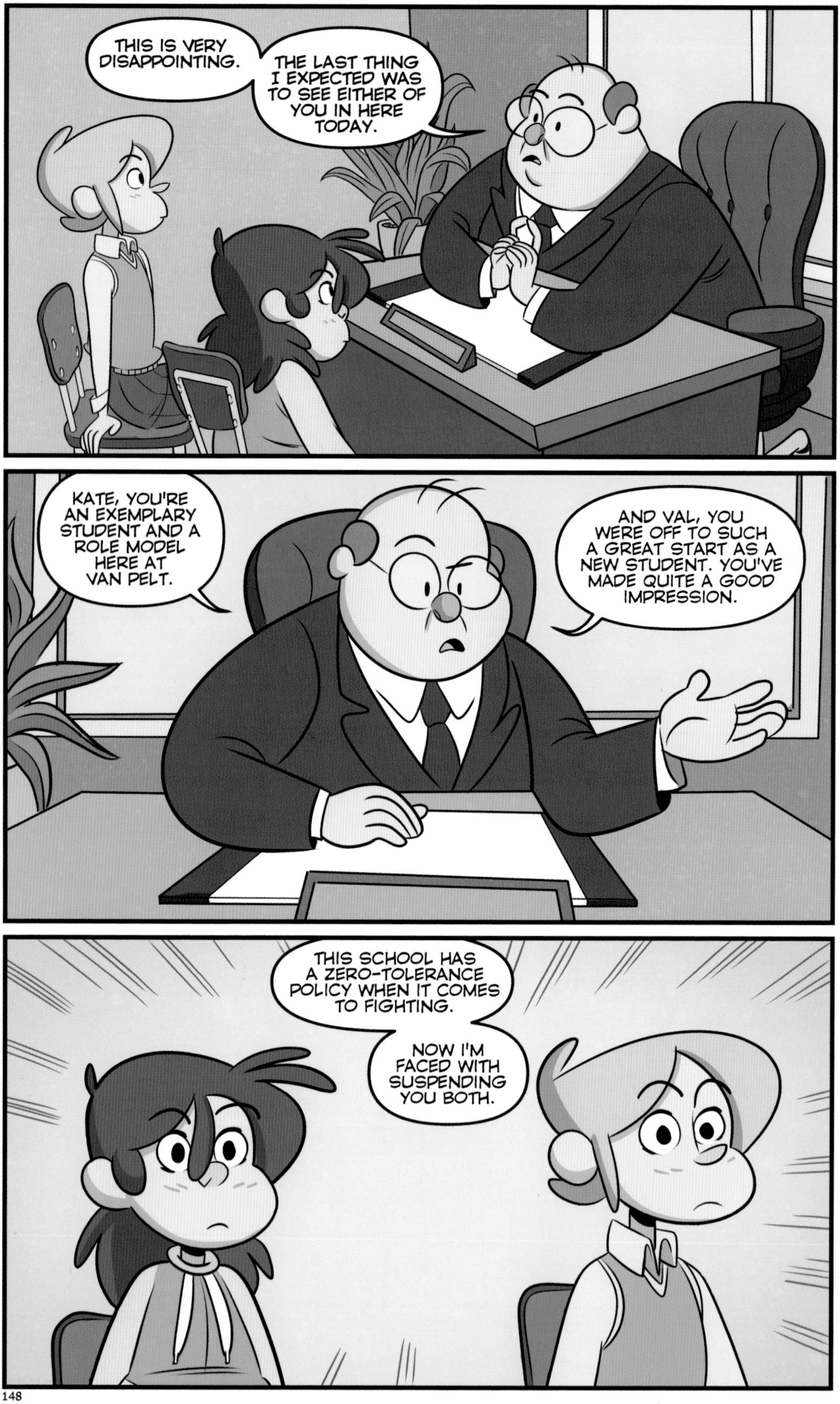
THIS IS VERY DISAPPOINTING.
THE LAST THING I EXPECTED WAS TO SEE EITHER OF YOU IN HERE TODAY.
KATE, YOU'RE AN EXEMPLARY STUDENT AND A ROLE MODEL HERE AT VAN PELT.
AND VAL, YOU WERE OFF TO SUCH A GREAT START AS A NEW STUDENT. YOU'VE MADE QUITE A GOOD IMPRESSION.
THIS SCHOOL HAS A ZERO-TOLERANCE POLICY WHEN IT COMES TO FIGHTING.
NOW I'M FACED WITH SUSPENDING YOU BOTH.

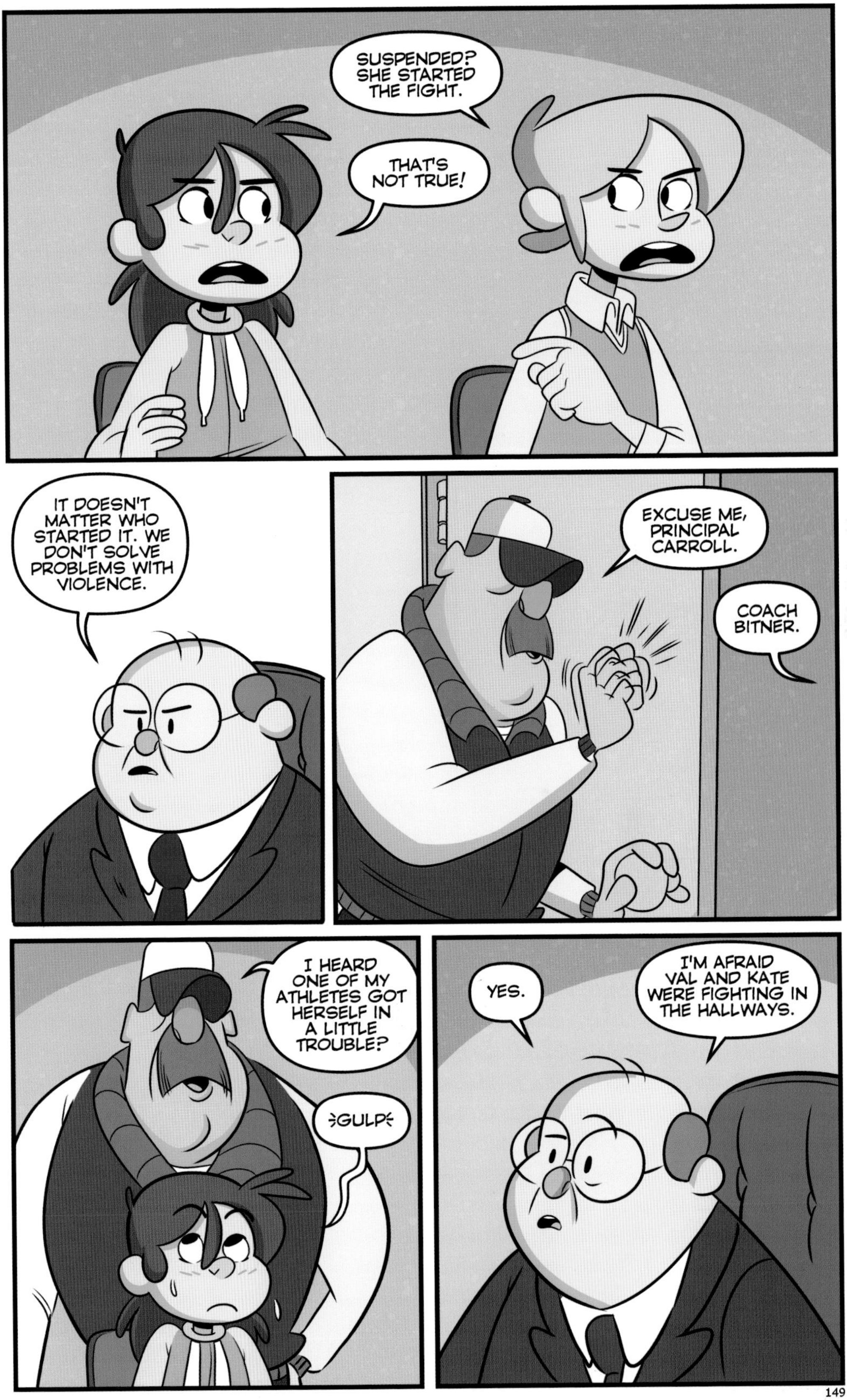
SUSPENDED? SHE STARTED THE FIGHT.
THAT'S NOT TRUE!
IT DOESN'T MATTER WHO STARTED IT. WE DON'T SOLVE PROBLEMS WITH VIOLENCE.
EXCUSE ME, PRINCIPAL CARROLL.
COACH BITNER.
I HEARD ONE OF MY ATHLETES GOT HERSELF IN A LITTLE TROUBLE?
GULP
YES.
I'M AFRAID VAL AND KATE WERE FIGHTING IN THE HALLWAYS.

FIGHTING, HUH?

THE WAY I HEARD IT, WINTERS WAS JUST SHOWING KATE HOW TO EXECUTE SOME WRESTLING MOVES.

I'M SORRY?

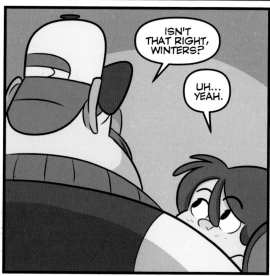
ISN'T THAT RIGHT, WINTERS?

UH... YEAH.

I WAS JUST SHOWING KATE HOW TO DO A SPINNING COBRA CLUTCH AND WE KIND OF GOT...

TANGLED UP.

RIGHT.

SEE? NO FIGHTING.

JUST SOME ATHLETICS THAT GOT OUT OF HAND.

RIGHT, GIRLS?

YES?

YEP!

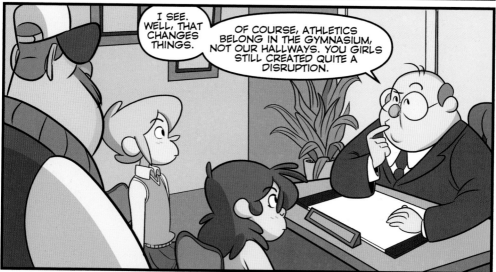

I SEE. WELL, THAT CHANGES THINGS.

OF COURSE, ATHLETICS BELONG IN THE GYMNASIUM, NOT OUR HALLWAYS. YOU GIRLS STILL CREATED QUITE A DISRUPTION.

WHAT DO YOU THINK WOULD BE AN APPROPRIATE PUNISHMENT FOR THAT, COACH?

OH...I CAN THINK OF SOMETHING.

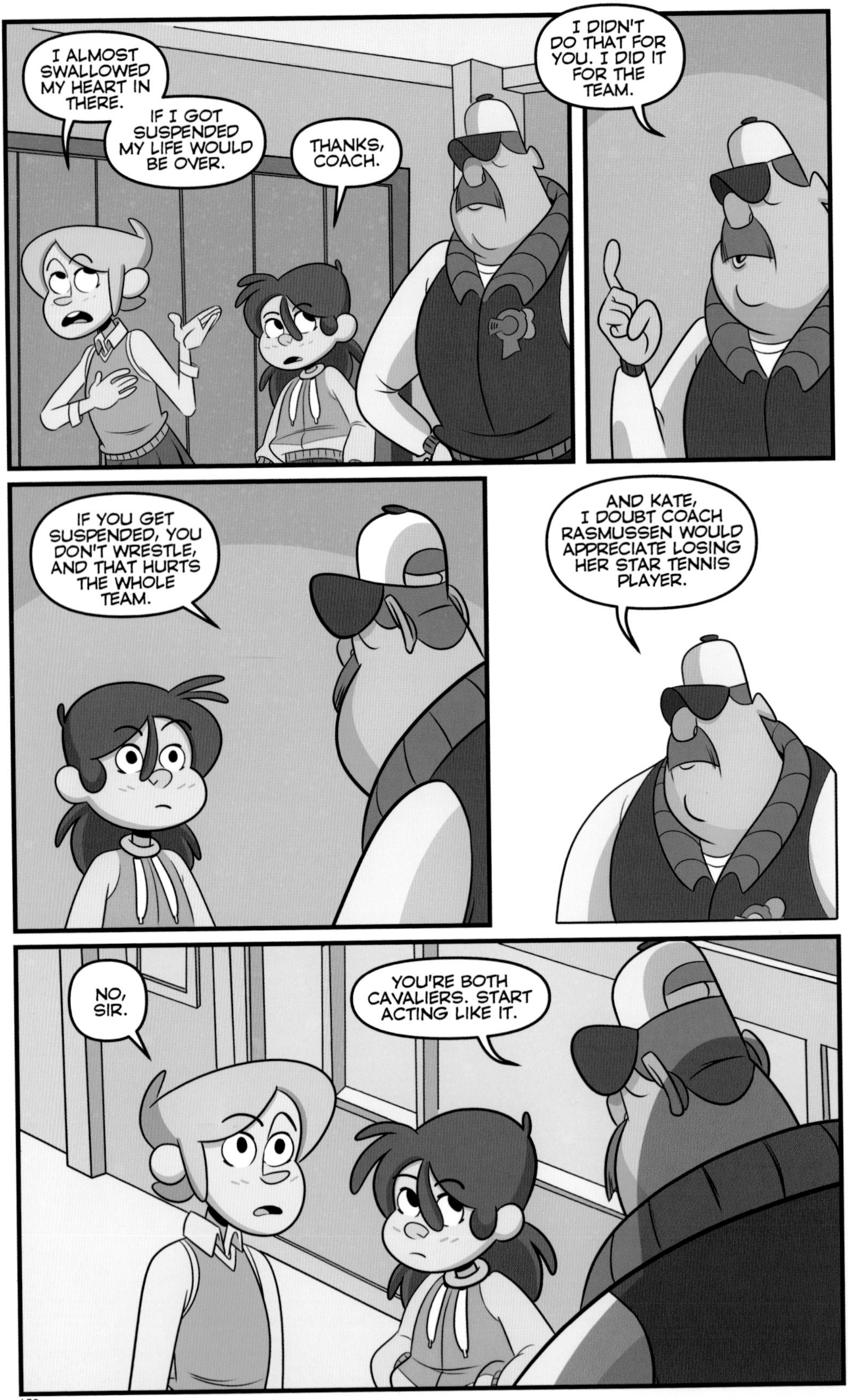
I ALMOST SWALLOWED MY HEART IN THERE.
IF I GOT SUSPENDED MY LIFE WOULD BE OVER.
THANKS, COACH.
I DIDN'T DO THAT FOR YOU. I DID IT FOR THE TEAM.
IF YOU GET SUSPENDED, YOU DON'T WRESTLE, AND THAT HURTS THE WHOLE TEAM.
AND KATE, I DOUBT COACH RASMUSSEN WOULD APPRECIATE LOSING HER STAR TENNIS PLAYER.
NO, SIR.
YOU'RE BOTH CAVALIERS. START ACTING LIKE IT.

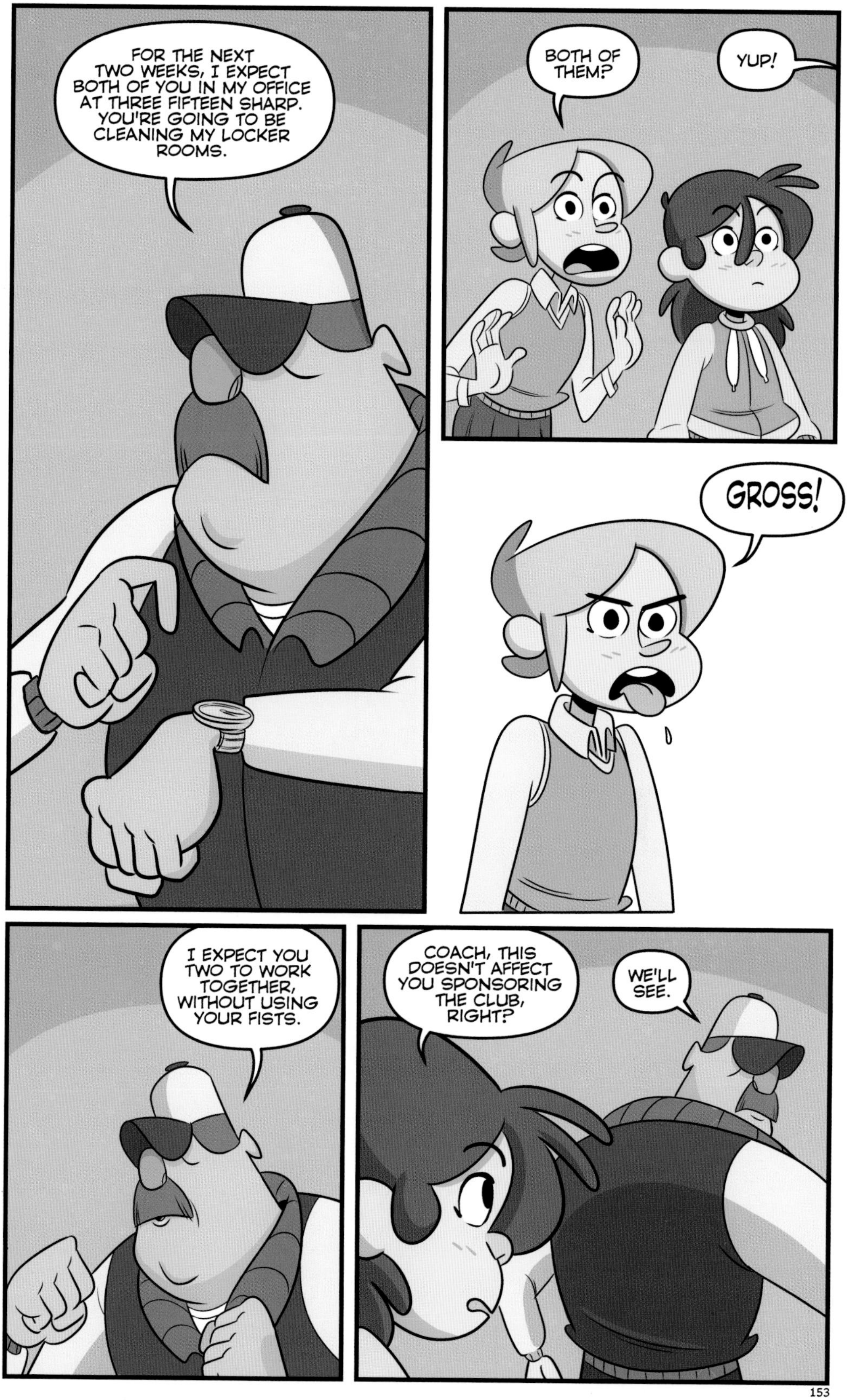
FOR THE NEXT TWO WEEKS, I EXPECT BOTH OF YOU IN MY OFFICE AT THREE FIFTEEN SHARP. YOU'RE GOING TO BE CLEANING MY LOCKER ROOMS.
BOTH OF THEM?
YUP!
GROSS!
I EXPECT YOU TWO TO WORK TOGETHER, WITHOUT USING YOUR FISTS.
COACH, THIS DOESN'T AFFECT YOU SPONSORING THE CLUB, RIGHT?
WE'LL SEE.

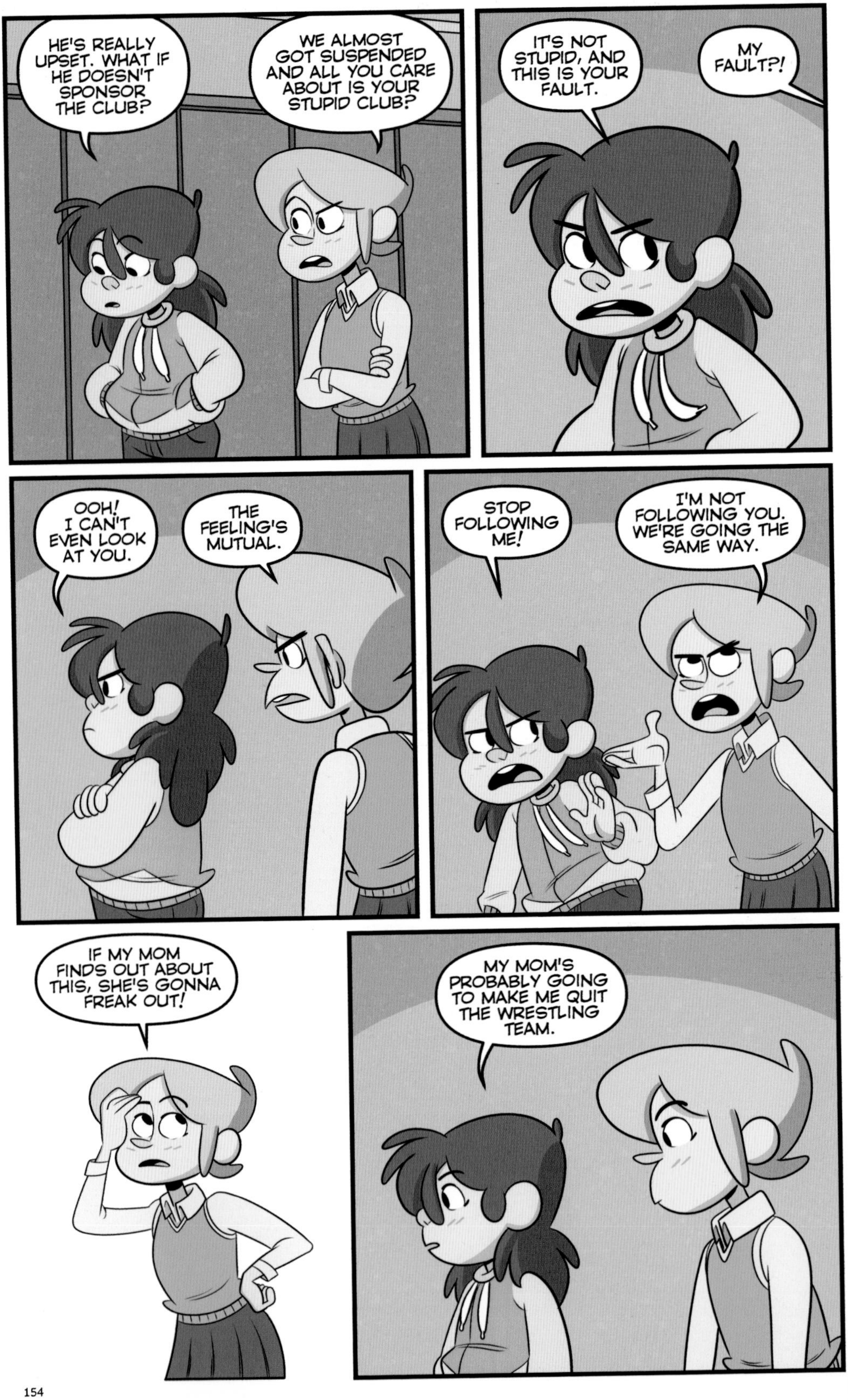
HE'S REALLY UPSET. WHAT IF HE DOESN'T SPONSOR THE CLUB?
WE ALMOST GOT SUSPENDED AND ALL YOU CARE ABOUT IS YOUR STUPID CLUB?
IT'S NOT STUPID, AND THIS IS YOUR FAULT.
MY FAULT?!
OOH! I CAN'T EVEN LOOK AT YOU.
THE FEELING'S MUTUAL.
STOP FOLLOWING ME!
I'M NOT FOLLOWING YOU. WE'RE GOING THE SAME WAY.
IF MY MOM FINDS OUT ABOUT THIS, SHE'S GONNA FREAK OUT!
MY MOM'S PROBABLY GOING TO MAKE ME QUIT THE WRESTLING TEAM.

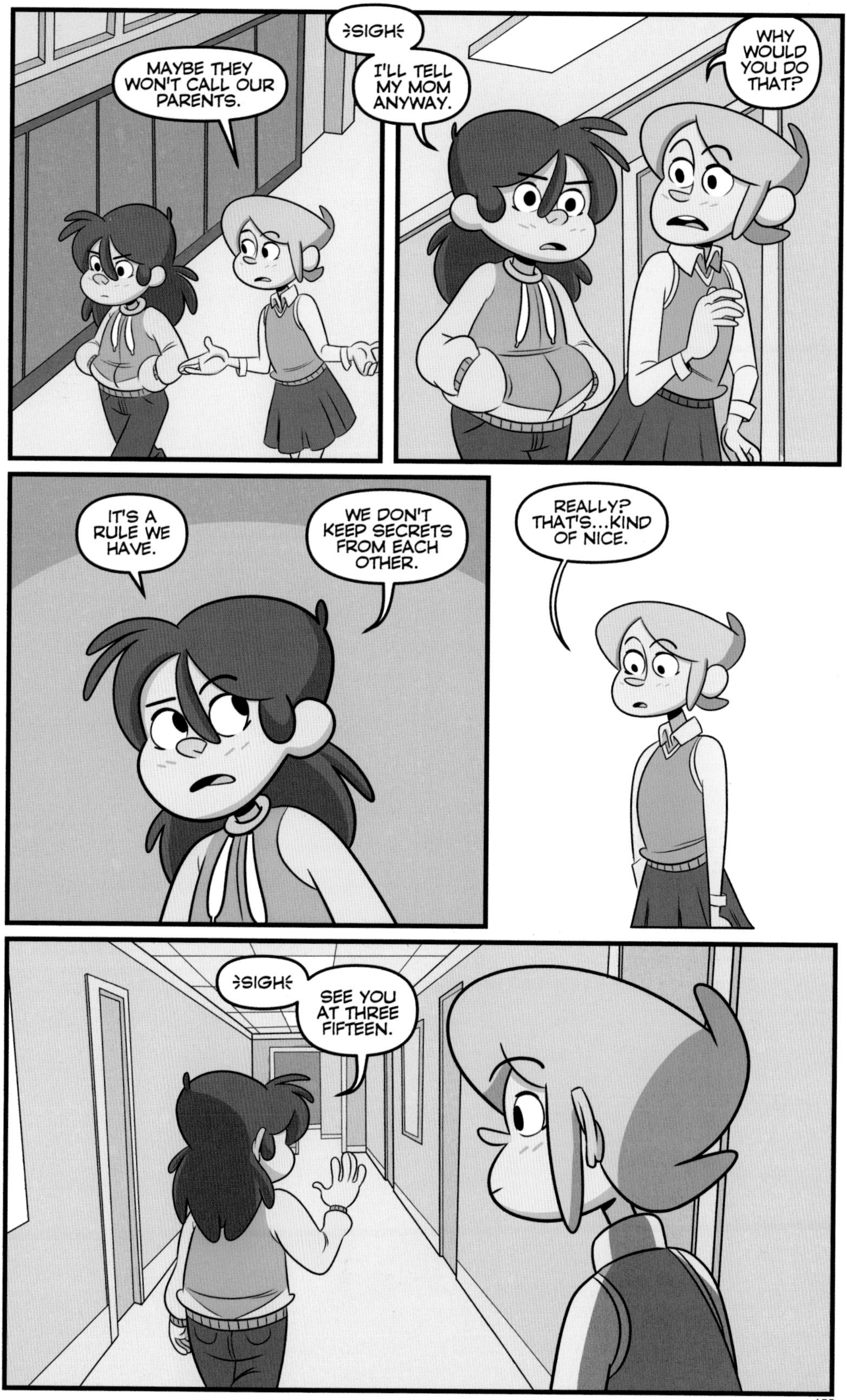
MAYBE THEY WON'T CALL OUR PARENTS.
SIGH
I'LL TELL MY MOM ANYWAY.
WHY WOULD YOU DO THAT?
IT'S A RULE WE HAVE.
WE DON'T KEEP SECRETS FROM EACH OTHER.
REALLY? THAT'S...KIND OF NICE.
SIGH
SEE YOU AT THREE FIFTEEN.

GEOMETRY CLASS

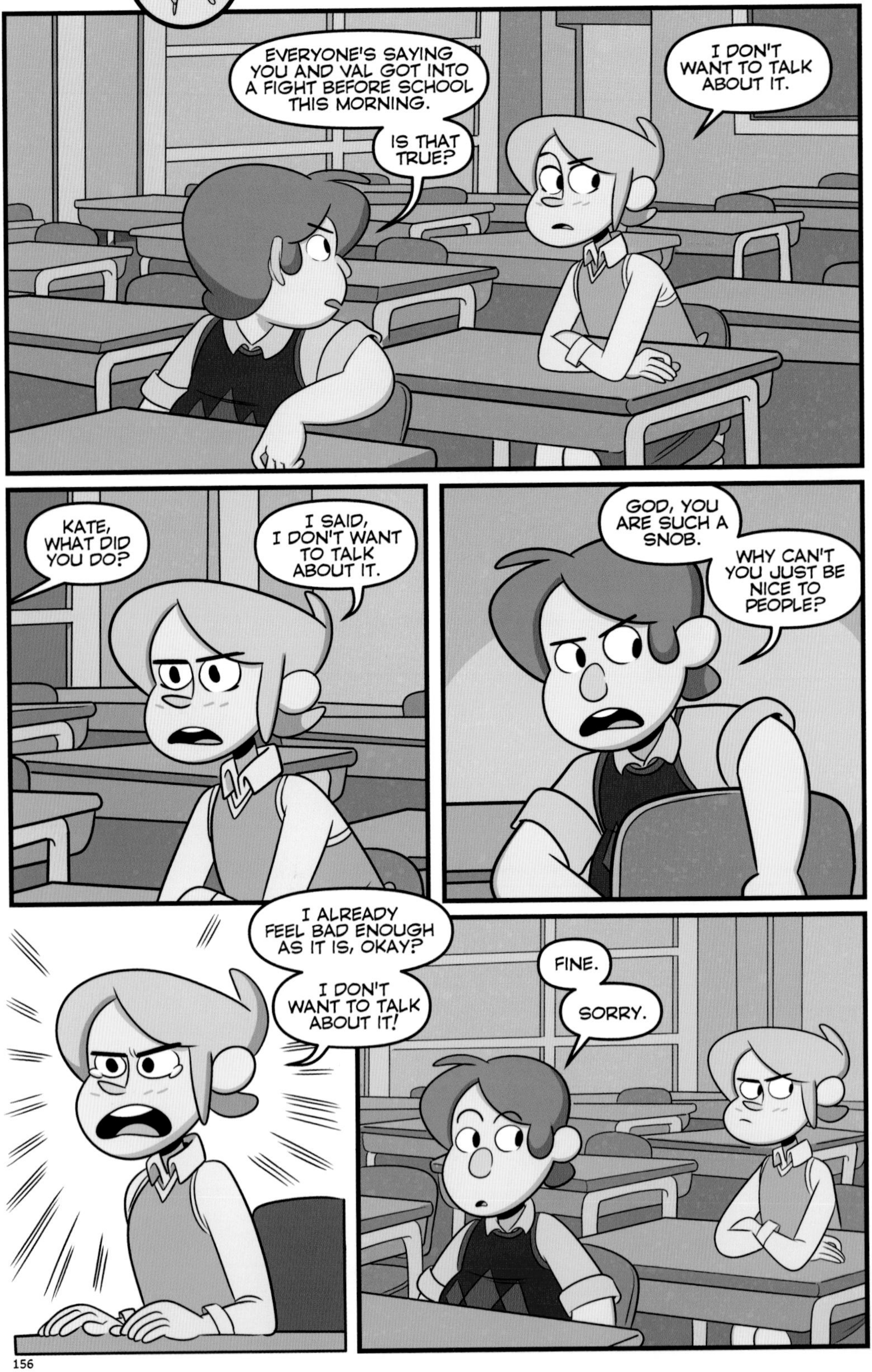

EVERYONE'S SAYING YOU AND VAL GOT INTO A FIGHT BEFORE SCHOOL THIS MORNING.
IS THAT TRUE?
I DON'T WANT TO TALK ABOUT IT.
KATE, WHAT DID YOU DO?
I SAID, I DON'T WANT TO TALK ABOUT IT.
GOD, YOU ARE SUCH A SNOB.
WHY CAN'T YOU JUST BE NICE TO PEOPLE?
I ALREADY FEEL BAD ENOUGH AS IT IS, OKAY?
I DON'T WANT TO TALK ABOUT IT!
FINE.
SORRY.

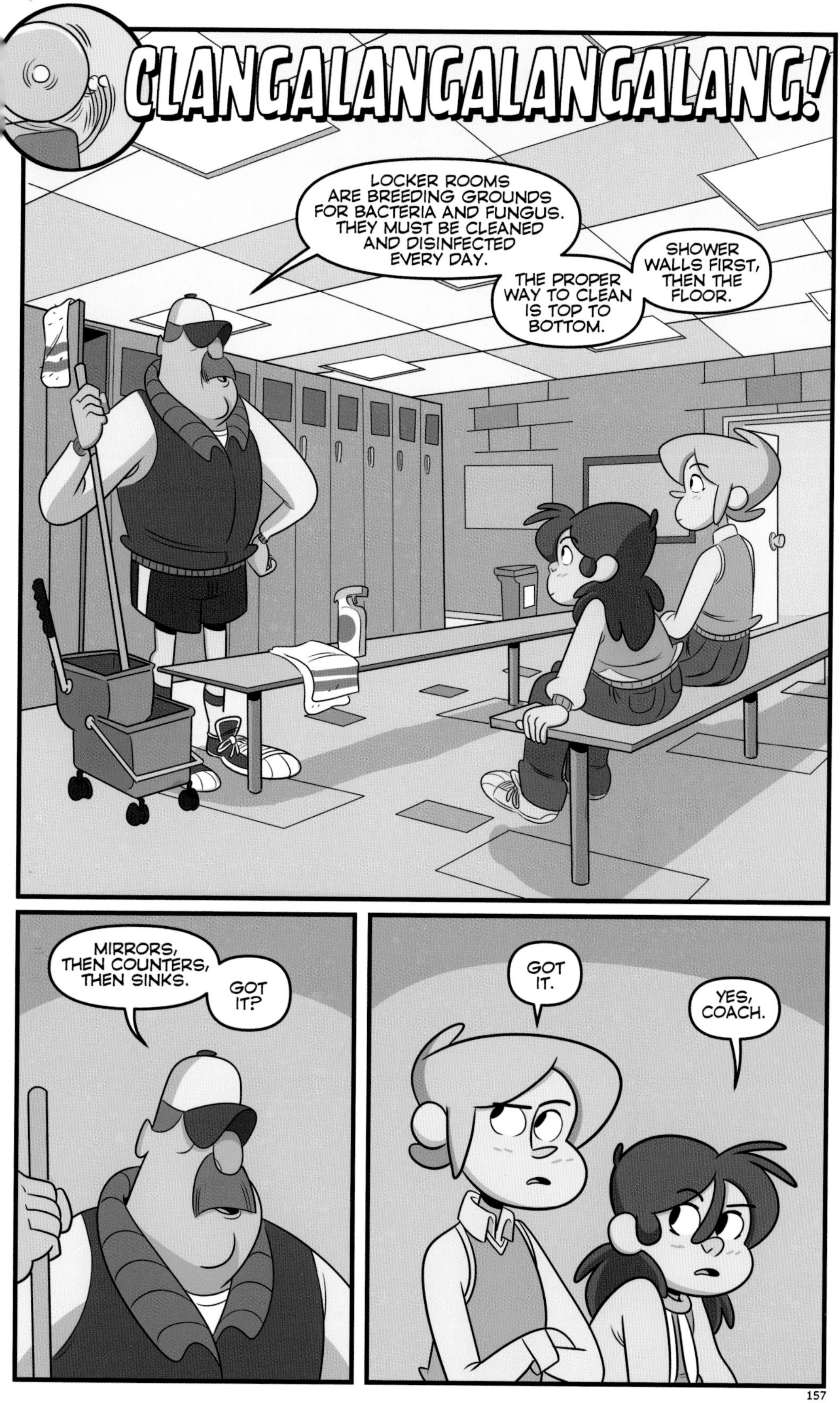
CLANGALANGALANGALANG!
LOCKER ROOMS ARE BREEDING GROUNDS FOR BACTERIA AND FUNGUS. THEY MUST BE CLEANED AND DISINFECTED EVERY DAY.
THE PROPER WAY TO CLEAN IS TOP TO BOTTOM.
SHOWER WALLS FIRST, THEN THE FLOOR.
MIRRORS, THEN COUNTERS, THEN SINKS.
GOT IT?
GOT IT.
YES, COACH.

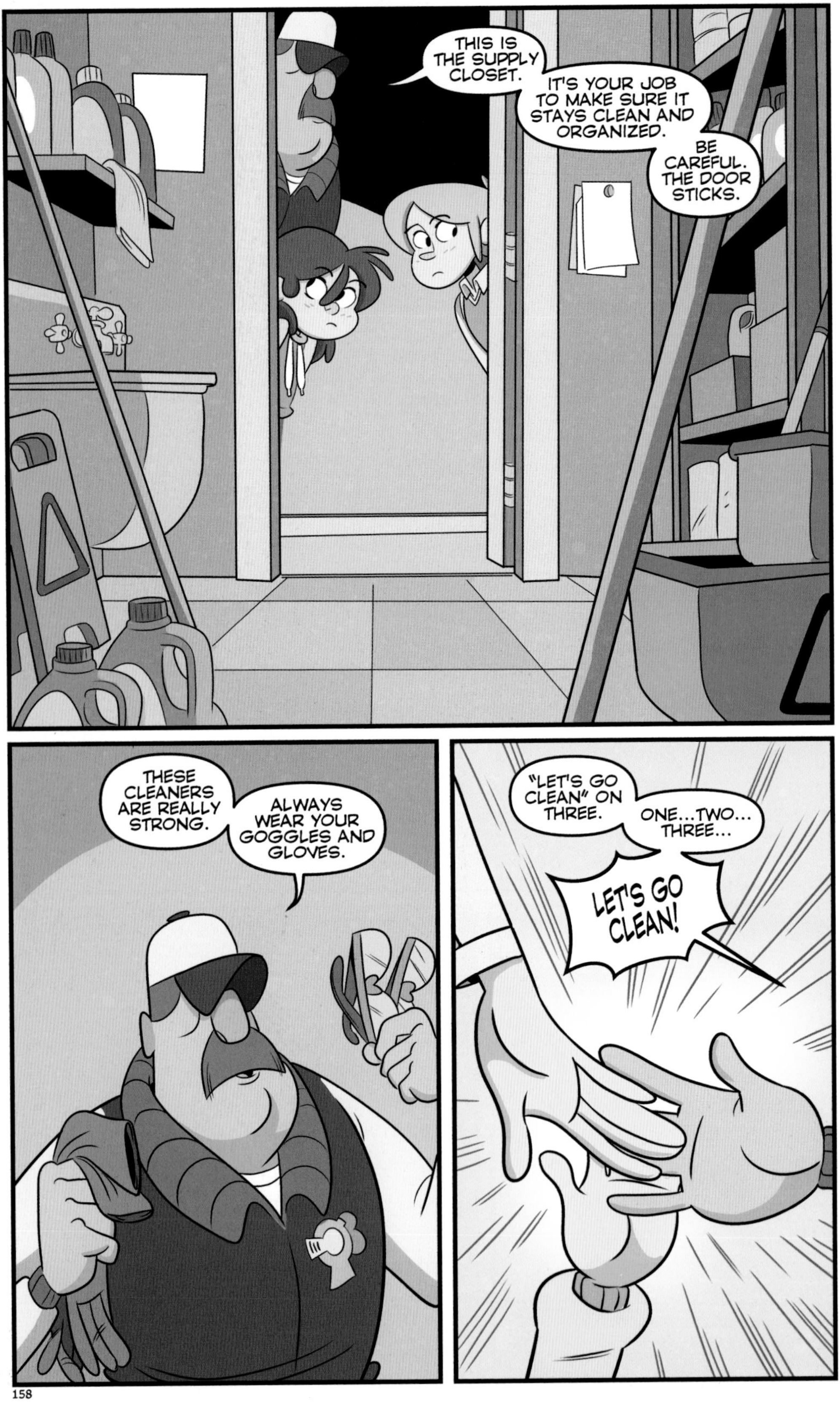
THIS IS THE SUPPLY CLOSET.
IT'S YOUR JOB TO MAKE SURE IT STAYS CLEAN AND ORGANIZED.
BE CAREFUL. THE DOOR STICKS.
THESE CLEANERS ARE REALLY STRONG.
ALWAYS WEAR YOUR GOGGLES AND GLOVES.
"LET'S GO CLEAN" ON THREE.
ONE...TWO... THREE...
LET'S GO CLEAN!

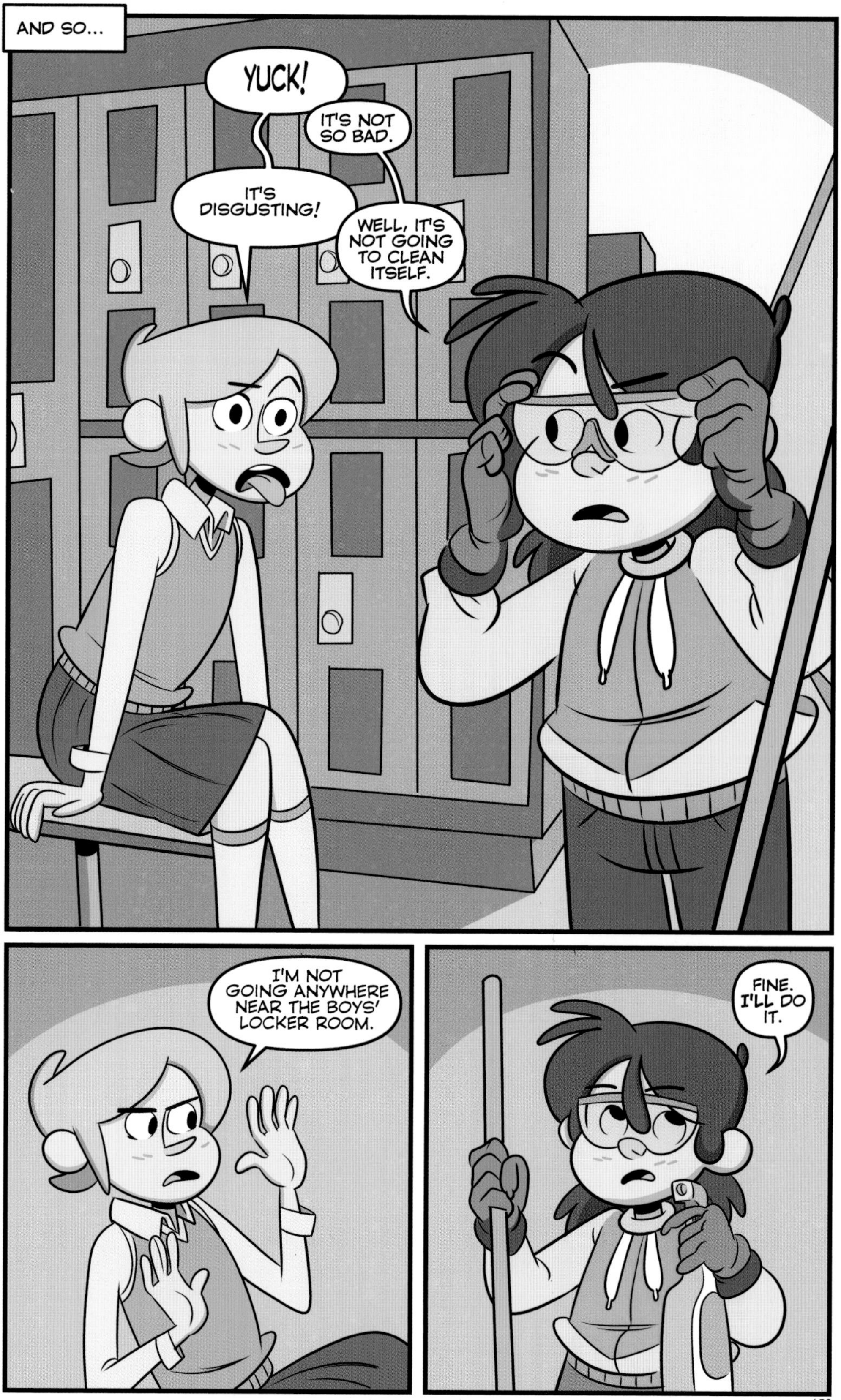
AND SO...
YUCK!
IT'S NOT SO BAD.
IT'S DISGUSTING!
WELL, IT'S NOT GOING TO CLEAN ITSELF.
I'M NOT GOING ANYWHERE NEAR THE BOYS' LOCKER ROOM.
FINE. I'LL DO IT.

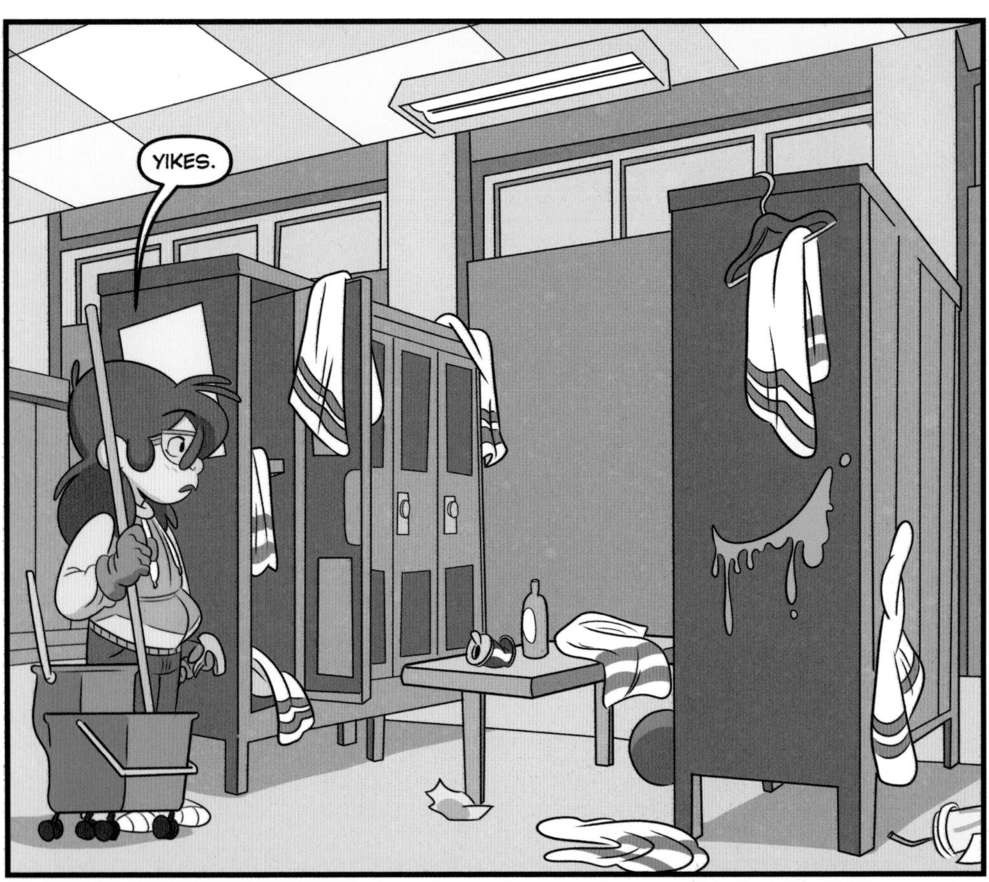
YIKES.

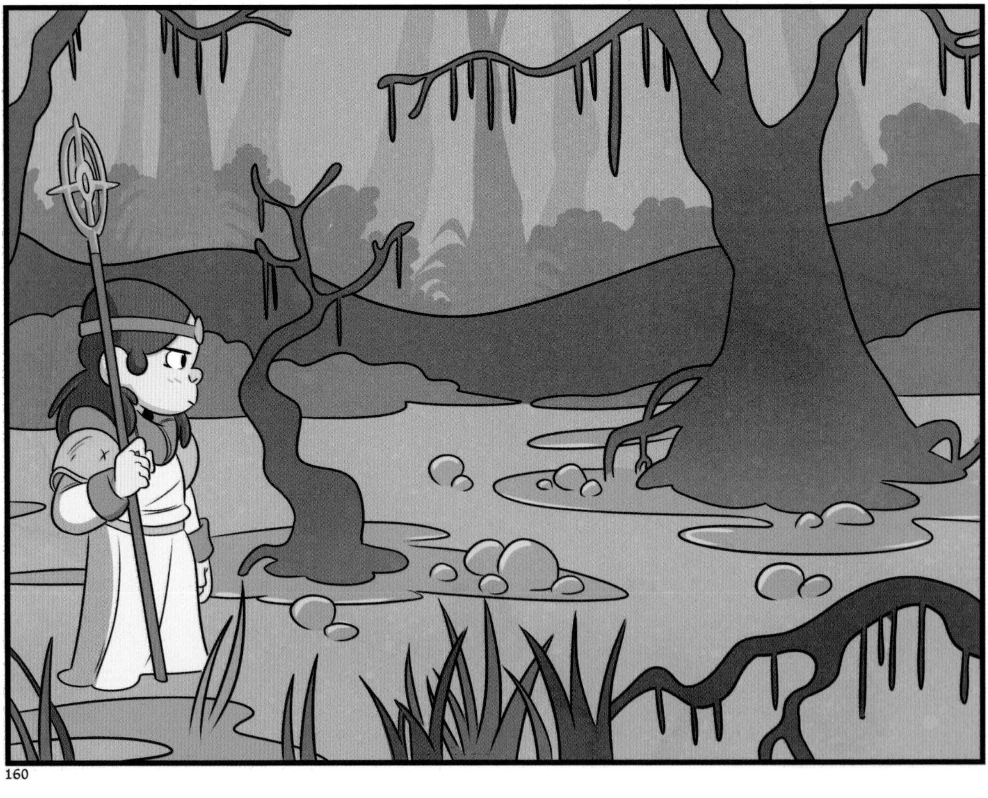

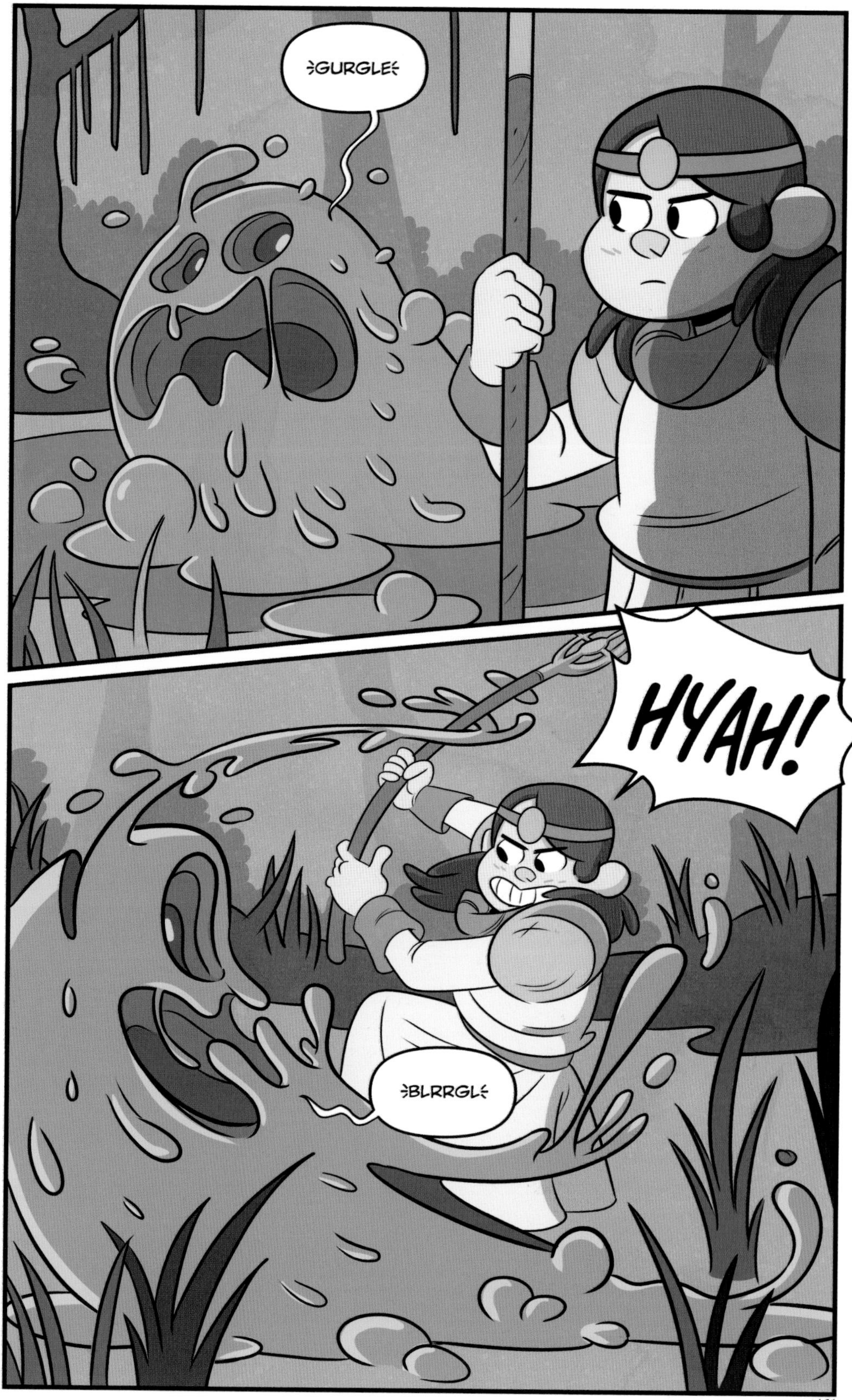
GURGLE
HYAH!
BLRRGL

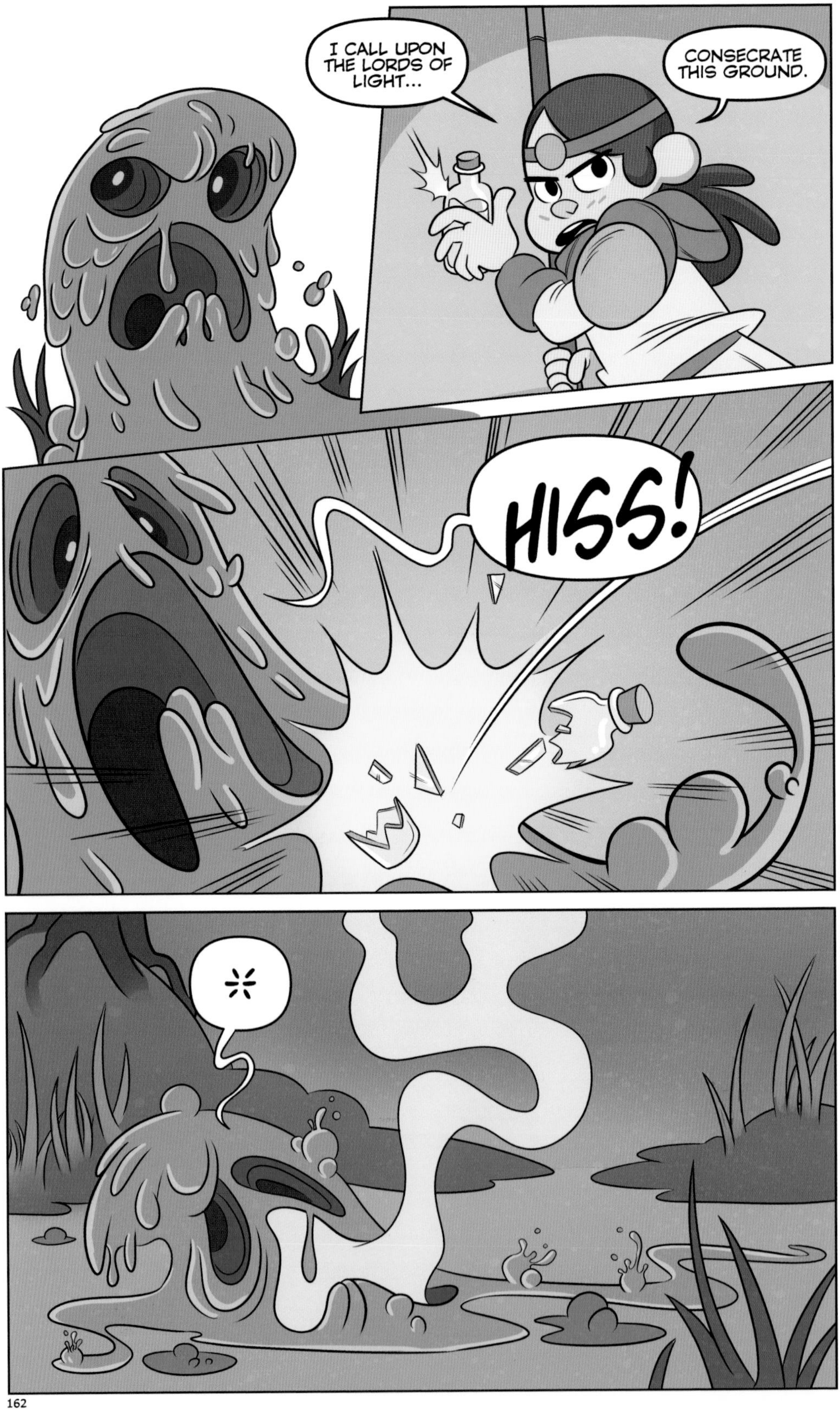
I CALL UPON THE LORDS OF LIGHT...
CONSECRATE THIS GROUND.
HISS!

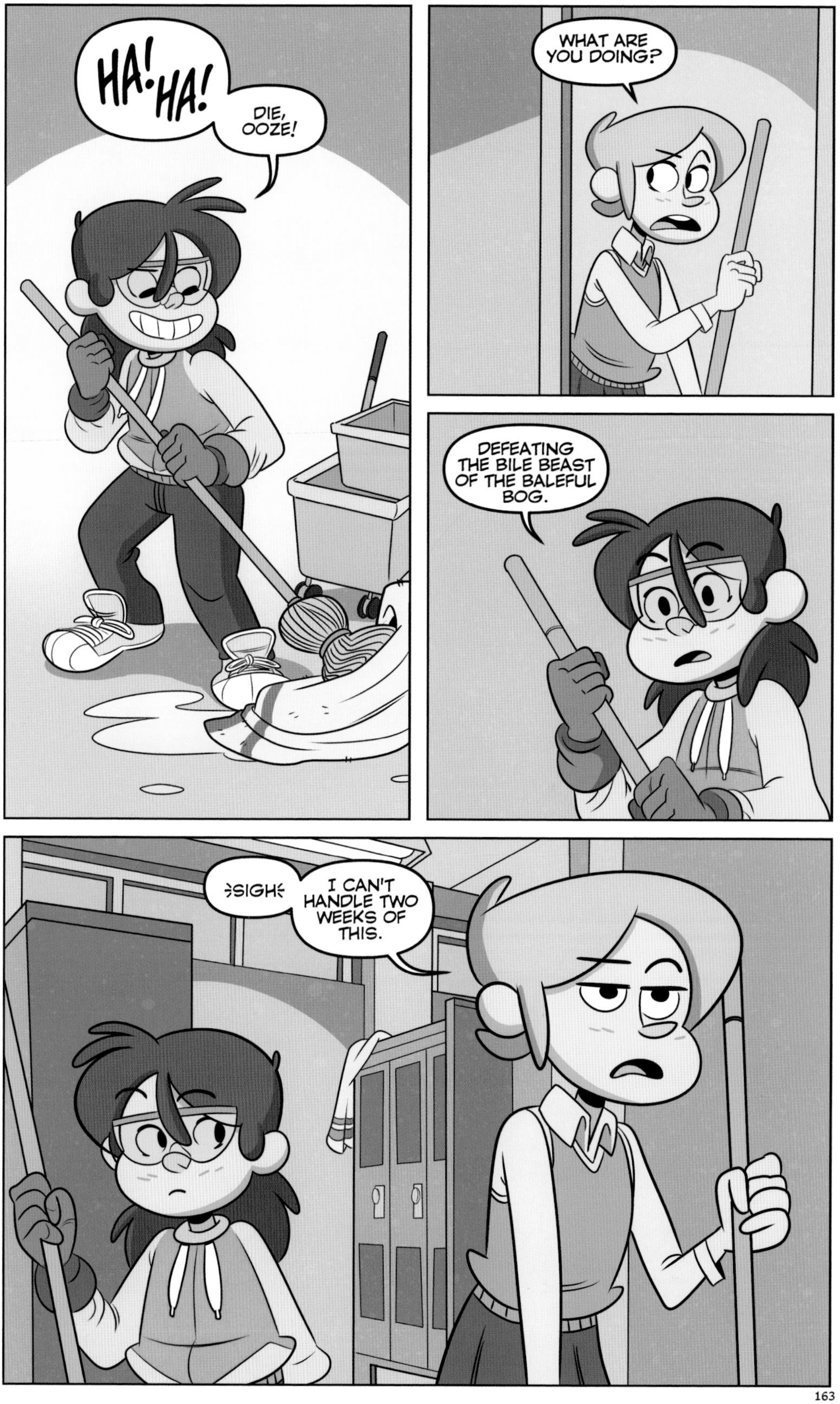
HA! HA!
DIE, OOZE!
WHAT ARE YOU DOING?
DEFEATING THE BILE BEAST OF THE BALEFUL BOG.
SIGH
I CAN'T HANDLE TWO WEEKS OF THIS.

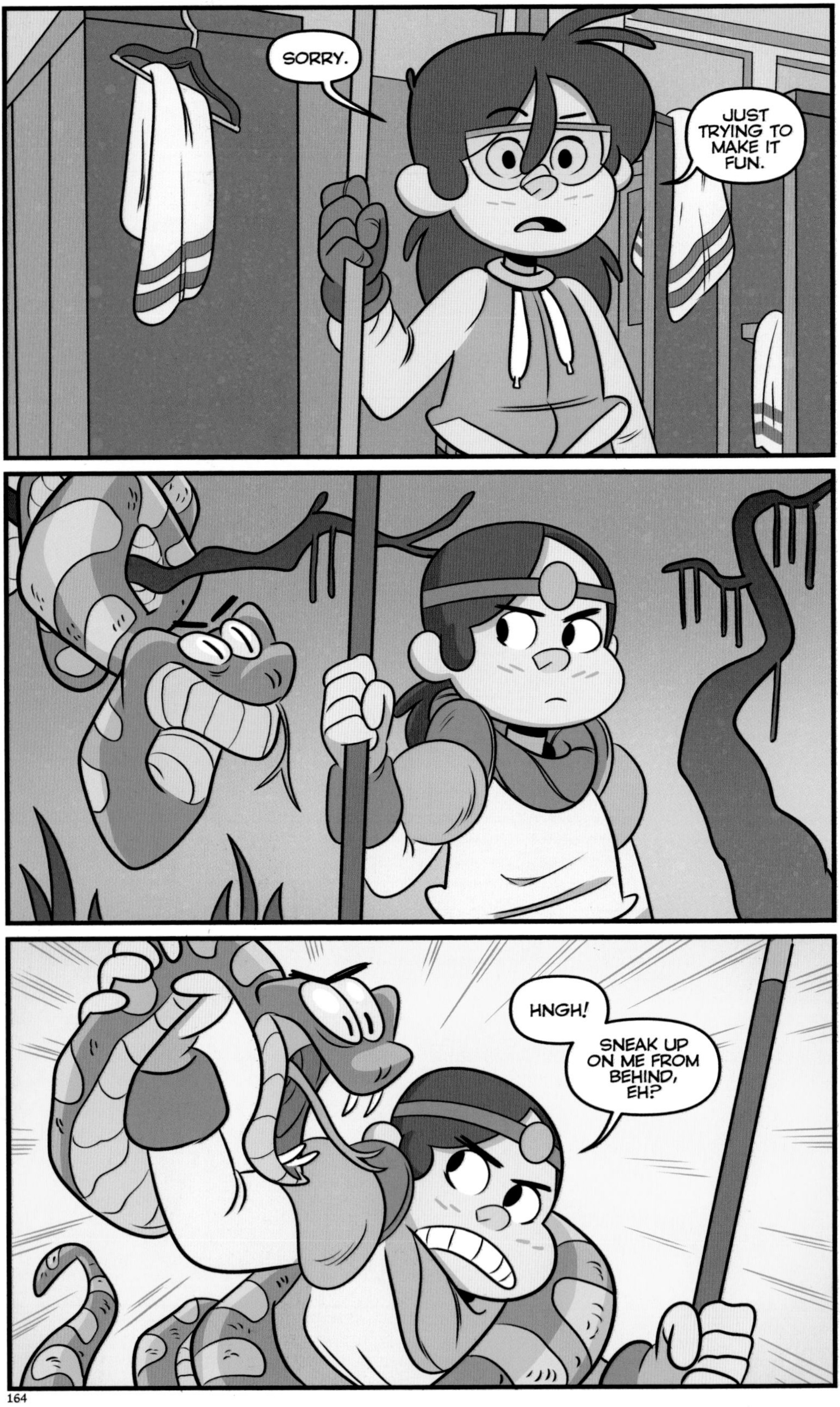
SORRY.
JUST TRYING TO MAKE IT FUN.
HNGH!
SNEAK UP ON ME FROM BEHIND, EH?

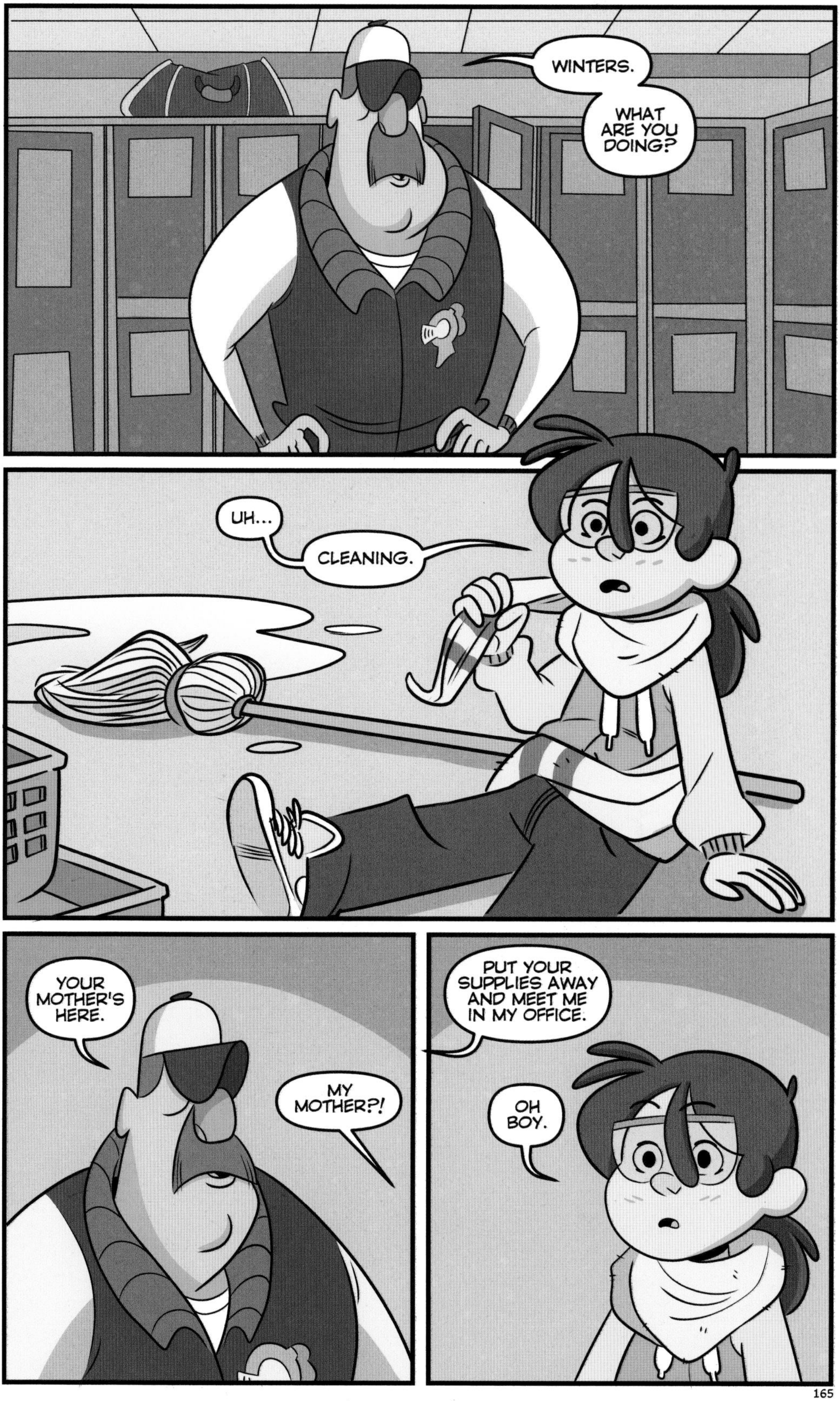
WINTERS.
WHAT ARE YOU DOING?
UH...
CLEANING.
YOUR MOTHER'S HERE.
MY MOTHER?!
PUT YOUR SUPPLIES AWAY AND MEET ME IN MY OFFICE.
OH BOY.

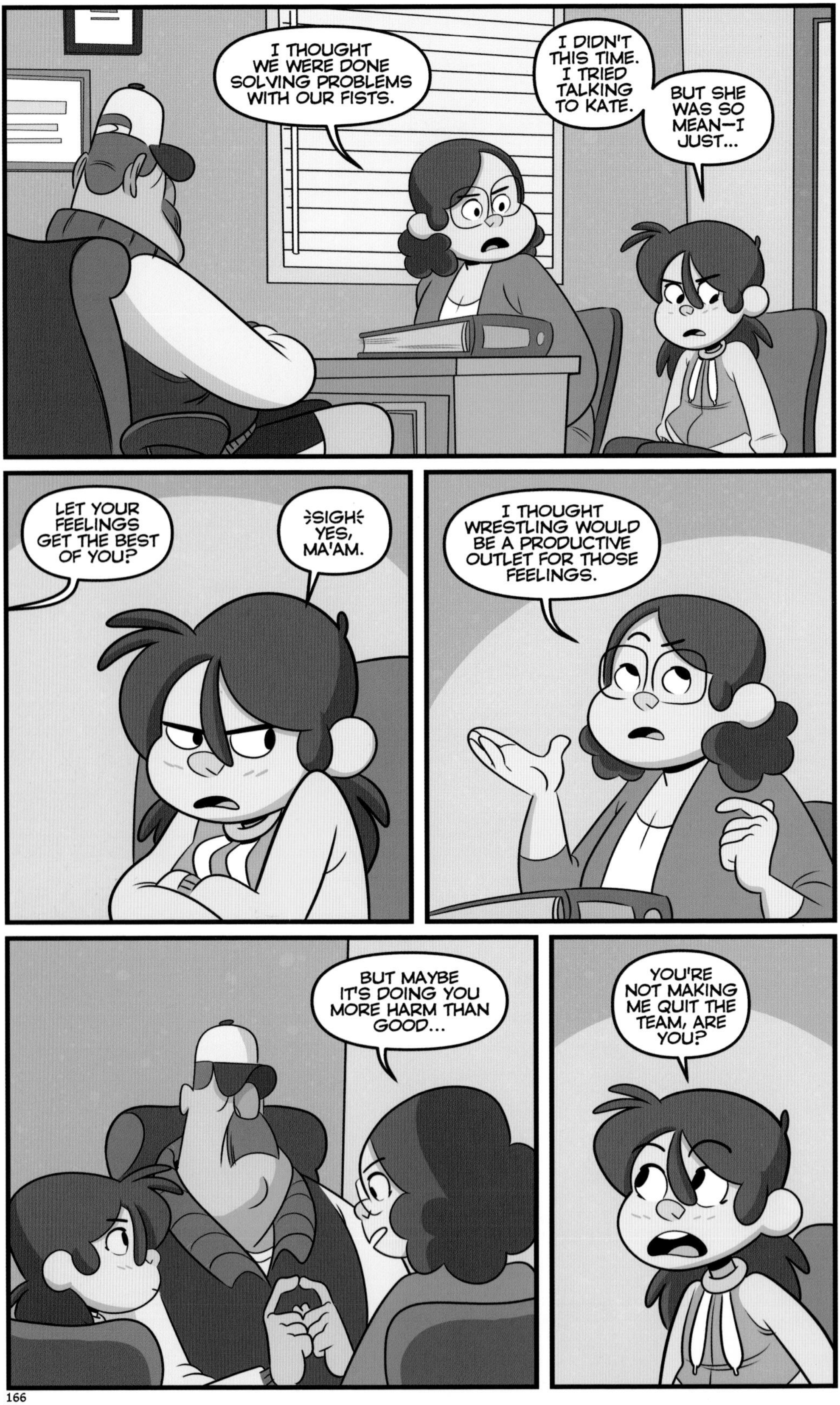
I THOUGHT WE WERE DONE SOLVING PROBLEMS WITH OUR FISTS.
I DIDN'T THIS TIME. I TRIED TALKING TO KATE.
BUT SHE WAS SO MEAN—I JUST...
LET YOUR FEELINGS GET THE BEST OF YOU?
SIGH YES, MA'AM.
I THOUGHT WRESTLING WOULD BE A PRODUCTIVE OUTLET FOR THOSE FEELINGS.
BUT MAYBE IT'S DOING YOU MORE HARM THAN GOOD...
YOU'RE NOT MAKING ME QUIT THE TEAM, ARE YOU?

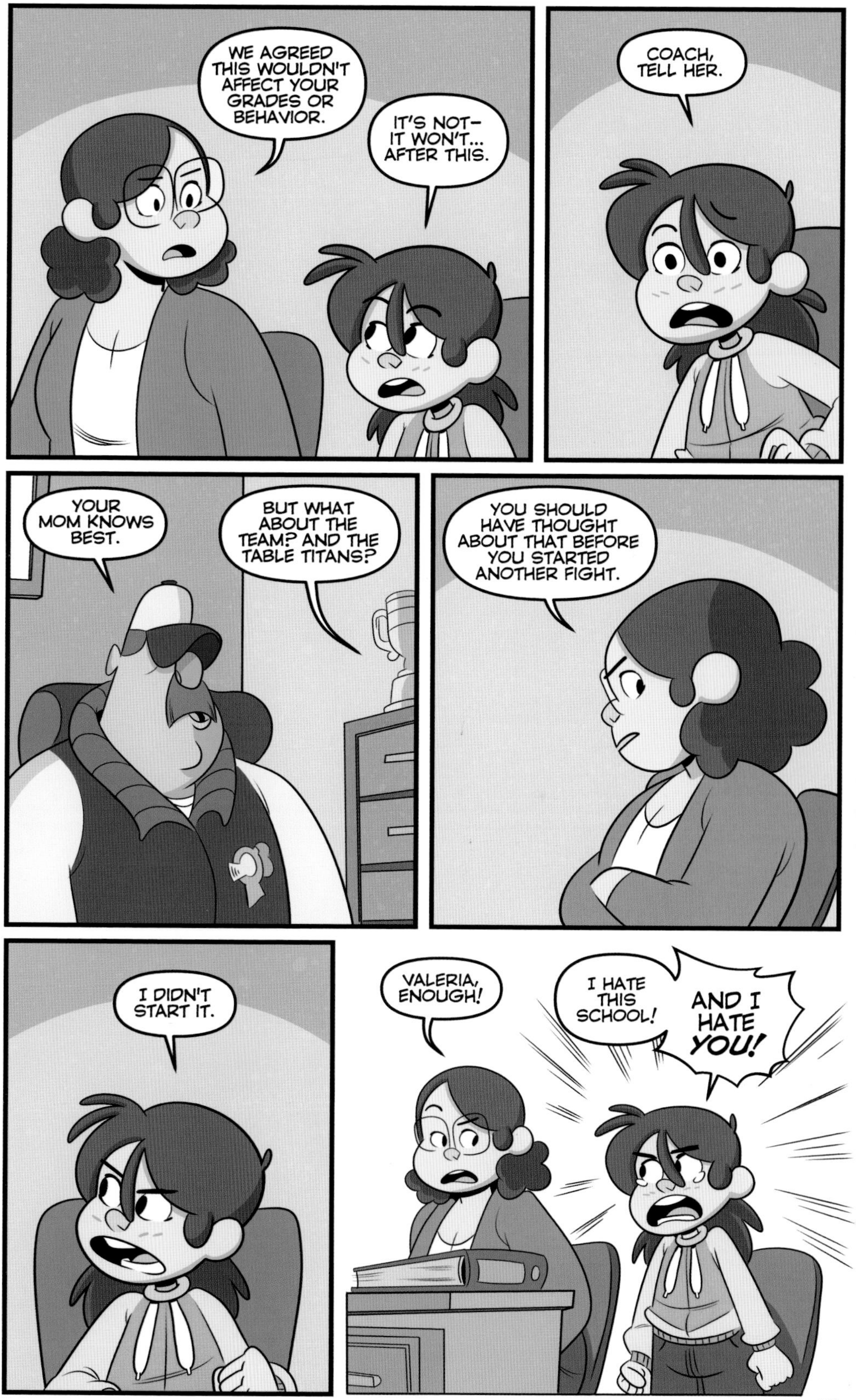

WE AGREED THIS WOULDN'T AFFECT YOUR GRADES OR BEHAVIOR.
IT'S NOT– IT WON'T... AFTER THIS.
COACH, TELL HER.
YOUR MOM KNOWS BEST.
BUT WHAT ABOUT THE TEAM? AND THE TABLE TITANS?
YOU SHOULD HAVE THOUGHT ABOUT THAT BEFORE YOU STARTED ANOTHER FIGHT.
I DIDN'T START IT.
VALERIA, ENOUGH!
I HATE THIS SCHOOL!
AND I HATE YOU!

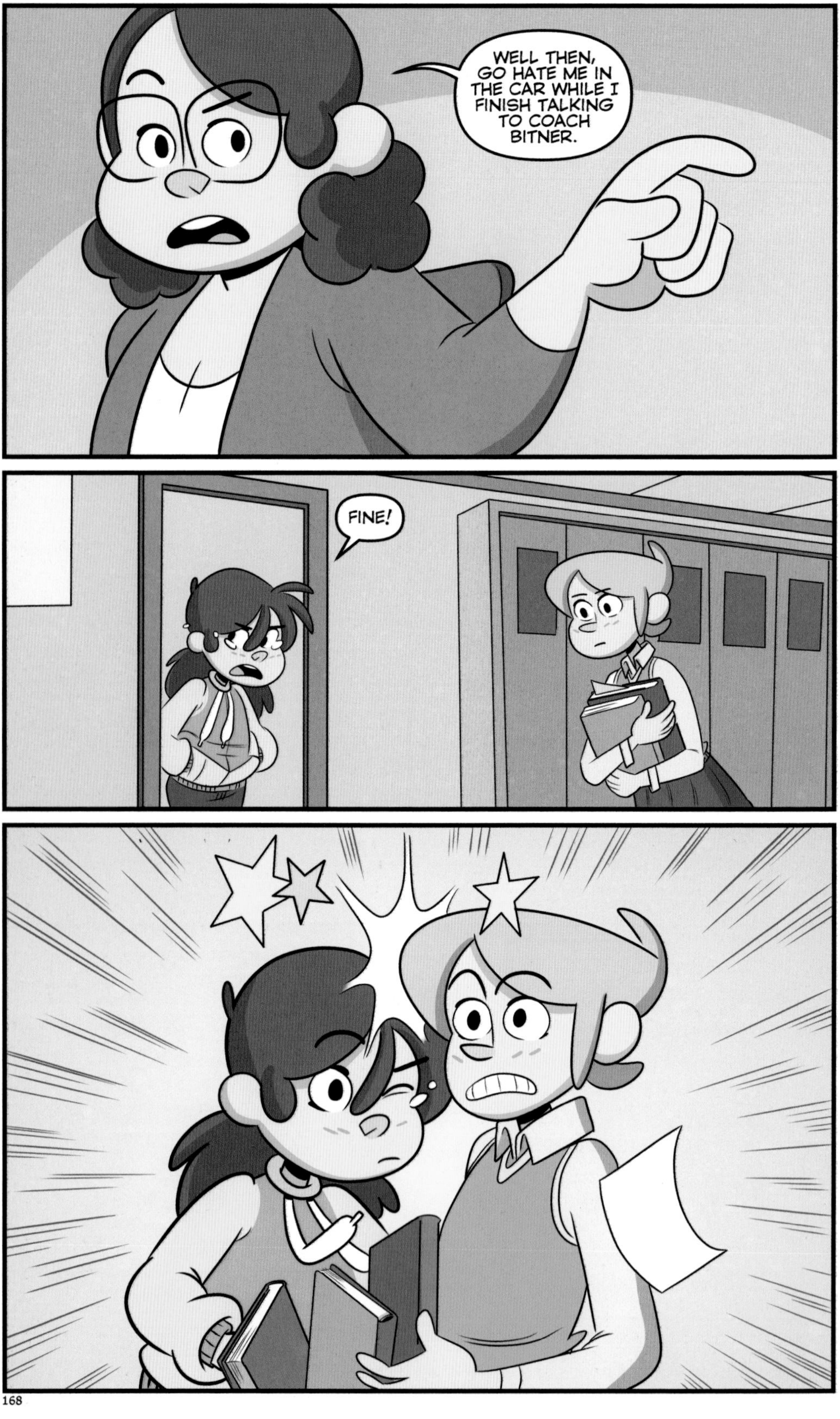
WELL THEN, GO HATE ME IN THE CAR WHILE I FINISH TALKING TO COACH BITNER.
FINE!

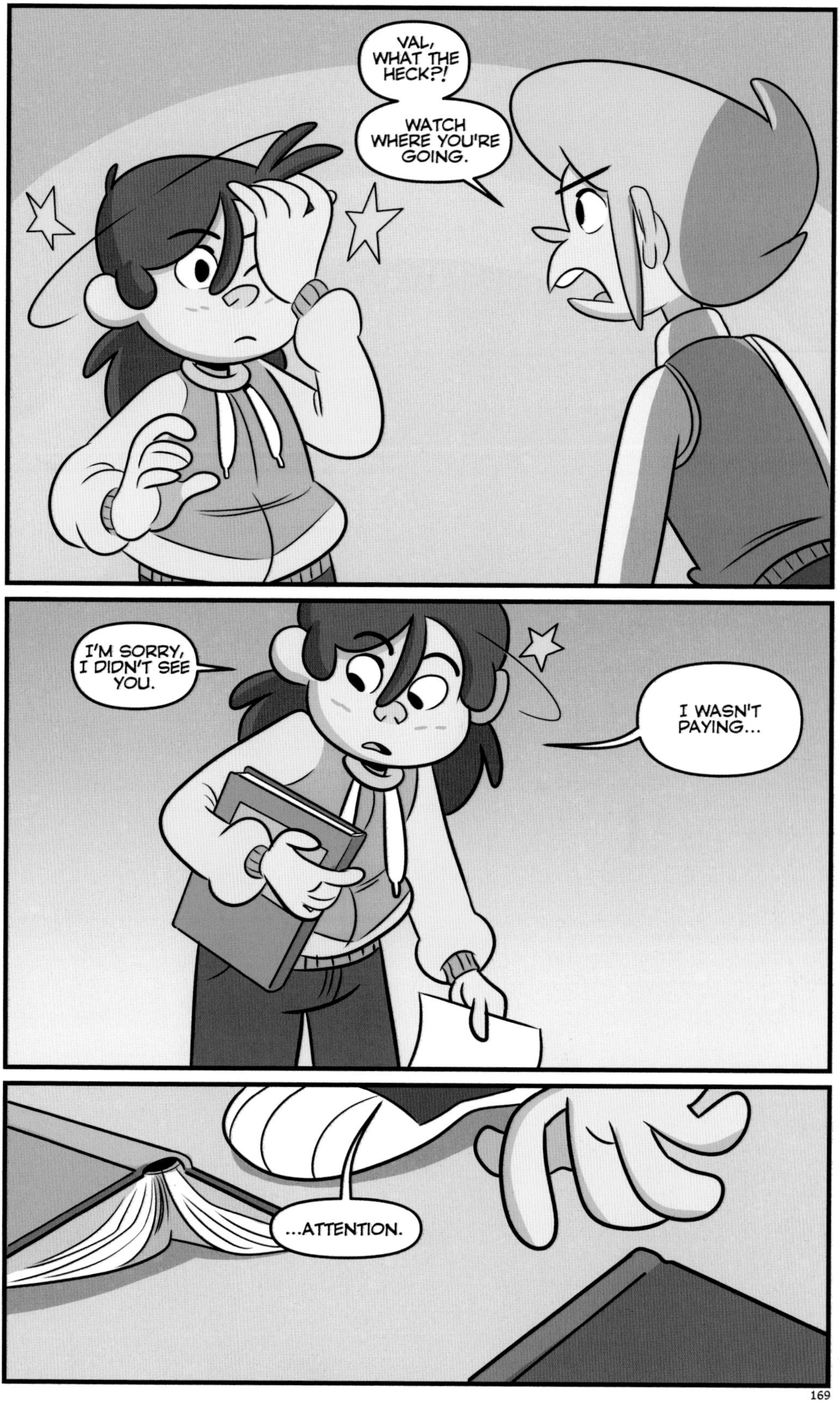
VAL, WHAT THE HECK?!
WATCH WHERE YOU'RE GOING.
I'M SORRY, I DIDN'T SEE YOU.
I WASN'T PAYING...
...ATTENTION.

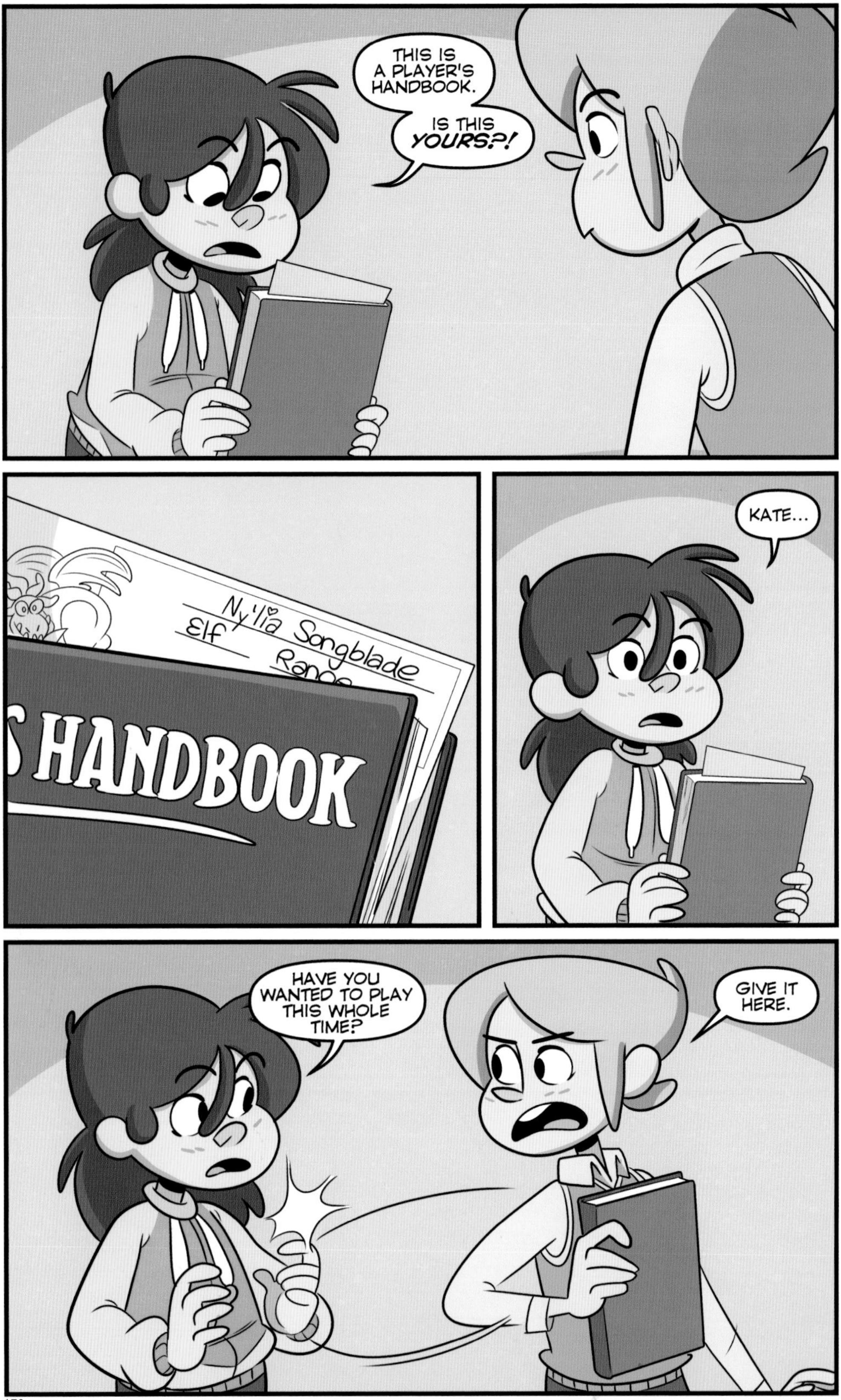
THIS IS A PLAYER'S HANDBOOK.
IS THIS *YOURS?!*
Ny'lia Songblade
Elf
HANDBOOK
KATE...
HAVE YOU WANTED TO PLAY THIS WHOLE TIME?
GIVE IT HERE.

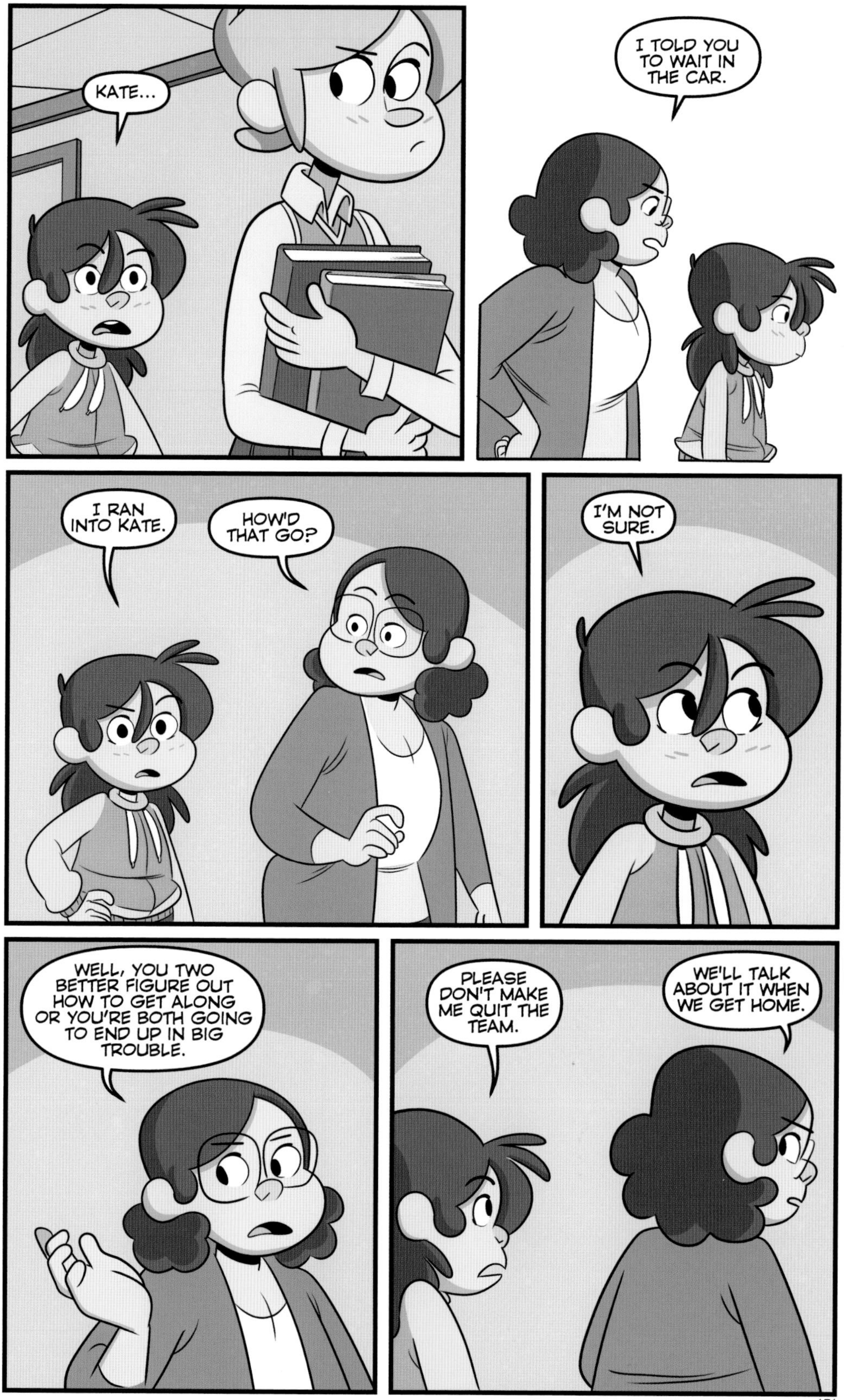
KATE...
I TOLD YOU TO WAIT IN THE CAR.
I RAN INTO KATE.
HOW'D THAT GO?
I'M NOT SURE.
WELL, YOU TWO BETTER FIGURE OUT HOW TO GET ALONG OR YOU'RE BOTH GOING TO END UP IN BIG TROUBLE.
PLEASE DON'T MAKE ME QUIT THE TEAM.
WE'LL TALK ABOUT IT WHEN WE GET HOME.

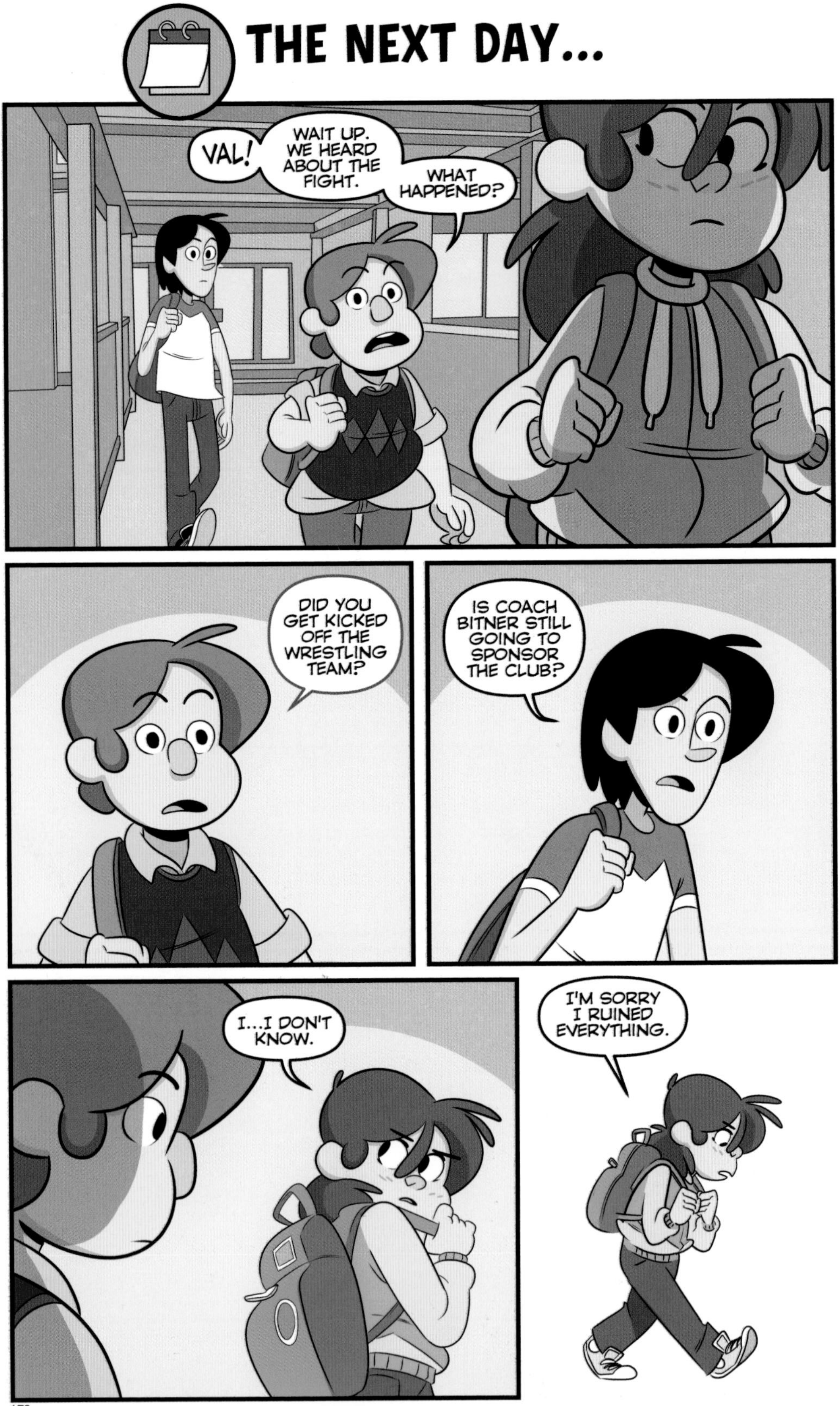
THE NEXT DAY...
VAL!
WAIT UP. WE HEARD ABOUT THE FIGHT.
WHAT HAPPENED?
DID YOU GET KICKED OFF THE WRESTLING TEAM?
IS COACH BITNER STILL GOING TO SPONSOR THE CLUB?
I...I DON'T KNOW.
I'M SORRY I RUINED EVERYTHING.

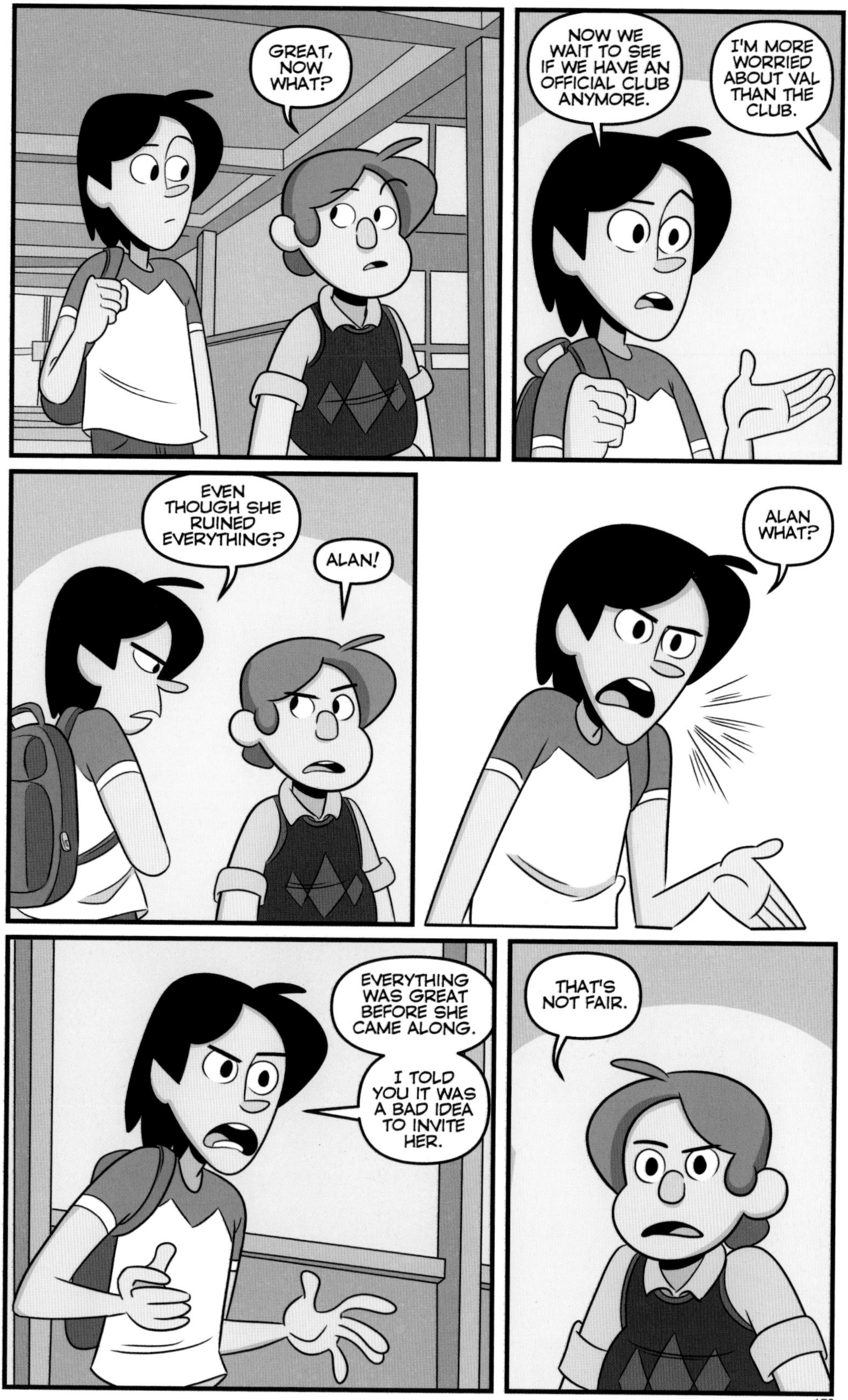
GREAT, NOW WHAT?
NOW WE WAIT TO SEE IF WE HAVE AN OFFICIAL CLUB ANYMORE.
I'M MORE WORRIED ABOUT VAL THAN THE CLUB.
EVEN THOUGH SHE RUINED EVERYTHING?
ALAN!
ALAN WHAT?
EVERYTHING WAS GREAT BEFORE SHE CAME ALONG.
I TOLD YOU IT WAS A BAD IDEA TO INVITE HER.
THAT'S NOT FAIR.

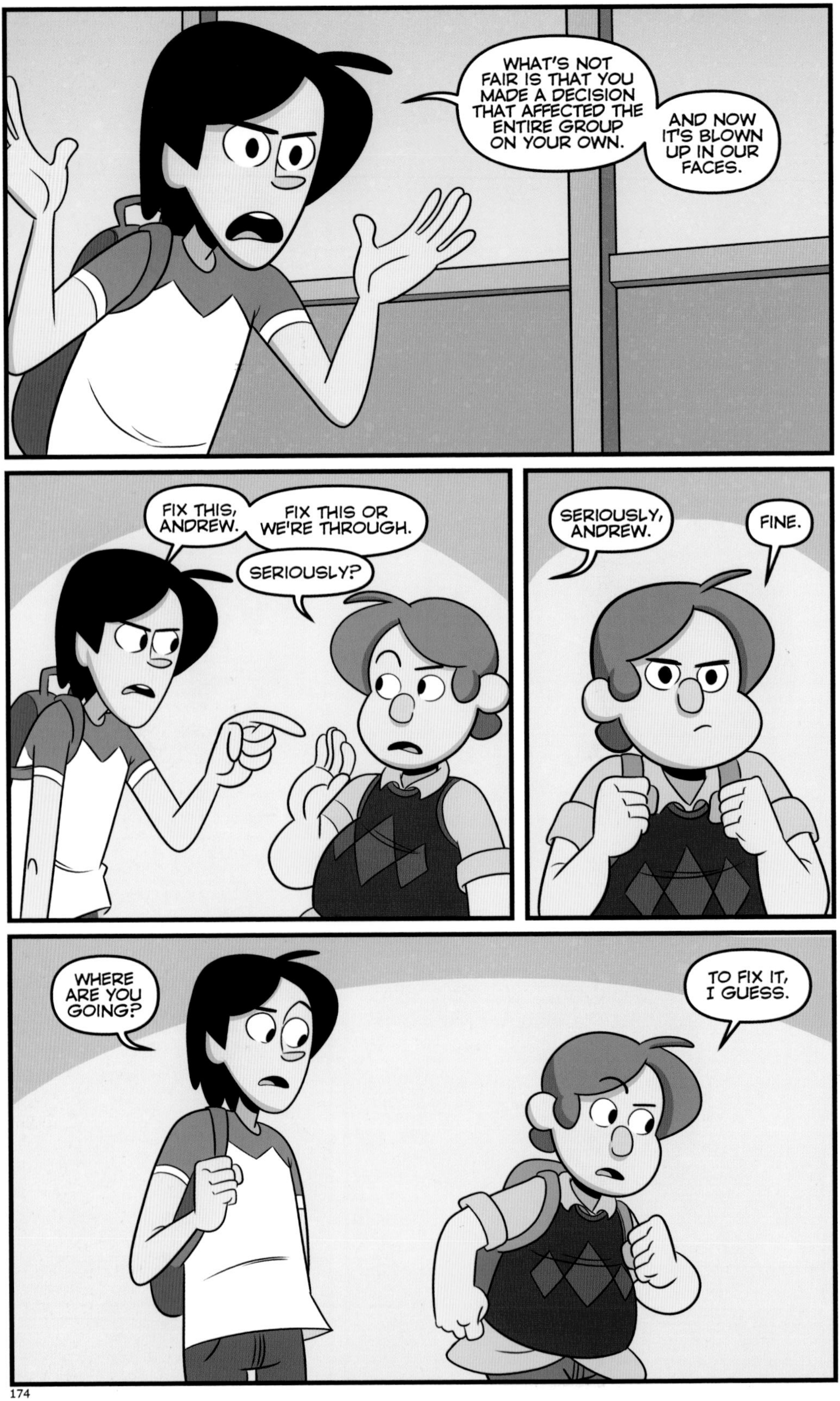
WHAT'S NOT FAIR IS THAT YOU MADE A DECISION THAT AFFECTED THE ENTIRE GROUP ON YOUR OWN.
AND NOW IT'S BLOWN UP IN OUR FACES.
FIX THIS, ANDREW.
FIX THIS OR WE'RE THROUGH.
SERIOUSLY?
SERIOUSLY, ANDREW.
FINE.
WHERE ARE YOU GOING?
TO FIX IT, I GUESS.

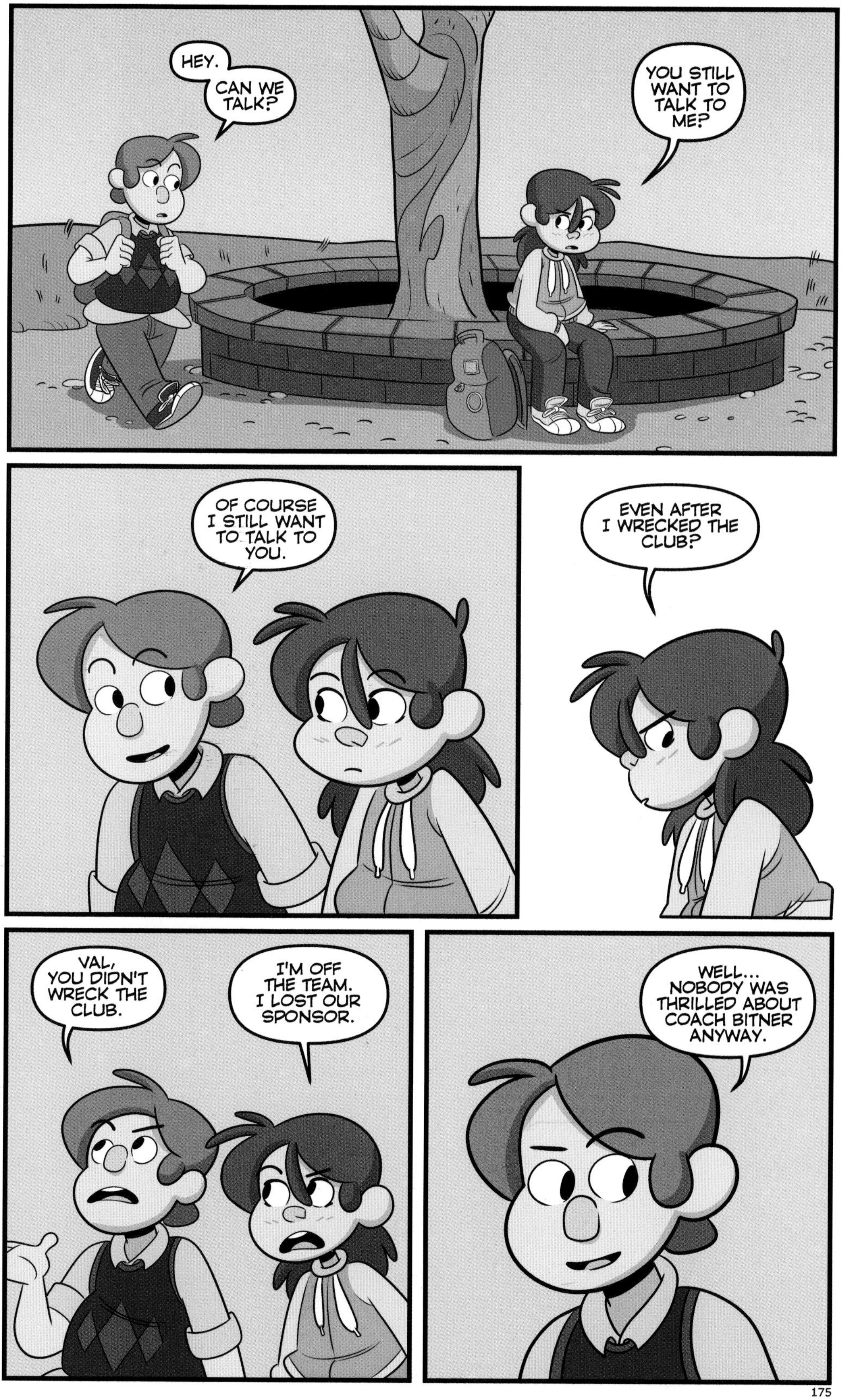
HEY.
CAN WE TALK?
YOU STILL WANT TO TALK TO ME?
OF COURSE I STILL WANT TO TALK TO YOU.
EVEN AFTER I WRECKED THE CLUB?
VAL, YOU DIDN'T WRECK THE CLUB.
I'M OFF THE TEAM. I LOST OUR SPONSOR.
WELL... NOBODY WAS THRILLED ABOUT COACH BITNER ANYWAY.

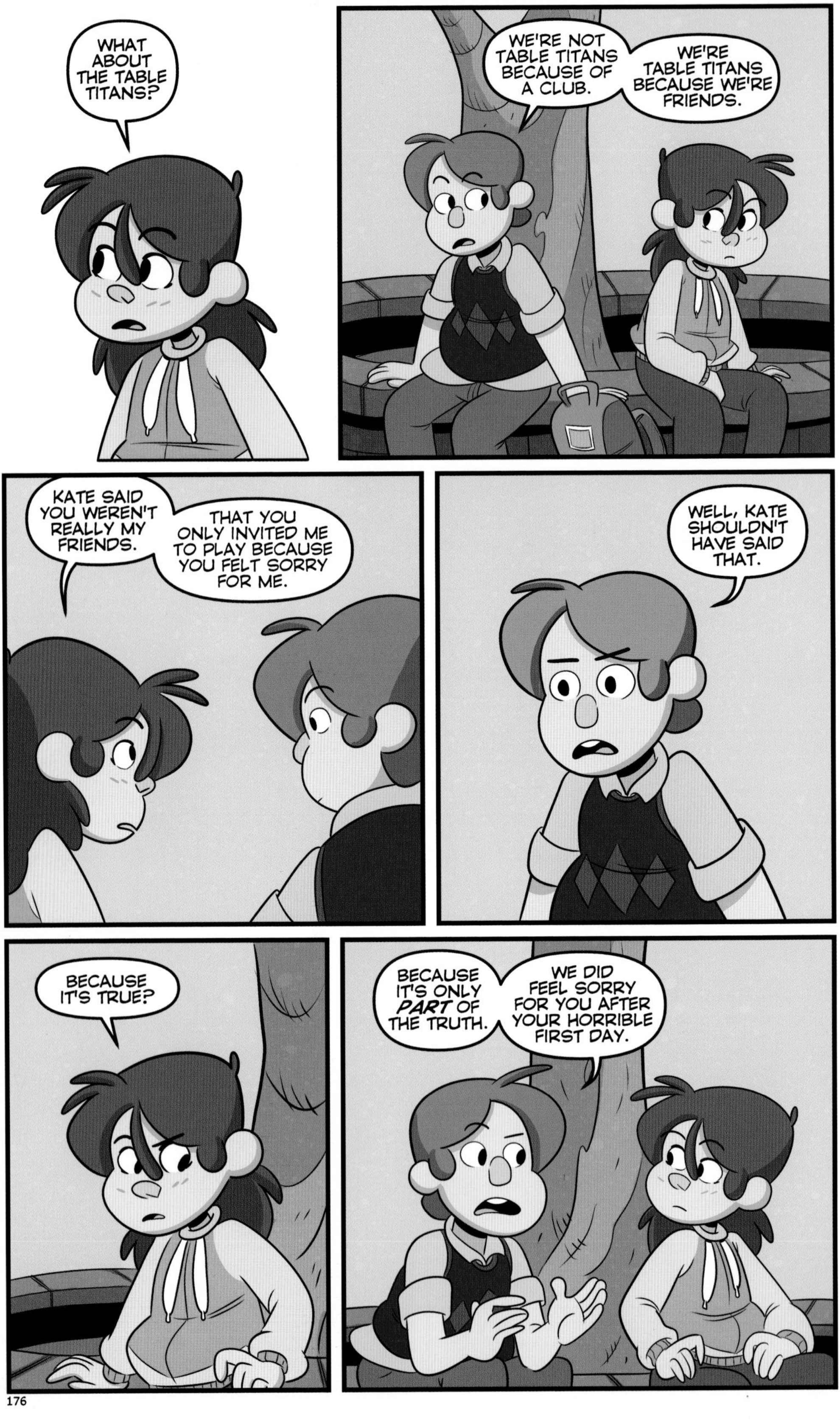
WHAT ABOUT THE TABLE TITANS?
WE'RE NOT TABLE TITANS BECAUSE OF A CLUB.
WE'RE TABLE TITANS BECAUSE WE'RE FRIENDS.
KATE SAID YOU WEREN'T REALLY MY FRIENDS.
THAT YOU ONLY INVITED ME TO PLAY BECAUSE YOU FELT SORRY FOR ME.
WELL, KATE SHOULDN'T HAVE SAID THAT.
BECAUSE IT'S TRUE?
BECAUSE IT'S ONLY *PART* OF THE TRUTH.
WE DID FEEL SORRY FOR YOU AFTER YOUR HORRIBLE FIRST DAY.

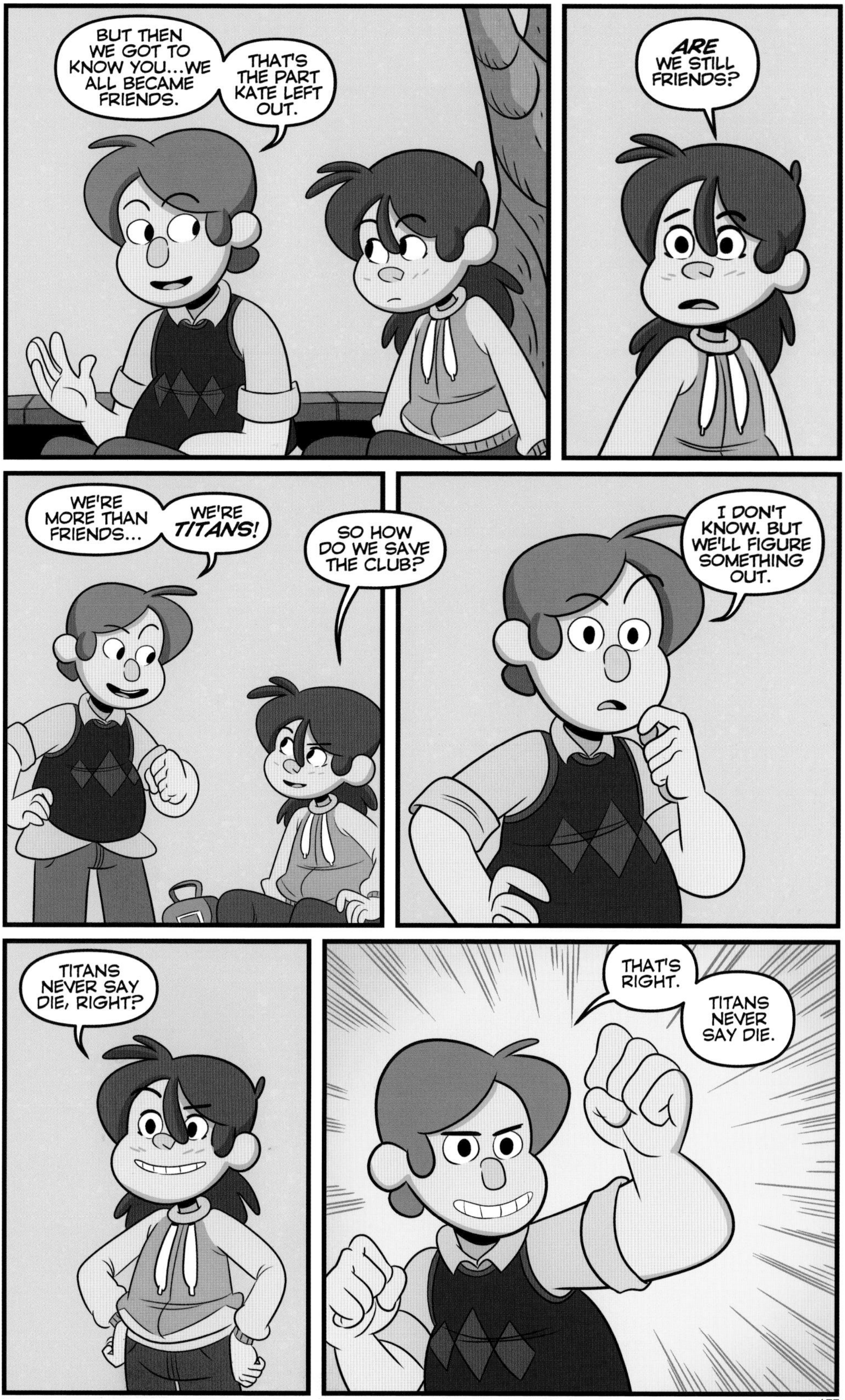

BUT THEN WE GOT TO KNOW YOU...WE ALL BECAME FRIENDS.
THAT'S THE PART KATE LEFT OUT.
ARE WE STILL FRIENDS?
WE'RE MORE THAN FRIENDS...
WE'RE TITANS!
SO HOW DO WE SAVE THE CLUB?
I DON'T KNOW. BUT WE'LL FIGURE SOMETHING OUT.
TITANS NEVER SAY DIE, RIGHT?
THAT'S RIGHT.
TITANS NEVER SAY DIE.

MEANWHILE, IN MR. KHOO'S ROOM...

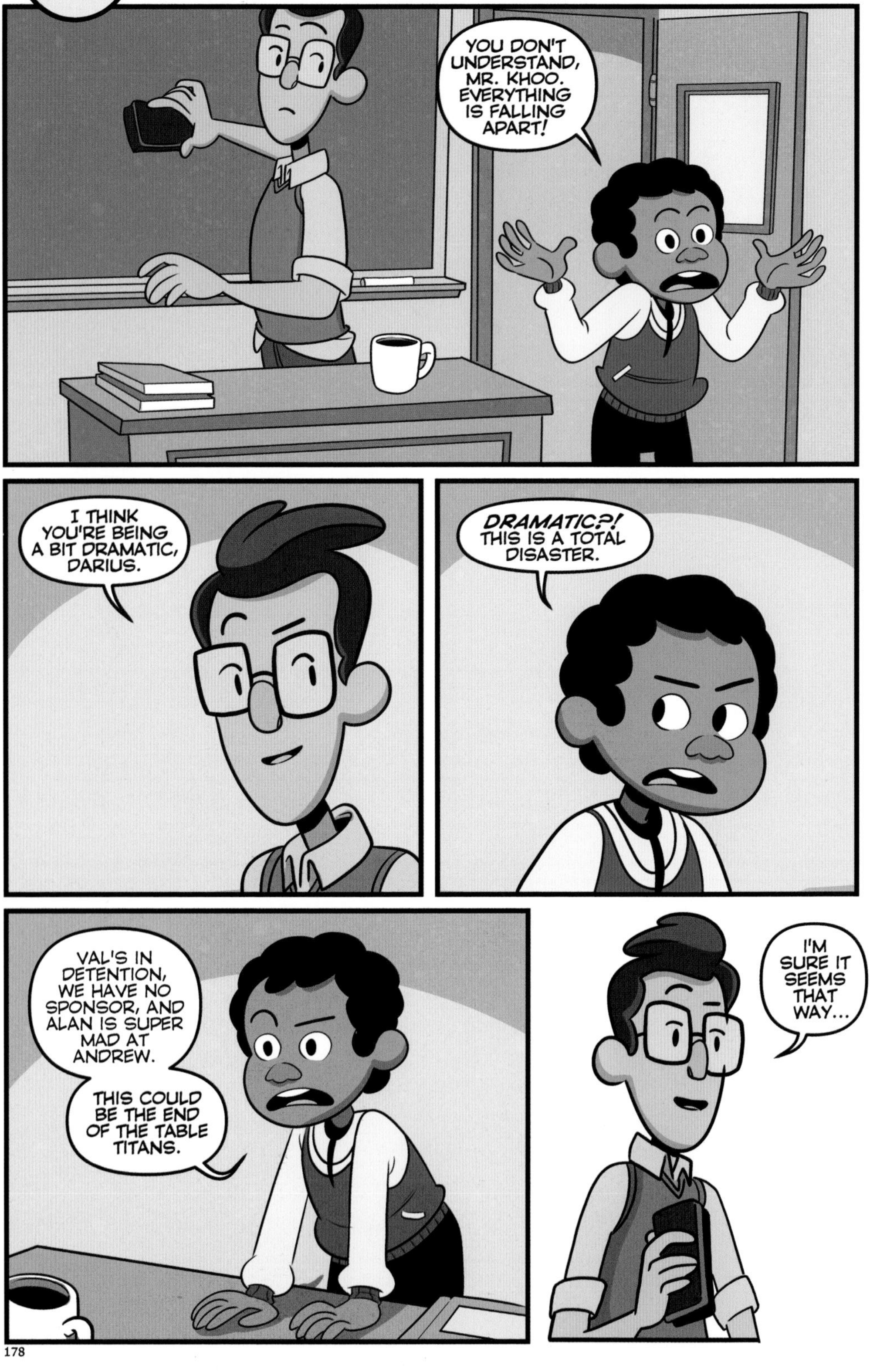

YOU DON'T UNDERSTAND, MR. KHOO. EVERYTHING IS FALLING APART!
I THINK YOU'RE BEING A BIT DRAMATIC, DARIUS.
DRAMATIC?! THIS IS A TOTAL DISASTER.
VAL'S IN DETENTION, WE HAVE NO SPONSOR, AND ALAN IS SUPER MAD AT ANDREW.
THIS COULD BE THE END OF THE TABLE TITANS.
I'M SURE IT SEEMS THAT WAY...

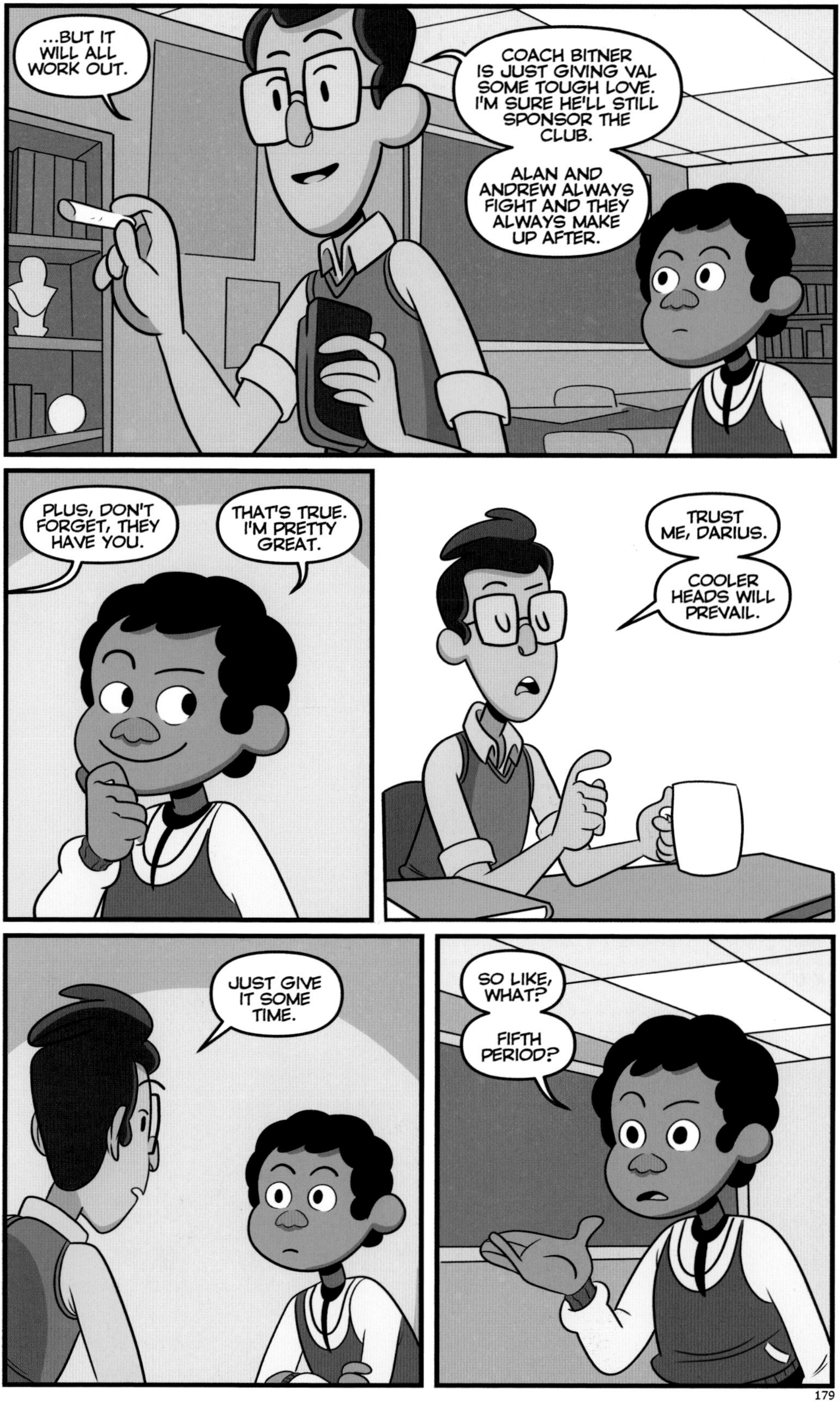
...BUT IT WILL ALL WORK OUT.
COACH BITNER IS JUST GIVING VAL SOME TOUGH LOVE. I'M SURE HE'LL STILL SPONSOR THE CLUB.
ALAN AND ANDREW ALWAYS FIGHT AND THEY ALWAYS MAKE UP AFTER.
PLUS, DON'T FORGET, THEY HAVE YOU.
THAT'S TRUE. I'M PRETTY GREAT.
TRUST ME, DARIUS.
COOLER HEADS WILL PREVAIL.
JUST GIVE IT SOME TIME.
SO LIKE, WHAT?
FIFTH PERIOD?

LOCKER ROOMS, 3:15 SHARP!

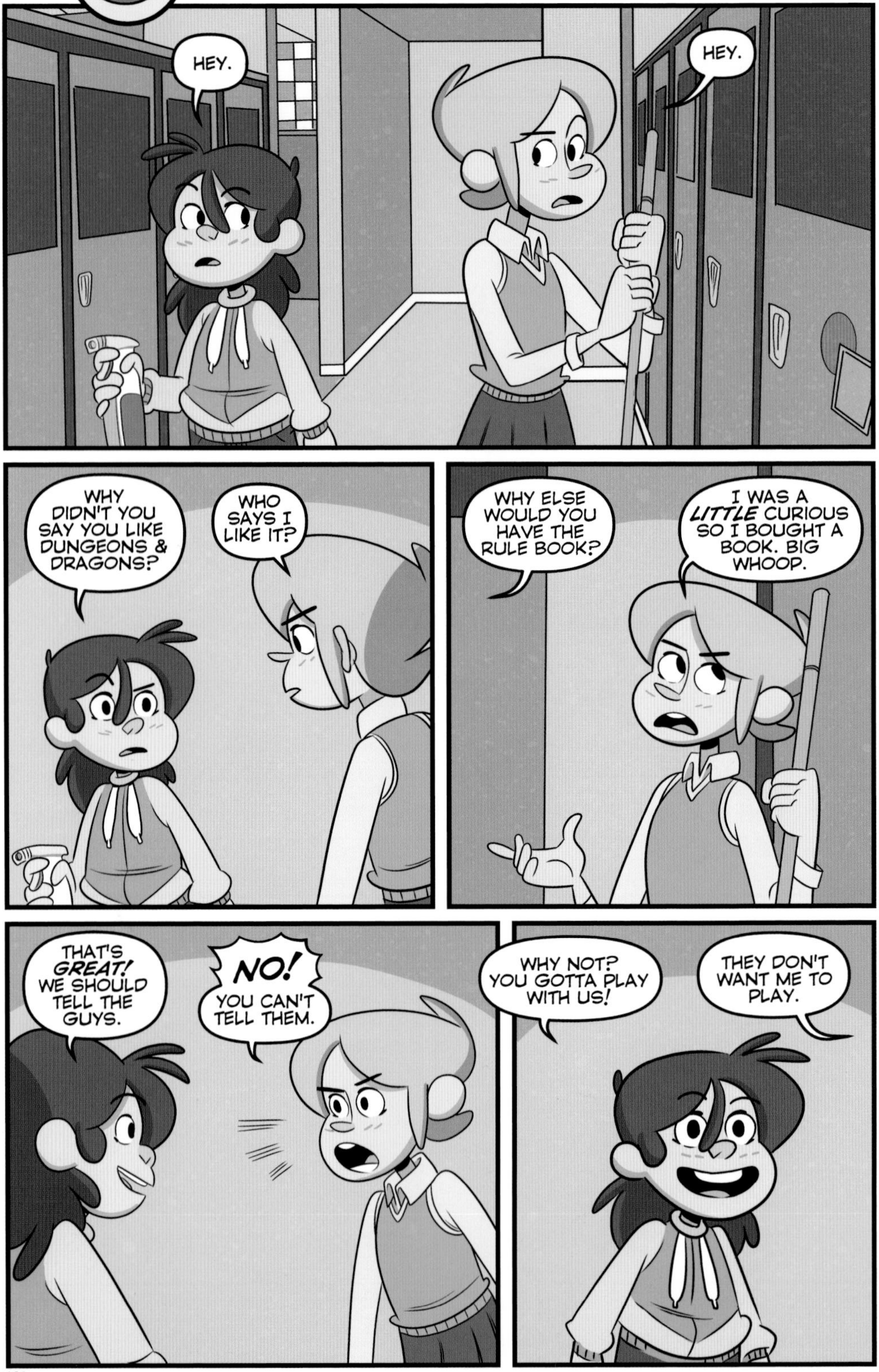

HEY.
HEY.
WHY DIDN'T YOU SAY YOU LIKE DUNGEONS & DRAGONS?
WHO SAYS I LIKE IT?
WHY ELSE WOULD YOU HAVE THE RULE BOOK?
I WAS A *LITTLE* CURIOUS SO I BOUGHT A BOOK. BIG WHOOP.
THAT'S *GREAT!* WE SHOULD TELL THE GUYS.
NO!
YOU CAN'T TELL THEM.
WHY NOT? YOU GOTTA PLAY WITH US!
THEY DON'T WANT ME TO PLAY.

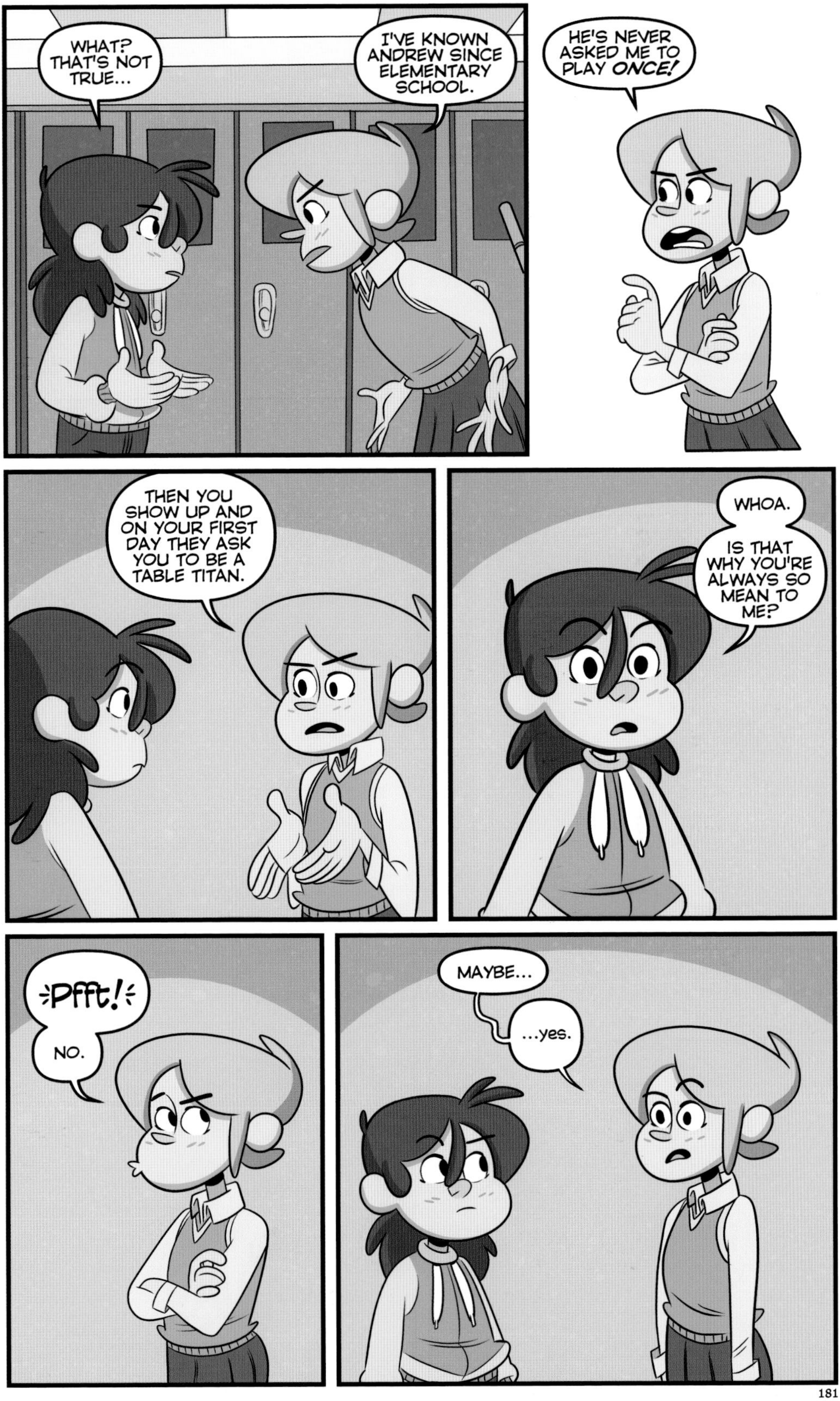
WHAT? THAT'S NOT TRUE...
I'VE KNOWN ANDREW SINCE ELEMENTARY SCHOOL.
HE'S NEVER ASKED ME TO PLAY *ONCE!*
THEN YOU SHOW UP AND ON YOUR FIRST DAY THEY ASK YOU TO BE A TABLE TITAN.
WHOA.
IS THAT WHY YOU'RE ALWAYS SO MEAN TO ME?
Pfft!
NO.
MAYBE...
...yes.

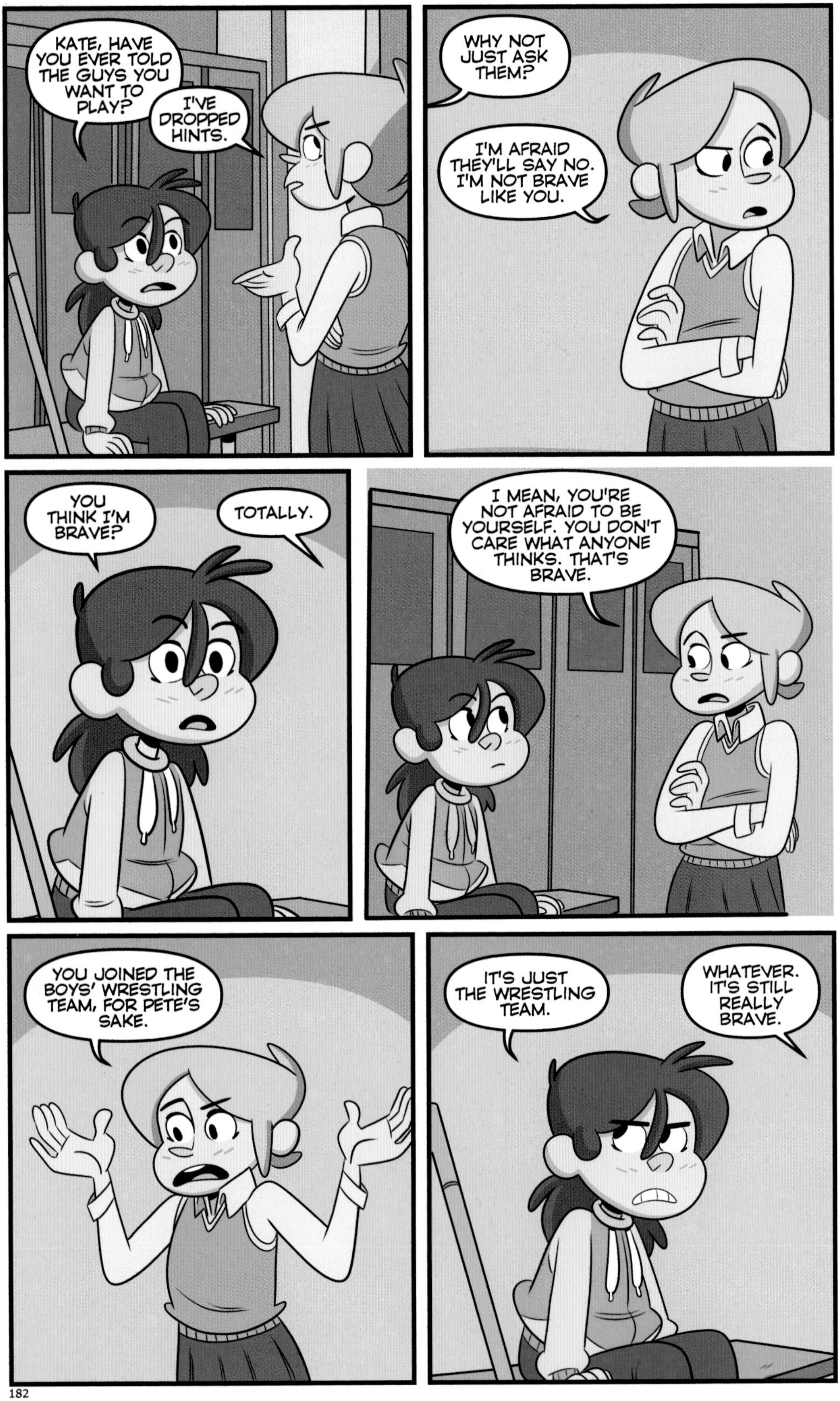
KATE, HAVE YOU EVER TOLD THE GUYS YOU WANT TO PLAY?
I'VE DROPPED HINTS.
WHY NOT JUST ASK THEM?
I'M AFRAID THEY'LL SAY NO. I'M NOT BRAVE LIKE YOU.
YOU THINK I'M BRAVE?
TOTALLY.
I MEAN, YOU'RE NOT AFRAID TO BE YOURSELF. YOU DON'T CARE WHAT ANYONE THINKS. THAT'S BRAVE.
YOU JOINED THE BOYS' WRESTLING TEAM, FOR PETE'S SAKE.
IT'S JUST THE WRESTLING TEAM.
WHATEVER. IT'S STILL REALLY BRAVE.

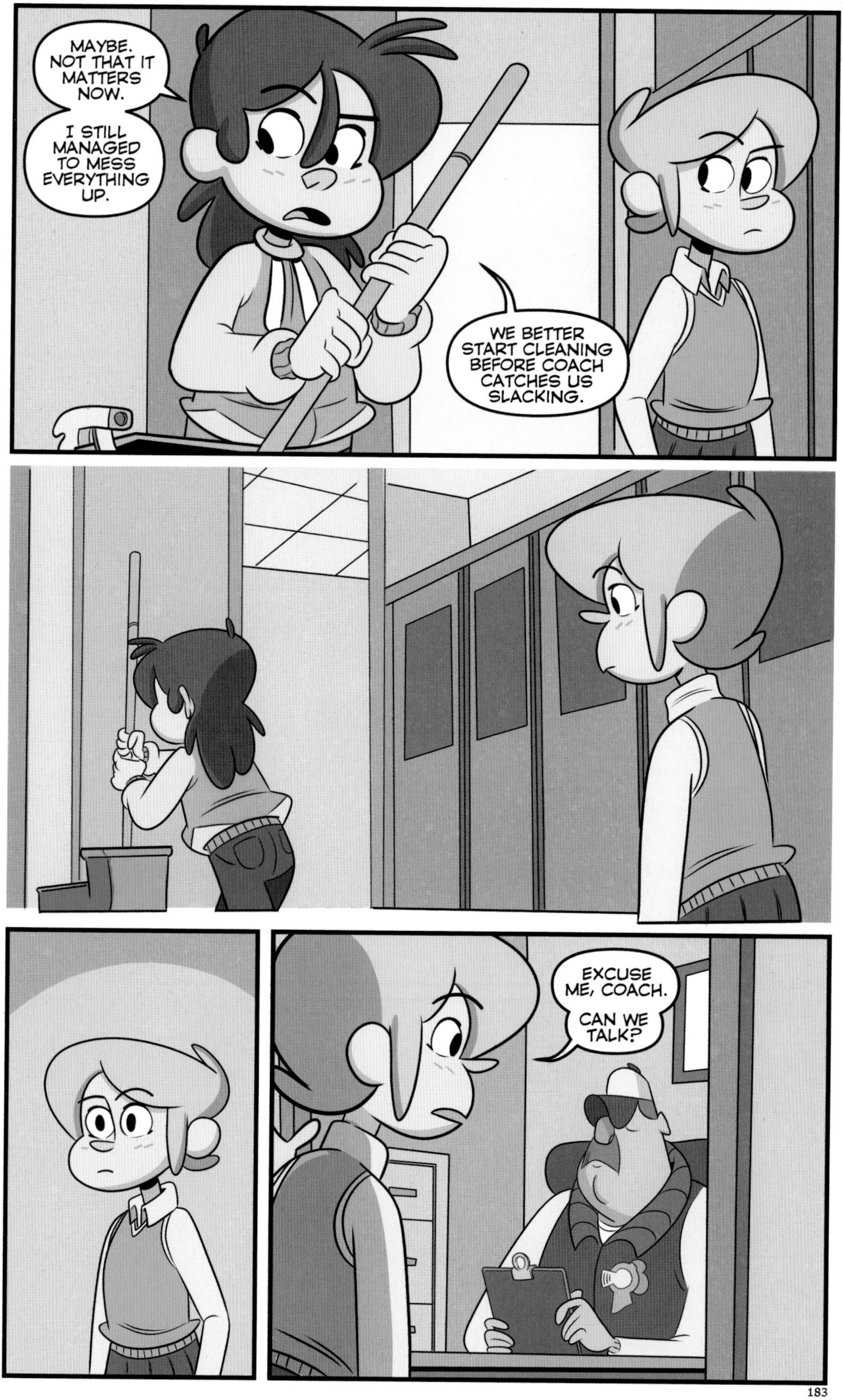
MAYBE. NOT THAT IT MATTERS NOW.
I STILL MANAGED TO MESS EVERYTHING UP.
WE BETTER START CLEANING BEFORE COACH CATCHES US SLACKING.
EXCUSE ME, COACH.
CAN WE TALK?

CHAPTER EIGHT

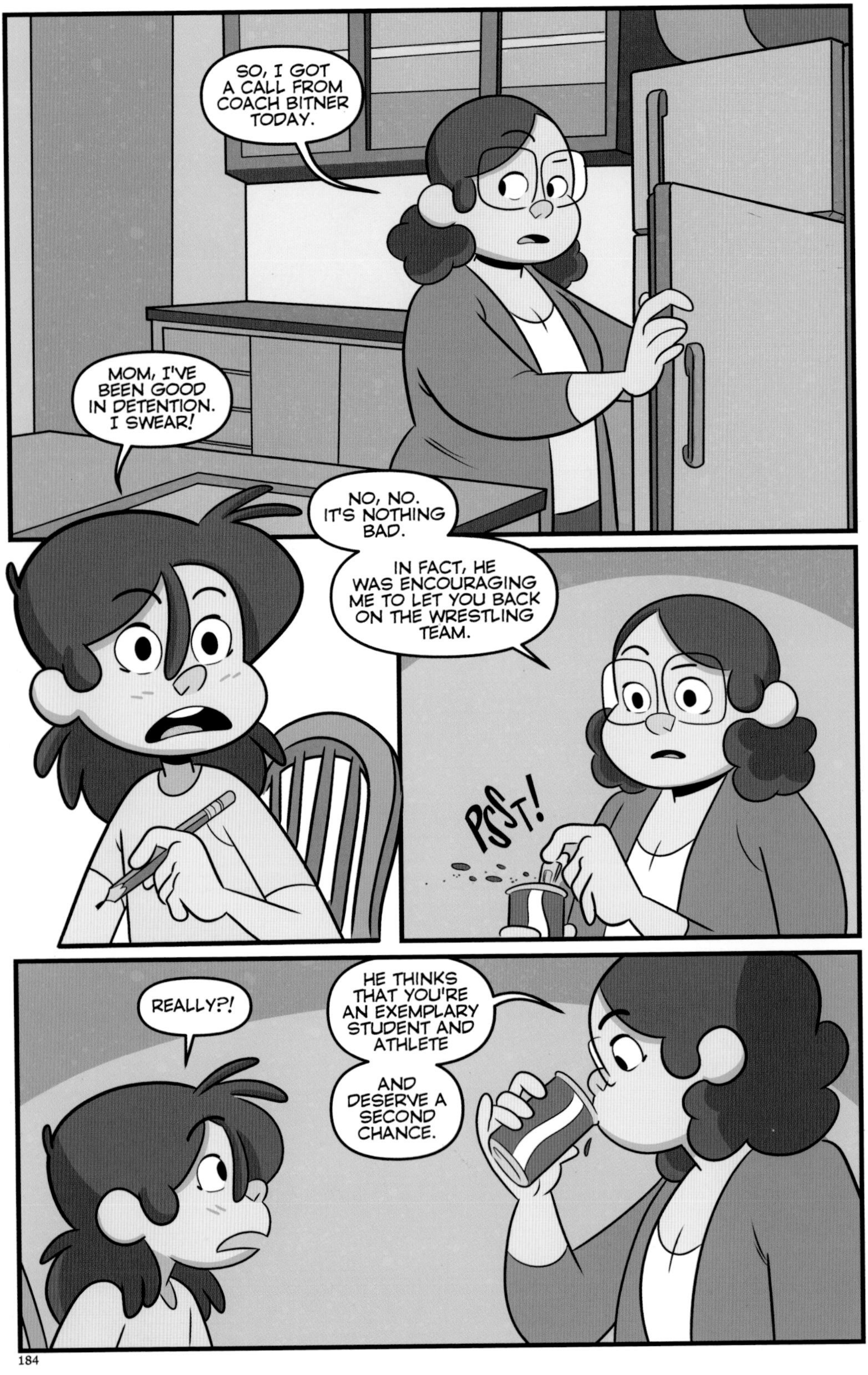
SO, I GOT A CALL FROM COACH BITNER TODAY.
MOM, I'VE BEEN GOOD IN DETENTION. I SWEAR!
NO, NO. IT'S NOTHING BAD.
IN FACT, HE WAS ENCOURAGING ME TO LET YOU BACK ON THE WRESTLING TEAM.
PSST!
REALLY?!
HE THINKS THAT YOU'RE AN EXEMPLARY STUDENT AND ATHLETE
AND DESERVE A SECOND CHANCE.

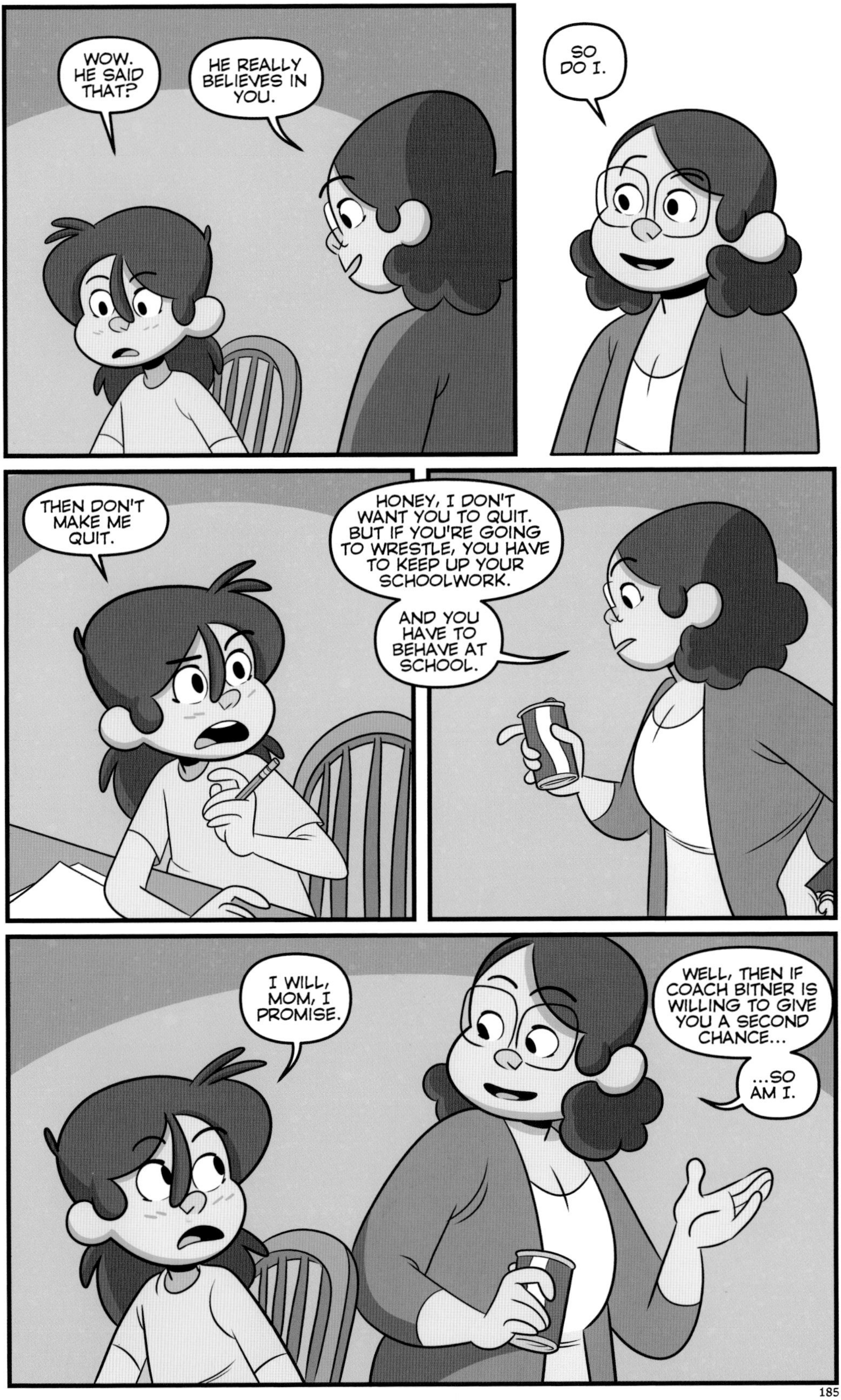
WOW. HE SAID THAT?
HE REALLY BELIEVES IN YOU.
SO DO I.
THEN DON'T MAKE ME QUIT.
HONEY, I DON'T WANT YOU TO QUIT. BUT IF YOU'RE GOING TO WRESTLE, YOU HAVE TO KEEP UP YOUR SCHOOLWORK.
AND YOU HAVE TO BEHAVE AT SCHOOL.
I WILL, MOM, I PROMISE.
WELL, THEN IF COACH BITNER IS WILLING TO GIVE YOU A SECOND CHANCE...
...SO AM I.

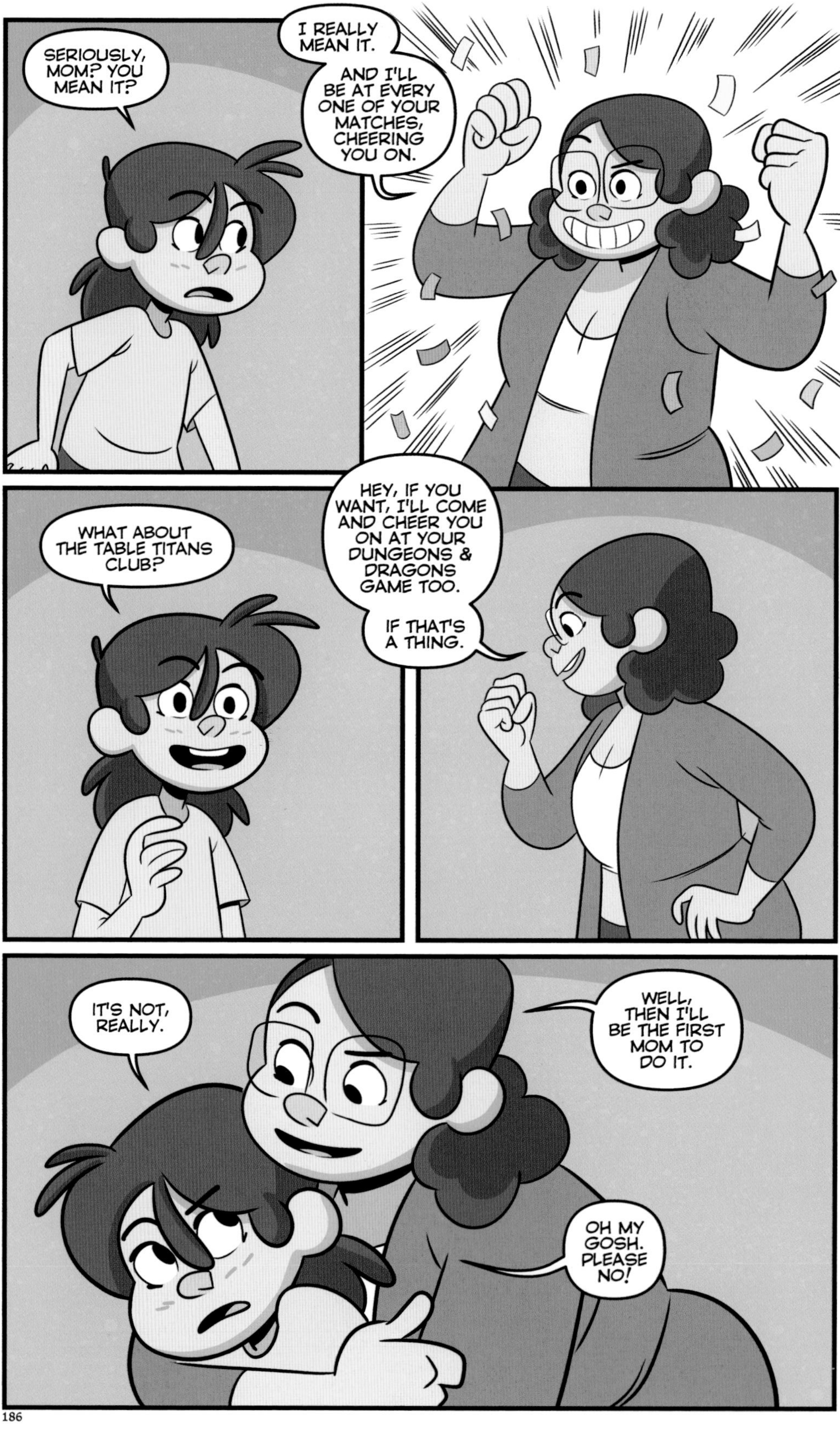
SERIOUSLY, MOM? YOU MEAN IT?
I REALLY MEAN IT.
AND I'LL BE AT EVERY ONE OF YOUR MATCHES, CHEERING YOU ON.
WHAT ABOUT THE TABLE TITANS CLUB?
HEY, IF YOU WANT, I'LL COME AND CHEER YOU ON AT YOUR DUNGEONS & DRAGONS GAME TOO.
IF THAT'S A THING.
IT'S NOT, REALLY.
WELL, THEN I'LL BE THE FIRST MOM TO DO IT.
OH MY GOSH. PLEASE NO!

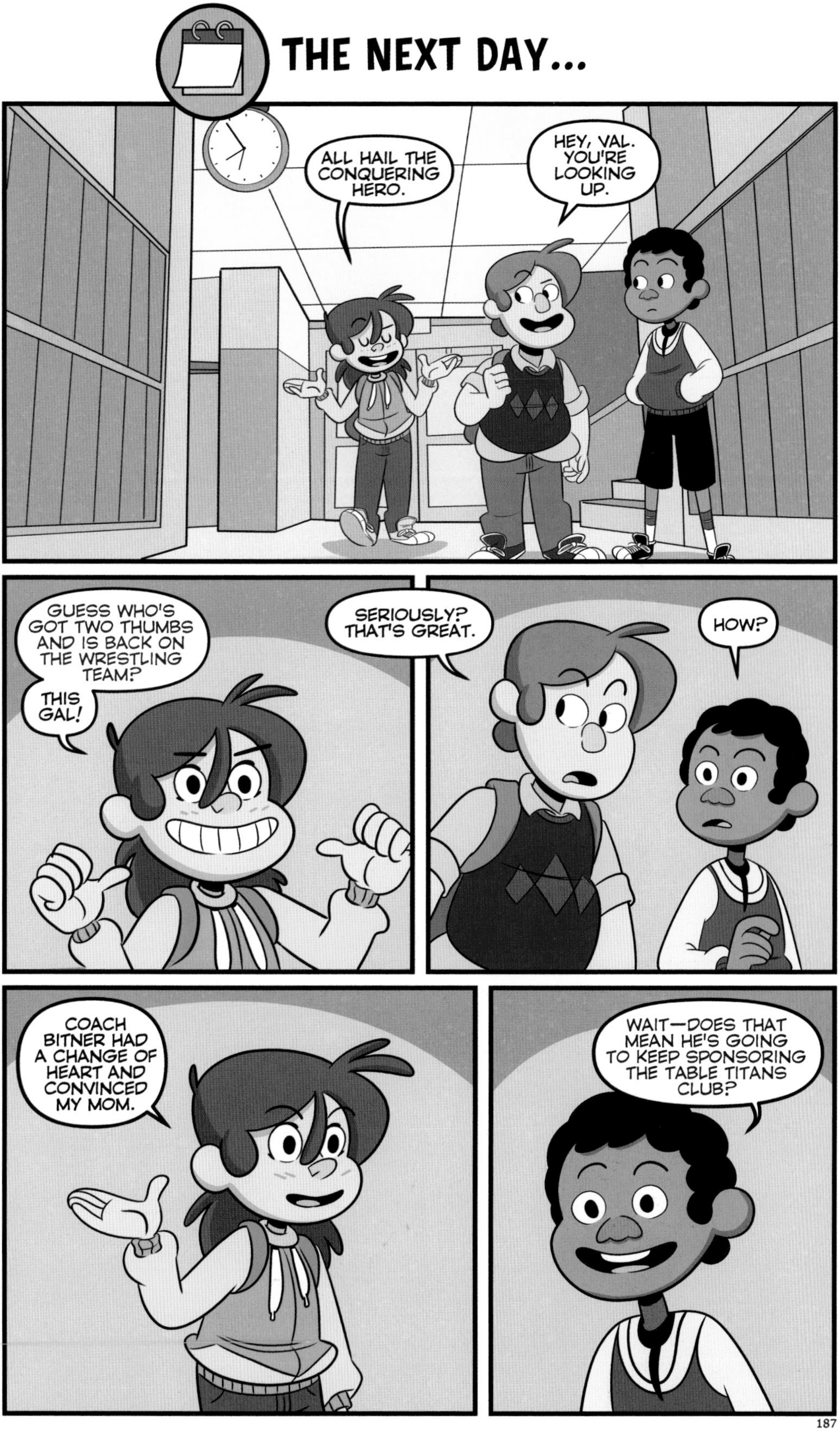
THE NEXT DAY...
ALL HAIL THE CONQUERING HERO.
HEY, VAL. YOU'RE LOOKING UP.
GUESS WHO'S GOT TWO THUMBS AND IS BACK ON THE WRESTLING TEAM?
THIS GAL!
SERIOUSLY? THAT'S GREAT.
HOW?
COACH BITNER HAD A CHANGE OF HEART AND CONVINCED MY MOM.
WAIT—DOES THAT MEAN HE'S GOING TO KEEP SPONSORING THE TABLE TITANS CLUB?

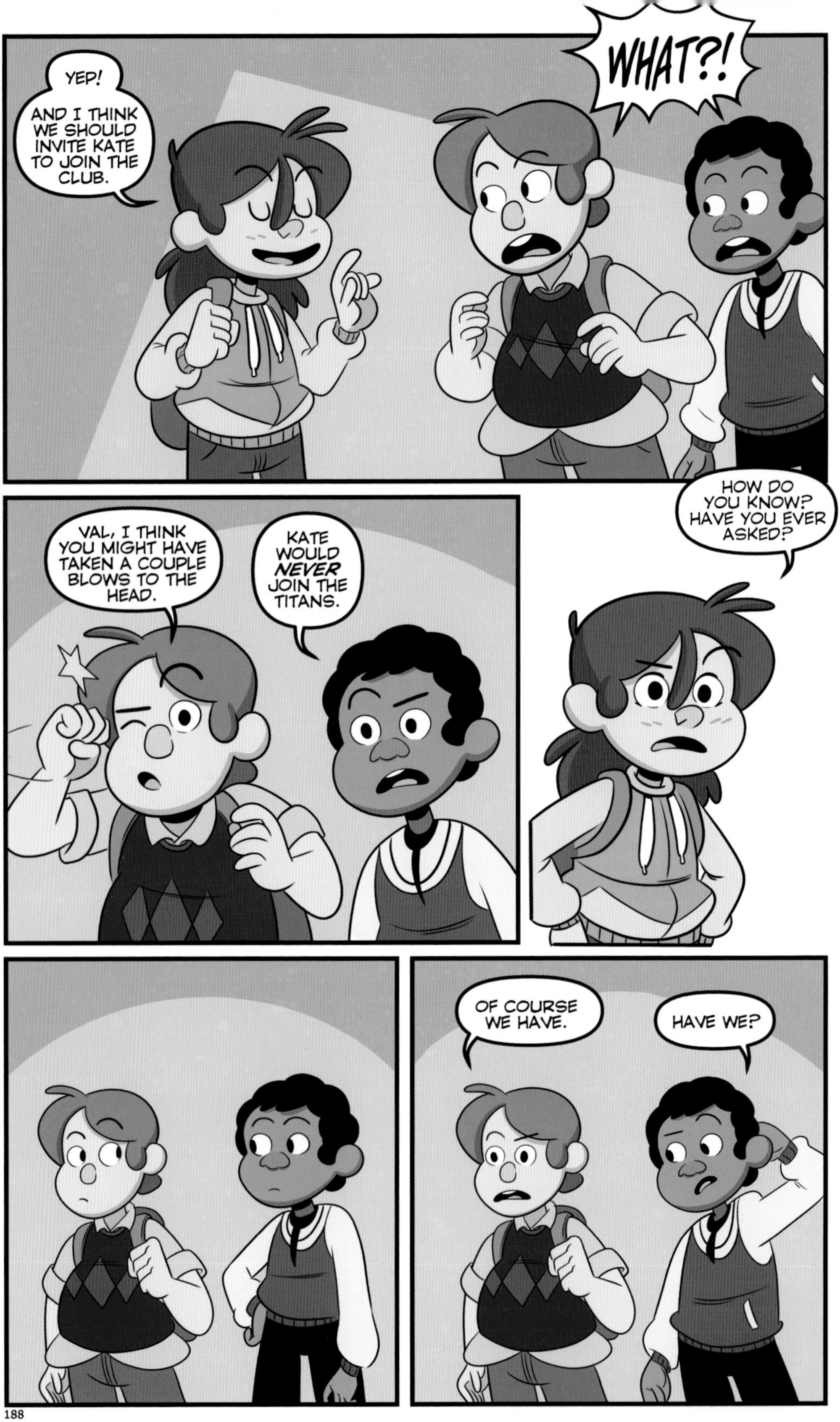
YEP!
AND I THINK WE SHOULD INVITE KATE TO JOIN THE CLUB.
WHAT?!
VAL, I THINK YOU MIGHT HAVE TAKEN A COUPLE BLOWS TO THE HEAD.
KATE WOULD *NEVER* JOIN THE TITANS.
HOW DO YOU KNOW? HAVE YOU EVER ASKED?
OF COURSE WE HAVE.
HAVE WE?

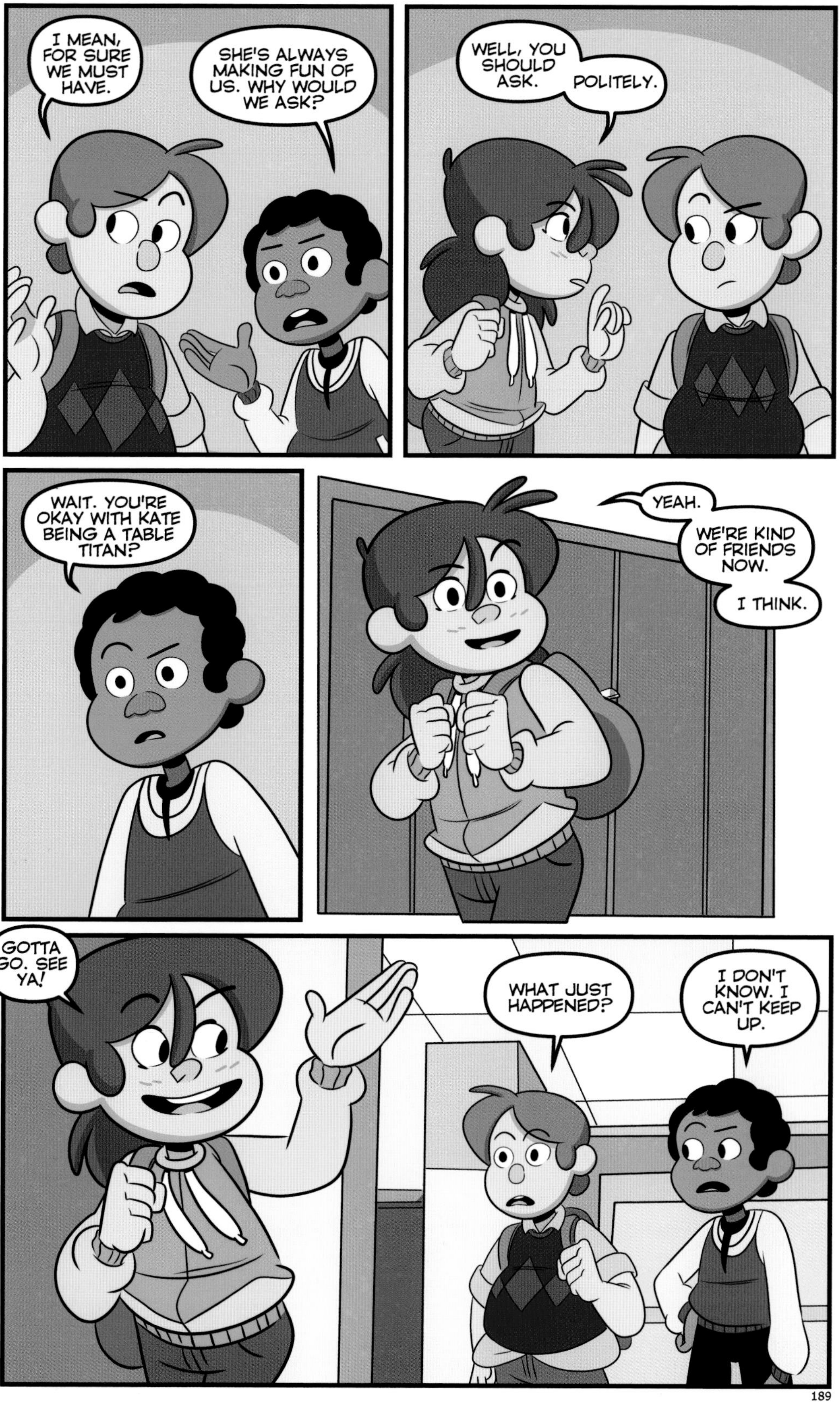
I MEAN, FOR SURE WE MUST HAVE.
SHE'S ALWAYS MAKING FUN OF US. WHY WOULD WE ASK?
WELL, YOU SHOULD ASK.
POLITELY.
WAIT. YOU'RE OKAY WITH KATE BEING A TABLE TITAN?
YEAH.
WE'RE KIND OF FRIENDS NOW.
I THINK.
GOTTA GO. SEE YA!
WHAT JUST HAPPENED?
I DON'T KNOW. I CAN'T KEEP UP.

WRESTLING PRACTICE

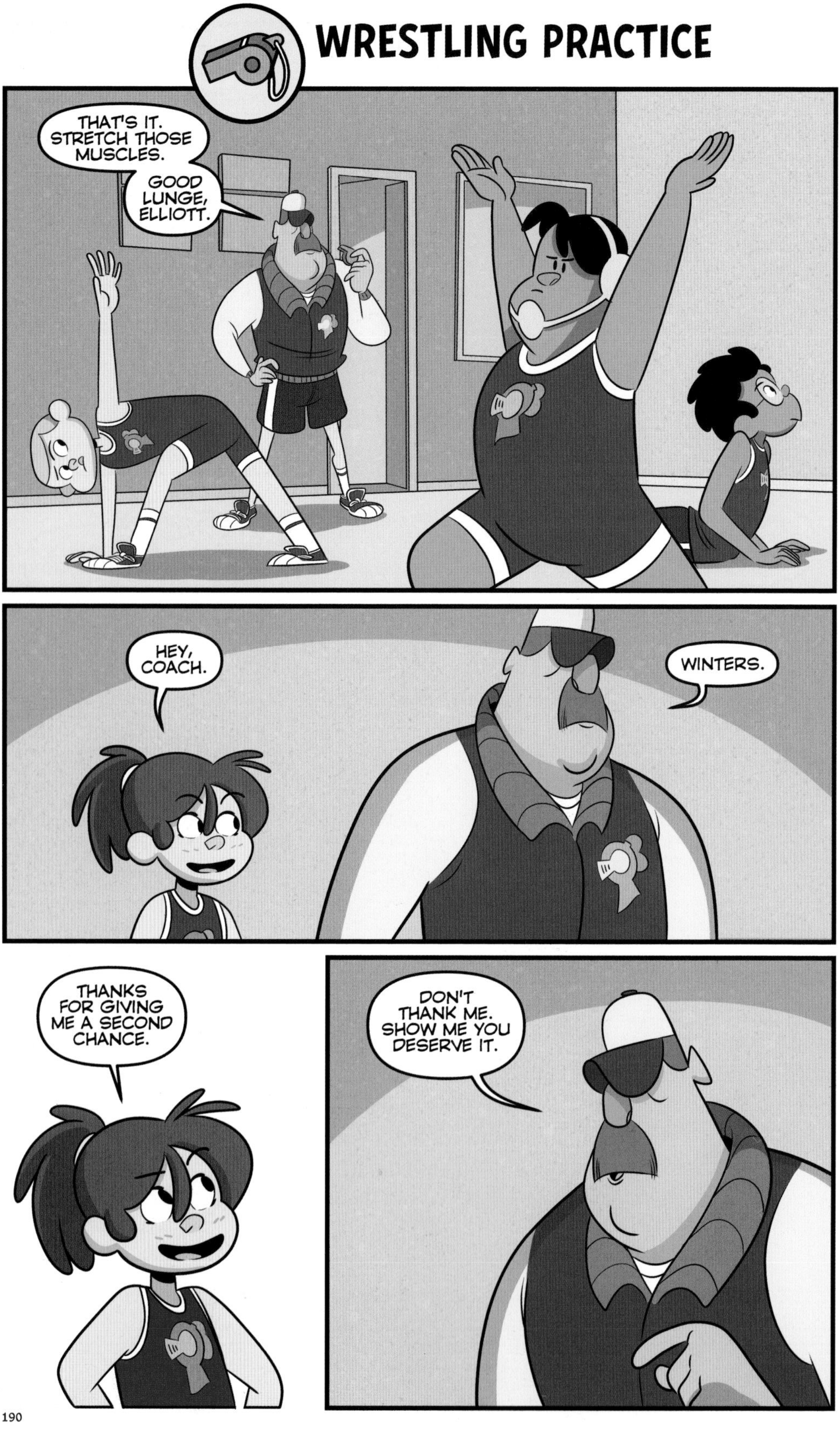

THAT'S IT. STRETCH THOSE MUSCLES.
GOOD LUNGE, ELLIOTT.
HEY, COACH.
WINTERS.
THANKS FOR GIVING ME A SECOND CHANCE.
DON'T THANK ME. SHOW ME YOU DESERVE IT.

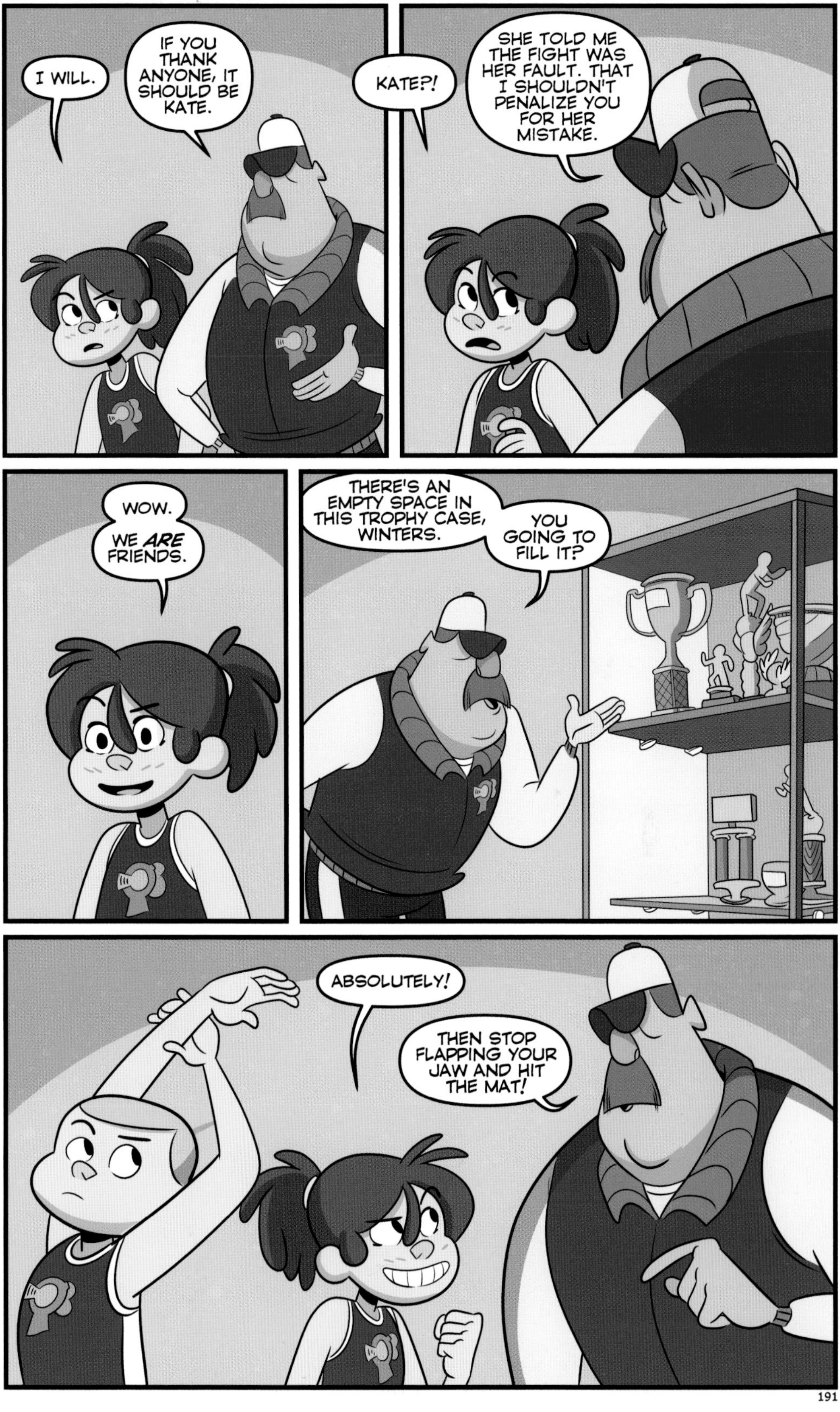
I WILL.
IF YOU THANK ANYONE, IT SHOULD BE KATE.
KATE?!
SHE TOLD ME THE FIGHT WAS HER FAULT. THAT I SHOULDN'T PENALIZE YOU FOR HER MISTAKE.
WOW.
WE *ARE* FRIENDS.
THERE'S AN EMPTY SPACE IN THIS TROPHY CASE, WINTERS.
YOU GOING TO FILL IT?
ABSOLUTELY!
THEN STOP FLAPPING YOUR JAW AND HIT THE MAT!

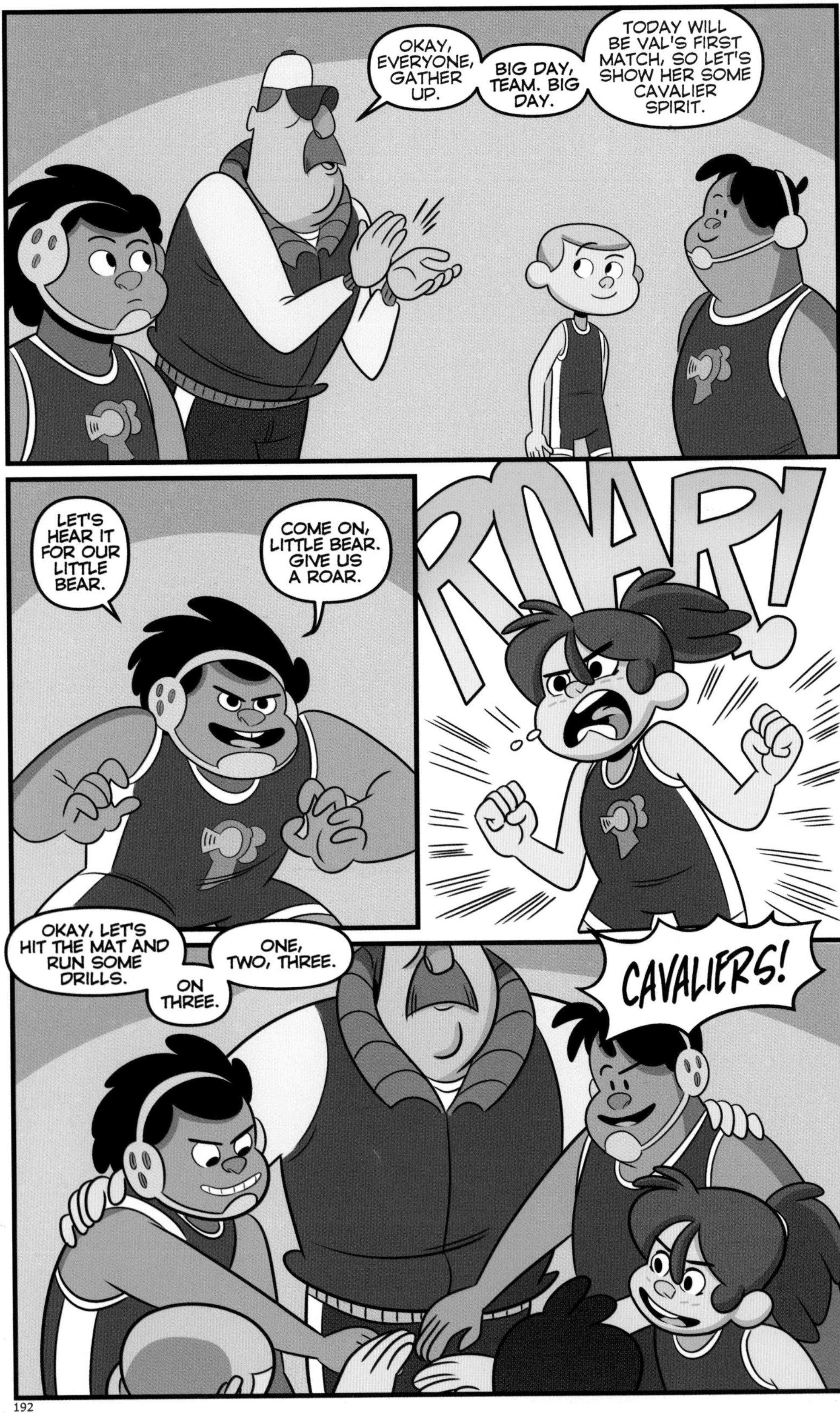
OKAY, EVERYONE, GATHER UP.
BIG DAY, TEAM. BIG DAY.
TODAY WILL BE VAL'S FIRST MATCH, SO LET'S SHOW HER SOME CAVALIER SPIRIT.
LET'S HEAR IT FOR OUR LITTLE BEAR.
COME ON, LITTLE BEAR. GIVE US A ROAR.
ROAR!
OKAY, LET'S HIT THE MAT AND RUN SOME DRILLS.
ON THREE.
ONE, TWO, THREE.
CAVALIERS!

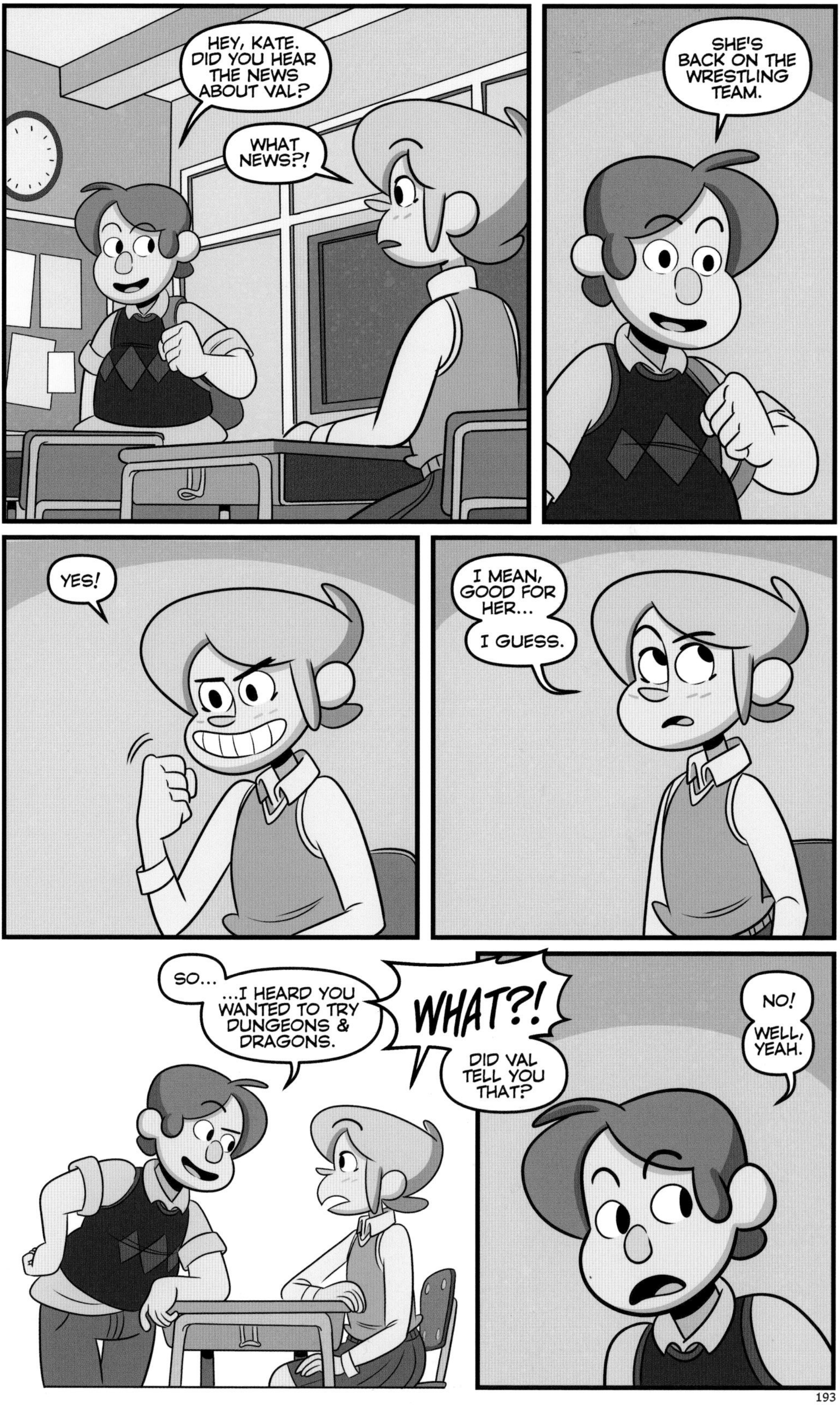
HEY, KATE. DID YOU HEAR THE NEWS ABOUT VAL?
WHAT NEWS?!
SHE'S BACK ON THE WRESTLING TEAM.
YES!
I MEAN, GOOD FOR HER...
I GUESS.
SO...
...I HEARD YOU WANTED TO TRY DUNGEONS & DRAGONS.
WHAT?!
DID VAL TELL YOU THAT?
NO!
WELL, YEAH.

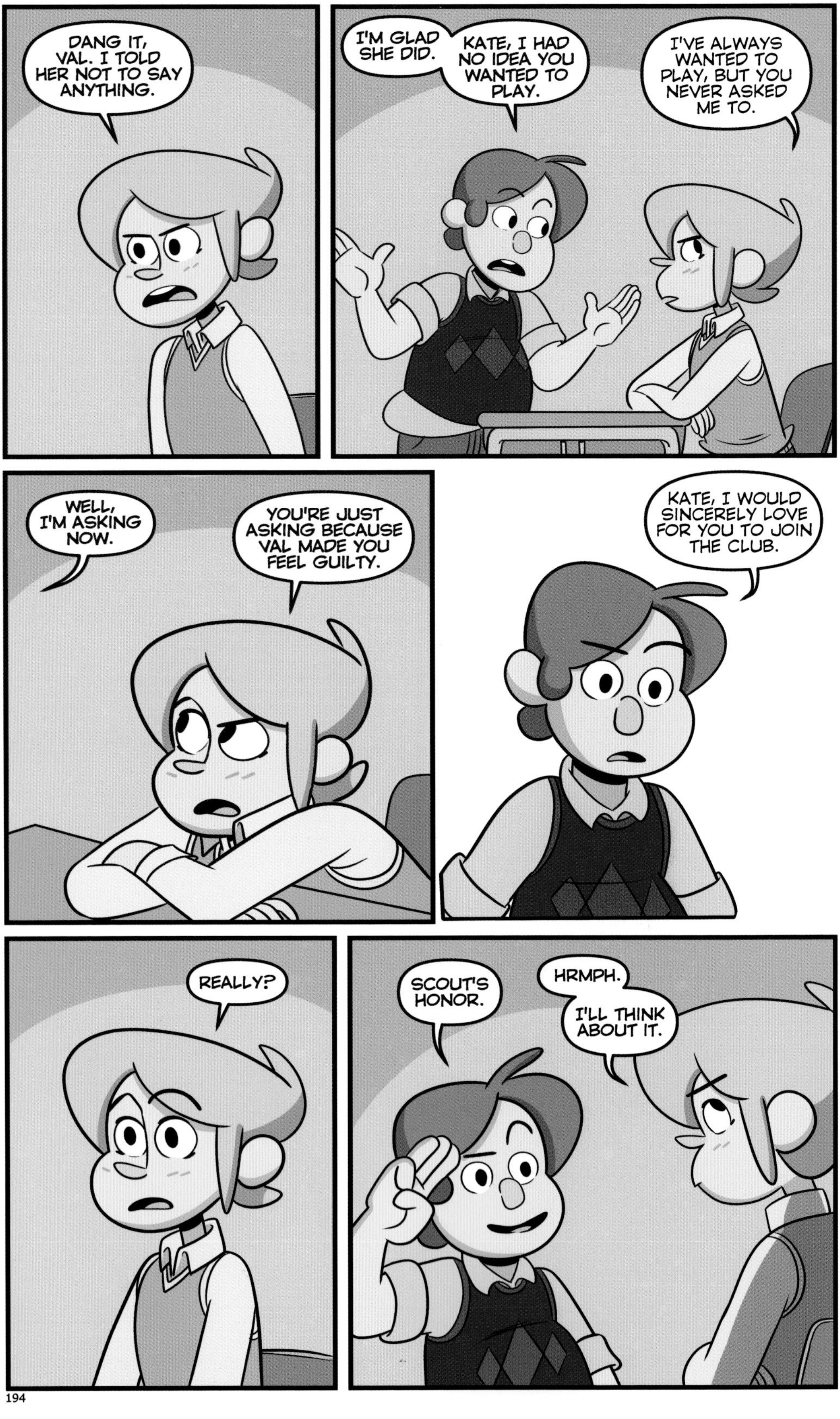
DANG IT, VAL. I TOLD HER NOT TO SAY ANYTHING.
I'M GLAD SHE DID.
KATE, I HAD NO IDEA YOU WANTED TO PLAY.
I'VE ALWAYS WANTED TO PLAY, BUT YOU NEVER ASKED ME TO.
WELL, I'M ASKING NOW.
YOU'RE JUST ASKING BECAUSE VAL MADE YOU FEEL GUILTY.
KATE, I WOULD SINCERELY LOVE FOR YOU TO JOIN THE CLUB.
REALLY?
SCOUT'S HONOR.
HRMPH.
I'LL THINK ABOUT IT.

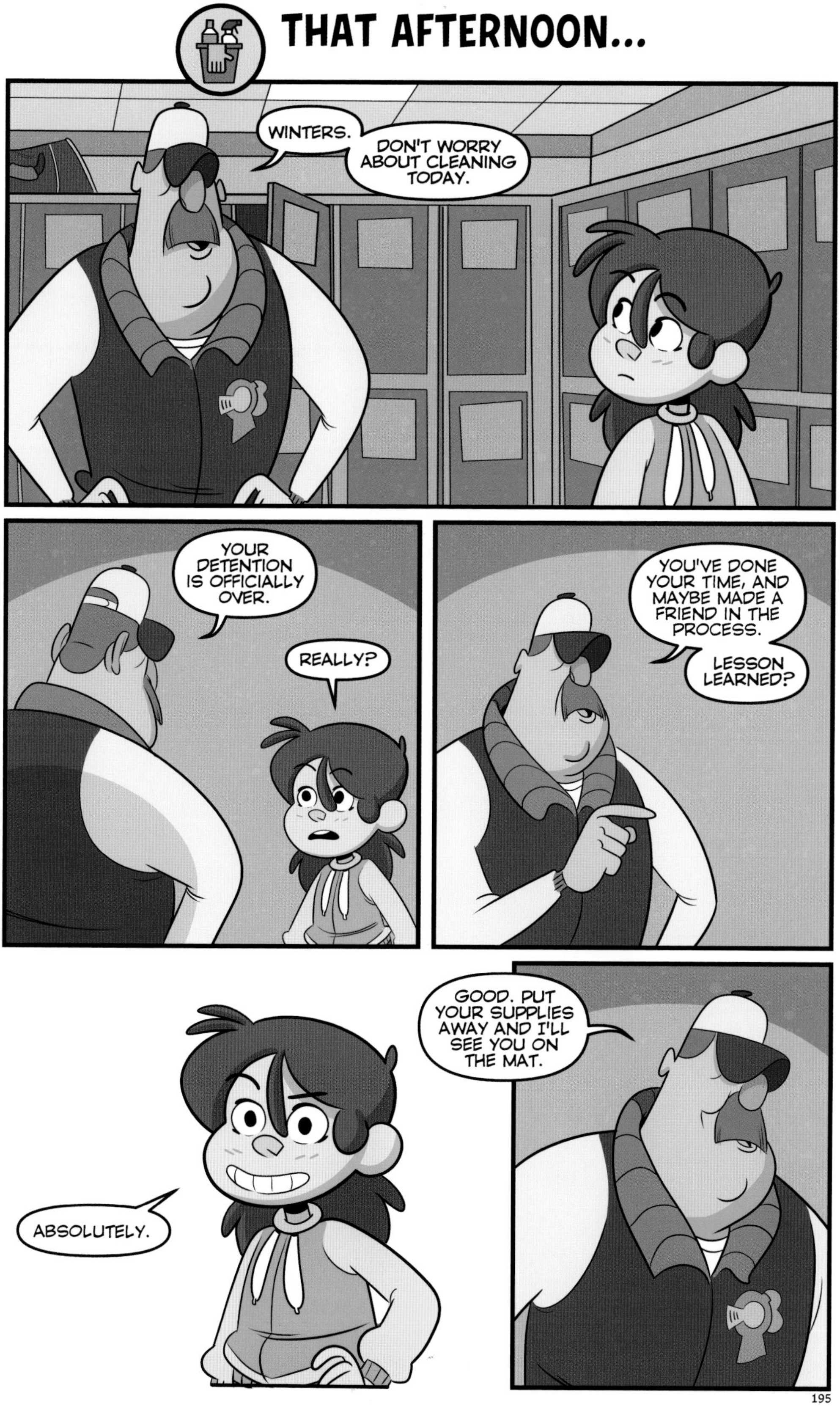
THAT AFTERNOON...
WINTERS.
DON'T WORRY ABOUT CLEANING TODAY.
YOUR DETENTION IS OFFICIALLY OVER.
REALLY?
YOU'VE DONE YOUR TIME, AND MAYBE MADE A FRIEND IN THE PROCESS.
LESSON LEARNED?
GOOD. PUT YOUR SUPPLIES AWAY AND I'LL SEE YOU ON THE MAT.
ABSOLUTELY.

THE BIG MATCH!

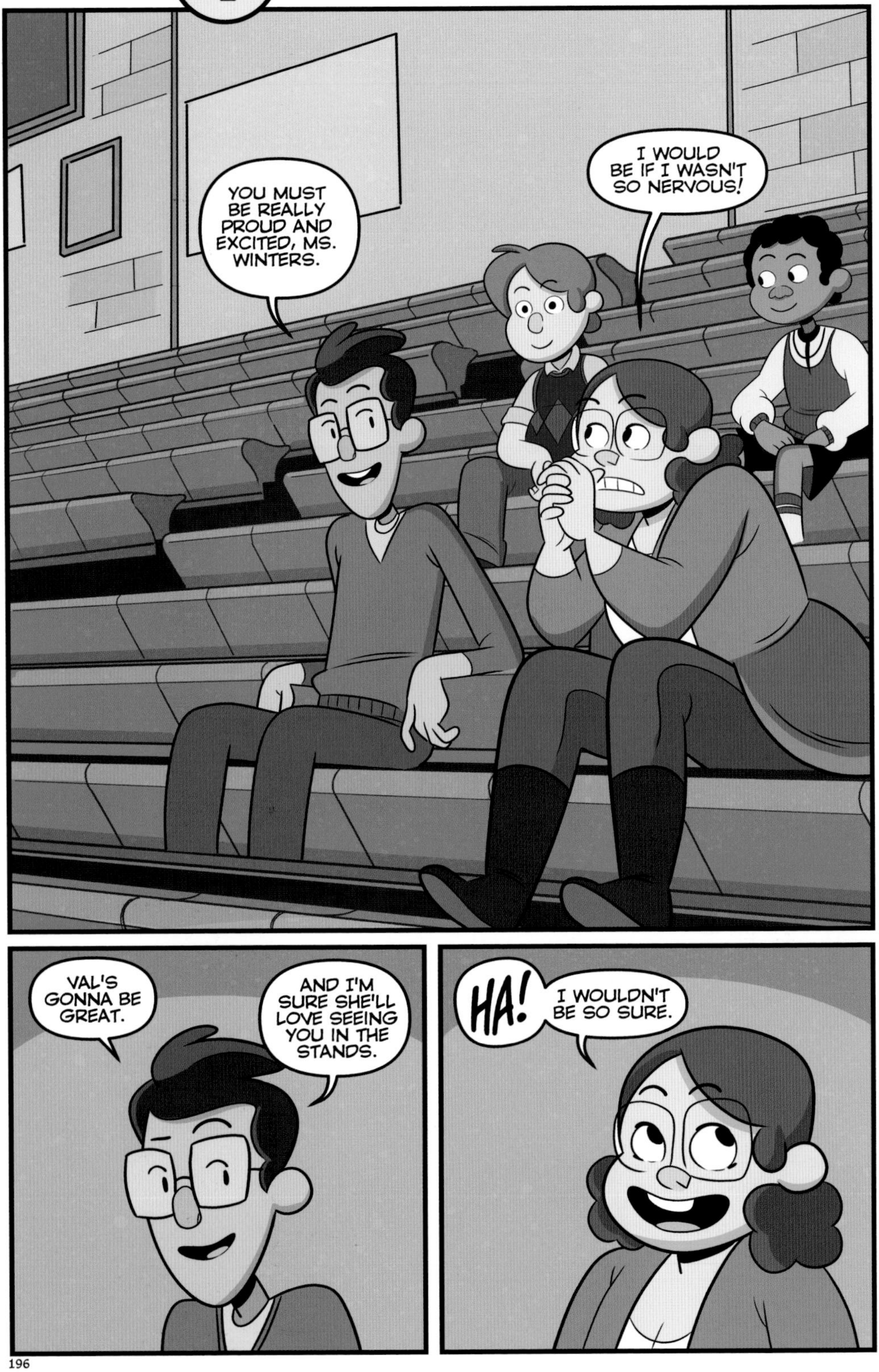
YOU MUST BE REALLY PROUD AND EXCITED, MS. WINTERS.
I WOULD BE IF I WASN'T SO NERVOUS!
VAL'S GONNA BE GREAT.
AND I'M SURE SHE'LL LOVE SEEING YOU IN THE STANDS.
HA!
I WOULDN'T BE SO SURE.

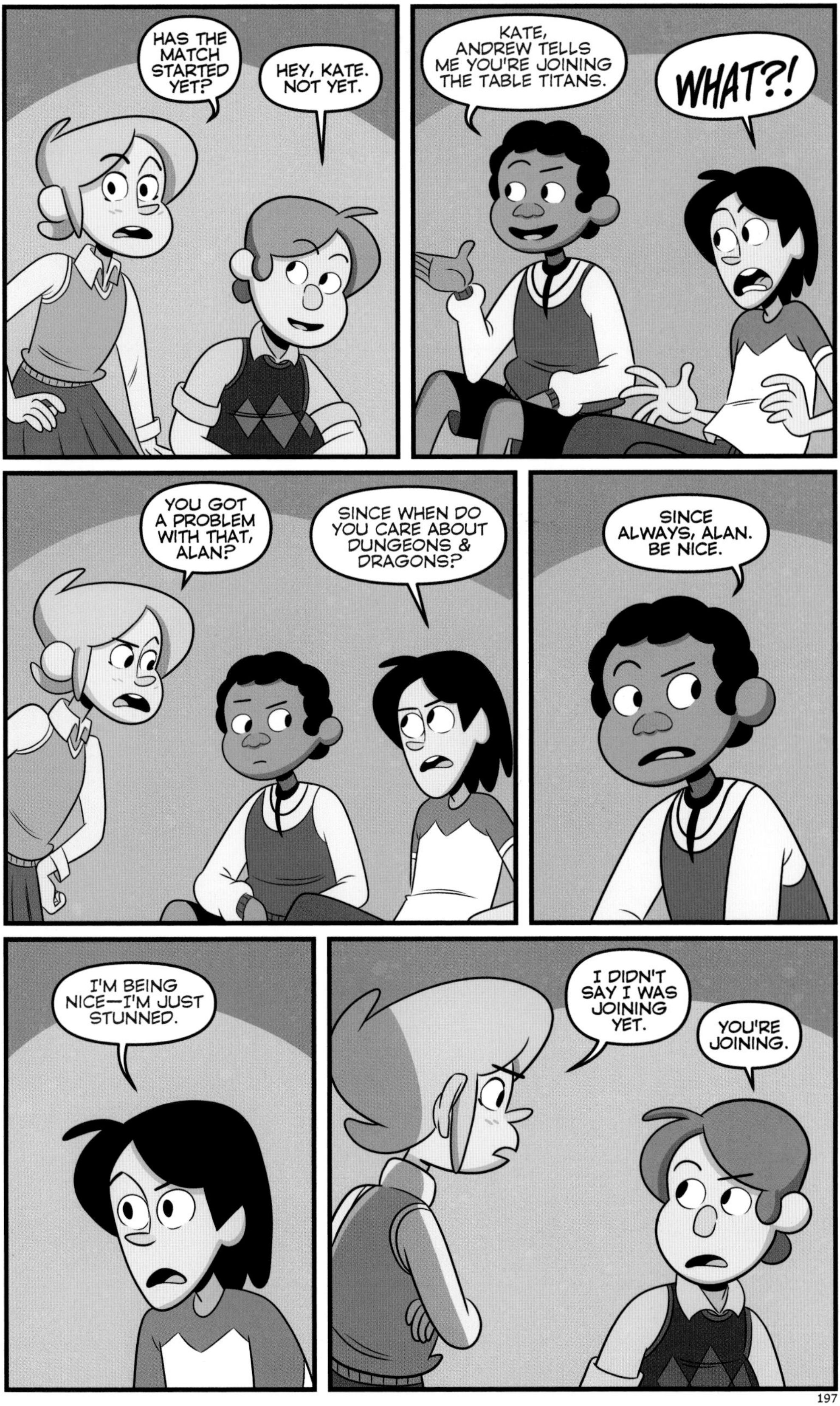
HAS THE MATCH STARTED YET?
HEY, KATE. NOT YET.
KATE, ANDREW TELLS ME YOU'RE JOINING THE TABLE TITANS.
WHAT?!
YOU GOT A PROBLEM WITH THAT, ALAN?
SINCE WHEN DO YOU CARE ABOUT DUNGEONS & DRAGONS?
SINCE ALWAYS, ALAN. BE NICE.
I'M BEING NICE—I'M JUST STUNNED.
I DIDN'T SAY I WAS JOINING YET.
YOU'RE JOINING.

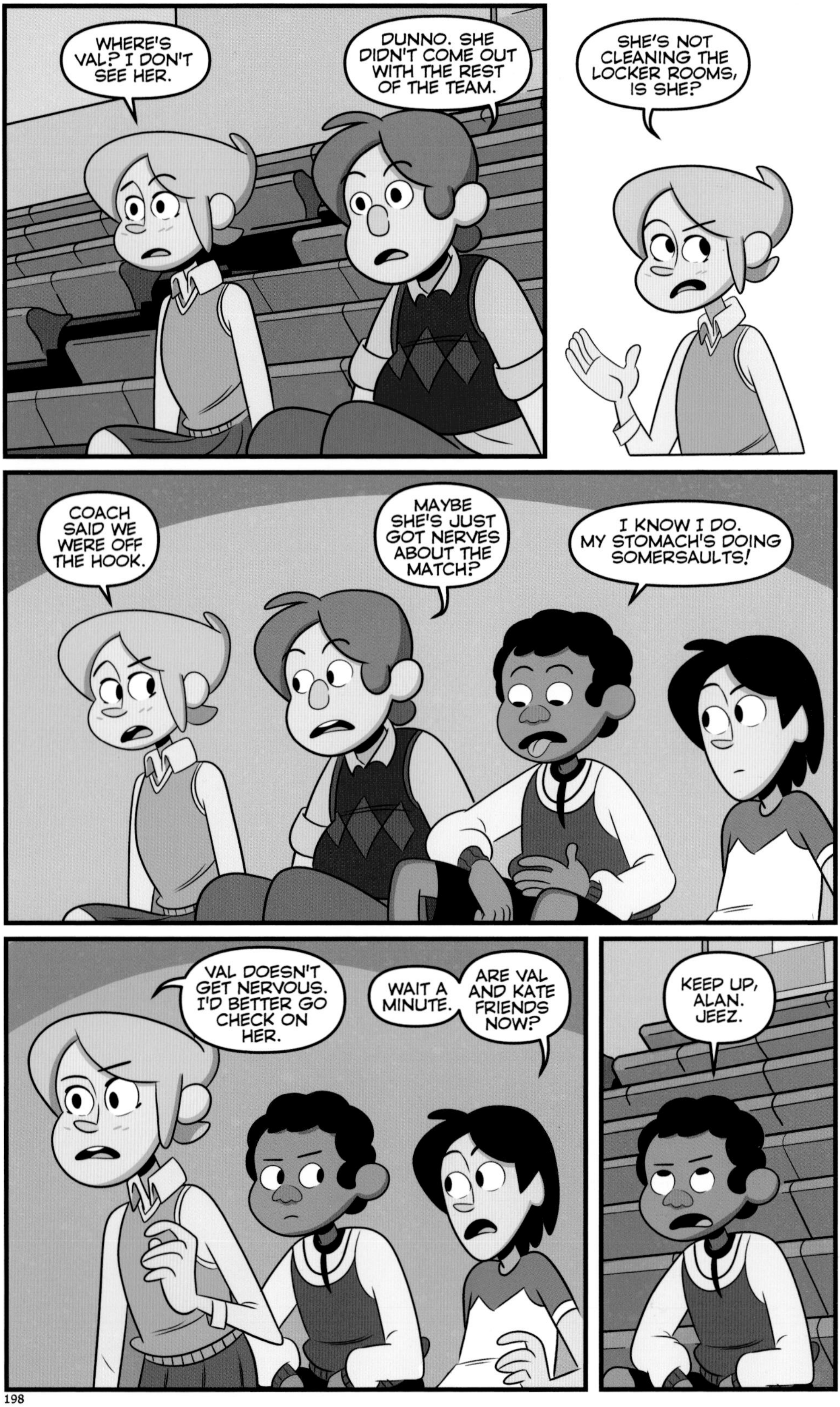

WHERE'S VAL? I DON'T SEE HER.
DUNNO. SHE DIDN'T COME OUT WITH THE REST OF THE TEAM.
SHE'S NOT CLEANING THE LOCKER ROOMS, IS SHE?
COACH SAID WE WERE OFF THE HOOK.
MAYBE SHE'S JUST GOT NERVES ABOUT THE MATCH?
I KNOW I DO. MY STOMACH'S DOING SOMERSAULTS!
VAL DOESN'T GET NERVOUS. I'D BETTER GO CHECK ON HER.
WAIT A MINUTE.
ARE VAL AND KATE FRIENDS NOW?
KEEP UP, ALAN. JEEZ.

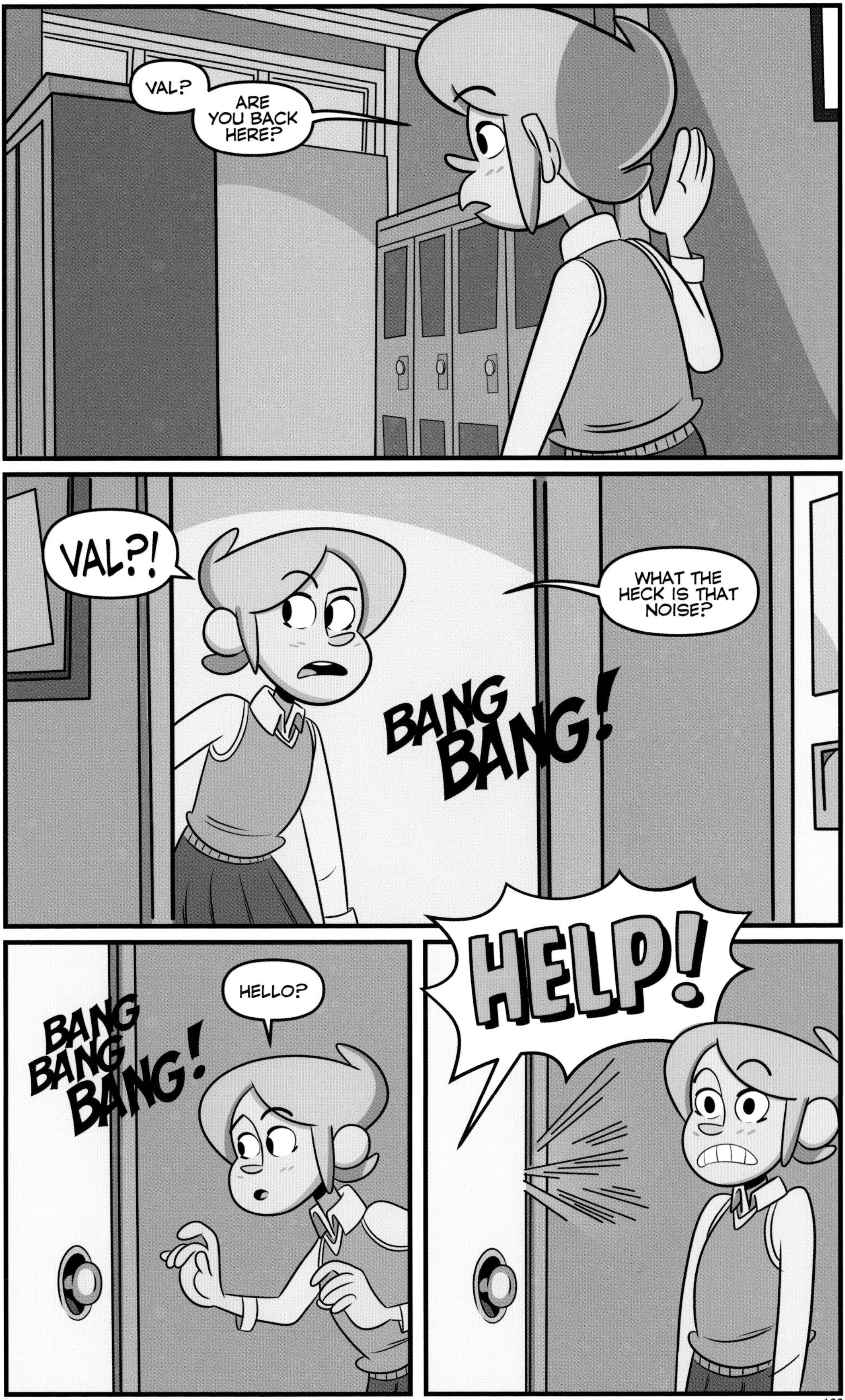
VAL?
ARE YOU BACK HERE?
VAL?!
WHAT THE HECK IS THAT NOISE?
BANG BANG!
BANG BANG BANG!
HELLO?
HELP!

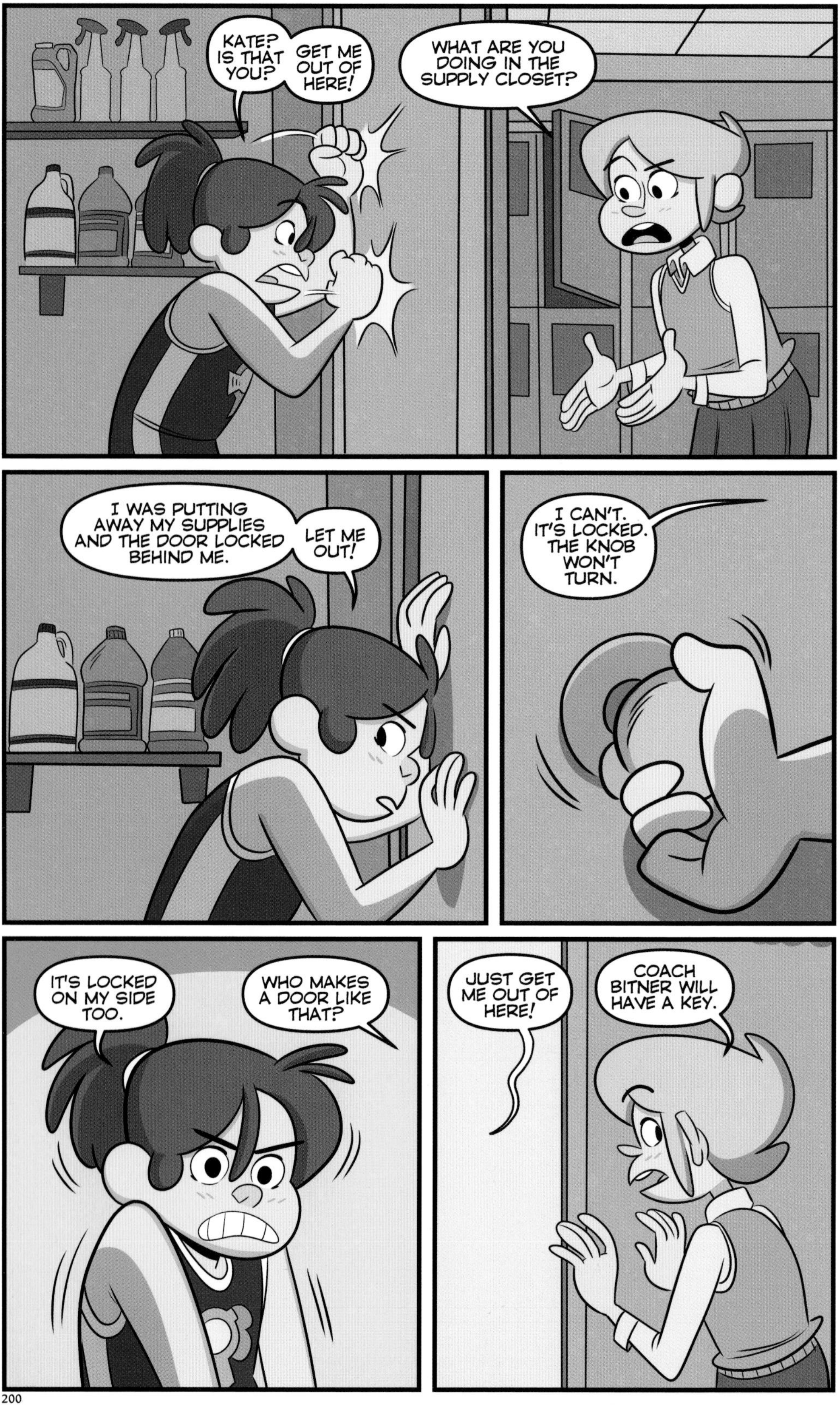
KATE? IS THAT YOU?
GET ME OUT OF HERE!
WHAT ARE YOU DOING IN THE SUPPLY CLOSET?
I WAS PUTTING AWAY MY SUPPLIES AND THE DOOR LOCKED BEHIND ME.
LET ME OUT!
I CAN'T. IT'S LOCKED. THE KNOB WON'T TURN.
IT'S LOCKED ON MY SIDE TOO.
WHO MAKES A DOOR LIKE THAT?
JUST GET ME OUT OF HERE!
COACH BITNER WILL HAVE A KEY.

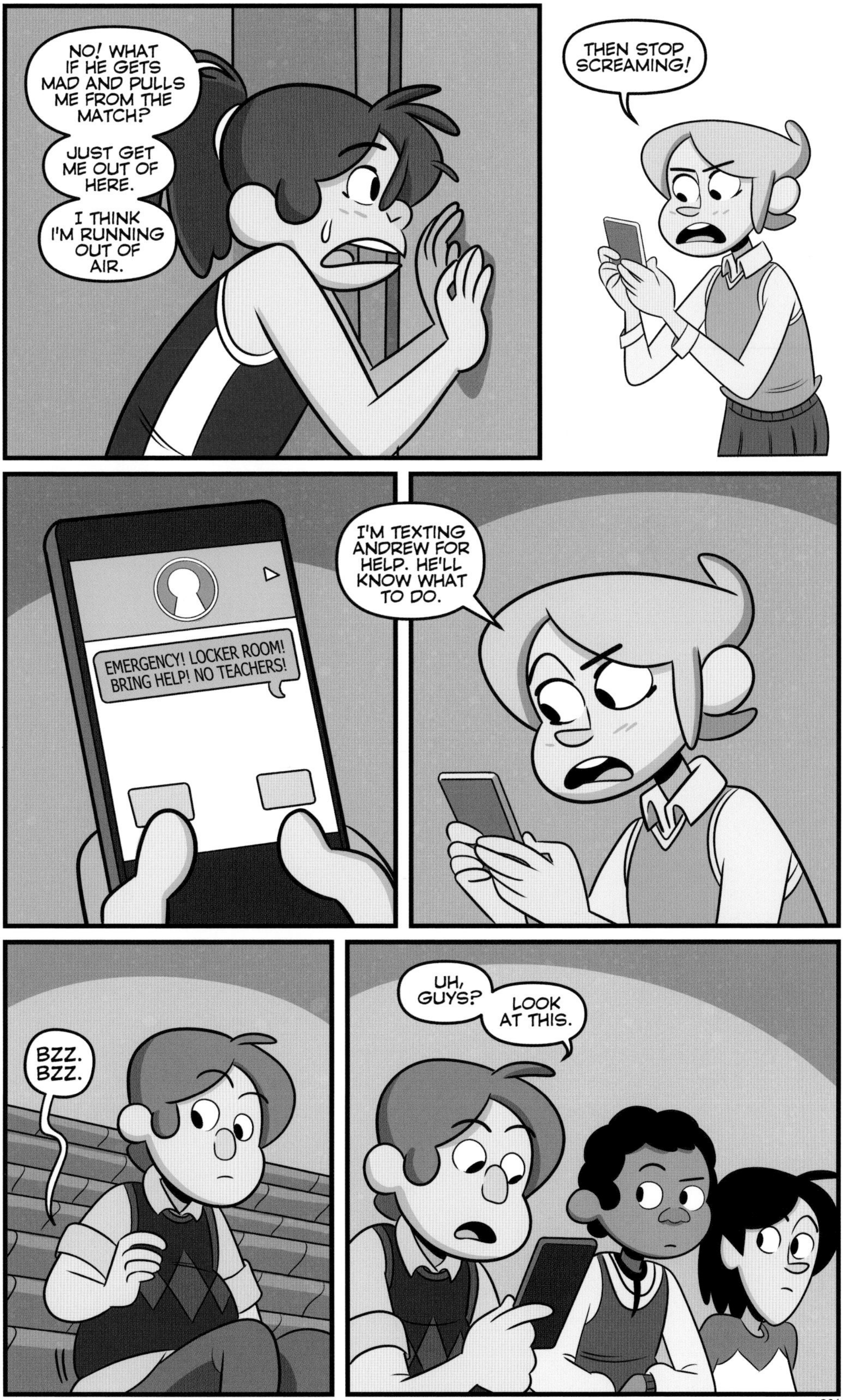

NO! WHAT IF HE GETS MAD AND PULLS ME FROM THE MATCH?
JUST GET ME OUT OF HERE.
I THINK I'M RUNNING OUT OF AIR.
THEN STOP SCREAMING!
EMERGENCY! LOCKER ROOM! BRING HELP! NO TEACHERS!
I'M TEXTING ANDREW FOR HELP. HE'LL KNOW WHAT TO DO.
BZZ. BZZ.
UH, GUYS?
LOOK AT THIS.

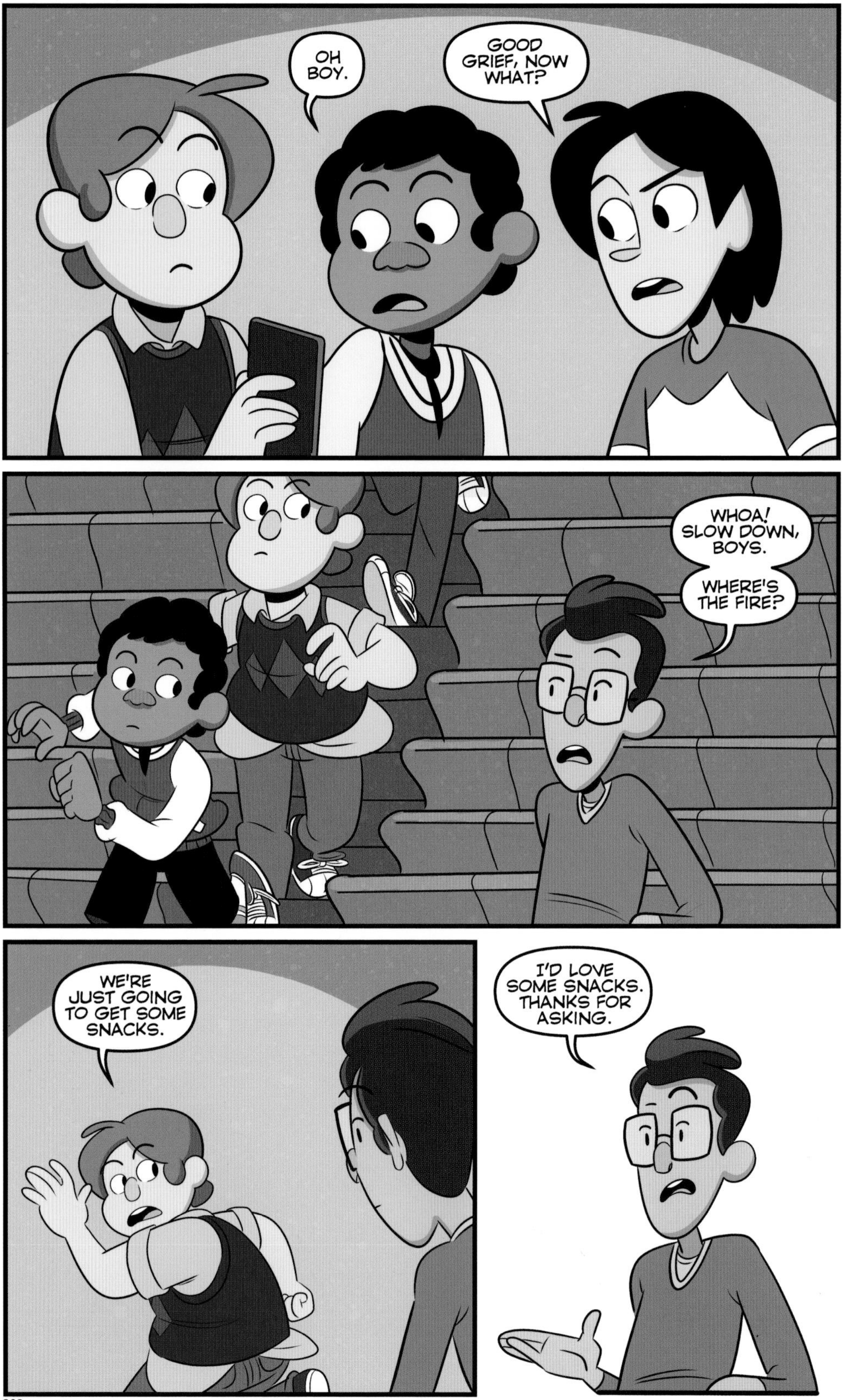
OH BOY.
GOOD GRIEF, NOW WHAT?
WHOA! SLOW DOWN, BOYS.
WHERE'S THE FIRE?
WE'RE JUST GOING TO GET SOME SNACKS.
I'D LOVE SOME SNACKS. THANKS FOR ASKING.

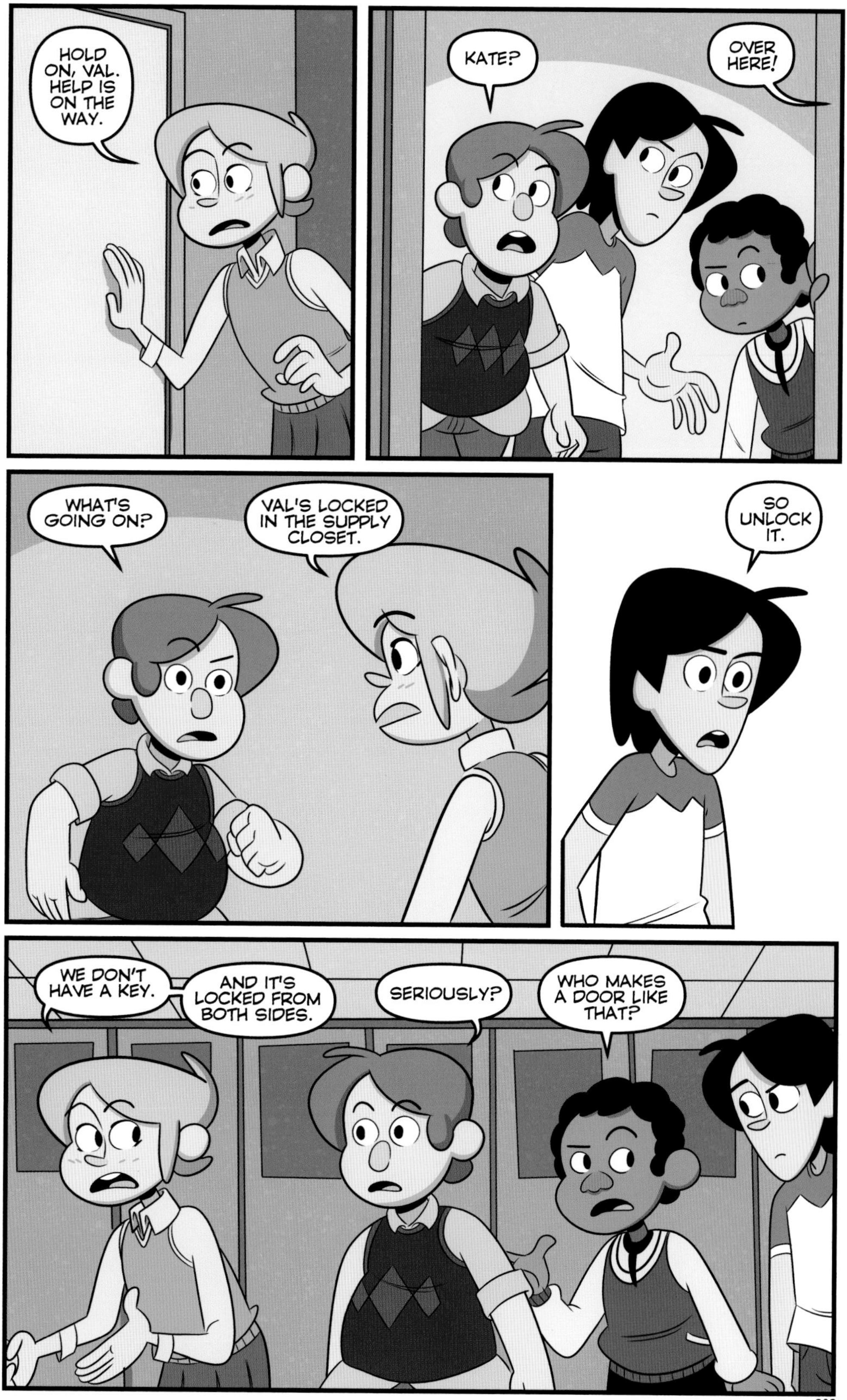
HOLD ON, VAL. HELP IS ON THE WAY.
KATE?
OVER HERE!
WHAT'S GOING ON?
VAL'S LOCKED IN THE SUPPLY CLOSET.
SO UNLOCK IT.
WE DON'T HAVE A KEY.
AND IT'S LOCKED FROM BOTH SIDES.
SERIOUSLY?
WHO MAKES A DOOR LIKE THAT?

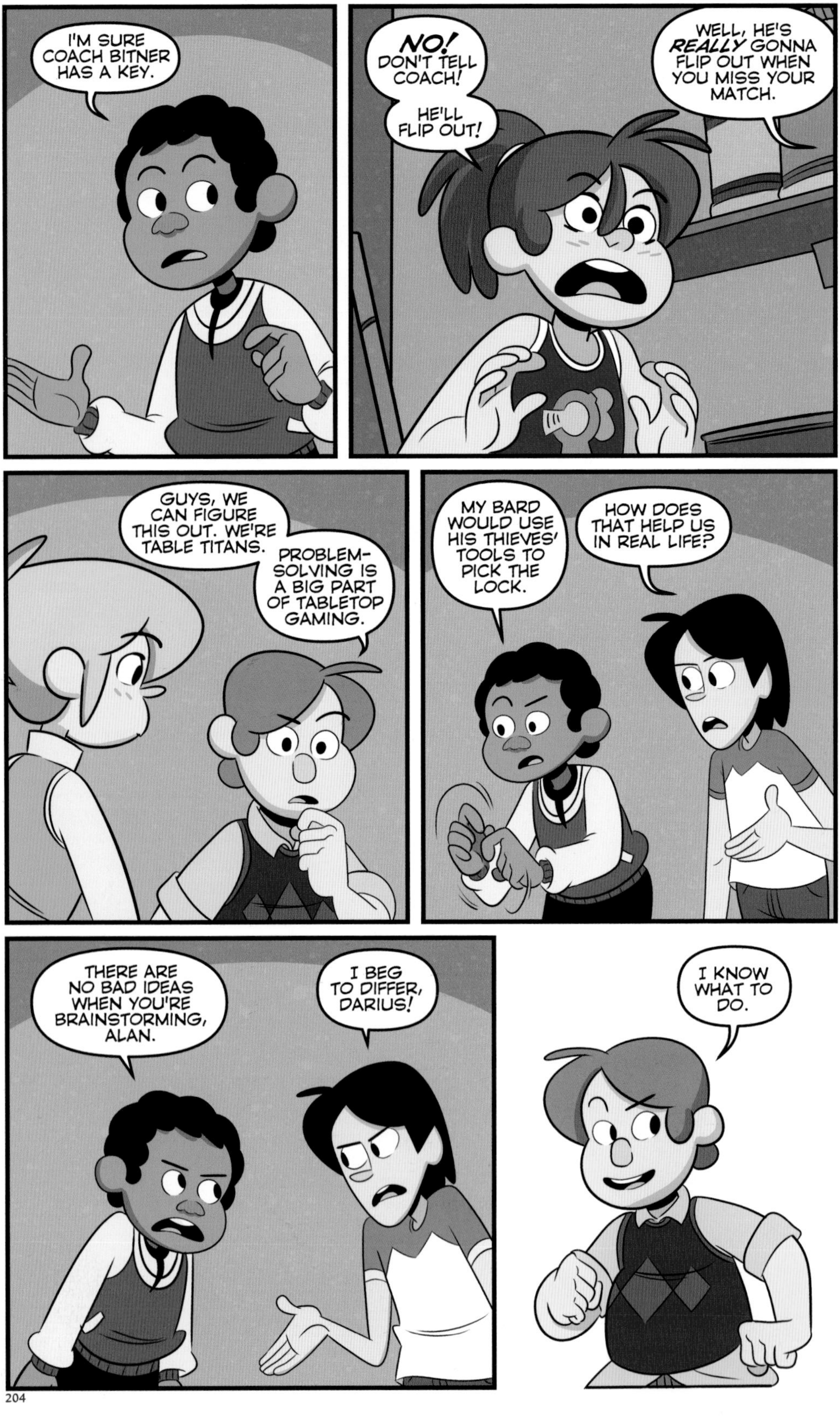

I'M SURE COACH BITNER HAS A KEY.
NO! DON'T TELL COACH!
HE'LL FLIP OUT!
WELL, HE'S REALLY GONNA FLIP OUT WHEN YOU MISS YOUR MATCH.
GUYS, WE CAN FIGURE THIS OUT. WE'RE TABLE TITANS.
PROBLEM-SOLVING IS A BIG PART OF TABLETOP GAMING.
MY BARD WOULD USE HIS THIEVES' TOOLS TO PICK THE LOCK.
HOW DOES THAT HELP US IN REAL LIFE?
THERE ARE NO BAD IDEAS WHEN YOU'RE BRAINSTORMING, ALAN.
I BEG TO DIFFER, DARIUS!
I KNOW WHAT TO DO.

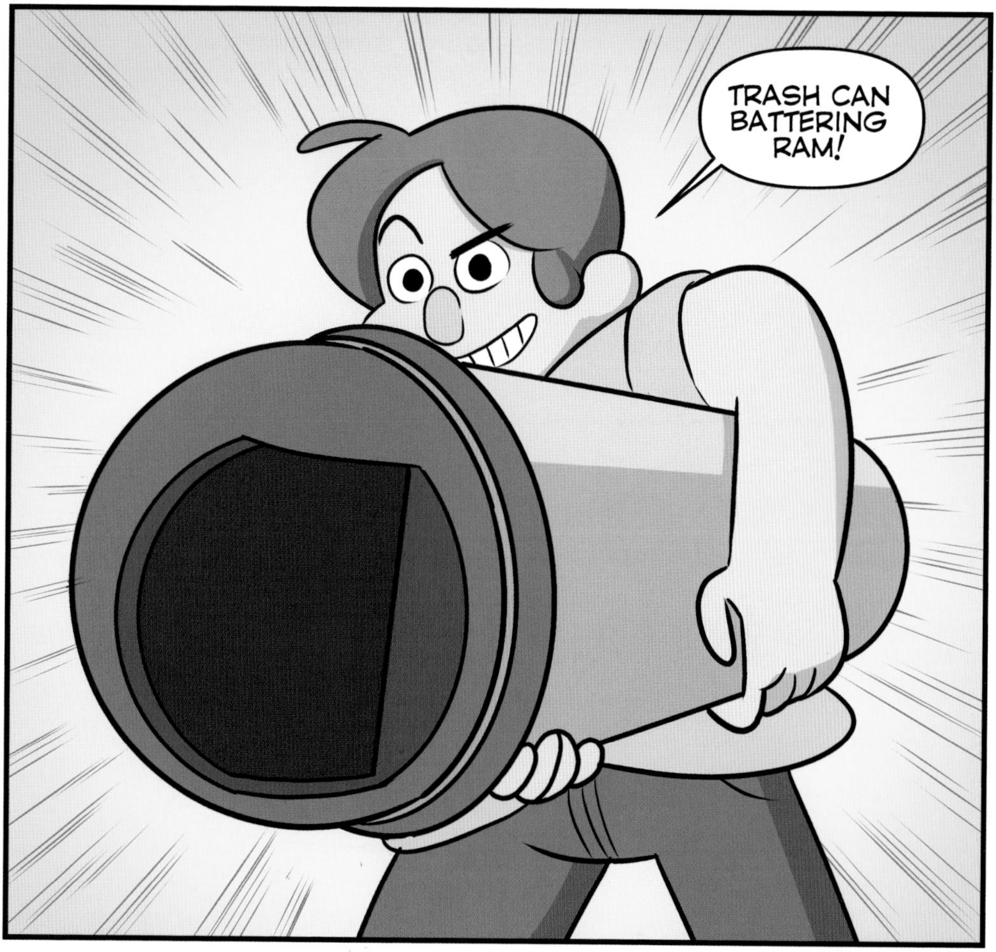
TRASH CAN BATTERING RAM!

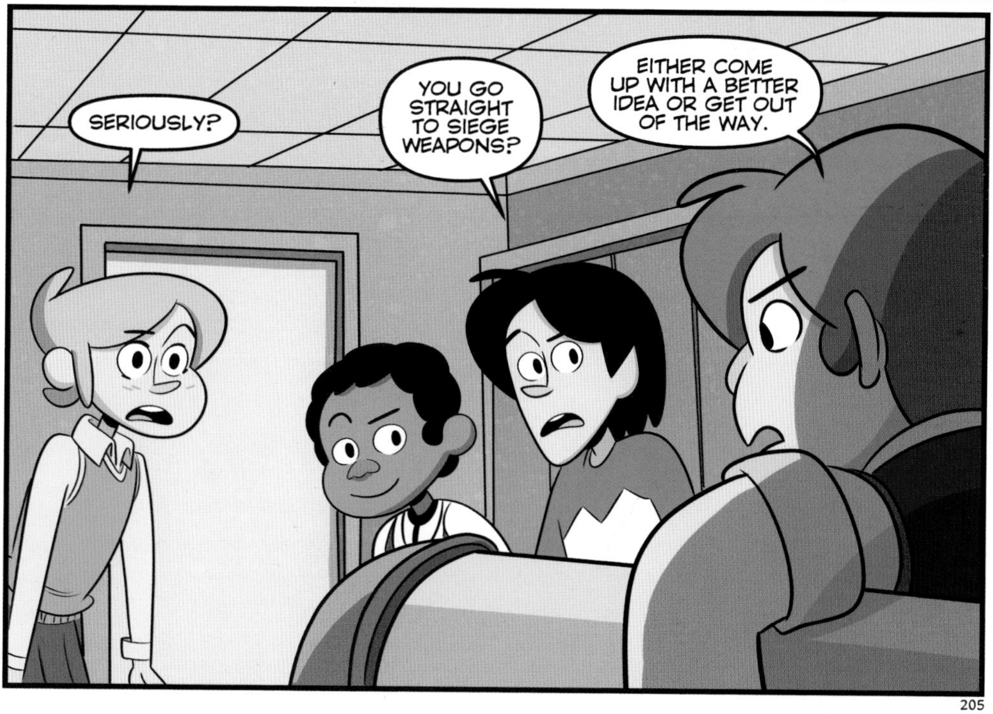
SERIOUSLY?
YOU GO STRAIGHT TO SIEGE WEAPONS?
EITHER COME UP WITH A BETTER IDEA OR GET OUT OF THE WAY.

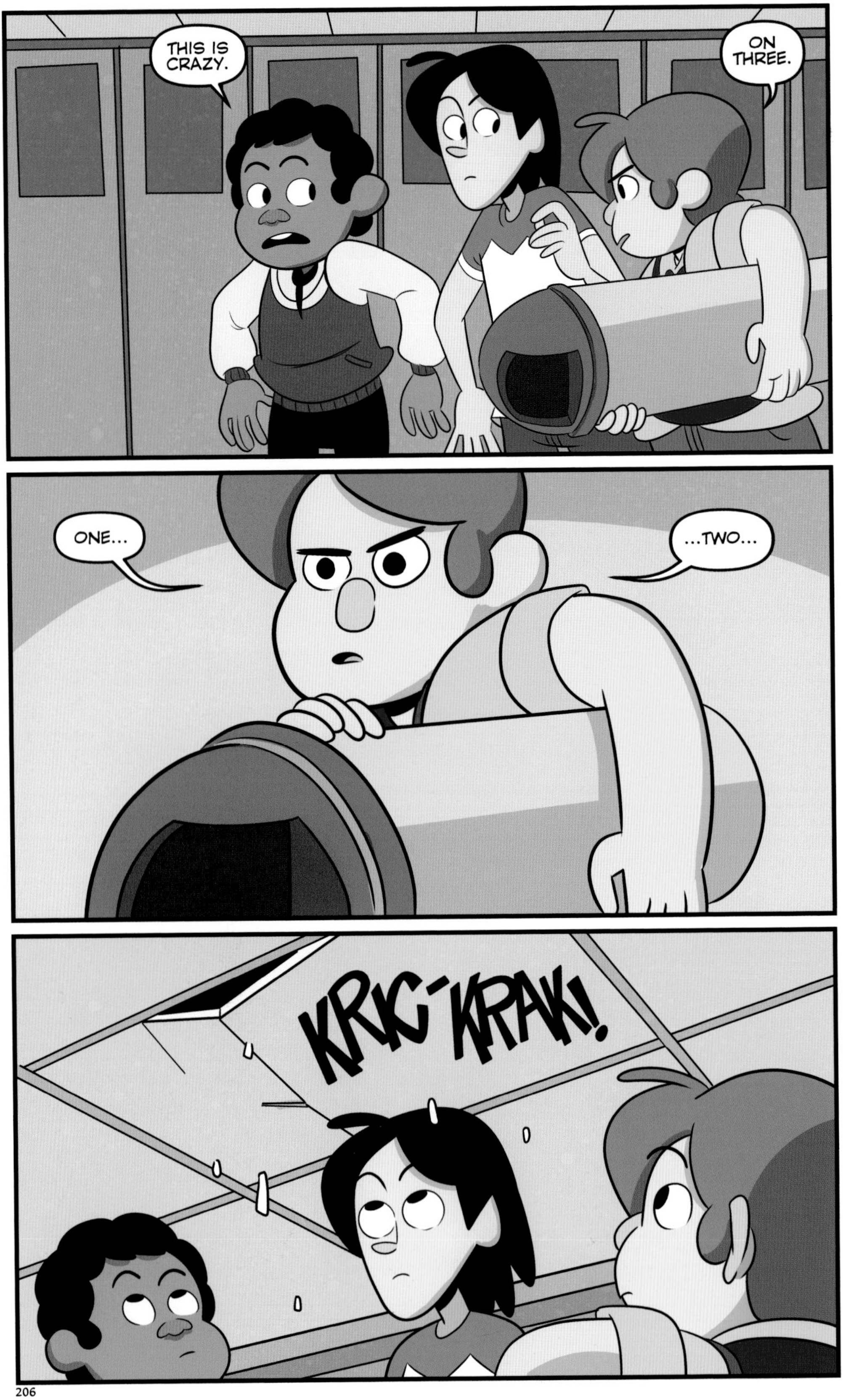
THIS IS CRAZY.
ON THREE.
ONE...
...TWO...
KRIC-KRAK!

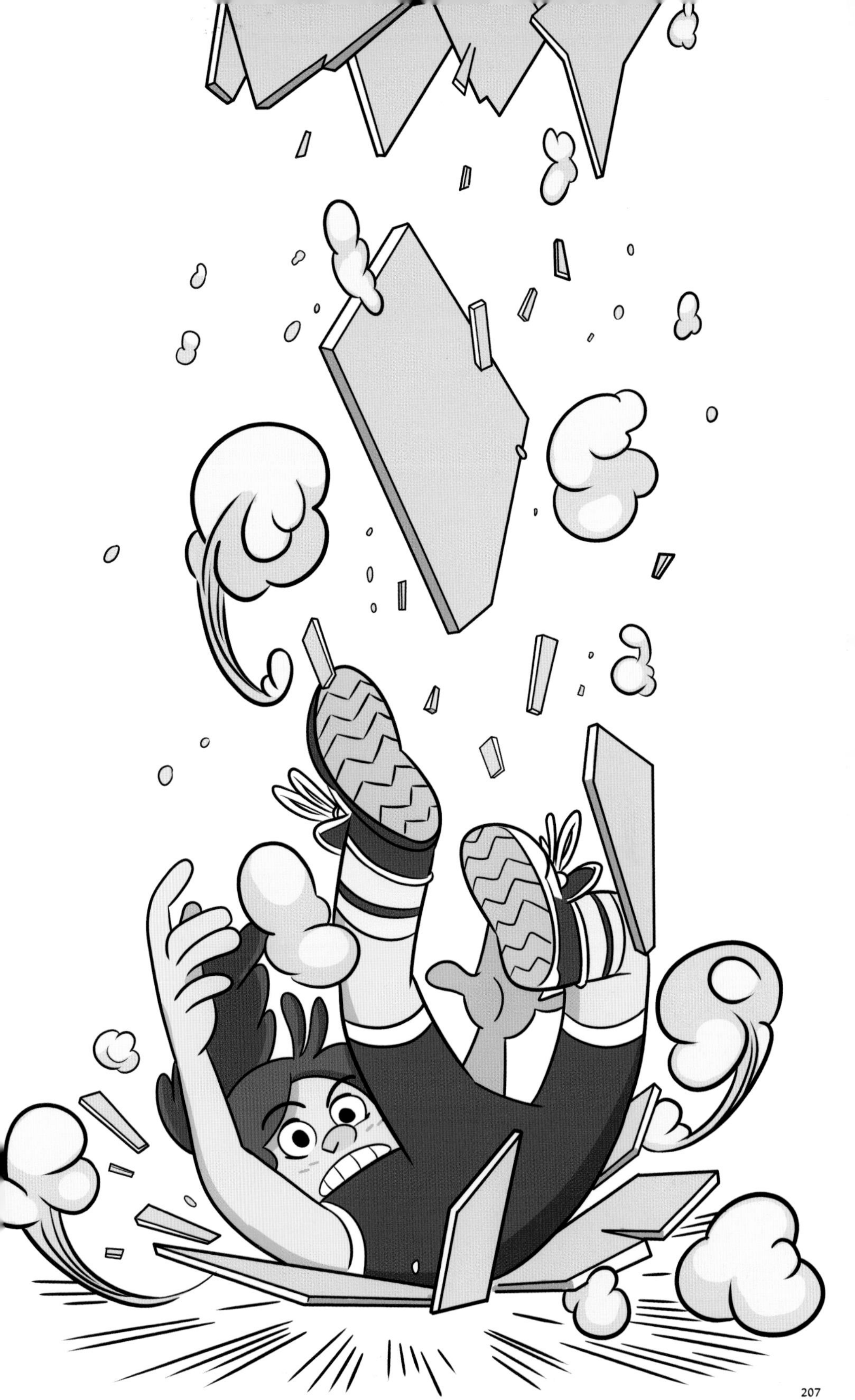

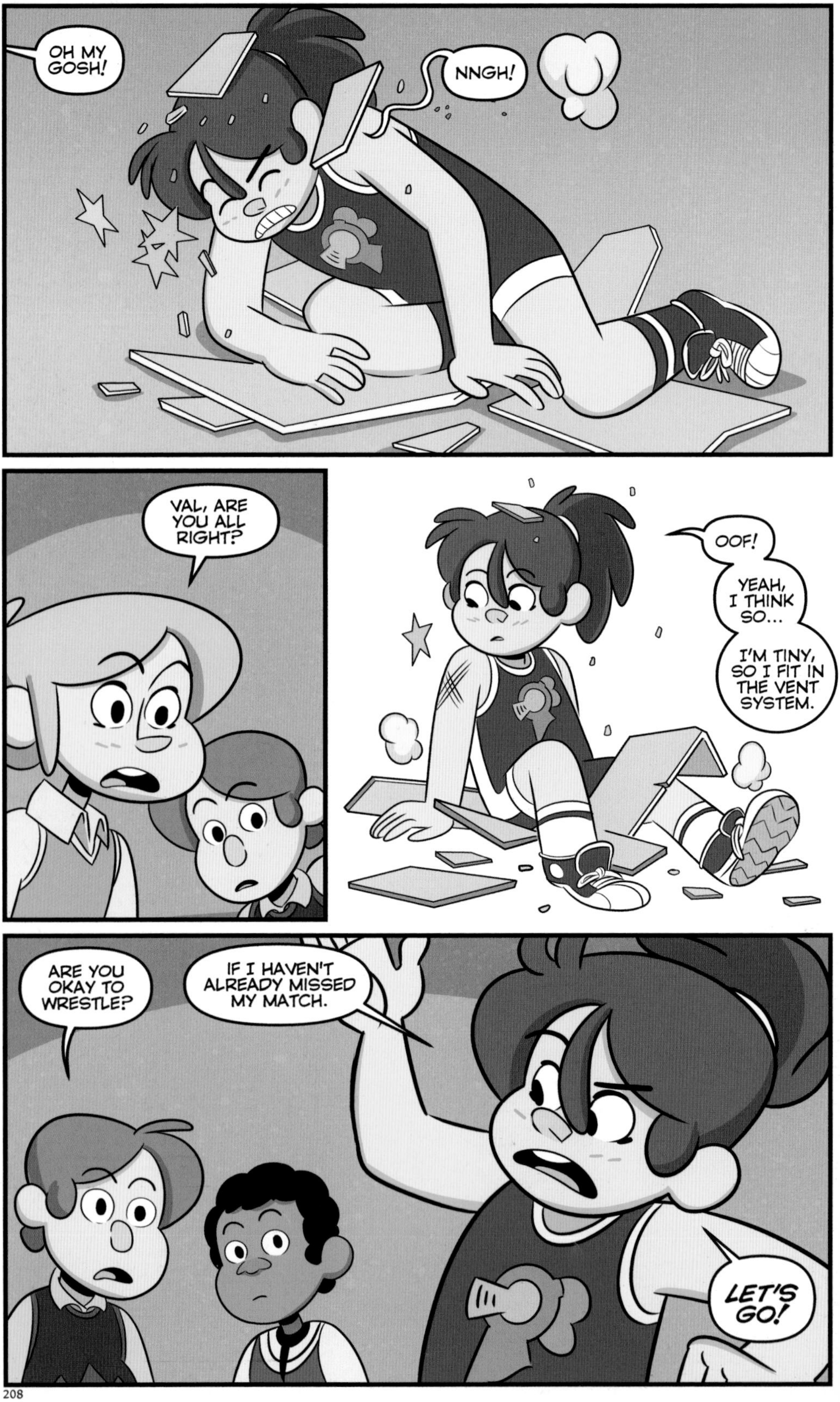

OH MY GOSH!
NNGH!
VAL, ARE YOU ALL RIGHT?
OOF!
YEAH, I THINK SO...
I'M TINY, SO I FIT IN THE VENT SYSTEM.
ARE YOU OKAY TO WRESTLE?
IF I HAVEN'T ALREADY MISSED MY MATCH.
LET'S GO!

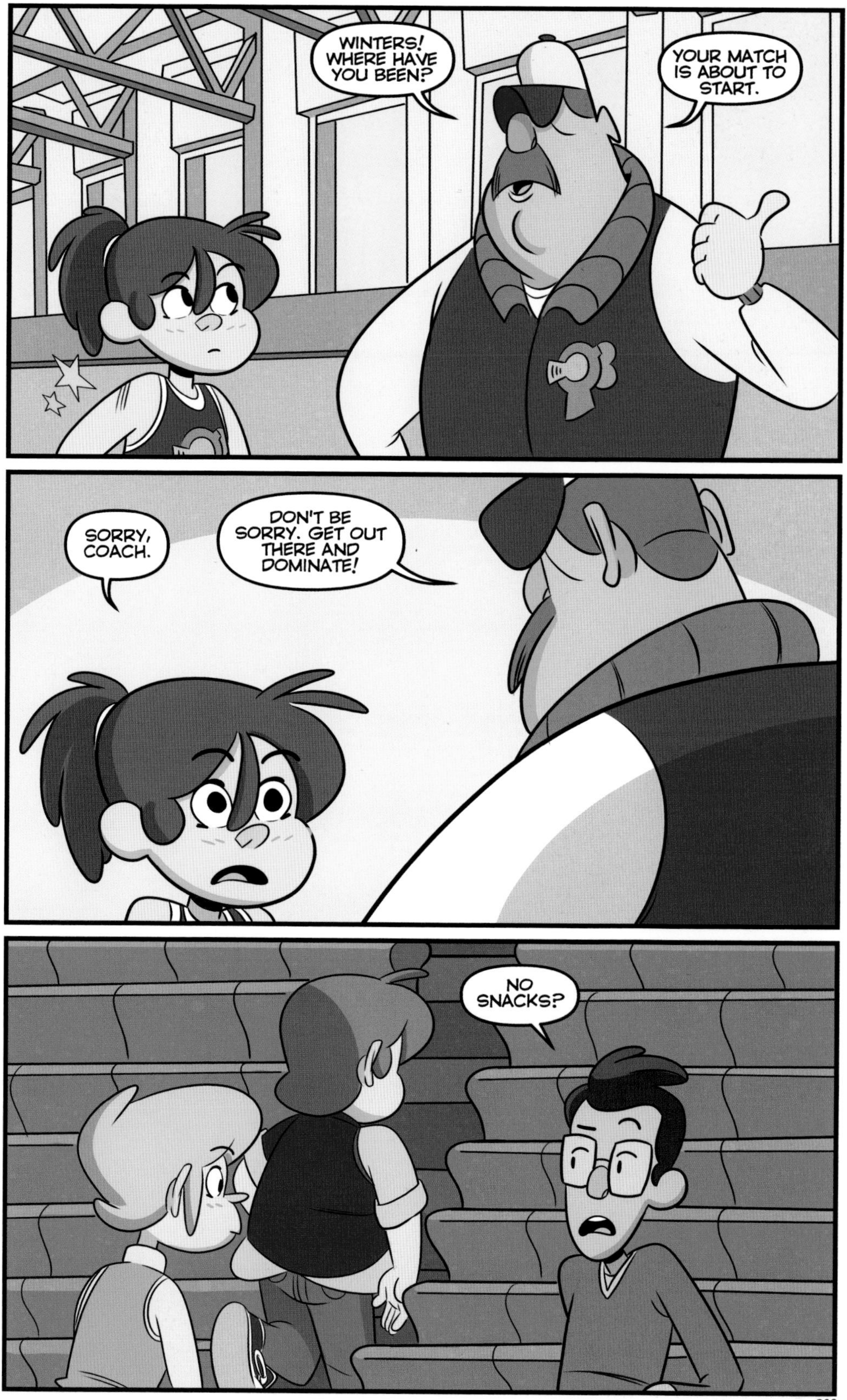
WINTERS! WHERE HAVE YOU BEEN?
YOUR MATCH IS ABOUT TO START.
SORRY, COACH.
DON'T BE SORRY. GET OUT THERE AND DOMINATE!
NO SNACKS?

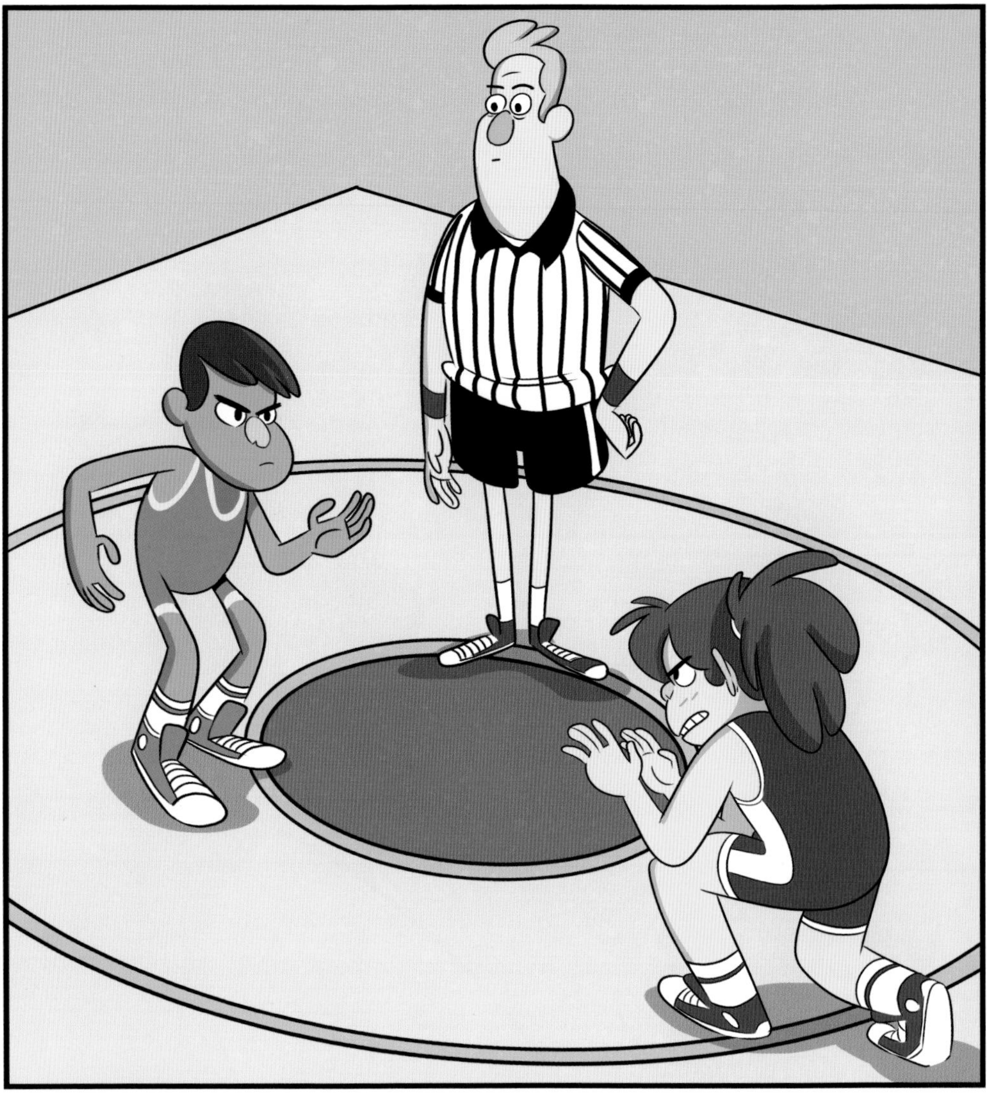

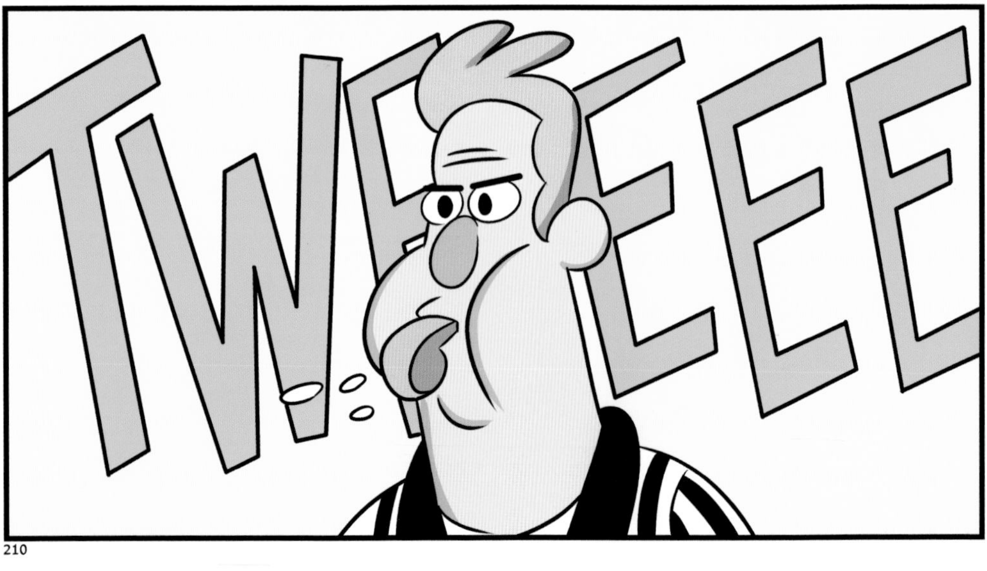
TWEEEE

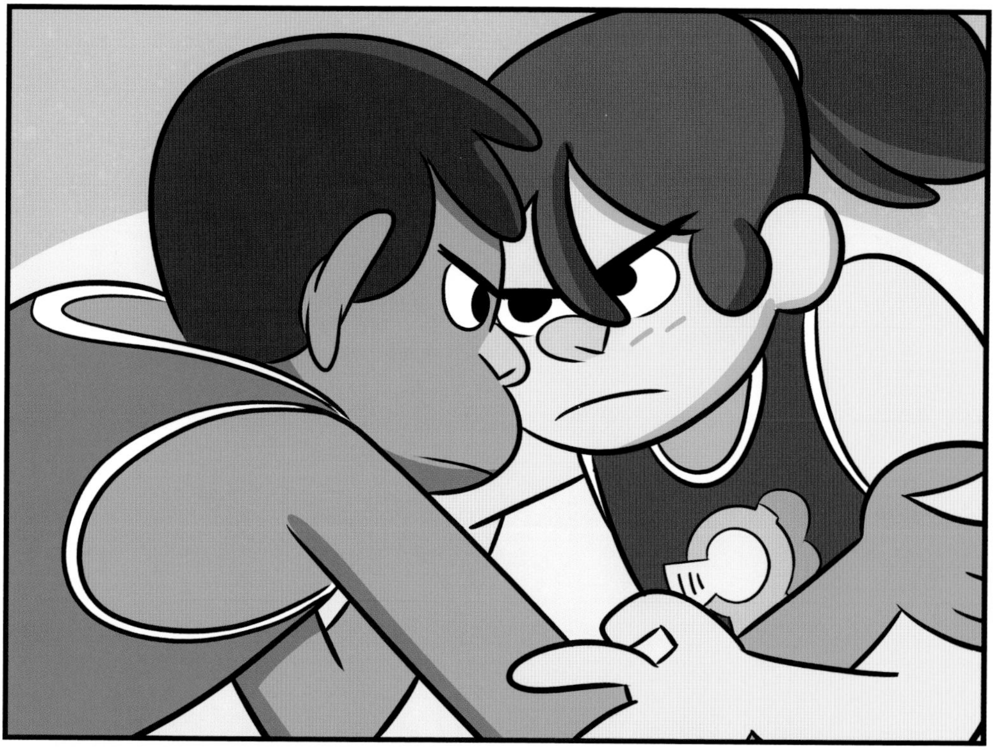

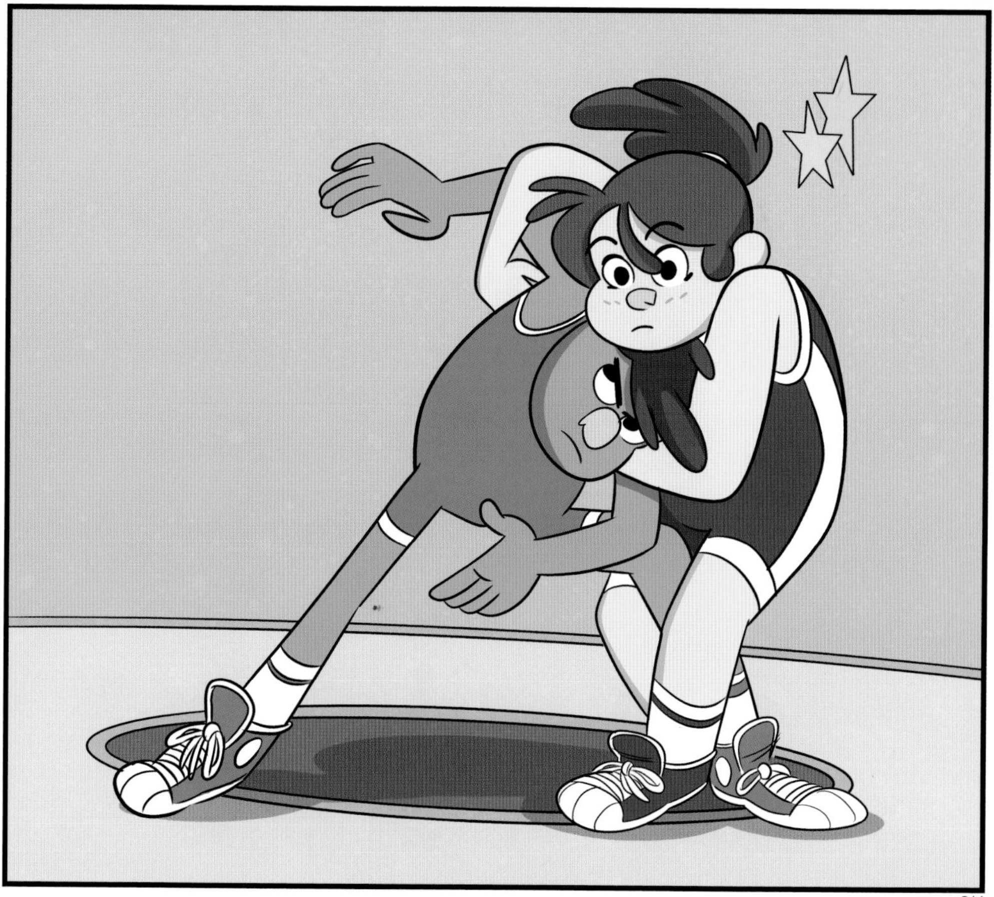

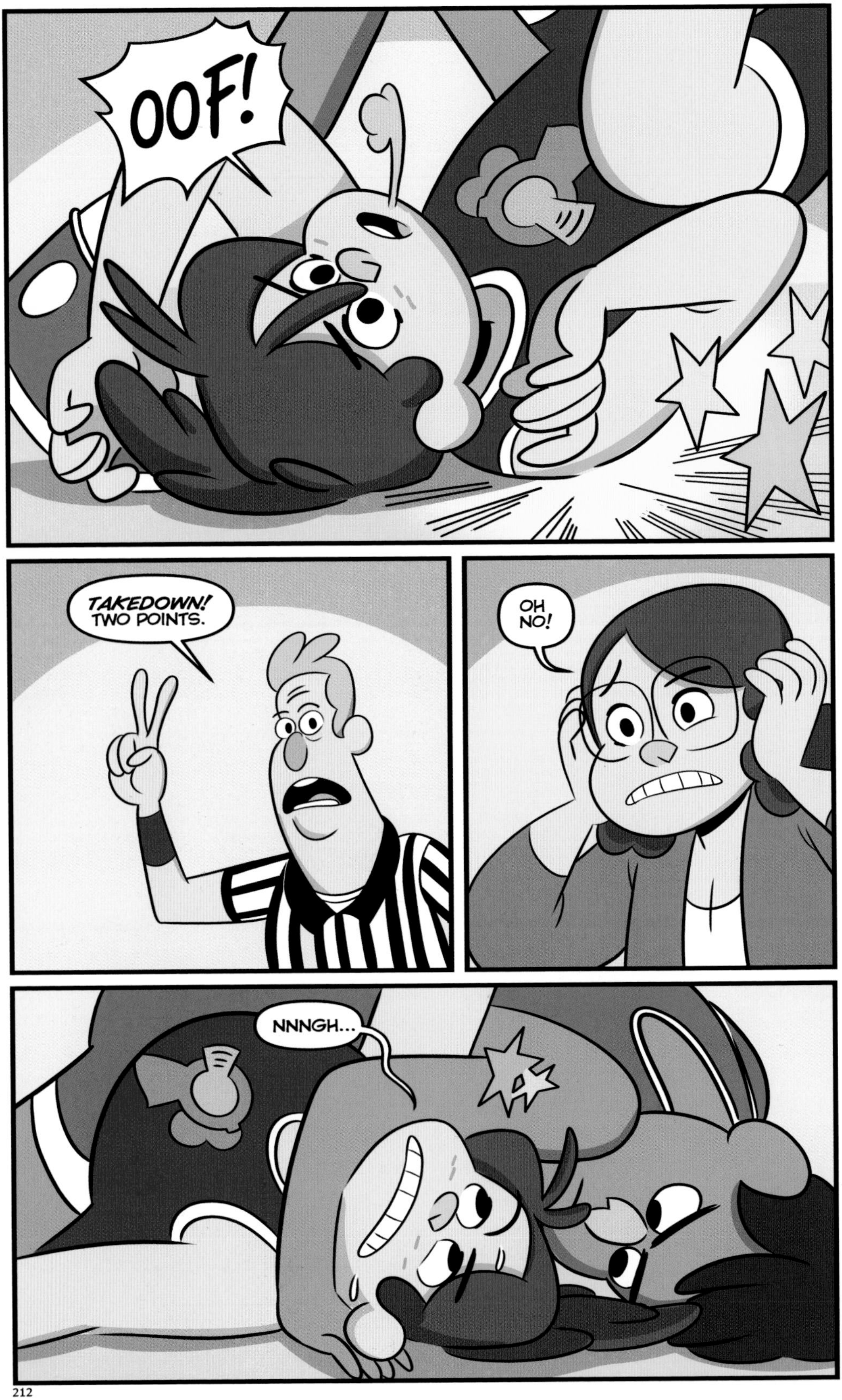
OOF!
TAKEDOWN! TWO POINTS.
OH NO!
NNNGH...

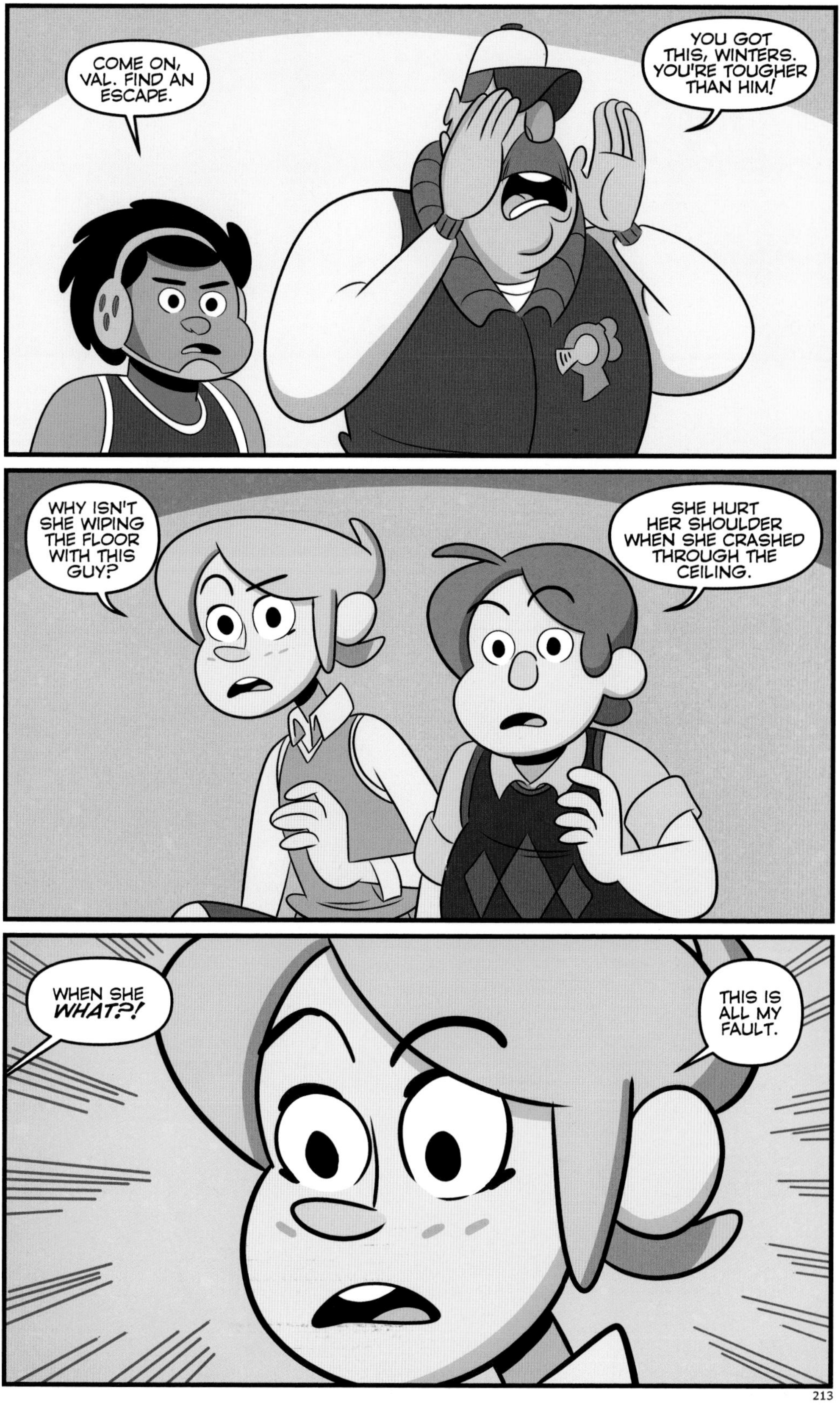
COME ON, VAL. FIND AN ESCAPE.
YOU GOT THIS, WINTERS. YOU'RE TOUGHER THAN HIM!
WHY ISN'T SHE WIPING THE FLOOR WITH THIS GUY?
SHE HURT HER SHOULDER WHEN SHE CRASHED THROUGH THE CEILING.
WHEN SHE *WHAT?!*
THIS IS ALL MY FAULT.

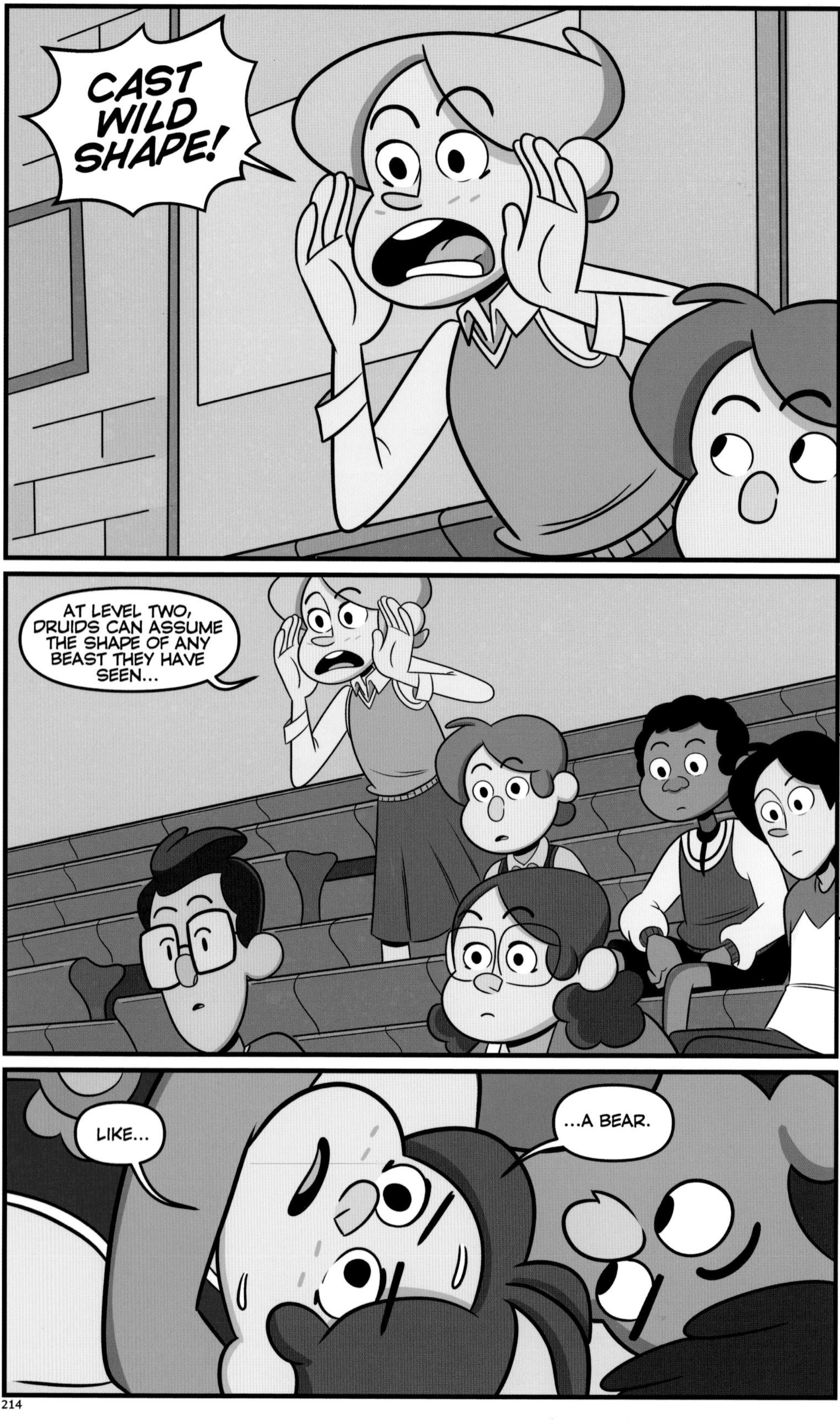
CAST WILD SHAPE!
AT LEVEL TWO, DRUIDS CAN ASSUME THE SHAPE OF ANY BEAST THEY HAVE SEEN...
LIKE...
...A BEAR.

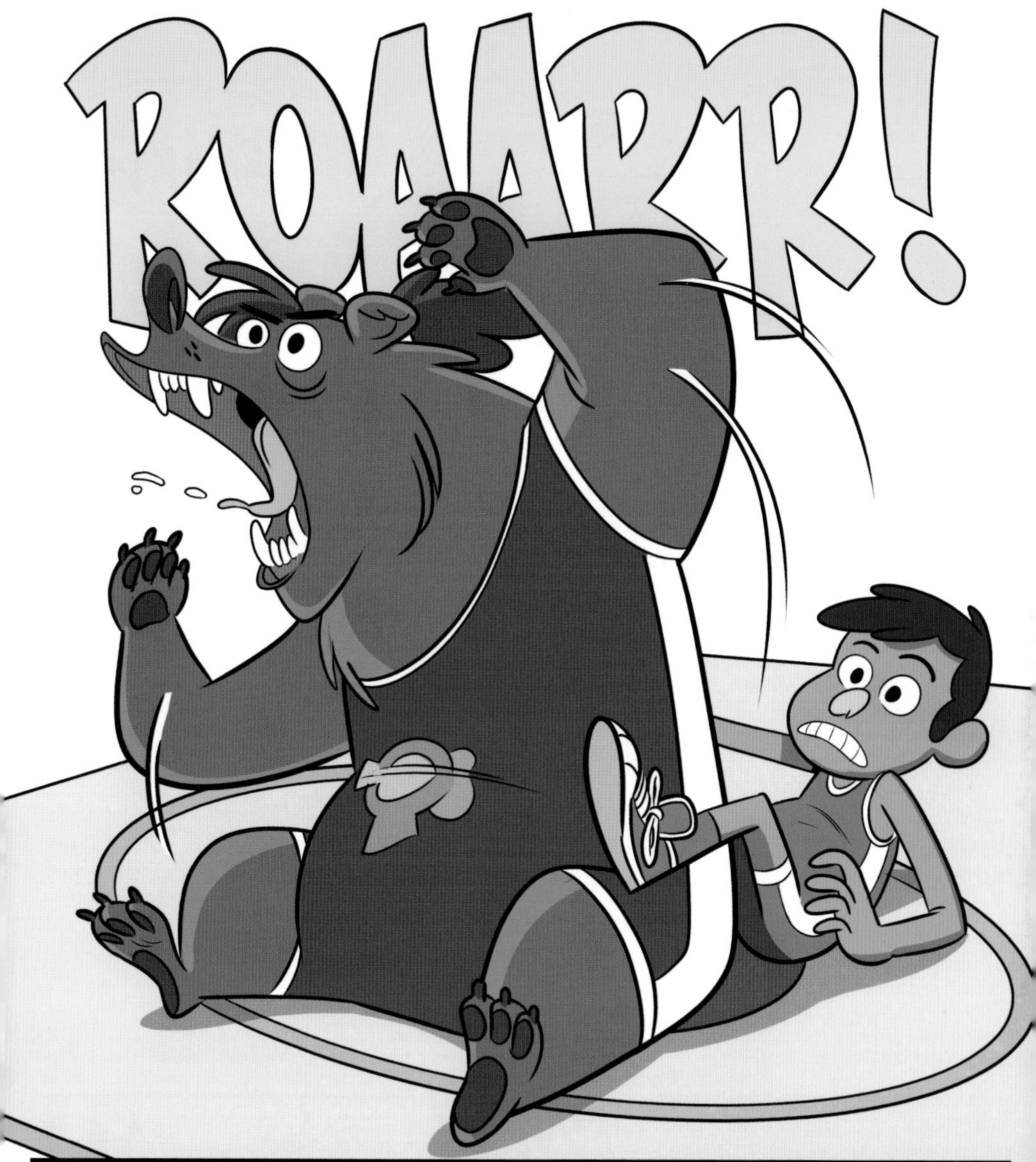
ROAARR!

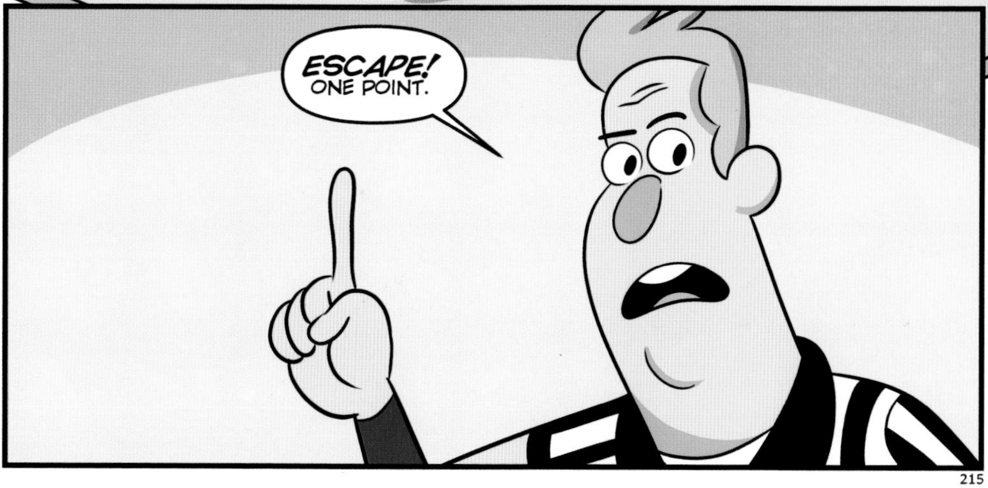
ESCAPE! ONE POINT.

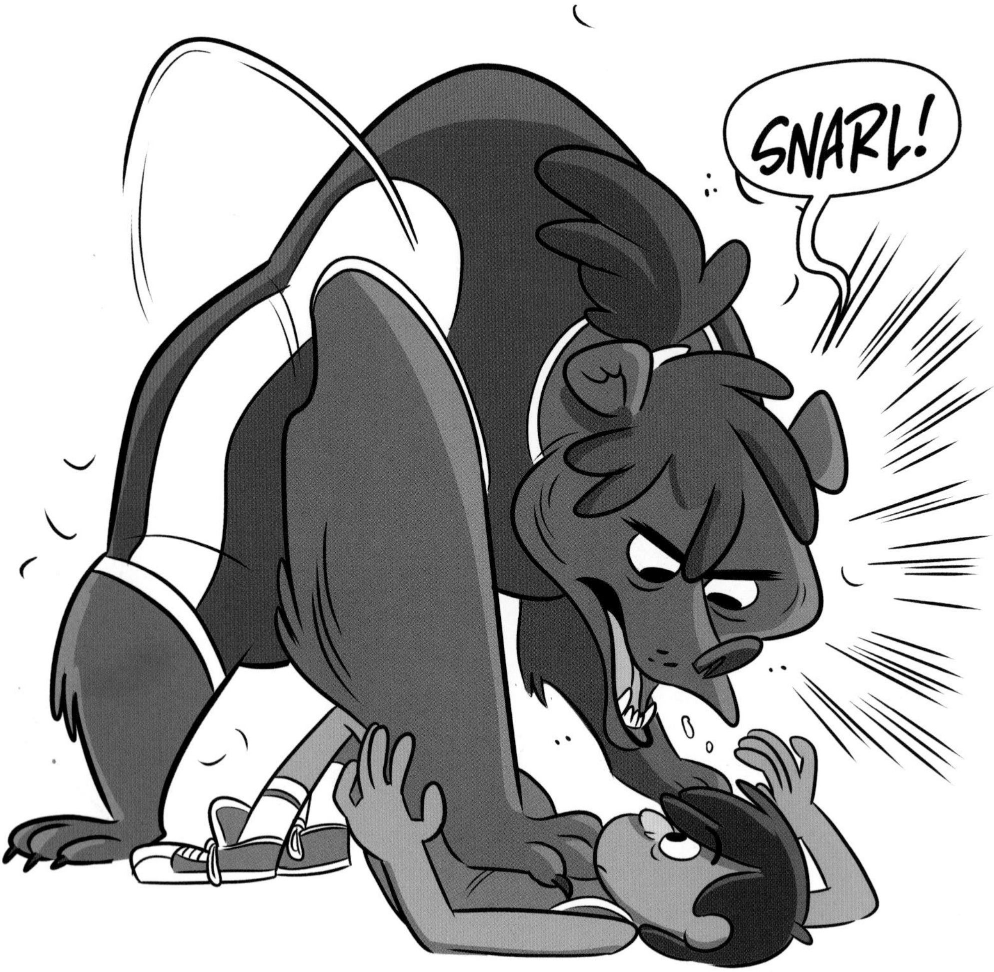
SNARL!

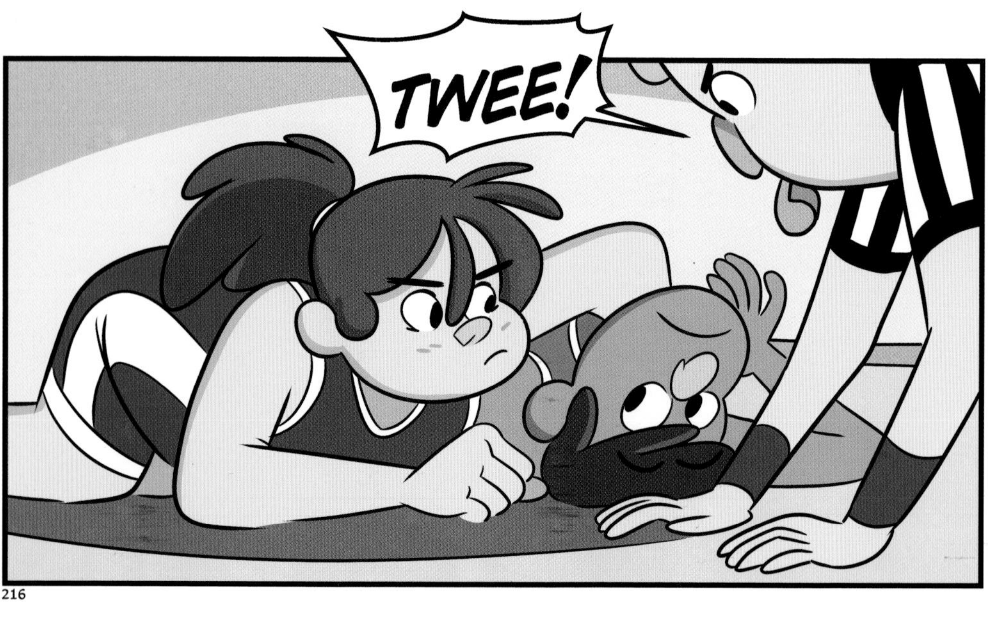
TWEE!

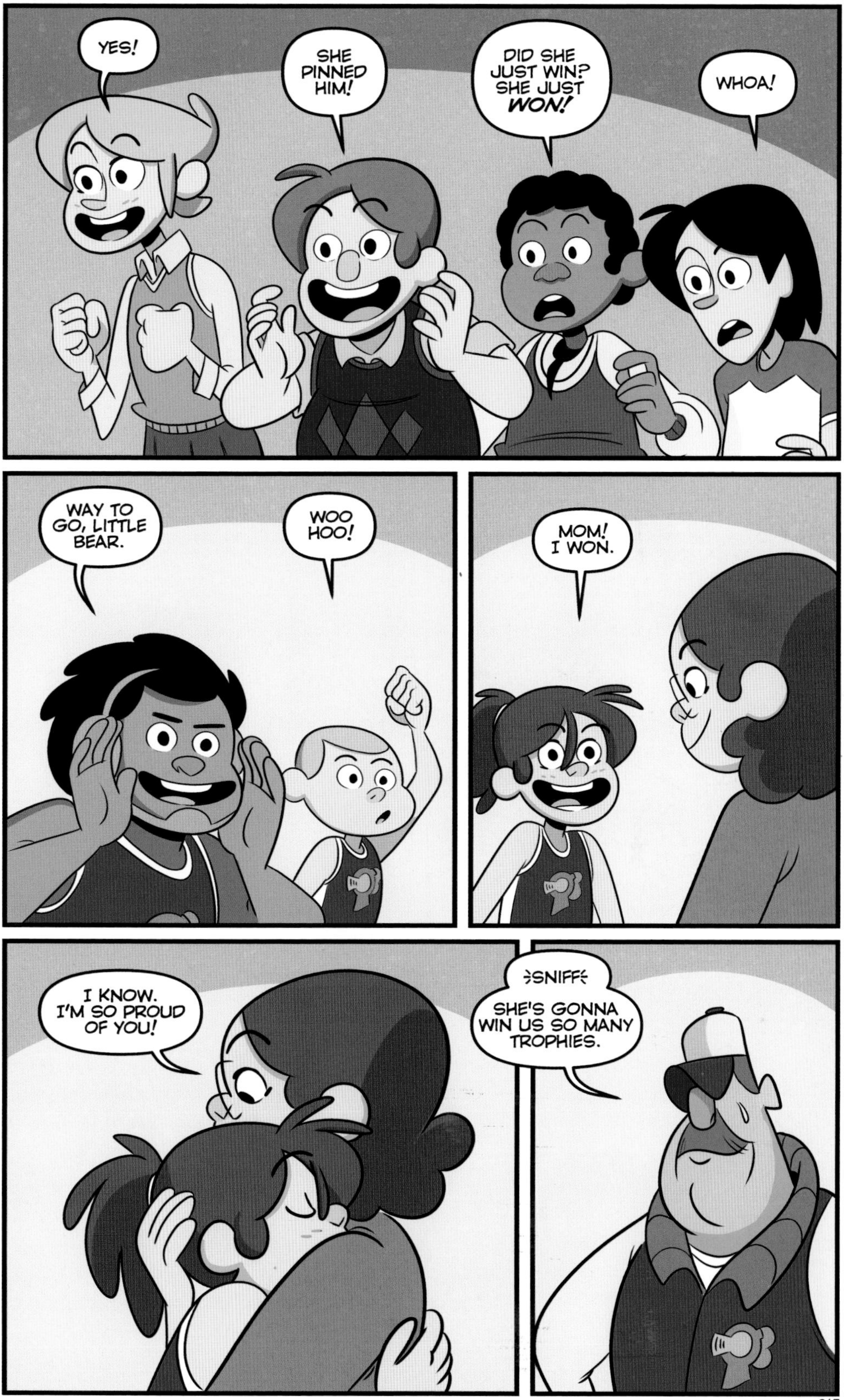
YES!
SHE PINNED HIM!
DID SHE JUST WIN? SHE JUST WON!
WHOA!
WAY TO GO, LITTLE BEAR.
WOO HOO!
MOM! I WON.
I KNOW. I'M SO PROUD OF YOU!
SNIFF
SHE'S GONNA WIN US SO MANY TROPHIES.

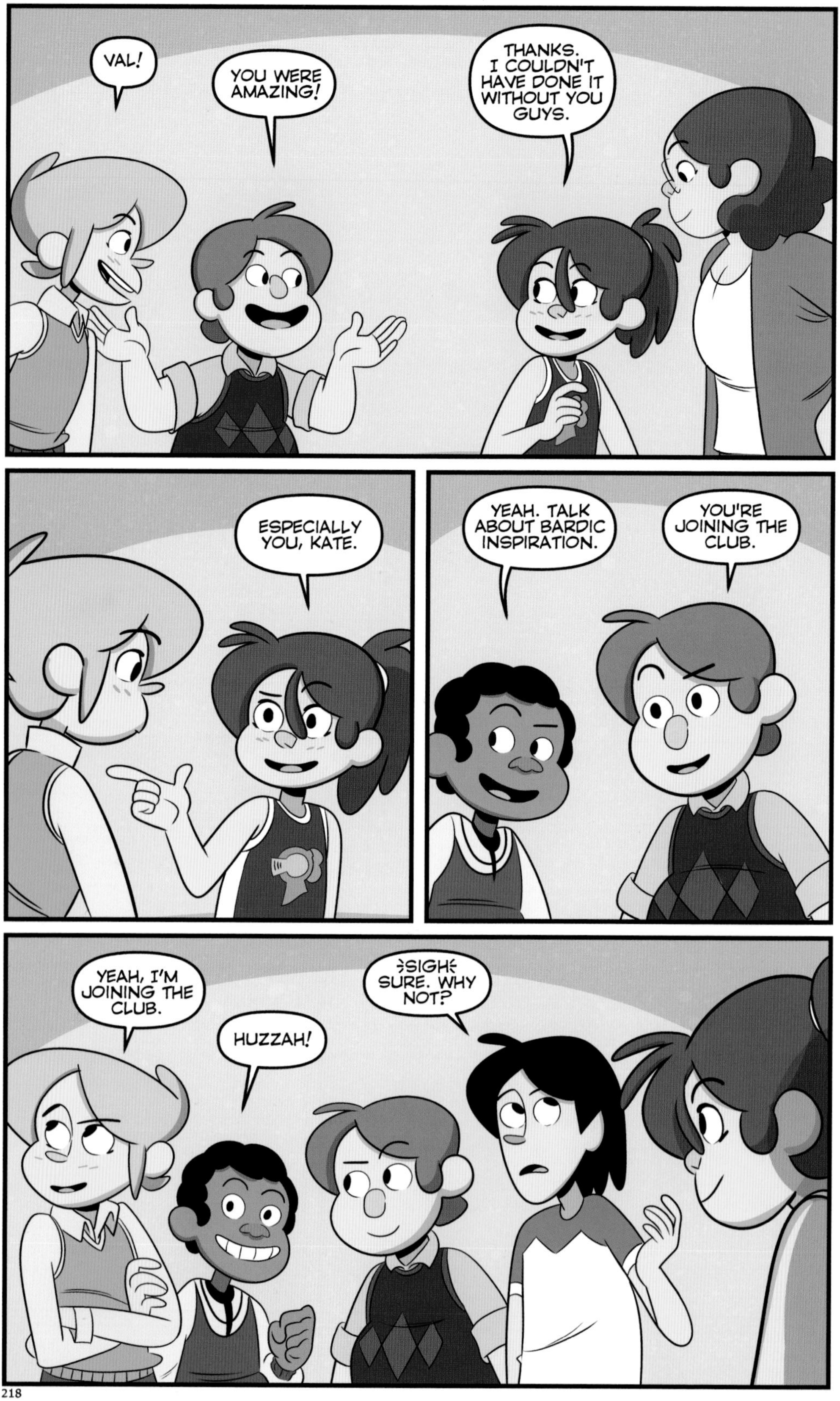
VAL!
YOU WERE AMAZING!
THANKS. I COULDN'T HAVE DONE IT WITHOUT YOU GUYS.
ESPECIALLY YOU, KATE.
YEAH. TALK ABOUT BARDIC INSPIRATION.
YOU'RE JOINING THE CLUB.
YEAH, I'M JOINING THE CLUB.
HUZZAH!
SIGH
SURE. WHY NOT?

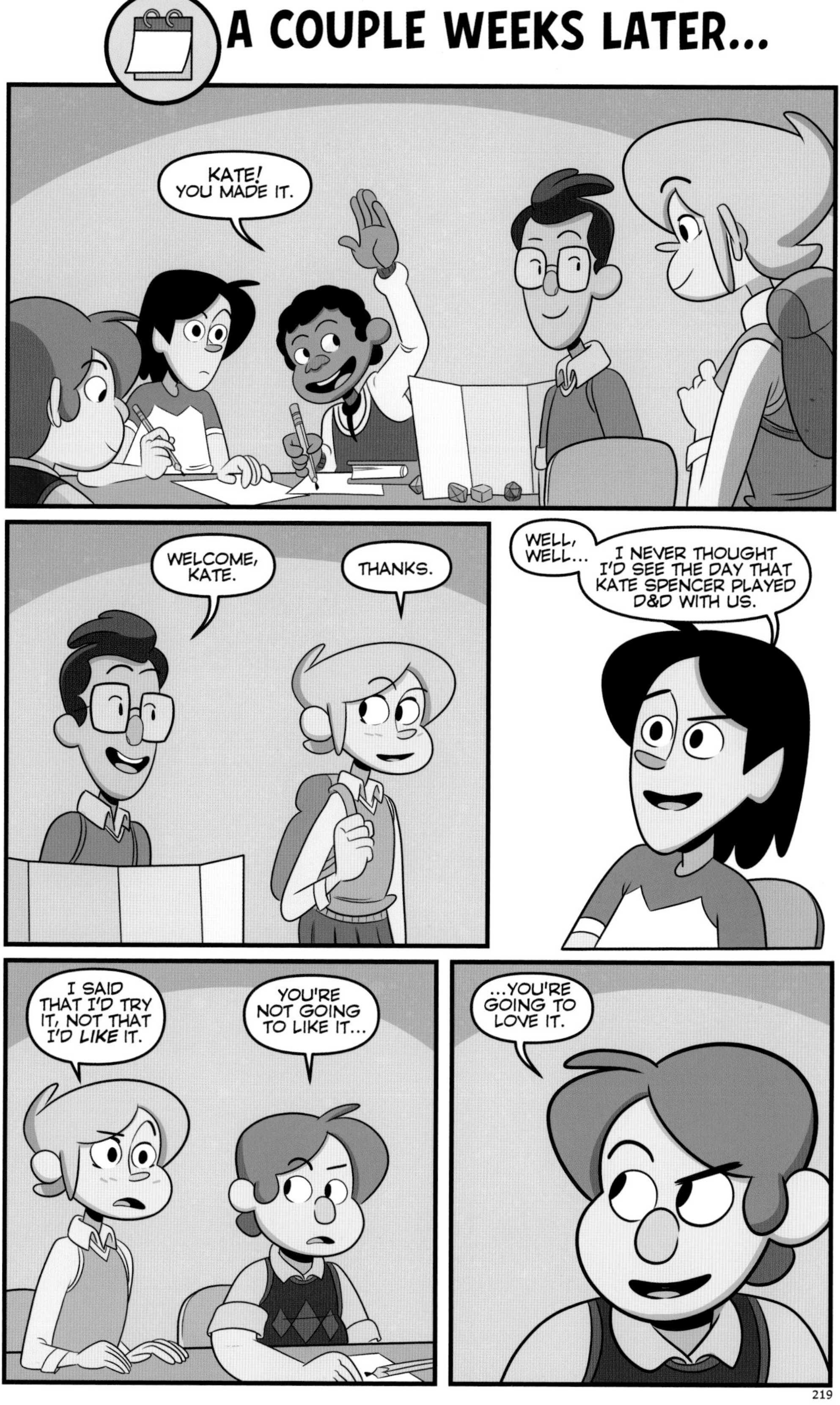
A COUPLE WEEKS LATER...
KATE! YOU MADE IT.
WELCOME, KATE.
THANKS.
WELL, WELL...
I NEVER THOUGHT I'D SEE THE DAY THAT KATE SPENCER PLAYED D&D WITH US.
I SAID THAT I'D TRY IT, NOT THAT I'D *LIKE* IT.
YOU'RE NOT GOING TO LIKE IT...
...YOU'RE GOING TO LOVE IT.

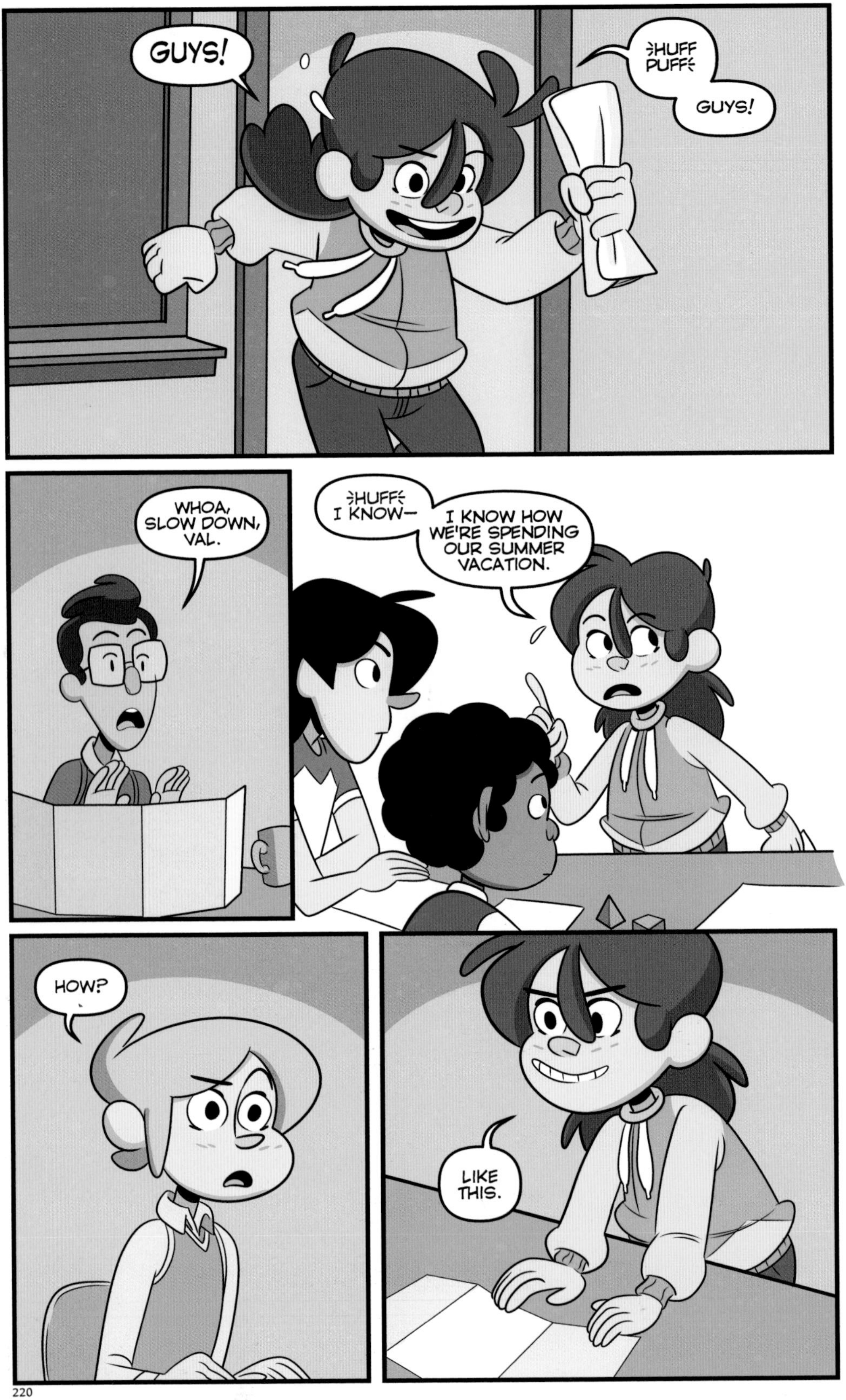
GUYS!
HUFF PUFF
GUYS!
WHOA, SLOW DOWN, VAL.
HUFF I KNOW—
I KNOW HOW WE'RE SPENDING OUR SUMMER VACATION.
HOW?
LIKE THIS.

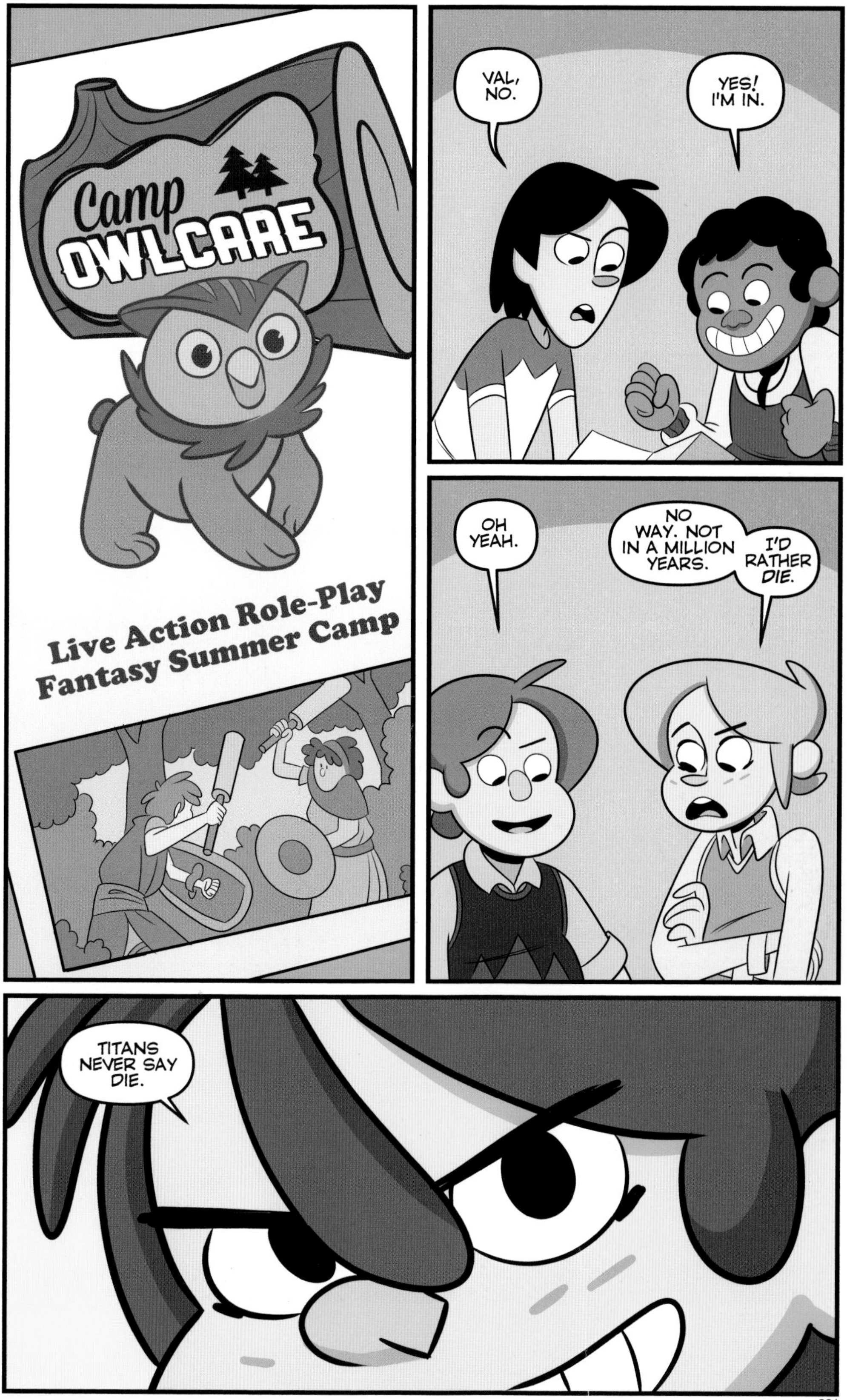
Camp
OWLCARE
Live Action Role-Play
Fantasy Summer Camp
VAL, NO.
YES! I'M IN.
OH YEAH.
NO WAY. NOT IN A MILLION YEARS.
I'D RATHER DIE.
TITANS NEVER SAY DIE.

Acknowledgments

Thank you to Rich Moyer, who helped me take my first steps toward kid lit (and for offering to show my stuff to his agent). Thanks to Tim Traviglini for taking me on and for guidance as I tripped my way over every step of this process. To Sally Morgridge for believing in this book and rooting for Val from the very beginning. To everyone at Holiday House for their hard work and support.

Thank you to Steve Hamaker for all your brilliant colors and for making my line art feel vibrant and alive. It wouldn't be a Table Titans book without you. Thanks to Cole, Faby, and Deon for killing it on an impossible deadline with your color assists.

Thanks to all my peers who read my early drafts and encouraged me to pursue this, especially Chris Schweizer and Shana Targosz.

Finally, thank you to my family: Angela, Brian, Regean, and Miranda for being there to pick me up, always believing in me, and refusing to let me doubt myself.